THE FIFTH HOSTAGE

It is 1980 and Iran is in turmoil. Fear grips the corridors of Whitehall: a Briton is being held in Teheran and the secret information he holds has catastrophic implications. The nation's most wanted man – and his devastatingly beautiful girlfriend – must be rescued, at all costs.

There is only one way to bring them home. Enter the SAS – 22 Special Air Service Regiment – a secret and elite fighting group, highly trained, determined, respected throughout the world.

A crack team is assembled and the mission is under way. It is a nail-biting race against time: the stakes are high and the dangers incalculable. It is not just the fittest who will survive.

Once again, Terence Strong has written a breathtaking thriller that takes you deep into the heart of Iran, the world of the SAS, and the private and service lives of these dedicated professionals. THE FIFTH HOSTAGE is a stunning and worthy successor to his previous bestseller, WHISPER WHO DARES.

**Also by the same author,
and available in Coronet Books:**

Whisper Who Dares

The Fifth Hostage

Terence Strong

CORONET BOOKS
Hodder and Stoughton

Copyright © 1983 by Terence Strong

First published in Great Britain 1983
by Coronet Books
Fifth impression, 1983

British Library C.I.P.

Strong, Terence
  The fifth hostage
  I. Title
  823'.914[F]   PR6039.T/

  ISBN 0 340 32120 2

*The characters and situations in this book are
entirely imaginary and bear no relation to any real
person or actual happening*

Printed and bound in Great Britain
for Hodder and Stoughton Paperbacks, a
division of Hodder and Stoughton Ltd.,
Mill Road, Dunton Green, Sevenoaks,
Kent (Editorial Office: 47 Bedford
Square, London, WC1 3DP) by
Cox & Wyman Ltd., Reading.
Photoset by Rowland Phototypesetting Ltd.,
Bury St Edmunds, Suffolk.

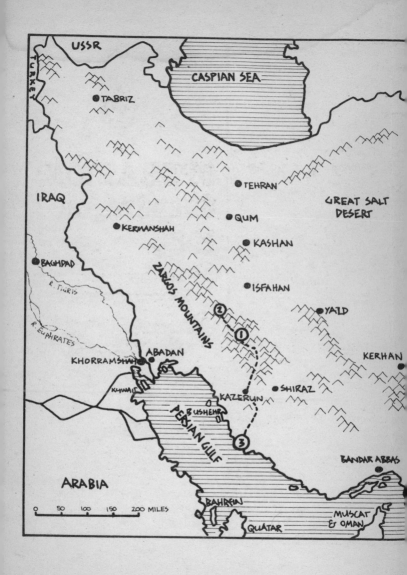

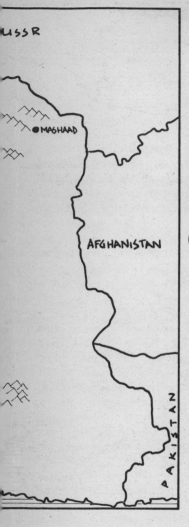

OPERATION: Snapdragon 1980

① Drop zone for Snapdragon

② Lordakam airstrip (disused)

③ Plan B pick-up point

---- Route taken

AUTHOR'S NOTE

After the brave but unsuccessful bid by the United States to rescue the 52 hostages from its Teheran embassy in 1980, many asked how Britain might have coped with a similar situation.

Certainly the British would not have had to cope with the unmanageable scale of operation faced by the Americans. But the basic logistics nightmare would have been the same. So what known and unexpected hazards might have been experienced by such a mission?

Undoubtedly it would have called for the multifarious talents of 22 Special Air Service Regiment. This elite and secretive British Army outfit had sprung to unaccustomed world attention earlier that year with the spectacular busting of the Princes Gate siege in London.

That, however, was a rare public display. This unorthodox regiment earned its first spurs back in the Second World War and subsequently in Malaya, Borneo, Oman, Ulster and the Falklands War – amongst many other, lesser known campaigns and assignments.

Mixing fact with fiction is fascinating for both writer and reader, particularly when it is realised that certain fact can *only* be more truthfully told as fiction. But there are dangers.

I feel it only right to make it clear that, to my knowledge, nothing like "Operation Fulcrum" was ever mounted by British intelligence services. However, the many possible reasons given as being behind it, are authentic. There is no doubt that these might have been considered valid by several interested nations and multi-national industrialists.

Indeed many think it strange that – in little over a year – a single religious agitator in exile could have risen from obscurity to absolute control of one of the most powerful countries in the Middle East.

Unfortunately the horrors and methods of that revolutionary Islamic regime are not imagined. Nothing has been invented. At the time of writing Khomeini still lives. Ayatollah Beheshti was blown apart by a terrorist bomb not long after the events described in this book. Thankfully, Judge Khalkali enjoys a little less influence nowadays.

The mission described in this book, too, is accurate. It was planned as an SAS operation from start to finish. The routes used, roads, pylons, telephone lines and gas pipelines described are where stated.

It *could* all have happened exactly as written.

But did it?

Terence Strong
London 1982

My thanks for unstinting assistance on some technical details go to: aviation writer Peter Gilchrist; the Royal Observatory; Jo Dennis of E. Leitz (Instruments) Ltd, and Terry Burnal of CSE Aviation Ltd who taught me how not to fly his beloved Jet Rangers.

For my parents.
And for the thousands
of now silent innocents
in a mystical land
that deserved better.

But specially
the lads of 22.

PROLOGUE

THE HAWK HUNCHED on the high outcrop, eyes hooded against the fierce Omani sun.

Waiting.

Watching. Ever patient.

The penetrating eyes blinked as they relentlessly searched the wadi far below. This year the rain-laden winds of the *Khareef* had waned early and already the river bed was reduced to a mere stream. Given time the prey would come, picking its way carefully through the patches of frizzled grass and stunted thorn bushes at the water's edge. Given time.

As the sun reached its zenith the heat took on a throbbing momentum of its own. The very air itself began to bake.

In the shadow of the outcrop a man moved. Leaving the radio, he quickly scaled the few feet to the peak. He was small, wiry and unkempt, despite the fact that he wore military fatigues. A greasy sweatband kept his wild hair in place.

"Boss?"

Major Alan Hawksby's eyes didn't leave the wadi. "Yes, Scottie?"

"Contact. A mile te the west, approachin' doon a finger-wadi."

Hawksby almost smiled. Unlike the Scotsman, the major looked very much an Arab. Firm distinctive bone structure. Prominent hooked nose. Luxuriant black beard. And the green *shamag* head-dress turned up to form a turban.

Only the hard blue eyes might make one question his origins. Yet when he spoke Arabic, all such doubts would evaporate. He was as much an Omani as Sultan Qaboos Bin-Said himself.

"Put everyone out of their misery," the major said.

It was only when he spoke English that those who did not know him realised he did not, in fact, have the slightest trace of Arabic blood in his veins. A fact he actually regretted.

He added: "Remind Dherdhir to follow our lead. I don't want any accidents this time. I want them in the trap *before* I close the door."

Corporal Hamish McDermid smiled. There was no danger of that. 'The Hawk' had made it plain to the unit of regular Sultan's Armed Forces, and their irregular Dhofari guides, that there was to be no repeat of the last time. There was still some antagonism between SAF troops and the Dhofaris which tempted them to outdo each other. That was how the last mistake had occurred.

The rivalry dated back to the early seventies when large numbers of Dhofari tribesmen had been formed into the Firqat Forces – 'firqat' meaning quite literally 'company'. Operating with the SAS, these irregulars had proved a potential weapon in the armoury of the Omani authorities. They had been spectacularly successful in the wild interior – to the chagrin of the regular SAF who had failed to establish themselves against an elusive enemy.

Although the Firqat Forces had now disbanded, their job done, enmity between the SAF and the few remaining firqat guides had not died. It was actually encouraged by some British officers on secondment to Oman, several of whom despised the tribesmen.

But not Major Hawksby who was idolised by the firqats. He actually enjoyed living, eating and sleeping alongside them. Their problems were his problems and, after a while, *vice versa*. He got things done for them because he had the ear of men in high places. He cared for them. In return they respected him, not least because they admired his qualities as a leader and a soldier. That was why they had been uncharacteristically quiet after the fiasco two weeks earlier.

They had been operating on a similar joint patrol from one of their bases, a high fortress of natural rock overlooking the stony desert in the west. Reports had come in of a column of men moving through the network of wadis on the jebel plateau. The ambush was expertly laid. Patiently they waited. For hours under the blistering sun. Then, in his enthusiasm, a firqat solider had opened fire prematurely against the infiltrators from neighbouring South Yemen. The enemy had bolted, leaving the major empty-handed and the firqats somewhat shamefaced.

The danger now, decided McDermid, was that both the SAF and firqats would leave it too late to open fire.

As the Scotsman disappeared from view, Hawksby slipped farther back into the discreet shadow of an overhang on the outcrop.

It was strange, he reflected, that today's action was a direct legacy of one of Britain's most successful but least-known military operations. Whilst the Americans had been winding down their unhappy anti-guerilla war in Vietnam, the British Army Training Team – or BATT as they were known to the firqats – had been stepping up theirs in support of the Sultan of Oman. From 1970 to 1976 the men from 22 Special Air Service Regiment who formed the BATT had been waging a war of similarity, if not of scale. But the results had been markedly different.

In July 1970 the tyrannical Sultan Said bin Taimur of Oman was deposed by his son. The young Qaboos had been educated in Britain and had passed through the Royal Military Academy at Sandhurst to be commissioned in the British Army. During this time his father had continued his despotic rule, which only helped to create the very threat he was trying to crush by ruthless means. Western goods and clothes were banned, and dancing, music and smoking were strictly prohibited on pain of prison or flogging. As collective reprisals, village wells were often filled in, with horrifying results.

There was a seething resentment amongst the down-trodden Dhofari tribesmen on the mountainous jebel interior that the Soviet Union was quick to exploit.

Department VIII of the KGB, responsible for the Middle East area, recognised the importance of this small country strategically placed alongside the jugular of the West's oil routes from the Gulf. They fuelled the explosive situation with propaganda, intimidation, arms and training through the Soviet-backed regime in adjoining South Yemen.

The brave move by the young Qaboos in ousting his father in a virtually bloodless coup came almost too late. When he took power the only place safe from the Marxist rebels was the palace itself at Salalah. Already the country was overrun and the situation seemingly irretrievable.

What followed was to be a classic counter-revolutionary campaign, masterminded by the BATT and drawing on previous lessons learned in Malaya and Borneo.

It was a 'hearts-and-minds' job from the start. The primary key to all was the formation of local Firqat Forces of loyal tribesmen who, it was argued, would be fighting for their own home territory. But initially, it was the promise of water wells that won their loyalty, rather than any genuine belief in the new Sultan.

The fearsome warriors operated under BATT command and also provided much intelligence about their rebel brothers on the jebel. These adoo, or enemy, were trained at special camps in South Yemen, through which also passed recruits for virtually every terrorist organisation in the world, including the PLO, Baader-Meinhof and the IRA.

Next came two other key factors: Civil Action Teams to bring water, medicine and schooling to the barren interior; and a constant flow of truthful counter-propaganda to convince the adoo that the new Sultan really meant to keep his promises. The CATs were also run by the SAS, assisted by more British servicemen who were seconded from other supporting units to provide transport, engineering, medical and veterinary expertise. It was a proven boast at Hereford that the regiment had saved countless more Omani lives than it had killed enemy.

Slowly, but surely, the plan worked, as more and more adoo came across to join the Firqat Forces. Over six years the firqats and small BATT teams, together with the regular Sultan's Armed Forces, gradually forced their way back onto the jebel from the south and east. And, as they re-established their presence in each sector, so the Civil Action Teams followed close on their heels. Eventually they pushed out the last rebel strongholds, back over the western frontier to South Yemen.

That, Hawksby recalled, was four years ago. And now, increasingly, those who had fled earlier to the Yemen were learning of the new Oman and returning for a better way of life. It gave him an immense feeling of satisfaction. Unlike so many Third World countries, the Omanis had done it for themselves – with a little help from their friends. At one time there had been a full squadron of eighty SAS men, now there were only a handful. Some were on secondment, like Hawksby, as liaison officers; others were on contract.

Suddenly two dark figures appeared around the junction between the tributary finger-wadi and the main river bed. Their outlines were stark against the sun-bleached rock. Hawksby raised his binoculars. Two women. Returning refugees or infiltrators? That was the problem. The Soviets never gave up. Having been defeated in conventional warfare, the Marxists were now starting to plant 'sleepers' who they hoped would burrow into the Omani community. The Lenin School at Al Ghayda still managed to turn revolutionaries off its production-line at a frightening rate.

Guerilla wars seldom had tidy endings and Oman was no exception. There were still stubborn and isolated groups of adoo virtually cut off in the jebel. They had no popular support so their existence was an unenviable and uncomfortable business. Nevertheless they still managed to cause trouble while the smallest trickle of supplies was getting through.

"What d'ye reckon, boss?" He hadn't heard McDermid's return. "Old Dherdhir reckons they're women and swears they're adoo."

Hawksby's beard parted to reveal a white grin. Firqat vision without binoculars never ceased to amaze him. But he had more doubts about their interpretation of what they saw. "Dherdhir always swears they're adoo. He misses the old days of the real shooting war."

McDermid gave an ironic smile. "Don't we all."

It was a tactless thing for the Scotsman to say. He knew the major deeply regretted having missed the main campaign. If he'd forgotten Hawksby's feelings on the subject, the brittle silence that followed reminded him.

Again Hawksby brought the binoculars up to his eyes. Finally he said: "Here come the rest of them."

Below, a plodding train of humanity trudged out of the finger-wadi. Men, women and some children. There were also half-a-dozen loaded donkeys and a small herd of scrawny goats.

Hawksby beckoned McDermid to his side. "Quick, Scottie, there's to be no shooting. I reckon these are returning refugees. Order the SAF and Dherdhir's men to approach with caution but not to open fire except in self-defence. We'll wait here in case of trouble."

McDermid nodded. For once the SAS philosophy 'Do unto others before they do unto you' was shelved. Dead civilians, accidental or otherwise, only served the enemy's cause.

In fifteen minutes it was all over. At a given signal the SAF troops and firqat guides emerged like wraiths from the rocks and shrubbery overlooking the wadi. Others approached the column from the front and more still came from the rear. The refugees froze in stunned horror. Despite the presence of the uniformed soldiers, the robes the firqats wore beneath their camouflage jackets made the refugees wonder if they were bandits. Hands moved slowly towards daggers and rifles.

Then Dherdhir, a big bull of a man, whose heavy silver belt emphasised the bulge of his stomach, strode forward in greeting, pushing aside his men and the SAF soldiers. It was a brave act that could have gone wrong if one of the refugees had panicked. As it turned out, it may have saved a needless massacre. Once he was amongst them the tension melted, the patrol lowered their arms, and the refugees relaxed. There were a dozen families and a few hangers-on from the same tribe. Tea was brewed and everyone began exchanging stories.

Yes, they'd fled in the early seventies. They had come because they knew that the stories of change and development were true, despite what they'd been told by the Yemeni authorities. They knew it was true because the Sultan's men could not command the jebel without the firqats. And they would not support the Sultan unless there had been real changes.

Hawksby stretched out his legs and began to fill his clay pipe. He felt at home as he applauded the tribesmen for making the right decision to return.

A sudden commotion took him by surprise. A fight had broken out between one of the refugees and a firqat who had been conducting a search of the donkeys.

"An adoo courier," Dherdhir hissed in Hawksby's ear.

The major scrambled to his feet and swiftly defused the situation by assuring the tribesman that he would come to no harm. The young man's eyes were furtive and wild as he looked around.

Hawksby and McDermid exchanged glances with Dherdhir. They'd seen too many fanatical adoo over the years to have any doubts about *this* young refugee's loyalties.

The firqat handed Hawksby the Arabic order-papers that he had found on the donkey. The major glanced quickly over them. They detailed a secret cache of arms in the hill caves to the north. A powerful surprise offensive was planned. Dhjerdhir was grinning fixedly. Although he'd been wrong about the refugees, he'd been right about the adoo. A perfect face-saver.

"That'll make interesting reading for the Int. boys," Hawksby said. He handed the papers to McDermid for safe-keeping, turning as he heard an excited voice beyond the group of seated refugees. A shabbily-dressed mullah was talking in impassioned tones to a group of young Omanis and pointing at the white soldiers.

McDermid frowned. "Tha' holy man seems te have a bee in his bonnet aboot somethin'."

Dherdhir shrugged. "He is Persian. He is travelling with the refugees to pass on the message of Islam, on orders from the Imam in Teheran."

For a moment Hawksby studied the ranting words of the mullah. His audience seemed unsure. Traditionally, tribal loyalty meant more to Omanis than their Islamic religion, but that was slowly changing. As travel improved over the new roads, the strength of ties to individual tribes would inevitably diminish. And what about these refugees, uncertain of their future? Perhaps they too would turn to Allah for comfort as the heady fire of Islamic fundamentalism swept through the Gulf from Iran.

"One of the Ayatollah's mob?" McDermid asked. "Spreading the gospel?"

Major Alan Hawksby nodded, solemnly. "What we've feared for the past eighteen months, Scottie, it's just beginning."

Part One

IN

CHAPTER ONE

TEHERAN: 0305 hrs, Monday 11th August, 1980

"Jon'i?" Eva Olsen was suddenly awake, her Norwegian accent heavy with sleep. "What iss it, Joni'i? What iss t'e matter?"

His whispered reply sounded loud in the absolute stillness of the darkened hotel bedroom. "Someone at the door."

"At t'is time?" She sounded incredulous. "It iss so late . . ."

Jonathan Blake glanced at the luminous face of his wristwatch. "Just gone three."

Beside him, Eva's naked body tensed with alarm. They had both heard stories about the nocturnal raids by revolutionary guards or, even worse, the zealots from the Centre for the Abolition of Sin whose mansion headquarters weren't a stone's throw from the hotel. But somehow Blake couldn't see them tapping meekly and waiting so patiently.

"You iss going to answer it?"

Blake reached for his dressing-gown lying on the bed. "I don't really think I've got much option."

The visitor was knocking again as Blake switched on the light.

"Jon'i, I'm scared."

Blake tried to look reassuring. It was unusual to see Eva anything less than brimming with self-confidence and bravado. Her nervousness now was just another symptom of the creeping paranoia and uncertainty that had paralysed Teheran since the triumphant return of the exiled Imam, Ayatollah Khomeini, earlier that year.

As Blake opened the door the movement and sudden brightness flooding into the dimly-lit corridor made the short man jump. The swarthy skin beneath his thinning black hair glistened with tell-tale perspiration. He regained his composure and smiled, hesitantly.

"Mr. Blake?" Light glinted on his thick-lensed spectacles.

"Yes." The irritation in Blake's voice masked his own nervousness.

The little man looked apologetic. "Forgive me, Mr. Blake. This is truly an impertinence." He fingered the crocodile document case that he clutched in both hands. "I am sure you understand that I would not call at this unearthly hour without good reason . . ."

Now he knew there was no danger, Blake's instinctive journalistic curiosity took over. "Don't I know you?"

The man looked genuinely pleased to be recognised. "We see each other on several occasions. At the Imam's home in Qum and more recently at his daughter's house. My name is Karemi. Sabs Karemi."

"You're on Khomeini's staff?"

A slightly indignant expression passed over Karemi's face. "It has been my honour to serve as an adviser to the Revolution for Islam."

Blake scratched his head. He still found Iranians every bit as inscrutable as the Orientals.

"But please," Karemi continued hurriedly, "is it possible that I could intrude on your tolerance just a little longer? In private? It would be dangerous for me to be seen here."

Blake hesitated. Despite the inevitable Persian courtesy, Sabs Karemi was obviously a very nervous man. Behind the glasses his eyes pleaded.

Reluctantly Blake stepped aside. "I'm sure this must be very important . . ."

Karemi needed no second bidding. "Blessings for your kindness," he muttered as he stepped quickly out of the corridor. Blake glanced outside, up and down the length of the well-worn carpet. He could see no one lurking in the shadows.

"May the Holy Prophet forgive me! To come between a man and his wife!"

Blake turned as he closed the door. With her usual childish

disregard for modesty, Eva was sitting naked on the bed, her legs curled elegantly beneath her. The long, pale hair framed a puzzled expression.

Angrily Blake snatched the red silk kimono from the bottom of the bed and thrust it at her. "For God's sake, Eva, show some respect for the poor man's feelings!"

She glared at him. "I am not expecting unannounced visitors, Jonat'on!" The way she rolled her tongue around his full Christian name, which she had difficulty in pronouncing, emphasised her annoyance.

He ignored her, returning quickly to Karemi. He was about to assure him that they were not married, when he thought better of it. Morality was a touchy subject in Iran nowadays. Instead he just said: "Feel no embarrassment, my friend. You interrupted nothing."

In fact, as he stood strategically in front of her while she dressed, Blake was more than a little irritated. Eva Olsen was one of the most sensual and sensational women he had ever met. She was the epitome of the cool Nordic blonde. If he had been describing her for the popular press back home he would have called her 'mean, moody and magnificent'. Although her body was almost painfully slim, to model-girl proportions, she still exuded an animal magnetism of universal appeal. Even the Iranians, who traditionally favoured meatier fare, seemed mesmerised when she walked by. It was something in the way she moved, with a tantalising colt-like elegance. And the way her small jutting breasts shifted freely beneath the thin cheesecloth shirts she always wore. In short, press photographer Eva Olsen – daughter of a leading Norwegian publisher – was the sort of girl that every man admired and yet hated. Unless she was his.

Almost anywhere else in the world Blake would have been proud to have her by his side. But in the revolutionary Iran of 1980 she was a downright liability.

Blake offered Sabs Karemi a seat and fetched a bottle of warm lemonade and two tooth mugs from the adjoining bathroom. "It's all the hospitality I can offer you," he apologised. He didn't mention the bottle of Scotch beneath the mattress; you couldn't be too careful.

The Iranian raised his hand. "May your kindness be rewarded on earth. You have already done too much. Let me, please, explain my intrusion. Then I can leave you in peace."

Blake couldn't resist a smile. No matter how harassed, the ordinary Iranian was incapable of dropping the traditional poetic courtesies of his language. It was all part of the natural warmth and charm that had cast a spell over him on his first visit to Teheran, five years earlier, as a junior reporter for the 'Insight' television news team. He had been surprised to discover the innate Persian hospitality, most noticeable away from the big cities. Steeped in a gentle religious tradition, the average Iranian would instinctively offer free refreshment and words of welcome to any traveller or stranger, no matter how poor the host. God, as always, had provided and it was only expected that much good fortune should be shared.

It was hardly the view of the nation held by the world at large, especially since the Shah had fled the country. But it was the face of Iran that Blake was determined the hostile outside world should know. When they were ready to look.

"You know the Imam well?" Karemi asked suddenly. Obviously he was more anxious than he pretended.

Blake nodded. "You know that, my friend. I consider myself privileged to be one of the few Western reporters to enjoy the Ayatollah's confidence. I do my best to explain the case for the Islamic Revolution"

"Quite so. It is my understanding that you have respect for the words of the Holy Prophet and the need for us to cleanse ourselves of centuries of influence from outsiders."

Blake was becoming impatient. "Look, Sabs – if I may call you Sabs? You know all about me, my faith in the Revolution and your people. But I know nothing about you, except that I've seen you in the Ayatollah's entourage. You're not a cleric?"

Krami smiled graciously. "No, I am not a religious man or a scholar. I am but a humble practitioner of law. I was part of the team which was working on the case for the extradition of the traitorous Shah. You know of this huge work?"

Blake nodded. He was well aware of the confusing, hastily-prepared 450-page dossier for the Panamanian government, intended to persuade them of the justification of extraditing the sick Shah. Under orders from Khomeini's Revolutionary Council, a team had been assembled to wring specific allegations from a mountain of seized government papers and financial records. The investigation had involved the Ministry of the Interior, which prepared details of SAVAK's unpleasant excesses under the Shah, the Foreign and Finance Ministries, and the Office of the Minister of the Imperial Court.

It had been a momentous undertaking that should have received years of painstaking research, checking and cross-referencing. By the time it was translated into French and then into Spanish, it was an even more incomprehensible mess. More importantly, it had missed the deadline set by Panama. To the world at large it looked like just one more example of Iranian bungling.

"I sympathise," Blake said truthfully. "It was an impossible job you set yourselves."

"With God's help, even the impossible is possible," Karemi replied evenly. "And it was under God's guidance, as I toiled, that I discovered papers that I wished I had not found."

"From t'e offices of t'e Shah?" It was Eva who spoke. She sat on the edge of the bed, long legs akimbo, toying absently with the expensive Leicaflex camera on her lap. The Iranian turned quickly, pleased at the opportunity to look on such forbidden Western beauty. "From the Shah's offices, yes, but also from SAVAK and the new administration."

He missed the faint, metallic click, but Blake didn't. One sixtieth at $F1.7$, he guessed, on Tri-X uprated to 1600 ASA. It was that sort of superb skill that won his professional admiration of the girl, despite his frequent irritation at her manner. It was a skill that had resulted in some of the most telling pictures to come out of Iran.

She hadn't even been looking at her subject as the shutter went; she was reaching for a pack of cigarettes.

"And you 'af discovered somet'ing in t'ese papers t'at you iss not expecting?" Her voice was clipped and calculating, exaggerating her difficulty with the pronunciation of *th*. The cigarette hung impudently from her lips, unlit.

Karemi felt under pressure and he didn't like it. Uncertainty flickered in his eyes.

"Look," Blake said. "I'm afraid you've just got to decide whether or not you can trust us." He was tired. His brain was cranking around with excruciating slowness and this whole nocturnal visit was beginning to seem preposterous. Unless, of course, he was being set up by someone. "Now, Sabs, just *what* is so important about your discoveries?"

Karemi hesitated for a moment then, as though suddenly coming to a momentous decision, he slapped the crocodile case on the coffee table in front of him. "It is all in here. Copies of documents and papers from many sources. A – how you say? – jigsaw which makes very unhappy reading. Evidence that does your own Satanic Government in Britain little credit. But, more important, evidence that heaps the shame of treachery on the Imam himself!"

"Khomeini?" Blake was astounded.

He exchanged glances with Eva. No wonder the Iranian was skulking about in the middle of the night like a frightened rabbit. He was evidently an intelligent man whose eminence as a lawyer was obvious by the fact that he'd been involved at all in the anti-Shah investigation. If he had unearthed material that was genuinely detrimental to Khomeini, he had every reason to be nervous. His indecision about sharing that information with strangers was totally understandable. Why he should even want to, though, was not.

Blake leaned forward. "What exactly is this connection between the British Government and Khomeini that's so earth shattering?"

"It is all in there. It is much too complicated to explain. But it is evidence that the Imam has betrayed his principles and his people. That, far from breaking away from foreign interference, he has allowed himself to be manipulated." He indicated the case on the table. "The evidence is all there."

"Written evidence?" Eva asked.

"Yes." Flatly.

26

"If this is true," Blake said slowly, "then why are you telling me? Your precious Revolution is likely to collapse around your ears."

"Alas, Mr. Blake, it is no longer *my* Revolution." He smiled uncomfortably. "Like most of my fellow countrymen, I loathed the regime of the Shah and supported the return of the Imam. Indeed, perhaps we welcomed him too blindly. We did not expect him to attract the worst zealots of Islam, many just interested in grabbing power and riches for themselves, like moths around a Holy candle.

"Everyone pledging allegiance to the Imam is acceptable. They persecute and terrorise in his Holy name. They quench their desire for revenge. Even the Palestine Liberation Organisation and ex-SAVAK policemen may join in the purge of anyone who has the vaguest connections with the West."

He looked at Eva and blinked hard. She noticed that the skin below his eyes was red and glistening. "The finger has even been pointed at me, for I number men from many nations amongst my friends . . . So I turned my back on them. For the sake of my family I have to. That has never been the teaching of Islam. But the Imam does not seem aware of this blasphemy. In fact he encourages it."

Karemi appeared to regain his composure as he continued: "The Imam seems to have his own interpretation of good and evil. Since he has imprisoned the people from the American embassy, all foreign aid and investment has dried up. Prices of everything soar like a bird. There are few eggs and little meat in the markets. No oil to cook with . . . Now many people are without work. That is why there are such crowds at the marches and demonstrations . . ."

"Look, Sabs," Blake said, "I can understand why you are a disillusioned man, but what makes you think I'm interested in these papers of yours? At the moment I'm able to get the sort of stories from Khomeini that other reporters would give their right arms for. I can demand any price I like for them on the open market. I've got dual nationality, which means that your Revolutionary Council can address themselves to my Swiss half and ignore the Satanic British bit. I've got it all going for me. Why the hell should I give it all up by getting involved with this yarn of yours?"

Karemi leaned forward so that his face was only a few inches from Blake's. His breath smelled faintly of sugared almonds. "You are a left-winger, are you not?" He nodded towards Eva. "And your wife?"

Blake raised an eyebrow. "We're both socialists, yes."

"And therefore it follows that you support the Mojahedin?"

"No, it does not *follow*!" Blake was angry at the man's simplistic assumption. "We support no special faction in this country. We like the people and I like what Khomeini set out to do. Including kicking out the Yanks."

"And you think the Imam's Revolution succeeds?"

Blake hesitated. "No, not yet. It's a mess, we all know that. But all revolutions take time. They need a period of settlement and adjustment."

Karemi said: "I am afraid I cannot wait that long, Mr. Blake. I weep for our entire nation, but I fear for my wife and daughter. I am taking my family away."

Blake was surprised. "When?"

"Tomorrow, God willing."

The journalist's eyes narrowed. "Do you know Eva and I leave for Switzerland tomorrow?"

Karemi smiled apologetically. "That is why I am here. To enlist your help. When you read the contents of the papers I think you will change your mind about this accursed Revolution. With regard to your present success with writing about the Imam's regime . . ." He held Blake's gaze unblinkingly ". . . The story you will now have to tell will make you a journalistic celebrity world-wide and probably give you a fortune to match."

Eva leaned over Blake's shoulder and studied the Iranian opposite. "And what iss it t'at you iss wanting us to do? To take out your precious document for you?" she asked.

A row of bright white teeth broke through the tense, perspiring face. "Not for me, Mrs. Blake. For Persia."

Outside the crumbling baroque facade of the Masnava Hotel, a red Peykan car was parked beneath the avenue of plane trees with its lights off. Inside an observer watched as one of the ornate double doors opened and a small man in a blue suit trotted down seven steps to the empty street. After glancing nervously to right and left, he stepped into the shadows and melted into the night.

Five minutes later the watcher climbed out of his car and walked slowly towards the telephone box situated a little farther up the street, outside a deserted tea-house. He picked up the receiver and dialled 112. When the police telephonist replied, he gave his pass code-number and asked to be put through to Colonel Najaf Murad.

Patiently the watcher waited while the call was re-routed through to the new SAVAMA headquarters, the replacement security apparatus for the SAVAK secret police. Still in its infancy, the new organisation was poorly administered and had yet to draw its teeth. But no one doubted that under its director Hussein Fardoust, an ex-SAVAK officer who had wisely changed sides, it would soon become as ruthless and depraved as its predecessor.

Colonel Najaf Murad, too, had served under the Shah. Now a quickly-reformed character, he headed a special section with exclusive responsibility for internal security of the ruling Revolutionary Council itself.

At last the watcher got through. "Yes, Colonel, he has now left the hotel. He did not have the document case with him." He listened for a moment, then hung up.

Lights came on in the tea-house as the owner stirred and began to prepare for the first customers of the day. To the north the towering outline of the magnificent Elburz mountains began to stand out in relief against a lightening sky.

Quickly the watcher returned to the red Peykan.

As it drove off, the man who had been watching the watcher stepped from the shadowy doorway of a second-hand shoe shop. He, too, knew that Sabs Karemi no longer had his crocodile document case.

The orange taxi swerved, braked hard and hooted its way through the crowded streets towards the airport.

Normally Blake would have enjoyed the hot and jolting trip, despite the discomfort, as he watched the fascinating mix of modern and ancient worlds jerk past like images from an early movie camera. A dented Mercedes growled angrily behind a weary column of unheeding donkeys; coppersmiths' workshops, bakeries and bazaars bustled on as usual in the lee of overshadowing modern office blocks; brown-cloaked mullahs jostled alongside long-robed merchants, students in jeans, and *chador*-masked women.

It was a world that had once captivated him, but today he stared out of the fly-splattered window, unblinking and unseeing. Nerves seemed to twist his intestines until they felt like knotted tree roots.

"You look worried, Jon'i." He felt Eva's hand on his thigh, reassuring.

He forced a smile. She looked as imperturbable as ever, her flowing blonde hair tucked beneath a silk scarf, her slender body cool in a white cotton drill shirt and knee-length skirt. For once unprovocative.

The amused look in those wide blue eyes irritated him. "I don't find it particularly funny, Eva. We've got plenty to worry about. And you more than me?"

She smiled and looked out of the window. "It iss my secret, Jon'i. Mine and yours. And no one iss going to know unless you tell t'em . . ." She turned back to face him. "Unless you give it all away by acting like a frightened child."

The gross driver, whose buttocks overflowed his seat, swung the fur-covered steering wheel and turned his taxi unnecessarily into Taleghani Avenue, recently re-named after a revered Muslim cleric. Unnecessary, because it wasn't on their direct route, but expected because it took them past the gates of the now world-famous American Embassy.

"Hey, see!" he bellowed. "This is the embassy of the Great Satan! This is the American spy centre where they plot against us! *Allahu akbar!*" He sounded jubilant but, as they passed the high walls, the scene was very much an anticlimax. The humiliated hostages had long since been moved, scattered in houses and prisons, many in other cities, and now only a small cluster of students and revolutionary guards hung around the gateway.

Nevertheless the sight had emphasised the danger of their own position. One slip now, and the two of them could share the same uncertain fate. Glancing at Eva, sitting cool and composed, Blake wondered if she had any nerves at all. Perhaps it was just imagination she lacked. For once he wished he did too.

Mehrabad International Airport is situated to the south-west of Teheran, encircled by ugly ranks of pre-cast apartment developments. It was outside one of the French-designed terminal buildings that the orange taxi squealed finally to a halt. As Blake and Eva struggled with their luggage through the plate glass doors they were immediately aware of the tense atmosphere. Fear hung so heavily in the air that they could almost smell it. There was none of the hustle and excited chatter usually found in airport departure areas. There were queues everywhere, winding in confused snakes across the vast tiled floor. But the seething mass of people was strangely hushed and expectant, like a column of mourners entering a mausoleum. It was unnerving. Only the children seemed unaware, scampering about in a make-believe world, their voices shrill in the echoing quietness of the place.

Eva smiled at the pinched, worried faces in a group of would-be travellers, vainly reassuring. They smiled back nervously and shrugged.

"It looks like t'ey play travellers' roulette," she observed quietly.

"Thank God we're not included in it," Blake replied, dropping their cases at the end of a long switchback queue to the passport desk.

Ever since the obsessive prosecutors in Teheran had declared their belief that pro-Shah counter-revolutionaries were smuggling out the country's wealth, travel for middle-class Iranian nationals had become decidedly hazardous. The airport's self-appointed Revolutionary Committee would wait like vultures for the people on their blacklist: those who had refused to contribute to the Revolution's 'Foundation for the Oppressed'. At the airport there was little chance of escaping the net, because Iranians intending to travel were first required to hand in their passports, several days in advance, with an application for an export visa. Only on the day of their flight did the would-be passengers discover if they were free to go. First the baggage check, then through the security gate, hopefully to pick up a passport. If it was not there, the traveller was immediately arrested and escorted to prison. It was a particularly spiteful manifestation of the corruption of absolute anarchic power.

Eva and Jonathan fell into a sullen silence with the others, shuffling slowly forward every few minutes for the next half-hour.

Suddenly a commotion broke out at the head of the queue. A small round man wearing a blue suit and spectacles was protesting loudly. From the angry gabble of Farsi, Blake realised that a passport was being withheld.

Eva nudged him. "Jon'i!" she whispered, "isn't t'at Sabs Karemi?"

"Sssh!" Blake hissed. "Don't draw attention to us."

She peered ahead as two men strutted forward from a slovenly group of revolutionary guards who had been standing around chatting and smoking. "It iss, Jon'i! T'e poor man! And, look, t'e woman in t'e red dress. T'at must be 'is wife. Wit' t'e little girl!"

"Eva, *please*!" Imploring.

Amidst howls of noisy protest, mostly from the woman in the red dress, Sabs Karemi and his wife were summarily arrested and force-marched into a side office. For a moment the daughter was forgotten, left standing in a state of childish panic before one of the guards turned back. He scooped her into his arms and followed after the others.

Blake looked sideways at Eva. Her face was deathly pale.

No one took any notice of them when they reached the passport desk. But the baggage search was a distinctly unnerving experience. Blake had no need to take out his notebook; he kept all relevant facts and information in his head. After all this time he knew Iran as well as he knew his native country. But Eva needed film and she watched, without expression, as the wall-eyed guard seized the rolls of Kodachrome she had wrapped in a pile of underclothes.

The lure had worked; the fascination of running his rough fingers through the silky soft material, that had been in intimate contact with such an attractive Western woman, proved too much.

"Please," she said quietly. "I iss a photographer. T'ose films iss my livelihood. T'e world wants to know of t'e progress of your Great Revolution."

Behind the wall-eyed guard, his unkempt, blue-chinned companion leered at the distinct outline of her brassiere through the thin material of her drill shirt.

"You want to tell the world, eh, lady?" said Wall-eye. "You tell them Ali says we managed for centuries without photographers. And we certainly don't need photographs from your damn American friend, Mr. Kodak."

Ali turned to his blue-chinned friend Iraj for recognition of his ready wit. He got it.

"I don't like America either," Eva replied, unperturbed, "and I 'af great faith in your Revolution. But I *need* my film in order to live."

"Ah, but God will provide!" said Ali, his eye suddenly fixing on the three camera cases around her neck. "You are a smart lady, yes? You take three pictures at once, eh?"

Iraj belly-laughed. Blake ground his teeth.

"Three cameras is a lot for one lady," Ali continued with a fixed smile. "Especially when a camera can save much precious film . . ." He grasped the rolls of film in his hand and held it out tantalisingly.

She exchanged glances with Blake, who nodded grimly. She shrugged and unlooped the strap of the battered 35 mm Leicaflex. Ali's smile widened as he reached out to take it; his attempt to charm her was spoiled by his yellowing teeth.

"I take pictures, too!" Iraj cried suddenly.

Ali pointed at the Hasselblad. "One lady one camera, eh? And much film, much money, eh?"

Eva raised an eyebrow, wondering if the confiscation

33

would be covered by her insurance policy, as she handed that over too. "And now you give me back my film?"

"Sure, sure," Ali replied gleefully, as he handed the camera to his companion. "We do not steal. It is against the law of Islam."

He made them wait another two minutes while he carefully unravelled each roll, held it up to the light, and proclaimed it 'innocent'.

He handed back the twisted coils of useless celluloid with an ingratiating smile. "Thank you, lady. You have taken no wickedness with your camera and you make a most generous gift to the Revolution! *Allahu akbar!*"

As they left to go to the counter to collect their Swissair tickets, Eva snorted: "Bloody little creep!" Only her accent softened the angry tone of her voice.

Blake didn't trust himself to speak. He just took a deep breath, thankful to get on to the security door for yet another check and to join the next queue building up for the Emigration desk.

An alert-looking middle-aged man in the crisply-pressed blue uniform of the National Police was scrutinising each passport with agonising thoroughness. It was quite noticeable that the scruffy armed guard beside him was interested only in Iranian nationals. One unfortunate, evidently identified as part of the bourgeoisie by his suede overcoat and gold wristwatch, was plucked away from his wife and young son. If he wished to rejoin them there would be a heavy 'contribution' to be made to the Revolution.

Blake shivered as he pushed forward. Next came the policeman in the glass booth who got the queue moving again as he rapidly examined passports, tickets and visas, and brought down his exit stamp with a flourish.

It was with sheer relief that they finally joined the tense, milling crowds in the Departure Lounge. Over the tannoy came an announcement for passengers for the Swissair flight to Zurich to make their way to the boarding gate. Through the window they could see the grubby blue airport bus waiting to take them to the aircraft. Here, everyone seemed happier, despite the fact that the place was littered with guardsmen in their Korean-made field-jackets and with anonymous agents of the Revolutionary Committee. All the time watching, waiting. A knowing look. A laugh that was too nervous . . . that was all it took. And every passenger knew it.

But as the crowd funnelled towards the gate, Blake and Eva exchanged glances, and smiled. They'd done it.

"Mr. Blake?"

His blood froze.

"Keep moving," Eva urged.

"Mr. Blake and Miss Olsen! If you please."

There was no way they could ignore the iron-haired man of military bearing who stood at the checkout desk. Behind him, their arms smugly crossed, waited Ali and Iraj.

Eva faltered. Blake's eyes were drawn towards the man in the smart grey mohair suit. His well-manicured hand stretched out for the passports, visas and tickets. "We'll look after those for you, shall we?" He stepped forward. "My name is Colonel Murad. I am security adviser to the Revolutionary Council."

Eva stood naked and defiant before the two women dressed from head to toe in black robes. Her lips were bloodless and pressed tight as their fingers probed and explored. One of them, her bright coal eyes gleaming behind a *chador* mask, pinched her breast maliciously.

Two tears rolled slowly down her cheeks until she could taste the salt. Still she did not flinch. Her clothes, each seam now carefully razored for concealed items, were thrown at her feet, and she was ordered to dress.

Then one of the women called out and Iraj came in, smirking as the Norwegian tried to button her ragged drill shirt. He was ushered out by the women and returned a few moments later with Blake. Judging by his dishevelled and uneasy appearance, Eva guessed that he had suffered a similar body search.

"You okay, love?" he asked.

She blinked away the tears from her eyes and smiled weakly. She couldn't speak, but anyway one of the women

35

nudged her with the barrel of a sub-machine gun. "Silence!" she spat.

At that moment Colonel Murad entered and the guards fell silent as he looked at the two prisoners in turn. When he spoke his voice reminded Blake of a heel being slowly ground in gravel. "You have both been arrested on very serious charges. Espionage and subversion against the state of Iran. You know what that means, don't you?"

Blake blustered: "I've told you a thousand times, we've done *nothing*!"

Murad continued, unperturbed. "We have information that you were brought a number of secret documents in your hotel room last night, and are attempting to smuggle them out for publication in the West to create a scandal for our country."

The journalist shook his head. "Rubbish! It's rubbish! I'm a friend – well, confidant, of the Imam himself. I've worked in this country on and off for five years. I *love* the place! I've a reputation here, a good one. The Imam likes my stories and the world wants to hear them. And that means a lot of money to me. Why the hell should I blow all that?"

Murad looked impassive.

Eva said: "You 'af found not'ing, alt'ough your witches 'af search very damn t'orough . . ."

The colonel raised his hand. "The guards realised that you deliberately stored film on top of your luggage so it would be found. Now we have, as suspected, found more film in the bottom lining of your case . . ."

Eva tried to sound exasperated. "T'ings iss always slipping down t'ere. It's torn."

"Perhaps, Miss Olsen, but it makes us very suspicious. Last night you were given state documents. Today you try to leave the country. And the documents . . ." He opened his hands forward, palms up. ". . . nowhere to be seen. Now, it follows that, if you are not trying to smuggle them out, you two know where they are. And you two alone."

Eva tried to speak, but the words caught in her throat.

"I now have no alternative but to report to my superiors in the Revolutionary Council. While they decide what is to be

36

done with you, you will be held in custody at Ghasr Jail . . ."

"For God's sake!" blurted Blake. Somehow he had never visualised events taking such a turn. He knew of Ghasr. Everyone did. It was run by the dreaded Khalkali. Ayatollah Sadeq Khalkali, the merciless Islamic judge who had made himself known to the world at large when he had gleefully waved bits of dismembered American bodies at the television cameras after the abortive rescue attempt in April.

Colonel Murad turned abruptly and left the small security room. A few moments later the revolutionary guards had handcuffed journalist Jonathan Blake and press photographer Eva Olsen and had marched them brusquely through the door. In the empty room a copy of the ubiquitous poster of a demonic-looking Ayatollah Khomeini glared down with stern approval.

CHAPTER TWO

LONDON: 2000 hrs, Friday 15th August

For a full five minutes the figure stood at the fifth-floor window of the twenty-storey Century House office block in Westminster Bridge Road. Thoughtfully he watched as a train wormed its way out of Waterloo Station at the start of its run to the south coast.

He glanced at his watch. Eight o'clock.

Now would be a good time, he decided. At least as good a time as any. If ever there could be a good time to bring such news to the attention of the Prime Minister.

But something had to be said about the top-secret report from the Deputy Head of the Directorate of Production 2, the Middle East section, that now rested on the kidney-shaped desk behind him.

He just hoped that no decision on action would be taken, despite the urgent demands of the Deputy Head of DP2 himself. It wasn't the first time they had disagreed and neither would it be the last. Anyway, once it was with the PM, the decision could go either way – his way with any luck.

Then the Director-General of the Secret Intelligence Service, otherwise known as DI6, or more popularly MI6, made a decision.

Reaching for the intercom, he buzzed his secretary. *"Sir Arthur?"*

"Rosemary, be kind enough to get the Cabinet Secretary and tell him that 'C' requests an urgent meeting with the PM, will you? Either tomorrow morning, or before close of play tonight if it's more convenient."

"Very well, Sir Arthur."

The meeting was to be that night. Matters of state security were ones to which the Prime Minister always gave the highest priority. Besides she enjoyed 'C's company: he was a dedicated Establishment man and shared her views concerning the prominent role Britain could still play in world affairs.

She awaited the arrival of the spymaster in the empty magnificence of the Cabinet Room on the second floor, seating herself at the long polished table by the fireplace. Above her hung an oil portrait of Britain's first Prime Minister, Robert Walpole.

Scarcely had she settled down when the Secretary to the Cabinet entered and announced a soberly-dressed Director-General of the SIS. Punctual as always.

"Hallo, Dickie," she said as he sat down next to her.

"Good evening, Prime Minister," replied Sir Arthur formally, ever mindful that familiarity was best avoided on such delicate occasions.

"And what has 'The Firm' been up to that warrants such urgent consultation?" She smiled. "Do I smell trouble abroad in the air?"

"At the moment, ma'am, it is just that. A mere whiff of trouble that may come to nothing."

"And what part of the world are we talking about?"

"Iran, ma'am, I'm afraid."

The Prime Minister's eyes flickered with interest. "I appreciate that there is unlikely to be anything other than bad news coming from that unhappy country for a while."

"You're so right, ma'am. In fact, it would appear that another British hostage has been taken," replied Sir Arthur, his voice deliberately flat. "I only heard two hours ago. Our man has been trying to get a message out since it happened five days ago."

The Prime Minister shook her head slowly. "Who is it this time? Another missionary?"

"No, ma'am, a journalist called Jonathan Blake. You may have heard of him. He used to be a regular reporter on the 'Insight' television programme, but lately he's been writing more frequently for left-wing magazines here and in Europe. Became a bit of an expert on Iranian affairs."

She nodded. "Yes, I know him. In fact some of his articles were brought to my attention last year." She paused, frowning. "But, if I recall correctly, he was basically pro-Khomeini. I seem to remember him giving quite a lucid explanation about things from the Iranian viewpoint. So why arrest him?"

Sir Arthur raised an eyebrow. "That is precisely what concerns me, ma'am. You see, one of our few remaining men in Iran has been seeking out new contacts, which is particularly difficult in a country where so many are being put before the firing squad or imprisoned for no apparent reason. One such man is a lawyer and legal consultant to Khomeini's Revolutionary Council, who is believed to have connections with the Mojahedin opposition movement. He had been involved in preparing the case against the Shah for extradition proceedings and therefore had access to many sensitive documents from several sources. Apparently he has stumbled across some evidence related to what we know as Operation Fulcrum."

The furrows deepened on the Prime Minister's brow. She had come across mention of it only occasionally in the yellow dispatch boxes that contained matters of intelligence, and had questioned its significance when she had first come to Number 10. "Dickie, you assured me that the matter was dead and buried." It was a statement, not a question.

He smiled thinly. "Oh yes, the operation was cancelled back in '78 when it had obviously become too successful. As you say, dead and buried. Unfortunately it doesn't prevent interested parties from exhuming the corpse."

The Prime Minister blanched. "And this Iranian is planning to conduct a post-mortem? My God, I certainly hope not!"

Sir Arthur tried to look confident but, under the Premier's penetrating gaze, he failed miserably. "Apparently he is now thoroughly disillusioned with Khomeini's regime and sees the publication of the details of Fulcrum as a means of bringing it down . . ."

"And us, too," the Prime Minister interrupted testily.

The Director-General of SIS continued, undeterred. "That is where our journalist friend comes in. The Iranian visited Blake the night before his arrest and, we surmise, persuaded him to smuggle the documents out of the country."

"But surely, if Blake is arrested, then it's too late to do anything about it? Details of Fulcrum will already be in the hands of Khomeini's people."

Sir Arthur raised his hand. "No, no. You see, our man followed the Iranian to his meeting with Blake at his hotel. Apparently he was also being shadowed by the secret police. But our man waited longer, in case Blake left the hotel and tried to make contact with someone else. In the event, he didn't, but about an hour after the Iranian left our man saw some movement in the alleyway beside the hotel. A sort of utility area where the waste bins are kept. Lo and behold, it was Blake. Our man took a look afterwards and found the relevant documents, torn to shreds and stuffed in amongst the kitchen garbage." Sir Arthur allowed himself a tight smile of self-congratulation. "Luckily, he had the good sense to destroy the evidence on the spot before the secret police decided to turn the hotel over – which they did after Blake was arrested at the airport."

The Prime Minister's eyes narrowed. "So you're saying that there is now no danger of Khomeini's people getting hold of the story?"

"Well not cohesive written evidence," the Director-General replied. "Not with the assembled document burnt."

"But what if Blake is made to talk? I understand their interrogation procedures can be pretty horrific."

"Ill-founded rumours about Fulcrum we can live with. Most accusations coming out of Teheran are treated as a joke. Besides, if Blake talks, it's likely to be the last thing he ever says. Khomeini won't want that story getting around. It would do him more damage than it would us."

"I doubt that," the Prime Minister observed bitterly. "But, tell me, Dickie, what will happen if Blake doesn't talk?"

"I suppose he could be left to rot for years. They don't

seem to be in such a hurry to let the Americans go. Or . . ." he hesitated. It was a mistake.

"Or he could eventually be released?" the Prime Minister suggested.

"Er, perhaps . . ."

"In which case we'd be faced with the difficult task of keeping him quiet about Fulcrum while in the full glare of the world's media?" She paused. "And I gather he's rather a determined and outspoken crusader against Western policy."

He shrugged. "If I may so so, ma'am, that's being a little speculative."

"It'll have to be considered eventually," she chided and then stared thoughtfully at the chandelier overhead. "What about the Iranian who put together the document? I suppose you won't tell me his name?"

Sir Arthur just smiled. It was traditional that the country's leader should never be concerned in details of espionage or even know the names of those involved in the elaborate maze of mirrors in which the world's secret services operate. "I don't recall his name, ma'am. But I can tell you that he committed suicide at Ghasr Jail the afternoon after his arrest. I gather they threatened to torture his wife and twelve-year-old daughter. He decided that a leap from the window would rather short-circuit their plans . . ."

"Good grief." The Prime Minister's eyes clouded and she shook her head slowly in disbelief. After a moment she said quietly: "The more I hear of events in that sad country, the more I am reminded of the terror of the Inquisition. All in the name of God and religion . . . I makes me sick to think of it. The more so when you realise that genuine missionaries have been seized by these people."

The Director-General nodded sympathetically, although he had little time for anyone who wasted his life in the thankless task of spreading the gospel where it wasn't wanted. To his mind, the world's peasantry already put too much faith in God, and not enough in themselves. The Prime Minister might distinguish between the two, but the Director-General had as little time for fearless Christian missionaries as he did for zealous Islamic mullahs.

His thoughts were interrupted by the Prime Minister. "Tell me, Dickie, what are the chances that we could persuade Teheran to hand over Blake to us quietly and without fuss?"

"A secret transaction, ma'am?" Sir Arthur ran a hand through his straight, iron grey hair. "As the Iranian secret police already seem to have wind of this business, I'd think none at all. Even if they haven't discovered the full implications of Fulcrum, I can't see them co-operating. Khomeini's regime is a law unto itself. There is no influence we could bring to bear to guarantee a straightforward, let alone a covert transaction."

The chair scraped as the Prime Minister rose to her feet and moved towards the mantelpiece, her hands clasped together before her in a wringing motion. "You know, Dickie, I will not allow Britain to be caught in the same trap as the Americans. Since their failed rescue attempt, they have become a laughing stock . . ."

The Director-General felt increasing alarm at the way the conversation was going. "I am merely reporting, Prime Minister. I was not recommending any particular course of action."

Her eyes blazed at him from beneath the upswept golden hair. "But someone has to consider what action is to be taken, Dickie. As I understand it, you recommend that we leave Blake alone in the belief that, if Khomeini's people do find out about Fulcrum, they'll be as anxious as us to keep it quiet . . ."

"The truth would destroy Khomeini's regime." Emphatic.

". . . Ah, the truth. But as we well know, the Iranians are not beyond bending the truth a little to sound *very* different! However, it is just possible that they will discover nothing, in which case, at some future time Blake will be released and, I am sure, will take an understandable delight in revealing the whole sorry story to a stunned world. A story, I might add, that in the course of events would totally shatter our relations with the Americans, the rest of NATO and the EEC."

"You paint an over-pessimistic picture, ma'am . . ."

Slowly, she said: "What does your Middle East Section say, Dickie?"

Sir Arthur hesitated. With uncanny ease she'd found his weak spot. "Well, ma'am, I must confess that the Deputy Head wants Blake out, but I . . ."

"Ah," she said triumphantly, "so at least someone in your organisation's not willing to abdicate the responsibility of putting right the catastrophic results of their own actions."

"But, ma'am, I . . ."

"Does the Press know about Blake?" Demanding.

"No. He has dual nationality, but mostly travels under a Swiss passport. No one's picked up the story yet. That's probably why. Besides, just recently, he's been working mostly for European publications."

"Can you do anything to help keep the news secret?"

The Director-General considered for a moment. "I'm sure there is something. Perhaps we could have some false stories filed in his name. We know the papers he was under contract to. I'll look into it."

She nodded, temporarily satisfied, and looked up at Walpole's portrait. "How many hostages do we now have captive in Iran, Dickie?"

He caught his breath. "Ah, well. There are the Colemans. The missionary nurse Jean Waddell." He hesitated. "Oh, yes, and the businessman Andrew Pyke."

The Prime Minister turned to look down at him. "So our Mr. Jonathan Blake is the fifth."

Sir Arthur thought quickly. He did not want to get the Service enmeshed in any sort of rescue bid. If things went wrong, as they undoubtedly would with such a complex and dangerous mission, there was one scapegoat obvious even at this early stage. Him.

"Prime Minister," he said, slowly and clearly, "although we have contacts in Iran, we have no SIS field agents in the country capable of participating in active service."

"Oh, course not, Dickie." The lady's smile was absolutely charming. "Just be ready for a further meeting tomorrow with the Foreign Secretary and Sir Anthony."

The Director-General rose slowly from his seat. He was

unhappy. A meeting with both the Head of the Joint Intelligence Committee and the Foreign Secretary meant that the Prime Minister saw need for very positive action.

She held out her hand. "Till tomorrow, Dickie. The Secretary will let you know what time as soon as possible."

"Good night, Prime Minister."

"Good night, Dickie." She left him at the door and began making her way slowly back to her private study. As she moved down the corridor, deep in thought, her mind crowded with images of earlier that year.

It was April. The Iranian Embassy siege had just ended. She was sitting, cross-legged on the floor, ecstatically happy as she watched the video tape action replay. Enveloped in the boisterous and good-humoured atmosphere, she had been surrounded by popping beer cans and soldiers of what had, overnight, become the most famous regiment in the world.

As she entered the empty study and seated herself at the leather-backed swivel chair, she turned the question over in her mind. Was it feasible? Was it just remotely possible to succeed where the massed might of the United States had failed?

OMAN: 1830 hrs, Sunday 17th August

"Good grief, man! Heard you'd gone native, but I'd never have believed it."

Major Hawksby was unloading his kit from the Land Rover at the wadi encampment, when he heard the distinctive gruff voice behind him. He turned in surprise, feeling suddenly naked in the sleeveless goatskin coat he wore over khaki shorts. The muscles twitched at the corners of Hawksby's mouth in an unsure smile. It was not every day that the Old Man dropped in at a remote desert outpost several thousand miles from the Hereford base.

"Welcome, boss, this is an unexpected surprise."

The colonel of 22 Special Air Service Regiment extended a short muscular forearm. Hawksby shook his hand.

"S'ppose we shouldn't salute while you're wearing that

45

damn turban arrangement, eh?" quipped the CO. "Sorry to shake you out of your lethargy like this. I got in on that damn chopper you ordered up for the casualty."

Hawksby nodded towards the Sultan of Oman's Air Force Bell 214B that had come to rest farther down the dried-up river bed and where a litter was being loaded. "One of the firqats stopped one in the leg," he explained. "Nothing serious if we get him to Qaboos Hospital soon enough."

"Bloody uncomfortable ride," the Old Man complained. "I thought these Omani pilots were British trained."

"He is British, boss. On contract."

The Old Man grunted. "S'ppose he's gone native, too, has he?"

Hawskby smiled. "It happens if you stay out here too long. The sun gets to you."

"You were keen enough to get out here again." Challenging.

Hawksby slung the Bergen pack over his shoulder and began walking slowly towards the tents. "I love it, boss. Converted to the nomadic life. Fully paid-up converted Arabist, that's me."

"Looks like I arrived in the nick of time, then, doesn't it?"

Hawksby shuffled to a halt. The dust swirled up around them. "Sir?"

"This isn't a social call, Alan." There was a hard edge to the CO's voice. "Something's in the wind. Something big. And it needs special talents."

Hawksby watched him carefully, but the Old Man's face remained impassive. "It must be important, boss, to bring you all this way?"

"Yes. And a pleasant change it makes to get out of HQ. Chance to get the old knees brown too. Besides, I thought it best to see you here, in case you want to select some men from your team here."

Hawksby started to speak, but the Old Man raised a hand to silence him. "Let's walk, Alan, my legs are stiff after all those hours cramped in choppers and VC10s. Dump your kit and I'll explain."

They left the tents as the rotors of the SOAF Bell started

working up a minor sandstorm prior to its journey back to Salalah. It was a hard climb up the steep sides of the wadi to where a noble-looking firqat warrior with a white goatee beard crouched on picket duty, his black *bishte* flowing in the breeze beneath a camouflage jacket.

The CO looked out over the monotonous sea of dry, rolling rock. "So, Alan, that's about it. Plan for a raid into Iran to snatch a British prisoner from a Teheran jail. Singe the old Ayatollah's beard, so to speak." His grey eyes looked un-cannily pale as he gazed into the shimmering northern sky. It was almost as though he was seeing the Iranian coast some thousand miles beyond the horizon of crumbling hills. "We've been ordered to make the fullest contingency plans, and by all accounts we need to treat it very seriously. Tricky job. And a bit of a challenge after all the trouble the Yanks had. I'm afraid it served to queer the pitch."

"But why me, boss?" Hawksby's penetrating eyes met the Old Man's.

"Do I have to spell it out? As you spent most of your childhood in Iran with your parents, you've a better know-ledge of the place than anyone else in the regiment. And you've been on exercises with the Iranian Army since. Both there and here in Oman when the Shah sent his troops over to help out. In short, you know better than anyone how they *think*." He sounded irritated at Hawksby's lack of enthu-siasm.

The major hesitated, choosing his words carefully. "Sir, you haven't yet had a chance to read my latest reports on the situation here. I've got details of a major infiltration planned by the adoo in six weeks' time."

The Old Man grunted. "The whole world knows South Yemen lost the war here back in '76. 'Pity *they* don't recognise it."

"They won't stop until the Russians stop paying out the roubles. And we know they won't ever stop that if they think there's the faintest chance of a return on their investment." Hawksby looked down at the ant-like figures in the wadi encampment below. "I'd like to ensure the Sultan's rede-velopment plans for Dhofar have a chance to work without the Russians stirring up trouble again . . . There must be half-a-dozen Farsi-speaking officers in the regiment able to handle this Iranian raid."

The CO's eyes were as hard as grey granite. "And there are *two dozen* able to handle your team here."

Hawksby opened his mouth and shut it again. The CO added: "If it's any consolation, Alan, we have information that Khomeini is planning to drag the rest of the Gulf into his blessed Islamic Revolution. There are already *agents provocateurs* at work in Saudi, Bahrain and other Islamic states. How long before he sets his sights on Oman with its loyalty to the West, do you think?"

Hawksby didn't reply. He knew that, as usual, the Old Man was right.

"You said two months, Alan?"

"Before the adoo offensive? Yes."

The colonel's granite face softened. "Then you'd better get cracking if you want to be back."

TEHERAN: 0800 hrs, Monday 18th August

Ayatollah Ruhollah Khomeini had been up an hour before the sun. As was his usual practice, he read the Koran for an hour until it was time for morning prayers. Then, following a light breakfast, he had received half-a-dozen local officials in the small room of his daughter's modest white village house in the old section of the mountain suburbs in north Teheran.

He had lived there since his heart attack in January, after which he had been advised to leave his own small house in the Holy City of Qum, some seventy miles to the south. Here he was happier, protected from the pressures of power by his immediate family, but free to continue his spartan lifestyle in the same way that he always had.

Slowly he had looked around and noted that there was not a foreign journalist amongst his visitors. In fact, there had not been for some weeks, except the Swiss reporter Blake. And now, he knew, that man would not be seen again here. His future was to be discussed that very afternoon. The

48

79-year-old Imam allowed himself a rare smile. Truth, as always, had found out the evil-doer. The snake in the nest had been removed, and would be destroyed.

He had found the meeting with the local officials tiring and had welcomed the noon prayers and the simple lunch that followed. It had included rice pudding, a dish to which he was particularly partial; and this had put him in a good mood. This was fortunate, because he knew the late afternoon meeting would make him weary and irritable.

The meal finished, he lay down on his blankets on the floor and began his afternoon nap. Deliberately he kept his mind free of all worries and refused to think about the decisions he would be asked to make when his ministers and Revolutionary Council members arrived later. For, despite his slow and serene manner, apparently untouched by the troubles of the human race, his heart attack had disturbed him deeply. He could not erase the memories of the uncertain fluttering deep within his chest during the two weeks of exhaustion before it struck. It still preyed on his mind. For the first time in his life, the implacable Gandhi-like leader of the Shi'ite Muslims had been frightened.

Hardly had it seemed that he had closed his eyes, than he was roused by his son Hamad.

Already he could hear the whispering of those gathered in the reception room. It was the loudest noise he had heard all day; there was not even a telephone in the house. But even the sound of voices ceased as the tall, stooping figure of Khomeini stepped with his usual slow deliberation into the room where four men waited. Nowadays, he did not normally see more than one visitor at a time. Today was an exception as a matter of state security was involved.

The five men seated themselves on scatter rugs on the plain blue carpet Khomeini had brought from his home in Qum. Tea was served to the men, two of whom were members of the mystical and all-powerful Revolutionary Council.

The odd man out was Colonel Najaf Murad of SAVAMA. He was invited to speak first. For a moment he waited, careful to choose his words so that they would offend no one.

Even he was aware of the precarious balance of power in the land, and the knife edge that was walked by everyone who aspired to the highest offices of state. It was quite literally a case of the higher one climbed, the farther there was to fall – and the more jealous people there were, all willing to give a helping push.

And the two other men in the room would have been happier than most to push anyone who got in their way. The squat Islamic judge, Ayatollah Sadeq Khalkali, who sat opposite like a sinister fat buddha, would have pushed anyone for the sheer pleasure it gave him. Which was the same reason he indulged occasionally in his unusual hobby of killing stray cats by crushing their heads in the nearest available door. Ayatollah Mohammed Beheshti, on the other hand, would get someone else to do the pushing.

Next to the Imam himself, the tall, imposing Beheshti was probably the most powerful man in Iran. Once one of his leader's most promising students in Qum, the cunning mullah had organised the Islamic Republican Party into the most powerful force in the land, evidence for which was its recent landslide victory at the first parliamentary elections since the departure of the Shah. Yet he took care to distance himself from the spotlight of politics, preferring to operate by manipulation and coercion of others, even – so his critics claimed – Khomeini himself. Whenever contentious and dangerous situations arose Beheshti would melt like a phantom into the background, steering events from a distance, away from the public gaze. Never, for instance, was he seen to be involved in the question of the American hostages, unlike the ill-fated new President Bani-Sadr and Sadegh Ghotbzadeh, the Foreign Minister. Instead he was working quietly behind the scenes to destroy them both. Bani-Sadr, because of his ever-increasing powerbase, and Ghotbzadeh, because his influence with Khomeini, were getting too strong for comfort.

Aware of this, Colonel Murad directed his gaze mostly towards the hook-nosed Beheshti, resplendent in his immaculate robes of fine imported cloth. "As directed by you, and with God's help, I have concluded the first part of my investigations into the lawyer called Sabs Karemi. All findings have been detailed in my report."

He held up a blue cardboard folder, but Khomeini waved dismissively. Rarely did he read state papers, preferring to rely on his God-given gift of divine infallibility. "So the man is a spy." It was a statement, not a question.

"*Was* a spy, *Agha*," replied Colonel Murad. "A few days ago he took his own life in prison while in the custody of Khalkali."

For a second the fat smirk on the judge's face vanished.

"Then the truth speaks for itself. God has passed judgment," murmured the Imam. "This man tried to purge himself with his own blood, but he will only drown in it."

Khalkali's fat smirk returned. Confident now that he was not to be chastised, he said: "There are many more who will drown in their own blood, with a little help from me. What of his accomplices, Colonel? Did this blasphemous scum not have fellow traitors in the Mojahedin?"

Murad ignored the rhetoric and met Beheshti's penetrating stare. "The man indeed had contacts with the Mojahedin terrorists, but I do not believe he was a dedicated member."

"Do dog fleas mind which dog they are on?" Khomeini asked.

The colonel smiled courteously. "Indeed, not, *Agha*. But this man felt driven to work with them because he was disturbed by what he discovered while working with secret state documents."

"Huh!" Khalkali snorted. "He was influenced by the devil, and driven by personal greed."

"Of course," Murad replied. "I am sure you are right. And that is why he approached the journalist Blake to take sensitive information out of the country for publication in the West."

Beheshti leaned towards the Imam. "You see I was right to recommend we stamp out all Marxists and liberal trouble makers. Your 'Cultural Revolution' was another measure of your wisdom."

The Imam nodded; there was nothing to disagree with.

Murad was intrigued to see Beheshti at work, influencing

51

Khomeini, at first hand. It had been he who had suggested the purge of all those 'who chewed gum and corrupted children' two months earlier. The first result had been the vicious confrontation on the Teheran University campus between revolutionary guards and left-wing students, but the mullahs had continued on to purge anything and everything in Iran that deviated in the slightest from a strict interpretation of the Islamic code.

Beheshti turned suddenly on Murad. "And you also have this messenger of the devil? This viperous man called Blake who slid into our Imam's presence and would twist his words in articles in the foreign press?"

"We have him," the colonel replied. "And his accomplice. A woman photographer."

Khalkali sneered. "Then she must have the soles of her feet beaten to purge her soul!"

"Quite," Murad said impatiently. "Her punishment, and his, must be your decision, Judge Khalkali. I am just a humble policeman charged with the security of the Revolutionary Council itself. And I have my work cut out establishing exactly what information the traitor Sabs Karemi had discovered that could discredit us so as to make it worth him taking his own life."

"You mean you do not know?" Khalkali screamed his incredulity.

"I am finding out." The SAVAMA officer raised his hand to stop the verbal tirade. "You see we could not seize papers from the traitor, otherwise he would not lead us to other accomplices. As indeed he did: the Swiss journalist Blake. His colleagues had pointed a finger of suspicion, so we observed him. Day and night, including the night he took his papers to the journalist."

"So, what happened to them?" Beheshti demanded.

"I do not know . . . yet. Neither the traitor nor the journalist had them when arrested. My men searched the hotel where they had the rendezvous and found a few scraps of paper in some garbage bins. But most of the papers . . ." He raised his hands ". . . had gone!"

"The journalist must know," Beheshti said.

Murad shook his head. "He says he threw them out because he refused to comply with the traitor's request. He says he did not read them and doesn't know what happened to them either."

"Convenient," Beheshti breathed, stroking his beard thoughtfully.

"I shall make him talk!" Khalkali declared enthusiastically. "And if he doesn't, I shall tear his tongue out!"

"Not a practical suggestion if you want to learn something from a man," the colonel retorted.

Khalkali, however, seemed not to appreciate the patronising rebuke. "He will be made to appreciate the truth of Islam!"

Murad continued: "And while he is learning his lesson, my men will go over all the government papers on which Karemi was working to try and find out what he discovered. Meanwhile Blake should be kept in custody in case he was a willing accomplice with the traitor."

Beheshti recognised that Khomeini was getting tired and irritated with the subject. He turned quickly to Murad. "The Swiss Blake shall be held in Khalkali's custody while you gather evidence. But you *shall* find that evidence, is that understood?"

Murad understood. His neck was to be on the block if he failed.

"You are hereby charged by the Imam and the Revolutionary Council to bring evidence that is beyond dispute." He gave Murad a withering look. "If, that is, you are any good as our personal guardian of security."

"I shall report back to you with the results of my findings within four weeks," the colonel replied quietly. "I shall give you evidence of the information the traitor had unearthed, and proof of Blake's guilt or otherwise." He dared to look pointedly at Beheshti. "Whether or not you want it."

After the intense claustrophobic atmosphere of the inner power cell of the Islamic Revolution, Colonel Murad was pleased to step out into the waning afternoon sun, and back into the twentieth century. He watched as Judge Khalkali was whisked away by his personal gang of bodyguards, and the elegant Beheshti climbed into the green Range Rover to be hidden from inquisitive eyes behind its sinister black-tinted windows.

Murad watched impassively as it drove away down the mountain road. The mullahs, he mused, through Beheshti's Islamic Republican Party, had the country buttoned up tight.

CHAPTER THREE

"Honestly, darling, the whole family's been dying to know if you were one of them." Even at this time of the morning, Caroline Hawksby's voice had the vivacity of a vintage champagne.

The major took out his irritation at her family by stabbing a plump kidney on the crested bone-china plate. She held her coffee cup delicately in the fingers of both hands, her elbows on the table's edge, and peered at him from under a flap of wavy fair hair. "I do believe you're embarrassed by all this attention, Alan."

He pushed aside the plate and looked out across the cropped straight mower lines of the lawn. In winter, from the lodge where he sat, you could see Greshmile Manor itself. But in August it was hidden behind an ornate screen of chestnut trees on the ridge. It was all so green after Dhofar.

"I thought your family had lost interest in my Army career after I left the Cavalry."

Again the sparkling laugh. "Silly, they didn't realise what the Special Air Service was. Daddy thought it was something to do with Forces mail. It was only after that embassy siege business in London that everyone twigged what you did."

Hawksby lay back in his chair and thrust his hands deep into the pockets of his dressing gown. It was silk, monogrammed, and a present from Lady Greshmile. And he hated it. Hated it like he hated everything about Greshmile Manor, the lodge where he lived with their daughter, and their entire flippant and affectatious lifestyle, which was comprised mostly of gossiping, eating, drinking and shooting defence-

55

less wildfowl. Sometimes he wondered if it had been worth all that just to get Caroline.

The memories of last night, when he had come home unexpectedly on a snatched twenty-four hour pass, put it all into perspective. Caroline had been leaving for a hunt ball as he arrived. She had greeted him with a delight that was so overwhelming that it made him doubt if it was genuine. She laughingly ignored his plea to spend a quiet evening in and insisted that he went with her as she couldn't – nor did she seem to want to – let down her circle of aristocratic friends.

Hawksby found the evening insufferable and he purposefully avoided everyone to whom Caroline tried to introduce him. It never ceased to amaze him how she managed to know so many people on Christian name terms. Although he shared her blue-blooded background, his father had not inherited any vast estate and actually worked for a living in the Diplomatic Corps. After a patchy education by private tutors of questionable qualifications in most Middle East countries, including Iran, Hawksby had spent only three years in an institutionalised public school back in Britain. By then he was a fully-developed loner and outcast, and was never to be quite accepted into the social circle of society that awaited him. He had also found he couldn't accept them. And last night's hunt ball had served to remind him of it.

Caroline knew it too, and had done her best to make it up to him. When they returned after midnight to the lodge, she had disappeared while he poured himself a nightcap. Wondering where she was, he had sauntered into the bedroom. There he found her waiting for him, kneeling at the foot of the bed. She was stark naked except for a pair of silk apricot French knickers, which emphasised her buttocks as she leaned forward and beckoned him seductively.

Six months of deprivation had risen in a sudden surge of wanton energy, and he had taken her then and there, like an animal, over the edge of the bed. He hadn't even waited to remove his clothes, or hers.

The demure daughter of British aristocracy had squealed with delight.

Now, as he reached out and poured another coffee from the

silver pot, again he wondered, if he hadn't turned up unexpectedly, if some other young noble buck from the ball might not have enjoyed Caroline's own exotic brand of nightcap.

Hawksby said: "I told you, I can hardly have been involved at Princes Gate. I've been based in Oman since February."

His wife looked impish. "Oh, come on, Alan. From what I gather your chaps whizz all over the place at the drop of a hat. Daddy was telling me . . ."

"I thought you said he thinks the SAS is a parcel-delivery service?"

"Oh, that was before! He was really interested and got all the gen from some of his chums at the club. They said the major who led them answered your description."

Hawksby smiled and killed the coffee in one gulp. It was luke-warm. "You remember Jeremy? I introduced him to you at last year's regimental Christmas party. He's the one your father wants for his son-in-law."

Caroline remembered the dashing major. Although, at thirty-eight, he was the same age as Alan, he was more gregarious and out-going, with a devilish sense of humour. He'd been an instant hit with her, chatting enthusiastically about fishing, shooting, yachting and ski-ing. Immediately she knew her father would have thoroughly approved of him, and she was enjoying herself until his wife, Susan, joined them. Having already been told that she was a portrait artist who had painted many of the Royal Family, Caroline felt at a distinct disadvantage when the major's wife started asking questions. Like a naughty girl caught red-handed at a candy jar, she had quickly made her excuses and withdrawn.

"Don't be silly, Alan. Daddy wouldn't change you any more than I would."

"Of course not," Hawksby said without emotion. "Anyway the word is Jeremy's making colonel shortly. Taking command of the Hussars in Germany, later this year."

Caroline whistled gently. "That's some reward."

Hawksby smiled. "The country doesn't always forget its heroes."

She reached out and squeezed his hand. "Well, you're *my*

hero. Even if you do spend all your time running round the desert like some latter-day Lawrence of Arabia! Mummy wouldn't change you either. In fact when she realised you were back last night she told me she's planning a surprise party for you. Tonight at the Manor."

"Oh, my God! This isn't VE day."

She ran her hand over his beard. "But I'm sure she'd like it if you could shave this awful thing off . . ."

Hawksby removed her hand. "I'm afraid that's out of the question. Odd as it may sound, I've actually been ordered to keep it." Then he lied, "And I have to reach Hereford by this evening."

"Oh, *no*, Alan." Caroline's eyes widened. "Mummy will be shattered. You didn't mention it last night."

"You didn't ask."

"Alan." Reproaching.

"I'm sorry. Really."

Caroline shrugged, disappointed. Then she smiled sweetly. "Let's go back to bed. Just a quickie? Please?"

Hawksby looked at her for a long moment. There was humour in his fierce blue eyes. "How could I refuse?"

Obviously they weren't to enjoy the luxury of the new brick-built quarters. It was a disgruntled Sergeant Forbes who dumped his kitbag outside Hut 26 at Bradbury Lines barracks. The door to the black-painted wooden building, which had been specially allocated to the operation's snatch team, was open and 'Big Dave' strolled straight in.

Six men were standing around the old coke boiler that served as the focal point to the dormitory – a habit which had developed during cold winters, and stayed even during summer months when the fire was out. Like himself, they were all in short-sleeved order, the light khaki material emphasising the tanned faces and forearms.

Forbes recognised most of the men by sight, but only one by name. That was a senior corporal, Hamish McDermid, a lean hard-faced Scot who had shared many a leave with the sergeant in the desperate search for liquor and women in some of the more remote outposts of the British Empire during their younger days. Now in their mid-thirties, they had both mellowed after long service with the regiment.

"Hallo, Scottie," Forbes said flatly. "You're the first bit of good news about this flap that's on. 'S'pose you *are* in, are you?"

McDermid smiled; a rare occurrence. "Y' ken as much as me, Davy. Two days ago I was having it off in a tent in the jebel wi' this Arab chieftain's daughter – a lovely little raver she was. Ach, and suddenly there's a priority message te get the next milk plane oot. Only just got in maself."

Forbes scowled across at a diminutive trooper from the East End of London he remembered from a pre-selection training cadre back in '76—Jim Perkis, more recently known as 'Worzel' or 'Nature Boy' for his newly-acquired interest in wildlife that had reached fanatical proportions.

The trooper, now a specialist driver/mechanic, waved across to Forbes, who nodded back.

"I've been pulled back from a cushy number in Belize," Forbes complained to McDermid. "Training with Gurkhas and a bunch of Anglian recruits new to jungle warfare. Great fun."

The Scotsman nodded in solemn commiseration: the SAS always enjoyed their regular training exercises with the Gurkhas, the only other soldiers in the world they really considered to be their equals. "We've got a gherkin in this op, Davy, did y' ken?"

The sergeant peered over at the gathering of men. "Didn't see the little bugger. Why's he kneeling down?"

McDermid chuckled. "He's noot. They only groo 'em tha' size. He reckons it's 'cause his old dad only had one ball."

Forbes was feeling better; Scottie hadn't changed. "See you've been ordered to grow your whiskers, too," he observed, indicating the thick stubble on the corporal's chin.

"It's disgustin' enit?" the Scotsman muttered. "If I'd wanted a full-set I'd 've joined the bleedin' Navy."

"Makes me itch just thinkin' about it," said Forbes, who normally sported only a drooping moustache. "I suppose this is the bright idea of your bloody Squad commander? He is leading this mystery tour, isn't he?"

McDermid's eyes narrowed. "Don't knock the Hawk, Davy. Leastways till y' meet him. Wee bit eccentric. Likes te get the sand between his toes, if y' ken me meaning? And he's a tough bastard. But good."

From Scottie it was praise indeed, but Forbes wasn't convinced. "If you say so, Scottie. But I've managed to avoid serving in his Squadron so far, and I'm not too pleased at getting seconded to this little lot. I've always had my suspicions about officers with aspirations to be Montgomery or Napoleon. Or T. E. Lawrence."

At that moment four more soldiers trudged into the hut. Forbes recognised Captain Johnny Fraser, whom he'd worked with for a long time in Ulster, and the three other men from the Squadron's Boat Troop.

"Hi, lads!" Fraser called out cheerfully. "We hear there's a party on. Can anyone come?"

"Gordon Bennett," muttered someone. "It's Kermit and his frogs."

"Are you deliberately trying to rub our noses in the shit?" demanded the American.

Ian Ferguson, a slim middle-aged Englishman, wrinkled his waxed moustache. Before he could answer, the band struck up a lively rendering of 'Oklahoma' which drowned all conversation in the first three rows of deckchairs around the Regent's Park bandstand. He motioned to his opposite number in the US Central Intelligence Agency to move to a quieter spot.

As they picked their way through the untidy sprawl of sun-bathing office workers and tourists, Ferguson said: "Just in time, Josh. The attendant was coming for the seat tickets. Not worth it unless we stay to hear the whole repertoire."

Joshua Gibbons, a powerfully-built 55-year-old with grizzled hair and a stiff-backed bearing that gave away his West Point training, laughed gently. "C'mon, Ian, you British are always pleading poverty, yet your firm is virtually answerable to no one. We blindly go on subsidising you, one way or another, just on your say-so that you're broke."

Ferguson stopped at the edge of the lake. "Since when is our word to be doubted?"

"On matters most secret," Gibbons replied, "or where money is concerned, always. And that's why I don't like the implications of your request."

Ferguson shrugged. "My request is simple enough. We'll need close-up satellite pictures of the terrain. You've got them, we haven't. We need them, you don't. It's what our masters are always trying to encourage. What they call two-way traffic."

The wrinkles deepened around the American's eyes as he looked out at the rowing boats on the lake. "You and I both know that there's only one possible reason why you would want such photographs. And you and I both know that there's no way the Administration is going to agree. They're trying to cool the situation over there. There's no chance of mounting another rescue bid, according to us and the Pentagon. So Carter's just goin' to have play it Khomeini's way. If no one rocks the boat we may still get 'em out." He turned back to the Deputy Head of SIS Middle East Section. "How the hell is it goin' to look if you limeys go charging in gung-ho and stir up the whole damn hornets' nest again?"

"Gung-ho is an American expression, Josh," Ferguson replied acidly. "It's not our way. Besides, we're only interested in one man, not fifty-two. It's a question of precision surgery, not full amputation. The patient won't even know it's happened."

"You bet?"

"I guarantee it."

"In writing?" the American snorted. "No, Ian, it's all too much of a risk. For our hostages and the current Administration – not to mention my career."

Ferguson turned angrily and stared back up the slope to the bandstand where the Parachute Regiment musicians were now beating out 'Oh, What a Beautiful Morning' to a soporific audience. "If you'd paid attention to my reports earlier, Josh, you might not be in this mess now. I hate to remind you of this, but I personally nodded you the wink on several occasions what was going to happen in Iran. And you chose to ignore it."

"So your crystal-ball turned out to be clearer than ours," Gibbons retorted. He bit his tongue to prevent himself from saying more. He had known Ferguson for a long time and liked him a lot. But he was of the 'Old School', a long-serving Colonial Office man, who had resented the merger with the Foreign Office in the late 1960s. That resentment had festered to the extent of becoming virtually gangrenous when an abrasive, arrogant outsider had been brought in from the FO to be Head of Middle East Section. In recent years reports from the new man and Ian Ferguson were at such variance that the CIA thought they were just being given the spent ammunition from an internal feud.

Ferguson said: "Your people had their chance, Josh, and I remember we gave them every assistance, particularly using our influence in the Arab world to smooth the way. But you blew it. No disrespect, it was just one of those things. But you blew it. And now we need to do something for one of our poor buggers."

"Which one?"

"The journalist called Blake."

"What about Dr. Coleman and his wife. And the others?"

The Englishman shook his head. "They wouldn't thank us. No doubt they'll want to go back some time. Assuming, that is, they ever get out."

"Then you must want Blake pretty badly. Can I ask why?"

"The PM wants him out."

Gibbons laugh was harsh. "That doesn't constitute an answer, Ian."

"We think he's uncovered Khomeini's plans to spread the Islamic Revolution round the Gulf," Ferguson lied, "and that's very much our business and yours. The whole lot could come down like a pack of cards. That's as much as I can tell you."

For a moment, Joshua Gibbons watched the red-bereted trooper move amongst the sun-bathers selling the Parachute Regiment's LP of famous marches. "There's a consignment of satellite pictures due over next week on Afghanistan. A misinterpretation of map-references could encompass Persia, I guess."

A ghost of a smile flickered on Ferguson's face. "It'll be appreciated."

Gibbons nodded. "In view of the reason behind the mission, I think it's justified. Well almost. But that's my personal assessment. Any co-operation from us is on a purely personal level and totally non-official. I'll deny everything."

"Don't we always?"

The two men laughed, then the Englishman said: "I know the Iranians got hold of a lot of details about your agents and safe-houses during your raid. But do you have anyone left who could assist? We've always thought of Iran as your patch, Josh, and we're a bit thin on the ground."

Gibbons' face set firmly. "What do you need?"

"I want to establish exactly where Blake is being held. And a contact for an escape-route if anything goes wrong."

"C'mon, Ian!"

Ferguson said mildly, "Methinks thou dost protest too much."

"You must have someone there yourself?" the American challenged.

"Not now," Ferguson lied. Sir Arthur had insisted that none of the Section's few remaining field-officers or paid help in the country should be put at risk in this particular 'sand bagging' operation. He could sense trouble and preferred to keep his powder dry; his people might be needed later.

"You drive a damn hard bargain, Ian. But I'll see what I can do. 'Though, understand, only if I can find an individual who will do it off his own bat. Nothing official."

The red-beret walked past them. As well as the Parachute Regiment's LP, he carried a few singles in a stark black-and-white cover.

"March of the Special Air Service," Ferguson explained. "The Paras recorded it for them."

"Don't they have their own goddamn band?"

Ferguson shook his head. "You can't shoot people with

63

trumpets. Besides, I told you, we British are hard up. Come on, it's hot. I'll buy you an ice cream."

"Big deal," said the American, and strode to catch up as Ferguson set off in the direction of the park cafeteria.

OSLO: 1512 hrs, Wednesday 20th August

At the editorial offices of *Idag-Imorgen*, the editor, Ove Gustavsen, stepped out of his glass-partitioned 'throne room' into the general office. He called over a pimply-faced, mousey-haired girl reporter who was the antithesis of the typical Scandinavian beauty beloved by the media. "Monika, have you heard anything from the Englishman Blake? I'm holding a slot for him on page two."

The girl looked up, dragging her eyes reluctantly away from the complex financial feature she was trying to sub-edit. "He has not phoned in yet, but he's sent a story."

"I thought he was flying out ten days ago?"

Monika shrugged. She didn't like the Englishman anyway, and she didn't care. "He must have changed his mind. Anyway, here's the MS."

Gustavsen took the manuscript back to his office and settled down to read it, noting that Blake had evidently bought himself a new typewriter.

He read it over three times, before finally sticking it on his spike in disgust.

There was nothing in it. It was wordy, rambling and, worse, two hundred words short. Blake must've been drunk when he wrote it.

Gustavsen opened the door again. "Monika, run me up a thousand words on Iran will you, child? Put together some extracts from Blake's previous pieces and find a new slant."

"Sure, Ove, why not," Monika replied and savagely put the blue pen through the best sentence in the article she was editing.

Hameda Gulistani wasn't hungry.

"I must go. I'll be late." She stood up, leaving the rest of her family sitting cross-legged around the plastic check cloth which had been spread over the faded arabesque carpet.

"Must you go in?" her mother asked. "It's your day off."

Hameda picked up her shoulder bag. "I know, but they have asked for extra help. There are so many people arrested nowadays, the prisons are bursting. Administration is months' behind and we're trying to catch up. I promised I'd go in."

She had worked as a secretary at the Ministry of Justice for the previous seven years. Her mother had given up hope that Hameda, at 26, would ever marry. However, her out-of-work teenage brother was more perceptive.

"More likely she's going to see her American boyfriend," Davoud said through a mouthful of yoghurt. Like most youths the world over, he enjoyed antagonising his elder sister.

"Do shut up, Davoud!" Hameda snapped, turning to glare at him with an angry toss of her wavy black hair. "And you've got food all over that moustache you're trying to grow!"

Not to be put down in front of the family he replied: "Everyone knows about your boyfriend. All my friends know, and the local guards. And everyone at the mosque. They *all* know you're flirting with an American."

Hameda diverted her eyes. "Everyone knows all the Americans have gone. He's French." She didn't look up. "Anyway he *isn't* my boyfriend. But he is charming and polite – which is something, Davoud, you will never be!"

"Now, now, my children," their mother chided.

"See, she even dresses like a damn Westerner," Davoud persisted, indicating the way her tight-fitting skirt clung to her fulsome hips. "You should wear a *chador*. It's good enough for your sister. The mullahs have said that women shouldn't dress to inflame men's passions!"

"I cover my head like we've been ordered," Hameda replied icily.

Davoud laughed. "Yes. In a Pierre Cardin scarf!"

Hameda turned on him. "Why don't you go and join the *Hezballahi* and jeer at people like me, if that's what you want!"

Her brother smarted. 'The Party of God' was a new militia of street louts who intimidated men wearing ties and women dressed in smart fashions – in fact, anyone who didn't conform to their narrow view of the Islamic code.

"I might just do that," he muttered darkly, as he watched his sister walk out in her high-heeled shoes.

Fifteen-year-old Shirin, who sat quietly in traditional dress, admired her sister's grace and wit and style. "You should respect your elders and betters," she said sharply.

Davoud just smouldered. Why did his family always side with his big sister? It was so unfair. It might even be anti-Revolutionary.

Outside, Hameda Gulistani suddenly felt as free as a bird as she scurried on her way to the Ministry, trying not to draw attention to herself.

It would not be easy to find the exact whereabouts of the Swiss reporter without raising the suspicions of her office colleagues. But if the Frenchman wanted to know badly enough, she reasoned, he might at last be willing to help her leave this damnable country that was being hauled, screaming, back into the fourth century. After all, she knew he had connections abroad.

And he had told her that he loved her.

For Jonathan Blake the waiting was the worst part.

From the first he had known he was receiving special treatment, because he had a cell to himself. It was an eight-foot concrete cube. Grey walls, grey floor, grey ceiling and a steel door. The chipped paint was grey. During the daylight hours the cell was lit from a small barred opening high on the wall that overlooked the courtyard. As there was no furniture, just a rotten mattress, there was no way he could look out. But then he didn't really want to, because the sounds alone were nightmarish enough.

Five in the afternoon was usually the worst time, when Judge Khalkali himself would tour the cells of Ghasr like a fat, toad-like Angel of Death, selecting prisoners at random, and dispensing his evil justice by whim. "Your turn today, my friend!" "You've had it!" "Outside you go!" The chubby bearded face would often smile cheerily. But the eyes, those dark eyes, through the horn-rimmed spectacles, were expressionless and lack-lustre. It was really the eyes that told you that you were next to die.

Blake shivered. Sometimes, at no special part of the day, he would hear the screams of those being lashed or beaten. Sometimes the noise of the firing squads in the courtyard would go on for an hour. Ghasr Jail had only been designed to hold four hundred prisoners, so with nearly two thousand inmates and dozens arriving daily, the firing squad was the only way to solve the accommodation problem.

He pushed away the plastic bowl of thin cabbage soup, which he knew he wouldn't be able to keep down without gagging. Fear and concern over what had happened to Eva, who he hadn't seen since their arrest eleven days ago at the airport, gnawed at his gut. It wasn't helped by the all-pervading smell of confiscated whisky and vodka that wafted up from outside, where the revolutionary guards used it to flush away the stench of blood.

His bowels gurgled violently and he knew that today he would again be tortured by the diarrhoea he'd had ever since his first meal at the prison. Slowly he crawled across to the mattress, beat off the cockroaches and climbed on. The material was damp and mildewed, but he didn't care. Sleep pressed in around him with the promise of escape into the shallow unreality of disturbed dreams.

Although an hour had passed, it seemed only seconds before he heard the footsteps and banging on the cell doors outside. Blake's eyes were gluey as he forced them open. He knew it would be Khalkali's personal chauffeur who showed an evil delight in telling the inmates that the judge had returned from his morning session at the newly-opened Iranian parliament, the Majlis. Somehow Blake had a premonition that today was his turn for a visit, and he was right.

His heart pounded as the bolts were slid back on the door. It was opened, he was sure, with deliberate slowness. Two revolutionary guards, Ali and Iraj, who had never been far away since the arrest, entered first. Blake suspected that it was their morbid interest in Eva that kept them around. That at least, he hoped, meant she was still alive.

The two men stepped aside, waving Blake back with their sub-machine guns, while a beaming Judge Khalkali entered, wearing forage cap and tunic that strained at the buttons around his belly.

He looked slowly around the cell and sniffed. The smile dropped like a stone. "It stinks in here. You don't appreciate what we do for you. In most cells there are six or eight men living. You see, we treat you well. Because you are a visitor to our country." The smile returned, and he kicked idly at the bowl of cabbage soup with his foot. "Still, you'll be going soon. Faster than you came." He laughed suddenly, forming the first two fingers of his right hand like a gun. "Bang, bang! You go, see, very quick from Iran."

Blake felt sick, but was determined not to let the man know he was scared witless. "I've done nothing, Judge. I just want to return home."

"Of course you do!" Khalkali chuckled. "But first you must confess. And then repent! You see we know what to do with spies!"

"For Christ's sake, I am *not* a spy!" Exasperated.

Again the smile dropped from Khalkali's face. "It is already decided that you are a spy. The only question that remains is whether you live or die. Do you want to die?"

"Of course not . . ." He bit his tongue, and restrained the overwhelming urge to spit in the man's eyes. "Judge, believe me. I want to live very much. I beg you for my life, and that of my associate, Miss Olsen."

The judge's face split into a wide grin. "That is good. Then you will sign this confession."

Blake ignored the paper that Ali suddenly waved under his

68

nose. "I haven't even had a trial, so how the hell can I sign a confession when I have done nothing?"

Khalkali sighed heavily. He looked bored. "Then you shall be executed. It is inevitable." He turned abruptly and walked out. The two revolutionary guards waved their weapons at him and, still grinning inanely, backed carefully through the door. It slammed shut with a decisive thud.

Blake's gastric juices gurgled audibly and he slunk back onto the mattress, clutching his stomach. Desperately he clenched his rectal muscles, but could do nothing to stop the vile wet patch spreading over his trousers.

One floor below Blake, in another identical grey concrete cell, Eva Olsen sat with her back against the wall, her long legs splayed out in front of her. Unlike the journalist, she had remained free from any stomach upset because she had made a point of eating only bread and ignoring all other concoctions of soup or stew that were thrust in on a plastic tray.

Even before the door of the prison had shut out the world, she was determined that she was going to get through the ordeal any way she knew how. With a more instinctive sense of survival than Blake, she had immediately discarded any pride or shame she felt. She smiled at the cell guards, talking to them in Farsi, and tried to keep them interested in her as a woman. This was particularly difficult as one of the first humiliations she had suffered on entering Ghasr was to have had her long, pale-blonde hair shorn with a pair of blunt scissors.

Steadfastly, Eva had refused to accept this insult to her femininity and overcame it by widening her eyes and forcing a sugar-sweet smile for the benefit of the men. She had, nevertheless, been careful not to be too brazen, in case she accidentally offended one who may have thought more of his God than his bodily lust. Besides, she had no desire to influence their black hearts and end up being raped by a gang of them. Instead, aware that there were frequently prying eyes at the spy hole, she would deliberately allow a bare breast or glimpse of grubby pants to show through her tattered clothes when she moved.

This, she reasoned, might at least persuade her captors that it was in their own personal interest to keep her alive, and to use their probably slender influence to divert unwelcome interest elsewhere.

So far the ploy appeared to have worked. It had quickly become a sort of ritual and everyone seemed happy with it, so much so that she had even been brought tea, cigarettes, and other luxuries. A comb and mirror, a half-used tube of mascara and extra food rations, which were evidently from the guard's own plate and marginally more palatable than those served to the prisoners.

However, her questions about Jonathan Blake had not brought any response from her captors. They were evidently under the strictest orders to say nothing, or simply did not know. Eva had therefore assumed that it was most likely that he was dead, and tried to put all thoughts of him from her mind. He was gone and she had herself to think about. And inevitably that meant, eventually, getting out with the film.

That, in all fairness, had been Blake's idea. Suspecting that the little Iranian, Sabs Karemi, might have been followed, he had told her to take a photograph of each page of the document on her miniature Minox LX camera. They had gone into the windowless bathroom, so that there would be no tell-tale lights visible from outside. Then they had steadily clicked their way through the thirty pages. It was nerve-chewing work that seemed to go on for hours. In fact, it only took forty-five minutes before Blake had been able to ditch the document in the hotel rubbish tip.

Eva had snapped off the half-inch plastic spool cassette containing the exposed film and carefully concealed it in a sanitary towel which she then wore. As she was not due for a period she had nicked her finger with Blake's razor and spread the blood over the towel to add authenticity if she was searched.

She was. And it had all worked, although for one dreadful moment she thought the cackling women at the airport wouldn't return it to her. Now she had the problem of keeping the cassette safe.

Temporarily she had resolved the problem by using a strip of used Sellotape from one of the guards' sandwich packs to hold it in place at the nape of her neck, hidden by the remaining tufts of her cropped hair.

Eventually, if she stuck to her story, she was convinced she would one day be put on a plane and sent packing. She had heard of foreign nationals being executed, but it was rare. Not rare enough, though, for Blake it seemed. Nevertheless, she would try to smuggle out the film and publicise the story in the same way that he had planned to grab the world's media headlines.

The door lurched open after a sudden clash of bolts. She looked up with a jolt at the shadowy figures in the darkened corridor. A scruffy guard, whom she did not recognise, stepped in waving an oil-smudged old machine-pistol. Eva climbed quickly and nervously to her feet and tried to disappear back into the concrete.

The man seemed angry, his eyes blazing. "You lie to us! You finished. You waste of time." His voice reached screaming pitch. "We KILL!"

She felt the spray of his words and the smell of his breath on her face as her eyes remained riveted on the large mouth with its discoloured teeth. It seemed enormous, big enough to swallow her whole.

The man twisted her right arm up behind her back and frogmarched her towards the door. A train of fluorescent tubes rushed along the endless corridor ceiling above her, bathing the long slabs of concrete in flat cold light. She was pushed roughly through the crush of people around the door. There seemed to be faces everywhere. White, blank faces under the stark light. Some she recognised, some she didn't. Some, including the guards she had got to know, seemed friendly now, even concerned. They were pushed aside.

"Please, you iss 'urting," she pleaded as unseen hands propelled her forward.

Blank grey doors flashed dizzily passed her on either side. Above, the continuous strip of light glared down like the anaesthetised view from a hospital trolley. Doors clanked open and shut. More corridors, more lights, more blank faces. Then stairs. Down, down. More corridors, more doors.

Suddenly she was in the cool night air.

Half-a-dozen revolutionary guards dressed in ill-fitting uniforms stood in the centre of the courtyard, idly fingering their rifles. A young mullah in brown robes and a turban waved and shouted instructions.

Her eyes darted around the high walls of the enclosure. Her gaze looked past the hooded figure, who stood with head bowed before the line of guards, to the unmistakable squat shape of Judge Khalkali. His face was impassive and his eyes, enormous behind his spectacles, seemed unaware of the scene being played out before him like a sinister mime.

Again the unseen hands manhandled her across to the lone, bent figure awaiting execution.

Something about him seemed familiar . . . Then, just as she realised Blake was still alive, the sack went over her head and abruptly plunged the world into utter blackness. She tried to call out to him, but the jute fibres caught in her throat. She gagged.

She heard the distorted order in Farsi and the cocking of the rifles. It was all happening so fast that she couldn't believe it. Eva couldn't feel her legs on the ground beneath her feet. Their muscles had wasted away in an instant. She began to topple.

Her silent cry suddenly found her vocal chords as the order to fire was given, but it was drowned in her own scream.

The six rifles emptied with a clash that sounded like thunder in the enclosed walls, the noise reverberating in a whirling cacophony that numbed the senses and deafened the eardrums.

Eva's slender and defenceless body trembled as she waited for the lash of shells to tear her flesh apart.

Two floors above the courtyard Colonel Murad let the window blinds drop back into place. Slowly he turned into the spartan concrete office and studied the slow revolution of the ceiling fan. But his retina still retained the image of the two hooded, sobbing figures on the ground below. He had seen enough mock executions to know they would both have soiled themselves. He also knew they wouldn't care. Their racing hearts would leave them in no doubt that they were still alive. That's all they would care about.

He reached into his jacket pocket, extracted a packet of forbidden Kent cigarettes and lit one of its contents with a monogrammed gold Dupont.

Perhaps now they would feel more like talking.

CHAPTER FOUR

HEREFORD: 1000 hrs, Saturday 23 August

"And that, gentlemen, is it in a nutshell. The job of this special team is to enter Iran, spring Blake from Ghasr Jail and make haste out of the country before the Ayatollah and his cronies know what's hit them . . ."

The Hawk's incisive tones seemed to hang suspended in the wooden rafters of Hut 26. Below, the eleven men of Operation Snapdragon sat on the two rows of chairs that had been turned to face the small wooden rostrum from which Major Alan Hawksby addressed them. Initial looks of surprise were gradually being replaced by faint smiles.

As usual, speculation had been rife as to the purpose of the hastily-assembled mission team. The choice of the Hawk was an obvious pointer to the Middle East, but no one had guessed its true purpose. Sergeant 'Big Dave' Forbes had got closest when, realising that both he and Hawksby spoke fluent Farsi, he had jokingly suggested they were being sent to bump off 'Crazy K and his mad mullahs'. Once the true nature of Snapdragon had been revealed, all the minor irritations and resentment felt by many at being pulled off current projects were evaporating fast.

With his baton Hawksby tapped the map of Iran pinned to the blackboard. "You can wipe those smiles off your faces, gentlemen. There's no room for complacency. You may think that a rag-tag bunch of religious guards will be no contest, but eighteen months ago Iran had one of the best-equipped armed forces in the Gulf and there's still a lot of expertise there, despite the purges. Luckily for us, the last one was only in July, as you may know. That means that morale amongst the professional forces must be at a pretty low ebb." Hawksby tapped the map again. "But it's a bloody big country, roughly six times the size of the UK, and the population is decidedly hostile. The terrain is uncompromising and the roads we'll be using are primitive when they're not non-existent. Then we have the problem of getting into and, more importantly, out of Ghasr Jail.

"So it's not going to be easy and we can't afford mistakes. In fact, if we put a foot wrong the entire world will blow up in our faces and we'll set Anglo-American relations back to the time of the War of Independence." This brought a few smirks from the audience who, predictably, had not been impressed with the US rescue attempt earlier that year.

"And we're going to have no heroes on this jaunt. Any of you who think this is in any way going to be a repeat of the Pagoda team's public relations exercise at Princes Gate can think again. A lot of people have gone to a lot of trouble to keep Blake's detention out of the newspapers, in the interests of national security. So, even if all goes to plan, as far as the rest of the world's concerned, it never happened."

"There goes my chance on *This Is Your Life*," someone muttered.

Hawksby's eyes flashed to the man concerned, but he didn't allow himself to be distracted. "We have not been told why Blake is wanted and it is not necessary for us to know. In fact, in case of accidents, it's best that we're all kept in the dark. The PM wants him out, and that's good enough for us."

"Good ol' Boadicea!" Johnny Fraser murmured.

McDermid gave him an icy stare. He didn't share the captain's and the regiment's general enthusiasm for the lady.

"Any questions?" Hawksby snapped.

Forbes raised a hand. "When do we leave, boss?"

The major swung his leg over a chair saddle-style and sat facing the men with his arms folded across its wooden back. "Two weeks from today. We've only just had Ghasr confirmed as the target, but Planning had already made a start on the assumption that Teheran would be our destination. So we're well advanced. Unfortunately, as Iran isn't our usual sphere of operations, it's all taking a bit longer. We need assistance from the Americans but it's had to be done through the back door, so to speak, and that takes extra time."

Hawksby sat up in the chair. "Now, although most of us know each other by sight, we haven't all worked together before. So let's introduce ourselves, reading from left to right, together with your special mission qualifications for the benefit of those who don't know you."

He inclined his head towards Scottie, who rose briefly from his seat. "Corporal Hamish McDermid."

"Mission qualifications?" someone asked.

McDermid scowled. "Glaswegian."

As the laughter subsided, the diminutive ex-Gurkha with the permanent broad grin stood up. "Jit Ratna. But you can call me 'Tiger'. Communications."

"Sit down, pussy cat!" one of the Boat Troop called out, provokingly.

On the rostrum, Hawksby's eyes shifted along the row to the next man, the cheerful-looking East Ender known to all as 'Nature Boy'.

"Trooper Jim Perkis. Driver." Another small man. Hawksby mused that the US Marines would probably have rejected half his crack force for being physically unsuitable for soldiering. But in the Special Air Service Regiment it was not appearances, but capability, endurance and experience that counted. Apart from being one of the regiment's top drivers, which meant that he could probably show the Monte Carlo Rally winners a thing or two, Perkis was a leading exponent of unarmed combat.

Next followed the two trained helicopter pilots on the team: Sergeant Dave Forbes, an SAS veteran who also spoke six languages fluently and three passably, and an Australian, Trooper Ian 'Kangers' Webster, who had originally joined the Australian SAS. He'd been flying since his early teens on his father's farm.

The serious, large Fijian, the second driving expert, stood up next. "Corporal Ramami Penaia." He was known amongst his closer colleagues as 'Pogo'. No one really knew why, it just sounded right.

A tall, slim trooper who had been seconded from D Squadron, which recruited exclusively from the Regiments of Guards, then raised his hand. "John Belcher. Trainee brain surgeon." In his late twenties, with hair cropped to disguise the fact that he was balding fast, 'The Butcher' was the team's bush doctor.

Finally Captain Johnny Fraser and his men from the Squadron's Boat Troop, which specialised in boat handling and general underwater operations, introduced themselves: Sergeant Turner, and two Corporals, Mark Benjamin and Bill Mather.

"You'll all get plenty of time to know each other better," the major said, "as between now and the mission start you're all in pre-op confinement.

"I'm dividing this small troop into three patrols. The patrols that will perpetrate the snatch will comprise Dave Forbes, who speaks Farsi like a native – so I'm told – and Kangers Webster. That gives us two chopper pilots. Then we'll have Tiger on the radio, along with myself. The theory is that, in case of trouble, Dave Forbes and I can talk our way out of it."

Hawksby paused briefly whilst the remaining eight men reconciled themselves to the fact that they would not have the dubious honour of penetrating the final bullseye of the target. There were some glum expressions.

As the chosen three in the audience nodded to each other with evident satisfaction, he continued: "Hamish McDermid will command the back-up patrol with our bush doctor, John Belcher, in case our hostage is in poor health. And, of course, our two drivers will have to find vehicles to spirit us away from the scene of our misdemeanour. If we manage to acquire helicopters, of course, this may not be necessary. It's early stages yet, so anything could happen."

Hawksby's keen gaze shifted to the four men from the Boat Troop. "Johnny Fraser's motley crew are here because we anticipate a wet entry for the rescue team, via the Caspian Sea." He rose from his chair and strode back to the blackboard. "For those of you who failed your GCE Geography, that's the big pond north of Teheran. And there's a damned great mountain range in the way."

"Wee bit close te the Ruskies ennit, boss?" McDermid observed.

A glint of humour flickered in the major's eyes. "Yes, it is, and the RAF are a bit uppity about it. However, I think they see that it's the only practical solution to a fast penetration and retrieval.

"Anyway it'll be Johnny Fraser's team's responsibility to make their own way in and complete the reconnaissance. McDermid's patrol will provide the reserve in case we need to switch the teams around."

He moved slowly back to the chair and, raising his booted left foot, placed it on the seat.

Forbes watched with interest. He was an imposing bugger all right. Tall and distinguished. The way he let his head drop between his shoulders, and the distinctly crooked nose, gave him the menacing look of a bird of prey that had earned him his nickname.

Hawksby continued: "When we dismiss I want to see Captain Fraser, Sarn't Forbes and Corporal McDermid for a meeting with Planning. As soon as our plans are finalised we'll have another full briefing." He looked slowly around at the team. He knew that many of them would be weighing him up in the same way he was them. So far they seemed happy enough, but he wondered if they would be when he finished. They were now all waiting for how the preparation would affect each one of them individually. They would not, he was sure, be disappointed.

"Commencing at 0400 tomorrow we'll be leaving for the secure enclosure of Sennybridge Camp for personnel mission preparation. The usual stuff with weapons training and an unarmed combat brush-up course, and some fast cross-country night hacks to loosen up those slack leg muscles. We'll select equipment and stores and establish load dispersal. In the second week the chopper pilots will go to Middle Wallop for a crash refresher course and the Boat Troop patrol can polish up its procedures for a night sea drop with the RAF. The rest of us will move to Capel Curig battle camp in North Wales for mountain driving and general mission manoeuvres. We'll then meet up for a full simulated exercise rehearsal involving all elements, including some Close Quarters Combat training on the mock-up that the engineers are starting to construct."

Hawksby took his foot off the chair. This bit, he knew, would not go down well. "From tomorrow morning, Sarn't Forbes and I will conduct our conversation only in Farsi. An expert from our Army Languages College at Beaconsfield will be visiting us and he'll attempt to teach the rest of you some basic phrases. The best one, I predict, will be: 'I am sorry I do not understand. I am deaf.'" This brought a low rumble of mirth from the team. "Planning has managed to collect a number of fairly recent travel books and tourist guides on Iran which will be circulated to you. I expect you to read them at every spare moment you have, so that you can get a good feel of the place. We are also trying to locate film footage from both the BBC and the private film libraries."

In the first row Forbes nodded to himself in silent approval. He was not afraid of hard work, especially on mission preparation, and appreciated the major's thorough approach. Perhaps, despite the rumours he had heard, the Hawk wouldn't be so bad a commander to serve after all.

His self-satisfied illusions were about to be thoroughly crushed.

"Now," Hawksby said, "I come to the question of personal preparedness. Before your medical this morning, I instructed the MO to give me a special report. This I have received and I am not at all pleased with what I find." He pulled a sheet of paper from his tunic pocket and studied it for a moment. "I expect my men not just to be fit, but to be the *fittest*" – he emphasised the final syllable with relish – "And that means able to run – not jog, *run* – five miles at the drop of a hat with a 30lb pack. And, as I don't want any of you dropping dead on me with coronaries, I expect to be able to pinch no more than half-an-inch spare midriff. That's a quarter inch out, and a quarter inch back – before you all start playing with yourselves." He looked around at the horrified gathering with a steady unsmiling gaze. "In other words, just about *fat free*! Men who've been serving with my squadron in Oman know my feelings on the subject and, I'm pleased to say, they appear to be least at fault. Those of you who have been seconded in, however, will have your work cut out!"

"*Jesus!*" breathed Forbes. McDermid smirked mischievously.

Hawksby held up his hand. He was aware that telling a professional SAS soldier that he wasn't properly fit was the biggest insult you could pay him. Virtually everyone did regular running and weight-training of their own volition, because they couldn't stand the excruciating agonies of trying to get fit the regiment way from a position of anything less than top physical shape. "You all know your lives may depend on it. But more importantly, so might mine." Hawksby smiled to let them know it was a joke; but no one seemed to appreciate it.

The Hawk stood up and handed the sheet to Sergeant Forbes, who took it reluctantly. "You're a big boy, Forbes, so I'll put you in charge of getting everyone in tip-top condition by the off. After all, as you'll see from the list, you've got more to lose than most. John Belcher will keep an eye on you all to check you're all alive in two weeks time, and not just pretending."

As Hawksby stepped back onto the rostrum it was a deeply hurt Forbes who turned to McDermid. "What's up with the guy, Scottie? Just 'cause *he's* as skinny as a rake, why does he expect the rest of us to look like a platoon of sodding Twiggies?"

The corporal shrugged. "Dunno, laddie. Someone told me t'was because his ma didna breast feed him as a bairn."

"He had a mother?"

"That's all, gentlemen," the major concluded. "We'll all meet on the parade ground at 0400 hours tomorrow for a nice slow five mile run before breakfast . . . to break you all in gently."

Hawksby closed his file with a snap. The first briefing was over.

That afternoon found the major, Forbes, McDermid and Captain Fraser making a start on the serious business of the mission: preparation.

The Planners, a specialist team detached from the Intelligence Corps, an SIS Middle East expert and members of the SAS's own 'Kremlin' intelligence unit, were already well-established in the Snapdragon operations centre which had strictly limited key-holder access.

Overlapping large-scale relief maps covered the far wall to represent the whole of Iran. They showed every city, town and village, every main and secondary road and track, together with all telephone, pipeline and electricity pylon systems, and all landmarks visible from the air. Civil and military airfields were all clearly marked, together with radar stations and navigational beacons.

"Of course, we don't know how much of this is still in operation." The man who spoke with a distinctive Oxford accent was a slim, dapperly-dressed civilian in an expensive light-grey mohair suit. When he smiled, with even white teeth, his thin lips curled upwards in perfect line with his thin up-turned waxed moustache. His hair was thin and black, parted just to one side of centre. As he looked to be in his late forties, Sergeant Forbes guessed he'd been at the Grecian 2000. But the rest of him looked genuine enough, including the wrinkled laughing eyes, and the firm warm handshake.

"Ian Ferguson," Hawksby introduced the man to the SAS leaders.

The man smiled. "I'm the Deputy Head of the Section at SIS. I'm pleased to meet you all. I've worked a lot with Major Hawksby in Oman, so I'm sure we'll all get on well."

For a moment the soldiers watched as two members of the planning team practised their uncanny skill in identifying wild landscape photographs from tourist guides and travel brochures. Initially guided by the captions, they read maps as easily as most civilians understood a daily newspaper. Within seconds they would pin the photograph at the side on the wall, with a line running to an exact point on the map. Such ground views of the terrain, over which the team would travel, would play a vital part in orientation and familiarisation when they were dropped into a hostile, unknown landscape.

Forbes turned to Hawksby. "What's the plan for entry, boss?"

As the major explained, Forbes stroked his moustache thoughtfully. At the moment the plan sounded a bit bald, but he knew that at this stage it was only a composite of a number of contingency plans held in constant readiness. These were a mixture of actual operations and fully detailed exercise plans that were constantly updated and reviewed. This was the only way the SAS was able to respond instantly and effectively to any emergency. In fact, the sergeant recognised the first element of the plan. He had actually been part of the Sabre team that, two years earlier, had dropped into the Baltic, off the coast near Gdansk, as part of a mission to rescue an important Polish government official whose days as a British agent were more numbered than he knew.

Still, this time preparations would take considerably longer. Iran had never been seriously considered as a possible sphere of operations and so more research than normal would be needed and, presumably, some outside help.

Ferguson confirmed this. "We don't envisage you having to go anywhere near the Iranian military. In fact we'd like you to keep as far away from them as possible." The waxed moustache flicked upwards to emphasise the smile. "There are plenty of helicopters still in Iran. The trick is to find one that's serviceable. And there we have some information from our American friends."

"The same source tha's confirmed Ghasr as the target?" McDermid asked.

"Yes, one of their few remaining agents whose cover hasn't been blown. Secret papers were left behind when the Americans had that mishap in the desert. Safe-houses, agents, codes and escape routes, the lot. It's one of the main reasons they won't try again."

"I'm surprised they've co-operated at all." Captain Fraser's view echoed all their feelings.

A ghost of a smile passed over Ferguson's face. "It took a little arm-twisting, I admit."

Forbes shook his head. "The Yanks think it's too dodgy, yet we're willing to try it. For God's sake, don't we have anyone of our own? I'd feel happier."

Ferguson looked uncomfortable.

"My feeling exactly," Hawksby said crisply. He'd already decided that there was no point in going over old ground and creating ill-feeling. "But our friends in SIS insist that we have no one of our own who can assist, so that's an end to it."

McDermid instantly recognised the message behind the major's tone; he had served with the Hawk too long not to. The wiry Glaswegian glanced sideways at Dave Forbes. Evidently, too, the big bluff sergeant wasn't as dumb as he made out.

HEREFORD: 0009 hrs, Wednesday 27th August

Despite the team's misgivings at having to rely on a contact from an obviously reluctant CIA, the American's help was to prove its worth within the next few days.

The most significant event was the arrival of the photographs taken by one of the US geo-stationary satellites covering the region of Iran and Afghanistan. Due to their low orbit above the target zone, gravity soon dragged the satellites down into the atmosphere: their short life therefore made them expensive. But, at an operational height of only eighty miles, the clarity and definition of the pictures was superb. So good, in fact, that it was often possible to read the number on a car registration plate.

Hawksby pored over them late into the night. Alone in the operations room, he laboriously moved the wire legs of the Stereoscope along the overlapping nine-inch sheets that covered their anticipated lines of approach and escape from Teheran. Whenever additional detail was demanded three-foot enlargements would be ordered and run under special magnification stereos. Peering into the twin lenses he could see the bird's-eye view of fields, bleak mountains and remote villages thrown into startling three-dimensional relief by the device. Every road and track could be explored in safety to see what advantage it offered, or danger it concealed. Once on the mission one wrong turning, judged from a map that was just a month out-of-date could prove disastrous: a bridge that couldn't take the weight of their vehicles; a recently resurfaced road that gave an unexpected bonus to pursuing enemy . . . Ah, debris from a landslide was blocking the hairpin mountain track completely.

Hawksby sat up and rubbed the back of his hand over his eyes. He glanced at his watch. Already it was an hour unto the new day and he was due to lead the cross-country run at 0400 hours. He plucked the red Chinagraph pencil from his breast pocket and carefully circled the position of the land-slide on the clearfilm surface of the photograph.

Later, he would check this and other points against the JARIC analysis. At RAF Brampton, the Joint Air Recon-naissance Intelligence Centre also had copies of the film which they were putting under intense scrutiny, translating every blob and blur into pin-point fact. With unbelievable ease, developed from years of practice, they would correct lense-angle distortions and establish exact heights of land-marks and the size of buildings or natural features. They would identify a water tower here, a mosque there, a water well and an abandoned car, a lump of camel dung or a hole in the road. They were at this moment assessing each of Snapdragon's routes foot by foot, so that the entire team, but particularly the drivers, would know more about the terrain than the natives who lived there.

These finite and detailed analyses would then be taken over by a round-the-clock team of resident map-makers at Hereford provided by the Royal Engineers. Hawksby antici-pated that the intricate map strips, which on the mission would be destroyed as each section was passed, would be ready by the end of the first week.

Shortly after, the model makers would reveal their awe-inspiring work in papier-mâché, plaster and flock: a com-plete, solid interpretation of the most intricate geographical aspects of the mission, including a cutaway model of Ghasr Jail, which would have to be memorised. A full-size version was already under construction, built like a film set to enable realistic assault training.

Hawksby finally lay back in his chair. He was mentally and physically drained. To go on now would be to invite mistakes. Others would check his work, as he would check theirs, but there was no point in provoking an error that might waste valuable time. There was precious little of it.

He stood up, stiff-legged, from the table. Tugging the short clay pipe from the deep pocket of the goatskin waistcoat he habitually wore over his drill shirt, he began filling the bowl with tobacco.

Eddies of blue smoke drifted over the pools of light that shone over the photographs and maps on the table. He only had to squint his eyes a fraction and he was there, seeing the two Pink Panther Land Rovers picking their way through the Iranian night on a boulder-strewn mountainside.

He killed the lights and took one last look into the darkened room. Inexplicably he thought of Caroline. For a moment he allowed his mind's eye to linger on the contours of her body. Funny, he mused, how always when he thought of her they were making love. Always.

"Just 'oo in the 'ell do you think you are?" bawled the NCO instructor. "Bloody Bodie and Doyle?"

The tall sandy-haired Kangers Webster, and Tiger Ratna stood back-to-back in the false corridor at the Close Quarter Battle (CQB) training centre and admired their handiwork.

They looked faintly ridiculous, the little Gurkha only half the size of the rangy Australian.

As the fog of gunsmoke subsided, the two cardboard cut-out figures that had sprung up in the open doorway, could be seen to have blackened 9 mm bullet holes in the target areas around the heart.

Kangers slipped the safety on the small Uzi sub-machine gun. "I call it bloody good shootin', Sarge. Looks like we got one each."

"And smoke very thick," Tiger piped in, his white teeth gleaming in the dirt-smudged face.

The instructor sighed. "Reckon you're a right couple of crack-shots, don't you, lads?"

Kangers grinned laconically. "Not bad."

"Then I hope t'God you two berks never have to rescue me." He tapped the full-size photographs of the faces stapled to the cut-outs. The first was one of an unshaven Iranian student taken from a press photograph; the other was of a bald man with a stubbly blond beard. "Because, my intrepid heroes, you have just shot the man you've come to rescue."

"Awe, c'mon," Webster said angrily. "Looks nothin' like him."

Tiger nodded, still grinning ferociously. "Kanger's right, Sarge. This guy's got no hair."

The instructor shook his head sadly. "We don't train 'em like we used to, do we? What the hell do you think Blake'll look like after a month in a Persian clink?" His eyes burned angrily. "They'll bleedin' shave 'is bonce and they ain't gonna 'and out razors to prisoners now, are they? Jesus, our photo retouchers 'ave got a better idea than you two cowboys!"

Kangers smacked his forehead hard with the palm of his hand. "Oh, bloody hell, I never thought of that."

For once Tiger's smile disappeared.

"C'mon," the instructor said patiently. "I think we'd better try again before we move on to live targets, don't you?"

Forbes read through the hastily-revised DIS document for the third time. He was not impressed.

The report had been prepared by the Defence Intelligence Staff in Whitehall, and comprised valuable but low-grade logistical, political and economic reports on the countries in which the British Armed Forces were expected to operate. It was compiled from information supplied by consulates, defence attachés and 'confidential' contributors. Much of it contained geographical and logistical information vital to the smooth running of an operation like Snapdragon.

Forbes tossed the stapled A4 folder aside. There were too many question-marks in this one. To start with, Iran wasn't reckoned to be within the British sphere of operations, the Americans always having had it well sewn up until recently. That meant the DIS info was only likely to be used for joint exercise purposes. It evidently hadn't been up-dated for several years. But, more importantly, the writers obviously didn't have a clue about the current political, economic or military state of the country. The entire document was full of loose ends, cautious generalisations, and dotted with reservations about factual accuracy.

"So much inspired guesswork!" Forbes muttered aloud.

"That's wha' I thought, Davy." McDermid came noisily into the operations centre carrying a bundle of folders. "Te be perfectly honest wi' ye, Davy, I think this'll be more use te us."

The sergeant immediately recognised the highly-classified coloured files which indicated that they contained transcripts of intercepted radio traffic from the Government Communications Headquarters at Cheltenham.

That, at least, was the best news he had heard all day. Although he had soon forgotten his initial resentment about being pulled back from Belize, as the magnitude of Snapdragon became evident, the lack of solid information on Iran was beginning to depress him. He was convinced it was going to be the most exciting mission of his life; he was also starting to think that it might be his last.

The Scotsman grinned. "I also understand there's a special consignment of Iranian television video tapes on its way te us from the BBC Monitoring Service at Caversham." He was obviously delighted. "The Hawk's arranged for us te sit down tonight an' go through 'em all. Including some long monologues from ol' Crazy K himself. Sorta see inte the mind o' the enemy, so te speak."

Forbes groaned, then thought better of it. Almost anything was better than the usual long chat with Hawksby in Farsi.

"Did you know that when the praying mantis mates, the female bites the male's 'ead off?" Jim Perkis asked casually. "Apparently it really gets 'im going."

"Oh, give over, Perkis," Trooper John Belcher said through a mouthful of sandwich. "I'm in the middle of eating my lunch!"

"Sorry, Butcher," the little East Ender said, jumping down from the bonnet of the Land Rover where he'd sat to have a brew-up of tea. "You're a bit squeamish though, aren't you? For a bleedin' bush doctor, I mean. 'Wouldn't fancy you extractin' a bullet from my arse. I'd 'ave bloody gangrene by the time you came round."

Belcher, a one-time failed medical student, who was the son of a Harley Street gyny specialist, did not take kindly to any slight on his skills as an SAS medic. Although he had treated hundreds of gunshot and knife wounds, splinted legs in the middle of the Malayan jungle, amputated limbs and immunised entire villages in remoter regions of the earth, John Belcher had never quite got over his father's obvious disgust when he announced he was giving up his medical studies to join the Army. He had made the decision after a particularly bad day in St Thomas's when it dawned on him that he'd rather kill half his snivelling, self-centred patients than cure them. So he left the medical profession before he did.

When at twenty-six, he had been accepted into 22 Special Air Service Regiment, he was surprised but pleased to find they valued his past experience. Two years later he was a fully qualified unqualified 'Bush Doctor' who knew more about practical surgery, osteopathy and tropical diseases than the average doctor would learn in a lifetime. Nevertheless, despite his undoubted medical prowess, Belcher still smarted at his father's stubborn refusal to accept that he had achieved anything more than being the Army equivalent of a male nurse.

He finished his sandwich and delicately licked the remnants of fish paste from his fingers. "Any more cheek from you, Perkis, my son, and I promise you that if ever I have to operate on you, it'll be without the benefit of an anaesthetic. It pays you to select your enemies very carefully in our line," he added with good-humoured menace.

"The Butcher's right," Pogo added solemnly as he began his third Mars Bar – a delicacy to which he was totally addicted. The serious big Fijian wasn't given to lightweight banter unless he could throw in some comment so deep and profound that the conversation tended to grind to a confused halt. "I had this friend in D Squadron who had much dental work done and couldn't pay the man for the work. Dentist much annoyed. When my friend come back on leave he find that when his wife went to have teeth fixed, dentist drilled out all her gold fillings while she under the gas."

Belcher ran a hand over his patchy crop of thinning hair. "That's disgusting, Pogo old boy."

"Would never 'appen on the National 'Ealth," Perkis quipped.

"Anyway, what's all this about the sex life of the praying mantis?" Belcher demanded. "You've got sex on the brain, man. Remind me to give you a thorough examination when we get back to camp."

"With your cold 'ands? Not bleedin' likely," Perkis laughed.

Pogo's eyes were very dark and serious beneath the frizzy mop of black hair. "It is because his wife has little one on the way, Butcher. He cannot get any jiggy on his leave, so his mind always turn to erotic things."

"Like biting the heads off insects?" Belcher was appalled. "Is this true, my lad? Your missus has got one up the spout?"

Perkis beamed. "Yep. All me own work."

Belcher shook his head. "Disgraceful. You should never be allowed on a mission like this, not with a pregnant wife on your mind. You'll be a positive liability."

Pogo thought he was serious and tried desperately to find a profound statement. He couldn't think of one, so he said: "I think it is time we get on."

The other two nodded their agreement and made their way back to the second Land Rover, parked behind the first on the windswept sunny slopes of the Brecon Beacons. Butcher climbed into the navigator's seat and picked up the clipboard that listed the manoeuvres they still wanted to practise that afternoon. Tomorrow it would be a visit to the Metropolitan Police Driving School at Hendon to brush up on high-speed pursuit driving. Then back to Hereford to plan the load distribution of provisions and equipment for the two vehicles.

He glanced sideways at Perkis' cheerful face. He was like a peacock with two tails out in the countryside, Belcher mused. After a childhood and a mis-spent youth in the brick and concrete confines of East London, the sudden adaptation to virtually permanent life in the field with the regiment had come as a shock to his system. Others, less kindly, had said to his brain.

He had looked about him with child-like wonder at the activities of birds, insects and general wildlife. It was as though the emphasis of training on survival and living off the land had suddenly pulled this mysterious world into sharper focus. It had given him a hobby for the first time in his life. For two years he had spent all his spare cash on natural history books, reading avidly every night until, from knowing less about nature study than the average squaddie, he had become something of an expert.

His amazement and awe had been infectious as he passed on his tit-bits of 'useless information' to all and sundry. Everyone had been fascinated, particularly as they themselves were frequently in a unique position of closeness to nature. After all, they were always observing and stalking the most cunning and dangerous animal of all.

Although nowadays, a marriage and four years' service later, Perkis rarely gave his naturalist's anecdotes, the 'Nature Boy' label still stuck. No doubt it always would.

"When did you say she was going to drop it, Perkis?" Belcher asked.

The driver switched on the engine. "That's no way for a doctor to be talking."

"I'm not a proper doctor, Perkis," Belcher replied, and waved to Pogo to follow them. "That's the difference. I'm a pilgrim first and a medic second."

Nature Boy shifted the Land Rover into first and let out the clutch. "Janet's due in about three weeks."

"Shame."

"Why?"

"I was going to offer to deliver it for you."

"You *must* be joking!"

CHAPTER FIVE

TEHERAN: 1100 hrs, Thursday 4th September

Curt Swartz Jnr. was a worried man. And he had good reason to be.

Sitting at the long table in the Alborz Tea House, he had the distinct feeling that the eyes of every man in the place were on him. It was ridiculous, of course. But the very fact that he was experiencing a paranoia he had not known since his earliest days in the CIA compounded his growing feeling of anxiety.

Curt baby, he told himself, at fifty, you are getting too old for this game. They may reckon back at Langley, Virginia, that experience is everything, but in truth age is no substitute for youth when it comes to innocence abroad. He knew too much and had seen too much. He *knew* that, despite elaborate precautions, things could go wrong. He *knew* that, when the chips were down, you couldn't even trust your own boss. And he *knew* that lightning could, and often did, strike in the same place twice.

As far as he was concerned, lightning had already come too close for comfort, following the series of raids by SAVAMA after the attempted US rescue bid. Luckily it was not planned for him to have a role in events; as an exceedingly experienced field agent in Iran he had been held 'in reserve'. If things went wrong, it was his responsibility to build up a new network of pro-American agents from the swelling number of Iranians who were disillusioned with Khomeini's Revolution.

It had been a precaution that had been proved necessary, and so far he had been reasonably successful without arousing undue suspicion – as far as he knew.

At least, as a fluent French speaker, he had an excellent long-established cover as the Teheran agent of a French-based carpet importers, although the office in the Boulevard St Germain was little more than a dead-letter drop.

It was also an advantage that he could easily be mistaken for an Iranian. He had a slightly swarthy complexion and close-trimmed black beard, although it was somewhat at variance with the tufty, prematurely white hair on his head. Due largely to disciplines instilled during his service in the US Marines, he was always impeccably dressed. Recently he had tried to look less conspicuous by dressing casually, but even in sweater and slacks, he managed to look smarter than the average Persian.

He had been reading the *Teheran Times* for the past half-an-hour, but he realised that he had not taken any of it in. Hameda was late, and that was unusual for her. She had sounded anxious on the telephone when she had implored him to meet her, although she had given no reason for her request.

Then he spotted her amongst the stream of pedestrians on the other side of the road. Heads turned as Hameda clattered over the uneven pavement in her awkward high-heeled shoes and tight skirt. In one hand she clasped her shoulder bag and she used the other to hold the expensive headscarf that threatened to lift off in the breeze. Curt shook his head disapprovingly. Time and again he had tried to impress on her not to dress in such a Western fashion, but still she persisted. A trail of frosty glares followed her along the road. In fact, her determination to shed all vestiges of her Persian background and to leave the country seemed to grow every time she met him. He blamed himself for letting her fall in love with him.

Curt paid for his tea and, with a nod to let her know he had seen her, followed Hameda into some secluded public gardens nearby. He found her waiting on a bench.

Casually he sat down at the opposite end and, unfurling his newspaper, began to read it. Her eyes seemed even wider than usual; wide, dark and beautiful, but frightened, like the eyes of a small child. Her knees were clamped tightly together, and both hands clutched tightly at the bag on her lap. Nervous. Distinctly nervous.

"Hallo, Hameda," he said, feeling absurdly like a ventriloquist as he spoke from the corner of his mouth. "What's the problem? Why did you need to see me so suddenly?"

"It's the Englishman. Blake." Her voice was faltering. "He has been moved. I only heard this morning."

Curt was disappointed. The failure of the US rescue mission had been bad enough, especially as it was now very unlikely that they'd try again. So the chance to help the British to hit back at the bastards ruling Iran was welcomed, even if he was going directly against official instructions from Washington. If this was starting to run into difficulties . . .

"When did this happen?"

"A couple of days ago."

"Do you know where he has been moved to?"

"Isfahan."

Curt thought for a moment. Isfahan was some two hundred miles to the south. Far away from the Turkish border. It was bound to mean a major change in any rescue attempt the British may be planning.

"Do you know where in Isfahan?"

"A house. It is specially fortified and will have its own force of revolutionary guards."

The American grimaced. In some respects it might be easier to penetrate a jail like Ghasr than a special detention centre guarded by fanatics.

"Do you know exactly where?"

Hameda shook her head. "No, but I shall try to find out tomorrow."

"Be careful. Don't put yourself in jeopardy."

She was puzzled. "Pardon?"

"At risk. Don't put yourself at risk."

"Curt?"

"Yes?"

"I am frightened, Curt. People in the office are starting to give me looks because of the questions I am always asking. And I have been told I must not stay late alone at the office."

Curt thought for a moment. "Then perhaps it is better that

93

I don't ask you to do any more. Anyhow, you've done enough."

For the first time she turned her head to look at him directly. "No, I want to help you."

She sounded alarmed and he knew why. While she was of use to him, she thought there was a chance he could spirit her away to the West. He had told her she was deluding herself, that this superiors would never allow such a move, but pathetically, her hope seemed to spring eternal.

He said harshly: "Your help isn't going to be much good if it gets us both arrested . . ."

Suddenly his voice faded.

He had been watching the group of youths at the other side of the vast lawn, since they had appeared from the trees a few minutes earlier. There were about ten of them; scruffy individuals, they gave the distinct impression they were looking for trouble as they slouched around, leering and calling out to people who walked by. Then one of them pointed straight to where he and Hameda sat and the group suddenly took on an air of purpose and menace.

"Time for you to go, Hameda," Curt said quickly, and began to curl his newspaper into a tight roll.

She looked up, seeing them for the first time. Instantly, the blood drained from her face. "It's my brother."

Curt was puzzled. If her brother was amongst them, then why did they look so distinctly hostile.

"Do you know his friends?"

Her voice was husky with fear. "I know Davoud's usual friends, and they aren't there. Those men are from the *Hezballahi*. The Party of God. There was a group of them at the house before I left. I was going to tell you . . ."

"Oh my God," Curt breathed. "Get up. For God's sake shift your goddamn ass and MOVE! Don't run, just walk quickly. I'll phone you at your office tomorrow."

"But . . ." she began.

"Don't argue!" he snapped. "Just shift it! Go!"

She glanced at him, her head shaking in uncertainty. Two large tears rolled down her cheeks.

"Hey, Western doll, come here!" came the taunt from one

of the approaching group. The words seemed to jolt Hameda into action. She took a deep breath, stood up and began walking away.

For a moment Curt followed the movement of her body in the thin material. She looked very composed, considering how terrified she must be. The girl's got guts, he thought, and felt a pang of pride in how she was coping with a world and home that had turned against her. He only wished he could believe that there would be some reward for the risks she was taking, but he knew there was none beyond the paltry retainer she was given. And while he needed her help, he couldn't bring himself to tell her that he was married.

"Hey, harlot, come back! Don't go! Let's talk!"

The excited voices were getting closer. Some of the youths broke into a run.

Curt Swartz Jnr. climbed to his feet, his newspaper clenched in his right hand, and began to saunter diagonally across the path of the approaching group so that he came between them and the retreating Hameda.

"That's him!" Curt guessed it was Davoud's voice.

"Hey, Frenchie! You come here. We teach you a lesson in Islam." The voice was high-pitched and excited, but Curt pretended not to hear. He strolled along, looking up at the ornate trees and breathing in the sweet air.

"Hey, Frenchie!"

The group was standing in his path. He stopped. Most had their eyes on him, although a couple were watching Hameda as she disappeared down the path. Some of them were grinning malevolently. Curt noticed that one youth held a length of metal piping behind his back.

Curt smiled, and wished them good morning politely. "*Subh-i shuma bikhair.*" Then he added: "Parlez-vous fran-çais?"

Some looked vague, but the ringleader, a tall, toothy individual with a bulbous nose nodded his head, meaning no.

"You speak English? *Inglizi midanid?*"

The ringleader sneered. "*Kami.*" A little.

Curt heard a rustling as the youth with the piping and two others worked their way round behind him.

The American still smiled broadly. "Good. Then perhaps you'll understand this ... LEAVE ME THE FUCK ALONE!"

The tightly-rolled copy of the *Teheran Times* jabbed forward in Curt's fist, its rigid end hitting the ringleader so hard in the ribs that the cracking of bone was distinctly audible.

In one practised movement, the American pirouetted around, his right elbow bent. It met the face of the man immediately behind him, dislocating his jaw-bone. A lump of piping thudded onto the grass.

As he continued to spin, Curt opened out his arm, so that his fist, still balled around the newspaper, hit the third man square on the nose. It crunched up like a ripe tomato, spurting twin jets of blood from his nostrils. The other man behind him was startled, hesitating a vital second too long before lifting the knife in his hand. The rolled newspaper jabbed again, into his right eye, pushing it three inches back inside his skull.

There was a wailing like tormented souls as the four members of the *Hezballahi* writhed on the grass. Slowly, the group began backing away, clumsily falling over each others' feet, as they kept their eyes fixed on the panting American.

At last, Curt Swartz Jnr. straightened himself up, and tucked the bloodied newspaper under his arm.

"*Khoda hafez*," he said quietly. Good day. He continued towards the park exit gates at a leisurely pace. His stomach was turning somersaults. It had been at least five years since he had last raised a fist in anger and he had been pleased with his reflex reactions. He may be fifty, he told himself, but he had the physique of a man twenty years younger.

Perhaps Langley was right after all: there was no substitute for experience. He just prayed that, after the sudden burst of exertion, his heart wouldn't give out before he reached the park gates ...

Hawksby watched as the men drew up the chairs in Hut 26 and positioned them in a rough semi-circle around the portable wooden rostrum. He was well pleased with what he saw.

Gone was the boisterous good humour of two weeks ago, replaced instead by a cheerful confidence and quiet anticipation of what lay ahead. Each man, he knew, would be alone with his thoughts: excited, concerned, engrossed, as a million and one items were ticked off on the mental check-list. And no amount of training would ever eliminate pre-op tension, even if it was just the irrational belief of the veteran that, one day, his luck would run out.

If there were such doubts in the minds of the gathered men, they remained well-hidden. The complex series of briefings and dry-run rehearsals over the past two weeks seemed to have served their purpose. Each man knew exactly what he had to do, and had had the opportunity to iron out problems to his satisfaction. Cementing the entire programme together, there had been the crash physical fitness course.

It had given everyone a physical target in addition to the mental ones set by mission preparation. It had ensured that everyone was too exhausted at night to lie awake fretting over the unknown weeks that stretched ahead. Most importantly, it had had the effect of squeezing out any dangerous feeling of complacency. Hawksby had deliberately kept all the physical targets slightly out of reach until, by a last super-human effort, they had been accomplished only the day previous to this final briefing. The first and biggest obstacle had been overcome right at the beginning when the men had discovered that the Hawk's idea of a daily five mile run with kit was not on roads or even track, but across rough country.

Hawksby smiled now as he recalled the looks of horror and anguish from men no longer used to being defeated by any man or natural barrier. For two weeks, the major had changed all that.

He looked round at the group as they settled down.

"Well, gentlemen," he began. "Just to put you all out of your misery, I can confirm that we leave at 0400 tomorrow morning for Turkey. By tomorrow night we shall – God and the RAF willing – be somewhere in Iran."

Mostly the faces remained impassive; there were just a couple of smiles. "When we've finished here, we'll drop into 'Q' who has a special treat for us in the shape of Iranian army uniforms. Oh, they're olive drab, for any of you who are fashion conscious. Like the Korean-made jackets so beloved by the dreaded Rev. Guards of Crazy K." He turned to the drivers. "Perkis and Pogo, I then want you to collect the two 'Rovers from the paint shop. They've been given the insignia of the 5th Iranian Infantry. Supervise their loading on the two trailers outside. I needn't remind you to make certain the tarpaulins are properly secured. I don't want a scare in tomorrow's papers with reports that the Iranians have invaded Hereford."

The laughs came a little too easily. Keyed-up. The atmosphere was charged with tension. Electric.

"Well, if there are no further questions, you'll be pleased to know that I'm putting the Mess back on limits for tonight. Don't overdo it. I want you to turn in for an early night."

At that moment the door of the hut opened abruptly. All heads turned to see the stocky figure of OC22 enter. He gestured quickly for the men to remain seated as he strode purposefully up to the rostrum. Beneath the fawn beret the florid face looked concerned.

He stepped onto the platform and spoke briefly to Hawksby, who had to stoop to catch the words of the shorter man. The major listened for a moment, a frown deepening across his forehead, then nodded.

The Old Man faced the men of Snapdragon. "I'm afraid I have some bad news for you all. The mission is to be postponed and revised for a new target destination. Our hostage has been moved to Isfahan. That, I'm sure you're aware, means that the plan as it stands just isn't on." He paused for a moment as the waves of disappointment ebbed over the two rows of seats. "We have also heard a whisper that a military coup is expected in Turkey. Therefore you could find yourselves returning to a country in the throes of a revolution of its own. I'm sorry, gentlemen, but there it is."

The CO nodded to Hawksby and left the rostrum.

"In view of this," the major said, "I think it's best that you all take forty-eight hours' leave as from now, whilst Planning and I sort out what needs to be done. Forbes, McDermid and Fraser, I'm afraid I'll require you here to help work out revised operational details." His eyes took on a hard, glazed look. "I do not intend that this setback should delay us more than a week."

"I suppose," Forbes said to McDermid, "this'll mean continuing with the Hawk's bloody morning marathons."

The Scotsman grinned. "Certainly in y' case, Davy. You didna' reach y' target weight, did ye? When the major finds that out, he'll be takin' a very special interest in you."

Forbes shook his head in disgust.

TEHERAN: 1800 hrs, Friday 5th September

Colonel Najaf Murad replaced the receiver.

On the other end of the line the Director of SAVAMA had sounded distinctly harassed. He had questioned the colonel harshly and had only stopped short of direct criticism. That in itself was uncharacteristic of Hussein Fardoust who had served with him for years and knew of his unquestioned efficiency at first hand. Evidently someone, somewhere, was putting on the pressure. Someone who didn't understand that such investigations necessitated long, painstaking and routine enquiries.

Probably it was Beheshti demanding results. But it could equally well be that fat toad, Judge Khalkali.

Murad grimaced. Clearly the vicious mullah was anxious to use Blake and his girlfriend for a showpiece trial and execution. The American hostages had been carefully kept from his grasp, but evidently he had high hopes of using the plight of the journalist to boost his public popularity.

So he would not be pleased when he learned that Blake and Eva Olsen had been moved to Isfahan on Murad's personal instruction. It had been the only way to ensure that the sadistic ayatollah didn't kill the prisoners out of sheer spite, boredom, or by accident. Even now the colonel awaited the inevitable furious 'phone call.

But Murad pushed the coming confrontation from his mind. He picked up the single sheet of paper from the green leather desk top. On it was written the word MULCRUF in capitals.

Turning the word over in his mind, he stood up and paced thoughtfully towards the window. Outside, the setting sun was casting the shadow of the Police Headquarters building into the grounds of the Archaeological Museum opposite.

Slowly he dipped into his pocket and brought out a packet of cigarettes. He shook one out of the wrapper and put it to his lips, unlit.

MULCRUF. A strange word. Perhaps it was a typing error?

In the four weeks since his investigation had begun, Murad's team of agents had been ploughing through the thousands of papers that the lawyer Sabs Karemi was believed to have worked on. Of course, it was impossible to tell if they were all there; in fact Murad had a distinct feeling that some might have been removed.

Only one item to date had raised any suspicion. It was an old report, dated 1978, from a SAVAK agent in Paris who had been keeping the home of the exiled Khomeini at Neauphle-le-Château under surveillance. Part of his brief had been to discover from whence the troublesome ayatollah was receiving support. The agent had intercepted some mail and discovered a payment cheque from the Mulcruf Foundation, a trust set up for the furtherance of Islamic studies and based in Geneva.

A red star had been marked in biro on the top right-hand corner by someone. Sabs Karemi? Or someone else?

By far the easiest course of action would, of course, have been for him to question the SAVAK agent who had filed the report. Unfortunately the man had backed the wrong side when Khomeini had made his triumphant return. By now the unfortunate's remains would be in an advanced state of decomposition somewhere in the grounds of the Comité Prison.

He went back to his desk and picked up the handset of the telephone. Within a few minutes he was through to one of his subordinates. "I wish you to check out a charitable trust in Geneva called the Mulcruf Foundation. Treat it as urgent and report back to me as soon as possible."

He hung up and sat back in his chair, staring at the pile of folders stacked in his IN-tray. Every day the list of suspect anti-revolutionaries grew like a cancer. His special responsibility was to deal with suspects working within government offices.

Idly, he picked up the first dossier and glanced at the badly-typed label. *Hameda Gulistani. Secretary. Age 26. Ministry of Justice.*

Angrily he threw the file back into the tray. They would just have to wait. He would simply recirculate them around the Ministry's bureaucratic maze and wait for them to turn up again weeks later.

The telephone began to sing shrilly and he snatched it up.

There was no mistaking the angry rasp of Farsi on the other end.

"My dear Judge Khalkali," Murad began soothingly. "To what do I owe the unexpected pleasure . . ."

OMAN: 2330 hrs, Saturday 13th September

On the throbbing flight deck of the giant C130 Hercules transport aircraft, Squadron Leader Michael Fontenoy completed the last of his power checks.

Outside, the dark void of the tropical Omani night pressed in on them, relieved only by the distant lights of the control tower that dominated the secluded military area at the western end of Seeb International Airport.

Some ten feet below, four figures in dark fatigues stood at the edge of the runway, watching. The up-turned faces looked pale in the glow of the machine's landing lights, grim and disappointed.

Under the hastily-revised plan for Snapdragon, Captain Johnny Fraser and his three men from the Boat Troop had lost their starring role. They were relegated instead to running the mission's new operations nerve centre which had been set up within the regular SAS headquarters at Salalah. Only if things went desperately wrong were they committed to a night dash across the Persian Gulf in a fast patrol boat of the Sultan of Oman's Navy.

But that was only in the direst of emergencies, and Fraser's men were under no illusions that such an eventuality was remote. They were bitterly down-hearted, and no amount of nonchalant bravado and caustic comment could conceal it.

Fontenoy glanced at his co-pilot, a doughty Flight Lieutenant from Yorkshire, and grinned widely. He had spent twenty years in the Royal Air Force and never had he been on a mission quite like this. It was as though his entire career had been preparing him for the next twelve hours.

Yorky's returning glance was less enthusiastic; he was a practical man and uncomfortably aware of the responsibility that such an operation demanded of him.

"The rpms are still unstable on No. 3," he muttered. "Wavering, but I think it'll stay within limits."

Mildly irritated at his companion's attitude, Fontenoy said, "Ground crew checked it over, didn't they?"

"Aye, but that sort of problem isn't easy to locate out here."

Fontenoy jerked his thumb over his shoulder towards the freight bay. "You want me to tell *them* we can't go because of a problem on No. 3?"

Suddenly their covert call-sign came over the radio. "*Control to Alpha Zulu. One-Zero-Seven. Control to Alpha Zulu. One-Zero-Seven. You are cleared for take-off. Over.*" Control's voice in the earphones was very British; very correct.

Yorky thought for a moment, sniffed again, and said, "No, skipper. Them mad idiots'd fly themselves in I reckon. And probably drop us out over Teheran for good measure."

Fontenoy laughed and, the ice broken, so did Yorky.

"Good evening, Control. This is Alpha Zulu. Permission

to take off now? May I have some runway lights, please? Over."

"Roger, wilco, Alpha Zulu." The runway lights suddenly came on like three parallel lines of fireflies stretching out before them. *"Good luck. Over."*

"Luck's nothing to do with it, Control," Fontenoy chuckled. "We'll be back before breakfast. Over."

"How do you like your eggs, Alpha Zulu?"

"Sunny side up, of course," the pilot replied.

"Cut it out!" A new stern voice came in. *"Please maintain proper radio procedure."*

"Sorry, Control. Alpha Zulu rolling. Out."

Fontenoy eased the row of power levers forward, gradually winding up the four huge Allison turbo props into their full combined eighteen thousand horsepower. The cockpit decking began to tremble under the strain as the engine pitch rose to a deafening crescendo. He exchanged glances with Yorky, who gave him a thumbs-up sign. Reaching forward, he released the brakes. Immediately, as the restrained force was unleashed, the unmarked Hercules began lumbering forwards. Once, twice, the aircraft jolted as the nosewheel tyres passed over the runway centreline. Then, as the momentum increased, the take-off run became faster, smoother. The engines screamed as the blades ripped into the torpid air and the runway lights began flashing past until they became one continuous blur of fiery ribbon.

"Vee One," Yorky reported. They'd reached decision speed. Now they were committed to take-off.

Fontenoy didn't have to check his instruments to know they'd hit 130 knots.

"Rotate." Yorky confirmed the safe flying speed.

The nose began to lift and Fontenoy eased the control column in towards his stomach and the aircraft's nose lifted as the broad-wing began to do its job. He felt a gentle thud as the front wheel left the tarmac; then a second as the low-slung main undercarriage followed.

The fat black belly skimmed low over the perimeter fence just as the undercarriage clunked up into the giant body.

"Gear up," Yorky verified.

Fontenoy grunted and eased the control column to port, gently dipping the giant bird on its wing as it turned, running parallel with the Sohar Road. As they straightened up he could just distinguish the landing lights on the strip. He settled down, clutching the controls loosely; they felt good in his hands. In a few seconds the shimmering Gulf would appear through the thin mist some hundred feet below them. They would remain at this height all the way into Iranian airspace. Beneath the all-seeing, ever-sweeping cone of the military long-range radars. Just above the wavetops. De-restricted wartime altitude flight.

Snapdragon was on its way.

CHAPTER SIX

Jonathan Blake felt drowsy.

He had been sitting in the hard-backed chair for three hours and the cords that bound him cut so deeply that the blood no longer reached his arms. He resisted the prickly sensation behind his eyeballs and forced the lids up. The glare of the interrogation lamps seemed to bore into his retinas.

He looked around the room, trying to make out some recognisable shape beyond the bright lights. He knew Ali and Iraj were there somewhere, but still they didn't speak. Finally his patience ran out. "Why are we waiting?" he demanded. "What's it for?"

He heard one of the guards but he wasn't sure which. "You shut up. We ask questions, not you. Colonel Murad is coming to see you. He tell us to make you sit up and wait like obedient dog." He laughed maliciously.

Sweet Jesus! And to think that when they came for him and Eva at Ghasr, he had actually thought they were going to be released. Even when he was bundled – stark naked as a deterrent to an escape – into the prison van, and learned that he was being transferred to some mysterious destination, he was actually relieved at having escaped the unpredictable Judge Khalkali.

How stupid he was to have thought things would improve. Now, an even more intense interest was being taken in Eva Olsen and himself. Harassment and intimidation continued day and night.

He guessed that they were in Isfahan, although no one would confirm this to him. And the big fortified mansion was typical of the riverside properties that had been confiscated since the Revolution. He had been kept in this cold, damp cellar and, although it must be well over a week, he had started to lose track of time. Days and nights all merged into one.

The only consolation was that he knew that Eva was still alive. Precious, wonderful Eva. They would never break her.

"Hallo, Jonathan." Murad's voice was as smooth as oil.

A shudder ran through Blake, developing into a physical tremor that he was unable to control.

Murad's hand, warm and dry, reached forward and rested on one of his shoulders. He could feel the heat of the palm on his cold skin. It was both comforting and sickening at the same time. He dropped his gaze, his head bent.

"Now, now, Jonathan," Murad's soothing tone continued. "That is no welcome for an old friend."

"You're no friend of mine," Blake rasped through clenched teeth.

"Oh, but I am, Jonathan. And the sooner you realise it, the better. Because I am the only one who can authorise your release. Indeed, I am the only one who *wants* to. If Khalkali had had his way, you'd have been dead by now. Only my actions have prevented it." The voice continued to drip like syrup. "So you see, to all intents and purposes, I am the only friend you have in the world."

Blake turned his eyes upward, just enough to see the lips moving around the perfectly formed teeth. He could smell the man's cologne. "Fuck off, Murad, you stink."

Murad didn't appear to hear him. "Jonathan, you told me that you never looked at the document Sabs Karemi handed you. I accept that. But you must have glanced at it, at least, in order to know that you wished to have nothing to do with it."

The journalist shook his head. "No, I didn't even glance at it."

Murad's eyes narrowed like a cat's. "Tell me what you know about the Mulcruf Foundation, Jonathan?"

For one vital, but fateful second Blake's eyes betrayed him, and that was all that the SAVAMA colonel needed. He had

106

spent too many years interrogating for the Shah's regime not to be able to read eyes like other men read books.

"Bring in the girl!" he snapped.

"For God's sake!" Blake protested. "It means nothing to me, nothing at all . . . believe ME!"

Murad rounded on him. "Tell me what I need to know, Jonathan, or shut up."

Blake's eyes began to burn with tears that wouldn't shed.

When the guards dragged in Eva Olsen, she didn't seem to have the strength to stand on her own. Still dazed and bewildered, she was hardly aware that she'd been violently woken from her sleep, before she was being strapped to the large wooden chair opposite Blake. The main interrogation light was swung round until she was full in its beam. The guards took no care for her modesty as her knees and ankles were tied to the chair legs. Then her wrists to the armrests. Murad noted with interest the way the light caught the perspiration that glistened, like a thin film of gelatine, between her breasts, where the ragged shirt had fallen open. He blew a steady stream of Kent tobacco smoke across the cellar. It burst silently against the damp stonework, disintegrating into a hundred writhing blue snakes.

He said: "Bring in the *Apolo*, quickly." Ali nodded quickly and left.

Murad watched the girl carefully. Getting her bearings, she was now glaring up at him with bright, hate-filled blue eyes from beneath the tufty mop of fair hair. Hard bitch, he thought. But beautiful, truly beautiful. They really should not have cut those flowing locks that way. He dropped his cigarette butt onto the floor and ground it out with his soft leather shoe.

No, that bitch would not break easily. Jonathan Blake would be the one to talk.

"Here, Colonel!"

Murad turned. Ali offered what looked like a bright red galvanised bucket.

The colonel shook his head. "Just hold it up for our two friends to see." The man obeyed.

"You have heard the famous story of *The Man in the Iron Mask*? Alexander Dumas, I believe."

"It's grotesque," mumbled Blake. The black eye-holes in the helmet seemed to be staring at him. How many poor souls had witnessed the depths of human depravity through its restricted apertures. He turned away, feeling the vomit rising.

"*Apolo* was invented by SAVAK," Murad said matter-of-factly, "but now it is used widely by the Imam's security forces. A simple device, but effective. It is just a hollow globe of steel." He nodded towards Eva. "Now just imagine the effect if we lock it onto your pretty accomplice's head . . ."

The girl's eyes widened.

"Of course," the colonel continued, "we could just hit the side of the mask with a hammer. It rings like a bell, you see . . . Can you imagine what it's like to be inside a bell when it rings . . ."

"You bastard!"

"But, no, instead we place electrodes on her body. You know, sensitive places. Usually the nipples, or inserted in the vagina . . ."

Eva began to shake her head like an automaton.

Something snapped inside Blake. "What the hell happened to God in your Revolution, Colonel? Or did you forget about Him in your rush to kill and torture innocent people!"

Ali and Iraj exchanged startled glances, but Murad just smiled gently. "We'll leave you and your girlfriend to worry about God, as she is deafened by her own screams. They will reach such a pitch of decibels, Jonathan, that she will probably have her hearing impaired for life. Can you imagine that? Deafening yourself. No, God will have his work cut out solving your problems without worrying about the way we conduct the Revolution."

Murad extended his hand. "Friendship, Jonathan, and freedom is what I offer? You will not be accepting it for yourself, but for Eva . . . Now, what about the Mulcruf Foundation?"

Blake began to sob.

At the precise moment that Colonel Murad stepped out of the riverside mansion in Isfahan, ready to begin his drive back to the capital, a black shadow passed over the Iranian coast some four hundred miles to the south.

Alpha Zulu's flight had been uneventful, the Hercules droning steadily westward across the starlit waters of the Gulf. At fifty feet it was as though you could reach down and pluck a handful of gems from its satin surface. But two hundred miles out from Saeb, the navigator had given a heading for the course alteration north. They had skirted the island of Sheykh Sho'eyb, just beyond the starboard horizon, and then passed over a remote stretch of coast virtually halfway between the two Iranian Navy bases: Bandar Abbas, two hundred miles to their right, and Bushehr, two hundred miles up the coast to the left, not far from where the blunt apex of the Gulf was joined by the Shatt Al-Arab waterway.

Idly, Squadron Leader Fontenoy wondered if the fleet of American helicopters and transports had also passed this way back in April. There was no way of knowing, but it was likely. He just hoped the Iranians, too, had a proverb about lightning and the same place. At least Snapdragon would not be breaking radio silence for some eavesdropping Israeli to pick up.

He pushed the hypothetical problems to the back of his mind; he had enough real ones to occupy him. "I wish to God we could go on to autopilot. This is bloody tiring." They were too low to benefit from that piece of modern technology.

Behind and below the raised cockpit, the eight-man team seated on one side of the cavernous cargo hold appeared unaware of the fliers' worries. They preferred to concentrate on what lay ahead at the target. Getting them there was the RAF's job.

"We're over the coast," Dave Forbes observed matter-of-factly.

Perkis, who was in the canvas seat next to him, looked surprised.

"How do you know, Dave? Like animal instinct, I suppose?"

"Animals have nothing to do with it, Perkis. The flying's gotten jerky. That means we've crossed the Gulf."

"'Ope it doesn't mean the Brylcreem boys is takin' a kip."

Forbes smiled to himself; that wouldn't surprise him. "It means, old son, we're into the Zagros Mountains. Crazy K, here we come."

He glanced down his shoulder at the small frame of his companion, who was forming steeples with his fingers. "Didn't know flying made you *that* nervous."

Perkis smiled uncertainly. "It don't, yer berk. No, Dave, I'm a bit worried 'bout Jannie to tell yer the truth."

"The missus?"

"Yeah. We got this little sprog on the way and, well, the 'ospital reckon there could be some complications. She's got this small pelvis apparently, which could mean she'll 'ave a caesar."

"Seizure?" It was difficult to hear above the roar of the engines. "Caesar, Dave. Short for caesarean. Touch of the ol' knifework."

Forbes nodded, trying to remember what his ex-wife had said about it. "Something about big tits, big pelvis, isn't it? Or is it feet?"

The trooper laughed this time. "Feet. Size of the feet can denote the size of the pelvis."

"What size feet has your missus got, then?"

"Size three."

The sergeant nodded sagely. "I can see why they're worried. Still, there's millions of kids born everyday whose mums have got problems. She'll be all right."

"I guess so."

They laped into silence, and Forbes' thoughts turned to Major Alan Hawksby. An unknown quantity. But what he did know he wasn't sure he liked. Except for the occasional lapse into dust-dry humour the officer remained aloof and unapproachable. Not the sort for Perkis to take his domestic worries to.

The sergeant didn't doubt the man's dedicated professionalism, but wondered if he wasn't too much of a loner for a regiment where an informal camaraderie traditionally existed between officers, NCOs and men. It wasn't unusual for officers to find it difficult to adjust to the SAS. Hawksby's full-time involvement had come late in life, but he'd previously been seconded in on several occasions for clandestine observations of Soviet reserve vehicle parks in southern Russia. As a Cavalry officer his knowledge of armoured vehicles had been first-rate. When he'd finally joined, his achievements had been nothing short of sparkling. But even now, coming to the end of his three-year tour, few had got close to him. Even Scottie, who had served in his squadron for a year, didn't know him. Oh, he knew his likes and dislikes, his whims and idiosyncracies. And he recognised his tactical military brilliance. But in 'The Family' you needed more than that.

No, Forbes reflected idly, you're a cold, condescending bastard, Major, with that cut-glass accent of yours. We may not be good enough for you, but you seem happy enough playing sandcastles with the Arabs. An odd fish all right.

He sucked on his moustache. Still, another few weeks and I'll be back in Belize. Out of sight and out of mind.

At the other end of the row of canvas seats Hawksby sat with arms folded and legs outstretched, the peak of the Iranian-style forage cap tipped over his eyes. To all intents and purposes he seemed asleep. Only the occasional puff from the bowl of the protruding clay pipe indicated he was very much awake. In the darkness he was absorbing the faintly oily smell of the aircraft and the steady vibrant rhythm of its engines. Becoming part of it. It helped him to accept the reality of it all; something he had often found hard to do on missions since he had joined the SAS three years earlier.

Suddenly, it was as though the weeks of planning had never really existed. Now he had started living through a chain of predestined events; the result of meticulous research, analysis and informal speculation, that had been conceived in the minds of a handful of men in an isolated camp thousands of miles away. Sustained by endless cigarettes, coffee and their over-active imaginations, they had determined each minute step of the operation to come.

He and his team would be walking through the scenario created in the pages of that report. It was uncanny and unnerving, and it was why he had to pinch himself mentally to be sure he was really here – living out the Planners' thoughts – and not just dreaming.

He opened his eyes and tilted back the peak of his cap. In the dim red glow of the interior lights the two long wheel-based Land Rovers, with their bizarre desert camouflage, were real enough. They sat firmly secured onto their para-chute pallets, like two trapped noble beasts eager to be free. As much a friend as the horse to the cowboy, the 'Pink Panthers' were very special fighting machines. With their reinforced chassis, 16 inch sand tyres and monstrous super-charged V8 engines, they would be the team's home for as long as the mission lasted. Aboard was everything they would need in the coming days: doss bags strapped to the vehicles' side-bins which carried tools, ammunition and equipment; jerry cans of fuel and water; provisions, personal kit, communications equipment – and a veritable arsenal of weaponry, not least the menacing L37 'jimpy' general pur-pose machine guns which were mounted on the vehicles, capable of tackling even low-flying aircraft, or light armoured vehicles.

The kit, Hawksby reflected, was probably the best in the world. The best even before the SAS engineer detachment began its own modifications.

He glanced sideways along the row of men. They too, he was satisfied, were second to none. McDermid he knew well: as tough as they come, but a fast thinker too, especially in a tight corner. 'Tiger' Ratna was an ex-Gurkha. Enough said, except that the tiny man from Nepal had served with him for a year in Oman and had a genius for coping with the communications problems caused by the crazy atmospherics experienced in the mountains and deserts. Iran had both. 'Nature Boy' Perkis, the Cockney wildlife freak, also hap-pened to be the second best driver in the regiment; 'Pogo' was the first – and was one of a long line of Fijian SAS recruits.

Next to Hawksby sat the bush doctor, John Belcher, scribbling thoughtfully in a small red notebook. Dedicated, with an insatiable thirst for medical knowledge and practical experience of every emergency he might ever be called on to contend with – as well as many he certainly wouldn't. Belcher also knew how to kill a man with one hand, and in fact, had. Twice.

That leaves Dave Forbes, thought Hawksby. A bit of an unknown quantity to me. Plenty of form though, and a pretty chequered history. A bit of a mascot in 'The Family', he was just coming to the end of his third tour of duty, which would be his first break since the unhappy year he spent desk-bound with an Intelligence Corps unit in 1977. Afterwards he had been offered the chance of 'a crown' up, but turned down the rank of Staff Sergeant in favour of remaining 'up the sharp-end'.

22 Special Air Service Regiment had cultivated a special 'rotation' system to avoid unnecessary wastage of skills that were expensive to acquire in terms of time and money. It was long proven that you couldn't keep a man in top fighting trim for longer than three years without his cutting edge becoming dulled. So the regiment would normally second him to another, less arduous, and totally different task for a year. Preferably he would acquire a new special skill or knowledge that would be useful when he returned. After his relaxing break, the soldier would come back refreshed and begin re-training back to his old peak.

Big Dave Forbes was one of those who couldn't keep away. He craved action like other men craved drink or women. Hawksby frowned. In fact, according to his record, the sergeant was pretty fond of both of those too!

On past occasions he had got pretty close to being RTU'd but, because of his exemplary combat record and glowing testimonials from his squadron commanders, he had escaped the SAS man's most feared punishment: to be Returned To Unit. An ordinary squaddie again.

Hawksby tapped out his pipe. You certainly couldn't describe Forbes as ordinary. Despite the caricature image of the oafish NCO he had cultivated, it was just a veneer to cover a sensitive soul. Or so he had been told. Certainly it managed to conceal successfully his obvious intelligence and brainpower. He was accomplished in languages, explosives and demolition, communications, and a qualified helicopter pilot into the bargain.

It was for that vast experience that Hawksby had wanted him. But, as a soldier in his team, he still wasn't sure. He had found the 35-year-old sergeant fit enough, but overweight and resentful of authority. Perhaps it was just *his* authority that rankled. Just an unfortunate chemistry clash. On the other hand, Forbes, perhaps you've finally burnt yourself out? You may be as good as they say you are, sergeant, but I'm not so sure. I'll be watching you carefully. Very carefully.

The rest of Alpha Zulu's run-in went like clockwork. There was just one fleeting moment of panic when the aircraft's specially-fitted radar warning receiver identified an airborne Iranian radar attempting to 'interrogate' them. But the signal disappeared as quickly as it came, losing the bulky aircraft in the 'ground clutter' thrown up by the hilly terrain.

Squadron Leader Fontenoy relaxed again as Alpha Zulu droned doggedly on to the designated drop-zone some ninety miles south-south-west of Isfahan. The DZ had not been selected for the pilot's benefit; far from it. It was no more than a remote three-mile-long triangular break in the Zagros Mountains range, on the edge of the salt lakes of the Qash-quai. Offering a gentle incline into the surrounding crags, through which ran one of the main tributaries to the Khersan River, it allowed Fontenoy's crew under two miles of level flight to set up for the jump. One second's miscalculation and Alpha Zulu would find itself face-to-face with a steeply rising 10,000 peak.

Fontenoy wiped the sweat off his palm onto the leg of his flying-suit. "Okay, Yorky, we're approaching the target area now. Tell the dispatchers to stand by. Time to run about ten minutes, now."

The call to action stations over the intercom signalled a sudden rush of activity. The air dispatchers began unshackling the Panthers' drop pallets. Strapping on their jump helmets, Hawksby's group gathered at the front of the bay beneath the flight deck. Without a word they went through the routine of checking each others' parachutes and ensuring that all their personal kit was securely fastened.

They all felt the aircraft begin to lift as it rose from 100 feet to clear the range of hills blocking their approach to the desolate triangle that formed their DZ.

Nearest to a portside window, at the front of the freight bay, Forbes peered out at the vague bulk of boulder-strewn hillside flashing past beneath them. It was faintly illuminated by a liberal sprinkling of stars in the black domed void.

"Hope that the pilot knows where he is!" he shouted above the noise of the engines. "All looks the bloody same to me! Not a light anywhere!"

He had forgotten Hawksby was behind him, and was almost surprised not to get a curt reply. "Probably still over the Gulf, Dave! Sure you can see land?"

Forbes gave a thumbs-up. "It's scraping the bottom of the plane! Is this a request stop?"

Hawksby's teeth glistened in the red light, as he grinned and leaned over the other's shoulder. The aircraft began to descend the far side of the range as the hills started flattening towards the tributary river bed. "See those black holes, Dave?"

"Huh?"

"Down the side of the mountain!"

Forbes squinted into the hazy light. It wasn't easy to see as the terrain was dropping away fast beneath them. Then he saw them, like a long line of molehills, each some four feet across, strung in a straight row at regular intervals down the slope.

"They're the irrigation *qanats*!"

"Look more like bleedin' great shell holes!" He nodded with approval. Back at Hereford he had been greatly impressed by the ancient Persians' traditional method of bringing fertility to their acrid land. A long series of vertical tunnels, sometimes 300 feet deep, were sunk into the lower hill slope, all converging with a main horizontal channel at the base. It served to carry the water, collected from condensation high in the mountains, to the villages in the valleys. Sometimes a *qanat* would run underground for as far as twenty-five miles, its course marked by the endless series of vertical shafts which had been used by the builders to extract the earth by hand during construction. It had been the one redeeming feature about Iran, decided Forbes. It took some guts and a lot of work for the peasants to dig through twenty-five miles of long passages just four feet in diameter, armed with a shovel and a goatskin excavation bucket.

The aircraft levelled out bumpily as it hit the 800 foot spot on the radio-altimeter. A slight crosswind buffeted the huge bulk as the pilot fought to hold a steady course. The giant ramp doors gradually opened under the tailplane like a great jaw.

There followed a few seconds of chaos at the sudden inrush of air. Dust, rubbish and loose rigging whirled crazily in the sudden maelstrom. As it subsided the inside of the aircraft became icy cold, as it filled with crystalline mountain air.

The red light blinked on, followed seconds later by the green.

As the pilot released the extraction chute, everyone watched with bated breath as the 100-foot line tugged at the first Panther pallet. It began accelerating fast over the deck rollers towards the yawning tail ramp.

"Load moving," the dispatcher reported solemnly into his intercom.

Gathering momentum, the first pallet rattled out into the night to the brisk snap of parachutes opening into the slipstream.

Above, on the flight-deck, Fontenoy grimaced as he held Alpha Zulu's speed steady at 115 knots. Seriously late in establishing a steady approach run across the triangular DZ, the Hercules had already gobbled up seven hundred metres of the precious thousand that remained.

The second pallet followed, immediately gliding across the spinning metal cylinders, over the ramp, and disappeared.

"Load gone." The dispatcher listened intently on his earphones to the instructions from the cockpit. Concern clouded his pale face. Hawksby met his gaze. 'WE'RE RUNNING OUT OF DZ, MAJOR! GO!"

Major Hawksby beckoned his men. "OKAY, LET'S GO!"

Grins broke through amid the line of blackened faces as they began their rush down towards the ramp and hurled themselves unhesitatingly out into the night sky.

Someone screamed: "GERONIMO . . .!" at the top of his voice, but the war cry was cut off abruptly by the slipstream.

Fontenoy died for the sixteenth time in as many seconds. Beside him, Yorky leaned forward, peering out through the screen as though he would see better if his eyes were watering with strain.

"We won't do it," he said stiffly.

Fontenoy blanched. There was no mistaking the solid black wall of mountain hurtling towards them. He was mesmerised. *Come on!*

"Stick gone!" At last the dispatcher's voice broke into Fontenoy's headset.

"Thank Christ!" He hauled the control-column towards him and palmed the power levers forward. On the radio-altimeter the needle had started registering the rapidly-rising ground. The protesting engines screamed like banshees and the deck canted violently as the nose of the C130 was dragged upward. The mountain filled the windscreen, blotting out the sky.

In the cargo hold the dispatchers grabbed for handholds as Alpha Zulu suddenly found its strength and began to surge upwards, reaching desperately for the stars. Just before the rear ramp closed, they caught a clear glimpse of the DZ triangle behind and below them. In the starlight it was just possible to distinguish the dark shapes of bobbing aerofoil parachutes strung out into the distance.

Yorky sat frozen and speechless as the mountain peak glistened a mere twenty-five feet below them. As the fear ebbed out of him, he felt a rush of pride. They had done it. Beside him Fontenoy sat nonchalantly. There was a smug, fat grin on his face.

The roar of Alpha Zulu's engines faded and the intense quietness of the Iranian night enveloped Hawksby as he swung gently earthwards. The only sound was a gentle singing of the wind in the canopy shrouds above his head.

Belcher, who had jumped with him, was veering to the north in one of the unpredictable mountain air currents, but was still in sight. The night was too dark to see anyone else, although vision would improve as their eyes became accustomed. Already he was just able to distinguish the ragged rim of the mountains against the ultramarine sky. He peered below for the earth that would suddenly swell up to meet him. There was no tell-tale sign of a tree or rocky outcrop that could so easily mean a fractured limb, or worse. Then he was there, the hard crust of barren soil just feet below him. He braced himself, bending his knees. It was such a clean landing that he surprised himself. Scarcely had his boots hit the ground, than he twisted the release ring at his stomach and stepped out of the harness. Swiftly he ran back round the fallen canopy in order to deflate it.

Then, in one practised movement he unslung the Uzi sub-machine gun and dropped to one knee. He squinted his eyes, trying hard to penetrate the utter blackness. Slowly he scanned the southern slope of the triangle where it dipped towards the valley. There came a soft crunch somewhere to his left. Fifty yards away John Belcher had made an untidy landing. He could hear the scraping as the man's boots were dragged across the shale for several feet before the canopy collapsed and the harness could be released.

Hawksby scanned again. His shoulders dropped slightly as he relaxed. So far, so good.

Within sixty seconds Belcher had retrieved and bundled the billowing black parachute silk. He then stood guard while Hawksby wrapped up his.

Suddenly Forbes came limping out of the darkness.

"You okay, Dave?" Belcher asked.

The sergeant grimaced. "Sprained my bloody ankle, that's all.'

Hawksby grunted. "Good job you lost that weight then. Otherwise you might have broken it."

Forbes glared.

"Never mind," Belcher interrupted quickly. "I have the technology to rebuild you."

The tension melted. Forbes elbowed him affably. "Piss off, Kildare."

They continued down the slope until they located the Panthers. The Fijian Pogo was already there and had started to drive one of them off the buckled pallet, the force-absorbing honeycomb platform having kept the vehicle intact.

Other members emerged from the towering shadow of the Zagros peaks.

Jim Perkis looked white. "I reckon this was a bleedin' close shave. I landed on a soddin' one-in-two slope."

"Get the 'chutes and pallets hidden," Hawksby ordered briskly. "We can stow them in those bushes."

"Quiet!" Tiger called suddenly.

He dropped to one knee, flicking the safety catch off his Uzi. Gently, everyone turned in the direction in which the little Gurkha was staring.

"What is it?" Perkis whispered.

"A noise," Tiger replied quietly. "Metallic. There it is again."

"Where?"

"Shut up!" Hawksby hissed.

There was a sudden movement in the gloom. Cocking handles rasped as eight Uzis with 280 9 mm rounds zeroed in on the shape growing out of the shadows.

Perkis' eyes widened. "It's a bleedin' sheep!"

Eight Uzis lowered as one.

"Before y' utter a word, laddie," McDermid said, "we dunna *care* what breed the little sod is."

"This place gives creepers-jeepers," Pogo Penaia said emphatically.

Hawksby shouldered his Uzi. "A sheep with a bell could mean a shepherd nearby. So let's get weaving."

Panther One careered around the outcrop in a four-wheeled drift. Perkis changed down for a better grip and let out the clutch. The heavy-duty tyres smoked and spewed pebbles as the treads bit deep and thrust them forward into the darkened landscape.

Beside the driver, Forbes felt bilious. It was no fun playing passenger on a night drive with invisible infra-red headlights, being hurtled blindly across country through the early hours of the morning.

"Steady on, Perkis. This isn't the M1."

He could see the driver's fixed grin beneath the khaki metal Common User Binocular frames. The CUBs were infra-red sensitive with their own power pack, which gave Perkis a distinct advantage over Forbes as he could clearly see the IR headlamp beams that prodded through the maze of rocks like illuminating fingers. The system was good but a bit out-moded. Nevertheless, on a 'deniable' mission, more modern identifiable night sights had been rejected.

"I know where we're goin'," Perkis reassured.

"I've only got your word for that. Bloody hell, we've only got to cover thirty-five miles before dawn."

"Yeah, but you're navigating Sarge."

"Charming!"

Forbes glanced down at the canvas case with the perspex face that held the detailed route maps prepared by JARIC. To the glow of a map-light he marked off the outcrop in Chinagraph. "Watch out for a land-slip debris approaching on your right." Perkis changed down.

After ten miles of rocky terrain they crossed over a dusty secondary road that ran due north and continued on at speed on a north-westerly bearing, skirting the edge of a vast salt bowl within the Zagros range.

At 0330 hours they crossed over another road that led south to the disused airfield at Lordakan. If all went well, Alpha Zulu would land there to pick them up in six days' time, but in the intervening period they would keep well clear of the rendezvous point, establishing their main base twelve miles to the north.

The early morning light was spreading across the eastern sky as the first of the two Land Rovers picked its way through the wooded river valley and up to a narrow ravine that cut into the mountains like a slice from a cake. Perkis hauled on the handbrake and killed the engine. He stepped out into the undergrowth as Panther Two nosed under the trees. As the noise of the second engine faded, the eight men looked round at their new surroundings. Dawn cast a pale golden glimmer. Birds began to chatter around the new arrivals. Insects called from the ferns, and fresh water tinkled musically from somewhere nearby.

Above them, the crumbling yellow face of the mountain was painted in the first wash of sunlight. From up there they would have a commanding view of the valley spread out below them.

"Welcome to yer new home, boys," Kangers Webster drawled.

"I'm shagged," Perkis said with feeling, leaning back in his seat.

Hidden deep in the Zagros Mountains, Snapdragon went to ground for the daylight hours. Isfahan was just one mountain range and seventy-five miles away.

CHAPTER SEVEN

TEHERAN: 0600 hrs, Sunday 14th September

The next morning found Colonel Najaf Murad of SAVAMA in pensive mood, pacing the carpeted floor of his Teheran office like a caged lion. He stubbed out his cigarette in the ashtray with slow deliberation before returning to his desk to read the signal from his contact in Switzerland for the fourth time.

> *Geneva 13/9/80*
> *Re: Inquiry of Mulcruf Foundation in Geneva.*
>
> *On investigation, I find that the above no longer occupies the stated premises. Those were comprised of one reception room in a quiet backstreet neighbourhood and were rented by Mulcruf from the period 3.1.78 to 19.11.78. They were normally unoccupied during that time, but someone would call in once a week to collect mail. No telephone or telex machine was installed.*
>
> *Mulcruf de-registered as a charity in late 1978. The two principals were recorded as having been an Iranian immigrant called Mr. I. Hassan-'Ali, an American citizen living in Florida and a Canadian named as Mr. J. Hussein of Toronto.*
>
> *If you wish me to conduct further inquiries, please advise.*

Murad snorted. Hassan-'Ali and Hussein. The Iranian equivalents of Smith and Jones.

He reached forward and pressed the play button on the cassette recorder. It was a slow and painful tape of the journalist Blake's knowledge of the Mulcruf Foundation.

If the man was to be believed, Sabs Karemi's report declared the Foundation to be a considerable source of political and financial support to Khomeini during his exile in Paris. Cheques would arrive regularly and, over a period, had mounted to several million dollars. In some of the very few letters sent by the Foundation, promises of international political influence were made and, apparently, these held good. That, Blake had protested, was the limit of his knowledge about the Mulcruf Foundation. Whoever they were, Hassan-'Ali and Hussein had access to some pretty powerful and wealthy people.

Still that word MULCRUF puzzled him.

He opened the top drawer of his desk and extracted a fresh sheet of paper.

Hurriedly he wrote out the word in full, leaving a space between each letter: MULCRUF.

Underneath that he wrote MURCFUL, then CRUM-FUL.

God, how he hated crosswords and anagrams.

He stared at the sheet for a full minute. His mind was a blank. Then, suddenly, he reached forward and underlined the letters FUL in red ink.

Very slowly he added . . . CRUM.

FULCRUM.

Murad looked at the word for a moment, then reached for the oak bookcase behind him. He drew out a battered English dictionary, with a leather binding that had seen better days. He flicked through it until he found the entry he wanted.

FULCRUM (pl. fulcra) (fulkRUM) n. pivot about which a lever turns; (fig.) means used to attain an end.

At least, he consoled himself, that was a recognisable word.

ISFAHAN: 0600 hrs, Wednesday 17th September

Three days after Colonel Murad had worked on the mysterious anagram in Teheran, two unkempt Iranian travellers were crossing the Zayandeh River in Isfahan by the magnificent Khaju weir bridge.

They had probably been there before, because they paid no heed to the ornate Safavid design, with its beautiful two-tier construction spanning twenty-four enormous piers, its arcade, or its central pavilion. They did not even spare a glance for the playful antics of the children splashing on the steps downstream.

Perhaps they were tired; they were certainly dirty from their journey, a thin layer of dust covering their worn jeans and jackets. Perhaps they were just intent on arriving at their destination.

The broader of the two men, who wore a woollen cap, waved cheerfully at a group of revolutionary guards gathered on the other side of the bridge. They called back: "*Allahu akbar!*" God is great.

The other man, taller and thinner, with a hawkish bearded face, inclined his head with approval.

"*Allahu akbar!*" he said, adding under his breath, "He sure is . . . to have got us this far."

"Just how I imagined it," Forbes muttered out of the corner of his mouth.

The SAS sergeant was feeling pleased with himself. He had kept up with Hawksby over the devastating two-night hack which had taken them over a mountain fold and into the flatter fertile plain around Isfahan. Earlier that morning they had left the other two members of the Sabre team, Tiger and Kangers Webster, at a temporary riverside hide, some twenty miles to the south-west. The two Farsi-speakers in the team had pushed on at night to the Russian-built steel mill complex on the outskirts of the new township of Riz. It had been easy there to hitch a lift on a flatwagon that threaded its way along the freight railroad, past the outlying villages and mines to the perimeter of Isfahan itself.

As dawn broke, they had mingled easily with the workers on their way to their daily toil. Their destination was a house in the labyrinth of narrow streets that made up the bazaar district to the north of the central Royal Square. The usual adornment of a black flag hung outside each crumbling house, signifying that its owner supported the Islamic Revolution.

Hawksby stopped outside a battered wooden door set in a high wall. There were no markings, no number and no nameplate.

"You sure this is it?" Forbes asked, nodding pointedly towards the limp flag.

Hawksby almost smiled. "Trust Allah." He knocked three times rapidly.

Almost immediately they heard a bolt shift and the door creaked open on its hinges. Both men were immediately aware of the beautiful dark eyes from the face slit in the black *chador* that covered the woman from head to foot.

Her voice was soft. "Peace be with you and your friend. Can I help you?"

"You are kind," Hawksby said, slipping into the fluent Persian identification code. "My friend and I are weary from travel. We seek rest and the name of a good silversmith, for I am here to do business."

The woman's eyelids fluttered as she glanced from the major to Forbes. "Then it is your good fortune to come to this door. My uncle is the best silversmith in Isfahan. But first you must rest and eat."

She stepped back, and the door in the wall swung open onto a small cobbled courtyard surrounded by shrubs. A solitary songbird hidden in the undergrowth emphasised the peace and stillness of the place. Water cascaded and gurgled in a small ceramic fountain.

The men looked around them while the woman re-bolted the door, then led them through an archway into a small whitewashed room beyond the fountain. A soft, intricately-patterned carpet covered the floor, and a white-haired man with a dark beard sat on one of the scattered cushions which had been thrown around a low table.

"Our guests have arrived, Curt," the woman said.

The American climbed to his feet and extended his hand in a firm handshake. "I'm Curt Swartz. You guys must've had one hell of a journey."

"It's had its moments," Hawksby admitted.

The woman released her face veil and pushed back the hood of her *chador*. Forbes was taken with her sultry beauty, immediately deciding that beneath the shapeless hang of her robes was the sort of full, firm figure he preferred.

"This is Hameda," Curt said. "She's been responsible for

finding out all the information about our friend Blake. At great personal risk to herself, I might add."

The girl looked embarrassed. Hawksby touched his forehead. "We're most grateful."

"Very," Forbes added with a grin that was in danger of becoming permanent.

"Forgive me if we dispense with full names, Curt," the major said lightly. "You may call me Alan and my colleague here is Dave."

"Of course, I understand. You guys certainly didn't get into this country by taking chances, and you certainly won't get out of it again if you do."

Hawksby looked out of the cool room at the contrasting brilliance of the courtyard. "Talking of precautions, may I ask who owns this place?"

It was the girl who replied. "It is my uncle's house. He really is a silversmith. He knows I am entertaining friends but, of course, he does not know who."

"I should hope not," Forbes muttered.

"He's a pro-Westerner?" Hawksby asked.

She shook her head. "Not really. But he is pro-me. He is a kind and lovely man and he is very fond of me. He paid for my education although he is not very rich." Hameda smiled bashfully. "But I would not wish to embarrass him. Abbas, that is his name, will be home at noon for a rest. It is best that we all be gone by then."

Hawksby said: "I'd like to leave as soon as possible."

"Not before you have eaten and are refreshed," Curt replied, smiling.

"You're getting too Persian for your own good," the major chided.

Curt shrugged. "In this country it's the only way to survive. Like the rest of the Middle East, you can't rush 'em. So you may as well drift along with the tide."

The girl went into an adjoining room and reappeared after a few minutes with a tray of food which she laid out on the low table. "I am afraid it is not much. Kebabs, cucumber and some yoghurt to drink. Oh, and, of course, melon. Isfahan is famous for its melons."

126

Forbes felt himself relaxing involuntarily after the rigours of the past few days. His mouth began to water at the sight of the food on two silver trays. Each had been intricately worked by hand, using just a hammer, gouging nail and a craftsman's eye. "It looks like a feast to me," he said appreciatively.

Hameda smiled and blushed. He was such a big man, this mysterious soldier from the West. In her mind, she could imagine his strength, and yet he seemed so gentle.

"These goddamn people would give you the last crust off their plate, Alan," Curt said, reaching for some meat. "Any passing traveller will get the same generous treatment. Until Khomeini arrived, that included Westerners. And if you say you like something, whatever it is you've been admiring, they're likely to give it to you. I've even known café owners to give free tea and bread when they're in the mood. Amazing goddamn place."

Hawksby agreed. "I lived here in my childhood, Curt. I know what you mean. You soon get attached to the place and the people."

"Not the sort of image it's got for itself at the moment," Forbes said through a mouthful of kebab.

"If I said in Washington now what I just said to you," Curt replied, "I'd be lynched on a bloody yellow ribbon. Those religious creeps have a lot to answer for. Poor goddamn peasants didn't know what they were lettin' themselves into. And it'll be one helluva job gettin' rid of the bastards now. They're clinging onto power like leeches and turning the whole of Iran into a virtual Gestapo police state."

Forbes frowned. "That's a bit of an exaggeration, isn't it?" He licked his fingers.

"I don't think so. These damn mullahs have been pretty quick to learn the black arts of suppression." The American held up his right hand, raising his index finger. "One. Where do these illiterate bastards get news and views of what's goin' on in the world? Answer: over half of 'em get it from one of the 80,000 local mosques. And that ain't exactly unbiased NBC reporting.

"Two. There's a unit of revolutionary guards attached to

each mosque and they're commanded by a mullah. And each mosque also acts as a bank, givin' interest-free credit. Those bastards provide finance for an entire quarter of the population, and they know *everything* about the poor little sods on their books! Khomeini and Beheshti have a built-in intelligence system, which is growin' like bindweed. Now children are being instructed by the mullahs in the old Nazi and Stalin tricks of spyin' and reportin' on the *misdemeanours* of their parents. Ah, shit, it makes me sick!''

Curt stopped in full flow and glanced up at Hameda. Suddenly the waterfall outside sounded very loud. ''Sorry, sweetheart, I shouldn't let off steam like that.''

She didn't smile. ''Allah will see that justice is done.''

''Perhaps we can give Him a little help,'' Hawksby said.

Curt laughed harshly. ''Anything to get rid of these bloodsuckers, Alan, anything. That's why I welcomed the chance to help you, although it's strictly against official orders. You know that?''

Forbes said: ''We know nothing.''

''Of course.'' The American sipped at his yoghurt. ''Hameda and I want to assist even if it doesn't help the case of our own hostages. The White House has been got by the short an' curlies, so it's got to kowtow to these shits in Teheran. But *you* don't have to. I welcome anything that will help to unsettle this regime and maybe topple it. Christ knows, even the bloody Commies would be better than this lot.''

On Curt's insistence, the two men took an hour's catnap and it was approaching noon before Hawksby and the sergeant stepped out from the door in the wall into the baking dusty street.

Forbes had to admit that he was impressed with Isfahan, not least because the garden city, despite being the second largest in Iran, was every bit as charming as Hawksby had promised it would be. A world of gold and blue domes and minarets. It was only the occasional sight of gaggles of revolutionary guards that shook him from his soporific mood.

Following Hameda's instructions, they crossed the central reservation of the crowded main south-north Tchahar Bagh Avenue and wove their way towards the plush residential district around Saeb Avenue. They had no difficulty in locating the villa they were looking for. Three guards were standing and gossiping under the plane trees outside its imposing twelve foot walls, along the top of which ran coils of barbed wire.

Slowly the two Iranian travellers sauntered past, engaged in a heated debate about the price one had paid for the other's goat. "You took advantage that I was sick." "Nonsense. As God is my witness, I did you a favour." "My wife does not know of such things. You tricked her!" "How was I to know how high the market price would go?"

They prodded each other's chests with mounting animosity as they stopped opposite the entrance to the villa. The guards watched with amusement as the men almost came to blows.

"Hey!" one called after a few minutes. "Why not go to your mosque and ask your mullah to adjudicate which of you is right?"

"Bah!" said the big bearded protagonist. "He would say we are both wrong and take the goat for himself!" The guards laughed amongst themselves as the two peasants strolled on.

"Twelve foot high gate," Hawksby said. "Pretty solid."

"Studded oak, I think," Forbes added.

"Need HE to shift it. A bit messy."

"Should've brought a rocket launcher after all."

"Still make too much noise. Don't forget we've got to get out of this place afterwards." Hawksby considered for a moment. "I think a more subtle approach is called for. Come on, let's have a look round the back."

They took a leisurely walk down to the start of the ancient Marnan footbridge, then turned left along the embankment of the Zayandeh river. The shade of the poplars provided relief from the hot afternoon sun.

The same high wall ran behind the treeline where the villa backed onto the water. Again the wicked coils of modern razor-edged barbed wire glinted in the sunlight. There were no gates or other apertures and only one guard was on the other side, evidently standing on a walkway or platform.

"That looks better for the initial approach," Hawksby decided. "Trees for cover and we can come straight across the river at night."

"That remote TV camera could give us trouble."

"If it works."

"That looks like the telephone cable. Did you see the power-line at the front?"

Hawksby nodded. "Yes, but why mess about? I'd rather knock out the whole city. Even here people have come to rely on electricity."

"Funny, isn't it?"

"What?"

"To think old Blake is sittin' somewhere behind that wall."

Hawksby sniffed. "I bloody well hope he is, anyway. Come on, let's cross the Marnan bridge. We might get a better view over that wall."

Their last task that afternoon was to visit Isfahan Airport on the south-east outskirts of the city. First changing into overalls they had been carrying in their holdalls, Hawksby and Forbes approached one of the security gates used by airport workers.

After a nerve-cracking few moments when the guard was evidently puzzled why he did not recognise the faces on the forged passes that had been supplied by Curt Swartz Jnr., they were in. Hawksby's explanation that they had been sent down from Teheran Airport to make up staff shortages seemed to satisfy the man.

Once inside the vast dusty airfield it was an easy matter to locate the helicopter park. There were plenty of the machines, as Iran had its own massive manufacturing plant at Shiraz and, with the vast distances to be crossed, flying was often the most viable means of transport for wealthier businessmen. So many had fled since the Revolution, the park was now filled to overflowing.

Hawksby approached a mechanic who was taking a much

extended lunchtime snooze in the shade of one of the machines.

"We've been sent to do a survey of serviceable helicopters," Hawksby said in an officious tone.

The man shielded his eyes from the sun as he looked up at the two strangers. "You're the fourth this year. You head office people don't know your left from your right hand!"

Hawksby peered disdainfully down his nose. "Your insolence has been noted. I am here to sort out the mess they made of the other three surveys. *This* time it will be correct. I want you to recommend the best six helicopters and we will test them."

"Now get up," Forbes growled. "If Allah had meant you to spend your life on your bottom he'd have given you the figure of a woman!"

Reluctantly the mechanic showed them along the long line of abandoned helicopters and selected half-a-dozen that he swore were airworthy.

Forbes then proceeded to try them in turn, revving up each until it was about to lift from the ground. Half were flying death-traps, some cannibalised of vital parts. Of the remaining three only one, a Bell JetRanger, had a full tank of kerosene.

"Will it get us there, Dave?" Hawksby asked.

Forbes shrugged. "It'll have to." He opened the engine cowl and extracted the igniter plug, placing it carefully in his overall pocket. "Short of actually taking off, I don't know what other surprises it may have. At least it's got fuel."

Hawksby seemed satisfied. "Even if it doesn't last the whole course, it'll get us out of Isfahan. And the Iranians don't like flying at night."

"Like the old American injuns?"

The major nodded.

"I just hope *they* know they don't like flying at night."

The twenty mile journey back to the Sabre team's hideout took until late evening. Hawksby and Forbes went by the same route they had used that morning, catching a return lift on a railway wagon bringing in ore from Zarand.

Alighting into railside shrubbery as the train neared the Arya-Mehr steel complex, they moved swiftly overland on foot for the remaining six miles.

"You see any of them voluptuous belly-dancers?" Kangers demanded of Forbes.

The sergeant was tired. "Haven't you learned anything during mission preparations, you ignorant bloody Aussie!" he snapped.

Kangers looked hurt. "Well you've been gone s' bleedin' long we thought you must've had your leg over somethin', yer miserable Pom!"

"You wouldn't say that if you saw the old bags we did," Forbes replied. "We now know why old Crazy K insists the women cover their faces. He can't stand the bloody sight of 'em!"

At precisely 1205 Tiger tapped out a high-speed coded Morse message on the radio: *Dragon One to Dragon Two. Tomorrow night Plan A. Over.*

Fifty-five miles to the south, deep in the Zagros Mountains, the four men of McDermid's Sabre team sat around Panther Two expectantly as Pogo operated the vehicle's radio. The big Fijian's face lit up as he translated the message.

McDermid grinned. "Canny bastards. I knew the Hawk'd pull it off." He nodded towards the transceiver behind the front seats. "Okay, just acknowledge, then put oot a long-distance to Oman."

Pogo nodded, his usual serious expression having returned.

The Scotsman stood up and breathed deeply on the chill night air. "I feel better fer hearin' that, laddies. I reckon we're as good as home'n'dry."

That night Forbes crashed out into an exhausted sleep. Hawksby, however, awoke in the early hours, his mind spinning with recollections of the past few days and worries about the challenge to come. He tossed around restlessly for an hour but couldn't get back to sleep. There were too many nagging questions at the back of his mind. Not least was why was Blake wanted and why was it so important not to tell at least the SAS team leader? That was fairly unusual. As old allies the secret service normally put the SAS in the picture. Or part of it. Not this time. Zilch.

During the day that followed a series of animated and heated discussions developed amongst the group as to how best to execute the operation. Each idea was carefully examined for faults or shortcomings, and then rejected or put to one side for possible use.

Having become closer to the major during their joint reconnaissance, Dave Forbes now found the distance between them growing again. The Hawk had stronger and more distinct views about how things should be done than most other SAS commanders under whom he had served. When Hawksby put forward his ideas, they were pitched in such a way that it dared anyone to challenge them. That acted like a red rag to a bull with the sergeant who proceeded to query every detail. It was as though he was part of an SAS officer training course, trying to upset a new recruit who was unused to having his orders queried.

Hawksby, although restrained, was becoming visibly more irritated with Forbes' endless criticisms. In the end, Kangers Webster said, exasperated: "For Chrissakes, Dave, what's gotten into you? D'ya want to plan the entire op by yerself?"

Startled by the outburst, Forbes looked sheepish. "Sorry, boys, I just want to be sure we've got it right." He glanced at Hawksby. "Sorry, boss, if I've been making heavy weather of things."

Hawksby looked quizically at the veteran SAS sergeant. "That's all right," he said quietly. "It's a nerve-racking time for all of us."

Kangers and Tiger Ratna exchanged glances.

TEHERAN: 1900 hrs, Thursday 18th September

The call from Paris that Colonel Najaf Murad had been so anxiously awaiting did not finally get put through until early evening.

At that moment the office was particularly quiet, and the sudden strident call made the SAVAMA officer jump. But his voice was as quiet and calm as always when he spoke.

"You took your time."

"The problems are at your end, Colonel. What's happened to our country? Communications seem to be a shambles like everything else."

Murad chuckled. "That's traitorous talk nowadays, my friend. Now tell me, what have you found out? Oh, wait a moment." He reached beneath his desk and turned off the tape recorder. "That's fine."

He listened patiently and without interruption as his ex-SAVAK colleague, who had been wise enough to keep out of the country since Khomeini's return, recounted his further investigations into the Mulcruf Foundation.

The two trustees had, as he suspected, vanished without trace back in 1978. A dead-end had been reached almost immediately on the American, Hassan-'Ali. He appeared not to have existed before or since he rented a short-lease apartment in Florida.

There was more luck with the Canadian, Hussein, who evidently supplied the money. He had opened an account at a Canadian bank with a cheque for $200,000, drawn on an unlimited British company called Zenith Exports with a registration address at a firm of solicitors in London's Whitechapel. That company's owner, a man called 'John Roberts', had subsequently disappeared from the face of the earth. However, Murad's diligent researcher had managed to establish that Zenith's main customer and benefactor was a small Wiltshire dairy products company with a farmhouse address. Two of the directors were a husband and wife; the third name was 'Ian Jones'.

A British private investigator had been hired to find out about the business, but it transpired that there was little to tell. A mutual friend had introduced the man called 'Jones', who persuaded the farmer and his wife to act as 'sleeping partners' in his dairy products business, although it appeared that they never actually sold so much as a pint of milk. 'Jones' had put in all the money in the two years of the operation, and they received a handsome £20,000 annual salary for just signing the necessary legal documents. They knew they were not to ask questions, and they didn't. Then, in 1978, the company was put into voluntary liquidation with all outstanding debts settled. Very neat, very clever, and all loose ends sewn up.

The couple had not seen 'Mr. Jones' from that day to this.

Pushing his investigations further, the private detective had managed to secure a blurred family album photograph of the farmer, his wife and two children in which 'Mr. Jones' appeared, evidently trying to get out of shot in the shadow of a tree. However, the distinctive black moustache was unmistakable.

Colonel Murad's agent had met Ian Stanton Ferguson, Deputy Head of the British SIS Middle East section too many times from his Colonial Office days not to recognise him instantly.

By the time the colonel had hung up his heart was pounding. Reaching forward he poured a glass of iced water from the crystal jug on his desk. He turned the implications of the discovery over in his mind. If Britain had been behind the Mulcruf Foundation it meant that they had also supported Ayatollah Khomeini in exile. It might even be said that they were instrumental in his return to power and the downfall of the Shah. He shook his head to clear his mind; it just didn't make sense.

If there was just the smallest grain of truth in the story, Britain would surely be desperate to keep it secret. After all, it would hardly endear them to the Americans, or their NATO allies. And how would the Imam and the Revolutionary Council react if they knew that the British – perhaps even with the connivance of the Americans – had secretly helped bring him to power? Just the whiff of such a scandal could be enough to bring Khomeini crashing down and throw the country into open civil war.

He thought of Blake, and the original discovery by Sabs Karemi. Just how much did the journalist know? He had had no real reason to disbelieve the man when he had admitted that he had read about the Mulcruf Foundation. After all, he had been under pressure of the torture threat to his girlfriend. Already he had been deeply shaken by the mock execution earlier, so his senses should have been so shattered as to find telling the truth painfully irresistible.

Perhaps, my friend, you are tougher than you look, Murad thought savagely. If Karemi was so sure that he could lure you into helping him, then in view of this new discovery, he must have thrown you a few more juicier morsels . . .

He did not give many chances for Blake's survival now. Once the Imam realised what the journalist knew he would insist on his execution – foreign national or not. And if he were ever to be released, then Murad was sure that the British would silence him. How could they risk the man on the loose with such information?

The colonel suddenly realised the momentous importance of his discovery. Now he was a party to that forbidden secret. He knew that in Iran the price of such knowledge could be death. But elsewhere? Elsewhere such knowledge could be profoundly rewarding. Before this went any further he would have to establish the fullest extent of Blake's knowledge. He would leave for Isfahan immediately.

Murad's aide burst in. "Trouble, Colonel. I think that Khalkali's still raging because you took his prisoners from him. He's been stirring up the Revolutionary Council and now they're baying for your blood. You are to report to them this evening and they expect answers!"

Damn! The colonel thumped his fist on the desk in a rare gesture of rage. Iced water slopped from the glass onto the leather top.

Being a perceptive young man, the aide thought it unwise to say more. Instead he just went to the OUT-tray and lifted the stack of files of suspected traitors and the signed detention orders.

The name on the third file from the top of the stack was *Hameda Gulistani*.

Ayatollah Khomeini closed his eyes and sat, cross-legged, in silence.

Beheshti's eyes burned darkly above the thin crooked nose as he watched his leader with increasing alarm. Such news could finally kill off the old man, such was his ailing state of health.

For once, even Khalkali was silent.

Colonel Murad, seated on the carpet before the trio, attempted to collect some saliva into his parched throat. Since deciding to reveal all that he knew, his body seemed to have dehydrated involuntarily. He could feel the sweat soaking into his silk shirt down the length of his back. His palms left damp imprints on his carefully pressed suit trousers.

He knew that if they didn't like what he had said, he could be a dead man by morning.

Suddenly Khomeini's eyes flickered open, his decision made. "It is a plot against us," he said with slow deliberation.

Beheshti and Khalkali leaned forward to catch his words.

"It is the work of the Great Satan America and its partner in crime Britain," the Imam continued. "It is all a snake's nest of lies. The venom must be removed and the reptiles put to death. God's truth must prevail."

Beheshi's eyes glittered. "*Agha*, might it not be unwise to kill the man Blake until the colonel has been able to extract more from him?"

The face of the old man looked tired, but it was set in an expression of grim determination. "Why extract more lies? Put him to death and his lies die with him."

"But it will also draw attention to him," Beheshti persisted. "We have not yet killed a foreign national, and the international furore would get everyone asking questions."

The Imam's wisdom was not to be so easily shaken. "You cannot ask questions of a dead man. My dear Beheshti, you should use those brains with which God has blessed you. Fill the snake-pit with acid. Destroy the purveyor of lies. The man Karemi is dead because he could not live with himself in the knowledge that he had committed blasphemy with his lies. Blake is like a messenger pigeon that has not left the cote.

If we do not let him leave the cote, then he has no message to deliver."

Murad suddenly got the distinct feeling that the old man knew. Knew that all the time he had been manipulated by foreign powers, but just didn't care. In his turn he had just accepted their money and influence, and made the most of it. The very thought chilled him.

Beheshti looked at Murad for inspiration, but was met with the man's professional mask of indifference. Unlike the Imam, he was unable to view life with the same medieval simplicity. It was, anyway, obvious that the wise old man would not last forever and it was he, Beheshti, as the unobtrusive power behind the Islamic Republican Party, who would have to contend with whatever trouble was brewing behind this whole Mulcruf Foundation affair. For all he knew the plot could involve the rivals of the Majlis in the conspiracy. He knew full well that the apparent British involvement could be just the tip of an iceberg. Maybe the pro-Soviet Tudeh Party or the Mojahedin were involved, or the Shah's supporters in exile. No, he must know more.

Khomeini waved his hand dismissively. "Ours is the world's first government of God and nothing must be allowed to blemish its name. I command you to destroy the man and the woman. Let that be an end to it. In all my long life I have never been wrong about what I say." He waved for his son Hamad to assist him to his feet.

When Murad stepped out into the cool night air, he found that Beheshti's green Range Rover was still outside, surrounded by his armed henchmen. Then one of the tinted windows was wound down, and the colonel saw the ayatollah signal to him.

"Colonel," said Beheshti, "you must obviously do what the Imam says. But the usual time for execution is dawn and it is now only eight o'clock. Go to the prisoner in Isfahan tonight. I am sure you can learn a lot before the sun rises. I should be most grateful." His dark eyes seemed to penetrate the security man's skull with their unblinking gaze. "Do I make myself understood?"

Without pausing for the reply, Beheshti wound up the

window. Murad was left standing in the swirling dust-storm as the Range Rover accelerated away.

For once in his life Colonel Najaf Murad felt uncertain, and very alone.

It was time to look for help elsewhere.

CHAPTER EIGHT

Well before nightfall everything was settled.

After a final briefing the Snapdragon team relaxed over a hastily-prepared concoction from self-heating Compo ration cans. A liberal sprinkling of curry powder made it almost edible.

Then the last-minute preparations began in earnest. Over dark green fatigues were slipped specially-tailored olive drab field jackets. These had been provided back at Hereford, based on recent photographs of what revolutionary guards were currently wearing. Although the garments looked the same, they had larger reinforced pockets and were cut loose in traditional SAS style with room for a lot of movement around the arms.

Each man wore a single belt-order rather than the mass of webbing carried by traditional British Army units, which becomes heavy and uncomfortable when wet. To this were fixed a number of large olive plastic respirator cases, in place of pouches, for medical kits, emergency dried rations and ammunition. In addition they took two metal water bottles apiece. All fittings used single popper-studs reinforced with self-cling Velcro.

The entire team was armed with Israeli-designed Uzis. Their simple, no-nonsense design made them ideal for desert conditions. They were easy to conceal, as well as offering a standardisation of ammunition with the soldiers' 9 mm Browning automatic pistols. Hawksby had insisted on the Uzis in preference to the cumbersome West German Heckler & Koch G3s which the revolutionary guards were now sporting. If anyone noticed that his men's guns were different, the obvious assumption would be that they were an elite unit. That suited Hawksby's plans well. The major didn't encourage prima donnas when it came to weapons selection, and he considered it crucial to standardise everything as much as possible. It may be fine in the movies with each man expert with a different weapon, but in a firefight, if you ran out of 9 mm ammunition, it was no good if your colleague could only offer 7.62 mm cartridges.

Everyone carried a standard fighting knife. Additional pump-action Remington repeater shotguns with snap-down skeleton butts were taken by Kangers and Tiger to deal primarily with locked doors and what the Australian euphemistically referred to as 'crowd control'. They packed their own 12-gauge solid shot and 1 oz slugs.

A minimum number of magazines were distributed amongst the men to keep down weight. It took only seconds for an expert to fill up an empty clip with loose rounds. A small selection of L2 fragmentation, smoke, incendiary and stun-grenades were handed out, together with illumination flares. As the explosives expert, Forbes had the additional burden of a dozen special 1 lb SAS-packs of PE4 and a variety of fuses. Far from complaining at the extra load, he was more anxious to have the chance to use the stuff.

Like the others, he stowed this additional paraphernalia for the mission into a small lightweight back-pack, along with flotation bags, toggle ropes, wire-cutters, line, and IWS Starlight 'scopes for night viewing. They also took a change of clothing that would be needed before the night was through.

All sleeping kit and camping equipment was discarded, buried in a pit deep in the river reedbeds.

Kangers took the Clansman radio for contact with the base team, but VHF Pye Pocketfones were worn by each soldier for secure short-distance communication amongst the four. The 'talking brooches' were discreet and uncumbersome, with a throat-mike and a small receiver earpiece.

With spirits high and the adrenalin pumping hard, the team ate up the six mile hack to the Arya-Mehr steel works in a mere thirty minutes, trotting most of the distance. Finally they were overlooking the vehicle compound that Hawksby and Forbes had earmarked during their earlier reconnaissance.

Tiger excelled himself as the team's master locksmith and was swinging open the tall gates within forty-five seconds. Selecting a nondescript 1½ ton Simca truck with a canvas cargo body, it took only a further minute under the bonnet for Forbes to get it started. Closing the gates behind them, they set off towards Isfahan ahead of schedule. To cheerfully disrespectful wolf-whistles from the rest of the team, Hawksby donned a white turban and brown mullah's robe. That done, they raised the canvas sidescreens to be in full view of everyone they passed.

The curfew situation was very fluid and uncertain, depending largely on the whim of the local Revolutionary Council, and Hawksby had decided that the best approach was to brazen it out rather than risk driving surreptitiously down the narrow streets. Iranian militia patrols, he reasoned, would not be so keen to apprehend an authoritative-looking mullah and his gun-happy henchmen.

The major's decision paid off, for they travelled without interruption to their first destination, a remote spot in the north-west of the town on the main Isfahan-Qum-Teheran road. The Simca pulled over into a roadside copse while Forbes busied himself strapping the green cardboard-covered block of PE4 to a pole that carried the main telephone link to the capital. He screwed the detonator of the clockwork time fuse into the small aperture in the pack of plastic explosive, checked his watch, and set the dial for exactly four hours and three minutes.

He gave his handiwork one last admiring glance. At precisely 0145 Iranian time Isfahan would lose all contact with the outside world. Unable to communicate with their superiors in Teheran, the local revolutionary guards and Gendarmerie would be running around like chickens who'd lost their heads.

The urgent squawk of the truck's hooter spurred the sergeant on. He hurriedly stowed his kit and returned to the others.

"You can't hurry a masterpiece like that," he grumbled, scrambling in as Tiger swung the vehicle onto the road.

"We can't allow for your artistic temperament, Dave. We've only got an hour to do the pylons," Hawksby said.

Forbes lit a cigarette, his mind still on the detonation he had just prepared. "That should roast Buzby's feathers for him, all right."

They continued north, taking the next left-hand turn which took them eastwards, arcing in a wide loop back towards Isfahan. It also took them past one of the massive pylons, on the edge of the outlying town of Homayunshahr. The giant steel legs carried the overhead power cables from the lakeside Zayandeh hydro-electric dam fifty miles to the west.

Laying a suitable combination of charges to bring down the pylon took Forbes and Kangers a full thirty minutes. Using twin packs of PE4 at each station, they set charges at two of the steel feet and two more up on the cross-bracings on the same side. Synchronising the time-fuses was tricky but, when they all went, the pylon would collapse to its knees. Forbes' nagging fear was that a spark would leap the necessary six feet to set off a charge prematurely.

They were still running to schedule when they climbed back into the Simca for the last leg of the journey back to Isfahan. They followed the river until they reached a quiet, dark side road, lined with plane trees. Tiger switched off the engine and beckoned Forbes to join the others in the back. Kangers and Tiger rolled down the canvas top over the cargo body frame, shutting off the outside world as they climbed in.

"Let's synchronise," the major said. "1155 hours."

Around him hunched figures nodded in agreement. In the dim light the pale faces looked tight and tense. There was no humour in anyone's eyes. For once, no one joked.

"That gives us five minutes," Hawksby continued. "Is everyone happy with what they've got to do?"

It was a perfunctory query. At this stage he would not expect anyone to have a question that hadn't already been discussed. Just an element of fine tuning, perhaps?

No one spoke. Glances were exchanged. Heads shook.

Everything settled. The plan clear. They were anxious to be going.

"Good. No last minute questions then?" Hawksby asked unnecessarily. He could feel the nerves flexing uncomfortably in his guts.

"Just one." It was Kangers.

Hawksby raised his eyebrows. Surprised.

"Can I be RTU'd now, please?"

The sudden choke of suppressed laughter was like the welcome relief of a safety-valve.

To Forbes' surprise, Hawksby grinned widely.

The Australian shrugged. "It was worth a try."

Hawksby slipped his back-pack over one shoulder beneath his robe, and gathered the folds of material around the Uzi. "Ready, Tiger? Give us five minutes, then you two leave. Okay?"

"Good luck, boss," Forbes said.

"Tashakkur," Hawksby replied with a smile. He leapt agilely over the tail board, with the small Gurkha close on his heels.

Precisely five minutes later, their faces and hands striped with camouflage cream, the sergeant and the Australian climbed out and melted into the shadows.

"Just the two of them then," Kangers Webster confirmed. He was studying the green semi-negative scene of the riverside mansion through the Starlight 'scope.

"One at the rear wall," Forbes said, "and one on the roof."

As if to emphasise the point a searchlight came on, blinding the 'shuftiscope'.

The faint whine stopped as the Australian turned off the night-sight and carefully replaced it in the waterproof carrying-case clipped to his belt. "That's a bit of a sod."

The sergeant's teeth glistened in the darkness. "You want it with cherries on?"

"I'm all for the easy life. Trouble is it's so damn cold, they'll be alert."

Forbes grunted. "They'll have to be."

"You want to change the plan? I mean you and that wop

144

can't share the roof. It just ain't big enough for the two of you."

"Stop talking like bloody Wyatt Earp." Forbes picked up the coil of nylon rope he had secured to the base of a willow tree at the water's edge. He shackled it to the harness belt around his waist.

"I suppose you can swim, Dave?"

Forbes swung the black polythene bag in a half-circle, filling the gaping mouth with air. "I got my proficiency badge in the Cubs."

"Anyone ever tell you you're over-qualified for this job?" Kangers said as he watched the sergeant's Uzi and back-pack disappear into the flotation bag.

Pausing with his parachute ankle boots in the water, Forbes said: "In case I get water in my mike, I'll just give three tugs on the line, right? Then you skin across."

"Check." He slapped the sergeant on the arm. "Keep your arse down. I always want to remember it like it is now."

"Piss off," Forbes replied, and waded into the gurgling, sluggish current of the Zayandeh as Kangers played out the blackened rope.

Within seconds the soldier's bulky form was lost from view as he paddled himself gently downstream behind the inflated bag. During this season of the year the river was very shallow in places and he found himself on hands and knees a lot of the way. He hardly noticed the chill temperature of the water, as the sense of danger and anticipation kept his own body heat high. His heavy boots caused the most discomfort, together with the cooling swirl around his crutch.

It took just ten minutes before his feet touched the pebbles on the other side of the river. Forbes estimated it to be about a hundred and twenty five yards at that point. Slowly and quietly he dragged his sodden bulk out of the water and rolled into the comparative dryness of a reedbed. Within seconds he had the Uzi in his hands as he began a systematic study of the approach to the rear of the villa. There was no one about and the only sign of life came from the parapet of the garden wall where a revolutionary guard occasionally played the heavy-duty searchlight along a span of the riverside walk. It was casual, careless and unprofessional. Forbes smiled to himself.

He reached down and gave the rope three hard tugs. Then he began winding in the slack as he felt movement on the other end.

Kangers' progress was much quicker until he reached the halfway mark. There he slipped the small lead weight over the rope. With a hiss and a ripple the rope submerged. After that the going was slower until he was almost at the water's edge.

"Okay?" Forbes whispered.

The Australian nodded, and began to extract the kit from his flotation bag. After a moment he tapped Forbes on the shoulder.

"Let's get on," the sergeant said. He began wading around the edge of the reedbed to avoid making an otherwise inevitable noise. Following behind, Kangers played out the slack rope.

One hundred yards upstream they found themselves directly opposite the villa wall. Now the rope to the opposite bank was running with the current.

Forbes checked his watch. 0130 hours. Fifteen minutes to go. Above them the upstretched hands of the riverside poplars rustled in the cool night breeze. The waters of the Zayandeh lapped around the shallow embankment. Somewhere on the other side of the mansion wall a man coughed. The noises of the secret insect world began to cocoon them as though some hidden hand had slowly turned up the volume. They settled down to wait. It was going to be a long fifteen minutes.

Iraj was not a malicious man. Despite his outwardly aggressive and surly manner, he was really a simple soul.

Although he could read and write, which gave him an advantage over the majority of Iranians, he was not very intelligent. He had easily fallen prey to the fervour and angry resentment that had swept the country during the Revolution. Irresistibly, he had been drawn into the rhetoric and petty viciousness of the new Islamic regime. His cruelty was that of the peasant boy to whom the killing of farm animals meant nothing, and that of other human beings conveyed little more. Led on by his cleric elders and fellow guards, he had not thought to question the conditions in which Jonathan Blake and Eva Olsen were held. Or the humiliations to which they had been periodically subjected. He saw himself in the forefront of a crusade to purge his country of internal and foreign parasites. Until he had been given the orders from Teheran to prepare the prisoners for 'intensive interrogation prior to execution' it had never crossed his mind that he might be debasing human dignity. Now he watched the girl through the peephole in the steel door to the bare basement cell as she paced up and down like a frightened caged animal. He compared her proud defiance of those early days of her arrest with her twitchy nervousness now.

Iraj knew that neither she nor her boyfriend had actually suffered physical torture. Even the mock execution at Ghasr had been purely psychological, and all other pressures had taken the form of threats and deprivation. He knew for a fact that his fellow countrymen had suffered worse. Foreign nationals, although they might not think so at the time, were treated with leniency.

But this new order changed all that. He had seen enough of the new regime to know that now the gloves were coming off. He knew that the mansion's doctor might have his work cut out keeping the couple alive until the execution at dawn. The list of ingenious torture apparatus he had been told to prepare turned his stomach. Most of it had been used before by SAVAK, and he wondered why the new regime, which was supposed to do away with all the torture and internment, need apply such fearsome techniques themselves?

He turned the key in the lock and heaved open the door. The girl looked round. Her eyes, sunken with fatigue, were suddenly bright with fear.

"It's all right, Miss Olsen." He tried to smile reassuringly.

She relaxed at the sight of the friendly face. "I t'ought it was Colonel Murad."

Iraj tried not to let her see him watching the slender body

that the patched and tattered clothes did little to hide. "He be here soon, but not yet. You cold?"

She hugged her arms and nodded. "It's freezin' in 'ere. Please, what iss time?"

"Nearly two o'clock."

"My God," she breathed. "Can't I wait in my cell? At least I 'af blankets."

Triumphantly he held up a tatty bundle of hairy mildewed material. "See, I bring for you! But you cannot go back. The colonel insist you are waiting when he comes. If I disobey . . ." He did a cutting gesture across his throat.

She took the blankets gratefully.

"Your hair grow." He smiled at her. "Look nice again, soon."

She almost wanted to laugh. "T'ank you."

"I make you tea. Warm you up inside. Quick before he comes. He is late already."

This time the smile came. "T'at really would be nice. You iss kind." She reached out and put a hand on his arm without thinking. He jumped back as though scalded.

"I'm sorry," she said, then suddenly thought how ridiculous it was that she should be apologising to him.

He, too, seemed to realise suddenly that the object of all his secret desires over the past weeks had actually *touched* him. He almost swooned, and stood grinning stupidly.

Then the lights went out.

Iraj laughed. "Electricity no good before Revolution, and no good now. Still we get the failures. The Imam doesn't like electrics."

Eva smiled. "Per'aps 'e is as wise as t'ey say."

The guard nodded. "I go now. Brew up your tea."

Happy for himself, but still concerned at what the future held for his beautiful Norwegian prisoner, he closed and locked the door.

Suddenly the searchlight on the mansion wall, which had been playing along the river bank, flickered and died. Cries of dismay in Persian drifted through the still air, followed by curses as someone stumbled. Far in the distance, Forbes' trained ear picked up the sound he had been waiting for: the dull thud of explosive.

Around them the twinkling lights of Isfahan faltered for a moment before the entire city was swallowed up by the black velvet night.

Hawksby's voice in the earpiece of the Pocketfone was decisive. "*Go!*"

"Roger," replied Forbes and tapped the Australian on the shoulder. "Move it!"

Together they slid into the darkened undergrowth like menacing black snakes. They moved surprisingly fast across the open expanse of embankment which was now bathed only in a gentle, eerie starglow. There were no tell-tale reflections on the kit of the two men as they continued their deliberate writhing motion through the long grass to the edge of the poplars. Hands and faces were thoroughly blackened, and all bright surfaces had been cautiously wrapped in matt black insulation tape or had been deliberately dulled with dirt. Nor was there any sound from the equipment which had been carefully hooked and attached around their bodies so that metal did not touch metal.

In the few short minutes it took to reach the lee of the twelve foot wall, both men were wringing with sweat from the exertion and the mounting tension as pounding hearts sent blood coursing through their veins.

Without a word Forbes slid the Uzi from his shoulder and, dropping to one knee, trained its long silenced snout on the section of wall where the guards had their observation platform, some forty feet to their right. Using the special L-clip, he had joined two 32-round magazines together, giving the weapon an oddly unbalanced look. But it gave him a devastating and prolonged blast of 9 mm firepower without the need to reload.

A mumble of complaining voices in Farsi came from the other side of the wall. Forbes strained to hear. Damn.

He held up his left hand with three fingers extended. Kangers wrinkled his nose in disgust. The sergeant gave him a thumbs-up, and they began the routine they had practised endlessly at a specially-built replica of the wall back at Hereford.

There were to be no 'James Bond' gadgets like extendable ladders or one-man helicopters. A twelve foot wall was easy to take in the time-honoured SAS fashion. Back against the wall, with knees bent, Forbes cupped his hands to take Kangers' weight as the Australian used him as a human ladder.

As the sergeant straightened up, Kangers was able to peer through the spiral of modern barbed razor-wire along the top of the wall.

Warfare, he mused, was definitely becoming more spiteful.

A few yards away he could see the outline of the wooden observation platform and the shapes of the three guards smoking and chatting beneath it. No one actually faced him: two had their backs in his direction, and the third was at an oblique angle.

He reached down a hand to snatch the padded combat jacket that Forbes passed up to him. With a quick flick of the wrist he threw it over the wire. He had already decided against cutting it. If the clipping sound hadn't alerted the guards, then the wanging spring of uncoiling razor-wire certainly would.

Instead Kangers threw himself smoothly over the jacket until he sat astride the wall. In one practised movement he unswung the Uzi from his shoulder and lined up the pip on the gunsight.

One of the guards, who had his back to the intruder, began to laugh and glance around the grounds. He shifted his position. That blocked the direct line of sight to the one man who was actually holding his carbine so that it could be quickly brought to bear.

"Come'n, my Islamic beauty," Kangers muttered under his breath. "Jesus wants you for a sunbeam."

The laughing man stepped back.

Phut! Phut! Phut! Phut!

Death slammed viciously and silently out of the night in three seconds of bewilderment and brief, lethal pain. Distributed in the SAS style of two shots per target. To be sure.

Phut! Phut! By the time the third man had hit the ground, Kangers was already pegging the razor wire so that it wouldn't unravel when the steel jaws of the cutters bit through it. Just two brief snaps and he was able to drop a length of the wicked stuff safely into a thick bed of vegetation.

Forbes had already threaded together four toggle ropes. Each six-foot length had a loop at one end of a four-inch wooden toggle at the other. Locked into each other, it gave a four-man Sabre team an instant twenty-four-feet scaling rope.

The sergeant tossed it up to Kangers and began his ascent. Within thirty seconds both men were in the mansion gardens – the guards eliminated and an escape route secured.

The Australian pointed to the inky silhouette of the building which grew out of the trees a hundred yards away. The cut-out shape of the flat roof, with its tall chimneys at either end of the central raised skylight section, were quite distinct. So was the outline figure of the patrolling guard who appeared to be hugging himself for warmth against the chill night.

"I could do a long-shot?" Kangers offered.

Forbes shook his head. He didn't want a dead body dropping to one knee, trained its long silenced snout on the outside the front door.

"Stay on station," he said briskly, "and negotiate anyone who gets too close until we're on the way out."

Kangers Webster nodded his understanding and then, waiting until the sergeant had disappeared towards the rear of the mansion, settled down to hold the snatch team's exit route.

The revolutionary guard on the roof was cold and he was hungry. Before Khomeini's return from exile he had been a professional soldier, but he had been one of the first to desert. Now his expertise was valued by the new regime and Colonel Murad in particular. He had been pleased to be assigned to these special duties, guarding the highly-prized foreign prisoners kept in the cellars. He would have preferred to be looking after the American hostages, some of whom were in another house not far away in Isfahan. There was more prestige attached to guarding them, especially as everyone thought the Americans might try another rescue attempt. No one seemed interested in the two foreigners below. No one, that was, except Murad.

The ex-soldier blew into his cupped hands. He really should have put on the extra jersey. He stamped his feet gently on the parapet and looked down into the darkened garden.

A dew drop formed on the end of his nose and he sniffed it back up into his nostrils. Funny, he thought, why hadn't those on the back wall turned on their torches. It looked like this was going to be one of the longer power cuts that they seemed to suffer so frequently, since the recently-built steel works had begun overloading the grid.

He looked up at the stars and, as he did so, forty feet below him a black shadow passed silently across the gravel path to the base of the drainage pipe at the side of the mansion.

In the shadow of the tall chimney stack, the SAS sergeant was aware that, like their civilian counterparts, soldiers behind the front-line never *really* thought that they were in immediate danger from the enemy. It was just an extension of the old 'It could never happen to me' syndrome. By the slack way the man was standing, Forbes also knew that he was tired and lacked concentration. Reaching forward, he eased a tiny pebble from the deep tread of his jump boot and tossed it towards the other chimney stack.

The picket looked across lazily to where he heard the scratching sound. A mouse? On the roof? A bird more likely . . .

That was the last thought he ever had.

There are three ways to kill a man quickly with a knife. Between the fifth and sixth ribs with a rapid up-and-twist motion to destroy the heart. But the blade can get jammed by muscle contraction. Another is to insert the blade below the left ear. Forbes went for the third option.

The powerful left forearm of the sergeant swung around the side of the guard's head and snapped close over his mouth like a steel vice. The man convulsed as he tried to cough up into the material that smothered him. His eyes nearly bulged out of their sockets as he saw the honed matt blade of the knife sweep up towards him. But he felt nothing as its scalpel point slid into the soft flesh under his chin and up into his brain. Nothing.

"One to Dragon Leader. In position. Over."

Sitting in the dirty green Peykan, which they had stolen forty-five minutes earlier, and was now parked in a side road opposite the villa, Hawksby smiled with grim satisfaction.

In the driver's seat beside him, Tiger was still watching the tall oak gates set in the high wall. There were no pickets outside, and the only sign of life was a solitary flickering light on a third-floor window.

Hawksby spoke into the mike clipped to the collar of his mullah's robe. "Someone's got a lamp on at the front. Can you see it? Over."

"Yes, I've had a look from the balcony. It's a radio room. They've got a hurricane lamp going. Leads run out to an aerial up here on the roof. Over."

Hawksby thought for a moment. There had been two advantages to be gained by knocking out the power. Obviously the opportunities for surprise were greatly enhanced, but it also meant that, prior to the attack at least, their opponents would have to use torches or lanterns to see their way around the building. As the SAS team had no way of knowing the internal layout of the place, or where the prisoner was held, the presence of lights enabled them to pinpoint areas of likely resistance.

He felt sure that for security Blake would be held on either the top floor or in the basement. Assuming that there would be a guard on duty at all times, it was likely he would want a light, even if the prisoner was kept in darkness. As the only light visible came from a communications centre, Hawksby felt fairly confident that they would find their prize in the basement.

"Proceed as planned, Dave. I think we'll probably find our hero below street level, so work your way down. But keep

your eyes peeled, because there's no guarantee he's there . . .
Dragon Two?"

"*Yes, boss?*" Kangers' voice crackled onto the network.

"Advance to the back door now, and keep the garden
sealed off 'til we get through."

"*Okay boss.*"

"Dragon One," Hawksby said quickly. "Put that radio
off the air will you, there's a good chap? Okay, let's go.
Out."

Forbes smiled to himself. It would be a pleasure.

He picked up the twelve-inch Schermuley Para-Ilum flare
from where he had placed it beside the one chimney that
smoked. Next to it he placed a No. 83 smoke grenade that
would ensure confusion by rapidly providing a seething and
impenetrable blue fog.

Holding the tube of the flare over the stack, he yanked the
pull-loop. There came a sudden *whoosh* of explosive as the
illumination flare rocketed down the chimney in a backlash
of flame and sparks. Imagining the scene of chaos below as
the Schermuley zoomed out of the fire and around the room
below, Forbes tossed in the No. 83, then quickly made his
way to the front of the building. Standing above the window
to the radio room, he extracted his knife again and sliced
through the cable to the roof aerial.

Colonel Murad was late. And he was furious. Tonight of all
nights his personal helicopter had developed a fault, and it
had taken the mechanics hours to fix. If only he had known, it
would have been quicker to have gone by car to Isfahan from
the outset.

That stupid mullah who had recently been put in charge of
the military airbase had refused point-blank to allow him to
use one of theirs, because he was worried about his pilots
crashing in the dark! Agitated, he strummed a tattoo on the
perspex canopy of the helicopter as it approached the airport
of Isfahan.

Next to him the pilot looked agitated. Beads of perspiration began to break out on his forehead.

"WHAT IS IT?" the colonel demanded above the clatter of the rotors.

"CAN'T FIND THE CITY! OR THE AIRPORT!" his voice verged on panic. "I THINK I'M LOST!"

Murad shook his head in disbelief.

Then, two thousand feet below, the emergency generator went into action and the lights of the runway and terminal buildings flickered on.

"PILOT, JUST GET THIS THING DOWN BEFORE I LOSE MY TEMPER!"

Part Two

OUT

CHAPTER NINE

Pandemonium broke loose within the villa.

"FIRE! FIRE!"

Ali looked up. He had just finished strapping Blake's wrists to the wooden arms of the upright chair which stood beside a long table strewn with interrogation apparatus.

Someone was banging wildly on the steel door. Quickly he picked up the hurricane lamp, crossed the concrete floor, and peered out through the spy-hole.

"Who's there? What's happening?"

He could hear people rushing around and colliding in the pitch black corridor that led up to the hall. Voices were raised in alarm.

Again someone shouted: "FIRE!"

Ali sniffed. Yes, he could smell smoke, too.

"Hey!" he cried. "Let me out!" He didn't intend to burn in hell or on earth, and certainly not trapped behind a locked steel door with a traitor. He shouted again, and this time the revolutionary guard who held the keys heard him.

"Let me out! What's happening?" Ali screamed.

The key turned and the door swung open. "There's a fire. It started in the kitchen. Apparently the tea vat on the stove just exploded!" Feeling more relaxed now that the door was opened, he laughed. "What's the cook put in it? Weedkiller and sugar. It tastes like it!"

The other man failed to see the funny side. "That's what he said. They're trying to stop the blaze spreading from the kitchen." More smoke began to tumble down the steps. "Hey, can I borrow your lamp? I can't see a thing out here with the lights off."

Ali was offended. "Certainly not. I'm looking after the prisoner."

A brass bell began to jangle fiercely at the top of the basement steps. The two men exchanged glances.

"Someone at the gate," Ali said. "It must be Colonel Murad. He'll be furious. The cook had better watch out!"

The guard grimaced and stumbled towards the steps, bumping into two more guards who were racing across the hall to the doors. The billowing smoke was thickening more than ever.

"Quick, get them open!" he shouted, "and let this smoke out. And for the sake of Allah find some more torches!"

The guard followed the others out through the doors, emerging on the front steps amid a mushrooming cloud of sickly smoke. His eyes streaming, he unshouldered his G3 as he ran down the path. Quickly he unbolted the gate and released the chains.

The hawk-nosed mullah looked imposing as the smoke wafted through the newly-opened hole in the wall and tumbled into the avenue.

"Colonel Murad?" the bewildered guard asked, trying to peer over the religious man's shoulder.

"Yes," Hawksby said gruffly. Whoever 'Murad' was, he was evidently expected and the opportunity was too good to miss.

The guard looked unsure, but Hawksby waved his gun aside with an elegant, commanding wave. Behind him Tiger looked sullen and arrogant in his spotless revolutionary guard's outfit.

"There are only two of you?" The guard looked out at the smoke now swirling in eddies around the trees in the avenue. "Hey, *agha*!"

He caught Hawksby by the sleeve. "Where's Colonel Murad?"

Hawksby brushed off his hand with an air of disdain. "He's coming. But it looks as though you have problems here. Quick! Lock the gate behind me! We don't want our prisoner escaping under cover of all this smoke!"

The guard looked surprised and ordered his two colleagues to secure the front entrance. "*Agha*, you know about the prisoner?"

"Of course," Hawksby answered imperiously.

"But I do not know *you*. I have never seen you before!"

Hawksby stared absently up at the gaping front door from which smoke continued to tumble. "Do you know our beloved Imam? Or our leader Beheshti?"

The man didn't know how to treat this authoritarian mullah. "You don't look like Beheshti," he ventured.

"Of course not," Hawksby replied. "I don't look like him because I am . . . his brother."

"Oh!" The man's mouth gaped and his eyes were wide with awe.

"Now we must take care that our important prisoner does not fry to death! Where is he?" Hawksby demanded, striding purposefully towards the steps.

"In the cellar, *agha*."

Hawksby said: "Fool! We shall put him in the rear garden. There he will not suffocate to death and he will be quite secure." He smiled sweetly at the perturbed guard. "Unless he is a monkey, eh?" The major paused. "Now, go and supervise the putting out of the fire, while I see to the prisoner."

Hesitating only for a moment, the man scurried off towards the kitchen, feeling thoroughly intimidated.

Harnessed to the chair in the cellar, Jonathan Blake was filled with black despair. The sense of foreboding had been gnawing at him since late afternoon when he had been informed that Colonel Murad was coming to conduct further interrogation. He realised by the tone of Ali's voice that the pressure was on. The screw was being turned. The guard gave no indication why, and indeed, Blake doubted if a peasant militant in such a lowly position would have been told anyway.

The journalist reasoned that he had been forewarned of the coming event so that he would have time to consider the consequences of his refusal to co-operate. It was like a prolonged wait outside a dentist's surgery with the sound of the drill whirring next door. His nerves felt frayed.

For some time now he had thought that he had got away with revealing only a limited knowledge of the Mulcruf Foundation, but nothing about its true significance. He had gambled that the Iranians would not really want to torture Eva, as they had threatened. Although he had heard many stories of nationals receiving such treatment under the mullahs, by all accounts they trod more cautiously with foreigners. Mock executions had been the vilest form of mental strain that had been used, he gathered, and victims of these had included some of the American hostages.

Evidently Murad wanted more now, and Blake knew that this time the silver-tongued interrogator would carry out his threat. If he was right, then he and Eva faced a new dilemma. To reveal all they knew might save them from the infliction of further pain, but it would also mean a certain death penalty. No one in Iran could know what he and Eva knew and be allowed to live.

He had spent the long hours of the night cursing Sabs Karemi's nocturnal visit and trying to work out a solution to his problem. But it was impossible unless he knew Eva's views. His brain felt as thought it was stuffed with cotton-wool, dulled and useless, paralysed with blind panic. And now, on top of everything, the fire. The guards seemed to be running around in chaos. Voices were raised in hectic frenzy as everyone shouted orders to everyone else. And no one seemed to be doing anything. Total bedlam.

It was then that he decided. As the smoke was getting worse, Ali would have to unshackle him from the chair. The cellar door was wide open. Outside the lights were out and everyone seemed confused. It was an ideal opportunity.

He looked at Ali's back. He was squinting into the corridor, his G3 slung carelessly over his shoulder. Could he overpower Ali? Blake was uncertain. The last time he had fought had been when he was eleven years old. It had been a playground battle over a myopic girl in pigtails. He had lost.

"Hey!" he called out on impulse. "I'm choking! Can't we get out of here until the fire's out?" He feigned a violent fit of coughing. Ali glanced back at the prisoner and considered.

The smoke was getting thicker, he was sure, but then if Murad had just arrived upstairs there could be hell to pay if Blake wasn't in his cell.

"You stay!" he called out.

He turned back to the corridor at the sound of heavy footsteps. A tall mullah emerged from the rolling clouds of smoke. He was followed by a squat, mean-looking revolutionary guard with slanted eyes that gave him a slightly Oriental appearance.

"Where's Blake?" the mullah demanded.

Ali was taken aback. He didn't know this man.

"Here," he replied without thinking. "Why, who wants to know?"

Hawksby ignored the question. "He is to be taken into the garden for safe-keeping. Otherwise he'll choke to death."

"On whose orders?" Ali was not sure. "Colonel Murad's?"

That name again. "Who else?" Hawksby replied aloofly, implying that the guard was a fool to think otherwise.

"I'll bring him," Ali replied. After all, it did seem a sensible thing to do. Blake would have to be a pole-vaulter to scale that wall.

"No," Hawksby answered quickly. "*We* will take him."

Again Ali looked uncertain. Then he shrugged and crossed to Blake, stooping to undo the arm straps and then the manacles that fastened his ankles to the chair legs.

No one had expected what came next. Summoning his courage and determination, Blake swung his feet upwards, catching Ali under the chin. The ferocity of it propelled him across the room in a half-somersault. Stunned for a moment, Ali lay on the floor. Then, seeing Blake leap from his chair, he reached for the G3 that had fallen by his side. For a man who had just been badly shaken his reactions were fast. He had the barrel trained before the journalist reached him.

But Ali wasn't fast enough. Flame spat silently from Tiger's unshouldered Uzi in a deadly one-second burst. Blake fell onto the Iranian with his hands about the man's throat.

Something warm and sticky pulsed through Blake's

fingers and he opened his eyes to see that Ali's face had gone. The 9 mm rounds had taken off his flesh like a bacon slicer, leaving behind an unrecognisable pulp of bone and red meat.

Hawksby hauled Blake from the dead guard. "Calm down, Jonathan. We're friends."

The sudden sound of the modulated English voice stunned Blake. He gaped up at the grinning bearded face in amazement.

"We'll have you out of here in a jiffy," the major continued. "Just play it cool and come along with us as though you are still a prisoner. Now turn around and put your hands behind your back." Roughly he spun the journalist and threaded some cord between his wrists. "This isn't tied, it's just for effect. We're going to take you through to the back garden. Should anything happen to us, or we get separated, make your own way if you can. One of our men is there and he'll see you're all right. Got that?"

Blake's mouth still hung open as he tried to comprehend the rapid burst of curt instructions. "You're British?"

Hawksby smiled reassuringly. "How d'ya, guess, old chap? Now shut up and come with us."

Blake resisted. "What about Eva?"

"Who?"

"Eva, my girlfriend. She's a press photographer. Eva Olsen. She's a prisoner here, too."

Hawksby was adamant. "No way, Jonathan. We've only planned on you. Now get weaving."

"NO!" Blake pulled away. "I'm not going without her."

"Look," Hawksby snapped, "you can come with us willingly or we'll carry you out unconscious. The choice is yours."

"You don't understand! She's got the film!"

"What film?"

Blake shook his head in despair. "*Please*! She *must* come. I can't explain . . ."

Hawksby hesitated.

Tiger, who had been keeping watch on the door, said: "You want me to get her, boss?"

Hawksby thought for a moment. "No, I'll go. Where is she?"

164

Blake inclined his head towards the corridor. "Two doors down."

Hawksby turned to Tiger. "Shut this door, and stay here until I get back."

The Gurkha nodded. "Better hurry, boss, this smoke thinning out. They must be gettin' fire under control."

Hawksby disappeared into the passage.

The major found the door to Eva's cell without difficulty. It was ajar and he peered in cautiously to see the unshaven, blue-chinned guard seated on an upturned orange box in the light of an oil lamp. He was drinking tea and talking to the girl. Hawksby was immediately struck by her beauty, particularly her bright violet eyes, despite the ragged blonde haircut and the old blankets she had around her.

She looked up as he entered, and the guard twisted around on his seat.

"Don't you know there is a fire?" Hawksby demanded in Farsi.

Iraj wasn't sure whether to challenge this stranger. "Someone said it's nearly out."

"Huh!" Hawksby retorted. "That's how much you know! This ceiling is about to collapse. I am taking this girl out the back to the garden."

Iraj misunderstood. He automatically assumed that the mullah meant that the prisoners were to go before a firing-squad. Several had been shot in the garden and buried in a quiet corner.

He climbed to his feet, deciding rashly that he wasn't going to let anything happen to this girl. It didn't occur to him that, over the weeks she had been his helpless captive, he might have become just a little infatuated with her.

"On whose orders?"

Hawksby used the name that seemed to impress everyone in the villa. "Murad."

Slowly the guard shook his head, as though making a difficult decision. He swung the G3 up into the firing position. "No, I will not permit it . . ."

The mullah's belly suddenly seemed to rip apart, the front of his robe bursting into blackened holes, as Hawksby squeezed the trigger of the concealed Uzi.

Eva gazed in amazement as the force slammed Iraj back against the wall. His spine hit the brickwork first, hard, so that his head jerked back sharply. There was an audible crack as his skull made contact with the hard surface. He slid slowly down the wall until he sat on the floor, his head slumped forward and his mouth slack, like a caricature of a sleeping man. Blood pumped from the sodden patch on his shirt.

Eva Olsen was horrified. Who was this ogre from whom even Iraj had tried to protect her?

"I've come to help you," Hawksby said quickly, reaching forward to take her arm.

She stepped back, her eyes wide with alarm. "What do you want with me?"

Hawksby frowned. "Norwegian?" He recognised the accent from the many times he had taken part in joint NATO exercises to reinforce the northern flank.

"Yes." Her voice was hoarse. "You iss English?"

He tried to be reassuring. "I'm not a mullah, I've come to get Blake out of here and you, too. Please don't hesitate, because we don't have much time before that fire is out."

"You start it?" Incredulous.

"A diversion."

"You'ss a secret agent?" Saying it like that made it seem like a joke. "A commando?"

"Sort of," Hawksby returned vaguely. "Now, *please!*"

She nodded. "But wait a moment." Turning, the girl rushed to a corner of the cell and, stooping down, eased a loose brick from the wall. She reached into the hole and pulled something out.

"Please, you can take it?" she said. "I 'af nowhere to keep it."

He accepted the small film cassette. Minox, he guessed. It was then that he realised that her filthy stained drill shirt and skirt were hanging in shreds beneath the blanket. "I can see your problem," he said, trying to avert his eyes.

Putting cord around her wrists, too, Hawksby pushed Eva into the passage, locked the door, and moved along to Blake's cell. To his double-knock Tiger opened it and ushered out the journalist. The smoke was now disappearing at an alarming rate and Hawksby led the party up the steps to the hall.

Forbes was waiting. He seemed to have four revolutionary guards under his command, rushing to fetch fire buckets as he bellowed instructions in Farsi. Hawksby couldn't resist a smile. It seemed that the qualities of an NCO were the same the world over.

"Slow it down," the major hissed at Forbes as they passed on their way to the back of the mansion, "the damn fire's nearly out!"

Once at the rear door, Hawksby swung it gently open to enable Kangers Webster to identify them. A sharp whistling note came from nearby shrubbery and the major saw the lean Australian emerge from the shadows. The Uzi waved them on urgently.

"Who *are* you people?" Blake murmured, not really expecting an answer.

Christ, they've taken their time, thought Kangers. But all he said was: "Straight down this gravel path, boss. Turn right at the wall. About ten metres along."

Hawksby guided the group forward, down between the fragrant flowering shrubs, past the three dead guards by the observation platform, and under the wall until they came to the scaling ladder.

Tiger sprang up it like a monkey, checked the other side, then leapt out of sight. Blake followed, swinging clumsily despite Hawksby's efforts to keep the ropes steady.

Kangers joined them as Eva began her ascent, making a better job of it than the journalist. The Australian glimpsed the exposed buttocks as she swung over the top of the wall.

He exchanged glances with Hawksby and a grin cracked his face. "Guess this job has it's compensations."

"Get over, you randy sod, and take them down to the crossing."

At the riverside, the weighted crossing rope was hauled taut and secured around the Australian's waist. Tiger went first to secure the opposite bank, then Blake was given a black flotation bag and clipped to the free-running shackle pulley.

Quickly he waded into the shallow water until he reached the deeper centre channel. There the current began to carry him downstream and across to the other side. Eva went next, followed by Hawksby.

Still outside the garden wall, Kangers glanced impatiently at the luminous dial of his watch. Where in the hell was Forbes?

Sergeant Dave Forbes was beginning to enjoy his role. He had never seen such a slovenly group of militiamen, and they seemed to be terrified at their first real taste of discipline. In their panic to obey this tyrannical Iranian NCO, who seemed to have sprung from nowhere, they were falling over themselves – sometimes literally – and shouting orders to each other. It all lent to the scene of uproar.

"But, *agha*," one diminutive student guard protested, "the fire is out now!"

"Nonsense!" Forbes bawled in Farsi. "Smouldering timbers can set the whole thing off again."

But, as the palls of smoke subsided, some sense of order was returning and the sergeant noticed that some of the more senior guards were starting to regain their composure and talk earnestly amongst themselves. Time for you to say your goodbyes, he thought to himself, and began backing surreptitiously towards the garden door.

One of the senior guards pointed to him. "Hey, you, I thought you said you were with Colonel Murad? I haven't seen him."

Forbes shrugged. "He was around. I expect he is upstairs somewhere."

"And what about the prisoners? Someone says your friend, the mullah, took them into the garden. Is that right?"

Forbes shook his head. "No, they took them out the front. Taking them back to Teheran."

Immediately he realised his stupid mistake. While he was so busy trying to confuse his enemy, he had confused himself. Iranians shake their heads for 'yes' and nod when they mean 'no'.

He heard the distinctive rasp of a cocking handle behind

him. Turning his head just a fraction, he glimpsed an intelligent-looking guard with a G3 pointed at the small of his back.

"I do not trust this stranger. Take his weapons, but do not get too close. I think he is dangerous." The man called to the others who were also lifting their weapons into the firing position. "Quick, go and check the garden. I heard the mullah saying they should take the prisoners there."

Christ, thought Kangers, the Hawk will kill me! He was angry with himself for his own indecision. Forbes was now five minutes behind the others, and yet he could not bring himself to cross the river and leave the sergeant to his own devices.

It was then he heard cries and shouts drifting through the still air from the wall. He could wait no longer. Grabbing the last flotation bag, which had been filled with all the left-over gear, he splashed into the chill water.

Simultaneously he heard the rifle crack and felt the sting-ing pain in his right arm. The shock of it on his nervous system made him drop the bag in a reflex reaction. Cursing, he stumbled farther into the water. More shots rang into the darkness and he saw tell-tale splashes around him.

Already the muscles in his right arm were beginning to numb and he knew he must be bleeding badly. He threw himself at the crossing rope, grabbing it fiercely with his left hand. Almost immediately he felt it being tugged in strong repetitive jerks. He knew instinctively that it must be Hawks-by and Tiger hauling him across from the opposite bank.

His vision was starting to blur. He gritted his teeth and tried to focus on his left hand. As he willed his concentration, his white strained fingers became an immovable steel claw in his mind. Even as they pulled him out on the other bank, his left hand still held a desperate grip on the rope. It was almost like a dead man's grip.

The helicopter carrying Colonel Murad landed heavily, fracturing one of the skis. However, he was not angry. He had been anticipating such a disaster and was just pleased to have got away with his life.

Bowing his head to avoid the slowing blades, he quickly left the pilot to worry about how to get the thing repaired.

Outside the terminal building a guard waited to chauffeur the colonel to the villa on the north bank of the Zayandeh. The man had gone to great trouble to impress his superior: freshly-laundered and pressed uniform and a field jacket he kept exclusively for his driving duties.

So he was greatly irritated when the colonel didn't even seem to notice him. In fact the SAVAMA officer only spoke once, when he asked about the lack of lights in Isfahan.

"Another power-cut I am afraid, *agha*," the driver replied respectfully.

Colonel Murad just gave an ill-tempered grunt and peered out of the side window at the dark streets flashing by.

Alan Hawksby was stunned by the speed at which everything had started to go wrong. It was bad enough Sergeant Forbes falling behind schedule. Possibly he had been overcome by the enemy, no doubt as a result of his own bull-headedness.

That would be typical of the man. But Kangers Webster's indiscipline in waiting too long for his companion was unforgivable. It was bad enough having to carry the semi-conscious Australian two hundred yards to the waiting Simca truck. But Webster's thoughtless action had cost Hawksby his second helicopter pilot. This was the problem foremost in his mind as he and Tiger thankfully rolled the Australian's deadweight onto the tailboard and hurried Blake and Eva Olsen inside.

Carrying the wounded man had lost them vital minutes. The guards must know that the team was headed south. Although they could not be sure of their quarry's destination, Isfahan Airport would seem a fairly obvious bet. Here, Hawksby's across-river escape route came into its own, providing a natural vehicle barrier. It was helped by the fact that the nearest bridge to the villa was for pedestrians only. By the time the guards reached the next bridge to the east,

Pol-e-Felezzi, the escaping truck should have had a head start. Now that lead might be only a matter of seconds.

Tiger had already substituted the Simca's headlamp bulbs with an infra-red set and, wearing the CUB viewer, Hawksby was able to drive at high speed down the darkened avenues to the airport. They managed to regain a few vital minutes on their planned schedule. By the time the Simca was parked opposite the airport's perimeter fence, Kangers was in less pain. Tiger had used one of the Australian's personal morphine syrettes, which he kept in a pouch around his neck. But he remained too weak to stand without assistance.

Disorientated by the unbelievable and fast turns of events, Blake and Eva followed the three SAS men in dumb obedience. The two prisoners were so stunned at their sudden freedom that they did not yet appreciate the difficulties that the snatch team were now in. Although emergency lighting was now on in the terminal buildings, the perimeter lamps were still out.

As Hawksby quickly stuffed his mullah's robes and turban into his back-pack he spoke to Blake: "I'm afraid, Jonathan, I need to enlist the assistance of you both. Tiger and I will go ahead through the wire. When he signals, I'd like you to help our wounded friend."

Eva glanced at Kangers who was sitting on the ground with his head in his hands, trying to shake off his double vision and feeling of nausea. "Will 'e be all right?"

"He'll survive," Hawksby replied curtly. "But on the first sign of any trouble just leave him and run through the wire in the direction of the helicopter compound. I'll show a small green light to guide you. Got it?"

Eva looked aghast. "Leave 'im, just like t'at?"

"Just like that."

She exchanged glances with Blake and shrugged.

Without waiting further, Hawksby and Tiger slithered across the intervening stretch of scrub to the fence. There the Gurkha kept watch with the cocked Uzi, while the major wielded the wire-cutters. In thirty seconds, a small section was removed and Hawksby wormed his way through. He moved in fast to where the Bell JetRanger would be waiting.

The compound was deserted and he had no difficulty finding the blue machine, although he had to waste valuable minutes locating a replacement igniter plug from another aircraft. Forbes still held the vital piece that had kept their getaway helicopter firmly grounded.

Quickly he switched on the cockpit lights and scanned the instrument panel, desperately trying to remember the brief course he had been on two years earlier. With bated breath, he pressed the starter button and waited for the engine to fire. The starter whirred discordantly. He tried again, 'cracking' the throttle open a fraction. This time there was a dull *whoof* and the great blades began their laborious sweep, gathering momentum at every turn. He fumbled for the signal lamp and flashed it once, briefly, in the direction of the perimeter fence.

Now the wait began. It seemed like an eternity. Scanning the surrounding darkness for signs of life, he laid the Uzi across his lap and flicked off the safety catch. Just in case.

After a few minutes he saw lights outside the terminal building. He squinted. Two of them. Damn! Dipped vehicle headlights. Turning in his seat, he peered behind. Blake and Eva were struggling across the tarmac with Kangers hung awkwardly between them. Obviously the Australian was making an effort but he didn't have the strength to raise his head. Twenty yards behind them, Tiger was walking unhurriedly backwards, cautiously sweeping the darkness with the snout of his sub-machine gun.

Hawksby reached over and pushed open the cockpit door. "For Christ's sake, hurry up! We've got visitors!"

Blake and the girl stumbled forward, bundling the soldier into the rear seat. Hawksby glanced back towards the terminal. The approaching headlamps seemed to burn into his skull. They were scarcely a hundred yards away. Eva fell in behind Kangers and Blake heaved at both of them as he tried to squeeze in. Tiger ran the last few feet. Hawksby twisted the throttle grip on the pitch lever. The finger on the dial crept towards 85. The gyrating blades began speeding to a blur. Above, the engine noise rose to a high-pitched whine.

Tiger leapt at the open door and hit the seat with a thud.

The machine began to tremble like a living thing. Dazzling white light from the nearing headlamps filled the cockpit, blinding Hawksby.

He twisted the throttle grip until the dial indicator passed the red line and prayed. For the life of him he couldn't find the correct speed.

Above the roar he heard the crack of gunshot. Somewhere something pinged against metal. The cockpit trembled again as he shifted the pitch lever so that the tilting angle of the blades would start to bite. Then, with agonising slowness he felt it start to lift.

Sod it! Wrong pitch.

In desperation he snatched at the lever and the helicopter left the tarmac like a rocket on a blast-pad.

Hawksby over-corrected the pitch, so that the gangling giant hoverfly dipped sickeningly. The gathering of guards from the airport jeep ducked instinctively.

The JetRanger seemed to find its height, bouncing comfortably in the air current. Hawksby's mind was a swirl of confusion as he tried to remember what the hell to do next.

"Kangers Webster," he cursed aloud, "I'm going to have your balls for breakfast!"

He eased the control stick away from him, increasing the pitch and rearward thrust. The machine dipped awkwardly as he began to take it forward and into an untidy circuit before breaking off in a southerly direction.

CHAPTER TEN

ISFAHAN: 0245 hrs, Friday 19th September

The revolutionary guards were going to take no chances with their new captive.

Anticipating the wrath of Colonel Murad on his arrival, they had secured Sergeant Dave Forbes in the cell that had previously held Jonathan Blake. To make certain that he stayed there, and wasn't sprung during a return visit by the strange mullah, they tied his hands behind his back and posted two guards on the door.

On the other side of it, Forbes seethed at his own stupidity. His feeling of frustration was aggravated by the fact that the guards refused to come in to silence him, despite his taunts and yells of protest. As the minutes passed he finally had to admit to himself that he had no chance of rejoining the others. He was on his own now.

He sat down on the stark wooden bench and considered his position.

Although there was a contingency plan for anyone who got cut off to make their way to the house of Hameda Gulistani's uncle, where they had first met Curt Swartz Jnr., there was no guarantee that help would be available in that direction for long. For all Forbes knew the American's French cover could already be under suspicion, and the snatch of Blake might just trigger off a wave of suspect arrests.

Therefore he had to move fast, and he was already prepared. Training in the Special Air Service instilled the point that it was invariably better to fight an adversary, however hopeless the struggle, because you never knew how weak he might be. The same principle applied to being held in captivity. Unless you needed time to recuperate from injury, you were to get out fast.

Behind his back, Forbes worked his hands ceaselessly until he felt the bindings begin to loosen. Each soldier in the regiment had a thorough knowledge of the techniques of muscle control and manipulation that had made a career for men like Houdini. A man who really understood ropes and knots might succeed in keeping an SAS soldier trussed, but he would really have to know his stuff. Hardly surprisingly, the revolutionary guards did not know their's.

Feeling the blood circulating around his hands again, Forbes began to relax. He looked up at the ceiling. That would be his way out, he decided, if he was going to be left for any length of time. It would be the one thing his captors wouldn't expect, yet it would be the easiest. Because it was not a purpose-built prison, the floor was a far weaker, and more flexible structure than the walls. Recalling the layout of the ground floor above he thought that he could gain access to a utility room which had bars fitted to the window. The hacksaw blade stitched into the collar of his field jacket would go through them like a knife through butter. It would then be a matter of using a conveniently placed tree to cross to the outer wall of the mansion. But he somehow expected that his first opportunity to get out would come much sooner. He was right.

Excited voices were heard outside, together with a scurrying of feet, before an unusual quietness fell over the place. Then there were heavy unhurried footfalls on the steps. After a few moments a wary eye peered in through the hole in the steel door. Forbes braced himself and stood up. He walked very slowly forward so as not to alarm anyone who was about to enter. If he waited a second too long, whoever was coming in would have time to have the door locked behind him immediately.

The sergeant deliberately slackened his facial muscles to take on an expression of dejected misery. As the lock turned and two guards stepped in, they were met with a pair of doleful spaniel eyes peering from a bowed head between hunched shoulders.

Pleased to see this arrogant giant so humiliated, one of the guards announced with a sadistic edge to his voice: "Now you see what Colonel Murad does to traitorous dogs."

But the man in the spotless silk suit who followed them in was more professional. Murad was only halfway through the door but he sensed the danger immediately. A desolate broken man cowers in a corner. However miserable he may look, he does not stand waiting for you to enter.

But before Murad could warn the two guards, it was too late. Aware that Murad was trying to back out through the door, Forbes stepped swiftly forward from his flat-footed stance in one fluid movement. His right leg bent upward, his booted foot then straightening out in a flicking kick that made contact with the first guard's knee like a pole-axe. Braced in a rigid position the man's joint shattered like matchwood, and he dropped to the floor with a squeal.

Forbes followed up on the second guard with a left-handed parry to the man's G3 carbine, as his right fist delivered a hard piston-punch to the solar plexus, throwing the man against the door and trapping Murad's right hand as the colonel tried to back out.

Winded, Murad swung his foot upward at Forbes' groin. It was an amateurish straight-legged attempt, which the sergeant countered by sweeping his arm upward, catching the offered leg and yanking it as high as it would go. Murad's back hit the floor with bone-shattering force, his skull cracking against the flagstones. He lay groaning, too dazed to move.

Picking up the dropped G3, Forbes slid through the door and turned the lock. He sped up the stairs to the entrance hall, taking five steps at a time. The guard on the front door gaped in amazement as Forbes emerged, cocking the first round into the breech of his carbine. Before the Iranian had time to unshoulder his own weapon, a two-second burst of 7.62 mm burst into his body and blew open the double doors behind him.

Forbes leapt into the garden from the top step and plunged down the path towards the gate. The single guard on duty, alerted by the gunfire, watched in disbelief as the sergeant levelled his weapon.

Only a forlorn click came as the firing-pin bit at an empty chamber. Forbes swore as he kept on running.

The barrel of the guard's gun dropped, waving from side to side in an effort to follow Forbes' weaving approach. A single shot added to the dying echoes of the previous outburst. Leaves fell over the path like confetti.

Forbes came up under the gun, pushing it aside with his own weapon and jamming the butt of it under the guard's chin, squeezing him back against the locked gate. The sergeant's knee slammed into the man's exposed crotch with eye-watering force. He stepped back to let the crumpled body slide down the gate into a sitting position.

Shouts of alarm came from the villa. In the darkness Forbes could hear orders being shouted and the menacing click of weapons being cocked for action. Quickly he tugged magazines of G3 ammunition from the pocket of the guard's field jacket. There was no time to hunt for more.

He glanced at the confusing tangle of locks, chains and bolts on the gate. Then, taking a rapid step back, he jumped onto the unconscious guard's slumped shoulders. Using the Iranian's head as a launch-pad, he vaulted up to the top of the gate. Ignoring the top edge of spike studs, he heaved himself up and over, and dropped the twelve feet into a deserted Saeb Avenue.

He landed heavily, bruising the bone in his left heel and the pain pulsed through his ankle. Ignoring the throbbing ache he sprinted across the road to where the green Peykan was parked in the side street opposite.

Going to the rear, he plucked the ignition key from the exhaust pipe, unlocked the door and climbed in. It took three turns to get the battered engine firing on at least three cylinders.

He engaged first and hit the accelerator.

It took Forbes half-an-hour to find his way to the bazaar district north of Isfahan's central square. He parked the car and made the rest of the journey on foot down the winding maze of narrow streets that were beginning to stir with life as early-risers prepared for work before the coming dawn. By the time he reached the unmarked door in the wall, the pain in his heel had become excruciating, and he was hobbling badly.

He fell back against the door with relief and, glancing up and down the dusty lane, knocked three times. Almost immediately the door opened.

"I am weary from travel . . ." he began in Farsi, then realised he had forgotten the agreed code. Stupid bloody idea anyway!

He felt a hand on his arm. There was no mistaking a woman's touch, even in the dark. "Quick, come in."

As soon as the door was bolted behind him, he was immediately aware again of the monastic tranquility of the secluded garden with its tinkling fountain. An oil lamp in the building shed a warm glow over the flowering shrubs; the scent of blossom hung heavily in the air. He breathed deeply on the heady smell. After the tension and violence of the past twenty-four hours, this perfumed garden was a welcome sanctuary from the mad world beyond its walls.

Behind the *chador* Hameda's eyes flashed with concern. "What went wrong?" she asked. "You are hurt?"

Forbes smiled at her and slapped his leg. "Just bruising. I'll tell you . . ." He froze.

Through the archway in the whitewashed room beyond the fountain he could clearly see Curt Swartz Jnr. seated on a cushion. He was in earnest conversation with a young Iranian who looked as though he was still in his teens. Instinctively Forbes raised the G3.

Hameda placed a restraining hand on his. He was aware of the warmth of her touch on his skin. "It is all right, Mr. Dave. That is my brother. He only arrived a few moments before you. You have nothing to fear," she said softly.

Forbes was not so sure. "You said nothing about friends and relatives. Just you and Curt."

Above the mask of the *chador* her eyes looked very beautiful. "Trust me."

Against his better judgment he dropped the G3 to his side. "Is your uncle here too? We could make it a party for the whole damn family."

"No. As I said, he is in Qum on business. He will not return until tomorrow."

"Why's your brother here?"

There was a fear in her eyes. "To warn me that the *Hezballāhi* are looking for me."

Forbes made a quick mental translation. "The Party of God?" He remembered mention of them before they left. "A sort of religious militia?"

"Yes. My brother was a member of them. That is how he heard that they suspect me. They have an order for my arrest. They have already visited my home in Teheran and my brother thinks they will come here in the morning. My mother is a foolish woman. She thought if she told them I was staying here they would be lenient with me."

Jesus, thought Forbes, that's all we need. He glanced up at the lightening sky. Their pretty Iranian accomplice may not have realised it, but the morning was about to announce itself.

They had just sat on a carved stone bench by the fountain when Curt came out of the room, leaving Hameda's brother by himself. Despite his welcoming smile, the American's bearded face was etched with concern. His eyes looked tired.

"Hi, Dave," he greeted. "But I can't say I'm pleased to see you."

"It went all right," Forbes assured. "I'm the only casualty."

Curt looked relieved. "Thank God for that. I somehow thought you guys might pull it off. You looked like a pretty tight team. Small is beautiful on this sort of exercise. How-'dya get left behind?"

"Let's just say I was playing tail-end Charlie. But I'm more concerned with what happens next."

Swartz looked embarrassed. "The plan was to get you out of here via Turkey or Pakistan."

"Was?"

"Well, I guess it still is, but now we've a few problems of our own. Has Hameda told you about Davoud?"

"Her brother?"

"Oh, don't worry, he knows nothing about you or your

179

operation. He just thinks you're a trusted friend." He indicated the sergeant's olive green uniform. "Although he is puzzled that we have friends in the revolutionary guards."

"I still do not understand why he's come to warn us," Hameda said. "Especially after that attack in the park by his friends."

The American shook his head. "He's young and confused. I reckon he's been carried along with this damn Islam Revolution like the rest of the youths in the country, and saw you as siding with the country's enemies. When he first told the *Hezbellahi* about us, I don't think he thought they'd harm us in any way."

"Jesus Christ!" Forbes was aghast. "You mean that pimply-faced yobbo in there was the one who shopped you?"

Anger flared in Hameda's eyes.

"Steady, Dave," Curt chided. "This detention order for Hameda is from the government. Earlier Davoud had tried to cause some mischief, but this country's in one helluva mess at the moment. It's on the brink of an all-out civil war and family loyalties are divided. But at roots your average Persian wouldn't hurt a fly, let alone a member of his own family. It's these goddamn mullahs who're turning tradition and religion on its head to suit themselves."

Forbes was determined not to get into a philosophical argument. "Look, Curt, we've obviously got to move on from here and quickly. What do you recommend?"

The American scratched thoughtfully at his beard. "Firstly I'll send young Davoud packing, and then we'll make our way by train to Kerman where Hameda has relatives who will help us. We'll be out of harm's way there, at least for a while, and we can complete plans to reach Pakistan. You will go with Hameda for safety's sake, and I will travel alone."

The girl's eyes brightened. "You mean I go to Pakistan too, Curt? Really?"

He grinned at her and squeezed her hand. "I reckon we're just about finished here now, Hameda. Now that you're being harassed, it will only be a matter of time before they're after me. If they aren't already. I'm sure my government won't try another rescue attempt of their hostages, so there's little point in me remaining." He threw a glance at Forbes. "And now I've a perfect excuse to take you with me."

She looked so happy that he tried not to think how he would eventually tell her about his wife and two children in Minnesota.

"I must say goodbye to Davoud," she said quickly.

"Don't say too much," Curt warned as she rushed inside.

"OPEN UP! GET THIS DOOR OPEN!" The harsh Farsi voice shattered the brittle stillness of the garden as fists thudded on the door in the wall.

Forbes and Curt looked at each other, disbelieving.

"THIS IS THE HEZBALLAHI! OPEN UP! *BIYA*!"

The SAS sergeant swung up the G3, but Curt reached out and put his palm over the breech. "No, Dave. We'll play for time. I'll keep them at bay while you make tracks with Hameda. She'll show you where we've guns hidden. A couple of Ingrams. Take Davoud with you, but leave him as soon as you can."

Forbes smiled. He'd had enough fighting for one day. "Sounds like a good idea, Curt." He handed over the G3 and two magazine clips. "Good luck."

Curt looked back to the door. "If I get caught and interrogated, I'll need to give them a plausible story to keep them away from your team until you've got out of Iran. Can you tell me where the pick-up's being made?"

Forbes felt uncomfortable. There was no way he would trust anyone with such information. It made sense in a way for Curt to be told the truth. Then he could survive any rough treatment by giving information that, whilst not a lie, was not exactly the truth. But Forbes didn't know the American well enough to be able to trust him that far. Even though he had just offered to put his life on the line without a second thought. The sergeant recalled the original Snapdragon plan which had been so hastily revised once Isfahan, and not Teheran, had become the target. "It's a flight in from Turkey, Curt. Low-level just this side of the Sov. border. The RV's at a disused airfield at Bu'in, about seventy miles west of Teheran."

Curt frowned as he checked over the weapon, and expertly

slid in a clip of cartridges. "I know it. We considered it for the 'Figbar' base in our own rescue attempt. But it's a long way from Isfahan."

"They'll make it," Forbes replied curtly.

"I'm sure they will." The American grinned reassuringly and motioned the sergeant to join Hameda and her brother. "Don't worry. I'll ensure they go huntin' for your friends a million miles from Bu'in."

Forbes shook his hand. "Have fun."

The noise of splitting timber filled the courtyard as Curt crouched down behind the stone bench. He levelled the G3 at the door in the wall. Forbes joined Hameda and the callow-looking youth in the archway to the building.

"Curt's staying?" she asked.

"Yes, he'll follow us as soon as he can."

She looked at him uncertainly. But somehow she felt she could trust this big dark soldier from another country. "There are stairs at the back. We can get out onto the roof and escape over the houses," she said quickly.

"Let's go."

The door finally ruptured to the ugly sound of rending timber. Curt squeezed the trigger gently as the first of the *Hezballahi* burst in through the shattered planks. The gun stammered noisily into action. Bodies fell headlong onto the cobbles. Others stumbled eagerly in behind them to take their place in the carnage.

Curt fired another measured burst in the soft mass of writhing flesh. Blood and entrails splattered onto the pure white walls. A returning shot was fired, a bright muzzle flash in the wreathing clouds of cordite. It was trapped like a mist in the enclosed space. A stray bullet hit the ceramic fountain behind the American. It fractured and shattered into the stone bowl. The delicate sound of water stopped abruptly.

Calmly Curt Swartz Jnr. pressed a fresh clip home into the carbine. The perfumed garden would never be the same again.

The JetRanger skimmed low over the mountain ridge and swept down the far side into the valley set deep in the Zagros range.

"It's nearby," Tiger asserted, concentrating the map-lamp beam on the chart on his lap.

Hawksby leaned forward to get a better view through the canopy. The sterile landscape through which the river bed coiled was bathed in pale starlight. Somewhere ahead, wreathed in mist, a wooded outcrop came steadily nearer.

"That's it," Hawksby said suddenly with a sense of relief. Twisting in his seat, he yelled back to Blake. "HOW'S OUR PILOT?"

The journalist leaned forward to shout his reply above the clattering blades. "HE'S CONSCIOUS, BUT VERY WEAK!"

Hawksby nodded. "PUT THE HEADSET ON HIM, WILL YOU!"

Blake nodded and withdrew.

"That's not it, boss." Tiger tapped the map with his forefinger. "I reckon we go on a bit farther."

Hawksby wasn't going to have his spirits dampened. "C'mon, Tiger, hasn't the regiment taught you anything about navigation? I'm sure this is it."

The Gurkha was emphatic. "*I've* taught the regiment a thing or two, boss. And this isn't it."

"It's how I remember it on the 3-D model they rigged up."

"Similar," Tiger agreed, "but not quite the same."

"*Hi, boss.*" Kangers Webster's voice suddenly came over the headset.

Hawksby, despite himself, was pleased to hear the familiar drawl again. "Thought you'd bought it, Kangers. You sound bright enough."

"*I feel effin' awful. Weak as a bleedin' kitten and I've got a touch of double vision. 'Must've hit my head somehow.*" He glanced around the cramped cockpit. "*Didn't know you could fly, boss.*"

Hawksby couldn't suppress a wry smile. "Oh, I can fly, Kangers, just. But I can't land the bloody thing. You'll have to give instructions."

The Australian chortled. "*I'll do me best, boss, but I'm seein' two of everything at the moment, and I'm half asleep."*

"So what's new?"

Hawksby eased up as the approaching outcrop took on a more distinguishable shape. "I'm still sure that's it, Tiger."

"Is that the fuel gauge, boss?"

"Huh?" He followed the pointing finger. "I think so. 'Must be. Oh, Christ!"

"What is it?" Kangers asked.

"Out of bloody fuel. There must be a leak."

Tiger peered again at the gauge. "Enough for another five miles, boss?"

Hawksby felt himself starting to panic. "How the hell should I know?" He didn't want to over-ride the Gurkha's legendary sense of navigation, but he was convinced in his own mind that they had reached their destination. "I'm going to take her down!" he announced.

"There's no signal from anyone," Tiger observed calmly.

Hawksby ignored him and slowed some more.

"Easy on the stick, boss!" Kangers said. *"And let the pitch lever down at the same time. But slowly!"*

The major obeyed, fumbling over the controls as he tried to co-ordinate his movements.

The helicopter dipped sickeningly and Eva Olsen let out a squeal of surprise.

"Lever up!" Kangers yelled.

Hawksby corrected and the helicopter hovered, but at an awkward tilt.

"What's below?" Kangers asked.

Hawksby peered over his shoulder. "Bare-arsed mountains."

"And bushes," Tiger added helpfully.

"You wanna land?"

"Of course, I bloody do . . ."

"Here, I mean. Is it flat?"

The major was getting impatient. "Just get us down, Webster, for cryin' out loud!"

"Okay. Just gently lower the lever." A frantic note crept into his voice: *"Not so bloody fast . . .!"*

The JetRanger dropped like a stone, then reared suddenly,

as Hawksby over-compensated, grabbing awkwardly at the lever. Then it plummeted again. As the Australian had suspected, the ground was far from flat, but in the eerie starlight it was impossible to see just how steep the slope was.

The first part of the helicopter to hit the ground was one of the hurtling blades. As the rotor embedded itself in the mountainside, what happened next was just a noisy, confused blur.

The rotor and transmission was ripped free of the rest of the fuselage which dropped fifteen feet farther down the slope. There was a violent cacophony of splitting metal and crackling perspex as the front cockpit burst apart like an eggshell. The engine screeched like an express train jamming its wheels on at full speed.

"TURN OFF THE FUEL COCKS!" Kangers yelled.

Stunned, Hawksby tried to find the switch while Tiger used his boots to kick open the jammed port side door.

The rear starboard door had burst open on impact and Blake and Eve were already helping Kangers out onto the rocky slope. Smoke began to stream from the engine cowling. Giving up his search for the fuel cocks, Hawksby dived after Tiger, rolling in a fast, rapid movement across the ground to the shelter of an uprooted boulder.

One of the electrical circuits blew in a shower of tiny sparks and the fuel tank went up with a whooshing roar of bright orange flame.

Hawksby felt the searing heat singe his eyebrows. The air was sucked from his lungs as the mushrooming pyre threw a stark aurora of light over the barren moonscape.

"Reckon you had more fuel that you thought, boss," Tiger observed dryly, and climbed to his feet. "And, by the way, this *is* the wrong ridge."

Hawksby stood up, brushing the dust and flecks of smouldering debris from his field jacket. He glanced across at the other three sheltering on the far side of the raging bonfire. "ANYONE HURT?" he called out.

"Just minor bumps and bruises," Kangers replied. Behind him, Blake and the girl looked pale and shaken. "Where're the lads?"

Hawksby grimaced. "Looks like Tiger was right. This *is* the wrong ridge."

Kangers punched the Gurkha lightly on the shoulder. "What's the Nepalese for smart-arse, Tiger?" He turned back to the major. "Personally, I don't give a monkey's where we are, as long as it's *terra firma*."

Hawksby raised an eyebrow. "You *will* do. I reckon we've got a few hours' walk to reach the others."

Blake approached, extending his hand. "I'm afraid I haven't had a chance to thank you yet."

Hawksby shook it. "I wouldn't thank me yet, Jonathan. This wasn't a scheduled stop and we've a long way to go."

Eva said: "It iss still better t'an being cooped up in t'ose cells. Wondering when we iss going to be tortured."

"Did they?" Hawksby asked. "Hurt you in any way?"

She shook her head. "We wass treated rough sometimes, but not'in' too serious."

"Good. I just hope you're up to a spot of hill-walking. Then we'll get our bush doctor to give you both a check over."

Eva was puzzled. "Bush doctor?"

"Our slang for a medic."

"You iss very organised." She smiled. "But we still do not know your name. Or who you people are. I 'ave 'eard your men call you 'boss'. T'at iss not a military expression, iss it?"

Hawksby laughed. "No, Eva, it's not, but then we're not a very orthodox outfit."

"You say you wass a commando back at t'e 'ouse."

"You said it, Eva," Hawksby corrected, "but that description is close enough. You can both call me Alan. No need to bother with formalities."

"No rank?" Blake asked.

"Still the journalist, Jonathan?" There was a sharp edge to Hawksby's voice. "I am a major in the British Army."

Eva looked impressed.

Blake said: "I'm not great fan of the military, Major, but for once I'm bloody pleased you turned up when you did."

"People usually are, Jonathan." This time there was no mistaking Hawksby's tone. "And I said the name is Alan."

"Yes, *sir!*" Blake mimicked.

"People call him 'The Hawk'," Tiger added brightly.

"Stow it," Hawksby snapped. He glanced at the dying flames of the wreckage that were now licking fitfully over the cockpit upholstery. "Let's get out of here before we get unwelcome visitors."

Above the crackling of the fire no one heard the distant whine of an Iranian Air Force F4 Phantom jet fighter. It was returning to its base at Shiraz after a night exercise.

TEHERAN: 0600 hrs, Friday 19th September

Despite his permanently severe expression, Ayatollah Khomeini was not given to fits of unreasoned anger.

But that morning, at the meeting of the inner caucus of the Revolutionary Council, the old man mercilessly flayed his fellow religious rulers and advisers with a barbed tongue. Vicious Persian rhetoric dripped like pure venom from each carefully selected word in a tirade of abuse and threat. It was directed at all those who had been responsible for the escape of the journalist Blake and the rescuer they had temporarily held.

Standing before the Council, with his head respectfully bowed, Colonel Murad allowed the verbal onslaught to wash over him. He knew that to have allowed the escape of such dangerous prisoners could easily have meant his own execution. However, he also knew that the capture of the American spy called Swartz in Isfahan had been his saving grace. Immediately the news of the *Hezballahi*'s fortunate find had reached him, he had had the prisoner held at the Isfahan mansion and had insisted that Judge Khalkali should take custody.

It had been a shrewd move; the best gift he could give to the mullah who desperately wanted to get his hands on an American, as he had been kept away from the US Embassy hostages. Murad's unexpected offer and co-operation had won the colonel Khalkali's tentative support in the Council. And now Murad needed it. Desperately.

The hook-nosed deputy leader Beheshti was also being subjected to the Imam's taunts and criticisms. He also was in no mood to condemn Colonel Murad. As the man shortly to inherit the leadership of Iran, Beheshti wanted this worrying puzzle fully resolved. And despite these latest upsets, he knew that the SAVAMA officer was the only one professional enough to do it.

At last Khomeini's voice slowed, like a record winding down on an old gramophone. Beheshti used the break to pursue his own line of questioning. "What, Colonel, is your opinion of the people who snatched Blake from Isfahan? Were they Americans?"

"Not necessarily, *agha*," Murad replied, "although the man Swartz was assisting them. They were using Uzi weapons which are Israeli, and the man we caught started speaking Hebrew when we had him in the cell."

Beheshti raised his eyebrows, although he was not altogether surprised. The Israelis had been good friends to the Shah's regime. "So they may have been agents of Mossad? The Israeli Secret Service?"

"Perhaps," Murad was non-committal. "But perhaps it was just a blind. Whoever actually carried out the operation need not be from the country behind it. Motive may tell us more than *prima facie* evidence." He paused, aware it was a dramatic gesture; he hoped not too much so. "I remind you that Blake has dual nationality of British and Swiss. Also there appears to be a strong British connection behind the Mulcruf Foundation."

The Imam seemed to have lost interest; he was looking drawn and weary. However, Beheshti's eyes were bright with curiosity. "This American, Swartz, will be able to confirm if these raiders came from Britain, Colonel?"

Murad inclined his head towards Judge Khalkali. "My good friend the mullah assures me of that, *agha*. And lots more besides. I have no intention of letting Blake out of the country. The helicopter his rescuers took from Isfahan airport had only a limited range, and I believe the American knows its destination. While we have him, we have a chance."

Beheshti's eyes narrowed like a cat's. "And he will tell you?"

Khalkali interrupted. "Even as we speak he is probably pouring out his soul to my men. I assure you he will tell us *all* he knows!" The judge was grinning as he spoke. Beheshti watched his display of enthusiasm with mild irritation, fascinated by the flecks of saliva that gathered at the corners of the man's mouth.

ZAGROS: 0700 hrs, Friday 19th September

The four-hour march had taken its toll.

It had been a tortuous journey along the uneven upper slopes of the valley in the darkness. But at least it had been better than the anxiety created when the rising sun radiated tentative fingers of light over the upper eastern peaks. It was almost as though the sun was deliberately trying to paint the group in stark relief against the barren landscape which offered no hiding place.

The rough ground over which they travelled was predominantly fawn in colour, but at each of the intersecting upper mountain valleys, the hue would change subtly to red or ochre, occasionally broken by a raw white gash of crumbled cliff. Vegetation was sparse and stunted but, way below, the valley walls became greener as they neared the wooded riverbeds. From that height, the lower slopes appeared to have the texture of brushed velvet.

To Hawksby and Tiger the trek had presented no problems. After the Brecon Beacons in Wales during winter, the gentle early morning climate made it seem like a nature ramble. It was a different matter for Kangers Webster, whose usual laconic good humour was noticeably absent as he stumbled after the others.

Blake had fared well for the first hour, but his generally poor state of health, the result of a deficient prison diet, had caught up with him after that.

The girl was in an even worse state as she had no shoes, and had to make do with the improvised sandals that Tiger had made out of torn strips of clothing with soles cut from the helicopter tyres. Despite his ingenuity, the soft skin of Eva's feet had begun to split after the first twenty minutes. By the end of the journey they were reduced to a blistered and bloody mess. She had finally fallen, exhausted, physically unable to put one foot in front of the other. It was then that Tiger, who seemed to have taken her as his personal charge, manfully lifted her onto his back and marched on steadfastly without slackening his pace.

There was a moment's scare when they were still thirty minutes' walk from the hide. A Land Rover broke cover a hundred yards in front of them. It appeared suddenly out of the wooded upper valley where the rest of Snapdragon was encamped.

For a second Hawksby was taken in by the olive green uniforms of the passengers. The way things had gone wrong in the past twenty-four hours, he could have believed anything. A welcome sense of relief swept over him as he recognised Panther One with Jim Perkis at the wheel.

"Am I glad to see you." It was the passenger, John Belcher, who spoke first as the vehicle slewed to a halt on the loose stones. "We saw the fire on the next ridge, boss, and thought it might be something to do with you. We could only identify it as wreckage of a chopper when daylight came up."

"Corporal McDermid's pulling 'is 'air out," Perkis added chirpily. "Thought you'd all gone up in a puff of smoke."

"We nearly bloody did," Hawksby replied. "You'd better radio him and put him out of his misery."

Belcher quickly surveyed the group. "No serious casualties then . . .?" His voice trailed off. "Where's Dave? He copped it?"

Hawksby's smile dropped. "I don't know. He got left behind."

"Jesus," Perkis murmured. "So he *could* be all right?"

The major seemed suddenly impatient. "Very probably. He can look after himself."

"He'll bloody well 'ave to, I reckon."

"And Kangers' looks none too bright," Belcher observed. "Messy arm wound?" As he climbed out to help the stragglers in the group, the medic noticed Eva Olsen for the first time. He had vaguely noticed that there was an unexpected addition to the party, but Eva's short hair and dishevelled appearance had led him to assume she was male.

"Stone me, boss, where'd you pick up that little trophy?"

Hawksby turned. Tiger was helping her the last few steps to the Land Rover. "Apparently she's a friend of Jonathan Blake here. So behave yourself and mind your language."

Folding his arms casually over the wheel, Perkis pushed up the peak of his forage cap and grinned blatantly at the Norwegian. "I reckon she's a pretty fair swap for ol' Forbsy, boss."

The major ignored him, addressing himself to Belcher. "You can stop ogling too, John. Presumably you've been sent to see if we need medical attention, so take a look at Kangers. The young lady's in no imminent danger."

The Butcher smiled. "Right-on, boss, I'll give her my *full* and undivided attention back at the hide."

"I've always wanted to be a doctor," Perkis muttered wistfully.

CHAPTER ELEVEN

TEHERAN: 0800 hrs, Friday 19th September

Colonel Murad felt better now.

An hour previously he had left the early morning meeting of the Revolutionary Council feeling distinctly nauseous. It was a combination of twenty-four hours without sleep and an uneasy feeling that he was losing his grip on the situation. Nevertheless he had made the decision to return to his apartment for a shower and some breakfast.

As his chauffeur drove him back to the headquarters building, he lit his first cigarette of the new day and began to marshal his thoughts. Perhaps things weren't so bad after all. The mysterious raiding party had been separated from one of their number, and the guards at the villa had claimed that a second had been wounded. Both factors, he reasoned, could force the raiders to change their plans. Or at least slow them down.

Then there was the timing of the raid. It was all well and good to attack in the early hours of the morning, when the streets were deserted and the enemy half-asleep, but it left little time to get out of the country – especially one the size of Iran – before daylight.

By the time the black Mercedes pulled up outside his office, Murad was convinced that the raiding party would be in hiding until the next night. Then there might be an attempt to fly in a long-range aircraft to pick them up.

That gave him all day to track them down. He had the authority to mobilise the entire Gendarmerie and traffic police network, which still existed – although with no real powers since the Revolution. Then he had the all-powerful, but hopelessly organised revolutionary guards who were attached to eighty thousand mosques the length and breadth of the country. With these he should be able to set up a check-point on every main road in the country. He would have investigations made in every hamlet, although it would take several days to reach settlements in the more remote regions.

But before he did, he must talk urgently to his team of investigators working on Sabs Karemi's research papers. That *must* come first.

As he took the stairs to his office two at a time, Murad also decided to approach the Army for assistance. There were still the remnants of three corps, based at Teheran, Kermanshah and Shiraz. He would ask the mullahs who now ran the military each to put their best infantry battalion at his disposal to search out the most likely areas for the raiders to be in hiding. They would follow up any leads the country's lethargic police force came up with.

"Good morning, Colonel!" his aide's voice greeted him brightly as he entered his office. "I have copies of all the reports you requested."

Murad grunted as he slipped off his jacket and rolled up the sleeves of his tailored white silk shirt. "Anything of interest?"

His aide shrugged. "There doesn't appear to be, but it's hard to say what incidents could be important."

"Let me see," Murad demanded, and moved over to the window as he flicked through the papers. Periodically he grunted as he scanned the error-ridden Telex printouts. "I see Isfahan Airport tracked the stolen helicopter on a south-westerly course, then lost it. Of course, that could be deliberately misleading. Hmmm. No reports of unidentified air traffic from other radar stations. And nothing in the way of interference that could be the result of jamming." He continued through the documents. "I see the Air Force has been busy."

His aide looked concerned. "There has been increasing concern about Iraq. We have stepped up our reconnaissance flights along the border. There are reports of troop and armour concentrations."

"That's no concern of ours," Murad scolded, "but it may mean that the military will be less than willing to spare aircraft for our purposes." In fact, he was certain of it. The Iranian Air Force was in even more of a shambles than the rest of the armed forces. Being better educated, and coming from wealthier families than most others in the military, many pilots had supported the Shah. A lot had discreetly walked out of their airbases and not returned. Of those who were left, hundreds were to fall victim to the mullahs' purges that followed. When the mullahs had taken command, their total ignorance of defence matters became obvious. Confusion degenerated into chaos. In fact, there was one famous incident of a mullah responsible for a major Air Force base who was informed as a matter of course, that Iran was under constant surveillance by US spy satellites. Angered, he immediately ordered the men of his new command to take off and shoot them down. They were still having difficulty in obeying that particular order, the colonel mused.

Suddenly a paragraph in one of the printouts caught his eye. "This fire seen in the Zagros mountains by a pilot from Shiraz?"

His aide shrugged. "A shepherd's fire?"

Murad chewed at his cigarette thoughtfully. "At three in the morning? And clearly visible for five miles?"

"Perhaps it got out of control?" came the helpful reply.

The colonel crossed to the large wall map and, picking up a large wooden chalk compass, drew a circle centred on Isfahan Airport. The distance represented 140 miles, or one hour's flying time for the Bell JetRanger helicopter.

He then worked out the grid reference given in the pilot's report and placed a cross in yellow Chinagraph on the map. The cross failed to intersect the circle by a whisker.

Murad grunted. "It could be significant, I suppose. Get me the officer commanding Third Army Corps at Shiraz. I'll see if they can't fly up some men to the site. It is just possible that it was a guidance beacon for a rescue plane."

The aide raised his eyebrows. "I never thought of that."

"I hope I'm wrong, though, because I'm counting on the fact that someone will attempt to land an aircraft tonight to pick them up." He glanced at his watch; it was eight-fifteen. "That probably gives us fourteen or fifteen hours to find the rendezvous position."

"What about the American?"

Murad smiled. "He is the only good news to come out of this whole sorry business. By now he'll be at Khalkali's tender mercies in Isfahan. As soon as I've finished here, I shall pay a visit – hopefully before the judge kills the man in his enthusiasm."

"You think he knows details of the plans?"

Murad's eyes narrowed and he studied the tip of his cigarette, blowing on it gently so that it glowed. "Believe me, if he knows, then so shall I before lunchtime."

The room suddenly felt chill to the colonel's aide. He left quickly to phone Third Corps at Shiraz.

Corporal Hamish McDermid was not happy.

As far as he was concerned, orders were orders, and if they included no mention of 'passengers' then there should not be any. Even if they were desirable Nordic blondes. Even worse was the absence of Forbes, a situation aggravated by the Hawk's apparent indifference to his loss.

The Scotsman had served with Hawksby for a year and admired him as a brilliant and often unorthodox soldier. But he had known Dave Forbes since they had been on the same training cadre on joining the Royal Corps of Transport in the mid-1960s. They had shared the same billet, the same enjoyment of a drink and a scrap. And not infrequently the same women. Forbes was a good friend who could be trusted when the chips were down. You could always rely on him being there with his boorish good humour. Ever since those early days, whenever their paths crossed, it was as though they'd never been apart. As far as McDermid was concerned, that was what friendship and the Army were all about.

"Hey, Scottie, what ya reckon on that crumpet the 'Awk's brought back, eh?" It was Perkis who had come across the clearing of the camp after assisting Belcher. "A wee bonnie lassie, eh?"

McDermid scowled. "I'm no sa keen on takin' women on this sorta exercise. Besides, I dunna like her hair. Looks like a bloody lavatory brush."

"C'mon Corp, that's a prison cut, ain't it? What 'ya expect, Vidal Sassoon?"

"She'll bring noot but trouble, Jim, mark ma words." He looked at the diminutive East Ender closely. "I'm more concerned about Big Davy than tha' bit o' skirt. I canna get nothin' from Hawksby on what happened. I ken they didna get on too well, but did Davy do somethin' stupid?"

Perkis shrugged. "According to Tiger, he just didn't turn up before the shootin' started and Kangers got hit."

The Scotsman grunted. "Doesna sound too good, does it, lad? I jest wondered if he'd been a wee bit foolhardy?"

"You know the 'Awk. 'Always bin a bit wary of Dave. They never worked together before, an' their styles are completely different. I mean, Dave's a bit laid-back an' plays it by ear, whereas the 'Awk's more of a planner. An' a stickler for discipline. They was chalk'n' cheese really."

McDermid nodded thoughtfully. "You're right, Jim, but I still canna get over the boss's indifference to losing Davy. I mean, even if he's alive an' free, it's no joke, is it? Stuck in the middle o' bleedin' nowhere wi'out a friend. I've worked wi' the major for a year on Oman and, well, he's a bit insular at the best of times. But never like this."

"Tiger reckons he thinks Dave is over the hill anyway. Past it like. An' 'im gettin' left behind backs up 'is theory. The 'Awk don't like second-raters."

"D'you reckon Davy's a second-rater? Past it?"

"Give over, Scottie." Perkis seemed genuinely hurt at the suggestion. "I first met Dave on me selection march. After that 'e was more of a dad to me than me old man. He looked after me, did Dave. 'E's the best . . ." He sniffed heavily.

McDermid felt the young man's sense of loss. "Let's no get maudlin', lad. Afore y' ken, we'll be weepin' like a coupl'a ol' soaks."

At that moment John Belcher strode across from the canvas stretcher bed where Kangers had fallen into an exhausted sleep.

He was grinning widely as he approached. "Got an errand of mercy for you, Perkis, my old chum. A favour for a lady."

Perkis grinned. "She still takin' a shower in the waterfall? Wants 'er back scrubbed, I suppose?"

"No, Jim, she wants your underpants."

"Eh?"

Belcher slapped him consolingly on the shoulder. "See, she didn't have time to pack when the Hawk bust in, so she's only got what she's standing up in. And after a few weeks in an Iranian prison, they can stand up by themselves."

"You're joking!" Perkis was incredulous.

The bush doctor smiled. "'Fraid not. You're the nearest to her size, so one pair of drawers, olive, if you please." He stood up. "Oh, an' she'll be needing your spare set of fatigues as well as a pair of boots . . ."

"Jesus H . . .!"

As Belcher turned away, the Scots corporal couldn't suppress his laughter. "I warned ye, lad, she'd be noot but trouble . . ."

At that moment a message came over the radio from Corporal Penaia, who had been posted on the rocky outcrop at the top of the ridge. From there, the Fijian had a panoramic view of the river valley, six hundred feet below them.

A voice yelled: "Everyone under cover!"

Perkis sprinted across the glade and snatched up a couple of jerry cans that could have been spotted from the air. Blake, who was sleeping blissfully in the sunlight, was unceremoniously booted awake by McDermid and pushed to the edge of the clearing where the two Land Rovers stood in the shade, draped with camouflage netting.

Woken with a start, Hawksby climbed out of his 'green maggot' sleeping bag. "What's up?" he demanded.

Tiger was still half-listening to the Fijian's sombre voice on the radio headset. "Pogo says chopper just landed, boss. Next to where we crash last night . . ." Hawksby went to speak, but was waved to silence by the Gurkha who was straining to catch the rest of the message. The major kicked impatiently at the tyre of Panther Two. It was never meant to have been like this.

At last Tiger took off his headset. "He says a second chopper dropping troops. Forming wide sweep across the valley . . ."

"What does that mean, Alan?" It was Blake, standing behind him.

Hawksby's eyes flashed with a glint of malevolence so mindful of a bird of prey. "It means that they know it was the helicopter we took from Isfahan last night. And it means they're determined to get you back. They must want you pretty badly."

Fear showed in Blake's eyes. "They do."

Hawksby leaned against the snub-nosed bonnet of Panther Two. "In fact, Jonathan, you seem to be in high demand half-way round the world. Looks like Crazy K and his mob want you as bad as our own people. What's a journalist have to do to be that popular? Most governments would rather see journalists of your sort shot for all the mud they dig up."

Blake gave a wry smile. "Maybe that's why they all want me. So that I can't talk."

Hawksby's lips were formed in a smile, but his blue eyes were hard like ice chips. "*I've* no orders to shoot anyone."

The journalist tried to diffuse the conversation by forcing a laugh that seemed to stick in his throat. "Thank God for that! You're the only friends I've got. And I'm not sure that's going to do me much good."

"Meaning?"

The man shifted uncomfortably. "No offence. It's just that things aren't going too well, are they? What with losing one of your men, and another wounded. Then crashing the chopper." He shrugged helplessly. "And now this . . . I wonder if we'll ever get out."

The major's eyes seemed to focus at some point beyond Blake. "We'll get you out." It was a flat satement that didn't invite contradiction, but as Hawksby turned, he felt as though he had been shot. He told himself it was just wounded pride, but it still hurt just the same. And coming from the two-bit journalist he'd risked his life saving didn't help.

"Oh, Major?" Blake called. Sensing that he'd managed to pierce the armoured reserve of this arrogant and mysterious rescuer, he felt an overwhelming urge to exploit the situation. "Haven't you been told the reason the British Government wants me out of this country?"

Hawksby turned slowly, determined not to betray his anger. Or his interest. "There's no need, Jonathan. I've no need to know. My orders are just to get you out, and that's what I intend to do."

Blake stared at the major's back as he began making his way up the steep incline to where the Fijian was keeping watch. He was annoyed that the soldier had refused to be baited. It was beginning to rankle that he had been rescued by exactly the sort of people he hated and had spent his professional career trying to expose and condemn. The military was the unacceptable sharp edge of the capitalist society he loathed. And, in that context, he saw the SAS as the finely-honed point. And he had little doubt that 'Major Alan' and his cronies were from the Special Air Service.

Neither did he doubt why the British Government wanted him out of Iran. For the same reason the Ayatollah Khomeini wanted him. They were determined to silence him once and for all.

Thoughtfully he shuffled to the southern edge of the glade, where the trees fell away towards the valley. Below, revolutionary guards were at that moment sweeping the woods.

He was equally determined that neither would succeed.

ISFAHAN: 1300 hrs, Friday 19th September

"AAAaagh!"

Curt Swartz Jnr. told himself that it was not his voice. Nor was it his body spreadeagled naked below him on the wire mesh bedstead. It could not be because, despite his fifty years, his body was in superb condition. It was lean and muscled and lightly bronzed from years of living in the tropics. The body now attached to his head looked pale beneath the single unshaded bulb. It was also ripped and torn and studded with livid weals where someone had attempted to stub out cigars on his skin.

His mind was on a higher plane, fixed to an image of his copper-haired wife Alison, and their two little girls in Minnesota.

It was one of those still mid-summer days when the air itself seemed to bake. He could hear Alison clinking crushed ice into the tall glass of lime by his sun-lounger. A droning bee was about the only thing that moved that fragrant, endless day. Except, of course, for the children. Rushing through the cool spray of the lawn-sprinkler.

He held the picture rigidly in his mind, until the sudden cry of laughter became prolonged and shrill, filled with the sound of pain.

He tried to conjure the picture of Alison again, but this time he couldn't see her eyes. Just the vague outline of her face. And then that, too, began to slip and the sound of a screaming child forced its way through, filling his head.

And then the picture in his mind fractured like delicate porcelain, and the sound of his own pain deafened him.

AAAAAGHH! Not a child's voice, but his own. A reluctant sound wrenched from him as the pain shot from his testicles and through the nerve tracts of his body. It burst out of his skin in a myriad tiny detonations.

The baton electrode was removed and the pain slowly subsided. But Curt knew it would begin again. He had finally lost the picture of Alison and the children forever.

He thought he had delayed long enough, but there was no way he could be sure.

He fixed his mind on what the SAS sergeant had told him. In his confused state of mind he knew he must not get it wrong. They were using Bu'in airfield, so he would tell them another one, in a different direction entirely. One he remembered that had been considered for the US's own rescue attempt. By the time they had got there, and found he was lying, the British would be away.

He tried to speak, but no sound came from his parched throat. His vocal chords felt like dried sisal and his lips had crusted over.

Someone pushed a tin mug to his mouth and he tasted the trickle of brackish water.

"Lordakan." The word was spoken so quietly he couldn't even hear it himself. More water. He felt the mucus in his throat begin to soften. "Lordakan. Disused airfield . . . They told me Lordakan . . . That's all I know . . ."

The bus jolted over a pot-hole on the sand-blown strip of tarmac road. It stretched ahead to the horizon where it melted into the gathering heat haze.

Forbes doubted that the ancient vehicle, packed with passengers and its roof piled high with luggage, provisions and market goods, would actually make the next twenty miles north to Qum. But Hameda, seated beside him in her *chador*, seemed to have no such doubts. And she wasn't tempted to glance out of the dirt-caked rear window for signs of a Gendarmerie car in hot pursuit. Her eyes were red-rimmed and moist, and he guessed she'd been brooding over Curt Swartz Jnr.'s fate.

Although many of the fly-spattered windows were cracked or missing, the flow of dusty air did little to relieve the oppressive heat, or the pungent mix of diesel, paraffin and perspiring bodies. After a while the cackling of poultry and the poetry recitations from some passengers, shouted above the noise of the bus, conspired to give him a dreadful headache. So, despite his desire to put as many miles between themselves and Isfahan as possible, he was relieved when the bus pulled in at a roadside village of mud-brick houses.

The driver had decided to take his lunch break at the wayside tea-house, and the rest of his passengers seemed pleased to pile out into the shade of some lemon trees. Like other countries in the Middle East, Forbes had found no sense of urgency here. All around them baskets and bundles were opened. Bread, grapes and cucumber spilled out over the parched grass. A gaggle of inquisitive geese waddled forward on a noisy reconnaissance mission.

For the first time since Forbes and Hameda had squeezed onto the overcrowded bus, they couldn't be overheard by their fellow travellers.

"Don't be so sad," Forbes said. "Curt told me you always wanted to leave the country, and this is your big chance."

Hameda studied him closely and he could tell that beneath the *chador* she was smiling. "You are kind, Mr. Dave." He felt her hand on his. "But I wanted to go with him. Not leave him in danger whilst I go with a stranger . . ."

"Of course. But I think Curt can look after himself."

"You think he is all right?" Her eyes were big and innocent.

"I'm sure of it," he lied. "By the time we get to your relatives in – where is it? – Kerman, I expect he'll already be waiting for us."

They could have caught a train direct from Isfahan to the eastern town of Kerman, where they could stay in safety before moving on through Baluchestan to Pakistan. However Forbes had preferred Hameda's suggestion that they mingle immediately with the locals and catch the first bus north to Qum. To the sergeant it felt a bit like putting his head in the lion's mouth, because Qum was the Holy City and the spiritual centre of the religious men who ran the Islamic Revolution. But, he argued with himself, in that respect it was probably the last place their pursuers from Isfahan would expect them to go. And at least it removed them from the immediate danger.

Once there, they would be able to wait with less trepidation for a train that would take them on eventually to Kerman, via the towns of Kashan and Yazd. Hameda felt certain that her relatives would lend them their car.

"If it is working," she added.

"You mean it might not be?"

She shrugged. "It is old. An Austin Cambridge? But it usually goes all right in the summer. If you avoid steep hills. And if we can get petrol."

"Petrol?"

"It is difficult since the Shah left. But I am sure my relatives know people. They will get us some."

"I hope so," he muttered, "it's a damn long walk to Pakistan."

At that moment one of the passengers, an old man with a

202

yellowing white moustache, hobbled towards them, leaning heavily on a stick.

The leathery face cracked open in a toothless smile. "You two do not eat?"

Quickly Hameda replied, "No, we left in a hurry. My husband here oversleeps. We rush to catch the bus and he forgets our picnic bag!"

The old man chuckled and fished a cloth bundle from his ragged overcoat pocket. "But you must be hungry! I have a little something here. Much too much for me."

He squatted beside them and spread out the cloth around a small mound of goat's cheese, a boiled egg and a green tomato.

"We couldn't possibly . . ." began Forbes, but Hameda raised her hand to silence him.

"You are too kind," Hameda said. "May your shadow never grow less."

Again the old man chuckled. "What are we if we cannot help a fellow traveller along life's troubled road." He reached into his pocket and drew out some nougat, and held it out for them. Forbes had heard that Isfahan was well-known for it. "And this will sweeten the taste of dust on the rest of your journey."

Unaccountably Forbes felt a warm prickling sensation behind his eyes. He didn't trust himself to speak. He was pleased when the bus eventually started again. As he peered back out of the rear window, he knew he would always remember that lunch under the lemon trees. The last sign of the place was a yapping mongrel dog scampering after them. Half-a-mile later it disappeared in the swirling wake of dust.

CHAPTER TWELVE

ZAGROS MOUNTAINS: 2200 hrs Friday 19th September

At precisely ten o'clock the two Land Rovers purred into life. To a gentle gurgle of exhaust and swish of rubber against long grass, Panther One led the way out of the hide. The only trace of Snapdragon's six-day occupation was the acrid scent of petrol lingering in the glade.

Although Pogo had watched the guards scouring the valley below from his vantage point in the crags above the hide, and had seen them leave at sunset, Major Alan Hawksby was taking no chances. The easiest route would have been a southward dog-leg journey around a ridge of mountains that blocked their way. It would have taken them fifteen miles along a river valley, then given them the benefit of an unmade road that had once served to link Lordakan airfield with a nearby oil exploration camp.

But Hawksby had taken the direct cross-country approach south, straight over the ridge. It was slow, tough going but no one would have expected anything to come from that direction.

It had been a wise precaution.

McDermid's Panther One, driven by Jim Perkis, and carrying Tiger and Kangers Webster, had been in the lead. Hawksby followed a hundred yards behind in Panther Two with the rest of the party. The idea was that, should the 'point' vehicle run into trouble, the second would have a chance to get away with Blake and Eva Olsen. If the opportunity arose they might even be free to mount a counter-attack.

"I think there's a wee problem, boss." There was no mistaking

McDermid's voice as it suddenly crackled in the Clansman radio head-set worn by Hawksby.

The major felt his heart sink. "What's up, Scottie?" As he spoke he tried to see where Panther One was located, but the dense blackness of the night defeated him.

"C'mon see for y'self," McDermid replied. *"Y're safe te advance."*

Hawksby nudged Pogo who sat next to him. The Fijian nodded and began to edge the vehicle slowly forward until they eventually drew alongside Panther One. McDermid was standing in the front seat scanning the airfield below with a Starlight 'scope.

He handed it across to Hawksby. "One, four and ten o'clock, boss. I'd say there's aboot four men in each party."

The strip itself was just a short unimproved stretch of level ground in a high mountain valley. There were no radars or navigational aids, just a derelict shed and rusting fuel tanks that once serviced the occasional light aircraft. Nearby were two mud-brick settlements used by a handful of shepherds who went to the uplands with their sheep for summer grazing.

The major studied each group of men in turn. They were concealed at the head of the airstrip and at either side. He could see the dull glint of gun metal as they shifted position. It was hard to tell from that distance, but he thought he could distinguish the long barrel of a heavy machine gun. After a full five minutes he lowered the Starlight 'scope. A nerve twitched involuntarily below his left eye.

"Some reception committee, eh, boss?" McDermid said, watching carefully for Hawksby's reaction.

Blake leaned forward from the open rear compartment. "How could they know?"

McDermid shot him a sideways glance. It was a question they'd all been asking themselves, and it was one that had a simple and unpalatable answer. Dave Forbes was in enemy hands and someone was putting on the squeeze. And if the veteran sergeant was talking, then someone was squeezing extremely hard. The Scotsman felt sick at the thought of it.

Swinging up onto the bonnet of Panther Two, Hawksby

scanned the airstrip again. "How they know is rather academic. It could be positive information or inspired guess-work." His voice was flat and unemotional.

For a moment McDermid considered the possibilities. "Y' mean Davy might noota said anything'?"

Hawksby's voice was icy. "You know him better than I do."

You bastard, McDermid thought savagely.

"You mean the man you left behind?" Blake challenged. He sounded very angry.

"Our men are trained to resist interrogation," Hawksby replied, lowering the 'scope.

McDermid eyed the journalist with disdain. "If someone puts y' balls in a steel vice an' spins t' wheel, ye tend te find anti-interrogation trainin' is no' all it's cracked up te be."

Hawksby cut in: "It's more than likely someone has put two and two together – and hit the jackpot. They know where the chopper landed and, after their search today, that there were no bodies. As Lordakan is only fifteen miles on a direct line, then there's a good chance it was going to be used for a pick-up." He glanced at his watch. "Looks like we've got just fifteen minutes before the Herc.'s due in."

"What a fucking cock-up," Blake muttered. It was hard to tell if his voice was quavering with anger, frustration or fear, or a mixture of all three.

"Keep it buttoned!" McDermid snarled.

"What d'ya reckon, boss?" Perkis asked. At least he sounded unperturbed.

Climbing down from the bonnet, Hawksby said quietly: "Well, as we've had contingency arrangements for just this sort of eventuality, I suggest we revert to Plan B."

In her seat next to Blake, Eva shook her head in slow disbelief. She was staggered at the calm way these soldiers were discussing the fact that their entire escape plan had blown up in their faces.

"T'is iss just a game to all off you, isn't it?" she challenged.

Hawksby threw her a hard, silencing glance, then moved away from the vehicles, beckoning McDermid to follow him out of earshot.

Although he appeared unruffled, the major's head was spinning with the implications of the ambush, and the horrendous problems they would face by having to execute the secondary plan. However carefully thought out, researched and rehearsed it had been, he had to admit that he had never really considered that it would ever have to be put into actual operation. He was uncomfortably aware that he was beginning to perspire. His mind ran over details of the alternative plan, examining each part for the flaws and difficulties that he was convinced must have been overlooked. Plan B had always been an academic exercise; just another training routine. He wished to God he'd been as thorough as he would have liked. If only there had been more time. If only the target hadn't been changed at the eleventh hour. If only . . .

McDermid joined him. "I dunna cherish the idea of a two hundred an' fifty mile dash south, te tell ye the truth, boss."

"It'll be no joy ride, Scottie, that's for sure. But let's tackle it one stage at a time." Hawksby looked up. Livid clusters of brilliant stars hung like tiny silver fruit in a cloudless night sky. "Our first problem is to prevent the Herc from getting shot up. If Crazy K's mob got their hands on an RAF crew, they'd have a field day. Someone's going to have to signal the abort code, but at the same time I don't want that lot on the airstrip to come galloping after us – and getting Blake back."

McDermid chuckled. "Aye, 't'would rather defeat the object."

"So I suggest you stay with Panther One and give the rest of us enough time to put some miles between us. To get south from here means going through the airstrip valley. So whatever happens it's going to be a tight squeeze. And that mob down there are regular Army, I think."

"It's noo a problem, boss."

Hawksby was relieved. "Good, then we'd best get weaving." He pulled a tight but grateful smile.

The two men returned to their respective vehicles. Almost before Hawksby was in his seat, Pogo Penaia was gunning. Panther Two's engine and swing the ¾ ton giant down the one-in-three boulder-strewn slope.

"So it's on then?" Perkis asked as McDermid clambered into his seat.

"I dunna ken why y're lookin' so pleased, lad. A four-day cross-country drive isna my idea of a picnic."

The Cockney adjusted his CUB nightsight. "It's okay when yer drivin', Scottie, you don't notice the bumps. It's you poor bleedin' passengers I feel sorry for."

Kangers Webster leaned forward from the back seat. "Listen, you bloody Pom, just make sure it's a smooth ride. I've gotta be treated real gentle. I'm wounded."

"You'll be bleedin' walkin' wounded if you don't shut up," Perkis replied affably.

McDermid wasn't in the mood for banter. "Jim, I want y' te get this thing down tha' goat track an' wait for me halfway doon the south slope by tha' gorse patch. When the Herc comes in, I'm goin' te warn 'em off. Then I want our friends down there te come lookin' for me. Up the quickest way . . ."

"The west slope?" suggested Kangers.

"Got it in one. While they're fallin' o'er themselves te get te me, I'll slip back te join y'. When they get up here we'll make a break fer t' road. Okay?"

"Sounds fun." Perkis' grinning mouth looked incongruous beneath the sinister CUB goggles.

"This isna a bleedin' training exercise," McDermid sneered.

The driver raised his hands in mock horror. "Don't spoil it for me, Scottie. You trying to put the wind up us?"

Exasperated, the corporal climbed out and delved into one of the side-bins. He extracted a green steel ammunition case of 9 mm cartridges, some grenades and coils of fuse wire, and rope. Finally he picked up the small radio transmitter and added it to the pile at his feet, together with a Verey signal pistol he would use as a last resort.

"Okay?" Perkis asked.

The Scotsman swung the strap of the Uzi over his shoulder. "Better get a move on, the Brylcreem boys 'll show in a few minutes." He turned briefly to the Gurkha who was seated next to Kangers in the rear. "If I dunna make it, just see if y' can navigate this silly bastard te the coast, will y'?

He's too young to die, an' he's got a bairn on the way . . ."

"Leave it out," Perkis protested. He palmed the gearstick into first. "Good luck, Scottie."

McDermid looked down at the arsenal by his feet and sniffed boredly. "Roll on death," he muttered, "and let's fuck the angels."

Panther One growled away and was swallowed up in the velvet night.

Using a small Vordic pencil torch to see, McDermid began snipping varying lengths of explosive Cordtex fuse, which he looped round several 9 mm cartridges, leaving a short gap between each cluster. He then taped the prepared Cordtex wires alternately with lengths of safety fuse. Once lit, the heat from the Cordtex would be sufficient to explode the cartridges at indeterminate intervals as the linked fuses burned through.

To the unsuspecting Iranians below, it would represent unnerving scattered gunfire that would continue for some time.

He repeated the process three more times, positioning each of the linked fuses in a different location.

Finally he took a trip-wire spool from a standard flare tin and rigged up two booby-traps on the most likely routes of approach. In each case he fixed one end of the trip-wire to an L2 fragmentation grenade which he taped to another rock. With a pair of pliers he squeezed the gap of the safety split-pin and partially pulled it. Just the slightest pressure against the trip-wire and the grenade would blow.

He glanced at his watch. If the Herc was on time, there were just two minutes to go.

Then he recalled the look on the Hawk's face when they had spoken earlier. He'd never seen the major look quite like that before. If he hadn't known him so well, he'd have said that the boss was showing signs of strain. Not panic, the SAS major was too much of a pro for that. But McDermid felt certain that he had detected an air of desperation.

Perhaps, after all, a year wasn't that long to get under the skin of a bloke like Alan Hawksby. In Oman he'd had it all his own way. He'd seized the initiative from the enemy in the beginning and kept it. He'd run rings round the rebel tribesmen and Yemeni troops, always planning and thinking ahead, always outwitting and, if necessary, out-fighting them. They never stood a chance.

Things were a bit different now though. Stuck in the middle of a hostile desert landscape, without support, knowing that the enemy was onto you, but not knowing just how far behind. And then problems exploding all around you like mortar shells. A bit different from Oman, all right.

McDermid squinted at the inky outline of the Zagros peaks beyond the airstrip below. No sign yet of Alpha Zulu.

His thoughts returned to the Hawk. Maybe that was it? Perhaps the major was really an HQ planner type? Okay when he was having it all his own way, but coming apart at the seams when the going got tough. He hoped not, because some sixth sense told him that things were going to get a damn sight tougher yet.

He dismissed the idea. Surely you didn't get to be a squadron commander in 22 if you couldn't take the rough with the smooth? The 'sickener' factor in all their training made sure of that. Everyone spoke of the Hawk with a respect bordering on awe. He was clever all right, and a bit distanced from his men, but never too much so. Perhaps he'd just had it too good for too long. After a spell with every assignment going like clockwork, he could be starting to believe his own publicity. McDermid hoped not. That would be a big mistake.

Then he heard the steady drone of the four giant Allison engines of the C130 Hercules at low level. Judging its whereabouts, though, was difficult. The noise was reverberating through the mountain range, bouncing from one peak to another.

He spoke into the radio: "Snapdragon te Dragonfly. Spider. Repeat. Spider. Over."

Nothing.

The regular beating sound grew louder until he was certain the heavy transport was coming in low from the far side of the strip. His eyes strained to pick up its shape against the irregular form of the mountains opposite. Then he caught sight of it, wheeling slowly in through a narrow valley like a giant black bat. It was a superb bit of flying, McDermid thought, as it levelled up on its approach.

He repeated his message. Still no response. Whether the radio was faulty or the mountains were playing their usual tricks with communications, he had no way of knowing.

He had forlornly hoped that the pilot would need confirmation of the strip, but evidently Fontenoy knew exactly where he was.

The sudden brilliance of the emergency runway flares after the absolute darkness momentarily blinded McDermid.

He couldn't believe his eyes. "The bastards!" he breathed.

They were actually illuminating the strip with marker flares to lure Alpha Zulu down. And it was going to work: he saw the heavy undercarriage unfold as the Hercules dropped height in line for a perfect first pass landing.

There was no alternative. He picked up the Verey pistol and squeezed the trigger. He watched as the shooting star blasted skywards in a twisting trail of smoke. It burst at one hundred feet, exploding into a dazzling aurora of red light.

Muzzle flashes blinked from either side of the airstrip as the Iranian ambush parties were startled into action. From McDermid's vantage point on the peak, the gunfire sounded no more menacing than firecrackers.

Alpha Zulu's heavy landing wheels bounced once on the overgrown strip, picking up festoons of tumbleweed, then lifted again as the pilot poured on the power. The engines screamed, sounding like a demonic laugh as their noise echoed around the valley. With agonising slowness the Hercules peeled away from the blaze of automatic fire. Its starboard wing just skimmed above the ground as it banked away.

McDermid could imagine the pilot's confusion as he fought to gain enough height to clear the looming peak. For a moment the wings and bulky fuselage glittered in the incandescent glow of the fading flare. Then its thunder was deafening as it swooped low over his position, its churning propellers clawing for altitude.

He felt the downrush of air blast over him, and heard the angry rustle of leaves being torn from their branches. His eyes followed the massive black bulk that seemed to blot out the sky, flattening him against the ground. Then he lost it as it vanished over the peak behind him, its receding roar seeming to make the very earth tremble. McDermid caught his breath and then allowed himself a smile of satisfaction as he realised that for the moment they'd got away. He was wondering if Alpha Zulu would now be able to make it undetected back to the coast when his thoughts were interrupted by the commotion down on the strip.

Voices were raised and, in the glare of the runway flares, he could see black shapes running. Arms pointed up to where the Verey pistol had been fired. Quickly the corporal lit the master safety fuse and rolled across the patch of open ground to where the vegetation began. The sparse shrubs would cover his rapid descent down to the near-vertical rock face. He had been scrambling down the south slope for some time before he heard the first of the 9 mm cartridges start exploding. Live shells fired haphazardly in all directions like demented catherine wheels.

After a few minutes he stopped, his feet jammed against the roots of a tree which overhung the bare chalk cliff that fell away three hundred feet below. The exact length of the 7 mm rope he carried. He forced himself to take a deep breath as he looked down. Below it was an inky void. A bottomless pit that even the starglow failed to illuminate. Fear suddenly rushed in on him. Were the JARIC maps spot on? Was the coil of rope he carried over his shoulder long enough? Would it leave him dangling short? He pushed the thought from his mind. It was too late to worry about that now. Already he could see the flash of torchlights moving away from the strip. The Iranian troops were beginning to make their way nervously up the western slope towards the hysterical burst of gunfire McDermid had set in motion.

Swiftly he fixed the first rope around the thin tree stump behind him. It would probably hold, he decided. If not, it would bring away an avalance of loose rock with it. Dead and buried all in one.

He threaded the rope in a figure-of-eight around the 'descender' friction-brake which he hooked onto his belt. Then, grabbing the trailing rope in his right hand, he swung back outward. Just one final downward glance and he pushed hard with his boots against the chalk face and lifted his right arm. The pressure swung him away and he dropped like a stone, his feet touching the cliff momentarily every twenty feet. Bend the knees and push out again . . . And again, all the time feeding the rope through the friction-brake.

A tiny black spider against the vast wall of chalk, he finally descended into the shadowy depths of the cliff.

He slowed down, aware he had abseiled far too quickly. The skin on his hands was scorched from the running rope and the friction-brake. But he was safe now, hidden in darkness. Blisters and weals were a small price to pay compared with a high-velocity round from some keen-eyed Iranian marksman.

McDermid took his time over the last few feet. He was careful not to sprain his ankle stupidly on the jagged scree at the valley floor. By the time he was unharnessed, the sound of detonating shells from the peak above his head had ceased. All he could hear were distant shouts in Farsi.

A sharp whistle split the immediate quietness. Two harsh notes.

It was Kangers Webster calling from the shapeless mass of nearby gorse bushes. Hurriedly he scrambled over the sea of fallen chalk and rocks until he could make out the stubby rear of Panther One.

"Pull yer finger out, Mac!" hissed the Australian. He was crouched behind the black shape of the L37 general-purpose machine gun that jutted menacingly out of the rear compartment. "Someone took an interest in your Spiderman impersonation. There's a vehicle comin' from the strip. Tryin' to cut you off."

"Shit!" McDermid clambered into the front passenger seat. The familiar smell of paint, leather and oil was comforting. He lifted himself in the seat and peered down the incline towards the strip. "How many men in it?"

"Don't know," Perkis replied tightly, slipping the gear into first, "but do you mind if we don't hang around to count 'em?"

Without waiting for a reply the East Ender let out the clutch. Panther One growled and all four tyres contemptuously kicked out chalk fragments as it jolted forwards like a startled animal.

"One to Two". In the rear Tiger was talking on the headset of the Clansman. "Moving now. Contact. One vehicle following. Out."

The SAS Land Rover broke from cover like a bat out of hell. With Perkis grasping the wheel at a relaxed ten-to-two position, the vehicle hit the dried grass flats of Lordakan airstrip flat out at sixty.

They had lost sight of the approaching Iranian vehicle and were astonished when they nearly collided with it coming the other way.

Although it was another Land Rover, it was no match for Panther One with its infra-red headlights and CUB night-drive gear. The three Iranians were shaken rigid as the totally blacked-out SAS vehicle shot past them out of the night.

By the time they had swung their vehicle round in a circle, Perkis had already launched his machine at the first of two dried-up river beds at full revs. The chassis hammered down into the wadi after leaving the ground with a squeal of protest from the heavy-duty shock absorbers. A fog of dust blasted up behind them as the sand-tyres bit into the cracked earth and found a purchase. Expertly, Perkis palmed the stick down into second, and they were away again, the airstrip disappearing fast behind them.

"Jesus!" Kangers swore. "If them mad mullahs don't get us, bleedin' Perkis will."

"Belt up!" McDermid hissed, feeling distinctly queasy. He'd never felt seasick on land before. But Kangers ignored him and continued making wisecracks that only Tiger could hear in the slipstream.

For a mile they kept well in front of the pursuing Land Rover, the drunken sweep of its headlights betraying its cumbersome progress. Then Perkis hit a problem attempting to cross the second wadi.

The far embankment rose up like a wall, almost vertical. Perkis slammed on the brakes and Panther One fish-tailed to a shuddering halt.

"Fuck," Perkis said, almost politely.

"Even you can't do that . . ." McDermid muttered. Then he was thrown forward in his safety-belt as the driver slammed the vehicle into reverse. Another hard brake and back into first. Kangers hit his head against the butt of the GPMG.

He felt the blood with his fingers. "Stone me, Perkis. I'll. . ." Whatever his threat, it was lost beneath the pounding roar of the engine as Perkis swung Panther One left, speeding south over the mosaic of cracked mud. Behind them the Iranians had gained. The probing fingers of light were now closer and more menacing. The gap began to close again as the driver took advantage of Perkis' misfortune.

At last the bank gave way to a shallow slope and Panther One was able to churn its way through a patch of soft ground to join the road south.

Perkis was shaking his head. "They're lighter than us. They'll catch us on the road."

McDermid swung around in his seat. "Slow down, Jim. Let 'em get close an' we'll give 'em a wee surprise. Shake up their liver a bit."

As Perkis eased up, the corporal reached over to Kangers Webster. "HOLD Y' FIRE TILL WE GET 'EM AT A HUNDRED METRES! OPEN UP WHEN I GIVE THE WORD!"

Kangers nodded and gave a thumbs-up, as McDermid motioned Tiger to hand forward the Clansman headset.

"One to Two?" he demanded. "Over."

"*Send sitrep. Over.*" It was Hawksby's voice. He sounded unperturbed, almost nonchalant. McDermid grinned as he heard the major add: "*You still in contact? Over*".

"Roger. Am slowing. Will engage. Over."

Hawksby's voice crackled again. "*Good luck. RV at two bridges. Out.*" That was some eighteen miles ahead.

More like the Hawk we know and love, McDermid thought. He handed back the headset to Tiger.

Now they had slowed to thirty and the Iranian Land Rover was gaining on them fast along the metalled road. McDermid put his full concentration on the widening eyes of light behind them.

Perkis had not wasted time when waiting for McDermid earlier. There were two fan-shaped dischargers on the rear of Panther One, each housing three firing tubes for L7 grenades that could be lobbed a full hundred metres, providing a blinding semi-circle of smoke to screen their escape. Perkis had replaced the contents with L5s. White phosphorus smoke that burned the skin and seared the lungs. More effective. His hand shifted towards the firing-button.

In the rear Kangers flipped up the breech lid of the GPMG and checked the feed-in of the first four rounds of the belt. Alternate two ball and one tracer. Lethal. And pretty. Bright fire-flies in the night that could mesmerise the enemy and tell you exactly where you were pouring in the deadly high-velocity shells. He cranked the cocking handle and lined his eye down the sight.

McDermid squinted into the brilliant dazzle. Waiting. Panther One seemed to have slowed almost to a halt. The slipstream all but faded, the engine unusually quiet. It seemed an age.

A shot cracked towards them from the Land Rover. No one heard where it went.

McDermid forced himself to count.

"Christ!" Perkis said. "Ain't they there yet, Scottie?"

"Stow it!" snapped the reply.

The Iranians hit McDermid's imagined hundred metre mark. "Okay, Kangers, give it 'em."

The stammering bark of the GPMG at close quarters was ear-shattering, as the Australian swung the blazing barrel in an arc across the bonnet of the approaching vehicle. Beneath his hands the trembling gun metal felt good. He was aware of the spent cartridges thudding into the canvas catch bags that hung beneath the weapon. It was good to strike back, he thought. Good to relieve the tension of the past weeks that left you feeling like an over-wound clock spring. Despite the oncoming headlights he had managed to shatter the bulbs. The world plunged into darkness but it was impossible to tell if anyone had been hit, because the vehicle kept on coming, and someone was alive enough to let rip a burst of returning fire. McDermid heard one of the shells zing against a side-bin. "Perkis!" he shouted.

The driver hit the switch. The blast of the six L5s detonating simultaneously seemed to jolt Panther One forward.

A billowing cloud of caustic white phosphorous smoke swirled up instantaneously, like some ferocious pantomime genie. In a split second the pursuing Land Rover was devoured in the gushing wall of smoke.

Kangers pumped another prolonged burst into the turmoil and they heard the vehicle's fuel tanks blow.

Still turned, McDermid felt himself pushed against the seat-back by the surge of power as Perkis accelerated away. All he saw was the vague shape of the vehicle in the middle of the inferno. One man broke through on foot, starkly outlined against the brilliant glow. His clothes were ablaze. Kangers killed him with the very last round of the complete belt he'd fed into the GPMG.

As they turned a bend in the road the only reminder of the brief and bloody encounter was a faint glimmer in the sky. It took just fifteen minutes for Perkis to cover the distance to the second bridge, travelling at a breakneck sixty miles an hour along the twisting mountain road.

Panther Two was parked at the far side of a deep ravine, spanned by an ancient stone bridge. It hardly looked capable of supporting even pedestrian traffic.

"We shook 'em off, boss," McDermid announced with an air of triumph as soon as they drew alongside.

Hawksby didn't share the Scotman's optimism. "There'll be more of them no doubt, but it's a good start. We've wired this bridge to blow in five minutes. That should cause a few problems to any vehicles trying to follow."

"It iss a shame to destroy such a beautiful old bridge." It was Eva who spoke from her seat in the back of Panther Two.

McDermid was amazed. "This isna Architectural Heritage Year in Iran, is it?"

"Leave it out, Scottie," Hawksby chided. He turned to address the occupants of both vehicles. "Now listen, all of you. Despite our setbacks we're still all together and ahead of the enemy. We've got the initiative and it's imperative to keep it if we're going to beat the odds. Our friends here will no doubt be pleased to know that we do have contingency plans to cover the sort of problems we've just encountered . . ." He went on, "I want to make good time for as long as night lasts, to put as many miles as possible between us. I intend, therefore, to make maximum use of these good roads, whilst the Iranians are still in a state of confusion. It's a calculated risk. But the farther away we get, the wider area the enemy will have to search. We'll keep heading south down this mountain road, turning left at Kalvart Olya where there's a junction with another road from the north. Ten miles south again there's another bridge which I also intend to take out." He turned to Eva. "Sorry about that."

She couldn't prevent the involuntary flicker of a smile.

He continued: "Some thirty miles beyond that we'll reach a large wooded valley, running alongside the Beshar River. It'll be as good a place as we're likely to find in this lunar landscape." He glanced at his watch. "Right, it's 0100 hours, so let's get weaving. We've a long way to go."

Despite herself Eva could not prevent a thrill of excitement at the major's words. As she'd already said, he seemed to treat the appalling catalogue of events as though it were a kind of game. Nevertheless, she had to admit it was a game he seemed to take seriously. His qualities of leadership were obvious and appealing. However crazy this adventure, which was wildly beyond anything she had ever experienced before, she felt safe under the protection of his hard-bitten team who seemed to thrive on adversity.

Major Alan Hawksby's manner, she decided, made a refreshing change from the evangelic convictions of Jonathan Blake. Whereas the journalist saw the world in shades of grey, Hawksby seemed to see it just as a series of immediate challenges to be met, fought and won.

He was a hard bastard, and no mistake. Idly she specu
lated on what made him tick; what it was inside that drove
him on?

These were the thoughts uppermost in her mind as Pogo
Penaia swung their vehicle into the dusty trail made by
Panther One as it took the lead on the road south.

ISFAHAN: 0100 hrs, Saturday 20th September

As Curt Swartz Jnr. came round, it was like surfacing after a
deep dive in clear waters. Then the pain hit him. He closed
his eyes against the burning force of the interrogation lamps,
but he didn't have to see to know the state of his tortured
body. His entire torso burned as though on fire.

Suddenly he became aware of a voice in his ear and could
smell almonds on the breath of his tormentor.

"You have done well, Mr Swartz." The modulated voice
was soothing like a balm. "We are most grateful for your
co-operation."

"I can't see."

"Of course." Considerate. "Turn off those lights."

Immediately the sun went out and Curt felt the throbbing
pain in his temples subside.

"Water."

"Let's not rush things, Mr. Swartz." Again the voice of
velvet. "You shall have something to drink, but first you
must help us some more."

Curt tried to focus his mind. As he did so, the voice went
on: "You were right about Lordakan airstrip, of course.
Please forgive me for having doubted your word. But, unfortunately, although we prevented the rescue aircraft from
landing, my men failed to apprehend your colleagues. So
now I want to know of their contingency plans." A pause to
let the significance soak in. "What would they do if their plan
failed?"

I don't understand. Correct about Lordakan? It was a
pack of lies. It couldn't be correct. I'd been told where it
really was. Have I betrayed them? Have I inadvertently got

it wrong? Had the SAS sergeant told me Lordakan after all and not Bu'in? Oh, God, no.

He felt sick. "Water." His parched plea was a scarcely audible croak.

"Water," commanded the velvet voice.

A tin mug was pressed to his lips, and he gulped eagerly. Suddenly he drew in his breath and spat it out. Salt!

"Tell us, Swartz, then you will have water. What was to be the plan if the Lordakan pick-up failed?"

"BASTARDS!" Curt screamed at the top of his voice, squeezing all the power in his lungs. But in the interrogation room all they heard was an incoherent mumble.

CHAPTER THIRTEEN

ZAGROS: 0230 hrs, Saturday 20th September

"Trouble, boss," warned John Belcher.

He was seated in the back of Panther Two with Blake and Eva. Hawksby swivelled round in the front passenger seat and glanced back along the road. The swirling dust reduced the distant headlamps to minute orbs of light.

"How far d'you reckon, John? Two miles?"

"Nearer three, I'd say."

As Hawksby reached to the radio, wedged behind the front seat, the headset came alive in his ear. It was McDermid who was riding point in Panther One. "*One to Two. Contact ahead, boss. Looks like a roadblock. Probably gendarmes. About a mile to half-mile ahead.*"

Hawksby glanced at Blake and Eva. "It never rains but it bloody well buckets." He spoke into the mike. "Two, Roger. Is there anywhere safe to pull off the road up there, Scottie?"

Instantly the voice came back. "*A derelict building on our left. Looks like it was once a tea-house. Over.*"

"We'll join you there in a couple of minutes, Scottie. Get well out of sight, we've just picked up a tail. Out."

He just caught sound of the Glaswegian blaspheming.

Five minutes later they found the collapsed mud-brick house and drove off the road into a shallow that was hidden from passing traffic. McDermid was watching the roadblock through a pair of binoculars. Although the police vehicles had their lights out, the flashing hand torches were like beacons in the vastness of the black landscape that dropped away to the south.

At least we can see them before they see us," Hawksby said as he accepted the proferred binoculars.

"It's still goin' te slow us doon too much, boss. It'll take a couple o'hours te pass them off the road. And we'll be sittin' ducks come daylight. We're still much too near Lordakan. They're boond te locate us if they organise an extensive search."

Blake had climbed stiffly down from his seat. "What d'you have in mind, Major?"

Hawksby resisted the temptation to accuse him of getting windy. "A diversion," he replied to no one in particular. "I seem to remember a pipeline marked on the map just before we stopped."

McDermid grinned. "Aye, boss, it's t' main gas link te the south. Mostly it runs undergroond, but I noticed the culvert aboot a mile back where it passes under t' road."

"Splendid," Hawksby replied.

"You don't think an explosion is going to stop them looking for us, do you?" Blake challenged.

"Have you ever seen a gas pipeline go up, Jonathan?"

"No."

"Then be a good chap, and reserve your judgment, eh?"

When the pipeline went it seemed like a thermo-nuclear blast to the gendarmes manning the roadblock.

It had taken McDermid and Tiger half-an-hour to return to the culvert and fix a charge of 1 lb of PE4 plastic explosive with a time fuse. On a last-minute impulse the Scotsman had insisted on giving the delay an extra couple of minutes. Having seen the four-foot diameter pipes close up, his imagination had begun to work overtime. There was over a million cubic feet of liquid gas between the two nearest shut-off valve stations on the pipeline.

As it turned out, it was to be a decision that saved their lives. On the return trip Tiger had sprained an ankle. It was only a minor injury but it slowed the pair of them down. Had they been caught in the open in the maelstrom that followed, they would have been blasted from the face of the earth. They had only just rejoined the others behind a giant shoulder of solid rock, when it blew.

It was hard to tell which came first. A momentous blast

lightened the sky like a gargantuan thunderbolt coming from deep within the ground. A mushroom of brightness radiated upward in a series of pulsing ripples, each more blinding than the last. The sound shook the earth beneath their feet and, despite the distance, the pain in their eardrums was intense. Almost immediately they heard something like a rolling barrage of heavy artillery as the pipeline ruptured on either side of the road. Great curves of steel pipework were spewed high into the air, amid a hail of earth and rock. The continuous roar went on, fed by the gas being pumped down the line.

Worst of all was the main blast which tore down the road as an awesome unseen force, uprooting trees and bushes as though they were mere bits of matchwood. They were nearly asphyxiated as the spiralling fireball sucked in the oxygen from the surrounding landscape.

"Jesus H . . .!" Perkis began.

"I reckon Paynes Fireworks might give us a job when we leave the Army, boss," McDermid murmured.

Behind them Blake and Eva were speechless.

Hawksby lifted the binoculars to his eyes and watched the gendarmes fight to get into their cars and race towards the mysterious apocalypse just behind the hill. "C'mon," he said. "Time we got going."

ISFAHAN: 0315 hrs, Saturday 20th September

A report of the gas explosion near the village of Meymand reached Colonel Murad at Isfahan exactly fifteen minutes later.

Despite the hysterical pleadings of the local commander of the Gendarmerie on the other end of the radio, he refused to be hurried. Wearily, he crossed the office to where his aide was studying the giant wall map.

The younger man stuck a pin into the spot where the gas pipeline crossed the road south. "That's where they are – the sons of Satan!" He turned to his superior. "Do we go now?"

Calmly Murad lit his umpteenth cigarette of the past

forty-eight hours. It tasted excruciatingly foul. "We are all tired, my friend. And that is when people make mistakes. These mysterious invaders have had time to rest. Obviously they are very experienced and are probably much fresher than us."

"But the explosion . . ." the aide protested.

". . . Serves no purpose," Murad cut in, impatient at the slowness of his aide to learn. "Except that it has our men on the spot flapping like a lot of old women. No doubt that was the intention. If we went there, I have no doubt that we would find the entire battalion at my disposal standing and staring at the damage . . . while our quarry slipped away."

The aide sighed and looked back at the map. "But where to?"

"If the American is to be believed, they will be moving south to the coast. Do not be down-hearted. Yesterday there was every chance they would get away. Tonight we have prevented that. Yesterday they could have been anywhere in Iran. Tonight – just fifteen minutes ago – we knew they were at Meymand. So why the gloom? The trap is closing in on them." Murad blew a smoke ring at the pin on the map. It hit the perspex covering and burst into a rolling blue wreath. "Now they do not have far to go before daylight. Then they will need shelter. Where would you go if you were them?"

"The forest?" The aide suggested, hopefully. "Shade and water from the Beshar River."

Murad smiled, his heavy eyelids almost closing. He drew a deep breath. "So let us forget about the gas blow-out. That is now the concern of the Energy Ministry. Let us arrange a roadblock on the outskirts of the forest valley to the south. That will cut them off. Then we shall fly down and take command of the search on the spot."

An hour later their army helicopter landed at the roadblock.

Although the personnel was composed of a motley collection of revolutionary guards, regular troops and gendarmes, a competent job had been made. Vehicles had been driven across the road, each nudging the next, so that any attempt to ram a way through would just lock them more tightly together. The area was some twenty-five miles south of the gas blow-out, which could still be seen as an incandescence on the horizon. The site had been carefully selected for the steep embankment on either side of the road. Two machine guns and supporting fire teams had been placed at the top of each bank. The entire perimeter of the roadblock had been sealed off with coils of barbed wire and oil cans.

The Army lieutenant in charge had deduced from reports of earlier clashes that the strangers were driving on infra-red lights and had been most insistent that none of his men used lights or smoked cigarettes. Murad at last felt guardedly optimistic. His headache was beginning to recede along with his fatigue.

Then they saw it. The brief flash of headlights.

"There!" the lieutenant cried. "On the crest of the hill."

The headlights had been dowsed as quickly as they had come on, but most of the men had seen them. A gabble of excited chatter broke out.

Murad frowned. "I thought you said they were using infra-red?"

The lieutenant shrugged. "Maybe they just wanted to get a better look at us?"

"No matter. Get half your men together and two vehicles, and come with me to the top of the hill." The soldier started to move but Murad restrained him. "For God's sake tell them to be careful. This enemy is good and could be setting a trap." As engines roared into life around him, Murad reflected bitterly that since the mullahs' purges there were few competent officers like the lieutenant left in the armed forces. He climbed into one of the vehicles. Not long now.

It took only moments to reach the top of the hill. A detachment of troops debussed from their vehicles to complete the approach on foot. The young lieutenant led.

There was nothing there.

Someone shone a torch beam on the dust-smeared tarmac. Murad knelt down and studied the tracks made by sets of heavy-duty sand tyres. "This is where they left the road. When we saw those lights flash, that must have been when they saw us. Just ten minutes ago."

225

The lieutenant looked pleased. "Two vehicles by the look of it. They cannot have got far."

Something was wrong, decided Colonel Murad, but what? For a moment he studied the smashed undergrowth at the west side of the road where the enemy vehicles had veered off to circumvent the roadblock. "Get your men organised with all the vehicles capable of cross-country travel. We shall begin a sweep as soon as you have them assembled."

The efficient young lieutenant who commanded the Iranian search detachment had never heard the anecdote about tracking SAS troops in snow. If he had, it might have occurred to him that he was organising his sweep in completely the wrong direction. On exercise in Norway, troops from the regiment had been known to cross snow-covered clearings by walking backwards to throw their pursuers off the scent.

Hawksby had used a similar ploy as soon as McDermid had located the position of the roadblock. Both Panther One and Two had pulled off the road, then reversed back onto it farther along, at the peak of the hill. They continued backward up the road, away from the roadblock, flashing a set of hand spotlights as they went.

As the Iranians and their vehicles left the road, moving westward like beaters on a pheasant shoot, the Snapdragon team was by-passing the roadblock to the east. When the six o'clock sun began warming the chill mountain air an hour later, the two SAS vehicles had drawn to a halt on the secluded upper slopes of the Beshar River valley.

Shafts of pale yellow light were slanting through the trees, as Hawksby stepped down wearily onto the thick carpet of pine needles. He glanced up at the canopy of branches, through which he could see fragments of powder-blue sky.

The foliage was a bit thin and he ordered his exhausted team to begin rigging the camouflage netting over the vehicles and the space between them that would serve as a tented living area. Hessian was used to kill the tell-tale glare of the windscreens and poles were erected to distort the vehicle shapes and support the leaf-cut rubber foliage of the netting.

No more than a few real branches were needed to add the finishing touches. A reconnaissance pilot would be hard pressed to spot a camouflaged vehicle at one mile. If he hadn't seen it by then, the speed of his approach would blur his vision to an extent that made identification impossible.

Hawksby stepped back to check the work. It was good, even from ground level. And if enemy aircraft were using ground-search radar, the signals would be absorbed by the specially-treated leaves of the netting so that the returning echo gave nothing away. Even if the Iranians were very crafty and used infra-red systems to pick up vehicle heat-spots amid the forest, the special paint pigment on the Panthers was designed to have identical reflective qualities to the chlorophyll in the surrounding natural foliage.

By now the sun was rapidly gaining in strength but Hawksby had decided that Blake and Eva should not be allowed to think they were passengers on some adventure holiday. With the promise of food later, they were dispatched under John Belcher's guidance to dig solar stills on the upper slopes of the valley. As they left the hide, Hawksby was sending out McDermid and Perkis on the first picket watch, to look out for anything approaching from the north or west. At the same time Tiger was scaling a tree, dragging up the 40-feet horizontal aerial of the A13 Skywave transmitter. This would eventually bounce their message off the iono-sphere on its long journey back to Britain.

As he trudged up the slope after Belcher, it was the sight of the Gurkha struggling in the trees, to unhelpful instructions from Kangers Webster on the ground, that started Blake thinking. He was so deep in thought that he hardly noticed the bone-hardness of the earth under the entrenching spade as they began the first of half-a-dozen small pits. Neither was he really listening as Belcher explained how they were designed to attract the moisture content from the ground. Each one, promised the soldier, would yield two litres of water by the end of the day.

Totally shattered, Blake prised away the last heavy scab of

compacted earth, and staggered back into the shade of a nearby tree. Eva, who had been given the slightly less arduous task of scooping out the loose pieces, peeled the damp hair from her forehead and stumbled over to join him. Her fatigues were black with sweat and clung to the contours of her body. She dropped down beside him. Too tired to speak immediately they watched as Belcher began spreading foliage around the cans he had placed in the centre of each pit.

At last finding her breath, Eva said: "It iss very clever. To find water in a place like t'is."

Jarred from his thoughts, Blake laughed harshly. "I'll remember that next time I'm stranded in a desert."

She looked at him, concerned. "What iss it, Jon'i? We iss free and on our way 'ome. I know t'ere iss dangers, but t'ese people are very capable. Yet you seem – I don't know – troubled."

He studied his outstretched feet. "I am troubled. Very troubled. And so should you be."

She was bewildered. "Why?"

Even dressed in baggy battle fatigues, she managed to look stunningly feminine. He found himself fascinated by the beads of perspiration glistening at the open neck of her shirt. He felt a need for her stirring in him. "I think they've been ordered to kill us."

Eva stared at him. "You iss mad," she accused. "T'ey 'af only just rescued us. Besides, t'ey iss British."

He gave a snort of laughter. "Don't you believe all the propaganda the British put out about themselves. The Establishment is as ruthless as anything in the world. And a damn sight more cunning than most. That's how they survive. They've been at it since medieval times. I know, I've been fighting them throughout my reporting career . . ."

"But why kill us?" It still seemed absurd.

"It's obvious we've been rescued because of Fulcrum. Somehow – God knows – they realise we have all the details."

She frowned. "It iss not because you iss a British hostage? Like the Americans."

"Act your age, Eva!" He almost spat out the words. "Have

228

you any idea of the cost of mounting a mission like this? I'll tell you: it's millions. And the risks! Jesus Christ, there are Englishmen languishing in some prison or other in every poxy country in the world, and they don't send out the SAS to get them back. For all her promises, Her Britannic Majesty just lets the poor bastards rot."

She watched unseeing as John Belcher started pegging out khaki-coloured plastic sheets over each hole, placing a heavy stone on the centre of each to form an inverted cone. "Obviously t'ey do not want t'e Iranians to know about Fulcrum. It would be embarrassing. T'at I understand."

Blake was losing patience. "And you think they'll allow us to tell the world when we get home?"

"We said we would. We agreed . . ." She began, suddenly realising what he was getting at.

"When we stopped at the camp earlier, I asked the major if I could have your roll of Minox film. He refused. Point blank. He said it would be safer with him."

Eva shrugged, unsure. "Maybe 'e iss right."

"Bullshit!" He glared out of the shade at Belcher who was completing his task, making sure that the presence of the stills would not be obvious from the air. "The major has denied he knows why we're wanted by his government, yet he's made no attempt to find out when I've baited him."

"Per'aps 'e 'as ot'er t'ings on 'is mind." She was being sarcastic and it rankled. "Per'aps 'e does what every soldier iss supposed to do. Get on wit' orders and not ask questions."

Blake shook his head vehemently. "If I was him and I *really* didn't know, I would try and find out something about why I was risking my neck."

"*You* iss a journalist," she reminded him. Belcher had picked up his spade and was returning wearily to them.

Quickly Blake said: "I'll put it to the test. I've had an idea. And I'll see if they can't let us carry arms. For self-defence . . ."

Eva went to speak but stopped as Belcher's shadow fell across them. "There you are, my beauties, that's how it's done! And, medically speaking, of course, water's more important than food. We'll have twelve litres of the stuff by

229

this evening. That'll help keep our reserves intact!" He was smiling broadly.

Blake smiled back. "Bloody brilliant!"

A look of uncertainty crossed Belcher's face. He wasn't sure how to take it.

Breakfast, when it came, was scarcely worth the long wait. Faces smiled with anticipation when the self-heating rations began hissing as water was added to the sodium carbide in the cans. The mood lightened as they gathered in the tented living area. But when the fluid stew was dolloped unceremoniously by John Belcher into the proffered mess-tins, faces fell.

Eva wrinkled her nose. "Iss t'ese edible?" she asked seriously. Already tiredness had caused a feeling of nausea, and the sight of the food didn't help.

Belcher got stuck in. "If it's good enough for the major's cat, then it's good enough for us," he enthused through a mouthful of the stuff.

Kangers looked at Eva in mock affront. "So what's wrong with kangeroo meat?" The SAS men laughed. Having eaten rat casserole on survival training exercises, the complaints were a mere ritual. Blake and Eva on the other hand, looked genuinely sick at the sight of it. The journalist ate a few mouthfuls then pushed it aside. He decided it was fear that had destroyed his appeite, and resolved to make an issue of their fate with Hawksby.

The major was pleased to find the rest of the group in such good humour. If ever that disappeared he knew he was in real trouble. Despite the setbacks, their morale seemed high and even the most unappetising meal was enough to restore their spirits. He reached for the aluminium kettle on the Gaz burner and poured the hot water over a teabag in a black plastic mug.

As the teabag was passed around the circle, Blake said casually: "I think, Major, that Eva and I should be armed. As it is we have no means of defence, and we could be a help if there's shooting."

Hawksby peered at him over the rim of his mug. "There're

230

seven of us with weapons, Jonathan. That's likely to be enough. It's dangerous having two inexperienced people wielding lethal firearms."

"You could instruct us," Eva suggested.

"It won't be necessary," Hawksby replied, wiping his mouth with the back of his hand. There was a finality to his voice. Subject closed.

The girl exchanged glances with Blake. He said: "Like it won't be necessary to give Eva back her film."

"I've told you, I feel happier if I keep it."

Blake's voice was edged with anger. "Then you must know what's in it." It was a flat statement.

The major ran a hand through his beard. It needed trimming. "I know it's important to you. And if it's important to you, then the chances are the contents are also of interest to the British Government. And they are paying the piper."

"Typical fascist attitude! So you're confiscating it?" Blake challenged.

"No, old chap. I'm looking after it, that's all."

"You *do* know what's in it!"

Hawksby was getting angry. "By the fuss you're making I know damn well you've something to hide." His eyes narrowed. "How about *you* telling me what's in it?"

The journalist's face contorted. "Piss off, Major!"

"Don't you trust me?"

"Frankly, I wouldn't trust you further than I can spit!" Eva placed a restraining hand on his arm. He shook it off. "It's got to be said. I think you're just waiting for the opportunity to kill me, aren't you? Shut me up for good and protect the lily-white name of the British Government!"

Hawksby's mouth dropped open in amazement. His tea spilled. The circle of SAS men exchanged glances, as though to check with each other that they weren't hearing things.

"Jon'i!" Eva warned.

For a moment the group sat in stunned silence.

Hawksby regained his composure. "I assume that this isn't your idea of a joke, Jonathan? But I wonder what in God's name you think we've been doing, risking life and limb to save your precious neck? It is not, I assure you, just for the pleasure of bumping you off."

Despite his conviction, Blake suddenly felt foolish. "I don't expect you to admit it."

"I wouldn't, Jonathan, because it's not true. And, if it was, we could have done it at anytime since we left Isfahan. Forget about any fairy tales you hear about the forces. War may be a different matter, but in peacetime we are under many constraints. Political assassination is not one of our tasks. For one, we just wouldn't accept such orders. And for another, we're too close to the government of the day."

"The boss is right," Tiger added. "If someone wants to get rid of you, they take out a contract with private outfit."

Blake eyed Hawksby suspiciously. "I've only got your word for that. I know the SAS is the strike arm of the Foreign Office."

"Not in that way," the major replied quietly. "And I am afraid you have only my word to trust. If you genuinely think our orders are discreetly to get rid of you, you're barking up the wrong tree. I promise you, if anyone made an attempt to take your life, he'd have me and my team to reckon with. That includes the Foreign Secretary, the Prime Minister, or even the Queen herself. My orders come direct from the Master." He paused, realising that Blake didn't understand. "That's our commanding officer. And he would not issue such an order . . ."

". . . But if he did?" Blake provoked.

It was Kangers Webster who spoke. "You'd be dead."

Hawksby flashed the Australian a daggers look that could have drawn blood. He turned back to Blake. "There is no such order, Jonathan. But if you even suspect that there might be, it reinforces my justification in holding onto that film."

Blake sneered. "And refusing us guns?"

The major's eyelids lowered and the journalist suddenly recognised the cold hawk-like expression. "Very much so."

"If what you say is true," Blake said after a moment's thought, "then I'd like you to send a message. You're going to make a transmission, aren't you?"

Intrigued by the reason behind the journalist's obvious fear, Hawksby began filling his clay pipe with tobacco. "Yes, we're set to transmit around noon. Whitehall will be shittin' bricks until they hear from us —" He turned to Eva apologetically. "I beg your pardon."

She shrugged and smiled.

"Then in your message tell them I know what their game is," Blake said savagely. "Tell them I know they want to kill me, and to keep their hands off!"

Hawksby was bemused as he drew on his pipe. "Verbatim?"

"Word for bloody word," Blake retorted. "Put the record straight. And let them know that you *also* know what I suspect."

A sweet smelling cloud of Dutch tobacco drifted through the living area. Thoughtfully Hawksby said: "If that's what you want, Jonathan? Yes, I'll do that for you." Taken aback, Blake stared at the major for a second. Then he relaxed. There was nothing more he could do. As he began picking at his meal in silence, Eva Olsen studied the expression on Major Hawksby's face.

At precisely 1204, Snapdragon's Morse message went out over the A13 Skywave transmitter. It was scrambled through the 'squirt box' attachment so that the high-speed broadcast was condensed to mere seconds.

Tiger switched to 'Receive' and glanced at the gathering of soldiers around Panther One. He smiled nervously. As usual, erecting the aerial coil through the treetops had been a pig of a job and there was no guarantee that any of the message would be picked up by the Government Communications Headquarters in Cheltenham. More likely was a partial atmospheric distortion, particularly prone to occur when transmitting from high mountainous terrain like the Zagros.

If they received no acknowledgment they would have to try again. And again. And with every transmission the danger of radio direction-finders in Teheran locating their position would increase.

Hawksby lay back in the front passenger seat, his forage

cap peak tilted over his eyes. The jutting clay pipe let out a twist of smoke. He tried with great deliberation to relax. After all, he had chosen Tiger because he was the best. Five minutes passed.

Jim Perkis, now replaced on his picket duty by Kangers Webster, tried to get to sleep, curled in his green maggot under Panther Two. Exhausted as he was, his mind kept turning, thinking of his wife Janet. The baby had been due yesterday. Earlier he had thought seriously of asking the Hawk to ask after her in his transmission. He had asked McDermid's advice. Not surprisingly, the taciturn Scot had said flatly no. Obvious really, it just helped to have a confirming opinion. He rolled over and covered his head with his arms.

Suddenly Tiger let out a whoop. "Eureka!" He pulled off the headset. "Acknowledged, boss. They will transmit confirmation of our request same time tomorrow. 1200 hours."

ISFAHAN: 1200 hrs, Saturday 20th September

Curt Swartz Jnr. curled in the corner of the bare cell like a frightened child. His knees were drawn up to his chest and he peered out at a hostile world with wide, blood-shot eyes. No one had come near him for the past five hours. They had told him they had finished with him. They had assured him they would not come back. He had done well, they said, but he didn't believe them.

He knew they would come back. It had taken immense concentration to concoct the cock-and-bull story about the contingency plans. His body had ached so abominably that it was impossible to think clearly. He had been confused and now he couldn't be certain exactly what he had told them.

He was only just beginning to remember what he had *meant* to tell them. That the rescuers had an emergency plan to escape by road to the south coast. It was the only thing he could think of. From what the SAS sergeant had told him – or what he *thought* he had told him – it was the most unlikely possibility.

Yet finally the interrogators had seemed satisfied. Someone had interrupted them. Something about a gas-pipe explosion. It was all confirmed.

You can go now. Have your glass of water. May Allah go with you.

Fuck Allah!

Curt felt as though he was coming round from an anaesthetic. Slowly, painfully, he lowered his knees.

Sun shone fiercely in through a barred window in the wall. In the corner of the spartan cell was a bed. Not a straw bundle, but a proper utility metal bedstead with a mattress. Beside it stood a small wooden table with a polythene bowl of water.

With agonising slowness he climbed to his knees. Then, clutching the wall for support, he shakily raised one leg. He didn't trust it to hold out. Using gentle shuffling movements he edged along the wall until he reached the bed.

He lowered himself onto the mattress. Beside him the clothes he had been arrested in had been laid out. On top of them was a small pile of his possessions. A handkerchief, a comb, a pair of sunglasses . . . a wallet. Snatching it up, he peered inside. No money. Only to be expected. No papers or visiting cards. No doubt any poor bastard whose address had been in his wallet would be receiving an unwelcome early morning call.

He thumbed open the back flap Yes! It was there: the photograph of Alison and the two children. He pressed it to his lips. It tasted almost sweet. He realised that he had succeeded. He was still alive. A physical mess perhaps, but he was still alive. After all there was something in the anti-interrogation techniques they had taught him at Langley. They must have learned something during Korea and Vietnam. Not all those young men, whose bodies were wickedly abused, had suffered in vain. Enough had survived to learn from their experiences.

He turned and looked through the window to the walled garden below. Beyond he could see a screen of poplars, and the glimmering surface of the Zayandeh River. It looked peaceful out there. Real. How life used to be.

235

The door opened with a jolt. He looked up startled as the revolutionary guard stepped in. The man was grinning inanely. "Hey! You nervous? What is your matter, huh? Those bruises! You have an accident?"

Curt said nothing. He just sat with his fists clenched on his knees. He averted his eyes. He was right: now it was going to start all over again.

"You should be more careful, son of Satan," the guard laughed. "Look where you are leaping, yes?"

The American glared at him, but the Iranian just laughed again. "Don't worry, we're not unkind. We look after you good. I get doctor to once you over, eh?"

Curt was puzzled, not knowing what to believe. The guard slouched towards the door. "I bring you tea. No coffee. No Carter's coffee, eh? A drink for evil men. I bring you tea." He wagged a warning finger. "Don't you try no funny business. It be shame to shoot you after you help us. You stay our prisoner but no more questions, eh? You relax. You sleep. Okay?"

Curt echoed in a whisper, "*Okay.*"

"And no salt in the tea, eh?" Chuckling the guard shut and bolted the door.

KERMAN: 1200 hrs, Saturday 20th September

Sergeant Dave Forbes and Hameda arrived at midday in the desert city of Kerman in the middle of a dust storm. The journey in the French-built turbo-train had been comfortable enough, but the strain of talking to ticket collectors and avoiding suspicious revolutionary guards, who took it on themselves to inspect everyone's credentials, proved nerve-fraying.

The vicious sand particles which swirled around them were the last straw, but at least they hid them from prying eyes. Hameda pointed out the blue domes and tiled wind tower around which eddies of sand scurried, but Forbes showed no interest. Even the mirror surfaces of the famous water gardens were shattered by wafts of grit brought in on a gusting wind. Blooms bowed in the flowerbeds. Above them cypress and pines creaked in protest.

"Is it far?" Forbes demanded, immediately inhaling a mouthful of fine sand.

More wisely Hameda didn't attempt to speak. She merely indicated the side street they were approaching.

He grinned at her. The thought of a few hours' rest, with salted cheese and unleavened bread, was welcome. However, as they turned the corner, the prospect of sanctuary died. Instantly. Hameda froze, but instinctively Forbes ushered her on on, twisting her arm so that she couldn't resist. He almost frog-marched her across to the shabby little tea-house opposite. As a result of his quick reaction, the surly-looking revolutionary guard who was standing outside the gate to her realtives' house, noticed nothing.

The owner of the tea-house was snoozing in the corner. He didn't hear them enter at first, their noise drowned by the gabble of Farsi from the transistor radio. He awoke with a start, evidently not expecting any customers while the dust-storm raged. Sniffing heavily so that his moustache twitched, he ambled across to the window bench where Forbes had parked himself to get a good view of the house opposite.

"Some tea and some food, if you please," he ordered.

The man didn't move. "No women."

Forbes looked up. He had forgotten that women were only reluctantly accepted at wayside tea-houses. Normally the places were a refuge for men, where they could discuss important matters. Mostly about women. Obviously Hameda realised, for she looked decidedly uncomfortable.

"Forgive us!" Forbes grinned broadly and made a show of extracting a fat wallet. "We are taking refuge from this infernal storm and we have travelled far." The man seemed unimpressed. "I see you have no other customers," he added. "And we shall be gone quickly."

"You are from the country?" grunted the owner.

"Yes."

"Obviously," the other replied. "Things are different now in the cities. I can get into trouble for allowing women in here."

"One woman," Forbes said smiling, and pointedly placed too much change on the table. "And five minutes."

As the owner shuffled off, the sergeant called him back. "By the way, why are there guards outside that house over there?"

"Last night they come," the man replied. "They take away the man, his wife and three children. They say they are traitors."

"They?"

He shrugged. "Everyone. A rich family. Shah-lovers. Bah, they get all they deserve. They never came in here . . ."

He tramped off.

Forbes turned to Hameda. He could only see her eyes in the *chador*, but they told him everything. They were full of despair, and tears were beginning to roll down the sides of her nose. "Now you know why I *must* leave this place," she said hoarsely. "It could be my entire family by now. In Teheran there is my mother, my grandmother, Shirin my sister . . . Davoud . . ."

Forbes stretched across the table and squeezed her arm. "Take courage. And don't jump to conclusions. It serves no purpose. We must concentrate on getting out of the country. There'll be plenty of time then to worry about others."

Her eyes looked suddenly angry. "You are a hard man, Mr. Dave. You sometimes frighten me."

Suddenly she cocked her head to one side, listening.

"What is it?" he asked.

Hameda frowned. "On the radio. A news bulletin." She strained to catch the distorted words from the tiny set on the counter. It needed new batteries. "Something about another American raid. To free their hostages."

"Huh?" Forbes listened, finding difficulty in picking up the rapid flow of Farsi rhetoric. News and patriotic religious comment all in one. Something about a helicopter stolen from Isfahan and a crash. Accusations of a second failure by the Americans.

It had to be Snapdragon. Forbes' heart sank.

"They ask for anyone who sees a strange group of men and

238

a fair-headed woman to tell police. Somewhere in the Zagros
. . . I did not catch the district.''

A smile flickered on the sergeant's face. "So they weren't
killed in the crash.''

"You mean they are not the Americans? They are your
people?''

He nodded. "No doubt about it. But I wonder *where* they
crashed. They were operating to a tight schedule. It wouldn't
take much for them to ruin the pick-up.'' And, he thought, if
the area was swarming with Iranian police, they could
hardly allow the RAF Hercules to land.

"Whatever their problems, it does not help us,'' Hameda
said moodily.

Forbes was deep in thought. "Without help getting to
Pakistan it *will* be difficult,'' he admitted.

"Then we give ourselves up?'' Her eyes were wide.

Forbes almost choked. "No way! But there's a chance . . .
if our team's been delayed, they might well try their contingency plan. Overland to the south coast . . .'' He peered
through the smeary window . . . "I just wonder if we could
make the pick-up.''

"By boat? When?''

"Three days from now.''

She thought for a moment. "There are no trains south
from here. We have to go by bus. But that is risky. Perhaps
the time-tables not tie-up. Depending on where we go there
may be no buses at all . . .'' She hesitated . . . "But what if
your friends did leave. And there is no one at the coast?''

Forbes shrugged. "We'll swim.'' He grinned. "Or steal a
fishing boat.''

The owner arrived with some white salted cheese and a
pancake of unleavened bread. Still glowering, he retreated
leaving the sergeant to pour out the fragrant Caspian tea. It
was scalding hot.

As he pushed a glass across to her, Hameda watched him
curiously, and said: "I expect your friends are missing you?''

"You just bet they are.''

239

CHAPTER FOURTEEN

"Well, ma'am, I thought you'd be pleased to hear . . ." As the Director-General of the Secret Intelligence Service stopped talking, the silence that followed was fragile.

It was a full thirty seconds before the Prime Minister, seated behind the desk of her study in Number 10, replied. Her mind seemed to be far away. "Oh, yes, of course. Thank you, Dickie."

"The last twenty-four hours have been rather nerve-racking," admitted Sir Arthur. "No news can be bad news."

"More nerve-racking for them, I think," she said reproachfully. "And, of course, it isn't exactly good news."

He shifted uncomfortably. "I've every confidence, ma'am, that the contingency plan will work."

"Four days in hostile territory across totally uncompromising terrain . . . I hope your confidence is well-founded, Dickie."

"It is, ma'am," he answered brusquely. "It's what the pilgrims are trained for."

The Prime Minister sat back in her chair and steepled her fingers together. Something was troubling her. "I am still curious about the message from Blake that was included in the transmission. Telling us he knows why we want him out, and warning us not to try to have him assassinated. Doesn't he realise – despite the wilder imaginings of thriller writers – Whitehall doesn't act like the Kremlin."

Sir Arthur smiled gently. "He's no fool. He knows we want him out, and he knows we mean him to keep silent."

The Prime Minister's eyes hardened, belying the polite smile. "There's nothing I don't know about, Dickie, is there?"

"No, ma'am. There is more than one way to shut someone up. No assassination, no lifetime in a mental institution. We just make sure no one will touch his work with a barge pole – in this country anyway. And we have many friends in America and Europe. My people are quite adept at this sort of thing. We merely isolate the subject in the appropriate manner.

"In Blake's case it will be a question of depriving him of his livelihood. Then, when he is beginning to get desperate, we engineer an opening for him. Like a drowning man he will clutch at it. It will be a good job with money he finds difficult to resist. Already we have a job in mind on a newspaper in a socialist African state. Well out of harm's way."

The Prime Minister nodded. Under the circumstances it seemed a good idea.

"What about this mysterious girlfriend?"

"All I know about her is that she is a photo-journalist of some repute. I've already put in hand an investigation. Maybe this African paper also has a vacancy for a picture editor. Either way, ma'am, they'll get no chance to cause trouble."

"See to it, Dickie. A slip-up would be indefensible. If word gets out about this it could lead to my government's fall. And that would be most unwelcome, especially as this whole business was begun by the Foreign Office under a previous administration!"

"Quite so," Sir Arthur replied. He was thankful that he could sense his audience coming to an end. "Rest assured. The Deputy Head of DP2 himself has made a personal request to meet Blake immediately he is out of Iranian territory. To ensure the matter can be dealt with satisfactorily. I have therefore given my consent."

At last the Prime Minister seemed satisfied. "I agree this deserves the attentions of a man of appropriate experience, Dickie. I am grateful. A frightened animal can be dangerous and, you know, Blake sounds very frightened. And that means he is potentially *very* dangerous."

Even as the Director-General of SIS was concluding his interview at Number 10, a priority coded signal was being flashed from HMS *Warrior*, the Royal Navy's underground operations centre at Northwood. It was received by the commodore aboard the County-class guided missile destroyer that was acting flagship to the three-vessel patrol steaming across the Indian Ocean towards Hong Kong.

Almost immediately a signal was made to the patrol frigate HMS *Antler* which followed behind the Royal Fleet Auxiliary tanker at the end of the line.

On the bridge of *Antler*, Commander Joseph T. Richmond, RN, was surprised to receive the order to break away from the patrol and head back towards the Gulf. He was also delighted. It looked like something interesting was in the wind.

At thirty-five years old he felt he had reached the peak of his career. Even though certain promotion lay ahead, sailing some desk in the dusty corridors of the Admiralty, he knew he would never again experience the exhilaration of commanding a newly-commissioned Type 21 frigate.

His Number One glanced down at the signal paper in the commander's hand.

"Trouble, Sir?"

Richmond looked down over the defiant snout of the 4.5 gun on the foredeck as he waited for the navigation officer to lay the new course. "We're diverting at all speed to the Gulf. We're to pick up a gentleman from the Foreign Office off Salalah. We'll receive further instructions from him."

Number One scratched his nose. "Sounds intriguing. The Gulf is a bit of a hot-spot at the moment."

Richmond gave his colleague a disapproving grunt for his obvious relish at the prospect of some excitement. But secretly he shared the other's enthusiasm.

Number One handed over the calculation. "Set a course bearing 270 degrees. Full ahead," Richmond ordered.

Number One grinned. "Aye, aye, Sir."

As the wake creamed out in a tight semi-circle behind her,

the rakish lines of HMS *Antler* looked breathtakingly sleek, her decks canting and the White Ensign thrashing wildly. By the time she pulled out of the turn and ploughed her nose into the north-westerly, she was already running a business-like twenty-seven knots.

Richmond glanced down at the signal and the name of the man he was to take aboard off the Oman coast.

Ian Ferguson.

At Snapdragon's operational headquarters in Salalah, Captain Johnny Fraser received the message to prepare for 'Operation Salvation' with mixed emotions.

He was not pleased to hear that the fall-back plan had to be implemented, because it meant the team was in difficulty. But, having already been deprived of a participating role in the very first rescue plan, he wasn't sorry to be needed now.

"So they've fucked up?" Sergeant Turner asked. He was a Brummie and an eternal pessimist, especially when it came to the abilities of officers. And with officers from the exalted ranks of the nobility like Hawksby, he considered disaster to be a foregone conclusion.

Fraser decided not to feed the NCO with additional fuel for speculation. "There's no detail how badly. But they're one man light."

"Who?"

"We don't know. But they're bringing out an additional passenger. A woman."

Sergeant Turner shook his head. Nothing could surprise him when aristocrats were involved. "I'll go and get things organised."

The door shut, leaving Fraser alone with his thoughts. Mostly these concerned the risks they were likely to be running. On balance, they should be negligible. That night they would leave in a fast patrol boat of the Sultan of Oman's Navy, commanded by a British officer. They would leave port early so that there would be no obvious connection with any trouble there might be in Iran.

Before dawn in three days' time the patrol boat would drop

243

them in two fast Rigid Raider assault craft over the horizon and away from the inquisitive ears of Iranian coastal radar. Immediately the Omani Navy boat would melt away and not return to its home port for at least a week.

This was not because of any reticence by the Omanis to get involved. London had determined that there should be no sign of their complicity – if trouble broke out over the pick-up. Having achieved their rendezvous with Snapdragon it would be a British ship that would be conveniently steaming past in the Gulf as the assault craft left Iranian waters.

Captain Johnny Fraser glanced down at the name he had scribbled on his pad.

HMS *Antler*.

The crew of the Iranian Navy anti-submarine Orion aircraft were not happy.

Like armed forces the world over there was fierce rivalry between the services, and the men aboard knew full well that they should be out over the Gulf, patrolling against incursion by Iraqi rebels. Everyone knew that war was imminent, although no one in authority wanted to admit it. Most certainly they knew that they should not be cruising over the Zagros Mountains on instructions from some jumped-up army colonel just because he wanted to make use of their highly-efficient infra-red night sensors.

It should not be allowed. The linescan screen operator watched the image of the mountains pass below him, his eyes flicking over the occasional blob that represented the heat-source of a vehicle moving along a road. There were few of these at this time of night and anyway he had been told to ignore them. Colonel Murad had made it clear that it was vehicles moving *off* the road he was interested in. Surely no one in their right mind would drive across the Zagros Mountains in daylight, let alone night time?

He was therefore astonished when he suddenly detected two tell-tale flickers far from any road, moving steadily southward.

They must be doing thirty miles an hour. Ridiculous.

Nevertheless the operator spoke into the intercom to the pilot. "I think I might have found what we are looking for."

Ever since they had broken camp at sunset to continue their journey south, Hawksby had felt an increasing sense of unease.

Perhaps it was the sense of foreboding that the professional soldier acquires over the years. Perhaps it was just battle fatigue, or even an over-active imagination. But it was just before midnight when he had confirmation that everything was not well.

Pogo Penaia had been negotiating Panther Two down a steep escarpment like a rider in a point-to-point, when his uncannily acute ears picked up the sound of an aircraft. The Land Rover engine had been almost idling at the time and the Fijian cocked his head to one side. Immediately he switched off the ignition. As the quietness swelled up around them, all eyes turned skywards. They tried to locate the source of the steady droning noise but the sky appeared empty.

They stopped twice more during the next hour. Each time the noise was still there – distant, muted, but strangely menacing.

"What you reckon, boss?" Pogo asked.

Hawksby shook his head slowly. "It's a turbo-prop job, I reckon. Heavy transport."

"You t'ink t'ey follow us?" Eva asked with alarm.

"It could be a coincidence," Blake suggested.

"I don't hold much with coincidence," Hawksby replied.

John Belcher leaned forward. "A reconnaissance patrol. Got to be." He added pointedly: "It's been with us on and off for the past sixty minutes. Maybe a Hercules."

"Not that sound." Pogo was insistent. They'd all been doing their homework.

"Then it's got to be an Orion," Hawksby decided.

"What's t'at?" Eva asked.

"A maritime patrol aircraft," Belcher explained. "They operate out of Bushehr in the west. They can track in the dark using infra-red. Not as effective overland, but in open terrain like this we'll show up like a boil on a bum." He grinned. "Sorry."

Hawksby reached for the radio. "I'll warn Scottie. But we've no option but to push on. Step on it, Pogo, will you. If we lose contact with Panther One, we'll really be up shit creek."

The Land Rover lurched forward, its growl swamping out the sound of the aircraft.

Putting himself in the position of the Iranians, Hawksby felt sure that the net was closing in. His diversionary tactics of the night before had worked well, but obviously the pursuers were not stupid. The likely presence of an Orion proved that. Once they were pin-pointed, it was just a question of time before the Iranians moved units up and sealed them off, like pieces on a gigantic chess board. Moving across country undetected, the SAS team held the initiative but once located, the Iranians had the advantage of helicopter mobility.

It was time for another navigational stop. Tiger had to take three star-sightings with the sextant, using a chronometer for precise timings. The slightest error and, by morning, they could be up to thirty miles off course. In mountain country the problems were compounded by the need to establish the angle of each star to the horizon, and the vehicle altimeter was notoriously unreliable.

Grimly Hawksby recognised there was absolutely nothing he could do except hope: hope that, despite his certainty to the contrary, the aircraft had not actually located them. And hope that they could fight their way out of any trouble. They just didn't have the time to go to ground.

Once Tiger was satisfied the two vehicles set off again. They were entering the flat-open mouth of a wadi, the sides of which began to rise more sharply with every mile they travelled. From the JARIC map they knew that eventually the walls would tower above them until the dried-up river bed narrowed to form a deep cleft in the mountain. Leading from that apex was a tortuous shingle track that wound up to higher ground. If they got that far. Like the infamous canyons beloved of Hollywood Apaches, it was an ideal place for an ambush.

In other circumstances Hawksby would have progressed with caution, sending reconnaissance squads along the top of each wall of the wadi. However there was no time to allow for such luxuries.

He discussed the dangers briefly with McDermid on the radio. The Scotsman didn't say much, but he was clearly concerned at the news of the persistent air patrol. They hadn't heard it, but they were well aware that danger could be imminent.

"There'll be more cover once we're out o' this wadi," McDermid said. *"We'll press on a wee bit faster. Out."*

Eva leaned forward as Hawksby finished his conversation. "What iss it, Alan. T'ere iss more trouble?"

Hawksby knew his voice lacked confidence. "No sign of activity ahead, so don't worry. It would take them some time to muster troops and dispatch helicopters."

"But t'at aeroplane iss been over'ead for at least an 'our."

He was suddenly aware of the closeness of her face to his. She was holding his gaze. In the darkness the whites of her eyes seemed large. Clear and bright. He tried to pick up the thread of their talk. Distracted, he said: "Yes. An hour is long enough. But we're still some distance away from any main base."

Hawksby began to feel uncomfortable and turned away, aware that he had revealed his interest in her. He could feel her shoulder rubbing against his as the vehicle bumped and thudded over the rough ground.

As she sat back in her seat, he felt himself relax. He must be getting old, he told himself. Earlier Scottie had jibed at him about Eva Olsen. He'd noticed her watching the major and had reported his observation. But behind the mischievous good humour, Hawksby realised that the corporal was firing a warning shot. He did not want their leader so besotted with one of their charges that it impaired his judgment.

On reflection he had to admit there was a fascination

about the girl. It would be surprising if there wasn't. She exuded animal sex-appeal like few women he had ever come across. His own wife Caroline was another, but he had already learned to his cost that it was a mixed blessing. It didn't necessarily cement a relationship.

He also recognised a quality in Eva that Caroline didn't possess. The Norwegian had a refreshing self-confidence that appealed to him. An air of determination and ruthlessness. It made Caroline, with her aristocratic disinterest and cultivated graces, seem as shallow and superficially beautiful as everything else about Greshmile Manor.

After years abroad in the Army, especially in the Middle East, he had slowly but surely begun to reject so-called 'civilised' society. Soft and diluted, it hardly compared with the harsh realities of life in the Gulf. There he'd been completely absorbed by the local languages, customs and way of life where everything was second in importance to water. Even in Iran, where he had spent so much time as a British adviser to the Iranian Army on armoured warfare tactics, water came first. Then food and procreation. Medicine and education came a poor third. Life there was raw, basic. *Real*.

Idly he wondered if he was being fair to Caroline. She could hardly be blamed for her own heritage. If only she'd *seen* more of the world, perhaps she'd understand how much there was to be done . . .?

"One te Two!" McDermid's voice was urgent.

Shaken from his thoughts, Hawksby switched on the mike. "Two. Send. Over . . .?"'

The reply was drowned by the thudding crescendo of a helicopter. It emerged suddenly over the rim of the wadi. Coming from downwind, its approach had been muted.

Simultaneously, gun flashes blinked from the high side of the river bed on the right. The noise rumbled back and forth, sounding like a distant avalanche, interspersed with whip-cracks of lightning. The heavy throb of the helicopter's twin rotors filled the air so that the very ground seemed to tremble. Then it disappeared over the right-hand wall of the wadi.

Fountains of dust sprayed up around Panther Two as a hail of shells stitched crazy patterns along the parched river bed. A second bank of muzzle flashes came from high up on the left as more rifle-fire poured into the wadi. Half-a-dozen rounds glanced off the vehicle's bodywork, the guns evidently fired from near maximum range.

Hawksby squinted forward, anticipating the presence of an enemy stop-group ahead. He was not to be disappointed. The stammer of the belt-fed machine gun and its infantry support came with a tell-tale flicker of flame that was spread like a winking necklace in the darkness before them.

Natural reaction in such circumstances is to dive desperately for cover. It is also a fatal reaction. While the victim is stunned and stricken with surprise, the attacker can pour in concentrated fire. Or close in. There are few ways to break an ambush. One is to pull back, fast. The other is to push straight on into it at all speed, and keep going. Regardless of casualties.

Countless hours of reaction-training made the Snapdragon team instinctively move as one to confound the Iranians. Seconds only had passed before Pogo had stabbed the smoke-button on the steering-wheel hub. Instantly both rear and forward smoke discharge ignited, hurling the L7 grenades forward and backwards in a defensive fan. They burst on impact, green smoke blossoming to blot out the landscape.

As Panther Two leapt forward into the protective fog, Belcher had yanked Eva and Blake to the floor below the vehicle's sidewalls. Already Hawksby had swung into action with the forward-facing twin-mounted GPMGs prising back the cocking handle of the machine gun in one practised movement. He readied himself for the breakthrough as the Land Rover lurched wildly into the curtain of smoke.

Then they were clear. Ahead, the wadi basin was illuminated in the harsh glare of an Iranian flare, creating the unreal quality of a science fiction movie set. Panther One was already racing at the enemy stop-group who had dug themselves in to form a line across the river bed. Sand clouds drifted everywhere. He saw Perkis swing the wheel to give his vehicle an unpredictable course.

McDermid was half-standing in the front passenger seat, crouching over their machine gun. Its long nose was spitting fire as wafts of cordite streamed in its wake. In the rear compartment, Kangers Webster hammered away with his L37 at positions on the left.

Instinctively Hawksby winced as he saw McDermid's Land Rover drive directly over one of the Iranian troopers. The man had no time to dig more than a shell-scrape in the hard-baked earth, and the heavy forward sand-tyre ground remorselessly into his belly as the vehicle struggled to get a grip. The SAS team's head-on attack had thrown the enemy completely. As Panther One surged past the machine gunner, the Iranian stood up, bewildered. He was obviously terrified that he would now be under attack from both sides at once. He was.

As Panther Two followed up, Hawksby blew him full of holes with a short burst from the GPMG. He then laced the remaining positions with a prolonged burst. Two Iranian guns fell silent.

The last remaining soldier climbed to his feet and began racing towards the side of the wadi. Pogo saw him and swung the wheel. The wing of Panther Two caught the man square in the base of the spine, carrying him forward like a ship's figurehead.

The body rolled away and Panther Two accelerated after McDermid into the shadows of the wadi.

"Christ!" breathed Blake, raising his head.

John Belcher unceremoniously pushed it down. "Keep the old arse-up position, Jonathan, there's a good chap. We're not out of this yet."

Hawksby snatched a fresh ammunition box from one of the side-bins. Hurriedly he broke the seal and ripped open the lid, then fed a new belt into the GPMG breech.

Although everyone in Iran had been expecting it, the news of the Iraqi invasion still came as a shock. Colonel Najaf Murad was no exception. As is the way of such things, official confirmation came at the most unexpected and unwelcome time. It had been the first time he had been able to snatch a few hours to himself since the journalist Blake had been snatched two days ago.

From that time he had survived on catnaps and the effects of exhaustion had increased until he no longer felt able to go on without at least four successive hours' sleep. He had managed to blackmail – quite literally, by putting pressure on an Iranian vice-admiral who had a penchant for teenage sailors – the naval authorities into giving him use of an Orion patrol aircraft. Then he had a detachment of *real* soldiers, not revolutionary guards, on standby with a heavy helicopter, under the command of a competent officer.

Having set his plan in motion, he had returned to his new smart apartment in Isfahan and the tender mercies of a high-class whore who had virtually lived with him back in Teheran.

Too tired to exert himself he had lain back on cool silk sheets, his mind a blissful blank whilst she had ministered to him. The expertise of her mouth and tongue had awakened his tired body, and then she had gently bored herself onto him in a series of slow, delicious movements. He felt the life force in him begin to move inexorably upward.

And then the bedside telephone began to shriek.

Wearily Murad stretched out and picked up the receiver. He signalled the girl to stop but, mischievously, she refused. Watching him with an impish smile, she reduced her pumping motion to a tantalising slowness.

The Iraqi offensive had begun in the early hours of the morning, the voice said. It was fractured with suppressed panic. The artillery duel which had been rumbling all summer across the border had erupted into a fierce, prolonged exchange. Armour was moving up. So was infantry. Assault bridging equipment and boats. Aircraft were in combat. Teheran was being hit by Iraqi MiGs.

Murad was dumbfounded. He could even discern the rumble of exploding bombs on the other end of the line.

Still the girl worked at him, now increasing the momentum.

The Orion maritime aircraft had been recalled by the Navy. All front-line troops were needed immediately. There, at the front-line itself, not charging after phantoms in the middle of the Zagros Mountains. If he wanted to continue his search, he would have to make use of local revolutionary guards. More bombs sounded in the background.

Murad was furious. But his stormy reply was interrupted by the excruciating sensation as his loins exploded. Momentarily he forgot his words.

Angrily he pushed the whore aside and swung his legs off the bed.

He shook the receiver. The telephone line from Teheran to Isfahan had gone dead.

CHAPTER FIFTEEN

Panther One appeared ahead at the apex of the wadi. It had begun to work its way up the track of stone debris to a higher level.

Pogo changed down gear and prepared to follow.

"Chopper!" Belcher yelled, swinging round the rear GPMG on its pintle mounting.

Hawksby looked up. It was the transport helicopter again. The giant Chinook disappeared over the wadi wall to disgorge more troops. Belcher loosed off a short burst, but the angle of elevation was too high. Panther Two began to rock from side to side like a boat in a heavy swell as Pogo followed the first Land Rover over the scree and onto the track. The veins in his forearms stood out like gnarled roots as he struggled with the wheel. His face glistened and his shirt was black with sweat. The white grin was fixed with determination.

Above, Hawksby could see shadowy figures scrambling over the lip of the wadi near where the helicopter had settled. He tried to count the bobbing shapes against the paler skyline. He reckoned three but couldn't be sure. Belcher had a better angle of fire with his machine gun, but the rocking motion of the vehicle threw his aim.

It took an age to crawl up the track, inching along.

"For God's sake, Pogo," Hawksby hissed. "Put your bloody foot down!"

The Fijian was unmoved. "It's better to arrive safe than never . . ." he said through gritted teeth. Hawksby grinned despite himself and dropped back into the seat. There was nothing more that he could do. However, now the small group of Iranian troopers had gained the advantage of height and, perched behind the protection of a rocky shelf overlooking the track, they posed an even greater threat. More muzzle flashes cut through the darkness, and an arc of fire swept over the two Panthers. Bullets twanged loudly on metalwork. Glass shattered.

Two dull *phut*-like detonations came from beneath Panther Two. The right side of the vehicle dropped sickeningly as though the suspension had collapsed An empty ammunition case dislodged and spun over the track. It disappeared noisily down the sheer drop into the wadi.

"Shit!" Hawksby swore. "Bloody tyres!"

Belcher's calm voice belied how he felt. "Time to abandon ship, I think." He grabbed Blake's arm. "C'mon, get to cover!"

Hawksby leapt into the rear compartment and seized Eva, hauling her roughly after him into the tight gap between the side of the vehicle and the wadi wall. More shells studded the earth above their heads, dislodging a shower of grit and stones. Hawksby lowered his Uzi sub-machine gun in disgust. He'd need more than that to shift the Iranians from their nest. They were shielded by rock, and even the heavy fire pouring from Panther One was having no noticeable effect.

Someone needed to gain a height advantage over them, but that wasn't going to be easy. The hail of fire was murderous if innaccurate. At least they didn't have night-sights. But still it would be impossible to root them out. Unless . . .

"Eva, that storage bin above your head," he said breathlessly. "Small grenades with fins."

She looked blank, her mouth agape with panic.

"Grenades! Quick, girl!"

Getting a grip of herself, she suddenly jolted into action, and peered into the side-bin. She extracted something. "T'ese?"

"Yes. And keep your pretty bloody head down," he snapped. "Or else it'll be just that." He grabbed the grenade from her and fitted it into the snout of the Uzi. Aiming high above the Iranians' position on the ledge, he squeezed the trigger.

The grenade hurtled skyward, lost in the blackness. Moments later it blew just below the ledge.

"Damn," he cursed. "Falling short. Just hasn't got the range. Still, it's given them something to think about."

The grenade did not keep the Iranians thinking for long. Another prolonged raking burst bit into the track and drilled into the bodywork of Panther Two. Hawksby flinched as dust and metal splinters lanced the air. Eva, petrified, pushed hard against him for protection, burying her head against his chest. He ruffled her hair consolingly. His eyes never left the ledge. They were well and truly pinned down.

Suddenly a fresh rattle of automatic weapons seemed to come from nowhere, but there was no mistaking where the deadly fire was being aimed. Shots from the Iranians on the ledge came to an abrupt halt. Clouds of dust swirled away from the position under the torrent of lead. Farther up the track Panther One's machine guns stopped. Only now it was possible to tell from where the surprise attack had come.

Hawksby glanced upward, wondering for a moment if one of McDermid's patrol had managed to scale the wadi to gain height over the ledge. He frowned.

"What iss it?" Eva asked breathlessly. The relief of the unexpected lull in the attack had affected her nerves. She began to tremble uncontrollably, as though in a fever.

Hawksby put his arm around her shoulder, as the crackle of gunfire died. "Kalashnikovs," he decided.

"What?" Eva's face was wet with perspiration.

"You can tell by the sound. Kalashnikovs. Not ours."

Belcher wriggled to him along the narrow gap. "I thought it might be Scottie," he said. "But you're right. They're Kalashnikovs, no danger."

Hawksby didn't need the confirmation. He'd heard too many of the Russian guns fired at him in anger by the Communist rebels in Oman to have any doubts. He reached for the Starlight 'scope in the passenger compartment and studied the ledge. There was no sign of life. Just a thin white hand protruding over the edge in a frozen farewell wave.

Then the shattering explosion came. It was a *whooshing* roar that rushed skyward in a giant spurt of flame above the lip of the wadi. One of the rotors of the Chinook helicopter came scything in slow-motion over the top like a gigantic boomerang. Whistling past them, the blade thudded upright into the floor of the wadi.

Belcher watched, fascinated. "Looks like bloody Excalibur."

Hawksby switched on his Pocketfone mike. "Scottie, for Christ's sake what's happening up there?"

"I dunna ken, boss," came the reply. *"A bunch o' peasants jest emerged from nowhere. Armed te the bleddy teeth. May be Kurdish tribesmen – anyhow they're irregular. All I ken is they've made mincemeat o' them Persians. An' jest blown the chopper into one giant monkey-puzzle. Over."*

Hawksby flipped the switch. "Watch 'em, Scottie and keep your guard up until we find out what their game is. I'll be right with you."

The major climbed to his feet and helped Eva out of the cramped space. She brushed the short fringe away from her brow. "T'ank you, Alan." She smiled nervously. Then, before he realised, she reached up and kissed him quickly on the mouth.

"Hey, this isn't the time, boss ..." Belcher said indignantly.

Hawksby flushed, stepping quickly back from the girl. Pogo was watching with a quizzical expression on his face.

"Forget it!" the major muttered, embarrassed.

"I iss really grateful," Eva said. "You save my life."

"Give it a rest, Eva." It was Blake who was the last to emerge from behind Panther Two. "You'll give the major ideas above his station."

Hawksby turned to Pogo. "Stay with 'em here, and don't let them out of your sight. John, come with me."

Belcher picked his Remington pump-action shotgun from the vehicle and set off up the track after Hawksby, who was disappearing from view, the Uzi ready for use.

"You have luck, my friend!" the big man boomed, chuckling as he rolled strands of tobacco into a liquorice paper. The small donkey he sat on emphasised his large frame. His bare feet only just cleared the ground Although the heavy Kalashnikov was still cradled across his forearms, it didn't interfere with the expert way he made the cigarette.

Hawksby shifted impatiently. Behind the big man stood three more donkeys. Each carried another tribesman, all in patterned woollen hats and tattered robes under well-worn sheepskin coats. And three more Kalashnikovs.

"Peace be upon you," Hawksby said warily in Farsi. He kept the Uzi pointing downward, just. He was aware that the stranger was weighing up the situation, but he had no desire to stand around exchanging niceties with renegade tribesmen who looked as though they'd sell their own grandmothers for a leg of mutton. Or another Kalashnikov. "I am in your debt, *agha*," he added.

In the quiet mountain landscape, the man's volcanic laugh sounded unnaturally loud. "Quite *so*, my friend! Quite *so*!"

He stuck the thin cigarette into the mass of tangled beard and cupped his hands as he lit a match. He coughed heavily, exhaling a pungent cloud of obnoxious smoke. Again he chuckled. "But you owe us nothing, soldier boy. You owe us nothing. It is a pleasure to help anyone who runs from the infidels of Qum!"

Hawksby's eyes narrowed. "You are Qashquai?" He was sure this giant and his motley crew were members of the nomadic shepherd tribes of the southern Zagros.

The man's eyes seemed to brighten. "Ah, then you have been to this district before, eh? Not a city dweller, eh?"

"You have no sheep with you?" It was a statement more than a question. Hawksby remembered that the Qashquai took their sheep up into the mountain pastures during the summer. Now, with the onset of autumn, they should be on their way back to the villages on the lower slopes with their flocks.

Carefully the man extracted some loose tobacco from the end of his cigarette with his teeth and spat it on the ground. It landed just before Hawksby's feet. "You ask many questions, stranger. That is not polite."

Hawksby's face was a mask. "If two strangers do not ask questions, then they will always be strangers."

For a moment there was tension in the air like an electrical charge. The moon came out from behind the clouds, its cold light glinting on the Persian's eyes. The three tribesmen behind him shifted on their donkeys.

Suddenly the man's laugh filled the air. "I see I have met a wise man! A man as wise as me!" In a sudden movement he kicked his left leg high over the donkey's head and allowed himself to slide from the animal's back.

"I am Mashallaha," he extended a hand. Hawksby shook it. It was like a paw, hard, calloused and twice the size of his own. The man's eyes fixed on the major's. "Now, so we do not remain strangers, I ask a question, eh? You are supporters of the Reza Shah? Why else do you flee from the Imam's infidels?"

Hawksby thought quickly. This man Mashallaha was unlikely to extend hospitality to any representative of authority, from either the late Shah's or Khomeini's new regime. Perhaps though, in Persia, there was still honour among thieves.

"We support no one. We want to be free men."

"Ah!" bellowed Mashallaha in triumph. "Deserters!"

Hawksby's expression didn't change. "We had a disagreement with our commanding officer."

The big man's beard cracked open to reveal a smile of decayed teeth. "Then you come to the right place. Here you can be free and we can put your vehicles to excellent use . . ." His voice tailed off.

He stepped closer to Panther One. He squinted. "A very unusual jeep, soldier boy. *Very* unusual. I do not see anything like this before. Very impressive. Dangerous. Veritably dangerous!"

McDermid still stood by the L37 GPMG. His finger closed slowly round the trigger.

"Your men," Mashallaha said. "They come from a deaf and dumb regiment? They don't say much!"

Just as well, thought Hawksby. Although they all knew a few sentences of Farsi, Forbes had been the only other fluent speaker in the team. And Perkis' Persian had to be heard to be believed.

"You like us give you some help?" Mashallaha directed his question straight at McDermid.

The Scotsman looked blank. He paused, then said: "*Hali-i shuma khube.*"

Hawksby winced. *How are you?* The idiot had got his phrases mixed up. Mashallaha frowned. The thick Glaswegian drawl dumbfounded him so much that it didn't register what had he said.

"Cleft palate," Hawksby said quickly. "From birth."

Mashallaha shook his head in dismay. "Today they take anyone in the Iranian Army! God save us!"

Although their transport helicopter had been destroyed, the Iranian detachment responsible for the ambush was not many miles behind. Even if they followed on foot, time for Hawksby's team was fast running out. Had it not been for the fortuitous arrival of the Qashquai brigands the operation would have been in serious jeopardy.

Panther Two had lost two tyres and McDermid's vehicle one. Both were precariously placed on the shifting shingle track, just a few feet from a sheer drop. However it was the resigned labours of the four donkeys that proved to be the real godsend. As an ex-Gurkha, Tiger had a lot of experience using the beasts in difficult terrain. But it took him some time to improvise harnesses to which tackle could be attached for hauling the Land Rovers onto solid, level ground.

The tribesmen themselves were worse than useless. Mashallaha sat on a boulder, smoking, coughing and laughing at the others as they tried to obey his contradictory directions. Only one of them, the thinnest, seemed willing to break sweat. The other two just made it look good with a lot of grunts and complaints. After a hot and exhausting twenty minutes, the SAS team went to work like a Formula One pit-stop crew, changing and repairing the wheels.

Hawksby and McDermid checked for other damage. Miraculously the only communications equipment damaged was the long-range Skywave set in Panther One, but this was duplicated in the major's vehicle. A couple of headlamps were shattered, but the bulbs were easily replaced and the lenses patched over with tape.

Most worrying was that there was now only one spare tyre between the two vehicles, and that was of dubious value as it too had been hit and now had a heavily-patched inner tube. Luck more than anything else would hold the thing together. The special water jacket on Panther Two, which was attached to the radiator on the outside, had been ripped beyond repair. Not only was the refrigeration effect lost, meaning probable overheating in the daylight desert driving conditions, but most of the water in the cooling system had been lost. By the time this was replaced, the team's water supply was down to an uncomfortably low level.

"You have women in your army, eh?"

Mashallaha's words jolted Hawksby from his concentration on repairs. Dressed in fatigues like everyone else and in darkness, he had not thought Eva would have been recognised as female. He had briefed everyone to treat her as though she were a man, until they were away from the Qashquai. Indeed she had determined to prove herself as useful as any of the others and now had a liberal coating of grease on her face and forearms.

But Hawksby realised it was hopeless to deny it. As she laboured with Perkis over the tyre levers to complete the repair, the over-large fatigue top revealed a gaping cleavage. Even in the moonlight, the provocative swing of her breasts as she worked was unmistakable.

Before Hawksby could reply, Mashallaha said: "When I served with the army, I do not remember women soldiers. Times have really changed! If I thought there were women now, I might even join up again!" His laughter petered out, his moist brown eyes becoming suddenly hard and cold. "But somehow I do not see our beloved Imam allowing it." He glanced around at the men at work. "And I do not recall having seen uniforms quite like yours before . . . And your vehicles! They are battleships of the desert . . . Remarkable!"

"We're a special unit . . ." Hawksby began, but he knew he sounded unconvincing. "See the insignia on the wing . . ."

"Ah, yes. Very good. Very good." Mashallaha laughed. "I

have the tattoo of an eagle on my arm, but it doesn't make me a damnable American! In fact, it is just the sort of trick Iraqi infiltrators use . . .!"

It was Blake who alerted the others. They had all begun to notice the changing tone of Mashallaha's Farsi gabble, but it was the journalist who strode forward to add weight to Hawksby's story.

"You talk like a mouse-eater, you infamous felon!" he challenged, insulting the Qashquai by suggesting he was an Arab. "Are you so dishonourable yourself that you cannot even recognise an honourable soldier when you see one?"

Hawksby stepped back in amazement. It was a valiant effort. It almost worked. He could see the doubt flashing in the Persian's eyes; then again they fell upon Eva as though to confirm his first suspicions.

"You stay and fight with us," he demanded, "or we keep your vehicles and the woman!"

Blake hesitated. He noticed that the three other tribesmen had stopped helping and were moving slowly back to join their leader. Slowly, very slowly, Kalashnikovs were being slipped off shoulders. Smiles took on a noticeably fixed expression. Blake was aware that Hawksby's hand was inching towards the Browning pistol strapped to his hip. From its position on Mashallaha's lap, it took only a split second for the muzzle of the tribesman's rifle to swing towards the major. Moonlight glinted on the curve of its magazine. Blake held his breath.

Hawksby knew the Persian was too close. Rule Number One: if you are armed, never get within arm's reach of an opponent. And Mashallaha was still seated.

As the major's left hand dropped to brush the barrel aside, his right struck with the speed of a snake, its edge catching Mashallaha full in the mouth. The Persian toppled backwards from his perch on the boulder. The Kalashnikov spun to the ground.

Mashallaha had fallen heavily and awkwardly onto the iron-hard ground, but he recovered almost immediately. For a moment Blake thought he was dazed, then suddenly realised that the Persian was extracting a revolver from inside his sheepskin coat. The journalist turned to warn Hawksby, but the major had found the flap stud of his holster jammed.

Hawksby looked up, realising he should have followed up immediately and killed the Persian by hand. As the snub-muzzled revolver was raised, he knew he had left it too late.

Mashallaha yanked at the trigger. Blinded by the sudden flash, Hawksby dropped to his knees. The Qashquai aimed again.

A Kalashnikov thundered into action, a wild zig-zag of shots raining furiously around the Persian's body. Several slammed into it, causing the torso to jerk involuntarily, shifting it along the ground for several inches.

Two of the other tribesmen lifted their weapons, but the full blast of Kangers' pump-action shotgun caught the first full in the face, taking it out like an eraser over a pencil sketch. As he fell dead the second reeled away, clutching his ear, desperately trying to stick it back onto the side of his head. Just as he began screaming, another 1oz slug blasted a fist-sized hole in his upper chest. The third man, paled, turned and fled.

Kangers Webster glanced at Hawksby. Reluctantly the major nodded, and averted his eyes as the third round slammed into the back of the running man.

The silence that followed was stunning in its intensity.

Blake, stunned, lowered the Kalashnikov that had saved Hawksby's life.

"Thanks, Jonathan."

Shaken back to reality, Blake opened his hands and let the weapon drop as though it had scalded him. For a second he studied it, mesmerised, then looked up at the quartet of corpses. He turned to face Hawksby. "Don't thank me, you fucking bastard. It was an impulse to save us both. It wasn't meant to let your soddin' execution squad go into action."

Hawksby's cheeks pinched. "Stow that sort of talk, Jonathan. It had to be done. It's not pleasant."

"Bullshit!" Blake snapped. "You didn't have to kill them all. The Australian didn't have to shoot that poor bastard in the back."

Kangers shouldered his Remington. "If the sod had had the guts to fight, he'd have been shot in the belly. It was his choice."

"Drop the wisecracks," Hawksby warned. He turned back to Blake. "It was my decision and it was based on orders to get you back in one piece. We're not going to do that if we leave a trail of witnesses behind us. Security must come first."

"Don't quote your fucking military jargon at me. You're just a cold-blooded thug dressed up in a uniform that makes you think you're God-all-fucking mighty!"

Hawksby's eyes narrowed. Quietly he said: "And just you remember it, Jonathan. Just you remember it."

Blake's eyes burned with anger. "Oh, I'll remember all right. I'll remember enough to see you cashiered when we get out of this!"

He turned on his heel and left Hawksby to study the scene of carnage. The men had started to clear up. Hawksby smarted. It was impossible to explain to a man like Blake that 'operational requirements' did, on mercifully rare occasions, dictate that even innocent parties sometimes must be killed. It was nothing to do with maliciousness or bloodlust. It was quite simply the age-old question of them or us, and on clandestine operations the principle had to be extended from an immediate enemy to the remotest threat to a mission's security. Blake would never understand that. Sometimes Hawksby found it hard to accept it himself. It left a bitter after-taste. He stooped to pick up the Kalashnikov. As he did so he felt a hand on his arm. The fingers were warm against his skin.

"I understand," she said. "I can see t'e 'urt in your eyes. But I'm t'ankful you do what 'af to be done." She smiled. "I seem just lately to be saying t'ank you a lot."

Hawksby turned to tell her to leave him alone. He was in no mood for soft words of consolation from anyone, even Eva Olsen.

But, when he looked down into the wide, blue eyes, his anger melted. He knew then that he wanted her.

Slowly he turned and began hurrying the others in their preparations to leave.

After the initial shock of the invasion news, Colonel Murad had moved fast. Using the temporary communications breakdown between Teheran and Isfahan base, he had contacted his aide with the ambush party in the Zagros.

He listened dispassionately to the news of the encounter and the loss of the transport helicopter. Mentally he dismissed the bad news. Far more important was the fact that contact had been made, even though his quarry had managed to break through the trap.

The mysterious snatch squad was still moving south, seemingly unstoppable. This was the confirmation he needed. They had to be making for a coastal rendezvous. He instructed his aide to commandeer local transport, but to avoid all contact with other military units. Only one radio was to be retained, netted to Murad's personal frequency. That way the High Command in Teheran would be unable to contact the men at all, let alone order them to the front.

"You smile," the whore said as he replaced the receiver.

Murad allowed himself a chuckle. "The idiots in the Revolutionary Council are mere beginners, my dear. I have been in this game a long time."

She allowed her naked breasts to swing towards him provocatively. "Come back to bed. It is nearly dawn."

"In a minute. And then it will be to *sleep*." He smiled as she pouted in feigned disappointment. "But first I must get reinforcements for my ambush party."

He dialled again and after a few moments an agitated voice came on the other end of the emergency military line to the General Staff. "Colonel Murad of SAVAMA here. Special security unit attached to the Revolutionary Council. I have highly-classified intelligence reports concerning an attempted landing of Iraqi infiltrators on the south coast. I must have a company of crack troops at my disposal with helicopter support and naval elements."

"Impossible!" crackled the voice at the other end. "Our units are falling back along the front! We have nothing to spare!"

"Do you want to be falling back from the south coast, as well, my brother? Do you want saboteurs to add to your worries?"

"I said it is impossible."

"Do you know," Murad said quietly, "that I am authorised to act on the personal instructions of the Imam himself?"

The man hesitated, a new respect creeping into his voice. "No, *agha*, I did not know."

"You may check with the Imam himself if you wish." Murad knew it was only partly true; mobilising troops and warships were *slightly* out of his jurisdiction. But equally he knew that the man at the other end would never dare to speak direct to the Imam or even the Council. Anyway, Murad's name was well-known and feared in military circles.

The voice was resigned. "Tell me what you require?"

KERMAN – BANDAR ABBAS ROAD: 0700 hrs, Sunday 21st September

Just what the hell was going on? Instinctively Forbes' hand closed around the stubby shape of one of the Ingrams he had in the travel-bag on his lap. There was no apparent reason for the bus suddenly to stop dead on a clear desert road heading south-west from Kerman. Beside him he felt Hameda tense.

The passengers looked expectant as the young bearded driver clambered out of his seat, waving a transistor radio above his head and shouting. His unruly mop of black hair added to the air of hysteria. Instantly the whole bus was in uproar, with people climbing to their feet and mouthing curses and obscenities to anyone who would listen. Amid the chaos, Forbes had found it difficult to catch what their driver had said. "A news broadcast on the radio," Hameda explained, "says the Iraqis have attacked. Iran has been invaded."

"Infidels!" bawled a peasant farmer at Forbes.

Forbes was stunned by the turn of events. "The sons of Satan," he agreed, hoping this would satisfy the passenger. It seemed to work. Muttering that the Iraqi president was a vampire and an atheist, he moved down the gangway to begin a heated argument with the driver.

Hameda glanced at Forbes. "What is happening to my country, Mr. Dave?"

The sergeant looked out at the early sunlight. "It's paying the price for international anarchy. While this country's in such a mess, you can expect enemies to try and take advantage."

"It is a terrible wicked world."

Forbes sat back in his seat. He laughed without humour. "It is indeed . . . But this might just work to our advantage."

Hameda looked puzzled.

"It might just help to take the heat off us."

At last the passengers settled down and the driver began again with a jolt. He was anxious to get to the next town so that he could volunteer to repel the invaders.

ZAGROS: 0800 hrs, Sunday 21st September

Despite the incident with the Qashquai brigands, the Snapdragon team had made good progress. The route, which threaded through a series of valleys in the Zagros range, had been kind to them.

As the first spread of dawning light rose in the east, at least they were another forty-five miles nearer their objective. They were in the midst of bare desert mountainside some twelve miles north-east of the town of Nurabad.

There was virtually no vegetation and very little cover of any sort. Jim Perkis led the two-vehicle convoy onto a north-facing slope that offered the protection of shadow and pulled up tight alongside a high overhang of fawn rock. It was here that the Panthers' bizarre pink camouflage should come into its own; there was nothing else between them and the inquisitive eyes of any overflying pilot.

They discovered that Panther One had sustained damage to one of its petrol tanks during the firefight with the Iranian ambush party. Thankfully it had not been a direct hit; a metal fragment had punctured it and petrol had been weep-ing steadily away since the incident. In the darkness it had been overlooked.

With this problem weighing on his mind, Hawksby had stolen away from the rest of the party and clambered down the six hundred feet to where a stream trickled fitfully over a stony bed. At his approach, a viper slinked away. It wriggled from side to side for a moment and vanished, sinking beneath the sand. Gone except for one evil black eye, like a small pebble, which continued to watch him.

Hawksby sat in the shade of an ancient footbridge. He eased off the Para jump boots which he wore without socks and sank his feet into the water.

"So t'is iss where t'e bossman come to get away from it all?"

He had been unaware of Eva's approach. Careless, he told himself. "Come in the shade. Then you can't be seen from the air."

She obeyed, moving under the bridge. "Don't you effer relax?"

"You can't afford to. We're only allowed one mistake."

"True." She smiled. "You iss clever to find water. I'm filt'y after all t'at driving and trying to wash in a t'imble of water your corporal allow us. Look at my 'air . . ." She laughed. "Or rat'er don't!"

It crossed his mind how Caroline would have reacted to having her hair shorn. Or having had to go days without washing. He decided a compliment would be appreciated. "It's growing. Anyway, it suits you short."

She held his gaze for a moment, a suppressed smile causing dimples in her cheeks. "You lie very beautiful. But I really do not need it."

Without a word she began to unbutton her fatigue top, and slipped it from her shoulders. The stark whiteness of her thin body in the gloom of the bridge arch whipped at his senses. Seemingly oblivious to him, she scooped up water in her cupped hands and splashed it on her body. He watched mesmerised as the water cascaded down between her small breasts.

"T'at iss better," she said and put the shirt back over her

267

wet torso, not bothering with the buttons. Then she seemed to notice him watching. "I'af make you uncomfortable? I am sorry, I do not t'ink."

Was it a game? "You surprised me, that's all."

She laughed. "T'at must be some achievement, to surprise super-trooper Major Alan." Then she added provokingly: "Besides what does you wife t'ink? . . . You iss married?" it was more a statement.

Thoughtfully he withdrew his feet from the water, and allowed eddies of wind to dry them off. "Yes, I am married."

"She do not mind t'at you iss always away. On dangerous secret missions?"

"She doesn't have to. She knew I'd be away a lot before she married me."

"Iss she pretty?"

Again Hawksby felt unaccountably embarrassed. Perhaps it was more resentment. He still wasn't sure if he was being deliberately chatted up. McDermid's warning was ringing loud and clear in his mind.

He said: "*I* think so."

Eva raised an eyebrow. There was something about the tone of his reply. "What iss t'e matter, Alan? You iss torn between two women."

"No," he said quickly, astonished at her suggestion, but not realising what she meant. "There're no other women in my life."

Eva smiled patiently. "I meant me," she said softly. He felt her hand on his forearm and before he could reply, she added: "I t'ink per'aps you iss not so 'appy wit' your wife as you would like. No, don't answer me. It iss not necessary. I 'af known many men and, well, I t'ink I understand t'em more t'an many women. Even mysterious Major Alan. Per'aps I am understanding a little about you. Your eyes gives away a lot . . ."

He scarcely heard a word she said. He was intrigued by the closeness of her mouth and the even white teeth. They seemed to be drawing him inexorably towards her.

CHAPTER SIXTEEN

KERMAN – BANDAR ABBAS ROAD: 0900 hrs, Sunday 21st September

The troops at the roadblock were very thorough.

Dave Forbes and Hameda Gulistani were the last ones off the bus. As they stepped down, grim-faced soldiers barged their way past to begin an intensive search of the vehicle. Seats were overturned and the pathetic bundles of market wares were opened, along with the tattered ranks of luggage fastened to the roof-rack.

A long line of passengers still led to the improvised checkpoint. In common with peasants the world over they accepted the interminable delay with resignation. The talk was of war and of Iraqi infiltrators. Some suggested it was part of a dragnet for Americans using the invasion as an opportunity to try again to rescue their hostages.

A toothy youth turned to Forbes, his eyes ablaze. "I go. I fight! I kill many Iraqi dogs! I die for my country and the Revolution!"

The sergeant smiled politely. Silly sod – hadn't he ever heard General Patton's famous, if less glamorous warcry? "Don't die for your country; make the other dumb bastard die for his." Something like that, anyway. It saddened him that the world was still full of political tyrants who could stir up enough hysteria to send off a nation of gullible youngsters to fight their wars, armed with no proper training and a belief in their own invincibility. He'd even heard someone on the bus say there were tablets that could make Iranian soldiers invisible.

"I do not like the look of this, Mr. Dave."

Forbes glanced at Hameda. "No. They seem to be very

thorough. I don't know if they're looking for us or Iraqis. Immaterial really."

Forbes gestured to Hameda to follow him into the shade of a large bush which shielded them from a direct view of the roadblock. On the other side of the bush a dusty track led away to a small village on the lower slope.

A sudden cry went up from the crowd. Fingers pointed. Forbes and Hameda looked up. High in the western sky the sun glinted on a fast-moving shape. From the distance it was impossible to identify it. If it was Iraqi, it was a long way from home. Probably at the limit of its combat range.

"Kill the aggressor!" someone yelled and everyone took up the chant.

As though in answer to their demand another aircraft, much higher, came from out of the sun, swooping in a power dive. One of them was probably a Phantom from Shiraz. There was a sudden puff of smoke. It looked like cotton wool from that distance, but no noise could be heard by the appreciative audience twenty thousand feet below.

"Kill the aggressor!" "Kill the aggressor!"

The tiny missile spiralled downward towards the unsuspecting jet. The noise was scarcely audible but it struck with a violence that could be felt even at that range. Trailing a greasy coil of smoke, the wreckage plummeted towards the dun-coloured hills in the distance, and a cheer went up from the crowd.

Forbes nudged Hameda. "These sods don't even know whose plane's been downed." He shook his head sadly. "C'mon, let's slip away while they're all celebrating."

As he led her down the rough stone embankment to the track, he could feel the strain of being so close to foreigners for a prolonged period begin to lift. For a few precious moments there was no fear of being discovered. No dread of breaking an unknown custom, or inadvertently saying the wrong thing. Such small mistakes, but such a big price to pay.

The noise of the crowd drifted away until all they could hear was the sound of their own feet on the dusty track. The peace and tranquillity affected Hameda too. She unhooked the facemask of her *chador*.

"One day," she said, "when all this is over, I think I will want to return."

Forbes lit a cigarette. It was locally-made and very strong, but he wasn't complaining; it helped to heighten the welcome sense of freedom. "I can understand that. I've been to many countries, Hameda, but this one's special." He blew a stream of smoke. "Mind you, this isn't exactly the best way to see it. In by parachute at the dead of night, hounded around by the local law and the army . . ."

She smiled, and he wondered if she was still thinking about the American. As if sensing his thoughts she said: "You know, Mr. Dave, I do not really think I have a future with Curt."

"No?" He tried to sound surprised.

Hameda looked straight ahead at some point in the distant heat-haze, beyond the village that they were approaching. "Since we parted, I realise that I have been used. Oh, I am willing, but I have been used. By America. By Curt. Even by you and your friends. I look at the world with the innocence of an adolescent.

"Curt never made promises, but I assume many. He was too kind to hurt my feelings. Too thoughtful to tell me the truth. He never really encouraged me to leave."

And you're still thinking like an innocent, Forbes thought grimly. But he said: "It's a tough old game that Curt's mixed up in. You have to make unpopular decisions. You know, you always hurt the ones you love. Like the song goes."

"Pardon?" Her eyes were big and dark.

He smiled. "Just a saying. It's easy to hurt those you're fond of."

"You think that Curt really was – how d'you say – fond of me?"

"He'd be a fool not to be. I'm sure he was," he said truthfully.

She laughed lightly, a pleasantly musical sound. "Always you say things to cheer me. You are a nice man."

Can't disagree there, thought Forbes, drawing himself up to his full height.

"Are you married, Mr. Dave?" He sensed it was a loaded question.

"No, not any more." The smile seemed to freeze on his face. "I'm divorced now. You know, separated."

"In Persia you can have several wives."

"One was enough."

"You did not like it?"

"It didn't work out," he replied stiffly.

He wanted to change the subject, but Hameda was intrigued. "And you have not been in love with another woman since?"

"In love?" he seemed surprised by her question. "Sort of. From afar. Although I don't think I realised at the time. The wife of another officer in my regiment." He paused. He hadn't meant it to sound dramatic. But it did. And, at the time, it had been. "She died."

"And her husband?"

Strange, thought Forbes, that the memory, even after all these years – how many, three, four? – could still hurt. Touch a raw spot. "He was my mate. My best friend."

"Not any more?" She seemed genuinely concerned.

"We're still mates," he said. "But we don't see much of each other now. Not since Trish died."

That was true. Since Trish died. Since then some secret bond between the two men had snapped. Captain Jack Ducane hadn't so much left the regiment as been kicked out. Security risk. That was a laugh. Jacko was the most dedicated pilgrim he'd ever come across: his only mistake was that his wife had been blackmailed into giving information to the IRA. Information she should never have known in the first place. Information that could only have come from her husband.

Really it was just a cruel twist of fate. It should never have happened, but it did. And she had paid the price with her life. Jacko had paid for it with his career.

Oh, they'd been nice about it at Hereford. Jacko and he had fought well, but still the price had to be paid. RTU'd. The dreaded punishment for any SAS man – to be returned to his original unit. It had been suggested to Jacko that he did

272

it voluntarily and he did. But it broke his heart.

Even returning to the Parachute Regiment with his majority had a bitter irony. After a year of no action and missing his past friends, Major Jack Ducane had left the Army altogether. And everything else. He'd sold up his home in Fulham and moved to an idyllic cottage in Devon, taking his daughter, Sarah, with him. Forbes had visited them once. A couple of years ago. Jacko had got a job as a security adviser with one of the several firms set up by past members of the regiment. He was amongst old comrades, but it wasn't the same.

They'd been having tea on the lawn. On a hot summer's day. Then young Sarah had walked in from playing with friends. In through the rose-arch.

Seven years old, and the living image of her mother.

Forbes hadn't been back since.

Hameda stopped walking. She turned and looked up to him. "I'm sorry to learn of your sorrow, Mr. Dave. You deserve more from God than that. I am sure He will give it to you."

Forbes felt his cheeks pink.

"I want you to know," she continued, "that if I do return here in the future, I'd be happy if you were by my side. No man should be without love for so long. I understand a man's needs. And I want you to know that if you want to make love with me . . ." She averted her eyes ". . . then I would be very happy for you." Again she looked back up into his eyes. "And me."

Forbes was stunned. It took a moment to overcome his paralysis and start walking again. He fixed his gaze dead ahead.

This was too much. How in the hell was he supposed to cope with this? As if they didn't have enough problems.

But, gradually, as they neared the village, his walk became a little more jaunty.

The wireless loudspeaker in the tea-house blared into the village square: "*People of Islam arise! Arise! Arise against the vampire Saddam Hussein! He collaborates with those twin Satans — the*

273

enemies of the Islamic Revolution – America and the Soviet Union. All three are each worse than the other!"

Forbes smiled at the illogical and ungrammatical curse as he drank tea with Hameda on a patch of grass outside the village hostelry. The place was packed out to hear the latest broadcast and call to arms.

"Now the devil is rattling at our gates! Arise, Islam! All able-bodied men! Gather yourselves together. Gather your lorries and your buses. Gather your courage! Gather God's spirit like armour! Come to the front . . .!"

The words were drowned in cheers.

Hameda said, "It looks worrying. I am afraid. It was bad for us before, but they say there are now roadblocks everywhere. Everyone is volunteering for the front and they tell them all to be aware of Iraqi infiltrators and sixth columnists."

"Fifth," Forbes corrected absently.

"I am sorry." She looked at him intently. "I am disturbing your thoughts, Mr. Dave."

God woman, you've disturbed them more than you think. "Drop the Mister, eh? Just Dave."

"Yes, Dave."

"Tell me, what's the going rate for one of these bashed-up old trucks we see all over the place?"

"I am sorry. Old trucks? What is 'rate'?"

"Price. How many toman for an old lorry?"

She shrugged. "Last year my cousin bought one for twenty-five thousand toman. But now petrol is difficult. Maybe prices are lower."

Forbes grinned. "Then let's lead a battle party to the front. I've ample cash to buy a jalopy. We can take some of these eager old men with us."

Her forehead creased in a frown. "You joke! Volunteer to fight Iraqis? You are crazy!"

Forbes said thoughtfully: "Not exactly what I had in mind. But at least it's in the right direction."

"You *are* crazy!"

He ignored her outburst. He'd overlook anything said by a woman who had just pledged her body to him. "I've got

274

green battledress in this bag, and two Ingrams. This lot'll be unarmed. Well, unless they bring their pitchforks with them."

"You cannot lead them!" she protested.

"You forget I'm a sergeant in the British Army."

Still she looked horrified. "They will question. They will find us out."

Forbes laughed. "You don't question *this* sergeant, luv. You don't argue. You just do what you're TOLD!" He raised his voice to illustrate the point.

Hameda shook her head in disbelief, but·at least she smiled. He knew then it could work.

ZAGROS: 1100 hrs, Sunday 21st September

Afterwards Hawksby was angry. With himself.

Through the rest of the day he had recurring visions of their brief and violent lovemaking in the cool shade beneath the bridge.

A collage of images flashed across his mind. The paleness of her skin, damp and cold with streamwater. He recalled the rampant eagerness with which he had taken her, her back jammed hard against the wet stones. And her delirious response, thrusting vulgarly against him, seemingly milking the passion from him. It had been over in minutes. Too soon.

Perhaps she had been putting on an act. But something about her tenderness afterwards suggested otherwise.

As if to reassure him she had said: "Don't worry, Alan, I do not make trouble. You 'af enough worries. No one will efer know about us." She was too confident. Kangers Webster and Pogo Penaia had come down to the stream to shave. They too had sought the obvious shelter of the bridge. Luckily Eva had brought down two black plastic jerry cans for water, so they looked as though they had been working.

The Australian noticed the smudges of sand that clung to damp patches on Hawksby's top. "What's up, boss? You fall in?"

Pogo gave an inscrutable Fijian smile. While Hawksby

helped Eva carry the cans back up the slope, she had asked suddenly: "You do not 'af a liking for Jon'i, do you?"

He squinted at the bright reflection of sunlight on the white scree. "He doesn't worry me."

"No, but you do not like 'im?"

"As a person, well, not much. But it's immaterial. It's just a job. To get him – well, both of you – out of here."

Eva stopped to rest and put down the jerry can. She looked down towards the valley stream, the gusting wind tugging at her fatigues. Below they could see the dust dancing. "And iss it just a job if you 'ad to kill us both?"

Hawksby looked at her darkly. "I don't make a habit of killing women I've just made love to. Besides, what have you two been up to that should make you think we'd be given orders to get rid of you?"

He had meant it as a rhetorical question. Although he still had a natural curiosity, he had no desire to get possession of information that Whitehall obviously considered he should not have.

She held his gaze. "Did you know t'at t'e British Government iss largely responsible for getting Khomeini into power in Iran?"

He raised his hand to stop her, but she was insistent. "It wass a scheme by your Foreign Office to – what d' you say? – fire t'e warning shot across t'e bows of t'e Shah . . ."

"Look, Eva, I really don't want to know all this."

"Per'aps you should, Alan. Understand why Jon'i and I iss so worried t'at you may 'af been ordered to . . . to . . . dispense wit' us. Yes? And if you do, you will be 'elping to cover-up an international diplomatic bungle of t'e 'ighest order."

"That would be nothing new."

She picked up the jerry can and started up the slope again. "Britain wanted to keep t'e Shah in power. But t'ey t'ought with 'is repressive measures t'at eventually a coup would come. Or a revolution will topple 'im. Also t'ey iss worried of t'e links t'e Shah 'af with Egypt. Imagine it. T'e two most powerful military nations in t'e Middle East? Forming an axis alliance? Your Arab friends in t'e Gulf iss very concerned. T'ey lead t'e area by economic might. Yes? Not military."

Hawksby crunched steadily up the slope. He didn't like what he was hearing; he got the distinct feeling he was getting the text of some top-secret Cabinet papers at Number 10.

"So your government decide to give t'e exiled Ayatollah some . . . what? . . . moral support," she continued. "And some finance. It iss t'ey who manages to put pressure on Iraqi Government to 'af 'im expelled. To somewhere t'ey will 'af more influence. So Khomeini go to Paris. And 'is organisation iss funded by your British Secret Service under t'e code-name of Fulcrum. I imagine t'at iss somet'ing to do wit' preserving t'e balance of power. It wass meant to get t'e Shah worried about a revolution to come. And t'en 'e become less oppressive."

"You're not suggesting Britain wanted to get rid of the Shah?"

She laughed bitterly. "You iss joking! Certainly not. T'ey just want to control Khomeini and turn t'e 'eat on t'e Shah when it suited. Make 'im, you say, toe t'e line. 'E wass an arrogant bastard, you know."

Hawksby reflected for a moment. "But it went wrong. Obviously?"

Indecision flashed across Eva's face, as she hesitated. "Yes. Khomeini iss given just enough money to keep 'im sweet. Enough to make loud bark, but no bite. But some'ow it got out of 'and. Too much money iss fed into t'e system, yes? Too many useful contacts go 'is way." They were now nearing the hide and she stopped, wanting to keep out of earshot. "T'e balance wass tilted. You know the rest. Khomeini stormed 'ome to Teheran in triumph. And t'e Shah . . . well, you see it iss not t'e sort of story t'at Britain iss wanting to get out. For a start t'e Americans would not be very 'appy . . ."

Hawksby had already examined the obvious aspects. Mentally he shifted the problems around, but something concerned him. Something didn't tie-up. He didn't mention it to Eva. Instead he said, "At a guess, you have some sort of evidence of this on that film?"

She nodded. "We 'af photographs of documents about t'is Fulcrum business. It iss not my imagination, yes? We 'af proof. Confirmation."

"And you think that, by me knowing this, it will prevent me from executing you and Jonathan?"

"I t'ink you iss an honest man, Alan," she said seriously. "And I 'af no doubt you would eliminate anyone if you wass told to. But you might 'esitate if you knew t'e reason why t'at order iss given."

"Look, I can now understand your reason for worry. But nothing's changed. We have *no* such orders. And if we did, they would be questioned, I promise you. We're not a Gestapo outfit." He looked into her eyes. "But there was no need to – to have it off with me just as some sort of insurance policy."

She looked hurt. "I make love wit' you because I wanted to, Alan." Then she pouted. "But per'aps it iss a little insurance. I 'af a natural instinct for self-preservation." She smiled.

"I'd noticed."

As the day progressed Hawksby's recollection of the conversation added to his increasing irritability. He was furious with himself for having succumbed to the Norwegian. Whether she was genuine in her affections or not was immaterial. He had compromised himself and given her a lever to use against him that could put the mission in jeopardy. Even to the extent of being almost caught in the act by Kangers Webster and Pogo. What would have happened, he asked himself, if they had been patrolling Iranian soldiers? Also he had added to his own vulnerability by listening to her account of their claimed discovery about British activities. Previously he would have carried out any orders; now he found himself questioning the whole reason for the mission itself.

He could understand how a well-intentioned secret service plan could back-fire. And why, as a result, Britain would want to prevent Blake's discovery from being made public. But what about Khomeini? He was hardly likely to broadcast the story. If it became known that Britain had helped get him to power, he and his precious Revolution would be finished.

So why risk a sensitive and highly dangerous operation like Snapdragon to rescue Blake? If Crazy K had found out about the journalist's discovery, then he and his girlfriend would have undoubtedly joined the hundreds being executed weekly in Iran's prisons. Why not let your enemy do your dirty work for you?

No, Hawksby decided, there was a missing element to the whole business. Someone, somewhere had another reason for wanting Blake out. But who? And why?

"Boss?" It was Perkis.

"What is it?"

Taken aback by the major's tone, the driver hesitated. "Er, it was about the transmission tonight."

"Well?"

Perkis flushed. He'd meant to stick to his earlier decision, but thoughts of his wife were starting to play on his mind. "Well, boss, I was wondering if you could slip in an enquiry about me missus? You know, she's expecting our first sprog. And, well, there was complications . . ."

Hawksby exploded. "Good grief, man! What in damnation do you think we're on, a bloody Sunday school outing? Our transmissions aren't Two Way Family Favourites, Perkis. Are you trying to have us located by Iranian listening stations? Act your age." His jaw set in a firm line. "Go on, get out of my sight. And just remember you're in the bloody Army. If you don't like it, get out!"

Perkis smarted. He'd never received such a dressing down since he'd been in 22 SAS. He could scarcely believe his ears. Suppressing his anger, he turned and walked away. His clenched knuckles showed white.

"Wee bit hard on the lad, boss."

Hawksby had been unaware of McDermid standing behind him. "Don't you start, Scottie. Mind your own business."

The Scotsman stood his ground. Everyone knew that with the 'squeeze-box' they could transmit the text of the entire Bible in a few minutes. A one line personal query would make no difference. "Look, boss, I dunna give a monkey's where ye dip y' wick, but dunna take et oot on us if she wasna up te much . . ."

Christ, thought Hawksby, Kangers has been blabbing. "Corporal, you are OUT OF ORDER! Now shut your mouth and keep it that way! That comment was untrue, unnecessary and, I repeat, *definitely* out of order! Got it?"

"Sah!" McDermid grated at the major's back as Hawksby turned and strode away.

He shook his head. "I've noo seen him like this afore."

KERMAN – BANDAR ABBAS ROAD: 1130 hrs, Sunday 21st September

"GET ABOARD! COME ALONG! YOU'RE IN THE ARMY NOW!" bawled the burly Iranian Army sergeant as he strutted alongside the neglected old lorry which still stank of its last consignment of citrus fruit. "I WANT DISCI-PLINE NOW WE'RE OFF TO FIGHT THE IN-FIDELS!"

No one in the remote village had seen where he'd come from. He just emerged at the tea-house as if from nowhere, along with a female revolutionary guard. Yet he certainly seemed to know what he was doing as he lined up the untidy rows of village volunteers to make his selection. To the surprise of many he asked each man in turn whether he had any military experience and told them to stand to one side – and promptly left them out of his force. He explained curtly that an Iranian Army officer would be along shortly to re-enlist them. He didn't seem the sort of man to argue with.

Women of the chosen ones began to weep. The village elders looked on, impressed. No one had dreamed that the Islamic war machine could be mobilised so fast. Before the wireless broadcast an hour earlier, no one had even known they were at war.

The thirty volunteers scrambled aboard with their hastily-grabbed bundles of possessions, the tailboard was bolted up, and the Iranian Army sergeant clambered into the cab alongside the woman.

There were cheers and waves and tears as he gunned the old vehicle out of the square. Even its irregular backfiring seemed symbolic of the war that lay ahead.

At the edge of the village, the sergeant pulled the lorry to a halt outside a shop where a carpet weaver was at work. He handed the woman a wad of notes. "Be an angel and buy me the best carpet you can get. Nothing too big, mind."

She looked astonished. "What?"

"When we get back I want proof that I got here." He winked at her. "It'll look good in the NCO's Mess."

ZAGROS: 2200 hrs, Sunday 21st September

The brooding atmosphere lasted until transmission time. Reception was poor but Tiger managed to pick up the confirmation signal for a rendezvous at last light the next day. Two Rigid Raiders, manned by Captain Johnny Fraser's Sabre Team, would come in through the treacherous coastal waters to the agreed RV. It all seemed so near, yet so far.

They were also given news of the Iraqi invasion. Everyone had plenty to think about.

At 2300 hours the two Land Rovers worked their way down the slope to the winding mountain road. Tonight was to be a fast dash with the idea of getting well clear of the previous night's pursuers if they were still in the area. The journey was uneventful, which only served to increase the tension. It was only relieved when they passed a small convoy of Iranian Army trucks travelling the other way. Hawksby decided to bluff it out and they honked their horns and waved as they passed. A cheer went up from the troops in the convoy and they brandished their weapons in the air. They were on their way to the front.

Twice the Panthers stopped at deserted petrol stations to see if fuel could be syphoned off, but on both occasions signs had been posted by the Gendarmerie. All fuel had been requisitioned for the war effort.

Not wishing to chance their luck further, they turned off

the road again. Finally they came to rest in the barren high ground north-west of Kazerun. By now their fuel had become critically low. With the aid of binoculars it was possible to distinguish some of the main features of the major town as the dark shapes of its skyline loomed out of the early morning mist some ten miles distant. It was on the national grid and had its own airfield. On the other side of the valley, beyond the maze of streets, there were water-pumping stations on the slopes of the towering Dovan mountain range.

Hawksby lowered the glasses. "If there's a chance of getting fuel, Scottie, it'll be there. I want a continual watch on activity in the town all day. Move a couple of chaps in for a closer look-see. Log all transport movement and note where all likely sources of fuel might be. There are also some decent JARIC photos of the place that might help. Tonight we'll see if we can't help ourselves to a gallon or two."

McDermid nodded in agreement. "Only thing tha' concerns me, boss, is tha' we've managed te throw 'em off our trail. If we go into Kazerun, we could stir up the hornets' nest again."

"That's a danger wherever and whenever we strike. And I don't see an alternative, d'you?"

McDermid shrugged. "Na doot ye're right. Aye."

"Look, boss," Kangers Webster said, prodding a finger at his notebook. "Five convoys of fuel moving through at a rate of one an hour. Most of the stuff is on the main road on the other side of Kazerun. Troops, ammunition trucks. Seem to be reinforcements from the Third Army Corps at Shiraz on their way to the front. It's all pretty damn congested. But some, mostly fuel, is coming this way. I reckon it's destined for the Navy base at Bushehr. If fightin's goin' on round the refineries at Abadan their usual fuel reserves could be cut off."

Hawksby studied the map. "Convenient," he muttered. It would make sense for the Iranians to grab any emergency reserves of fuel from inland if their main fuel source on the border with Iraq was threatened. Anyway, the reason was immaterial. A convoy on the open road was a more tempting proposition than crawling around Kazerun on their hands and knees all night, trying to find a fuel dump that hadn't been requisitioned.

"It wouldna be a clever idea te take on an entire convoy." McDermid was thinking aloud. "We need a way of getting t' fuel tankers away from the escorts."

Perkis said suddenly: "I've an idea what might work . . ." Almost immediately he shut up again. He didn't feel inclined to get another dressing-down from Hawksby who, unlike other SAS commanders, didn't take kindly to ill-conceived suggestions, however well-intentioned. Apart from that he didn't feel like suggesting anything to the major, except where to stick his arrogance.

Sensing his hesitation, McDermid said: "Spit it out, lad. Let's see what them CSEs did fer y' education."

"Well, it ain't nothin' that wonderful. I just thought we could take a coupla 'eadlights out of one of the Panthers. As we're runnin' on IR, it don't matter. An' then set 'em up on a battery. Just round a bend."

"How'd y'reckon that'd work?" Kangers asked, intrigued.

Perkis told them. Everyone seemed impressed. All attention turned to Hawksby for judgment, watching the hooded eyes as they peered over the thin hooked nose at the demonstration diagram scrawled in the sand.

After a moment, he said slowly: "Okay, chaps, we'll give it a whirl."

From the other side of the mountain hide, Eva Olsen watched the discussion group with interest. But her main attention was fixed on Hawksby. During the day he'd changed into baggy khaki shorts for comfort. The combined effect of the large Para boots emphasised his height and lean build. She noted there was not a spare ounce of fat on his body which glistened with perspiration. His stomach was flat and hard, the wiry muscle patterns knotted around his shoulders as he sat in his familiar hunched position. She could see now why the men called him the Hawk. It wasn't just a play on the name.

The jutting beard and the brown cloth sweatband around the wild black hair gave him a distinctly piratical look.

Physical desire for him suddenly throbbed in her, as she remembered the way he had taken her the day before. Ruthless. Animal.

"Can't you take your bloody eyes off him?"

Blake's harsh words made her jump.

"Jon'i! You surprise me. And do not be silly. Where am I supposed to look? Stare at t'is bloody desert all day. Or t'e sky. Do I 'af to watch you all t'e time?"

Blake sat beside her on the Land Rover's bonnet. "Don't kid me, Eva, I know you too well. Remember? You've only had eyes for your soldier boyfriend lately. Never give me a second glance. It gets noticed, y'know. I heard a couple of the others joking about it yesterday."

"Yes?"

"You can look like that if you like, but it's true."

"T'ey just 'af soldiers' fun. T'ey iss just jealous, I expect. I 'af been known to interest men before, you know."

Blake sneered. "Don't I just."

"Alan iss all right. Maybe very British officer type, but 'e iss okay."

"Just because he's promised not to bump you off."

Eva was exasperated. "*Neither* of us, Jon'i. I told you 'e said 'e 'ad no such orders. 'E says they iss not Nazis. 'E did not even know why we are being rescued."

"Balls!"

"I believe 'im, Jon'i."

"You'd believe anyone who gave you one."

She stepped away. "You make me sick sometimes. I 'af not been near 'im."

"What about the comments by that bloody uncouth Aussie and the others?"

Her eyes glared like an angry cat's. "I tell you. Soldiers' rumours. Armies are running on rumours, or 'adn't you 'eard? God, it wass *you* who wanted me to find out what 'e know about us."

"And what about your film?" he demanded.

"What about it? 'E told you 'e iss keeping it."

"Don't you realise? If we don't get it back, we'll never see it again."

"*You* know what t'e documents said, Jon'i," she challenged.

"Yes, but that's *not* evidence!"

Eva curled her lips in a snarl. "Jon'i, you iss getting to be a real pain in t'e arse. I am beginning to wonder what it was I efer saw in you."

Blake scowled after her as she turned away. Bloody randy cow, he thought savagely. I know what you saw in me all right. The only bloody Englishmen in Teheran with prick enough to satisfy you! He kicked at the wheel of Panther One. From the other side of the hide Perkis glowered at him.

CHAPTER SEVENTEEN

KAZERUN – BUSHEHR ROAD: 2230 hrs, Monday 22nd September

The driver of tanker No. 396 hadn't heard the two low-velocity shots fired from a silenced muzzle at the roadside. So he couldn't understand why the tanker was slowing down. He couldn't see that two of the four heavy-duty tyres on the rear-axle were spinning uselessly, their traction gone.

"We're falling behind the others," his companion observed lethargically. "Step on it, can't you?"

The driver frowned. It must be these unmade mountain roads. They were hopeless with a heavy load like this in a truck meant for metalled surfaces. His was the last tanker in the convoy and, behind him, the driver of the escorting armoured personnel carrier hooted angrily. In front, the tail end of the tanker column had disappeared around a tight left-hand bend. The road began to run downhill, flanked by a steep embankment on the left.

That's better. Good gradient. They were speeding up now.

Lazily the driver manhandled the big wheel, nosing the huge tanker around the bend. He was expecting to see the red trailer lights of the next vehicle some way ahead. He didn't. He was just suddenly aware of the blazing headlights of the oncoming vehicle right in front of him!

He hit the brakes. He spun the wheel. He cried out. There was no way he could miss it! He shut his eyes.

He heard the crack of the impact and the tinkling of glass and saw the dazzling headlights go out as he hurtled off the road. The forward momentum of the tanker came to a juddering halt as it ploughed axle-deep into soft sand. The driver braced himself against the wheel. But his companion wasn't so lucky. The man's head smashed against the windscreen.

Dazed, the driver saw soldiers running towards him in the glare of his own lights. The cab door was yanked open and he found himself looking down the ugly snout of a sub-machine gun. His mouth dropped open in surprise, and stayed open as the SAS man's gun spat twice.

Meanwhile the slab-sided M113 personnel carrier had ground to a halt on the road. The commander, amazed at the sudden disappearance of the tanker in front of him, opened his hatch and peered out.

Obviously there had been some sort of accident. He could distinguish the oval shape of the tanker's rear end jutting from the verge on his right. But the wreckage on the road puzzled him. A roadblock?

He was not expecting the thump immediately behind him as Tiger dropped down the embankment to land on the flat top of the carrier. The commander tried to twist round in his turret. His eyes caught the glint of razor steel as the Gurkha's long, curved *kukri* knife scythed through the air.

There was no cry as it hooked into the Iranian's wind-pipe, almost severing his head, until it met the resistance offered by the neck bone. Withdrawing the blade, Tiger stamped hard on the man's head, stuffing the limp body inside the vehicle. Withdrawing an L2 fragmentation grenade from his belt pouch, the little SAS corporal extracted the pin and let it topple in after the hapless commander.

Grabbing the bloodied *kukri* he'd let fall, the soldier just had time to drop to the road before the grenade ignited.

The contained explosion shook the carrier like a living thing. The blast spat off the unbolted hatch cover with contempt. By the time Tiger had doubled back to the tanker the carrier's fuel tanks had ignited, adding to the raging pyre.

"That your idea of a quiet disposal job?" Kangers asked sarcastically. He was helping the rest of the team fill the jerry cans from the tanker.

Tiger's white teeth grinned beneath the ever-cheerful eyes. "I get carried away."

"Right, that's it," Hawksby said and spun the tanker tap to the 'Off' position.

"Want me to charge it?" Kangers offered. "Make a lovely blaze, it would."

The major started back to Panther One. "No point in being unsporting. I reckon the poor buggers have got enough on their plate with the Iraqis. Besides, Tiger's beacon is quite enough."

Shaking his head sadly, Kangers said, "Boss, you're goin' soft in yer old age."

ISFAHAN: 2300 hrs, Monday 22nd September

He wasn't going to die.

Curt Swartz Jnr. was determined of that. But he knew if he remained captive at the Isfahan villa, it was a foregone conclusion.

He didn't pretend to understand his tormentors' ploy, but he knew they were up to something. The sudden friendly approach, food, drink and sleep . . . it was all an elaborate trick to get him off guard, and make him feel grateful to the nice guy. The old hard man, soft man technique that worked so well.

Yet it was all so stupid. If *he* knew he was lying, so must they by now. So, coolly and calmly, Curt had decided that he wasn't going to wait. Now that his tortured body was starting to heal, he could concentrate his mind above the lingering pain. He could recall his exhaustive training and summon the determination and incentive to live.

That was the easiest part. He had an intense yearning to make love to Alison again, even if it was for just one more time. And to hold the kids. The thoughts of putting them through the emotional mangle endured by the relatives of the embassy hostages was just too much.

And there was Hameda. Sweet innocent Hameda. He would dearly like to square things with her.

He had more incentive to survive now than he'd ever had in his life before.

His initial plan to mix kerosene and detergent to form a crude explosive mixture had been thwarted for the simplest of reasons. Iran's economy was in such dire straits that the guard was unable to buy any. Or so he said. Curt would just have to put up with the regular power cuts and do without a lamp. And he'd have to put up with dirty clothes for a few more days.

It was the electricity problem that gave Curt his second idea. He shouted to the guard, "Hey! My light's gone out! Is that another damn power failure? Hey, guard!" Outside there was the reluctant shuffle of feet. "Hey, guard!"

"What you want?" Followed by a yawn.

"Is there a power cut?"

"No. Go to sleep."

"My light's gone out. I'm trying to read."

Impatient. "Night is for sleep. You sleep."

"Be fair, I'm in too much pain to sleep. Please."

The small grille in the door slid back. A torch beam cut into the blackened room. "American, you stand back. No funny business."

Curt sat on the bed. A face appeared at the aperture. The nose wrinkled in disdain. "You piss? I can smell." The acrid stench of urine was strong.

"An accident. I kicked the can in the dark."

Come on, you bastard.

There was a faint clank of metal as the lock turned. A sliver of light played along the coiled length of bedspring that ran from the door handle to the empty light socket.

The second coil came down from the socket to the floor where the pool of urine lay just behind the door.

As the guard turned the handle and stepped in, the suddenness of the arcing blue light was as stark and brilliant as forked lightning, illuminating the look of frozen horror on his face. He pitched forward onto the floor. The wire swung back and forth across the urine puddle, fizzing and spitting a shower of sparks.

The 110 volts had only stunned him and Curt had to move fast to break the man's neck by stamping hard.

Quietly Curt picked up the dropped carbine, checked it

over, and slipped out onto the landing. It was deserted. He limped across to the head of the stairs and peered down. The entrance lobby, too, was empty. He breathed a sight of relief.

So far so good.

It took a long time to descend to the ground floor. Each footstep was agony, reviving the livid bruises that had swollen the soles of his feet after the thrashing with rubber hoses. He pushed the thought from his mind. That was all over now. A few more minutes and he would be a free man, able to start the long-planned escape route to Turkey.

"Hussein?" It was the dead guard's name. The inquiring voice came from somewhere below. Silently Curt backed into an alcove on the turn of the stairs. A portrait of Ayatollah Khomeini frowned down from its pride of place above his head. "HUSSEIN!" Below, the guard wandered into view and peered up the stairs. "Are you up there?"

The man shrugged and lit a cigarette. He went to walk away, then hesitated. He moved to the bottom of the stairs, leaning on the banister. "If you're asleep, Hussein, then Murad will pull your ears off with pliers. Don't let him catch you!" He chuckled.

Then the mirth died on his lips. He saw a slight movement in the alcove. A nervous smile. "Hussein? You playing stupid games? I can see you." The incident with the kitchen fire and the strange mullah a few days earlier had played on his nerves. Cautiously he unshouldered his carbine.

The Heckler & Koch G3 came alive in Curt's hands, trembling violently as it spat out its contents. Dying echoes reverberated around the hallway as the American stumbled down the stairs to the main door. He tried it – it was locked and bolted. Shit! A step back. The muzzle of the G3 drew level to the lock casing. Curt's fear and anger poured out through the weapon as he squeezed the trigger and blew the doors open. Cool, sweet night air rushed in.

"Hey, you!"

Curt spun round. Half-a-dozen guards were emerging from doors around the hall. He fired a long raking burst that sent them scurrying back under cover. Plaster fell in lumps to the floor. Shells richocheted haphazardly from wall to wall.

His heart pounding in his chest, the American launched himself into the garden, ignoring the agony of his feet. Grimacing, he pounded down the path to the gate but one look at the mass of bolts, chains and padlocks told him he couldn't shoot his way through. He would have to scale it.

Suddenly he was aware of the pain. Deep in his chest. A pain that felt like a knife being twisted. Something seemed to explode. He felt the stabbing sensation radiate to his left shoulder. His arm felt numb. His G3 clattered onto the stone slabs.

Then he heard it. The voice. Not here! Impossible. Alison couldn't be here.

He realised he was on his knees. The pain was consuming him. His whole body was just one throbbing, excruciating pain.

He opened his eyes. He had not been mistaken. Through the red mist he saw her come.

As she reached him, she leaned forward, concerned. He saw the worry in her eyes. But then he saw that her eyes were not blue but brown. And her skin was swarthy. She had bad teeth. She was a man.

Curt Swartz Jnr. was dead.

ZAGROS: 0045 hrs, Tuesday 23rd September

Jim Perkis drove like a man possessed.

As Panther One had led the way south yet again, McDermid had casually mentioned that during the earlier transmission from their hide overlooking Kazerun, Tiger had picked up a special message from London.

Apparently, after the blazing row the day before, the Hawk had thought better of his decision, because the message was a personal one for Trooper James Perkis: *Wife Janet says your son Jeremy, weight 7lb 6ozs, wants you home soonest. Please ask colleagues for advice on intensive nappy training before return. Baptism due on 27 Sept.*

"Jesus," McDermid had said. "Y'canna call the wee laddie Jeremy. Tha's a bleddy officer's name!"

Perkis looked immensely serious. "I know! I told 'er that

was no good. I wanted Bill. William, you know. And *she* knows that! That's why she's 'aving 'im baptized early. When? Gawd! That's in only four days' time! What gratitude after me worryin' over 'er."

"Perkis, laddie."

"Yes, Scottie?"

"I reckon tha' wife'n yours is pullin' y'pisser."

But Perkis didn't care. It was fantastic news, and with their coastal rendezvous only hours away, and no sign of the enemy, he'd have cheerfully pushed Panther One all the way. As it was he hummed an infuriatingly tuneless version of 'Where Will The Baby's Dimple Be' during the entire fifty mile cross-country dash.

The high folds of rock had flattened out completely now to become a vast undulating mountain basin. It was good going for the Land Rovers, only the occasional shallow wadi causing them to slow. The sky, too, added to the sense of exhilaration. Dark clouds scudded over angrily, threatening rain to break the heavy humidty of the past few days. On the distant mountains fork lightning stabbed viciously at the peaks. After fifty hectic miles on a southern trajectory, the vehicles swung westwards, skirting the edge of a mountain ridge, and continued flat out across the bare dusty plain towards the coast. Another thirty miles would see them near the village of Kalameh, which guarded the winding mountain pass through the last major natural barrier thrown up by the Zagros range. Once through that, they would be in the more fertile coastal strip.

Hawksby glanced at his watch. It was nearly 0100 hours, and already they had covered almost sixty miles. They were averaging almost thirty miles an hour across country; at this rate they would hit the pass by two in the morning.

Add an hour for skirting Kalameh and the more difficult terrain, and that would allow one hour before dawn to travel the sixty miles by road through the coastal farmland. The many scattered farms and hamlets in the narrow strip meant there was no alternative cross-country route to offer better security. Bravado and speed, Hawksby decided, would be the best way.

Despite the hold-up caused by the need to acquire fuel, he reckoned they would make their RV with Johnny Fraser's four-man Sabre team from the Boat Troop by dawn. The following nightfall they would be slipping out into the Persian Gulf on the evening tide.

In fact, Hawksby reflected, at that very moment two Rigid Raider fast assault boats should be creaming into the Persian shoreline beneath the leaden night sky.

PERSIAN GULF: 0100 hrs, Tuesday 23rd September

Captain Johnny Fraser scowled out from the wheelhouse. Before him the sleek prow of the Omani fast patrol boat nudged its way through the choppy black waters of the Persian Gulf.

Beside him the British officer who commanded the vessel looked remarkably relaxed for a man approaching the hostile coast of a country at war. "Nine knots is about right," he said. "If we get picked up by a coastal radar or one of the PBs, at least they're less likely to shoot first if they think we're a fishing boat."

Fraser grinned. "That sounds like a good theory." He glanced up at the star clusters in the vast sweep of tropical sky. "But I'd be happier with more cloud cover."

The officer smiled gently. He was satisfied that the makeshift canvas awnings, which had given the vessel an ugly, stunted silhouette, would confirm to anyone on visual reconnaissance that this was, indeed, a fishing boat. Besides, if they did look too closely, he knew he could rely on its makers, Brooke Marine in England, to live up to their reputation, and deliver the necessary horse-power. And its recently refitted Exocet ship-to-ship missiles meant it could tangle with anything the Iranians cared to throw at them.

However, the SAS captain had other problems. As the officer reminded him: "I think that Met report means you'll get all the cloud cover you want, Johnny. There appear to be local atmospheric storms all down the coast. The glass is already starting to drop like a brick."

"How far now?"

"Twenty minutes," the officer replied. "That'll see us just outside coastal radar range."

Fraser nodded. Another fine theory. Like the whole of 'Operation Salvation' it hadn't taken into account the fact that Iran and Iraq would be at each other's throats in a full scale war. Heading for a stretch of deserted coast between two major naval bases left plenty to chance.

He said: "I'll get prepared."

"Call in at the galley. I ordered them to brew up to celebrate your departure. I'm sure you'll find the rest of your men there."

"Food we can do without. Sleep and ammunition . . . but tea . . .?" Still chuckling, Johnny Fraser left the wheelhouse.

In fact, having all but drained the tea-urn, the rest of his Sabre team were already assembled at the stern. The two Rigid Raider assault craft were at an advanced stage of readiness, having each been mounted with a giant 40hp Evinrude outboard.

The men had all trained with the Royal Marines Special Boat Section at Poole. Whilst the elite SBS concentrated on secret beach surveys in preparation for Royal Marine assault landings, obstacle demolition, and more lately, oil-rig protection duties, the SAS Boat Troops used the same training both as another 'means of arrival' and as a support service to the full Squadron they served. And this time, Johnny Fraser's team would be making use of the full range of their skills.

First would come the approach to within three miles of the beach in the low-profile glass fibre craft.

Once off-shore, two members of the Boat Troop would go over the side and make a 'wet' approach. After surfacing to survey the beach with image-intensifier nightsights from the sea, they would land to check for enemy positions, patrols, or the unexpected they had encountered on other missions: fishermen, smugglers and, once, a nudist colony.

After confirming that the beach was secure, the two Raider craft would drift in silently on the tide. Then it would be a race against the clock as the four men excavated the deep hole in the centre of the cove and positioned the upturned craft to form a solid roof. Finally, dry sand would be sprinkled carefully over the dun-coloured hulls until they merged in as just two more undulations in the beach dunes.

Fraser pulled on the black rubber hood of his wet-suit and walked across the deck to where Sergeant Turner was preparing to slip the first Raider over the side.

"All set, Brummie?"

"As we'll ever be, boss." He squinted towards the horizon off the starboard beam. Dim flashes lit the distant skyline where the tropical storm raged. "It's going to be no millpond."

Fraser's teeth gleamed white against his blackened face. "If I didn't know you better, Brummie, I'd say you were a born pessimist."

ISFAHAN: 0015 hrs, Tuesday 23rd September

At the Isfahan villa where Blake and Eva Olsen had been held captive, Colonel Murad had a small office from which he and his aide had been running the dragnet that now covered a vast tract of southern Iran.

Covering most of one wall was a close-detail map of the territory on which the known route of the mysterious rescue team had been plotted. Red pins marked the course, beginning at the crash site of the stolen JetRanger. It then meandered on a southward bearing until it stopped at the wadi site of the abortive ambush attempt.

It was now just after midnight and the carefully-typed label beside the ambush pin was dated 21/9/80. The night before last.

Murad stood in front of the map, sipping slowly at a glass of tea. He had already received confirmation that one of the Navy's fast patrol boats from Bushehr had been put under his personal command, and that a replacement Chinook transport helicopter and platoon of seasoned troops from Shiraz were on immediate notice to embark.

There was no mention of the survivors of his ambush party. They were already out of contact with High Command, who no doubt had been desperately trying to reach them to divert them to the front. Murad, of course, knew exactly where they were: out hunting, travelling south in a commandeered bus. Wherever the elusive enemy was, his men, travelling faster, could not be far behind.

The door opened, and his young aide entered. Just recently, especially since news of the Iraqi invasion, he had looked tired and unusually humourless. Now, however, he was smiling.

"I think this will cheer you, *agha*." He handed over a cipher sheet. "I have just come from the radio room."

Murad studied it, a ghost of a smile forming on his face. "Ah, a fuel convoy just outside Kazerun, eh?"

"It could be an Iraqi attack," the aide suggested.

"And what would they want with fuel in the middle of the Zagros? They'd have destroyed *all* the tankers. No, this bears all the hallmarks of our friends."

He walked across to the map and added a new red pin. Right behind it was a blue pin: his men in the bus. Just sixty miles to the left was another blue pin. His new detachment at Shiraz. Seventy miles to the south-west, just off the coast was yet another pin. His fast patrol boat.

"They could walk to the coast from Kazerun," Murad observed. "In that terrain it would take maybe three days. Hardly worth the risk of stealing petrol. So they must be going farther south. Steering clear of Bushehr."

The aide looked over his master's shoulder. "Do you think we have them?"

Murad's ghost of a smile remained. "Let us say that they are walking into an inescapable trap. All we have to do now is close it."

"And wait?"

"And wait."

Then the telephone rang. The aide snatched up the receiver. Almost immediately he handed it over to Murad. "It is your investigators on Sabs Karemi's research. They've found something." He looked hurt. "They insist on talking only to you."

At last the narrow pass through the last limestone folds of the Zagros melted away into the inky blackness behind them. And with it the fear of being ambushed or trapped in the confines of the Zagros' rocky canyons. As the ground dropped steadily down towards the Gulf the increase in humidity was noticeable. The warm, moist atmosphere was oppressive and uncomfortable.

They steered south, running parallel with the coast into the wide, gently sloping valley of the Rud-e-Shur. It was formed by the last of the main inland Zagros range on their left, and a forty-mile-long scab of high and thinly-wooded coastal hills. It was almost the only area in south Iran that enjoyed any rainfall, Hawksby mused. A meagre two or three inches a year, and it looked as though they might get it all today.

"I dunna' like this, boss." McDermid's voice came over the Clansman. *"This place is alive wi' bleddy people. Over."*

It was an exaggeration, but dawn was approaching fast and local farmworkers were starting towards the mud-walled fields to begin their day's toil. No doubt the threat – or promise – of precious rain had spurred them on. Hawksby tried to sound light-hearted. "Just push on, Scottie. All we can do is brazen it out. They'll think we're reinforcements for the front. Over."

"One wee thing, boss. We're goin' t' wrong way for tha'. Over."

Hawksby grinned. "A technicality, Panther One, a technicality. Out."

Eva leaned over from the back. "Do you t'ink we make it before daylight, Alan?"

"Not if you don't keep down, we won't. And keep that blonde hair of yours well-covered. Turn up your collar."

She wrinkled her nose. "Yes, boss!"

Suddenly Pogo Perkis hit the brakes.

"What is it?" Hawksby demanded, but with the improving light he could answer his own question.

Thunder rumbled like heavy artillery as the tropical storm gathered its strength out over the Gulf. In the occasional lightning flash, the major could distinguish Panther One a few hundred yards ahead. Perkis had stopped behind a queue of scrawny cattle. The weather had made them jittery and the old herdsman couldn't stop them from blocking the track completely.

McDermid was first to realise that the hold-up had been a blessing in disguise. Even as he began to radio back to Panther Two, Hawksby saw half-a-dozen Iranian troopers emerge from the cluster of mud dwellings ahead.

Pogo nudged him. He pointed to a copse of scraggy acacia trees beyond the dwellings. The big Chinook helicopter had been parked carefully, out of view from the road. But its unmistakable outline shape was impossible to hide in the first glimmerings of dawn light.

Hawksby cut through McDermid's warning: "I know, Scottie. They're waiting for *us*! We're backing up, follow as best you can. Out."

His words were drowned by the grating of gears and the shriek of the propshaft as Pogo went hard into reverse.

Blake pointed behind them. "We crossed a bridge about a quarter of a mile back! It crossed over a wadi! Could we use that?" His voice ended in a scream to make himself heard.

Hawksby thought for a moment. It made good sense. Their destination was a sheltered cove on the other side of the coastal high ground. There the Boat Troop team would be waiting. Rather than go round it, they would use the dried-up river bed to go up it. And then make their way down the other side to the sea. At least it would by-pass the Iranian reception party.

They drew level with the old stone bridge and Pogo peered over the parapet. Twelve feet below just a thin trickle of water slurped over the stony river bed. "Looks okay, boss," he reported.

Hawksby nodded. "Right, lead on. Scottie can come up the rear."

The Fijian shoved the gear into first and swung over the embankment, his face set in a grim mask as the heavy vehicle half-drove and half-slid down the soft, sandy gradient. Ahead the wadi wormed its way up to the coast hills.

Colonel Murad had spent the rest of the night on a canvas camp-bed in his small office at the villa in Isfahan.

It had been an uncomfortable time, but it had been more than compensated for when he awoke to the urgent shout of his aide.

"News, *agha*! News!"

Wearily Murad lifted his feet from the bed and placed them on the floor, before he looked up at the grinning face of the young officer.

"What's all the excitement? I hope it's worth waking me at this unholy hour."

"Just minutes ago, *agha*, we spotted our mysterious enemy," the aide announced proudly, as though it had been his personal achievement. "Down on the coast near the village of Berid. A herdsman was interrogated and reported seeing them heading west along a wadi into the hills overlooking the Gulf. It was only minutes previously."

Murad carefully buttoned up his trousers. He didn't wish to rush with unseemly haste at what might turn out to be another false alarm. "Point the exact position out on the map, my friend."

Eagerly the aide obliged. "Here, *agha*, here!" He jabbed a finger at the coast, just north of Lavar Kabkan.

"Mmmm," Murad said thoughtfully. "I see there is a cove on the other side of those hills, which may be a suitable place for a landing. Their destination perhaps?" He turned quickly. "Do we not have a helicopter in the area?"

"We do, *agha*!"

"Good, then we can make use of it. I want our men hard on the heels of our mysterious friends, and our patrol boat brought up to cut them off at the cove."

Slowly and with a distinct hint of menace in his voice, he added: "At last, we . . . *have* . . . them!"

CHAPTER EIGHTEEN

ZAGROS: 0600 hrs, Tuesday 23rd September

"CHRIST! They're gaining on us!" Kangers Webster yelled.

McDermid twisted in his seat to make his own assessment. There was no disagreeing with the Australian. The pursuing Iranian jeep was making a determined effort to catch them, helped by its lighter load. Its almost reckless speed along the wadi was only possible because of the relatively smooth surface.

"Shall I blast 'em, Scottie?" Kangers demanded.

"No! I dunna want their friends knowing our location." He thought for a moment. Hawksby's vehicle was some way ahead and it was possible that the enemy didn't realise there were two Land Rovers. He nudged Perkis. "Could y' shake 'em off, Jim?"

The driver didn't look too happy at the suggestion. "I dunno, Scottie. Bleedin' risky."

"It might give t'others a wee chance." Coaxing.

"Aw, blimey. You can bloody soft-talk me into anything. 'Old tight, everyone . . .!"

As he finished speaking he snatched the handbrake and swung the wheel. Panther One bounced up the shallow embankment of the wadi and onto the hillside slope. Anxiously he looked for a suitable spot to turn, and as he found it, he ground the accelerator into the floorboards. A cloud of dust spewed up behind the thrashing rear wheels. He approached a particularly steep incline and began to execute a careful three-point turn as though he was taking a civilian driving test, but taking care to reverse up the slope.

The fast-approaching Iranian jeep was close behind, and

the driver suddenly realised that the strange pink Land Rover was trying to out-manoeuvre him by doubling back on itself.

The Persian saw that his only chance was to close the gap by cutting directly across the slope. Had he been properly trained in mountain driving, he would have known the dangers of turning a vehicle round on a steep slope. He would also have understood why the driver of the strange vehicle was making such a careful straight-line manoeuvre. Swinging the wheel, so that the jeep was straddled horizontally across the slope, he instantly realised his mistake. The uppermost wheels gently lifted as gravity took command and the vehicle began to topple. Both driver and passenger, taken by surprise, lost their grip and were poured out of the vehicle in an ungainly heap. The upturned machine rolled over them, crushing their bodies remorselessly as it began barrelling down the slope.

Perkis had stopped and watched, fascinated by the macabre sight. "Gawd, Scottie. That was 'orrible."

"I blame you." McDermid was grinning. "C'mon, y' great fairy, let's see if y' canna catch up wi' t' Hawk."

Seconds later, Panther One was bouncing hard across country, running alongside the wadi. After ten minutes the familiar shape of the other Land Rover appeared ahead down in the wadi. It was stationary. Perkis slammed on the brakes. "What's up?" McDermid asked.

Two figures were crouched by the rear offside wheel of Panther Two. It was John Belcher who turned around. "We've fucked up the rear axle, old lad! Bloody great pot-hole."

Perkis killed the engine and scrambled down the wadi embankment. "Let's 'ave a look-see . . ."

Hawksby stood up from examining the damage. "Forget it, Jim. I'm afraid this old charabanc isn't going any farther."

The Cockney glanced up the slope, tilting his head to one side, his eyes alert. "Hey boss, none of us is goin' any place if we don't get out!"

Hawksby listened. Water. Dammit! It was always a risk to use the dried-up river beds at the start of the rainy season.

But using them to keep out of view of their pursuers had levelled the odds. Until now. Somewhere in those distant hills it must have rained. Heavily.

He grabbed Eva and hauled her out of her seat. "Quick, up the embankment! And you, Jonathan, MOVE IT!"

They stared at him as though he was mad, not comprehending. Then they saw the urgency with which the others began off-loading vital equipment.

Pogo Penaia said solemnly: "I'll set a charge."

"Be sharpish," Hawksby replied, pushing Blake towards the embankment.

Belcher scrambled up the wadi side, loaded down with weapons and a medical bag while Hawksby scooped up the few remaining secret papers and ciphers. There were few maps left, as it was routine practice to destroy each one once they had crossed the territory concerned.

Perkis smashed the Skywave set and the vehicle's Clansman.

Pogo was sorting out a fuse. "Hey, Jim, take my gun and that bag. I got my last Mars bar in it."

Perkis obliged and headed for the edge of the wadi.

Then it happened.

Hawksby had seen it before in Oman. Perkis had only heard about it. He knew how it happened and the speed with which it occurred, but still it took him by surprise. Pogo, too, had witnessed once what happened when a dried-out watercourse, that had been bone hard for months or years, was suddenly fed with water from distant hills. But he had never thought of it happening to him.

Until the last moment the noise of the approaching torrent had been muted by the distant thunder. Only as the solid wall of mud-brown water rounded the bend like a mammoth helter-skelter did he realised it was upon him.

"POGO!" Perkis screamed.

A giant ten feet high fist of water smashed the Fijian square in the face as he looked up from setting the fuse. Its sheer force hurled him before it as contemptuously as a rag doll. The streaming eruption passed on regardless like an express train on a downhill run. Water creamed around

Perkis's legs, trying to pluck him in too. Kangers yanked him to safety and the vortex swirled past, dragging Panther Two with it. For a moment it was as though the trusty Land Rover had a mind of its own, determined to resist. Then it began to shift and move away with the current. A dead sheep floated after it.

"Oh, my God," Blake breathed. "Poor bugger didn't stand a chance."

Eva Olsen opened her mouth. She could find no words.

No one else said a thing. Hawksby felt sick.

Perkis stared after the raging torrent in disbelief. Then he looked down at the canvas bag by his feet, and the Mars bar that had tumbled out.

As they climbed aboard a heavily over-laden Panther One there was a dull distant *crump* and a flicker of brightness farther down the reborn tributary as Pogo's demolition charge blew on the lost Land Rover. Even in death the Fijian had done no less than what was expected of him.

It was in grim mood that Perkis drove the vehicle westwards up the lower slopes of the coastal hills. An irrational feeling was growing at the back of his mind that he would never get to see his new son. He tried to ignore the evidence that the enemy was closing in, but he couldn't dispel his fears. There had been one cock-up after another; it was as though the fickle gods of war were conspiring against them. First Forbsie and now Pogo Penaia. God knows how many SAS-hardened years of battle experience and training behind them. Unflappable, indestructible. That's how they had always seemed.

In the regiment you were trained to fight against everything, starting with your own human frailties. Coping with adversity and turning it to advantage was a stock-in-trade. But what could you do if fate and luck were stacked against you? He knew the very thought was a blasphemy, and the fact that it had even entered his head had appalled him. But noticing the solemn silence that had fallen over the others, he knew he was not alone. Even the Hawk looked pale and drawn, and there was a weariness in those normally penetrating and alert eyes.

The silence was broken by McDermid. "Chopper!" he shouted suddenly.

Dawn had brought another day of harsh, tropical sunlight. It was against a deepening ultramarine skyline that they saw the heavy Chinook transport helicopter hovering like a giant insect. Hawksby had been studying his last remaining map of the area. "Pull over, Jim," he said quickly. "Let's find some cover."

The driver had already located a likely spot, a hollow in the gradient that would screen them from the troops disgorging from the helicopter. He picked his way into the shelter of the rock and switched off the engine.

Instinctively, all eyes turned towards Hawksby. He sounded confident as he spoke. "I'm afraid it's time to destroy the vehicle and finish the job on foot. Now the sun's up there's precious little cover in these hills. If it's any consolation, it's only about ten miles to the RV."

"Not exactly downhill though, is it?" Blake said, looking at the distant ridge. He felt exhausted just thinking about the trudge under the Gulf sun.

McDermid nudged him. "It'll make a man o' ye!"

Hawksby suppressed a grin. It was good to have the tough Glaswegian with them. His dour humour, when it could be understood, was a palatable tonic. No one else felt much like joking, but now the major could sense the mood of the group lightening.

Eva asked: "Do you t'ink t'ey know where we iss? I mean t'at 'elicopter wass putting men down . . ."

Hawksby didn't want to harp on negative aspects. After losing Pogo, morale was low enough. "They only know our rough position, otherwise we'd have come under fire by now. But even if they close in on us on the coast, we'll be at our destination. And that means as good as out. So cheer up. All is not lost." He smiled reassuringly at everyone, but the returning expressions showed doubts. "Okay," he added suddenly, "we'll take only vital kit and distribute it between us all. Jonathan and Eva, I hope you don't mind taking something?"

"Do we have a choice?" Blake asked. He hadn't meant it to

sound carping, but it did.

"Not really," Hawksby replied, smiling, and handed him spare water carriers.

"How's your arm?" John Belcher asked Kangers.

The Austrian was taken aback. "Thought you'd forgotten about that. Bloody decent of you t' ask. Why, you gonna carry me to the RV?"

Belcher shook his head sadly. "Afraid not, old boy. If you're too weak to walk, I'm afraid we'll have to shoot you."

"I do believe you mean that, Butcher," the other drawled. "Thanks, but I'll manage."

The journey was less strenuous than nerve-racking. It was conducted in a series of slow leopard crawls between the patches of meagre cover offered by the bald, desiccated landscape. Hawksby and Perkis led the way, moving to each point offering shelter, where they would wait with firearms cocked to give covering fire in the event of attack. Once they were in position, Eva and Blake followed with McDermid, who hissed instructions on the elbows-and-knees movement and constantly warned them to keep their backsides down.

When they had joined the party on 'point', the end-group of Belcher and Kangers would wait, with weapons readied, until Hawksby and Perkis had wormed their way on to the next resting place. All the SAS troopers had smoke grenades at the ready in case the helicopter decided to make a nuisance of itself. If it had, the streams of green smoke would have obliterated the landscape long enough for Blake and the girl to make a dash for freedom.

That was a risk to be taken only in dire emergency. To prevent such a surprise Tiger had gone solo, remaining at the bottom of the hillside to watch for any elements in pursuit. The little man from Nepal had immediately volunteered for the role and no one argued. However much they trained, they'd never quite match the stealth and natural aptitude of the Gurkha. It was quietly understood by all, although no one actually admitted it. While he waited, Tiger set a timed demolition charge with the remaining plastic explosive that would vaporise the abandoned Land Rover.

After an hour of reasonable progress, Hawksby indicated back down to McDermid to approach with added caution.

The Scot's big hand slapped hard down on Eva's bottom as she wriggled across the tract of exposed hillside.

Keeping her belly touching the earth she strained painfully on, trying to keep her mind off her upper thighs, which felt as though they were going to part company with her groin. As she reached the patch of scrub, she turned back to face McDermid as he joined them. There were tears of pain in her eyes. "You, Corporal, iss a bastard!"

He grinned and put a finger to his lips, anxious to find out the reason for Hawksby's warning. "There's a whole line of 'em, Scottie," the major said. "They've fanned out since the chopper dropped them. Now they're combing down the hillside towards us. Nearest one's about a mile away."

He turned back to the others. "I've been looking at the map. There might be a way round them." McDermid frowned. It was unusual for the Hawk to hesitate if he had a bright idea. Although, for the life of him, the Scotsman didn't see what the exposed windswept landscape had to offer.

The major pointed out a large natural indentation in the hillside a quarter of a mile from where they sat. "There's a *qanat*, Scottie. Over there. It runs right under the hillside for miles. It would bring us up behind those Iranians as they come down."

McDermid knew then why Hawksby had hesitated. His blood ran cold.

"I dunna ken I've got t' bottle fer this, boss," McDermid muttered as they scrambled down to the sheltered *maqsam*: artistically-laid bricks formed a neat archway around the mouth of the *qanat*, from which the cool water cascaded, splashing into a shallow stone pool. At the far end of it a series of low, dividing piers separated the water into channels to serve different villages in the valley below.

"Blimey," Perkis said, sitting in the shade of the solitary mulberry tree. "'Ow far d'you say it goes boss?"

"This one is just seven miles," Hawksby replied. "Horizontal and straight into the hillside. Then, of course, it's joined by the vertical down-shafts. I plan to go up the last one of them, which will bring us out near the peak."

"Jesus wept," Kangers breathed. "That'll be like climbin' up a bleedin' waterfall."

Hawksby shook his head. "No, *qanats* aren't natural rivers as such. They don't tap springs or anything. They just collect condensation from the high ground and bring it together in one place to irrigate the farms. Damn clever really. Those vertical shafts were used by the builders to take out excavated earth. And for maintenance, of course. And they're used as wells . . ."

"Still," Kangers muttered, "having seen what happened to that wadi, I betcha they're goin' to be a bit wet. It's been rainin' somewhere round here, that's fer sure!"

"It'll be a bit damp," Hawksby conceded.

McDermid took a deep breath. He'd always loathed the flooded waterpipe in training. Everyone had a pet fear and his was tunnels. Tunnels were the things he had 'bad dreams' about. For others it was something different. Kangers Webster, he knew, had made over a thousand parachute jumps, but he still couldn't sleep well the night before.

At that moment Tiger emerged from the vegetation that grew alongside the irrigation canals. He didn't look too happy. "They closing, boss," he said simply. "But they come slow. Cautious. With luck we have maybe half-hour."

Hawksby took stock. Just thirty minutes before troops moving up the valley met those coming down. Then they would realise that their prey had disappeared somewhere in between. The *qanat* would be an obvious hiding place, but not necessarily an obvious route of escape.

"I'm afraid," the major said, "that if we attempt just to hide until nightfall, we'll be found. Our only chance is to move deep inside the hills and scale one of the wall shafts." Blake gave Eva a reassuring hug, but both looked apprehensive. "It'll be no worse than potholing. These *qanats* are centuries old, and we'd have to be pretty unlucky for the whole thing to collapse. The biggest danger is from panic, so for God's sake, try and keep your heads no matter what." He addressed himself to Blake and Eva. "We've all done caving, so you're in safe hands. As long as you do *exactly* what you're told. Remember, if anything does go wrong, there are shafts at regular intervals both in front and behind you. Any collapse is unlikely. And a collapse that blocked all means of escape would be damned unlucky."

"What if we get stuck in t'e 'ole?" Eva asked. Earnestly.

"No' much chance o' tha' wi' ye, lassie," McDermid replied. He'd meant it to sound comforting; it just sounded lewd.

Hawksby ignored the remark. "The body does swell when immersed, but muscle control is the more important factor. That's why I said you must keep calm. We'll send the biggest chap through first though, just to make sure."

"Thanks a million," Kangers muttered. "Have you noticed how the English always put us Aussies or the Scots in every bloody spearhead . . ."

"Stow it!" McDermid hissed. The prospect of this burrowing operation was preying on his mind; the sooner they got started, the sooner it would be over.

"The biggest threat is from the rains," Hawksby continued, "but last night's storm appeared to be out at sea, although it looks like those hills caught some of it. As we saw, the streams take the brunt. However, as moisture soaks through, it might affect this *qanat*. By how much we can only guess. Nevertheless, at the first sign of a rise in water level, we'll stay put at a well-shaft. Again, I remind you that they are spaced fairly closely, so don't get alarmed unduly." Hawksby turned to Kangers. "Don't worry, I'll be right behind you. We'll give our belt-orders to the others, so we're carrying as little as possible. Especially anything that can get us jammed in a tight spot."

"Sweet Jesus," Blake breathed. "This can't be happening."

But within a few minutes, the weird expedition had begun. Kangers Webster led the way into the dark mouth of the *qanat*, wading against the noisy flow of clear water and playing his rubberised torch over the six feet arch. Immediately behind came Hawksby, then Tiger. As the team's most proficient mountaineer, the task of scaling one of the well-shafts would fall to him.

Next followed John Belcher, loaded with a bundle of straightish branches hewn from the mulberry tree at the *maqsam*. These would be used to cross any deep troughs in the tunnel, or for shoring-up any suspect sections, or even as angle-joists to be wedged across the well-shaft, providing footholds for the ascent.

Blake and Eva Olsen followed next, carrying the leading members' belt-packs. McDermid and Jim Perkis brought up the rear, their Uzis at the ready in case they were followed into the tunnel.

It was an eerie sensation as the bright light of the entrance hole receded and finally disappeared around a bend. Torchlight threw distorted shadows on the crumbling walls. The only sound was the urgent gurgle of water around their knees and the occasional sound of equipment brushing against the earth sides. The smell of damp soil filled the air.

Imperceptibly the muddy bed began to incline, but the roof stayed level, forcing the column to walk at a slight crouch. It made the going more difficult, but no one complained. The absence of a speaking voice heightened the sense of isolation. It was the concentrated silence of unspoken fear. The walls of the *qanat* seemed to press in again. Hunched shoulders were rubbing against the moist earth of the roof. Despite the torches it seemed very dark and it was getting darker.

Ahead someone let out a yelp of surprise. A wild flapping sound resounded down the tunnel.

Instinctively Eva ducked. "God! What wass t'at?" Behind her, McDermid, too, had reacted in the same way. He could have well believed it was some subterranean beast unknown to mankind. "Jest a bat, I expect," he said.

"Oh, God, I 'ad never t'ought of t'at!" she replied.

"It was just a bird, luv," Perkis' voice piped up from the back. "S'pect 'e was more frightened than us."

"Speak fer y'self, lad," McDermid hissed.

Perkis played the light from his torch over the roof above their heads. "Look, them's the bats. 'Undreds of the little bleeders. No bigger 'n butterflies."

Eva shrieked.

"Cut it OUT!" McDermid thundered. "We can do wi'oot y' nature lessons, thank y', lad!"

The girl was down on her knees in the water, splashing about, trying to brush imagined bats from her hair.

"It's all right, Scottie," Perkis protested. "They'll stay put if we don't disturb 'em."

McDermid helped Eva to her feet, feeling distinctly queasy himself. "I'll bleedin' disturb ye, Perkis, if y' dunna shut y' gob!"

Stumbling around the next bend, they saw the welcoming dazzle of sunlight from the first well-shaft. Relieved, they clambered forward as the tunnel opened out.

"There, see!" Perkis was delighted. He splashed across to a rocky ledge where a bird's nest had been built. He peered in. "Eggs. Pied Wagtail, I reckon. Ol' Kangers must've scared 'er off. Don't reckon it matters. Too late in the season. Probably won't 'atch any'ow."

"I dunna care if it's a bleedin' dodo's nest y've discovered, lad. Just get on, will y'?"

The light relief was short-lived. Once they had left the well-head, the pool of light had quickly disappeared and, once again, the tunnel closed in. The flow of water had increased noticeably and they frequently found themselves wading waist high in water. They came across more well-shafts, but now the sunlight failed to penetrate. At each one the circle of sky above became smaller as they moved deeper and deeper under the hills.

Ahead, Kangers Webster came across the first real obstacle. He discovered that the floor of the tunnel dropped away deceptively beneath the black surface of the water. Gingerly, he put a foot forward and placed it down. It didn't hit bottom and Hawksby caught him in time to prevent him falling.

"Reckon it goes to the centre of the bleedin' earth," the Australian observed.

Swimming the thirty feet of collapsed floor was a gruelling business which left everyone soaked and depressed. It also served to slow them down considerably – a delay they could ill afford.

As they pressed on, it was Perkis who first saw the outline of someone's head peering over the rim of a well-head high above. It was so far distant that it was impossible to tell if it was a child from a local village, or an adult. But as he heard something dropped, bouncing noisily against the sides of the shaft, he feared the worst.

"Someone at the well-head!" he hissed at McDermid. "Tell 'em to speed it up." But, before the message reached the front of the column, there was an explosion behind them that set their ears ringing. The shockwave from the blast expanded down the tunnel, forming a solid wall of displaced air. It toppled everyone forward like ninepins, as loose stones and smoke chased them into the darkness. Shrapnel sang in the confined space.

Perkis cursed as he felt the metal slivers whip at his back. Something stung behind his right knee and his leg gave way, pitching him face-forward into the water.

"Oh, stuff me . . .!" McDermid could hardly believe his eyes as the fragile roof soil started to shower into the stream behind them. "COLLAPSE!" he warned, feverishly hauling Perkis from the water. Blake lent a hand while Eva repeated the warning to the rest of the party, who had disappeared from sight. Thick clouds of dust rolled towards them.

For McDermid, it was coming face-to-face with his one and only personal phobia. As the blanket of dust enveloped them, blotting out the torchlight and working its way into ears, nose and mouth, he felt as though he would suffocate. For a moment, he panicked, tempted to leave Perkis at his feet and run. He was brought to his senses by the plaintive, choking voice of Eva. "Corp-or-al Sc-ott-ie!"

Sand-blind, he finally hauled Perkis clear of the water. Summoning strength beyond the natural capabilities of his wiry frame, he heaved the hapless trooper forward. "Put somethin' round y' mouth, lassie!" he cried, unable to follow his own advice. He collided with Eva in the swirling, orange murk. She reached forward to help, but Blake pushed her aside.

311

"Join the others, quick!" he said and grabbed Perkis' other arm.

"I'm obliged," McDermid muttered, as he struggled on with the body.

From some distance ahead came another deep-throated roar. The whole tunnel trembled. Earth trickled from the roof.

"Christ," Blake said, "Was that another grenade?"

McDermid spat sand from his mouth. "Aye, lad, reckon they're tryin' te bury us alive."

"Looks like they've succeeded." Blake was surprised at the calm resignation in his voice. Like most people, he had wondered how he would face death whenever it came to him. He'd never guessed it would be like this – that he could accept it so quietly.

The tunnel was wider now. The flow of water had been stopped and much of the dust had settled thickly on the surface, rapidly turning it to liquid sludge. He managed to get Perkis' arm around one shoulder. The young Cockney tried to shake off the numbness in his head. He knew he was concussed and he knew he'd swallowed a gallon of water. Stupidly, he recalled the small fish he'd seen in the stream and wondered if he'd swallowed any. He tried to say thanks to whoever was carrying him, but when he opened his mouth, he just felt sick.

"Okay, don't talk," Blake said kindly. "We'll have you out of here in no time."

McDermid was surprised by the journalist's attitude. It wasn't in keeping. "We will?"

Blake laughed harshly – an incongruous sight in a mud-and-blood-streaked face. "Course we will – Corp. What is your lot's motto: 'Dare to be great'?"

"Somethin' like tha'."

Light glowed through the dust-laden air. It was Hawksby. "Are you all right?" he demanded, shining his torch.

"Your driver's been injured," Blake replied.

"It's nothin' much," McDermid added.

Perkis managed a weak laugh. "I'll be the judge of that . . . What's happened up front, boss?"

Hawksby waved aside the choking clouds. "Like what

happened back here, I imagine. A collapse. But Tiger and Kangers are trying to dig a way through."

"What iss our chances?" Eva asked. She didn't sound hopeful.

"Ask again in ten minutes," he answered tersely. "Meanwhile it'll help if we can join the others and form a crocodile to clear away the debris where they're working."

"I use stave to make hole," Tiger reported. "I get through to other side of fall. At least now we get air."

"Thank J.C. for that," Kangers muttered as he struck his entrenching tool into the soft silt. His back was dripping with sweat. McDermid was frustrated that there was barely room for two to work at a time. "It'll take Rolf Harris here a month-a bleedin' Sundays to get through. Put y' back into it, lad, y' no diggin' the Piccadilly Line extension."

"Sod off, Mac," Kangers replied. "We're through now, anyway."

Thankfully he slung down the short spade and shone his torch through the aperture.

"Well?" McDermid demanded impatiently. He was convinced that the entire tunnel would collapse at any moment.

"It's not the well-shaft," Kangers mumbled, half to himself. "The wall's collapsed into the shaft, I reckon, and created a new pocket. Sorta by-pass. I think . . . yes . . . I think we can get back into the tunnel at the other end. Bit dodgy though. This pocket is just loose soil. One sneeze 'n' the lot'll come down."

Hawksby was relieved. "You volunteering, Kangers?"

The Australian chuckled. "Threatenin' me with RTU, eh? Okay."

He wormed his way into the eighteen-inch hole and through the newly-created chamber. The others followed gingerly, not daring to look up, ignoring the constant sprinkling of soil from the unsafe ceiling.

Hawksby was last through. "Hellfire, I don't *ever* want to do *that* again!"

"Nonsense, boss," McDermid said, his bravado returning. "Ought te make it standard induction trainin' in future."

At least from the well-head above, it would appear as though there was no way past the shaft. Hawksby consoled himself with the thought. But if they had been given a reprieve, they had also been given another problem. With the *qanat* now blocked in two places, the water level was rising dramatically. It was happening too fast for them to have a chance of reaching the next shaft before the water reached the roof of the tunnel. They were also slowed by a wounded man.

Just beyond the collapse, the tunnel fanned out into an elongated cavern. At least it gave them the chance to rest and to look at Perkis' injuries. While they were doing that, Hawksby sent McDermid and Tiger back to try and create a new watercourse around the collapse.

"A piece of shrapnel's pierced a ligament," Belcher said, inspecting the back of Perkis' knee. "Not much I can do here, except strap it up tight. His back looks worse than it is. Peppered with steel fragments, but nothing serious. His son and missus can spend many happy hours picking the pieces out for years to come."

"Don't soddin' talk about me as if I ain't 'ere, Butcher!"

Belcher smiled mischievously. "Just think yourself lucky, old man, you didn't get yourself an impromptu vasectomy back there."

"Leave it out, yer bleedin' quack. Just get on wiv it." Perkis purposely ignored the medic, and turned instead to Blake. "Thanks, mate, by the way. It was pretty 'airy back there an' I'd 'ave understood if you'd just bolted an' left me to it."

Blake looked embarrassed. "I reckon all this derring-do rubs off after a while." He tried to make light of it. "Mind you, I still reckon you blokes must be bloody mad to do this sort of thing for a living."

Ten minutes later, Hawksby decided to risk it to the next well-shaft. The water level had not risen for some time, and it was worth a gamble. There was no way back and, if the water rose any more, they would be entombed three hundred feet below Iranian soil in a watery grave. Not a pleasant way to go.

Only one serious obstacle came between them and the next well-shaft. A stretch of the *qanat* had obviously suffered a cave in at some earlier time and the tunnel was reduced to a mere eighteen-inch circle. Swollen by the earlier storm, the onrush of water filled it completely. It was Tiger who volunteered to try and get through. He was the smallest and undoubtedly the best swimmer. For a full minute the little Gurkha thrashed in the flooded tube before he reached the other side. It had been touch and go. But now, roped to each other through the hole, it was just possible to be hauled through in half-a-minute. Provided, of course, that the swimmer did not panic.

Surprisingly, only Perkis did. His crippled leg dragged behind him, slowing him down until he felt that his lungs would explode. Hawksby had ducked in after him and given a mighty shove which sent the younger man bobbing up through the surface of water of the tunnel beyond.

"Now keep quiet everyone," Hawksby warned. "We're nearing the well-shaft and sound travels down here. I don't give a damn what happens – even if you're attacked by water snakes – scream in *total* silence."

Tension at the thought of escaping from their underground confinement charged the humid atmosphere of the *qanat*. Tiger edged forwards to where the faint glimmer of distant daylight outlined the mouth in the roof of the tunnel. Stepping nimbly onto Kangers' cradled hands, he reached up for a handhold on the rocky side of the vertical three hundred foot shaft.

When his feet were astride the shaft, he began moving up like a ferret in a rabbit-hole, selecting foothold after foothold with remarkable agility, occasionally showering those below with dislodged earth. Every now and again he would stop and use the string of interlinked toggle ropes to haul up one of the staves. They had been a hellish nuisance on the trip, but now they proved their worth, jammed across the shaft to provide welcome security and steps for the inexperienced climbers.

Belcher muttered to no one in particular: "I hope he remembers to come back for the rest of us."

Tiger Ratna had other things on his mind as he approached the last twenty feet below the well-head. The dazzling brightness of the sky was a welcome sight, but he was more concerned with what might be waiting for him at the top. He slowed his pace, feeling increasingly confident as he edged his way up the last few feet, the blade of the *kukri* clamped between his teeth. Vaguely he wondered if his late father could see him now? Wondered if he had felt the same cool self-assurance and superiority over the enemy when he had stalked Japs in the Burmese jungle. Now Tiger continued the family tradition, an almost monastic existence devoted to soldiery; the warrior caste from the foothills of Nepal.

He caught the body scent in his nostrils. Downwind. Not far. A prickle of anticipation crawled down his spine. Very slowly he shifted his left foot to a new position, resting on a protruding knob of rock. His muscles tightened to take his weight and he inched upward.

Then he caught another waft. Cigarette smoke. Cheap. Tinged with something else. The liquorice smell of graphite oil. That meant guns. Guns that had been recently cleaned and checked. Good men. He heard someone chuckle. Maybe not that good, he thought. Finally Tiger's hair appeared, encircled in the camouflaged bandana. But with his head tilted right back so that he could look down his nose, there was precious little of him to see. After a while what there was dipped out of sight again.

For a moment he thought about the scene indelibly etched in his mind's eye. A barren, sun-scorched hillslope sizzling in the unrelenting midday haze. Not a breath of wind. Sky more white than blue. Patches of shrivelled scrub almost as brown as the dun-coloured earth. Next to the well-head the simple wooden windlass, like a giant frame-constructed bobbin, which lowered the goatskin bags down into the *qanat*, had been cast aside. Two men sat on the ground, supporting their backs against one of the struts. The soldiers had their backs to him, facing away down to the distant river valley. Farther down the slope dark specks were gathered around another well-head. No doubt it was where the grenades had been thrown in. From that distance he couldn't be sure, but he had the impression someone was being lowered down.

Presumably they were only expecting to find corpses, because the two troopers in front of him were obviously not thinking anyone would crawl out this far up the *qanat*. Not for the first time, Tiger wondered at the stupidity of professional soldiers around the world. Even in peacetime their lives could depend on vigilance. They were in the profession dedicated to the destruction of the most cunning, savage beast on earth: fellow man. Yet everywhere they had the arrogance to assume that no one would dare to strike them down.

Dimly he recalled his father's words, many years before. 'When you join the Gurkhas you marry into the martial arts. For your life will never be the same as for other men. You will never cease to be watchful and wary. You will go about your business with a respect and single-mindedness that will astound others. And you will practise and refine your skills with dedication and the ferocity of a mountain cat. Because you know that you are better than any warrior pitted against you, you will not fear.'

He slid over the rim of the well-head on his belly like a snake, swinging his feet up clear of the surrounding stones. Now crouched, he stepped forward tentatively. A basking lizard, which was perfectly camouflaged, scuttled away from him and into the cover of some rocks. He froze. The two soldiers appeared not to hear the movement; they continued chatting in low voices. In total silence, he unslung the Uzi sub-machine gun. He had already decided that was how he was going to deal with them. There was no one else in immediate earshot and trying to tackle two with the *kukri* in total silence left room for mistakes. And Tiger Ratna did not make mistakes. As his father had always warned him, a Gurkha only ever made one mistake. His last.

Phut! Phut! The first seated soldier suddenly lunged forward awkwardly, half thrown by the force of the silenced 9 mm rounds that smashed into the back of his head. For a split second the other soldier thought his companion had fainted. He reached forward for him. Then he caught a glimpse of the dishevelled figure hidden behind the windlass. *Phut*! The third shot missed its mark. As he opened his mouth to speak, he caught the fourth round squarely in the temple.

Tiger advanced quickly but with caution, kicking the Iranian's weapons out of arm's reach. The first soldier was stone dead. The second was still breathing.

He'd known it happen before. A bullet could pass in one temple and out through the other side, leaving the victim blind but alive. Without hesitation, Tiger took the *kukri* still clenched between his teeth and cut the man's throat with one deft blow.

It took the Gurkha only a few minutes' struggle to position the windlass back over the well-head and drop down the rope. It made the climb much easier for everyone, especially Eva, Blake and Perkis, who had little control over his right leg. At stages, they could rest on the cross-members formed by the staves before continuing the ascent.

Hawksby glanced at the corpses of the two Iranian soldiers. "No trouble?" he asked Tiger.

"No, boss. Them as good as gold."

"Get them out the way. I don't want to advertise our presence. Throw them down the well."

Blake protested. "That's village drinkwater."

"If you've got a better place," Hawksby said, glancing over the barren landscape, "it's fine by me. Don't worry, they'll soon find 'em when they start a search."

Blake glanced at Eva for support, but none was forthcoming. She was past the stage of caring and just wanted to be gone from this oven-baked land.

A mile farther up the hillside, the unbroken desolation of the lower slopes gave way to a thin covering of spindly acacias and poplars which provided some welcome shade and cover. They trudged on over the ridge, through a flooded watercourse that ran between two peaks. Beyond, the land fell away in a series of low, undulating hillocks to the Gulf, blinding white in a shimmering sea mist.

CHAPTER NINETEEN

From their hide beneath the upturned Raiders on the rendez-vous beach, Captain Johnny Fraser's Sabre team maintained watch on the approaches with mounting tension.

Mark Benjamin, a good-humoured Jewish corporal with a mop of unkempt black hair, turned away from the observation periscope. "How long overdue are they, boss?"

"Five or six hours," Fraser replied. He was seated by the radio, anxiously awaiting the expected signal from Hawksby.

"They *must* have run into problems," Sergeant 'Brummie' Turner said emphatically.

"Hark at Cheerful Charlie!" Corporal Bill Mather added in disgust. An SAS veteran, he wasn't given to worrying unduly when missions didn't go to plan. As usual he took his mind off things by going through the unnecessary ritual of cleaning his gun. He'd only checked it over an hour earlier.

"Might be having transmission difficulties," suggested Benjamin, now back at the periscope.

Bill Mather wasn't convinced. "Not with Tiger on board. Signals wizard. Unlikely."

"Hey-ho," Benjamin said suddenly, pressing his eye closer to the rubber socket of the periscope. "It's party time, folks. A bleedin' great chopper's just landed with a couple o' dozen of Crazy K's men. Leapin' about all over the shop."

"*You're joking!*" Fraser was stunned. He had heard nothing above the noise of breaking surf.

"I don't make jokes about business," Benjamin answered evenly.

Already Mather and Brummie had begun rapidly stowing their kit ready to move. It was unlikely they'd be waiting for nightfall now. Suddenly the earpiece of Fraser's Pocketfone, lying discarded by the larger Clansman set, crackled. He snatched it up.

"Snapdragon to Neptune, do you read? Over."

"Hawksby? Is that you?" Fraser demanded in disbelief.

"Sorry if I made you jump, Johnny. Our last Clansman got bent while we were pot-holing. Thank God you had the sense to keep this on. Over."

"Christ," Fraser said. "You must be close! How far? Over."

"About a mile," Hawksby replied. *"Transmission's a sod in these hills. Why d'you sound distraught? Over."*

"Two seconds ago a party of Iranians started stamping their big boots all over the RV area. Are you in trouble? Over."

"Just footsore. But we had a few close shaves. I'll tell you about it in the Mess one day. Your visitors must be the mob we shook off earlier. What's their position? Over."

"Hold on." Fraser said, and spoke to Mark Benjamin. "Hello, Snapdragon, listen. They've taken the high ground to the north of the cove. Appear to be setting up an ambush position. Right over your line of approach to us. Over."

A pause as the significance sank in. Then: *"Oh shit!"*

The Iranians had taken the high ground dominating the sandy cove and they directly overlooked the footpath that wound down through the scrub to the beach.

Whilst Hawksby was grateful for Johnny Fraser's timely warning, it hadn't solved the problem of how to get access to the RV, which itself lay directly under the enemy guns – although they did not yet appreciate that.

Fraser knew the ground well and had quickly made a suggestion that appeared to provide the only solution in the circumstances. Top priority must go to getting Blake and Eva Olsen out safely, but Hawksby did not want to leave anyone behind. And that looked like proving difficult with Perkis. Nevertheless, Hawksby decided, they would have to grin and bear it, and negotiate the rocky outcrop on the seaward side of the footpath, until they reached the beach. Although it was overlooked by the high ground, at least it offered substantial hard cover, and was probably the least expected, and certainly most uncomfortable, route of approach.

As the SAS major and Fraser finalised their battle plan by radio, it was decided that only Hawksby and McDermid would remain near the path. They would offer diversionary fire whilst the remainder of the group began working their way around the outcrop. At the last moment the two remaining men would make a dash – straight down the path to the beach and, hopefully, board one of the Rigid Raiders before they left the shore.

Fraser had called up HMS *Antler* to advise them that the plans had been advanced. The commander was not amused. The rescue operation was meant to be in the dead of night, a secret and relatively safe operation, free from the risk of attack and international repercussions. Not least of his problems was that he was still cruising fifty miles offshore.

Hawksby glanced down at the pile of ammuniton by his feet. It had been grudgingly donated by the rest of the group, who now had no more than a single magazine apiece.

"Not a lot," McDermid observed.

"Better than nothing."

"I suppose we could always throw stones."

Hawksby settled down in the *sangar*, the circle of rocks which formed a natural fortress, and thumbed the last spare 9 mm rounds into a magazine. "Where are the others now?"

"I caught a glimpse o' the lassie's bum a coupla seconds ago. 'Boot halfway I'd say." He added appreciatively: "She's a tasty lass, boss, 'n' no mistake. Y'll have y' work cut oot wi' tha' one."

Absently Hawksby said: "Let's not bring that up again, Scottie."

"Aw, c'mon, boss. Mission's over, near enough. Good luck te ye, tha's what I say."

Hawksby half-smiled to himself. McDermid seemed sure enough they'd get out. He wished he could share the Scotsman's dogged confidence. Even more he wished they hadn't been forced to leave behind all the flares, grenades and plastic explosive. He understood then why sub-machine guns were termed 'small arms'. Suddenly they seemed exactly that. Small.

He said: "I'd like you to know, Scottie – just in case we don't all get out of this – that I've been very pleased with the team. Despite the few ups and downs. Very pleased."

McDermid grunted as he studied the Iranian positions overlooking the cove. "We'll get out, boss, no trouble."

"I just wanted you to know. That's all."

The Scotsman twisted his lean sunburnt face around to look straight at Hawksby. His dark eyes were hard, the skin around them drawn tight and etched with exhaustion. "Y've been in this outfit quite a while, Major, but y've still a thing or two te learn aboot the men, if y'll forgive me for sayin'. An' aboot y'self."

Hawksby felt his own teeth grind. "Careful, Scottie, the mission might be over. Just be sure it's not your career as well."

McDermid snorted. "I'm no gettin' younger, boss. My time is limited, but y' might be leadin' future ops. So I dunna really give a damn."

The major said nothing. He stared unseeing at the Iranian positions. The corporal spoke slowly, selecting his words, "Y're respected throughout the regiment, Major, but it doesna make y' another Stirling. Ye like givin' orders an' dunna like listenin' te ideas from others. Y've messed up on aspects of plannin' and in some parts of the op itself. If y'd listened an' discussed more, maybe we'd have been out o' here b'noo. Y'canna handle the unexpected too well. Like now. Y're best when y've got the initiative. Bloody good. Like when I was wi' y' in Oman. So my advice is . . ." He hesitated.

Hawksby watched him, mesmerised by the clarity and perception of the Scotman's observations. He didn't like what he heard, but he knew it was largely true. Then he realised that McDermid was waiting for permission to finish. To give his verdict.

"Well?" the major said stiffly.

"Get te know y' men better, Major, and dunna frighten

'em off wi' tha' goddamn reserve o' yours – Sorry." Apologetic in case he'd gone too far. "Just trust us an' listen te us a wee bit more. An' y'll be as good as y' reputation. Hawk."

Quietly Hawksby said: "That it, Scottie?"

"Jest one more thing," McDermid said. "I hope we'll be servin' t'gether back in Oman soon."

Hawksby felt the very reserve that McDermid had criticised begin to form a defensive barrier. For once, he ignored it. "You think we could stand another tour together?"

McDermid almost smiled. "I think maybe we're just gettin' te know each other, boss."

Hawksby did smile. Perversely, he felt better.

"Comin' up fer time," McDermid reminded, glancing at his watch.

Grabbing his Uzi, Hawksby scrambled up to the wall of boulders. He exchanged glances with the Scotsman and nodded.

The languid air of the Persian Gulf was torn apart by the violent, staccato chatter of automatic fire. Opposite, an Iranian soldier, who had been peering down to the footpath for sight of the expected enemy, did a spectacular Hollywood stuntman dive down the rockface.

After a few seconds' delay, the Iranians began returning fire. It was sporadic at first, but rapidly gathered momentum. Dust plumes rose in the rocky *sangar* and ricochets whistled around them, terrifyingly close. The two men dropped back behind cover.

"That's woken them up," Hawksby observed.

"Bleedin' woken me up too," McDermid replied.

The Iranian firepower gathered in ferocity, raining about them. It was professional and concentrated, but at least it diverted the enemy's attention away from the party on the outcrop. In a few minutes the rest of Snapdragon would reach the cove itself. After a while the gunfire melted away as the troops sought confirmation of whether their targets had been hit. Plans would be made to work around behind them, cutting off their retreat to the sea.

Hawksby peered around a slab of rock and let off a three-second burst. "Just to let them know we're still here."

Then they knew the main group had reached the beach. There were shouts in Farsi as someone raised the alarm. Orders were yelled. They could hear shots going in a new direction, the sound more muted.

Then came the real surprise for the Iranians. On the cove in front of them a yawning hole appeared in the sand, as if from nowhere. As the men from the Boat Troop lifted up the two Rigid Raiders that had formed the improvised roof of the hide, the lightweight mortar inside belched rudely into action. It had been Johnny Fraser's idea to bring it for just such an emergency, despite the extra weight it added. It was planned to give a blast of covering fire until the few rounds they carried between them were exhausted.

The 60 mm Hotchkiss-Brandt commando mortar was wildly inaccurate when hand-held, but it was good enough to lob three phosphorous bombs into the base of the high ground. Instantly an impenetrable curtain of smoke wafted skyward. The Iranian positions disappeared from view.

Hawksby and McDermid sprayed their remaining ammunition into the smoke as the Hotchkiss-Brandt began to discharge high-explosive bombs in a high arc, disappearing into seething white fog in a series of bright flashes. Below them in the cove, Tiger and John Belcher were helping Fraser's men down to the water's edge whilst the others sought what cover they could in the rockpools. The shrill whirr of heavy-duty outboards drifted across the beach.

Hawksby nudged McDermid, who was loosing off his last clip. "C'mon! Time to join Fraser's frogs!"

The Scotsman slung down the spent Uzi and followed Hawksby over the *sangar* wall and down the steep slope to the footpath.

The last six feet was a sheer drop onto soft sand and sparvo grass. The high ground climbed away above their heads, still streaming white smoke from Fraser's last mortar bombs. They sprinted down the path, muscles pumping, hearts pounding and minds blank to everything except the need to get down the footpath and onto the open sand.

Then, as they reached the beach, the ground opened up

before them in a blinding flash. Wicked shrapnel fragments seared in all directions. Staggering under the impact, both men toppled into the smouldering mortar crater.

"Jesus!" breathed Hawksby. Blood was streaming from a deep cut in his forehead. He tugged at the steel splinter embedded in the bone. "What the sweet fuck's happened to Johnny's aim?"

McDermid peered out of the crater. "It isna our mortar. It's the soddin' mad mullah's." As if in confirmation, two more bombs detonated in close proximity. The earth trembled and more debris showered over them.

Hawksby looked out of the crater rim, through the drifting ribbons of smoke, to the shore-line. Already one Raider was standing clear of the beach. Eva's blonde hair was unmistakable. The second waited impatiently, bobbing in the swell, held by a cluster of men knee-deep in water. One of them was yelling, but his words weren't carrying. Nevertheless, the meaning was clear enough.

"They've zero'd in on us, Scottie," Hawksby rasped. "Move from here and we'll be cut to blazes." To emphasise the point, thick fire from a heavy machine gun ploughed into the sand ahead of them.

Momentarily McDermid shut his eyes. He always knew it would have to end sometime. In a second the smoke would clear and the Iranians would just have to adjust the mortar settings. A piece of cake.

"We'll have to chance it," Hawksby decided.

McDermid desperately tried to think why they shouldn't. His mind was blank. Small arms fire clattered high up on the inland slope. At that distance it sounded deceptively ineffectual. Hawksby frowned. He hadn't remembered seeing Iranian troops up there. Perhaps they'd spread out during the smoke bombardment?

"There's a truck up there," he muttered half to himself. Fraser had mentioned a helicopter, so these must be reinforcements. They must have come along the old coastal camel track.

"Oh sod," McDermid groaned. "There's another two dozen of t' bastards. Swarmin' all over t' fuckin' place."

Hawksby looked puzzled. The Iranian mortaring had ceased abruptly. "Why've they stopped?"

McDermid shielded his eyes from the sun. "Fuck me, they're shootin' at t' bloody mullah's lot! Stupid soddin' goons."

A smile creased Hawksby's lips. This was unbelievable luck. But, sure enough, a ragtail platoon of men were working their way down the slope, waving all manner of improvised weapons in the air. Only a couple of them appeared to have firearms, but they were putting them to good effect. The new arrivals were directed by a big bearded scruff who was standing apart from them with a rolled bundle over his shoulder. Beside him stood a woman, her flowing black *chador* looking strangely macabre against the sun-bleached rocks.

Hawksby nudged McDermid. "Whoever they are, it's a bloody godsend, Scottie. Let's get to the boats!"

They rushed out of the crater and pounded across the hard wet sand to the waiting Raider. The sound of crashing surf, dazzling in the sunlit mist of spume, filled their ears. They began wading out to where the SAS captain stood holding the bucking craft.

"COME ON!" Johnny Fraser yelled. "THIS IS THE LAST BUS TODAY!"

"I HAVNA GOT BLEEDIN' FLIPPERS!" retorted McDermid, losing his balance as a breaker foamed around him. He threw himself into the Raider. Willing hands grabbed him and hauled him unceremoniously aboard.

The outboard roared, throttling up. Hawksby jumped, helped by Fraser who followed him expertly over the side.

"Christ!" McDermid bawled. "HANG ON! IT'S FORBSY! I DUNNA BELIEVE IT! LOOK! IT FUCKIN' WELL IS!"

Hawksby couldn't believe his ears. Already the Raider was starting to tear a wake through the rollers, drenching them all in salt spray.

"TURN ROUND!" Johnny Fraser ordered.

Mark Benjamin threw the tiller, bringing them broadside-on to the beach. They crawled up the side of a wavecrest which threatened to turtle them. The trough opened up and they swept into it, bracing themselves for the thunderous crash of the next roller.

Hawksby's eyes stung so he could hardly see. He could feel his skin already caked in salt. Two dark figures lumbered out from the shoreline, struggling against the tide. The water tugged at the woman's sodden *chador*, threatening to drag her back to the beach.

"TAKE IT BLOODY OFF!" There was no mistaking Forbes' voice. He was striding out behind her, a large bundle over his shoulder.

McDermid grinned broadly. "Soddin' typical!" He stood up in the craft. "ATTABOY, DAVE!" Fraser hauled him down again.

Free of the flowing robe, the woman struck out, now making better progress. She was strikingly dark and attractive, thought McDermid. Hawksby recognised Hameda immediately. Inching towards the Raider riding on the swell, she threw herself at the gunwhale. The craft dipped as she hooked herself over the edge, the hem of the black silk slip riding high over her voluptuous buttocks. Forbes, grinning widely, slapped them appreciatively, as he rolled her over onto the decking. He threw in the bundle from his shoulder.

McDermid was incredulous. "A bleddy Persian carpet? Christ, he coulda bleddy *flown* out!"

Forbes hauled himself up after the girl. McDermid and Hawksby grabbed him. Suddenly he stiffened. His eyes looked wide with surprise.

"What is it, man?" Hawksby demanded.

"Oh, shit, boss." He shut his eyes and bit his lower lip. Hard. "I've just bought one."

In the clamour of the raging surf, they could no longer hear the gunfire from the land. Benjamin threw open the throttle as Forbes was dragged aboard. Within moments, the craft drew along side the second and, together, looking like a pair of madcap dolphins, they slammed out hard against the incoming rollers. Out into the Persian Gulf.

"So where'd ye get y' wee private army, Davy?"

"Give us another swig of that brandy, Scottie, and I'll tell you." Forbes was propped against the gunwhale of the Raider, his leg outstretched on the deck at a curious angle as Belcher did his best to strap it up. The sheer elation of being out of Iran and the liquor combined in a potent anaesthetic. Despite Belcher's protests he took another swig. "We recruited them way back inland. Volunteering for the front. You know, repel the Iraqi aggressors. We've been on the road for days. 'Course they didn't know which way I was going. Well, if they did suspect, no one said anything!

"Then, when we got here, we saw you lot in the middle of a raging bloody firefight." He threw a punch at Scottie and missed. "Can't leave you alone for a bloody minute, can I? Bloody Glaswegians 're all the same."

"How'd y' persuade 'em te attack?"

Forbes tapped his nose. "Told 'em the Iranians were a bunch of Iraqi infiltrators. Hell, they didn't know! Just did what I told 'em." He paused, took another draught, and sniffed. "Pity that. They were a nice bunch. Once you got to know 'em. Willin' fighters."

"Pity?" McDermid asked.

Forbes' eyes misted. "Our two Ingrams and a lot of sticks an' stones against a pro-Army detachment. That's the pity. Poor little fuckers'll be torn to bits. Won't stand a snowball's."

John Belcher looked up. "That's the best I can do, Dave. I'm afraid it's a right old Blighty one though."

Forbes ignored him. He was feeling woozy and hugged Hameda to him. She looked very fetching in the sodden slip that clung to her ample contours. "It'll heal," he said absently, and kissed her.

Belcher exchanged glances with Hawksby. The medic grimaced and shook his head. Modern high velocity rounds easily ripped off limbs. The sergeant would be lucky to keep his leg. The time had come for Dave Forbes and 22 Special Air Service Regiment to part company for good.

At last his head slumped between his shoulders and Belcher wrote the letter M for morphine on his forehead, the time and dosage.

Now that they were in calmer waters, Hawksby ordered

Benjamin to draw alongside the other craft so that he could go aboard.

"I t'ought we wass going to lose you t'en," Eva said, helping him to a seat.

Blake laughed. "That *would* be a shame, Major, after all this!"

Hawksby was pleased to see the journalist in good spirits. "I've avoided our Boat Troops for years, Jonathan. I get rotten sea-sick on a bloody pond."

Eva nudged Blake. "T'at would've put paid to your t'eories about the major's outfit, eh? Maybe t'ey iss 'uman after all, yes?"

"Just," conceded Blake good-humouredly. "Still, I can't pretend I won't be pleased to see the back of all of you."

"What will you do once you're back on *terra firma*?"

Blake looked puzzled. "That rather depends on you."

"Not on me, old boy," Hawksby replied. "My bit's finished. Perhaps the FO will want a word or two, but I guess you'll be free to go your own way."

"I hope you're right. If so, it'll be bath and meal. And a holiday, I guess."

"With Eva?"

The girl looked hard at the major. "You know t'e answer to t'at."

Hawksby felt uneasy. The others were watching. "Do I?"

Her eyes were bright. "Don't soldiers take 'olidays?"

His voice was firm. "Sometimes. With their wives."

But beneath the seat, out of view, her hand squeezed his. A silent question. He squeezed back. Long and hard.

"AIRCRAFT APPROACHING!" Benjamin shouted suddenly. "BEARING SOUTH-WEST. UNDOUBT-EDLY HOSTILE!"

Before everyone had realised what was happening, the F4 Phantom was on them. It came screeching down in a shallow dive, pulling up just feet above the water, skimming the wavecrests as it approached. All eyes upturned as it flashed alongside, a mere fifty feet away, the exhaust blast from its twin engines thrashing up a storm in its wake. Spray scattered over the two craft.

"Iranian markings all right," Hawksby confirmed. He watched as the Phantom sped away, gaining height and tilting its wings to take it back towards the coast. Without an order being given everyone who had a weapon began loading it with magazines handed out by Fraser's Sabre team. If the aircraft came back to strafe, they had every intention of taking the pilot to the bottom with them.

But the Phantom did not return. Instead, for fifteen uneasy minutes, it served to remind them all that they were far from safe yet.

The next hurdle did not come from the air, but from the sea.

"Either that's a tornado coming up behind us," Fraser observed drily, "or a fast patrol boat."

Heads turned. "Was that a joke?" Hawksby asked.

Fraser smiled back. "Depends on your sense of humour. That pilot must have reported our position." Since leaving the shore they had been travelling at half-speed to conserve fuel. There was no guarantee how far they'd have to travel before a rendezvous with HMS *Antler* could be managed. Now they would have to go for all they were worth, regardless of their fuel reserves. Beneath them, the fibreglass hulls seemed to come alive, the wedge-shaped bows rising out of the water as the Evinrude monsters flexed their muscles, biting deep and hard.

Despite the unbridled surge of power, the menacing shape astern was increasing in size. The patrol boat was closing the gap.

"Didn't think the bloody Frogs knew how to build ships," Brummie Turner muttered in disgust. "That bastard's shifting fast enough!"

"Got a following wind, that's all," quipped Corporal Bill Mather, swinging the second Raider away from the first to spread the target offering.

It turned out to be a fortuitous move. A distant boom was heard above the bumping crash of the cavorting craft. A bright wink of light appeared on the patrol boat's fo'c'sle.

"INCOMING!" Mather bawled, reaching forward to pull Eva from her seat to the deck. They heard the whine of the

76 mm momentarily before the huge fountain of explosive and displaced water erupted between the two Raiders.

"Sod it," Turner said. He'd been drenched. "They tryin' to re-fight Trafalgar?" The sergeant was angry. There was nothing worse than being dragged back into a fight, just when you thought you'd left it. As Mather began a zig-zag course to throw the aim of the enemy gunner Turner rummaged in one of the storage compartments for a distress flare. He crawled to the stern, pulled the ring and let the clouds of red smoke gush out in their wake.

Hawksby looked on with an almost detached interest. It was out of his hands now. Sergeant Turner's move had been smart, but was largely foiled by the sea-breeze. Its direction was carrying the smoke screen across the stern of the neighbouring craft, but it left them fully exposed. And, whilst the evasive course kept the Iranian Navy gunner guessing, it also allowed the charging patrol boat to gain headway.

Two more booms followed in quick succession, the first sending a plume of spray up just forty feet in front. The second was only a few yards behind it. A huge wave of seawater slopped over the transom. They were filling rapidly, the bilges awash.

Hawksby was considering letting the patrol boat come alongside, close enough to set a small charge of plastic explosive on the hull, when the unexpected happened.

Suddenly a huge waterspout mushroomed mere feet away from the nearing patrol boat. The Iranian helmsman evidently spun the wheel on reflex, the sleek craft keeling hard over in a tight turn.

Instantly, Turner said: "Christ! Where did *that* come from? It was a big one, all right . . ." The deep-throated noise of a 4.5 inch shell rolled through the sea haze ahead like distant thunder. Another shell landed just short of amidships of the careering Iranian vessel.

A grin of satisfaction spread across Turner's face. "They've decided not to risk it."

Hawksby turned his gaze from the retreating patrol boat, the scorch marks on its paintwork clearly visible, and towards the distant grey shape. HMS *Antler* emerged like a wraith from the haze some two miles off, the smoke still wafting from her 4.5 inch gun.

At the masthead, the White Ensign flapped excitedly.

On the bridge of *Antler*, Commander Joseph T. Richmond, RN, was miffed. Secretly, he'd hoped the Iranian fast patrol boat would put up a bit of a fight. And he'd dearly have loved to have given the order to 'Break out the battle ensigns' before the engagement. But in the event, there had been no time. Also, with the man from the Foreign Office standing beside him on the bridge, he would have been odds-on for a court-martial had he not obeyed the precise instructions to the letter.

As it was, Ferguson seemed well pleased. Throughout the ship's mad dash, his pale face had been as waxen as his neatly curled moustache. Now he allowed himself a faint smile. "Well done, Commander. A classic eleventh-hour touch."

"Thank you, sir," Richmond replied courteously, then turned to his Number One, "Make-ready to receive our guests."

"No," Ferguson interrupted, "not just yet. I'd like you to wait. Circle or something, whatever the expression is."

Richmond was amazed. "For God's sake why? There's a patrol boat around and our friends must be low on fuel."

Ferguson smiled. "Trust me. If Snapdragon makes for us, it can't be construed that we're rescuing them. We have to think of the international implications of openly associating with these people."

The commander went to speak again, then thought better of it. Instead he passed on the instructions to begin a port turn at slow ahead.

At the corner of the bridge, Lieutenant Colin Horne, the Senior Watchkeeper, lowered his binoculars. "That damn ship's turned up again, sir. The one that picked up our tail after we left Salalah."

Richmond crossed to his side. "I thought she'd given up chasing us around. Now what in the hell can she want?"

"Whatever it is," Horne said, "she's closer now than she's

come before. Her present course will cut between us and the Raiders."

Johnny Fraser was cheerful. "Looks like they've sent the whole damn fleet to meet us."

"Should think so," Benjamin said. "Only right they should show their appreciation." He followed the team leader's gaze towards the second ship that had cut in from the port side, now wallowing majestically in the troughs, hiding HMS *Antler* from view. He squinted against the dazzling shimmer. "What is she? A Type 21?"

"*Amazon* class?" Hawksby asked. Warships weren't his strong point.

Fraser nodded. "Probably. She's making a signal. Hold on, let me see . . ." All eyes turned to the brilliant signal lamp blinking out its message. "*Well done . . . Please send . . . cargo . . . across in one boat . . . We will take good care of them . . . Make your way . . . in second boat . . . to Antler . . . Again our thanks . . .*"

Hawksby and Fraser exchanged glances. The major shrugged. He could only assume that they wanted to give any pursuing Iranians a choice of targets to add to the confusion.

"I don't like it," Blake said flatly.

Hawksby wasn't in the mood to row. "Our's is not to reason why."

Eva's eyes clouded with concern. "Alan, you promise t'ere would be no danger to us. Now we do not 'af your protection."

"Don't start all that again. You're dealing with the Royal Navy. They'll look after you, don't worry. There could be a hundred and one reasons why they want to separate us. We might be needed for a new assignment. This ship may have a helicopter on board ready to spirit you away . . ."

That seemed to satisfy Blake. "Makes sense I suppose."

Eva still looked unhappy. Hawksby squeezed her arm. "As soon as I'm aboard, I'll check out the reasons for the split, all right? And I'll get an assurance as to where you are being taken."

She nodded and smiled resignedly. "Okay, Alan, I 'af trust in you."

He turned to Fraser. "Okay, Johnny, you'd better acknowledge. Meanwhile let's get all our gear into the one craft."

"I'm not sure I can handle this," Blake said, frowning at the outboard. It was an intimidating size.

"No sweat," Benjamin assured him, "just set it on low throttle and take your time to line up alongside the ship's ladder. When you're thirty feet away, cut the engine and coast in. Don't worry about the paintwork. Besides, they're experts at this sort of thing."

"All stowed," Sergeant Turner reported and clambered into the Raider alongside, taking the remaining items of SAS kit with him.

"Alan," Eva said suddenly.

Hawksby turned. "Yes?"

She scrambled across the deck to his side. "T'ank you for all you 'af done. Jon'i and I. Well, we are grateful. We might not 'af show it always, but truly we iss."

He tried to make light of it. "All part of the service."

She smiled, but her eyes were moist and betrayed her real feelings. "Some'ow I feel we do not see you again. T'at you disappear as fast as you come. Into a different world. We meet soon again, yes?"

Looking into those beautiful blue eyes, Hawksby felt no doubt in his mind. "Soon," he assured. He meant it.

Reluctantly she let go his arm. Benjamin was already aboard the second Raider, holding both craft together so that the gunwhales rubbed noisily. Hawksby stepped across.

Apprehensively, Blake opened up the throttle. Free from its heavy load, the boat sprang forward eagerly towards the waiting grey outline of the Type 21. He waved. Hawksby just caught Eva's call to 'Take Care!' before the words and sound of the outboard were whisked away by the light breeze.

It was suddenly very quiet in the cramped and heavily-laden craft. Everyone was aware of the lazy slap of the waves against the hull.

"So," McDermid said slowly, "it's all over." He sounded down.

Surprisingly only Dave Forbes sounded cheerful. He'd

come round during the gunfire and had remained conscious despite the effect of the morphine and brandy. He contentedly hugged Hameda to him. She looked around, embarrassed, but didn't offer any resistance. "Looks like I'm the only one who's got anything left to show for this little expedition."

"I guess someone's got te get the girl," McDermid muttered disparagingly.

"An' the carpet," Forbes reminded. "You've got to admit it'll look good in the Sergeants' Mess."

No one could disagree with that. And no one had the heart to point out that Forbes wasn't likely to be visiting the Mess much longer to enjoy his own trophy.

Johnny Fraser coaxed the Raider forward. Hawksby watched from the bows as the tiny speck he knew to be the other craft went alongside the distant grey bulk. He saw the vague shapes of sailors helping them aboard. It looked as though Blake had made a reasonable job of it.

He was surprised he wasn't feeling the casual quiet satisfaction of an assignment completed. That sensation of mild elation that made you recognise that all the hard training and planning had, after all, proven worthwhile. Time to reflect that you'd won through and were still alive. That inexorable weariness that swept over you when you knew it was all over, and the adrenalin stopped pumping. And that overwhelming desire for a square hot meal, a beer and a bath . . . oh, of course, and that blessed long sleep. Undisturbed.

He wondered if the others were feeling that way now. Probably. No doubt they were already looking forward to reminiscing in the secure sanctum of the Hereford Mess.

But he knew he wasn't sharing that this time. He realised he'd reached a crossroads in his life. There was a fork in the road and it was up to him which track he took.

He could take the easy way to maintain the *status quo*: return to the regiment and try to make a go of his marriage to Caroline. But he knew that if he couldn't prise her away from her family and her lifestyle, it would be doomed to failure.

Or he could plan to leave the Army. McDermid's words back at the cove had cut him deeply. He knew instinctively that what the Scotsman had said was true, and he sensed that the others felt the same. But he wasn't sure he could change. He was thirty-nine – a bit old for new tricks.

Alternatively there was Oman. He knew he'd be welcomed as a commander in the Sultan's forces. Amongst the Arabs he knew he'd be content, with a real purpose and aim in life. Equally he knew that Caroline could never take it. Pink gins and hunt-balls were few and far between in Salalah.

The new dimension was Eva Olsen. A tough and resourceful lady, if unpredictable. She shared his sense of self-preservation. She'd had a genuine belief in the cause of the Iranian people, although that must have waned over the past few weeks. Perhaps she would find the struggle of the Omanis equally worthwhile? He knew he could have a damn good try persuading her.

He settled back, a half-smile on his face, recalling the warmth and animal passion of their illicit encounter beneath the remote Iranian bridge. He shut his eyes and felt the sun and the sea air against his face. Delicious. Peaceful.

"Something's wrong boss." There was deep concern in Johnny Fraser's voice.

Hawksby dragged himself away from the soft edge of sleep. "What's up, Johnny?"

The SAS captain pointed at the grey shape of the warship making headway off the starboard bow, now allowing them to see the elegant profile of HMS *Antler* beyond. "That bastard is not a sodding Type 21! It's only a bloody Koni! An effing Russian frigate. God, their lines are similar! The fore-gun fooled me. I just assumed . . ."

Hawksby was dumbfounded. All eyes turned in sheer disbelief as the haze-shrouded Soviet ship began dissolving from view. A group of sailors, like model railway figures in the distance, waved from the stern.

At last Hawksby began to grasp what had happened. "Quick, Johnny, make a signal to *Antler* and tell her to intercept . . ." Even as he spoke, he realised how stupid the words were. The Royal Navy intercept a Russian ship on the high seas? And to get back the prize of an illegal operation? It was hopeless. Slowly, he said: "Just inform *Antler* what has happened. The commander must make the decision."

Fraser picked up the Aldis. "Why the hell didn't *she* do something?"

A sudden thought occurred to Hawksby. "Has anyone seen my belt-pack? The one I gave to Blake back at the *qanat*?"

"'E's still got it, boss." It was Perkis. "Poked me in the eye with it earlier."

The Hawk stared after the spyship. It had melted into the haze as though it had never been there at all. And with it had vanished Jonathan Blake and Eva Olsen.

They had disappeared off the face of the earth, together with the only evidence of the reasons behind the mission. The filmed documentary details of Operation Fulcrum.

He shook his head slowly. "I don't believe it. I just don't bloody believe it."

EPILOGUE

CASPIAN COAST: 0700 hrs, Wednesday 24th September

The fisherman stood on the ancient stone jetty and stared out at the battered, paint-flaked fishing boat that struggled in from the Caspian Sea.

He looked a pathetic figure, alone in a vast grey seascape, where the brooding sky seemed to reach down and touch the sea. The collar of his old coat turned up against the blustery wind, he waited patiently. A travel-worn kit-bag was at his feet, filled with all his worldly possessions.

As the boat wallowed into the shore he watched with interest. It looked no different from the dozens of other craft used by the locals to catch sturgeon off the north Iranian coast. But he knew this was the one sent for him.

Absently he dug into his pocket. In the dullness of the late dawn, the bright flash of gold was unmistakable, as he cupped his hands around the flame of the Dupont lighter. His last Kent cigarette. He reflected that the only thing he would miss about Iran was his mistress. He himself had long since out-grown his own nationality. Years ago he had rejected the obsessive preachings of its religion and the blind obedience to the Islamic cause. He had become a true international and found that, in the big world outside, there were people willing to pay – and handsomely – for the benefit of his experience and many talents.

Colonel Najaf Murad's job was done, and he would go now to his new masters on the far shore of the Caspian. Masters whose own creed had no room for gods or political weakness, only an all-consuming lust for world domination, however long it might take. And those masters were not slow in handing out rewards to those who helped them further their aims.

Already he had sampled some of those rewards. Even in Teheran and Isfahan he had lived well, enjoying standards of living comfortably higher than those expected by SAVAMA, and previously SAVAK, personnel. Beyond the Iranian frontier, in a numbered Liechtenstein account, the accumulated wealth of payments had steadily mounted into a veritable personal fortune.

His masters, he was sure, were well pleased. After all, he had played his part in the downfall of Reza Shah. In his influential position within the country's security apparatus he had been ideally placed to help manipulate events. It had not been difficult to encourage excesses by the secret police and make sure their misdemeanours became known around the world. While at the same time he cultivated new friends amongst the holy men of Qum.

At each secret meeting with his Russian masters he began to realise, through protracted hours of exhaustive discussion, why they were willing to pay so highly for his continued co-operation. With the possibility of an Islamic Revolution they could eventually bring the pro-Western regimes of the Middle East tumbling to the ground from within. Implosion. From a nation's grass-roots upwards. So much more sinister, effective and long-lasting than overt interference, as they were learning in Afghanistan.

And in the chaos, confusion and instability that would inevitably follow, the seeds of Soviet influence and expansionism would germinate. Within a few years the flowers of Communism would rise naturally from the ruins, offering the only alternative to continued religious anarchy. As Lenin had put it, the Russians would be able to pick up the power lying in the streets.

He appreciated the importance his masters would put on his continued influence over the unpredictable mullahs.

For years he had known the extent of the Soviet destabilisation programme for Iran in readiness for 'the big push' to topple it into the hands of the Eastern bloc. Only recently, with his discovery of Fulcrum, had he learned how it was finally achieved. And that rankled.

His pride had been wounded because his masters had not put him fully in the picture. Not trusted him completely. Treated him like some Persian peasant, despite all he had done for them. However, he was well aware that Iran's Armed Forces and security organisations had been thoroughly penetrated to their upper echelons. He also knew that the Moscow-line Tudeh Party had a strong power-base at Teheran University ready to mobilise student unrest. But that was the easiest part, and hardly enough to transform overnight a long-established capitalist society into an enthusiastic socialist state.

It was only when his contact had unearthed the extent of the British intelligence involvement in Fulcrum that he accidentally stumbled across the first clue to how it was being done. But his first reaction had been to tell his masters of his discovery. He felt sure they would be willing to pay handsomely for such precious information.

Immediately after the meeting with Khomeini, when the Imam had demanded Blake's execution whilst Beheshti had pressed for more information, he had made contact with a vice-consul at the Soviet Embassy: a man from KGB Department VIII. Murad had been stunned by his reaction. Whilst the Russian was grateful for the news of Blake's arrest, he was furious that Murad's investigations had already revealed so much. The man demanded that the journalist and his girl-friend be eliminated immediately, before they said any more. Murad explained that Khomeini had ordered that they be executed next morning. That seemed to satisfy him. However it did not satisfy Murad. He was curious. What more *was* there for Blake to tell?

Then that night had come the dramatic rescue at Isfahan, like a bolt from the blue. That had rocked the boat. His masters were not amused.

But, whilst the chase ensued, he had directed his team of investigators going over Sabs Karemi's research to dig deep into the dirt for a Soviet connection with Fulcrum. With such a vital new clue, it had not taken them long.

Their first discovery had shocked him the most. Ayatollah Khomeini had been amongst the top five Soviet agents in

Iran for years, reporting through a highly-placed Iraqi official to Warsaw, thence Moscow.

He had sold them on the concept of using Islamic fundamentalism as a revolutionary force, using the clergy's influence on the common Persian man as a stepping stone to Communism.

The idea hadn't been the Imam's originally. It was first put to him as part of the Fulcrum plan by the British, and he had suggested to Department VIII that it might fit in well with Moscow's plans. Back in the days before the American-inspired coup of 1953, that had been how the British occupation forces had sustained control and continuing influence for decades. Through the powerful religious system that touched every home in Iran. It had worked then, the British reasoned, so why not now?

It was just the start of Fulcrum. Just the start of a brilliant British programme that had inadvertently given Moscow the way to achieve its own ends.

No wonder Khomeini had insisted on Blake's execution when he knew of Fulcrum's discovery.

Now Murad knew it all. An indictment of his professionalism.

He understood how Khomeini's influence had grown so inexorably, beyond the wildest predictions of the world's political pundits. Behind it all, he now knew, lay a British plan that had been mercilessly infiltrated and manipulated by his masters across the Caspian. The rest was history.

That was what the man Blake could not have understood. He never had a chance. Men who have the power to shape history to their own ends are not easily deterred. Not only was the journalist wanted by Khomeini and the British, but also by Moscow.

In the end, although he had not resolved the matter of Blake's escape to the Revolutionary Council's satisfaction, his masters were well pleased. And that was what mattered. It was a measure of his far-sightedness that he warned them that, if his own men failed, he was confident that an attempt would be made to pick-up the journalist off the south coast of Iran. They were immediately able to confirm the presence of a Royal Navy ship. And, naturally, one of their own nearby. No, they were well pleased. Now the shaping of this particular piece of history could continue uninterrupted . . .

The fishing-boat was changing course to come alongside the jetty. He could clearly see the two crew: one man in the wheel-house and the other on the fo'c'sle, preparing to take a line ashore.

In the open aft well-deck stood a lone third figure. Against the upturned collar of the black gaberdine raincoat, the man's face was deathly pale and gaunt. His short blond hair bristled in the breeze.

Idly, the fisherman on the jetty speculated where he might be going to next. Iraq, perhaps, now that the war had started? If Iraq won, the mullahs would fall and the Communists would be ready to step into the power vacuum. If Iraq lost, the Ayatollah's religious crusade could set the entire Gulf aflame. His masters couldn't lose.

The boat was alongside. He ground out his cigarette on the rough-hewn stone beneath his feet.

He was glad that they had arrived. Peace of mind wouldn't come to him completely until he'd left these troubled shores. Deliberately he had ignored the signal summoning him to the Revolutionary Council. Instead, he'd departed from Isfahan immediately, leaving instructions for his aide to attend in his place. The poor man's fate was sealed. He would feel the full avenging fury of the displeased mullahs, of that there was no doubt.

But then, thought the fisherman as he picked up the old kit-bag and moved slowly towards the waiting seaman, there always had to be losers.

The fisherman stood on the well-deck and watched as the Iranian coast disappeared over the horizon. There was a stink of diesel and fish in the boat, and it was choppy away from the shelter of the land. He felt a little uncomfortable.

Turning to the man in the black raincoat beside him, he smiled and asked: "Excuse me, comrade. I wonder if I could trouble you for a cigarette?"

"I do not smoke," replied the gaunt man. He did not smile.

Then a seagull swooped low over the stern, screeching loudly as it passed. And when it had gone Colonel Najaf Murad lay dead, his blood running into the bilgewater that slopped between the deckboards.

The seaman replaced the smoking machine-pistol in the stowage compartment and lifted out two lead fishing-weights.

He looked down at the body thoughtfully, then wiped his nose on his sleeve. "Who was he, anyway?"

Still looking out to sea, the gaunt man said: "Just a man who knew too much. A nobody who thought he was somebody."

OMAN: 1800 hrs, Wednesday 1st October

Major Alan Hawksby was in a buoyant mood as he stepped out of the fierce Omani sun and into the welcome cool of the Ops room.

"Well done," Fraser said from his seat by the desk. "I gather it was a hundred per cent successful."

Thankfully Hawksby slung his Bergen pack into the corner and dropped into the wicker armchair beneath the ceiling fan. "A classic, Johnny, if I say so myself. We killed six before they decided they'd had enough. Twenty wounded and the rest of the adoo scarpered like the very devil was after them."

"He was." Fraser grinned. "Any spoils?"

"Enough to re-arm the whole of the Gulf, I'd say. Rifles, grenades, mortars, the lot. We gained total surprise when we hit them. I don't think we'll see them on the jebel for a while to come. When will they realise that their methods are out of date?" He felt exhilarated. "Fancy a beer, Johnny? Got to celebrate. Reckon my stars are in the ascendancy after all!"

Fraser didn't smile. "I've had another signal from Hereford. Last night. Definitely no more excuses. Adoo or no adoo, you're on the next flight back."

Hawksby scowled. "So that bugger Ferguson still wants blood, does he?"

"He still reckons we should have done something to stop

344

Blake going aboard that Soviet ship. Says we should have realised that she'd blocked *Antler*'s view so they couldn't see what was going on."

"And he's beaten a path to the Old Man's door to nail the blame on us, I suppose. Searching hard for a scapegoat for him losing his charge."

Fraser shrugged. "Well, the CO does seem pretty keen to see you. In person. And soon."

Hawksby lay back in the chair and shut his eyes. Blindly, he pulled his clay pipe and tobacco pouch from his goatskin waistcoat. Absently, he said: "You realise what this is going to mean, Johnny?"

"Maybe."

"If the FO is after blood, I'll be *lucky* to get RTU'd. More likely it'll be a dishonourable discharge." He opened his eyes and looked down at the pipe he'd begun to fill. "But I tell you, Johnny, if we're working for buggers like Ferguson, I'd sooner jack it in anyway."

Suddenly Fraser said: "Before you get too despondent at the thought of kicking the sand out of your boots, I'd like you to have a look at these."

"What's that?" Hawksby replied, sucking on his pipe as he attempted to light the tobacco.

Fraser handed across a fan of photographs.

"In Farsi," Hawksby said, puzzled. "Documents in Farsi." He shuffled through the prints. "Where'd you get these from?"

"Just after you left for the jebel, Alan. Brummie Turner was cleaning out the Raider when he came across a Minox film cassette. Under some ropes.

Hawksby sat up. "You know what this is?"

The captain was grinning. "Must have dropped out of your belt-order. Probably when Blake was scrambling aboard."

"I don't care how we got it, Johnny!" His voice was almost hysterical. "It might just save my bloody bacon. A pretty good second prize, I'd say!"

"Might be more than that," Fraser said quietly.

"How d'you mean?"

"Those prints are just those I thought looked the most promising," Fraser replied, watching the major's reaction carefully. "There's a stack still be done." He prodded the top print in Hawksby's hand. "I've put a yellow chinagraph around the interesting passages."

Hawksby's pipe had failed to light, but he was unaware of it, as his eyes scanned the elegant Farsi script.

The noisy squeak of the overhead fan seemed to fill the heavy silence. Fraser glanced up. Like his predecessors he had never got around to oiling it.

A long, low whistle escaped Hawksby's lips, but he didn't look up.

"Enlightening, eh?" Fraser prompted. "You know about the British Fulcrum business?"

"What?" Hawksby tapped the prints with his pipe stem. "Oh, well a little. Eva gave me an inkling. I guessed there was more to it. But *this* is unbelievable." He looked up. "Or rather the opposite. It all fits into place. I mean this report is fundamentally an Iranian intelligence summary by this guy Sabs Karemi, with a lot of documentary evidence. There must be some guesswork, but he seemed certain about the Ian Ferguson connection."

Fraser nodded. "I've done a little discreet homework while you've been away, and it all fits. Ian Ferguson is a long-serving Colonial Office man. Usual story, resented the merger with the FO in the late '6os. He moved over to intelligence work but got increasingly peeved as he was overlooked for promotion. He was just about the only voice in SIS to warn about the threat of a grass-roots Islamic overthrow in Iran. Been predicting it for years.

"So, when they wanted someone to head up the Fulcrum operation, he seemed like the natural choice. Only I reckon he was only too keen to make it work."

Hawksby nodded sagely, trying to form a mental picture of the dapper Ferguson with his waxed moustache. "A chance to prove the oracle was right."

"Too bloody true, Alan," Fraser confirmed. "According to that report, the Foreign Office idea was that Fulcrum should just shake up the Shah a bit by putting some weight behind old Khomeini's movement. You know, get a few reforms through, loosen up on the old human rights bit. Similar sort of thing to what Carter was up to. There was real concern that the Russians would gain ground if the Shah didn't take steps to appease his critics.

"But old Ferguson had other ideas. And he had a few influential friends in the City and in Europe who thought the same. When the word leaked out that the Shah was ill, and with no mature successor, they saw it as a heaven-sent opportunity to kick the Yanks out for good."

Hawksby found it hard to believe that there could be such a build-up of resentment to American influence in Iran. "Did Ferguson really think he could turn the clock back? Britain wasn't doing so badly out of the Shah, trade-wise."

Fraser shrugged. "Not according to some. Before the Americans pushed their way in, back in '53, Britain was very strong there. And since the oil boom the Americans have pushed everyone else out. They've dominated totally and flogged billions of dollars of arms to the place. Like a salesman with a housewife who can't say no. A lot of countries were getting pretty pissed off."

"So Ferguson didn't find it hard to get support in Europe?" Hawksby suggested.

"Damn influential support, Alan," Fraser replied, warming to his subject. He'd been studying the report thoroughly. "Nothing official, but some powerful political and industrial lobbies. He persuaded the French to allow Khomeini to set up camp there. That was the real achievement. I mean, who's going to listen to some religious twit prattling away in some backwater like Iraq? In Paris old Crazy K had the attention of the world's media . . . with a little help from Ferguson.

"Then, in Germany, interested parties started inciting the Iranian students over there in support of Khomeini and the overthrow of the Shah. That's where it all started really."

Hawksby shook his head. "I don't really understand why. I mean were the pickings really worth it?"

Fraser gave a short snort of laughter. "Ferguson thought

so. He evidently believed Britain would benefit along with his cronies in the City. For a start they could see the oil contracts coming up for renewal in 1979 and reckoned it would be a better deal with their man on the inside. Khomeini. And arms. Buy cheap oil in return for expensive arms. Both Britain and Germany had big expectations in that direction. I'm sure Ferguson found plenty of takers in high places."

Hawksby realised that he still hadn't lit his pipe. He struck a match and began blowing slow rings of smoke as he considered the other implications of the revelation. He was well aware that the breaking of Iran's military strength would have pleased many of Britain's friends in the Gulf. Several Arab governments, he knew, were becoming increasingly nervous of an all-powerful Iran–Egypt axis, with a ruthless Israel friendly to both. Ian Ferguson would have been well aware of that too.

Fraser continued: "If Sabs Karemi's to be believed, Ferguson wasn't aware that Khomeini was on the Soviet's payroll. Had he been, he might have been more concerned when the Soviets started to take an interest in Fulcrum. As it was, I think he welcomed their interest. They've been wanting to get rid of the Shah for years, and Ferguson thought he could make use of their vast funding reserves to finance the venture out of all proportion to the initial Foreign Office plan. And they could mobilise an anti-Shah student protest. It also avoided any embarrassing use of Western currency, and it would be virtually impossible to trace where it had come from."

"So that's why the Mulcruf Foundation was set up," Hawksby observed dryly. "As a collection point and to launder all the funds from whatever source. No wonder no one in SIS or the Foreign Office realised that Fulcrum had grown so large."

"Until it came too late," Fraser pointed out. "Then friend Ferguson got a bit of a shock, too. Finding his stooge Khomeini storming to power – surrounded by PLO henchmen supplied by Moscow! The Soviets had the whole thing set up, just waiting for such an event. They'd established power-bases in the student movement, the Armed Forces and in the clergy through Khomeini.''

Hawksby stared down at the photographs in his hands. "What tangled webs we weave," he muttered, still finding it hard to digest the enormity of the revelations from Sabs Karemi.

Fraser said: "Of course, when Crazy K did establish himself, he immediately tried to shake off the Kremlin and paddle his own canoe. Those old mullahs aren't as daft as they look . . ."

"It doesn't matter, Johnny," Hawksby said. "In the bloody chaos we found over there, the Commies will have a field-day eventually, and they know it. I bet they were even expecting Khomeini to do the dirty on them once he was in power. They're a patient bloody lot. They won't mind waiting to ride in on the back of a religious uprising."

Fraser looked thoughtful. "I wonder what the Foreign Office think of Ferguson now? I mean, as far as they know, he just ran the operation according to orders. Hardly his fault it was taken over by those wicked Russians. Still, can't have done his reputation much good."

Hawksby allowed himself a smile. "I don't know. After all, you said he'd been predicting the revolution for years. Proved his point now. And, don't forget, a lot of people are going to be pleased the Americans are out of Iran. Fulcrum might not have been planned to go as far as it did, but now it has, the Foreign Office is going to make the best of it. I bet we do our damnedest to fill the vacumm left by the States. Politically and industrially. Falling over ourselves to appease Khomeini. In a way Britain's almost obliged to finish off Ferguson's private plan, just to stop the Russians from establishing themselves."

"Bet old Ferguson would have retired in bloody splendour with an OBE or some such," Fraser muttered in disgust. "With thanks from Her Majesty for being such a far-sighted smart-arse. Not to mention pay-offs from his industrial friends . . . Of course our chum Blake rather upset the applecart."

Hawksby nodded slowly. "A slight understatement, I'd

say. Ferguson knows he'll get no prizes if the Foreign Office finds out he deliberately caused the damn revolution. Christ, not only did Blake have us after him, but Khomeini's mob and the bloody Soviets."

"And look who won the jackpot again," Fraser observed sourly.

Slowly Hawksby rose out of the wicker chair. "Well, it explains one thing I never could quite fathom."

"What was that?"

"Why we were ever sent in the first place. Khomeini knew he'd been set-up, but then he wouldn't care if Blake had the story. The mullahs already had him under lock-and-key. So why should we go in to rescue him so he'd be free to make real trouble for Britain if he shot his mouth off?"

"Pressure from certain parties in the FO?" Fraser suggested. "Ian Ferguson again?"

Hawksby lit his pipe again. "Who didn't want anyone to know that he'd allowed the Soviets to take over the Fulcrum apparatus. Sweet Jesus, no wonder Blake thought we'd been sent to kill him."

"Did he really?" Fraser was amused.

Hawksby didn't see the funny side of it. "Well, Johnny, he was bloody well right, wasn't he?"

"How d'you mean?" He blinked rapidly. "What, the Soviet ship?"

Sometimes, Hawksby thought, even SAS officers can be incredibly slow. "We as good as handed Blake and Eva over to the Russians on a plate. We were manipulated, Johnny, bloody manipulated. I don't know if Ferguson told the Russians when and where we were coming out, but *someone* must have done! If he didn't plan it, he jumped at a heaven-sent opportunity. There's Ferguson demanding my head, when it was him aboard *Antler* who made bloody sure the Russians got them first. If they hadn't turned up, he'd probably have arranged to have them assassinated *anyway*."

Fraser's brows knitted. "In fact, if it was Ferguson who was pressing all along for our mission to be sent, then we might as well have been working for the bloody Kremlin for the past few weeks . . ."

Hawksby stared up at the fan. It looked as though he was thinking. In fact he was trying to stop tears of emotion breaking out. His mind's eye was filled with the vision of Eva's face. The fascinating lilt of her Norwegian accent was ringing in his ears. At last he managed to speak, his voice cracked. "At least in Oman you know who the bloody hell you're fighting."

A shadow suddenly filled the doorway, a man's shape silhouetted in the frame of harsh sunlight.

"Ah, Major Hawksby, there you are!" Ian Ferguson sounded pleased to see him.

Hawksby froze, turning slowly, wondering what the hell the SIS man had heard. Somehow he managed to control the tone of his voice: "I thought you were back in Blighty."

Ferguson, neatly dressed in a pale blue tropical suit and knitted tie, wandered across to the wicker chair. "I was until yesterday, Major. Then I heard a rumour that your chaps had got hold of some Foreign Office property." He gave Hawksby a withering glance. "I'm surprised such rumours are allowed to emanate from the revered headquarters of our illustrious Special Air Service Regiment. You, of all people, ought to know that careless talk costs lives . . . Anyway, I took the first flight out."

He glanced down at the sheaf of prints splayed out on the seat of the chair where Hawksby had left them. "Ah, I see the rumours were correct. Very naughty of you."

Fraser said quickly: "The film didn't turn up until after you'd left for the UK. We didn't realise its importance."

Ferguson picked up the prints and smiled. "Oh, its of no importance outside my office, Captain. None at all. It's just the principle. Government property and all that. You have the film safe, I trust?"

Reaching in the desk drawer, Fraser picked up the Minox cassette and tossed it across, hard. It was a test of wills. Ferguson caught it with a snatch.

"Right, gentlemen, thank you. You can forget all about it now." He started towards the door, then paused. Turning to face Hawksby, he said: "By the way, Major, I'm glad you're back from your trip to the jebel. Your Commanding Officer

351

and I would like a very thorough word with you back in the UK. As soon as you can, right?"

Beneath the waxed moustache, the lips creased into a sarcastic smile, but his eyes glittered without humour. Hawksby's eyes hooded, the muscles in his narrow cheeks hardening in suppressed anger.

"Why wait, my dear chap?"

Ferguson and Hawksby turned, stunned at the sound of the familiar clipped voice coming from the bead curtains behind the desk. The stout, florid-faced man in the immaculate drill uniform was no mirage. There was no mistaking the granite-eyed face of the colonel of 22 SAS.

"Sorry if I made you jump, chaps," the CO said lightly. "Truth is I've been doing a little earwigging with the kind permission of Captain Fraser here. Very interesting it's been too. Worth the long trip. Same flight as you actually, but I move faster . . ."

Ferguson's mouth dropped.

Hawksby glanced at Fraser, who shrugged apologetically. "I thought I ought to use my initiative." He grinned. "And the CO needed to be sure you really hadn't been negligent."

Ferguson's eyes darted towards the door. The Old Man read the signal. "Don't even think about thinking about it, old son. From now on you're in Major Hawksby's custody until a Special Branch escort can get out here."

The Hawk said, through clenched teeth, "Permission to blow the prisoner's brains out, sir?" He wasn't joking.

"Whilst trying to escape, eh?" The Old Man hesitated, his eyes glinting mischievously. "No, I don't think so. Permission refused, Major."

Ian Ferguson breathed again.

TOM CLANCY

Op-Centre

LINE OF
CONTROL

TOM CLANCY'S
Op-Centre
LINE OF
CONTROL

CREATED BY

Tom Clancy
AND
Steve Pieczenik

WRITTEN BY

Jeff Rovin

HarperCollins*Publishers*

HarperCollins*Publishers*
77–85 Fulham Palace Road,
Hammersmith, London W6 8JB

www.fireandwater.com

Special overseas edition 2001
This paperback edition 2001
1 3 5 7 9 8 6 4 2

First published in the USA by
Berkley Books 2001

A catalogue record for this book
is available from the British Library

ISBN 0 00 651399 9

Printed and bound in Great Britain by
Omnia Books Limited, Glasgow

Acknowledgments

We would like to acknowledge the assistance of Martin H. Greenberg, Larry Segriff, Robert Youdelman, Esq., Tom Mallon, Esq., and the wonderful people at Penguin Putnam Inc., including Phyllis Grann, David Shanks, and Tom Colgan. As always, we would like to thank Robert Gottlieb, without whom this book would never have been conceived. But most important, it is for you, our readers, to determine how successful our collective endeavor has been.

—Tom Clancy and Steve Pieczenik

TOM CLANCY'S

Op-Centre

LINE OF CONTROL

PROLOGUE

Siachin Base 3, Kashmir
Wednesday, 5:42 A.M.

Major Dev Puri could not sleep. He had not yet gotten used to the flimsy cots the Indian army used in the field. Or the thin air in the mountains. Or the quiet. Outside his former barracks in Udhampur there were always the sounds of trucks and automobiles, of soldiers and activity. Here, the quiet reminded him of a hospital. Or a morgue.

Instead, he put on his olive green uniform and red turban. Puri left his tent and walked over to the front-line trenches. There, he looked out as the rich morning sun rose behind him. He watched as a brilliant orange glow crept through the valley and settled slowly across the flat, deserted demilitarized zone. It was the flimsiest of barriers in the most dangerous place on earth.

Here in the Himalayan foothills of Kashmir, human life was always in jeopardy. It was routinely threatened by the extreme weather conditions and rugged terrain. In the warmer, lower elevations it was at risk whenever one failed to spot a lethal king cobra or naja naja, the Indian cobra, hiding in the underbrush. It was endangered whenever one was an instant too late swatting a disease-carrying mosquito or venomous brown widow spider in time. Life was in even greater peril a few miles to the north, on the brutal Siachin Glacier. There was barely enough air to support life on the steep, blinding-white hills. Avalanches and subzero temperatures were a daily danger to foot patrols.

Yet the natural hazards were not what made this the most dangerous spot on the planet. All of those dangers were nothing compared to how humans threatened each other here. Those threats were not dependent on the time of day or the

1

season of the year. They were constant, every minute of every hour of every day for nearly the past sixty years.

Puri stood on an aluminum ladder in a trench with corrugated tin walls. Directly in front of him were five-foot-high sandbags protected by razor wire strung tightly above them from iron posts. To the right, about thirty feet away, was a small sentry post, a wooden shelter erected behind the sandbags. There was hemp netting on top with camouflage greenery overhead. To the right, forty feet away, was another watch post.

One hundred and twenty yards in front of him, due west, was a nearly identical Pakistan trench.

With deliberate slowness, the officer removed a pouch of ghutka, chewable tobacco, from his pants pocket. Sudden moves were discouraged out here where they might be noticed and misinterpreted as reaching for a weapon. He unfolded the packet and pushed a small wad in his cheek. Soldiers were encouraged not to smoke, since a lighted cigarette could give away the position of a scout or patrol.

As Puri chewed the tobacco he watched squadrons of black flies begin their own morning patrol. They were searching for fecal matter left by red squirrels, goatlike markhors, and other herbivores that woke and fed before dawn. It was early winter now. Puri had heard that in the summer the insects were so thick they seemed like clouds of smoke drifting low over the rocks and scrub.

The major wondered if he would be alive to see them. During some weeks thousands of men on both sides were killed. That was inevitable with more than one million fanatic soldiers facing one another across an extremely narrow, two-hundred-mile-long "line of control." Major Puri could see some of those soldiers now, across the sandy stretch between the trenches. Their mouths were covered with black muslin scarves to protect them against the westward-blowing winds. But the eyes in their wind-burned faces blazed with hatred that had been sparked back in the eighth century. That was when Hindus and Muslims first clashed in this region. The ancient farmers and merchants took up arms and fought about trade routes, land and water rights, and ideology. The struggle became even more fierce in 1947 when Great Britain abandoned its empire on the subcontinent. The British gave the rival Hindus and Muslims the nations of India and Pakistan to call their own. That partition also gave India control over the Muslim-dominated region of Kashmir. Since that time the Pakistans have regarded the Indians as an occupying force in Kashmir. Warfare has been almost constant as the two sides struggled over what became the symbolic heart of the conflict.

And I am in the heart of the heart, Puri thought.

Base 3 was a potential flashpoint, the fortified zone nearest both Pakistan and China. It was ironic, the career soldier told himself. This "heart" looked exactly like Dabhoi, the small town where he had grown up at the foot of the Satpura Range in central India. Dabhoi had no real value except to the natives, who were mostly tradesmen, and to those trying to get to the city of Broach on the Bay of Cambay. That was where they could buy fish cheap. It was disturbing how hate rather than cooperation made one place more valuable than another. Instead of trying to expand what they had in common they were trying to destroy what was uncommon.

The officer stared out at the cease-fire zone. Lining the sandbags were orange binoculars mounted on small iron poles. That was the only thing the Indians and Pakistans had ever agreed on: coloring the binoculars so they would not be mistaken for guns. But Puri did not need them here. The brilliant sun was rising behind him. He could clearly see the dark faces of the Pakistans behind their cinderblock barricades. The faces looked just like Indian faces except that they were on the wrong side of the line of control.

Puri made a point of breathing evenly. The line of control was a strip of land so narrow in places that cold breath was visible from sentries on both sides. And being visible, the puffs of breath could tell guards on either side if their counterparts were anxious and breathing rapidly or asleep and breathing slowly. There, a wrong word whispered to a fellow soldier and overheard by the other side could break the fragile truce. A hammer hitting a nail had to be muffled with cloth lest it be mistaken for a gunshot and trigger return rifle

3

fire, then artillery, then nuclear weapons. That exchange could happen so fast that the heavily barricaded bases would be vaporized even before the echoes of the first guns had died in the towering mountain passageways.

Mentally and physically, it was such a trying and unforgiving environment that any officer who successfully completed a one-year tour of duty was automatically eligible for a desk job in a "safe zone" like Calcutta or New Delhi. That was what the forty-one-year-old Puri was working toward. Three months before, he had been transferred from the army's HQ Northern Command where he trained border patrols. Nine more months of running this small base, of "kiting with tripwire," as his predecessor had put it, and he could live comfortably for the rest of his life. Indulge his passion for going out on anthropological digs. He loved learning more about the history of his people. The Indus Valley civilization was over 4,500 years old. Back then the Pkitania and Indian people were one. There was a thousand years of peace. That was before religion came to the region.

Major Puri chewed his tobacco. He smelled the brewed tea coming from the mess tent. It was time for breakfast, after which he would join his men for the morning briefing. He took another moment to savor the morning. It was not that a new day brought new hope. All it meant was that the night had passed without a confrontation.

Puri turned and stepped down the stairs. He did not imagine that there would be very many mornings like this in the weeks ahead. If the rumors from his friends at HQ were true, the powder keg was about to get a new fuse.

A very short, very hot fuse.

ONE

Washington, D.C.
Wednesday, 5:56 A.M.

The air was unseasonably chilly. Thick, charcoal-gray clouds hung low over Andrews Air Force Base. But in spite of the dreary weather Mike Rodgers felt terrific.

The forty-seven-year-old two-star general left his black 1970 Mustang in the officers' parking lot. Stepping briskly, he crossed the neatly manicured lawn to the Op-Center offices. Rodgers's light brown eyes had a sparkle that almost made them appear golden. He was still humming the last tune he had been listening to on the portable CD player. It was Victoria Bundonis's recording of the 1950s David Seville ditty "Witch Doctor." The young singer's low, torchy take on "Oo-ee-oo-ah-ah" was always an invigorating way to start the day. Usually, when he crossed the grass here, he was in a different frame of mind. This early, dew would dampen his polished shoes as they sank into the soft soil. His neatly pressed uniform and his short, graying black hair would ripple in the strong breeze. But Rodgers was usually oblivious to the earth, wind, and water—three of the four ancient elements. He was only aware of the fourth element, fire. That was because it was bottled and capped inside the man himself. He carried it carefully as though it were nitroglycerin. One sudden move and he would blow.

But not today.

There was a young guard standing in a bullet-proof glass booth just inside the door. He saluted smartly as Rodgers entered.

"Good morning, sir," the sentry said.

"Good morning," Rodgers replied. " 'Wolverine.' "

That was Rodgers's personal password for the day. It was left on his GovNet e-mail pager the night before by Op-Center's internal security chief, Jenkin Wynne. If the password did not match what the guard had on his computer Rodgers would not have been allowed to enter.

"Thank you, sir," the guard said and saluted again. He pressed a button and the door clicked open. Rodgers entered.

There was a single elevator directly ahead. As Rodgers walked toward it he wondered how old the airman first class was. Twenty-two? Twenty-three? A few months ago Rodgers would have given his rank, his experiences, everything he owned or knew to be back where this young sentry was. Healthy and sharp, with all his options spread before him. That was after Rodgers had disastrously field-tested the Regional Op-Center. The mobile, hi-tech facility had been seized in the Middle East. Rodgers and his personnel were imprisoned and tortured. Upon the team's release, Senator Barbara Fox and the Congressional Intelligence Oversight Committee rethought the ROC program. The watchdog group felt that having a U.S. intelligence base working openly on foreign soil was provocative rather than a deterrent. Because the ROC had been Rodgers's responsibility he felt as though he'd let Op-Center down. He also felt as though he had blown his last, best chance to get back into the field.

Rodgers was wrong. The United States needed intelligence on the nuclear situation in Kashmir. Specifically, whether Pakistan had deployed warheads deep in the mountains of the region. Indian operatives could not go into the field. If the Pakistanis found them it might trigger the war the United States was hoping to avoid. An American unit would have some wiggle room. Especially if they could prove that they were bringing intelligence about Indian nuclear capabilities to Pakistan, intelligence that a National Security Agency liaison would be giving Rodgers in the town of Srinagar. Of course, the Indian military would not know he had that. It was all a big, dangerous game of three-card monte. All the dealer had to do was remember where all the cards were and never get busted.

Rodgers entered the small, brightly lit elevator and rode it to the basement level.

Op-Center—officially the National Crisis Management Center—was housed in a two-story building located near the Naval Reserve flight line. During the Cold War the nondescript, ivory-colored building was a staging area for crack flight crews. In the event of a nuclear attack their job would have been to evacuate key officials from Washington, D.C. With the fall of the Soviet Union and the downsizing of the air force's NuRRDs—nuclear rapid-response divisions—the building was given to the newly commissioned NCMC.

The upstairs offices were for nonclassified operations such as news monitoring, finance, and human resources. The basement was where Hood, Rodgers, Intelligence Chief Bob Herbert, and the rest of the intelligence-gathering and -processing personnel worked.

Rodgers reached the underground level. He walked through the cubicles in the center to his office. He retrieved his old leather briefcase from under the desk. He packed his laptop and began collecting the diskettes he would need for his journey. The files contained intelligence reports from India and Pakistan, maps of Kashmir, and the names of contacts as well as safe houses throughout the region. As he packed the tools of his trade Rodgers felt almost like he did as a kid growing up in Hartford, Connecticut. Hartford endured fierce winter storms. But they were damp storms that brought packing snow. Before putting on his snow suit Rodgers would get his bucket, rope, spade, and swimming goggles and toss them into his school gym bag. His mother insisted on the goggles. She knew she could not prevent her son from fighting but she did not want him getting hit by a snowball and losing an eye. Once outside, while all the other kids were building snow forts, Rodgers would climb a tree and build a snow tree house on a piece of plywood. No one ever expected that. A rain of snowballs from a thick branch.

After Rodgers had his briefcase packed he would head to the "Gulf cart" parked at the back door. That was what the military had christened the motorized carts that had shuttled officers from meeting to meeting during both Desert Shield and Desert Storm. The Pentagon bought thousands of them just before what turned out to be the last gasp of face-to-face strategy meetings before secure video-conferencing was created. After that, the obsolete carts had been distributed to bases around the country as Christmas presents to senior officers.

The Gulf cart would not have far to travel. A C-130 Hercules was parked just a quarter of a mile away, in the holding area of the airstrip that passed directly behind the NCMC building. In slightly under an hour the hundred-foot-long transport would begin a NATO supply trek that would secretly ferry Rodgers and his Striker unit from Andrews to the Royal Air Force Alconbury station in Great Britain to a NATO base outside Ankara, Turkey. There, the team would be met by an Indian Air Force AN-12 transport, part of the Himalayan Eagles squadron. They would be flown to the high-altitude base at Chushul near the Chinese border and then choppered to Srinagar to meet their contact. It would be a long and difficult journey lasting just over twenty-four hours. And there would be no time to rest when they reached India. The team had to be ready to go as soon as they touched down.

But that was fine with Mike Rodgers. He had been "ready to go" for years. He had never wanted to be second-in-command of anything. During the Spanish-American War, his great-great-grandfather Captain Malachai T. Rodgers went from leading a unit to serving under upstart Lt. Colonel Teddy Roosevelt. As Captain Rodgers wrote to Mrs. Rodgers at the time, "There is nothing better than running things. And there is nothing worse than being a runner-up, even if that happens to be under a gentleman you respect."

Malachai Rodgers was right. The only reason Mike Rodgers had taken the deputy director's position was because he never expected Paul Hood to stay at Op-Center. Rodgers assumed that the former Los Angeles mayor was a politician at heart who had eyes on the Senate or the White House. Rodgers was wrong. The general hit another big bump in the road when Hood resigned from Op-Center to spend more time with his family. Rodgers thought Op-Center would finally be his. But Paul and Sharon Kent Hood weren't able to fix what was wrong with their marriage. They separated and Hood came back to Op-Center. Rodgers went back to being number two.

Rodgers needed to command. A few weeks before, he and Hood had ended a hostage siege at the United Nations. Rodgers had directed that operation. That reminded him of how much he enjoyed risking everything on his ability to outthink and outperform an adversary. Doing it safely from behind a desk just was not the same thing.

Rodgers turned to the open door a moment before Bob Herbert arrived. Op-Center's number three man was always announced by the low purr of his motorized wheelchair.

"Good morning," Herbert said as he swung into view.

"Good morning, Bob," Rodgers replied.

"Mind if I come in?"

"Not at all," Rodgers told him.

Herbert swung the wheelchair into the office. The balding, thirty-nine-year-old intelligence genius had lost the use of his legs in the Beirut embassy bombing in 1983. The terrorist attack had also taken the life of Herbert's beloved wife. Op-Center's computer wizard Matt Stoll had helped design this state-of-the-art wheelchair. It included a computer that folded into the armrest and a small satellite dish that opened from a box attached to the back of the chair.

"I just wanted to wish you good luck," Herbert said.

"Thanks," Rodgers replied.

"Also, Paul asked if you would pop in before you left," Herbet said. "He's on the phone with Senator Fox and didn't want to miss you."

Rodgers glanced at his watch. "The senator is up early. Any particular reason?"

"Not that I know of, though Paul didn't look happy," Herbert said. "Could be more fallout over the UN attack."

If that were true then there was an advantage to being the number two man, Rodgers thought. He did not have to put up with that bullshit. They had absolutely done the right thing at the United Nations. They had saved the hostages and killed the bad guys.

"They're probably going to beat us up until the secretary-general cries uncle," Rodgers said.

"Senator Fox has gotten good at that," Herbert said. "She slaps your back real hard and tells your enemies it's a lashing. Tells your friends it's a pat on the back. Only you know which it is. Anyway, Paul will deal with that," Herbert went on. He extended his hand. "I just wanted to wish you well. That's a remote, hostile region you're heading into."

Rodgers clasped Herbert's hand and grinned. "I know. But I'm a remote, hostile guy. Kashmir and I will get along fine."

Rodgers went to withdraw his hand. Herbert held it.

"There's something else," Herbert said.

"What?" Rodgers asked.

"I can't find out who your contact man is over there," Herbert said.

"We're being met by an officer of the National Security Guard, Captain Prem Nazir," Rodgers replied. "That's not unusual."

"It is for me," Herbert insisted. "A few calls, some promises, a little intel exchange usually gets me what I want. It lets me check up on people, make sure there isn't a double-cross on the other end. Not this time. I can't even get anything on Captain Nazir."

"To tell you the truth, I'm actually relieved that there's tight security for once," Rodgers laughed.

"Tight security is when the opposition doesn't know what is going on," Herbert said. "I get worried when our own people can't tell me exactly what is going on."

"Cannot or will not?" Rodgers asked.

"Cannot," Herbert said.

"Why don't you call Mala Chatterjee," Rodgers suggested. "I bet she would be delighted to help."

"That's not funny," Herbert said.

Chatterjee was the young Indian secretary-general of the United Nations. She was a career pacifist, the most vocal critic of Op-Center and the way they had taken over and resolved the crisis.

"I talked to my people at the CIA and at our embassies in Islamabad and New Delhi," Herbert went on. "They don't know anything about this operation. That's unusual. And the National Security Agency does not exactly have things under control. The plan has not gone through the usual com-sim. Lewis is too busy housecleaning for that."

"I know," Rodgers said.

"The usual com-sim" was a computer simulation that was run on any plan that had been approved for the field. The sponsoring agency typically spent days running the simulations to find holes in the main blueprint and also to give backup options to the agents heading into the field. But the National Security Agency had recently been shaken up by the resignation of their director, Jack Fenwick. That occurred after Hood had identified Fenwick as one of the leaders of a conspiracy to help remove the president from office. His replacement, Hank Lewis, formerly assistant to the president, coordinator of strategic planning, was spending his time removing Fenwick loyalists.

"We'll be okay," Rodgers assured him. "Back in Vietnam my plans were always held together with spit."

"Yeah, but there at least you knew who the enemy was," Herbert pointed out. "All I want you to do is stay in touch. If something seems out of whack I want to be able to let you know."

"I will," Rodgers promised. They would be traveling with the TAC-SAT phone. The secure uplink would allow Striker to call Op-Center from virtually anywhere in the world.

Herbert left and General Rodgers picked up the files and diskettes he wanted to take. The hall outside the door was getting busier as Op-Center's day crew arrived. It was nearly three times the size of the skeletal night crew. Yet Rodgers felt strangely cut off from the activity. It was not just the focused "mission mode" Rodgers went into before leaving the base. It was something else. A guardedness, as if he were already in the field. In and around Washington that was not far from the truth.

Despite Rodgers's assurances, what Herbert said had resonated with him. Herbert was not an alarmist and his concerns did worry Rodgers a little. Not for himself or even his old friend Colonel Brett August. August would be commanding Op-Center's elite Striker unit. Rodgers was worried about the young multiservice members of Striker who would be joining him in Kashmir. Especially the ones with families. That was never far from any commander's mind. Herbert had helped to give it a little extra volume.

But risk came with the uniform and the generous pension. Rodgers would do everything he could to safeguard the personnel and the mission. Because, in the end, there was one inescapable truth about actions taken by men like Mike Rodgers and Brett August.

The goal was worth the risk.

TWO

Srinagar, India
Wednesday, 3:51 P.M.

Five hours after giving a false name to officials at the Foreigners' Regional Registration Office at Srinagar Airport, Ron Friday was walking the streets of what he hoped would be his home for the next year or two. He had checked into a small, cheap inn off Shervani Road. He'd first heard about Binoo's Palace the last time he was here. There was a gaming parlor in the back, which meant that the local police had been paid to keep the place secure. There, Friday would be both anonymous and safe.

The National Security Agency officer was happy to have gotten out of Baku, Azerbaijan. He was happy not only to get out of the former Soviet Republic but to be here, in Srinagar, less than twenty-five miles from the line of control. He had been to the capital of the northern state before and found it invigorating. Distant artillery fire was constant. So were the muted pops of land mines in the hills. During early morning there was the scream of jets and the distinctive whumping sound of their cluster bombs and the louder crashes of their guided missiles.

Fear was also in the air day and night. The ancient resort city was governed and patrolled by Indian Hindu soldiers while commerce was controlled by Kashmiri Muslims. Not a week went by without four or five deaths due to terrorist bombings, shoot-outs, or hostage situations.

Friday loved it. Nothing made each breath sweeter than when you were walking through a minefield.

The forty-seven-year-old Michigan native walked through the largest open-air market in the city. It was located on the eastern end of the town, near hills that had once been fertile grazing areas. That was before the military had appropriated the hills as a staging area for helicopter flights and convoys headed out toward the line of control. A short walk to the north was the Centanr Lake View Hotel, which was where most foreign tourists stayed. It was located near the well-kept waterfront region known collectively as the Mughal Gardens. These gardens, which grow naturally, helped give the region its name Kashmir, which meant "Paradise" in the language of the Mughal settlers.

A cool, light rain was falling, though it did not keep away the regular crowds and foreigners. The market smelled like nowhere else Friday had ever been. It was a combination of musk—from the sheep and damp rattan roofs on the stalls—lavender incense, and diesel fuel. The fuel came from the taxis, minibuses, and scooter-rickshaws that serviced the area. There were women in saris and young students in western clothing. All of them were jockeying for position at the small wooden stands, looking for the freshest fruits or vegetables or baked goods. Merchants whipped small switches at sheep who had been driven from adjacent fields by depleted pasturage or by soldiers practicing their marksmanship. The strays tried to steal carrots or cabbage. Other customers, mostly Arab and Asian businessmen, shopped at a leisurely pace for shawls, papier-mâché trinket boxes, and leather purses. Because Srinagar and the rest of Kashmir were on the list of "no-go zones" at the State Department, British Foreign Office, and other European governments, very few Westerners were here.

A few merchants hawked rugs. There were farmers who had parked their trucks and carts at one end and were carrying baskets with fresh produce or bread to various stands. And there were soldiers. Except in Israel, Friday had never seen a public place where there were nearly as many soldiers as there were civilians. And those were only the obvious ones, the men in uniform. He was sure that there were members of the Special Frontier Force, which was a cocreation of the CIA and India's Research and Analysis Wing, their foreign espionage service. The job of the SFF was to disrupt the flow of matériel and intelligence to and from enemy po-

14

sitions. Friday was equally sure the crowd included members of Pakistan's Special Services Group. A division of the army's Directorate for Inter-Services Intelligence, the group monitored actions behind enemy lines. They also worked with freelance operatives to commit acts of terrorism against the Indian people.

There was nothing like this in Baku, where the markets were quiet and organized and the local population was small and relatively well behaved. Friday liked this better. One had to watch for enemies while trying to feed one's family.

Having a desk at the embassy in Baku had been interesting but not because of the work he was doing for Deputy Ambassador Dorothy Williamson. Friday had spent years working as an attorney for Mara Oil, which was why Williamson had welcomed him to her staff. Officially, he was there to help her draft position papers designed to moderate Azerbaijani claims on Caspian oil. What had really made Friday's tenure exciting was the undercover work he had been doing for Jack Fenwick, the president's former national security advisor.

The broad-shouldered man had been recruited by the NSA while he was still in law school. One of his professors, Vincent Van Heusen, had been an OSS operative during World War II. Professor Van Heusen saw in Friday some of the same qualities he himself had possessed as a young man. Among those was independence. Friday had learned that growing up in the Michigan woods where he went hunting with his father for food—not only with a rifle but with a longbow. After graduating from NYU Friday spent time at the NSA as a trainee. When he went to work for the oil industry a year later he was also working as a spy. In addition to making contacts in Europe, the Middle East, and the Caspian, Friday was given the names of CIA operatives working in those countries. From time to time he was asked to watch them. To spy on the spies, making certain that they were working only for the United States.

Friday finally left the private sector five years ago. He grew bored with working for the oil industry full-time and the NSA part-time. He had also grown frustrated, watching as intelligence operations went to hell overseas. Many of the field agents he met were inexperienced, fearful, or soft. This was especially true in the Third World and throughout Asia. They wanted creature comforts. Not Friday. He wanted to be uncomfortable, hot, cold, hurting, off balance.

Challenged. Alive.

The other problem was that increasingly electronic espionage had replaced hands-on human surveillance. The result was much less efficient mass-intelligence gathering. To Friday that was like getting meat from a slaughterhouse instead of hunting it down. The food didn't taste as good when it was mass-produced. The experience was less satisfying. And over time the hunter grew soft.

Friday had no intention of ever growing soft. When Jack Fenwick had said he wanted to talk to him, Friday was eager to meet. Friday went to see him at the Off the Record bar at the Hay-Adams hotel. It was during the week of the president's inauguration so the bar was jammed and the men were barely noticed. Fenwick recruited Friday to the "Undertaking," as he had called it. An operation to overthrow the president and put a new, more proactive figure in the Oval Office. One of the gravest problems facing America was security from terrorists. Vice President Cotten would have dealt with the problem decisively. He would have informed terrorist nations that if they sponsored attacks on American interests their capital cities would be bombed flat. Removing fear from Americans abroad would have encouraged competitive trade and tourism, which would have helped covert agencies infiltrate nationalist organizations, religious groups, and other extremist bands.

But the plotters had been stopped. The world was once again safe for warlords, anarchists, and international muggers.

Fortunately, the resignations of the vice president, Fenwick, and the other high-profile conspirators were like cauterizing a wound. The administration had its main perpetrators. They stopped the bloodletting and for the time being seemed to turn attention away from others who may have assisted in the plan. Friday's role in setting up the terrorist Harpooner and actually assassinating a CIA spoiler had not been uncovered. In fact, Hank Lewis was trying to get as much intel as possible as fast as possible so he could look ahead, not back. NSA operatives outside Washington were being called upon to visit high-intensity trouble spots and both assist in intelligence operations and report back first-hand. That was why Friday left Baker. Originally he tried to get transferred to Pakistan, but was moved to India by special request of the Indian government. He had spent time here for Mara Oil, helping them evaluate future productivity in this region as well as on the border between the Great Indian Desert in India's Rajasthan Province and the Thar Desert in Pakistan. He knew the land, the Kashmiri language, and the people.

The irony, of course, was that his first assignment was to help a unit from Op-Center execute a mission of vital importance to peace in the region. Op-Center, the group that had stopped the Undertaking from succeeding.

If politics made strange bedfellows then covert actions made even stranger ones. There was one difference between the two groups, however. Diplomacy demanded that politicians bury their differences when they had to. Field agents did not. They nursed their grudges.

Forever.

THREE

Washington, D.C.
Wednesday, 6:32 A.M.

Mike Rodgers strode down the corridor to the office of Paul Hood. His briefcase was packed and he was still humming "Witch Doctor." He felt energized by the impending challenge, by the change of routine, and just by getting out of the windowless office.

Hood's assistant, Stephen "Bugs" Benet, had not yet arrived. Rodgers walked through the small reception area to Hood's office. He knocked on the door and opened it. Op-Center's director was pacing and wearing headphones. He was just finishing up his phone conversation with Senator Fox. Hood motioned the general in. Rodgers made his way to a couch on the far end of the room. He set his briefcase down but did not sit. He would be sitting enough over the next day.

Though Hood was forty-five, nearly the same age as Rodgers, there was something much younger-looking about the man. Maybe it only seemed that way because he smiled a lot and was an optimist. Rodgers was a realist, a term he preferred to pessimist. And realists always seemed older, more mature. As an old friend of Rodgers's, South Carolina Representative Layne Maly, once put it, "No one's blowin' sunshine up my ass so it ain't showin' up between my lips." As far as Rodgers was concerned that pretty much said it all.

Not that Hood himself had a lot to smile about. His marriage had fallen apart and his daughter, Harleigh, was suffering from post-traumatic stress disorder, a result of having been taken hostage at the United Nations. Hood had also taken a bashing in the world press and in the liberal American media for his guns-blazing solution to the UN crisis. It

18

would not surprise Rodgers to learn that Senator Fox was giving Hood an earful for that. The goddamn thing of it was nothing helped our rivals more than when we fought among ourselves. Rodgers could almost hear the cheering from the Japanese, from the Islamic Fundamentalists, and from the Germans, the French, and the rest of the Eurocentric bloc. And we were arguing after saving the lives of their ambassadors.

It was a twisted world. Which was probably why we needed a man like Paul Hood running Op-Center. If it were up to Rodgers he would have taken down a few of the ambassadors on his way out of the UN.

Hood slipped off the headphones and looked at Rodgers. There was a flat look of frustration in his dark hazel eyes. His wavy black hair was uncharacteristically unkempt. He was not smiling.

"How are you doing?" Hood asked Rodgers. "Everything set?"

Rodgers nodded.

"Good," Hood said.

"How are things here?" Rodgers asked.

"Not so good," Hood said. "Senator Fox thinks we've gotten too visible. She wants to do something about that."

"What?" Rodgers asked.

"She wants to scale us back," Hood said. "She's going to propose to the other members of the COIC that they recharter Op-Center as a smaller, more covert organization."

"I smell Kirk Pike's hand in this," Rodgers said.

Pike was the newly appointed head of the Central Intelligence Agency. The ambitious former chief of navy intelligence was extremely well liked on the Hill and had accepted the position with a self-prescribed goal: to consolidate as many of the nation's intelligence needs as possible under one roof.

"I agree that Pike is probably involved, but I think it's more than just him," Hood said. "Fox said that Secretary-General Chatterjee is still grumbling about bringing us before the International Court of Justice. Have us tried for murder and trespassing."

"Smart," Rodgers said. "She'll never get the one but the jurists may give her the other."

"Exactly," Hood said. "That makes her look strong and reaffirms the sovereign status of the United Nations. It also scores points with pacifists and with anti-American governments. Fox apparently thinks this will go away if our charter is revoked and quietly rewritten."

"I see," Rodgers said. "The CIOC acts preemptively to make Chatterjee's action seem bullying and unnecessary."

"Bingo," Hood said.

"Is it going to happen?" Rodgers asked.

"I don't know," Hood admitted. "Fox hasn't discussed this with the other members yet."

"But she wants it to happen," Rodgers said.

Hood nodded.

"Then it will," Rodgers said.

"I'm not ready to concede that," Hood said. "Look, I don't want you to worry about the political stuff. I need you to get this job done in Kashmir. Chatterjee may be secretary-general but she's still Indian. If you score one for her side she'll have a tough time going after us."

"Not if she passes the baton to Pike," Rodgers said.

"Why would she?" Hood asked.

"Back-scratching and access," Rodgers said. "A lot of the intel I have on Kashmir came from the CIA. The Company works very closely with the Indian Intelligence Bureau."

"The domestic surveillance group," Hood said.

"Right," Rodgers said.

Under the Indian Telegraph Act, the Indian Intelligence Bureau has the legal authority to intercept all forms of electronic communication. That includes a lot of faxes and e-mail from Afghanistan and other Islamic states. It was IIB that blew the whistle on Iraq's pharmaceutical drug scam back in 2000. Humanitarian medicines were excluded from the United Nations sanctions. Instead of going to Iraqi hospitals and clinics, however, the medicines were hoarded by the health minister. When shortages pushed up demand the drugs were sold to the black market for hard foreign currency that could be used to buy luxury goods for government officials, bypassing the sanctions.

"The IIB shares the information they collect with the CIA for analysis," Rodgers went on. "If Director Pike helps Chatterjee, the Indians will continue to work exclusively with him."

"Pike can have the trophy if he wants," Hood said. "We still get the intelligence."

"But that isn't all Pike wants," Rodgers said. "People aren't satisfied just winning in Washington. They have to destroy the competition. And if that doesn't work they go after his friends and family."

"Yeah—well, he'll have to get a task force for that one," Hood said quietly. "We Hoods are kind of spread out now."

Rodgers felt like an ass. Paul Hood was not living with his family anymore and his daughter, Harleigh, spent a lot of time in therapy. It was careless to have suggested that they might be at risk.

"Sorry, Paul. I didn't mean that literally," Rodgers said.

"It's all right," Hood replied. "I know what you meant. I don't think Pike will cross that line, though. We've got pretty good muckrakers and a great press liaison. He won't want to take any rivalry public."

Rodgers was not convinced of that. Hood's press liaison was Ann Farris. For the last few days the office was quietly buzzing with the rumor that the divorcée and Paul Hood were having an affair. Ann had been staying late and the two had been spotted leaving Hood's hotel together one morning. Rodgers did not care one way or the other as long as their relationship did not impact the smooth operation of the NCMC.

"Speaking of family, how is Harleigh doing?" Rodgers asked. The general was eager to get off the subject of Pike before leaving for India. The idea of fighting his own people was loathsome to him. Though the men did not socialize very much, Rodgers was close enough to Hood to ask about his family.

"She's struggling with what happened in New York and with me moving out," Hood said. "But she's got a good

21

support system and her brother's being a real trouper."

"Alexander's a good kid. Glad to hear he's stepping up to the plate. What about Sharon?" Rodgers asked.

"She's angry," Hood said. "She has a right to be."

"It will pass," Rodgers said.

"Liz says it may not," Hood replied.

Liz was Liz Gordon, Op-Center's psychologist. Though she was not counseling Harleigh, she was advising Hood.

"Hopefully, the intensity of Sharon's anger will diminish," Hood went on. "I don't think she and I will ever be friends again. But with any luck we'll have a civil relationship."

"You'll get there," Rodgers said. "Hell, that's more than I've ever had with a woman."

Hood thought for a moment then grinned. "That's true, isn't it? Goes all the way back to your friend Biscuit in the fifth grade."

"Yeah," Rodgers replied. "Look, you're a diplomat. I'm a soldier. I'm a prisoner to my scorched earth nature."

Hood's grin became a smile. "I may need to borrow some of that fire for my dealings with Senator Fox."

"Stall her till I get back," Rodgers said. "And just keep an eye on Pike. I'll work on him when I get back."

"It's a deal," Hood said. "Stay safe, okay?"

Rodgers nodded and the men shook hands.

The general felt uneasy as he headed toward the elevator. Rodgers did not like leaving things unresolved—especially when the target was as vulnerable as Hood was. Rodgers could see it in his manner. He had seen it before, in combat. It was a strange calm, almost as if Hood were in denial that pressures were starting to build. But they were. Hood was already distracted by his impending divorce, by Harleigh's condition, and by the day-to-day demands of his position. Rodgers had a feeling that the pressure from Senator Fox would become much more intense after the CIOC met. He would give Bob Herbert a call from the C-130 and ask him to keep an eye on Op-Center's director.

A watcher watching the watcher, Rodgers thought. Op-Center's intelligence chief looking after Op-Center's director, who was tracking Kirk Pike. With all the human drama

22

gusting around him the general almost felt as if it were routine to go into the field to search for nuclear missiles.

But Rodgers got his perspective back quickly. As he walked onto the tarmac he saw the Striker team beginning to assemble beside the Hercules transport. They were in uniform, at ease, their grips and weapons at their feet. Colonel August was reviewing a checklist with Lieutenant Orjuela, his new second-in-command.

Behind him, in the basement of the NCMC, there were careers at risk. Out here men and women were about to buy their way into India using their lives as collateral.

The day that became routine was the day Rodgers vowed to hang up his uniform.

Stepping briskly, proudly, Rodgers made his way toward the shadow of the plane and the sharp, bright salutes of his waiting team.

FOUR

Kargil, Kashmir
Wednesday, 4:11 P.M.

Apu Kumar sat on the old, puffy featherbed that had once been used by his grandmother. He looked out at the four bare walls of his small bedroom. They had not always been bare. There used to be framed pictures of his late wife and his daughter and son-in-law, and a mirror. But their house-guests had removed them. Glass could be used as a weapon.

The bed was tucked in a corner of the room he shared with his twenty-two-year-old granddaughter Nanda. At the moment the young woman was outside cleaning the chicken coop. When she was finished she would shower in the small stall behind the house and then return to the room. She would unfold a small card table, set it beside her grandfather's bed, and pull over a wooden chair. The bedroom door would be kept ajar and their vegetarian meals would be served to them in small wooden bowls. Then Apu and Nanda would listen to the radio, play chess, read, meditate, and pray. They would pray for enlightenment and also for Nanda's mother and father, both of whom died in the roaring hell that was unleashed on Kargil just four years ago. Sometime around ten or eleven they would go to sleep. With any luck Apu would make it through the night. Sudden noises tended to wake him instantly and bring back the planes and the weeks of endless bombing raids.

In the morning, the Kargil-born farmer was permitted to go out and look after his chickens. One of his houseguests always went with him to make sure he did not try to leave. Apu's truck was still parked beside the coop. Even though the Pakistanis had taken the keys Apu could easily splice the

24

ignition wires and drive off. Of course, he would only do that if his granddaughter Nanda were with him. Which was why they were never allowed outside together.

The slender, silver-haired man would feed the chickens, talk to them, and look after any eggs they had left. Then he was taken back to the room. In the late afternoon it was Nanda's turn to go out to do the more difficult work of cleaning the coop. Though Apu could do it, their guests insisted that Nanda go. It helped keep the headstrong young woman tired. When they had enough eggs to bring to market one of their houseguests always went to Srinagar for them. And they always gave the money to Apu. The Pakistanis were not here for financial profit. Though Apu tried hard to eavesdrop, he was still not sure why they were here. They did not do much except talk.

For five months, ever since the five Pakistanis arrived in the middle of the night, the physical life of the sixty-three-year-old farmer had been defined by this routine. Though daily visits to the coop had been the extent of the Kumars' physical life, Apu had retained his wits, his spirit, and most importantly his dignity. He had done that by devoting himself to reading and meditating on his deep Hindu beliefs. He did that for himself and also to show his Islamic captors that his faith and resolve were as powerful as theirs.

Apu reached behind him. He raised his pillow a little higher. It was lumpy with age, having been through three generations of Kumars. A smile played on his grizzled, leathery face. The down had suffered enough. Perhaps the duck would find contentment in another incarnation.

The smile faded quickly. That was sacrilegious. It was something his granddaughter might have said. He should know better. Maybe the months of incarceration were affecting his reason. He looked around.

Nanda slept in a sleeping bag on the other side of the room. There were times when Apu would wake in the small hours of the night and hear her breathing. He enjoyed that. If nothing else their captivity had allowed them to get to know each other better. Even though her nontraditional religious views bothered him, he was glad to know what they were. One could not fight the enemy without knowing his face.

There were two other rooms in the small stone house. The door to the living room was open. The Pakistanis stayed there during the day. At night they moved to the room that used to be his. All save the one who took the watch. One of them was always awake. They had to be. Not just to make sure Apu and Nanda stayed inside the house but to watch for anyone who might approach the farm. Though no one lived close by, Indian army patrols occasionally came through these low-lying hills. When this group of Pakistanis first arrived they had promised their unwilling hosts that they would stay no more than six months. And if Apu and Nanda did what they were told they would not be harmed after that time. Apu was not sure he believed the four men and one woman but he was willing to give them the time they asked for. After all, what choice did he have?

Though he would not mind if the authorities came and shot them dead. As long as he did not cause harm to befall them it would not affect his future in this life or the next. The shame of it was that as people they would all get along fine. But politics and religion had stirred things up. That was the story of this entire region from the time Apu had been a young man. Neighbors were neighbors until outsiders turned them into enemies.

There was one small window in the room but the shutters had been nailed closed. The only light came from a small lamp on the nightstand. The glow illuminated a small, old, leatherbound copy of the Upanishads. Those were the mystical writings of Apu's faith. The Upanishads comprised the final section of the Veda, the Hindu holy scriptures.

Apu turned his mind back to the text. He was reading the earliest of the Upanishads, the sections of verse that addressed the doctrine of Brahman, the universal self or soul. The goal of Hinduism, like other Eastern religions, was nirvana, the eventual freedom from the cycle of rebirth and the pain brought about by one's own actions or karma. This could only be accomplished by following spiritual yoga,

26

which led to a union with God. Apu was determined to pursue that goal, though actually achieving it was a dream. He was also devoted to the study of the post-Vedic Puranas, which address the structure of life in an individual and social sense and also take the reader through the repeating cycle of creation and end of the universe as represented by the divine trinity of Brahma, the creator; Vishnu, the preserver; and Shiva, the destroyer. He had had a hard life, as befitted his farmer caste. But he had to believe that it was just a blink in the cosmic cycle. Otherwise, there would be nothing to work toward, no ultimate end.

Nanda was different. She put more trust in the poet-saints who wrote religious songs and epics. The literature was essential to Hinduism but she responded to the outpourings of men more than the doctrines they were describing. Nanda had always liked heroes who spoke their minds. That had been her mother's nature as well. To say what she believed. To fight. To resist.

That was what had helped cost Apu his daughter and son-in-law. When the Pakistani invaders first arrived, the two sheep farmers made Molotov cocktails for the hastily organized resistance fighters. After two weeks both Savitri and her husband, Manjay, were caught transporting them inside bags of wool. The bags were ignited with the couple bound in the cab of their truck. The next day Apu and Nanda found their bodies in the blackened ruins. To Nanda they were martyrs. To Apu they had been reckless. To Apu's ailing wife, Pad, they were the final blow to a frail body. She died eight days later.

"All human errors are impatience," it was written. If only Savitri and Manjay had asked, Apu would have told them to wait. Time brings balance.

The Indian military eventually pushed most of the Pakistanis out. There was no reason for his children to have acted violently. They hurt others and added that burden to their spiritual inventory.

Tears began to fill his eyes. It was all such a waste. Though, strangely, it made him cherish Nanda all the more.

27

She was the only part of his wife and daughter that he had left.

There was a sudden commotion in the other room. Apu shut his book and set it on the rickety night table. He slid into his slippers and quietly crossed the wooden floor. He peeked out the door. Four of the Pakistanis were all there. The houseguests were working on something, arms and heads moving over something between them. The backs of three of the men were toward him so he could not see what they were doing. Only the woman was facing him. She was a slender, very swarthy woman with short black hair and a frowning, intense look. The others called her Sharab but Apu did not know if that was her real name.

Sharab waved a gun at him. "Go back!" she ordered.

Apu lingered a moment longer. His houseguests had never done anything like this before that he was aware of. They came and went and they talked. Occasionally they looked at maps. Something was happening. He edged forward a little more. There appeared to be a burlap sack on the floor between the men. One of the men was crouching beside it. He appeared to be working on something inside the bag.

"Get back!" the woman yelled again.

There was a tension in her voice that Apu had never heard before. He did as he was told.

Apu kicked off his slippers and lay back on the bed. As he did he heard the front door open. It was Nanda and presumably the fifth Pakistani. He could tell by how loud the door creaked. The young woman always opened it boldly, as if she wanted to hit whoever might be standing behind it.

Apu smiled. He always looked forward to seeing his granddaughter. Even if she had only been gone an hour or two.

This time, however, things were different. He did not hear her footsteps. Instead he heard quiet talking. Apu held his breath and tried to hear what was being said. But his heart was beating louder than usual and he could not hear. Quietly, he raised himself from the bed and eased toward the door. He leaned closer, careful not to show himself. He listened.

He heard nothing.

Slowly, he nudged the door open. One of the men was there, looking out the window. He was holding his silver handgun and smoking a cigarette. The Pakistani glanced back at Apu.

"Go back in the room," the man said quietly.

"Where is my granddaughter?" Apu asked. He did not like this. Something felt wrong.

"She left with the others," he said.

"Left? Where did they go?" Apu asked.

The man looked back out the window. He drew on his cigarette. "They went to market," he replied.

FIVE

Washington, D.C.
Wednesday, 7:00 A.M.

Colonel Brett August had lost track of the number of times he had ridden in the shaking, cavernous bellies of C-130 transports. But he remembered this much. He had hated each and every one of those damn flights.

This particular Hercules was one of the newer variants, a long-range SAR HC-130H designed for fuel economy. Colonel August had ridden in a number of customized C-130s: the C-130D with ski landing gear during an Arctic training mission, a KC-130R tanker, a C-130F assault transport, and many others. The amazing thing was that not one of those versions offered a comfortable ride. The fuselages were stripped down to lighten the aircraft and give it as much range as possible. That meant there was very little insulation against cold and noise. And the four powerful turboprops were deafening as they fought to lift the massive plane skyward. The vibrations were so strong that the chain around Colonel August's dog tags actually did a dance around his neck.

Comfort was also not in the original design-lexicon. The seats in this particular aircraft were cushioned plastic buckets arranged side by side along the fuselage walls. They had high, thick padded backrests and headrests that were supposed to keep the passenger warm. Theoretically that would work if the air itself did not become so cold. There were no armrests and very little space between the chairs. Duffel bags were stowed under the seats. The guys who designed these were probably like the guys who drew up battle plans. It all looked great on paper.

Not that Colonel August was complaining. He remembered a story his father once told him about his own military days. Sid August was part of the U.S. 101st Airborne Division, which was trapped by the 15th Panzer Grenadier Division shortly before the Battle of the Bulge. The men had only K rations to eat. Invented by an apparently sadistic physiologist named Ancel Benjamin Keys, K rations were flat-tasting compressed biscuits, a sliver of dry meat, sugar cubes, bouillon powder, chewing gum, and compressed chocolate. The chocolate was code-named D ration. Why chocolate needed a code name no one knew but the men suspected the starving Germans would fight harder knowing there was more than just dry meat and cardboardlike biscuits in the enemy foxholes.

The airmen ate the K rations sparingly while lying low. After a few days the air force managed to night-drop several cases of C rations and extra munitions to the soldiers. The C rations contained dinner portions of meat and potatoes. But introducing real food to their systems made the men so sick and flatulent that the noise and smell actually gave their position away to a German patrol. The airmen were forced to fight their way out. The story always made Brett August uneasy with the idea of having too much comfort available to him.

Mike Rodgers was sitting to August's right. August smiled to himself. Rodgers had a big, high-arched nose that had been broken four times playing college basketball. Mike Rodgers did not know any way but forward. They had just taken off and that nose was already hunkered into a briefcase thick with folders. August had flown with Rodgers long enough to know the drill. As soon as the pilot gave the okay to use electronic devices, Rodgers would pull some of those folders out. He would put them on his left knee and place his laptop on the right knee. Then, as Rodgers finished with material, he would pass it to August. About halfway over the Atlantic they would begin to talk openly and candidly about what they had read. That was how they had discussed everything for the forty-plus years they had known each other. More often than not it was unnecessary to say anything. Rodgers and August each knew what the other man was thinking.

Brett August and Mike Rodgers were childhood friends. The boys met in Hartford, Connecticut, when they were six. In addition to sharing a love of baseball they shared a passion for airplanes. On weekends, the two young boys used to bicycle five miles along Route 22 out to Bradley Field. They would just sit on an empty field and watch the planes take off and land. They were old enough to remember when prop planes gave way to the jet planes. Both of them used to go wild whenever one of the new 707s roared overhead. Prop planes had a familiar, reassuring hum. But those new babies—they made a boy's insides rattle. August and Rodgers loved it.

After school each day the boys would do their homework together, each taking alternate math problems or science questions so they could finish faster. Then they would build plastic model airplanes, boats, tanks, and jeeps, taking care that the paint jobs were accurate and that the decals were put in exactly the right place.

When it came time to enlist—kids like the two of them didn't wait to be drafted—Rodgers joined the army and August went into the air force. Both men ended up in Vietnam. While Rodgers did his tours of duty on the ground, August flew reconnaissance missions over North Vietnam. On one flight northwest of Hue, August's plane was shot down. He mourned the loss of his aircraft, which had almost become a part of him. The flier was taken prisoner and spent over a year in a POW camp, finally escaping with another prisoner in 1970. August spent three months making his way to the south before finally being discovered by a patrol of U.S. Marines.

Except for the loss of his aircraft, August was not embittered by his experiences. To the contrary. He was heartened by the courage he had witnessed among American POWs. He returned to the United States, regained his strength, and went back to Vietnam to organize a spy network searching for other American POWs. August remained undercover for a year after the U.S. withdrawal. After he had exhausted his contacts trying to find MIAs, August was shifted to the Philippines. He spent three years training pilots to help President Ferdinand Marcos battle Moro secessionists. After that August worked briefly as an air force liaison with NASA, helping to organize security for spy satellite missions. But there was no flying involved and being with the astronauts now was different from being with the monkey Ham when he was a kid. It was frustrating working with men and women who were actually getting to travel in space. So August moved over to the air force's Special Operations Command, where he stayed ten years before joining Striker.

Rodgers and August had seen one another only intermittently in the post-Vietnam years. But each time they talked or got together it was as if no time had passed. When Rodgers first signed on at Op-Center he had asked August to come aboard as the leader of the Striker force. August turned him down twice. He did not want to spend most of his time on a base, working with young specialists. Lt. Colonel Charlie Squires got the post. After Squires was killed on a mission in Russia, Rodgers came to his old friend again. Two years had passed since Rodgers had first made the offer. But things were different now. The team was shaken by the loss and he needed a commander who could get them back up to speed as fast as possible. This time August could not refuse. It was not only friendship. There were national security issues at stake.

The NCMC had become a vital force in crisis management and Op-Center needed Striker.

The colonel looked toward the back of the plane. He watched the group as they sat silently through the slow, thunderous ascent. The quick-response unit turned out to be more than August had expected. Individually, they were extraordinary. Before joining Striker, Sergeant Chick Grey had specialized in two things. One was HALO operations— high-altitude, low-opening parachute jumps. As his commander at Bragg had put it when recommending Grey for the post, "the man can fly." Grey had the ability to pull his ripcord lower and land more accurately than any soldier in Delta history. He attributed this to having a rare sensitivity to air currents. Grey believed that also helped with his second skill—marksmanship. Not only could the sergeant hit whatever he said he could, he had trained himself to go without blinking for as long as necessary. He'd developed that ability when he realized that all it took was the blink of an eye to miss the "keyhole," as he called it. The instant when the target was in perfect position for a takedown.

August felt a special kinship with Grey because the sergeant was at home in the air. But August was close to all his personnel. Privates David George, Jason Scott, Terrence Newmeyer, Walter Pupshaw, Matt Bud, and Sondra De-Vonne. Medic William Musicant, Corporal Pat Prementine, and Lieutenant Orjuela. They were more than specialists. They were a team. And they had more courage, more heart than any unit August had ever worked with.

Newly promoted Corporal Ishi Honda was another marvel. The son of a Hawaiian mother and Japanese father, Honda was an electronics prodigy and the unit's communications expert. He was never far from the TAC-SAT phone, which Colonel August and Rodgers used to stay in touch with Op-Center. The backpack containing the unit was lined with bullet-proof Kevlar so it would not be damaged in a firefight. Because it was so loud in the cabin Honda sat with the TAC-SAT in his lap. He did not want to miss hearing any calls. When he was in the field, Honda wore a Velcro collar and headphones of his own creation. They plugged directly into the pack. When the collar was jacked in, the "beep" was automatically disengaged; the collar simply vibrated when there was an incoming call. If Striker were on a surveillance mission there was no sound to give them away. Moreover, the collar was wired with small condensor microphones that allowed Honda to communicate subvocally. He could whisper and his voice would be transferred clearly to whoever was on the other end.

But Striker was more than just a group of military elite drawn from different services. Lt. Colonel Squires had done an extraordinary job turning them into a smart, disciplined fighting unit. They were certainly the most impressive team August had ever served with.

The plane banked to the south and August's old leather portfolio slid from under his seat. He kicked it back with his heel. The bag contained maps and white papers about Kashmir. The colonel had already reviewed them with his team. He would look at them again in a few minutes. Right now August wanted to do what he did before beginning every mission. He wanted to try and figure out why he was here, why he was going. That was something he had done every day since he was first a prisoner of war: take stock of his motivations for doing what he was doing. That was true whether August was in a Vietcong stockade, getting up in the morning to go to the Striker base, or leaving on a mission. It was not enough to say he was serving his country or pursuing his chosen career. He needed something that would allow him to push himself to do better than he did the day before. Otherwise the quality of his work and his life would suffer.

What he had discovered was that he could not find another reason. When he was optimistic, pride and patriotism had been his biggest motivators. On darker days he decided that humans were all territorial carnivores and prisoners of their nature. Combat and survival were a genetic imperative. Yet these could not be the only things that drove us. There had to be something unique to everyone, something that transcended political or professional boundaries.

So what he searched for in these quiet times was the other missing motivation. The key that would make him a better soldier, a better leader, a stronger and better man.

Along the way, of course, he discovered many things, thought many interesting thoughts. And he began to wonder if the journey itself might be the answer. Given that he was heading to one of the birthplaces of Eastern religion, that would be a fitting revelation. Maybe that was all he would find. Unlike the mission, there were no maps to show him the terrain, no aircraft to take him there.

But for now he would keep looking.

SIX

Srinagar, India
Wednesday, 4:22 P.M.

There was a two-and-one-half-hour time difference between Baku and Kashmir. Still on Azerbaijan time, Ron Friday bought several lamb skewers from one of the food merchants. Then he went to a crowded outdoor café and ordered tea to go with his dinner. He would have to eat quickly. There was a dusk-to-dawn curfew for foreigners. It was strictly enforced by soldiers who patrolled the streets wearing body armor and carrying automatic rifles.

Though the rain had stopped, the large umbrellas were still open over the tables. Friday had to duck to make his way through. He shared his table with a pair of Hindu pilgrims who were reading while they drank their tea. The two men were dressed in very long white cotton robes that were tied at the center with a brown belt. It was the wardrobe of holy men from the United Provinces near Nepal, at the foot of the Himalayas. There were heavy-looking satchels at their sides. The men were probably on their way to a religious shrine at Pahalgam, which was located fifty-five miles south of Srinagar. The presence of the satchels suggested that they were planning to spend some time at the shrine. The men did not acknowledge Friday as he sat, though they were not being rude. They did not want to interrupt his tranquillity. One of the men was looking over a copy of the *International Herald Tribune*. That struck Friday as odd, though he did not know why it should. Even holy men needed to keep up with world events. The other man, who was sitting right beside Friday, was reading a volume of poems in both Sanskrit and English. Friday glanced over the man's forearm.

37

"Vishayairindriyagraamo na thrupthamadhigachathi ajas-ram pooryamaanoopi samudraha salilairiva," it said in Sanskrit. The English translation read, "The senses can never be satisfied even after the continuous supply of sensory objects, as the ocean can never be filled with a continuous supply of water."

Friday did not dispute that. People who were alive had to drink in everything around them. They consumed experiences and things and turned that fuel into something else. Into something that had their fingerprints on it. If you weren't doing that you were living, but not alive.

While the pilgrims sat at the table they were approached by a Muslim. The man offered low-price shelter at his home if they wished to stay the night. Often, pilgrims had neither the time nor the money to stay at an inn. The men graciously declined, saying they were going to try and catch the next bus and would rest when they reached the shrine. The Muslim said that if they missed this bus or one of the later ones he could arrange for his brother-in-law to drive them to the shrine the next day. He gave them a card with his address handwritten on it. They thanked him for his offer. The man bowed and excused himself. It was all very civil. Contact between the Muslims and Hindus usually was cordial. It was the generals and the politicians who provoked the wars.

Behind Friday two men had stopped for tea. From their conversation he gathered that they were heading to the night shift at a nearby brick factory. To Friday's left three men in the khaki uniforms of the Kashmir police force were standing and watching the crowd. Unlike in the Middle East, bazaars were not typically the scene of terrorist attacks in Kashmir. That was because as many Muslims as Hindus frequently mingled in marketplaces. Hindu-specific sites were usually targeted. Places such as homes of local officials, businesses, police stations, financial institutions, and military bases. Even militaristic, aggressive groups like the Hezb-ul Mujahedeen guerrillas did not typically attack civilian locales, especially during business hours. They did not want to turn the people against them. Their war was with the Hindu leaders and those who supported them.

38

The two pilgrims quickly finished their tea. Their bus was pulling up three hundred yards to the right. It braked noisily at a small, one-room bus stop at the far western side of the market. The bus was an old green vehicle, but clean. There were iron racks on the roof for luggage. The uniformed driver came out and helped passengers off while a luggage clerk brought a stepladder from inside the bus stop. While he began to unload the bags of riders who were disembarking, ticket-holders began queuing up beside him to board. For the most part the line was extremely orderly. When the two men were finished they both entered the small wooden structure.

The two pilgrims at Ron Friday's table had put away their reading material and picked up their big lumpy bags. With effort, the men threw the satchels over their shoulders and made their way onto the crowded street. Watching them go, Friday wondered what the punishment was for stealing. With customers packed so closely together and focused on getting what they needed, the market would be a pickpocket's heaven. Especially if they were going to get on a bus and leave the area quickly.

Friday continued to sip his tea as he ate the lamb from the wooden skewers. He watched as other pilgrims rushed by. Some of them were dressed in white or black robes, others were wearing Western street clothes. The men and women who were not wearing traditional robes would be permitted to worship at the shrine but not to enter the cave itself. A few people were pulling children behind them. Friday wondered if their hungry expressions were anxiety about getting onto the bus or a physical manifestation of the religious fervor they felt. Probably a little of both.

One of the police officers walked toward the bus stop to make sure the boarding process was orderly. He walked past the police station, which was to his left. It was a two-story wooden structure with white walls and green eaves. The two front windows were barred. Beyond the police station, practically abutting it, was a decades-old Hindu temple. Friday wondered if the local government had built the police station next to a temple in an effort to protect it from terrorists. Friday had been to the temple once before. It was a dvi-bheda—a bidivisional house of worship that honored both Shiva, the god of destruction, and Vishnu, the preserver. The main portal was fronted by the five-story-tall Rajagopuram, the Royal Tower. To the sides were smaller towers over the auxiliary entrances. These white-brick structures were trimmed with green and gold tile and honored the two different gods. The walls were decorated with canopies, roaring lions, humanlike gatekeepers in what appeared to be dancing poses, and other figures. Friday did not know a great deal about the iconography. However, he did recall that the interior of the temple was designed to symbolize a deity at rest. The first room was the crest, followed by the face, the abdomen, the knee, the leg, and the foot. The entire body was important to the Hindus, not just the soul or the heart. Any part of a human being without the other part was incomplete. And an incomplete individual could not manifest the ultimate perfection required by the faith.

However fast they were going, each pilgrim took a moment to turn to it and bow slightly before continuing on. As important as their individual goals were, the Hindus understood that there was something much greater than they were. Other pilgrims were exiting the temple to catch the bus. Still other Hindus, probably local citizens, as well as tourists were moving in and out of the arched portal.

A block past the temple was a movie theater with an old-style marquee. India made more motion pictures than any nation in the world. Friday had seen several of them on videotape, including *Fit to Be a King* and *Flowers and Vermilion*. Friday believed that the dreams of a people—hence, their weaknesses—could be found in the stories, themes, and characters of their most popular films. The Indians were especially drawn to the three-hour-long contemporary action-musicals. These films always starred attractive leads who had no names other than "Hero" and "Heroine." They were Everyman and Everywoman in epic struggles yet there was always music in their hearts. That was how the Indians

40

viewed themselves. Reality was a disturbing inconvenience they did not choose to acknowledge. Like an oftentimes cruel caste system. Friday had a theory about that. He had always believed that castes were an embodiment of the Indians' faith. In society as in the individual there was a head, feet, and all parts in between. All parts were necessary to create a whole.

Friday glanced back at the market proper. Movement continued unabated. If anything it was busier than before as people stopped by before dinner or on their way home from work. Customers on foot and on bicycles made their way to different stalls. Baskets, wheelbarrows, and occasionally truckloads of goods continued to arrive. The markets usually remained open until just after sunset. In Srinagar and its environs, workers tended to be very early risers. They were expected to arrive at the local factories, fields, and shops around seven in the morning.

Friday finished eating and looked over at the bus. The driver had returned and was helping people board. The bus stop employee was back on his stepladder loading bags onto the roof. What was amazing to Friday was that amid all the seeming chaos there was an internal order. Every individual system was functioning perfectly, from the booths to the shoppers, from the police to the bus. Even the supposedly antagonistic religious factions were doing just fine.

A fine drizzle started up again. Friday decided to head over to the bus station. It looked as if there were new construction there and he was curious to see what lay beyond. As Friday followed the last of the pilgrims he watched the bus driver take tickets and help people onboard.

Something was not the same.

It was the driver. He was not a heavyset man but a rather slender one. Maybe he was a new driver. It was possible; they all wore the same jackets. Then he noticed something else. The clerk who was loading bags into the rack was being very careful with them. Friday had not gotten a very good look at the clerk. The exiting passengers had blocked his view. He could not tell if this were the same man.

41

The bus was still two hundred yards away. The American quickened his pace.

Suddenly the world to Friday's left vanished, swallowed in a flash of bright white light, infernal white heat, and deafening white noise.

SEVEN

Washington, D.C.
Wednesday, 7:10 A.M.

Paul Hood sat alone in his office. Mike Rodgers and Striker were on their way and nothing else was pressing. Hood's door was shut and a file labeled "Working OCIS" was open on his computer. The "working" part of the heading indicated that this was not the original draft but a copy. The OCIS was a clickable chart of Op-Center's internal structure. Under each division was a list of the departments and personnel. Attached to each name was a subfile. These were logs that were filed each day by every employee. They outlined the activities of the individual. Only Hood, Rodgers, and Herbert had access to the files. They were maintained to allow the Op-Center directors to track and cross-reference personnel activities with phone records, e-mail lists, and other logs. If anyone were working at cross-purposes with the rest of the team—cooperating with another agency or even another government—this was the first line of security. The computer automatically flagged any activity that did not have a log entry ordering or corroborating it.

Right now Paul Hood was not looking for moles. He was looking for lambs. The sacrificial kind. If Senator Fox and the Congressional Intelligence Oversight Committee wanted cutbacks he had to be prepared to make them. The question was where?

Hood clicked on Bob Herbert's intelligence department. He scrolled through the names. Could Herbert get by with just daytime surveillance of e-mail communications in Europe? Not likely. Spies worked around the clock. What about a single liaison with the CIA and the FBI instead of one for each? Probably. He would ask Herbert which one he wanted to lose. Hood moved the cursor to the tech division. What about Matt Stoll? Could he survive without a satellite interface officer or a computer resources upgrade manager? Matt could outsource the work he needed whenever they had to eavesdrop on foreign communications satellites or change hardware or software. It would be inconvenient but it would not be debilitating. He double-clicked on the upgrade manager and the position disappeared.

Hood's heart sped up as he checked the next department. It was the office of the press liaison. Did Op-Center really need someone to issue news releases and organize press conferences? If Senator Fox were afraid that the National Crisis Management Center was too visible, then the press officer and her one assistant should be the first to go.

Hood stared at the computer. Never mind what Senator Fox thought. What did he think?

Hood did not see the list. He saw the face of Ann Farris. After years of flirting the two had finally spent a night together. It was at once the most wonderful and devastating encounter of Hood's life. Wonderful because he and Ann cared about each other, deeply. Devastating because Hood had to acknowledge that a bond existed. It was even stronger than the one he had felt when he encountered his old lover Nancy Jo Bosworth in Germany. Yet he was still married to Sharon. He had his children's well-being to consider, not to mention his own. And he would have to deal with Sharon's feelings if she ever found out. Though Hood loved being close to Ann this was not the time for another relationship.

And what would Ann think? After a rough divorce of her own, Ann Farris was not a very secure woman. She was poised when meeting the press and she was a terrific single mother. But those were what psychologist Liz Gordon had once described at an employee "Job vs. Parenting" seminar as "reactionary qualities." Ann responded to external stimuli with good, natural instincts. Inside, where she had allowed Paul to go, she was a scared little girl. If Hood let her go she would think he was doing it to keep her away. If he kept her she would think he was playing favorites, protecting her.

.Personally and professionally it was a no-win situation. And Hood was not even considering how the rest of Op-Center would react. They had to know what was going on between him and Ann. They were a tight-knit office and an intelligence group. This had to be the worst-kept secret on the base.

Hood continued to stare at the screen. He no longer saw Ann Farris's face. He saw only her name. The bottom line was that Hood had to do his job, whatever the consequences. He could not do that if he let personal feelings interfere.

Hood double-clicked the mouse. Not on a name but on an entire two-person department.

A moment later the press division was gone.

EIGHT

Srinagar, India
Wednesday, 4:41 P.M.

Ron Friday felt as though someone had jabbed tuning
forks in his ears. His ears and the inside of his skull seemed
to be vibrating. There was a high-pitched ringing and he
could not hear anything except for the ringing. His eyes were
open but he could not tell what he was looking at. The world
was a cottony haze, as though a still fog had moved in.

Friday blinked. White powder dropped into his eyes, causing them to burn. He blinked harder then pushed a palm into
one eye, then the other. He opened them wide and looked
out again. He still was not sure what he was looking at but
he realized one thing. He was lying on his belly with his
face turned to the side. He put his hands under him and
pushed up. White powder fell from his arms, his hair, his
sides. He blinked it away. He tasted something chalky and
spit. His saliva was like paste. The chalky taste was still
there. He spit again.

Friday got his knees under him. His body ached from the
fall but his hearing was beginning to return. Or at least the
ringing was going away; he did not hear anything else. He
looked to his left. For a moment he felt as if he were inside
a cloud that was inside a cloud. Then the dust that had been
shaken from his body began to settle. He could see what he
had been looking at a moment ago, what had made no sense
to him.

It was wreckage. Where the temple and the police station
had stood there was now a hodgepodge of rubble between
jagged walls. Through the mist of the powder he could see
the sky.

46

The ringing continued to subside. As it did, Friday heard moans. He put a hand on his knee, pushed down, and began to rise. His back ached and he was trembling. Then his head grew light and his vision darkened. He settled back down on his knees for a moment. He looked ahead and saw the bus through the hanging dust. He also saw people coming toward him.

Suddenly, behind the people, the area around the bus turned yellow-red. Time seemed to slow as the colors exploded in all directions. It was followed by another loud crack that quickly became a rumble. The bus seemed to jump apart. It looked like a balloon that someone had stepped on—stretched out at both ends and then gone. Most of the pieces flew out, away, or down. Some shards skidded along the ground, moving fast and straight like vermin. Larger chunks such as the seats and tires tumbled away, end over end. The people standing nearest the bus were swallowed whole by the fire. Those who were farther away were thrown left, right, and back like the bigger pieces of the bus.

He continued to watch as a charcoal-gray cloud surged forward. Like lightning, flashes of blood and flame punctuated the rolling darkness.

Friday removed his hands from his ears. He rose slowly. He looked down, checking his legs and torso to make sure he had not been hurt. The body had a way of shutting off pain in cases of extreme trauma. His side and right arm ached where he had hit the asphalt. His eyes were gummy from the dust and he had to keep blinking to clear them. Except for the coating of dust from the blasted temple he appeared to be intact.

Papers from books and offices had been lofted high by the blast. They were just now beginning to return to earth. Many of them were just fragments, most were singed, some were ash. A few of the more delicate pages looked like they had belonged to prayer books. Perhaps they had been part of the Sanskrit text the pilgrim had been studying just minutes before.

The gray cloud reached Friday and engulfed him. Nine or ten feet high, it carried the distinctive, noxious smell of burning rubber. Beneath that smell was a sweeter, less choking odor. The stench of charred human flesh and bone. Friday drew a handkerchief from his pocket and held it over his nose and mouth. Then he turned away from the stinging cloud. Behind him the bazaar was still. People had flung themselves to the ground not knowing what might explode next. They were lying under stalls or behind wheelbarrows and carts. As his ears began to clear Friday could hear sobbing, prayer, and moans.

Friday turned back toward the remains of the temple and the police station. The drizzle was helping to thin the cloud of smoke and douse the few fires that had been ignited. No longer light-headed, he began walking toward the rubble. He just now noticed that the police officers who had been standing outside were dead. The backs of their uniforms were bloodied, peppered with shrapnel. Whatever did this had been a concussive device rather than incendiary.

It was strange. Besides the bus, there appeared to be two blastways, the fanlike spray debris followed from the epicenter of an explosion. One line led from the front of the police station. The other led from deep inside the temple. Friday could not understand why there had been two separate explosions on this site. It was unusual enough for two religious targets to be bombed, a temple and a busload of pilgrims. Why was the police station attacked as well?

Sirens cut through the cottony quiet as police who had been on patrol began to arrive. Other officers, who had been out on foot, began to run toward the toppled buildings. People began to get up and leave the bazaar proper. They did not want to be here if there were more explosions. Only a few people headed toward the rubble to see if they might be able to help pull out any survivors.

Ron Friday was not one of those people.

He started walking back toward the inn where he was staying. He wanted to get in touch with his contacts in India and Washington. Learn if they had any intel on what had just happened.

There was a sound like bowling pins falling. Friday looked back just as one of the surviving back walls of the temple crashed onto the rubble. Thick balls of dust swirled from the new wreckage, causing people to step back. After the blocks stopped tumbling, people started moving forward again. Many of them had dustings of white on their faces and hands, like ghosts.

Friday continued walking. His mind was in overdrive.

A police station. A Hindu temple. A busload of pilgrims. Two religious targets and one secular site. Friday could imagine the temple being brought down by accident, collateral damage from an attack on the police station. A lot of terrorist bomb makers were not skilled enough to measure precise charges. A lot of terrorist bomb makers did not care if they took down half a city. But there were those two blast lines suggesting concurrent explosions. And the bus proved that this was a planned assault against Hindus, not just against Indians. Friday could not remember a time when that had happened. Certainly not on this scale.

Yet if Hindus were the target, why did the terrorists attack the police station as well? By striking two religious sites they were obviously not looking to disguise their intent.

Friday stopped walking.

Or were they? he thought suddenly. What if the attack on the temple and bus were distractions? Maybe something else was happening here.

Explosions drew crowds. What if that were the point? To get people to a place or away from one.

Friday wiped his eyes and continued ahead. He looked around as he walked. People were either hurrying toward the disaster site or away from it. Unlike before there were no eddies within eddies. That was because the choices were simple now. Help or flee. He peered down side streets, into windows. He was looking for people who did not appear to be panicked. Perhaps he would see someone, perhaps he would not. The bag on the bus could have been planted at a previous stop. Explosives could have been set to go off with a timer in a suitcase or backpack well padded to take the bumps of the road. Maybe the passenger who was carrying the luggage got off here, deposited additional explosives in the temple and police station, and walked on. Perhaps the bomber was someone who had been masquerading as a pilgrim or a police officer. Perhaps one of the men Friday had been sitting with or looked at had been involved. Perhaps one or more terrorists had been killed in the blast. Anything was possible.

Friday continued to look around. He was not going to see anyone. In terrorist terms, years had passed. Whoever did this was dead or long gone. And he could not see anyone watching from the street, a room, or a rooftop.

The best way to deal with this now was with intel. Collect data from outside the targets and use it to pinpoint possible perpetrators. Then move in on them. Because this much was clear: Now that Hindu targets had been attacked, unless the guilty parties were found and punished, the situation in Kashmir was going to deteriorate very, very quickly. With nuclear war not just an option but a real possibility.

NINE

Srinagar, India
Wednesday, 4:55 P.M.

Sharab was sitting forward in the passenger's seat of the old flatbed truck. To her left the driver sat with his hands tightly clutching the steering wheel. He was perspiring as he guided them north along Route 1A, the same road that had brought the bus to the bazaar. Between them sat Nanda, her right ankle cuffed to an iron spring under the seat. Two other men were seated in the open deck of the truck, leaning against the bulkhead amid bags of wool. They were huddled under a tarp to protect them from the increasingly heavy rain.

The windshield wipers were batting furiously in front of Sharab's dark eyes and the air vent howled. The young woman was also howling. First she had been screaming orders at her team. Get the truck away from the market and stick to the plan, at least until they had additional information. Now she was screaming questions into her cell phone. The young woman was not screaming to be heard over the noise. She was screaming from frustration.

"Ishaq, did you already place the call?" Sharab demanded.

"Of course I placed the call, just as we always do," the man on the other end informed her.

Sharab punched the padded dashboard with the heel of her left hand. The suddenness of the strike caused Nanda to jump. Sharab struck it again but she did not say a word, did not swear. Blaspheming was a sin.

"Is there a problem?" Ishaq asked.

Sharab did not answer.

"You were very specific about it," Ishaq went on. "You wanted me to call at exactly forty minutes past four. I always do what you say."

51

"I know," the woman said in a low monotone.

"Something is wrong," the man on the telephone said. "I know that tone of voice. What is it?"

"We'll talk later," the woman replied. "I need to think." Sharab sat back.

"Should I turn on the radio?" the driver asked sheepishly. "Maybe there is news, an explanation."

"No," Sharab told him. "I don't need the radio. I know what the explanation is."

The driver fell silent. Sharab shut her eyes. She was wheezing slightly. The truck's vents had pulled in slightly acrid, smoky air from the bazaar blast. The woman could not tell whether it was the air or the screaming that had made her throat raw. Probably both. She shook her head. The urge to scream was still there, at the top of her throat. She wanted to vent her frustration.

Failure was not the worst of this. What bothered Sharab most was the idea that she and her team had been used. She had been warned about this five years ago when she was still in Pakistan, at the combat school in Sargodha. The Special Services Group agents who trained her said she had to be wary of success. When a cell succeeded over and over it might not be because they were good. It might be because the host was allowing them to succeed so they could be watched and used at some later date.

For years Sharab's group, the Pakistan-financed Free Kashmir Militia, had been striking at select targets throughout the region. The modus operandi for each attack was always the same. They would take over a house, plan their assault, then strike the target. At the moment of each attack whichever cell member had remained behind would telephone a regional police or military headquarters. He would claim credit for the attack on behalf of the Free Kashmir Militia. After that the FKM would move to another home. In the end, the isolated farmers whose homes and lives they briefly borrowed cared more about survival than about politics. Many of them were Muslim anyway. Though they did not want to cooperate and risk arrest, they did not resist the FKM.

Sharab and her people only struck military, police, and government offices, never civilian or religious targets. They did not want to push or alienate the Hindu population of Kashmir or India, turn them into hawkish adversaries. They only wanted to deconstruct the resources and the resolve of the Indian leaders. Force them to go home and leave Kashmir.

That was what they were trying to do in the bazaar. Cripple the police but not harm the merchants. Scare people away and impact the local economy just enough so that farmers and shoppers would fight the inflammatory presence of Indian authorities.

They had been so careful to do just that. Over the past few nights one member of the party would go to the bazaar in Srinagar. He would enter the temple dressed in clerical robes, exit in back, and climb to the roof of the police station. There, he would systematically lift tiles and place plastique beneath them. Because it was in the middle of a night shift, when this section of the city was usually quiet, the police were not as alert as during the day. Besides, terrorist attacks did not typically occur at night. The idea of terrorism was to disrupt routine, to make ordinary people afraid to go out.

This morning, well before dawn, the last explosives were placed on the roof along with a timer. The timer had been set to detonate at exactly twenty minutes to five that afternoon. Sharab and the others returned at four thirty to watch from the side of the road to make sure the explosion went off.

It did. And it punched right through her.

When the first blast occurred Sharab knew something was wrong. The plastique they had put down was not strong enough to do the damage this explosion had done. When the second blast went off she knew they had been set up. Muslims had seemingly attacked a Hindu temple and a busload of pilgrims. The sentiments of nearly one billion people would turn against them and the Pakistan people.

But Muslims had not attacked Hindu targets, Sharab thought bitterly. The FKM had attacked a police station.

Some other group had attacked the religious targets and timed it to coincide with the FKM attack.

She did not believe that a member of the cell had betrayed them. The men in the truck had been with her for years. She knew their families, their friends, their backgrounds. They were people of unshakable faith who would never have done anything to hurt the cause.

What about Apu and Nanda? Back at the house they had never been out of their sight except when they were asleep. Even then the door was always ajar and a guard was always awake. The man and his granddaughter did not own a transmitter or cell phone. The house had been searched. There were no neighbors who could have seen or heard them.

Sharab took a long breath and opened her eyes. For the moment, it did not matter. The question was what to do right now.

The truck sped past black-bearded pilgrims in white tunics and mountain men leading ponies from the marketplace. Distant rice paddies were visible at the misty foot of the Himalayas. Trucks bearing more soldiers sped past them, headed toward the bazaar. Maybe they did not know who was responsible for the attack. Or maybe they did not want to catch them right away. Perhaps whoever had framed them was waiting to see if they linked up with other terrorists in Kashmir before closing in.

If that was the case they were going to be disappointed.

Sharab opened the glove compartment and removed a map of the region. There were seventeen grids on the map, each one numbered and lettered. For the purposes of security the numbers and letters were reversed.

"All right, Ishaq," she said into the phone, "I want you to leave the house now and go to position 5B."

What Sharab really meant was that Ishaq should go to area 2E. The *E* came from the *5* and the *2* from the *B*. Anyone who might be listening to the conversation and who might have obtained a copy of their map would go to the wrong spot. "Can you meet us there at seven o'clock?"

"Yes," he said. "What about the old man?"

"Leave him," she said. She glanced at Nanda. The younger girl's expression was defiant. "Remind him that we have his granddaughter. If the authorities ask him about us he is to say nothing. Tell him if we reach the border safely she will be set free."

Ishaq said he would do that and meet the others later.

Sharab hung up. She folded the cell phone and slipped it in the pocket of her blue windbreaker.

There would be time enough for analysis and regrouping. Only one thing mattered right now.

Getting out of the country before the Indians had live scapegoats to parade before the world.

TEN

Siachin Base 3, Kashmir
Wednesday, 5:42 P.M.

Major Dev Puri hung up the phone. A chill shook him from the shoulders to the small of his back.

Puri was sitting behind the small gunmetal desk in his underground command center. On the wall before him was a detailed map of the region. It was spotted with red flags showing Pakistan emplacements and green flags showing Indian bases. Behind him was a map of India and Pakistan. To his left was a bulletin board with orders, rosters, schedules, and reports tacked to it. To his right was a blank wall with a door.

Affectionately known as "the Pit," the shelter was a twelve-by-fourteen-foot hole cut from hard earth and granite. Warping wood-panel walls backed with thick plastic sheets kept the moisture and dirt out but not the cold. How could it? the major wondered. The earth was always cool, like a grave, and the surrounding mountains prevented direct sunlight from ever hitting the Pit. There were no windows or skylights. The only ventilation came from the open door and a rapidly spinning ceiling fan.

Or at least the semblance of ventilation, Puri thought. It was fakery. Just like everything else about this day.

But the cool command center was not what gave Major Puri a chill. It was what the Special Frontier Force liaison had said over the phone. The man, who was stationed in Kargil, had spoken just one word. However, the significance of that word was profound.

"Proceed," he had said.

Operation Earthworm was a go.

On the one hand, the major had to admire the nerve of the SFF. Puri did not know how high up in the government this plan had traveled or where it had originated. Probably with the SFF. Possibly in the Ministry of External Affairs or the Parliamentary Committee on Defence. Both had oversight powers regarding the activities of nonmilitary intelligence groups. Certainly the SFF would have needed their approval for something this big. But Puri did know that if the truth of this action were ever revealed, the SFF would be scapegoated and the overseers of the plot would be executed.

On the other hand, part of him felt that maybe the people behind this deserved to be punished.

A "vaccination." That was how the SFF liaison officer had characterized Operation Earthworm when he first described it just three days before. They were giving the body of India a small taste of sickness to prevent a larger disease from ever taking hold. When the major was a child, smallpox and polio had been fearful diseases. His sister had survived smallpox and it left her scarred. Back then, *vaccination* was a wonderful word.

This was a corruption. However necessary and justifiable it might be, destroying the bus and temple had been vile, unholy acts.

Major Puri reached for the Marlboros on his desk. He shook a cigarette from the pack and lit it. He inhaled slowly and sat back. This was better than chewing the tobacco. It helped him to think clearly, less emotionally.

Less judgmentally.

Everything was relative, the officer told himself.

Back in the 1940s his parents were pacifists. They had not approved of him becoming a soldier. They would have been happy if he had joined them and other citizens of Haryana in the government's fledgling caste advancement program. The Backward Classes list guaranteed a gift of low-paying government jobs for underprivileged natives of seventeen states. Dev Puri had not wanted that. He had wanted to make it on his own.

And he had.

Puri drew harder on the cigarette. He was suddenly disgusted with his own value judgments. The SFF had obviously viewed this action as a necessary extension of business as usual. Trained jointly by the American CIA and the Indian military's RAW—Research and Analysis Wing—the SFF were masters of finding and spying on foreign agents and terrorists. For the most part, enemy operatives and suspected collaborators were eliminated without fanfare or heavy firepower. Occasionally, through a specially recruited unit, Civilian Network Operatives, the SFF also used foreign agents to send disinformation back to Pakistan. In the case of Sharab and her group, the SFF had spent months planning a more elaborate scheme. They felt it was necessary to frame Pakistan terrorists for the murder of dozens of innocent Hindus. Then, when the Pakistani cell members were captured—as they would be, thanks to the CNO operative who was traveling with them—documents and tools would be "found" on the terrorists. These would show that Sharab and her party had traveled the country planting targeting beacons for nuclear strikes against Indian cities. That would give the Indian military a moral imperative to make a preemptive strike against Pakistan's missile silos.

Major Puri drew on the cigarette again. He looked at his watch. It was nearly time to go.

Over the past ten years more than a quarter of a million Hindus had left the Kashmir Valley to go to other parts of India. With a growing Muslim majority it was increasingly difficult for Indian authorities to secure this region from terrorism. Moreover, Pakistan had recently deployed nuclear weapons and was working to increase its nuclear arsenal as quickly as possible. Puri knew they had to be stopped. Not just to retain Kashmir but to keep hundreds of thousands more refugees from flooding the neighboring Indian provinces.

Maybe the SFF was right. Maybe this was the time and place to stop the Pakistani aggression. Major Puri only wished there had been some other way to trigger the event.

He drew long and hard on the cigarette and then crushed it in the ashtray beside the phone. The tin receptacle was

58

filled with partly smoked cigarettes. They were the residue of three afternoons filled with anxiety, doubt, and the looming pressure of his role in the operation. His aide would have emptied it if a Pakistani artillery shell had not blown his right arm off during a Sunday night game of checkers.

The major rose. It was time for the late afternoon intelligence report from the other outposts on the base. Those were always held in the officers' bunker further along the trench. This meeting would be different in just one respect. Puri would ask the other officers to be prepared to initiate a code yellow nighttime evacuation drill. If the Indian air force planned to "light up" the mountains with nuclear missiles, the front lines would have to be cleared of personnel well in advance of the attack. It would have to be done at night when there was less chance of the Pakistanis noticing. The enemy would also be given a warning, though a much shorter one. There would be no point in striking the sites if the missiles were mobile and Pakistan had time to move them.

Around seven o'clock, after the meeting was finished, the major would eat his dinner, go to sleep, and get up early to start the next phase of the top-secret operation. He was one of the few officers who knew about an American team that was coming to Kashmir to help the Indian military find the missile silos. The Directorate of Air Intelligence, which would be responsible for the strikes, knew generally where the silos were located. But they needed more specific information. Scatter-bombing the Himalaya Mountains was not an efficient use of military resources. And given the depth at which the silos were probably buried, it might be necessary to strike with more than conventional weapons. India needed to know that as well.

Of course, they had not shared this plan with their unwitting partners in this operation.

The United States wanted intelligence on Pakistan's nuclear capacity as much as India did. The Americans needed to know who was helping to arm Islamabad and whether the missiles they had deployed could reach other non-Muslim nations. Both Washington and New Delhi knew that if an American unit were discovered in Kashmir it would cause a diplomatic row but not start a war. Thus, the U.S. government had offered to send over a team that was off the normal military radar. Anonymity was important since Russia, China, and other nations had moles at U.S. military installations. These spies kept an eye on the comings and goings of the U.S. Navy SEALs, the U.S. Army Delta Force 1st Special Forces Operational Detachment, and other elite forces. The information they gathered was used internally and also sold to other nations.

The team that was en route from Washington, the National Crisis Management Center's Striker unit, had experience in mountain silo surveillance going back to a successful operation in the Diamond Mountains of North Korea years before. They were linking up with a NSA operative who had worked with the the Indian government and knew the area they would be searching.

Major Puri had to make certain that as soon as the American squad arrived the search-and-identify mission went smoothly and quickly. The Americans would not be told of the capture of the Pakistani cell. They would not know that a strike was actually in the offing. That information would only be revealed when it was necessary to blunt international condemnation of India's actions. If necessary, the participation of the Striker unit would also be exposed. The United States would have no choice then but to back the Indian strike.

Puri tugged on the hem of his jacket to straighten it. He picked up his turban, placed it squarely on his head, and headed for the door. He was glad of one thing, at least. His name was not attached to the SFF action in any way. As far as any official communiqués were concerned, he had simply been told to help the Americans find the silos.

He was just doing his job.

He was just carrying out orders.

ELEVEN

"This is not good," Bob Herbert said as he stared at the computer monitor. "This is not good at all."

The intelligence chief had been reviewing the latest satellite images from the mountains bordering Kashmir. Suddenly, a State Department news update flashed across the screen. Herbert clicked on the headline and had just started reading when the desk phone beeped. He glanced with annoyance at the small black console. It was an outside line. Herbert jabbed the button and picked up the receiver. He continued reading.

"Herbert here," he said.

"Bob, this is Hank Lewis," said the caller.

The name was familiar but for some reason Herbert could not place it. Then again, he was not trying very hard. He was concentrating on the news brief. According to the update there had been two powerful explosions in Srinagar. Both of them were directed at Hindu targets. That was going to ratchet up tensions along the line of control. Herbert needed to get more information and brief Paul Hood and General Rodgers as soon as possible.

"I've been meaning to call since I took over at NSA," Lewis said, "but it's been brutal getting up to speed."

Jesus, Herbert thought. That's who Hank Lewis was. Jack Fenwick's replacement at the National Security Agency. Lewis had just signed off on the NSA's participation in the Striker mission. Herbert should have known the name right away. But he forgave himself. He had a mission headed into a hot zone that had just become hotter. His brain was on autopilot.

"You don't have to explain. I know what the workload is like over there," Herbert assured him. "I assume you're calling about the State Department update on Kashmir?"

"I haven't seen that report yet," Lewis admitted. "But I did receive a call from Ron Friday, the man who's supposed to meet your Striker team. He told me what you probably read. That an hour ago there were three powerful bomb blasts in a bazaar in Srinagar."

"Three?" Herbert replied. "The State Department says there were two explosions."

"Mr. Friday was within visual range of ground zero," Lewis informed him. "He said there were simultaneous explosions in both the police station and in the Hindu temple. They were followed by a third blast onboard a bus full of Hindu pilgrims."

Hearing the event described, Herbert flashed back to the embassy bombing in Beirut. The moment of the explosion was not what stayed with him. That was like running a car into a wall, a full-body hit. What he remembered, vividly, was the sickness of coming to beneath the rubble and realizing in a sickening instant exactly what had happened.

"Was your man hurt?" Herbert asked.

"Incredibly, no," Lewis said. "Mr. Friday said the explosions would have been worse except that high-impact concussive devices were employed. That minimized the damage radius."

"He was lucky," Herbert said. HiCon explosives tended to produce a big percussive center, nominal shock waves, and very little collateral damage. "So why is Friday so sure the first two hits were separate blasts? The second one could have been an oil or propane tank exploding. There are often secondary pops in attacks of this kind."

"Mr. Friday was very specific about the explosions being simultaneous, not successive," Lewis replied. "After the attack he also found two very similar but separate debris trails leading from the buildings. That suggests identical devices in different locations."

"Possibly," Herbert said.

An expression from Herbert's childhood came floating back: He who smelt it dealt it. Op-Center's intelligence chief briefly wondered if Friday might have been responsible for the blasts. However, Herbert could not think of a reason for Friday to have done that. And he had not become cynical enough to look for a reason. Not yet, anyway.

"Let's say there were three blasts," Herbert said. "What do your nerve endings tell you about all this?"

"My immediate thought, of course, is that the Pakistans are turning up the heat by attacking religious targets," Lewis replied. "But we don't have enough intel to back that up."

"And if the idea was to hit at the Hindus directly, why would they strike the police station as well?" Herbert asked.

"To cripple their pursuit capabilities, I would imagine," Lewis suggested.

"Maybe," Herbert replied.

Everything Lewis said made sense. Which meant one of two things. Either he was right or the obvious answer was what the perpetrators wanted investigators to believe.

"Your Strikers won't be arriving for another twenty-two hours and change," Lewis said. "I'm going to have Mr. Friday go back to the target area and see what he can learn. Are there any resources you can call on?"

"Yes," Herbert said. "India's Intelligence Bureau and the Defense Ministry helped us to organize the Striker mission. I'll see what they know and get back to you."

"Thanks," Lewis said. "By the way, I'm looking forward to working with you. I've followed your career ever since you went over to Germany to take on those neo-Nazis. I trust men who get out from behind their desk. It means they put job and country before personal security."

"Either that or it means they're crazy," Herbert said. "But thanks. Stay in touch."

Lewis said he would. Herbert hung up.

It was refreshing to talk to someone in the covert community who was actually willing to share information. Intelligence chiefs were notoriously secretive. If they controlled information they could control people and institutions. Herbert refused to play that game. While it was good for job security it was bad for national security. And as Jack Fenwick had demonstrated, a secretive intelligence chief could also control a president.

But though Ron Friday was a seasoned field operative, Herbert was not quite as willing to bet the ranch on his report. Herbert only believed in people he had worked with himself.

Herbert phoned Paul Hood to brief him on the new development. Hood asked to be conferenced on the call to Mike Rodgers whenever that took place. Then Herbert put in a call to the Indian Intelligence Bureau. Sujit Rani, the deputy director of internal activities, told Herbert pretty much what he expected to hear: that the IIB was investigating the explosions but did not have any additional information. The notion that there had been three explosions, not two, was something the IIB had heard and was looking into. That information vindicated Ron Friday somewhat in Herbert's eyes. Herbert's contact at the Defense Ministry told him basically the same thing. Fortunately, there was time before Striker reached India. They would be able to abort the mission if necessary.

Herbert went into the Kashmir files. He wanted to check on other recent terrorist strikes in the region. Maybe he could find clues, a pattern, something that would help to explain this new attack. Something about it did not sit right. If Pakistan were really looking to turn up the heat in Kashmir they probably would have struck at a place that had intense religious meaning, like the shrine at Pahalgam. Not only was that the most revered site in the region but the terrorists would not have had to worry about security. The Hindus trusted completely in their sacred trinity. If it was the will of Vishnu the preserver then they would not be harmed. If they died violently then Shiva the destroyer would avenge them. And if they were worthy, Brahma the creator would reincarnate them.

No. Bob Herbert's gut was telling him that the Hindu temple, the bus, and the police station were struck for some other reason. He just did not know what that reason was.

But he would.

TWELVE

C-130 Cabin
Wednesday, 10:13 A.M.

When he first joined Striker, Corporal Ishi Honda discovered that there was not a lot of downtime on the ground. There was a great deal of drilling, especially for him. Honda had joined the team late, replacing Private Johnny Puckett who had been wounded on the mission to North Korea. It was necessary for Honda, then a twenty-two-year-old private, to get up to speed.

Once he got there Honda never let up. His mother used to tell him he was fated never to rest. She ascribed it to the different halves of his soul. Ishi's maternal grandfather had been a civilian cook at Wheeler Field. He died trying to get home to his family during the Japanese attack on Pearl Harbor. Ishi's paternal grandfather had been a high-ranking officer on the staff of Rear Admiral Takajiro Onishi, chief of staff of the Eleventh Air Fleet. Onishi was the architect of the Japanese attack. Ishi's parents were actors who met and fell in love on a show tour without knowing anything about the other's background. They often debated whether knowing that would have made a difference. His father said it absolutely would not have. With a little shake of her head, her eyes downturned, his mother said it might have made a difference.

Ishi had no answers and maybe that was why he could not stop pushing himself. Part of him believed that if he ever stopped moving he would inevitably look at that question, whether or not a piece of information would have kept him from being born. And he did not want to do that because the question had no answer. Honda did not like problems without solutions.

What he did like was living the life of a Striker. It not only taxed him mentally, it challenged him physically.

From the time he was recruited to join the elite unit there were long daily runs, obstacle courses, hand-to-hand combat, arms practice, survival training, and maneuvers. The field work was always tougher for Honda than for the others. In addition to his survival gear he had to carry the TAC-SAT equipment. There were also tactical and political sessions and language classes. Colonel August had insisted that the Strikers learn at least two languages each in the likely event that those skills would one day be required. At least Honda had an advantage there. Because his father was Japanese, Honda already had a leg up on one of the languages he had been assigned. He selected Mandarin Chinese as the other. Sondra DeVonne had chosen Cantonese as one of her languages. It was fascinating to Honda that the languages shared identical written characters. Yet the spoken languages were entirely different. While he and DeVonne could read the same texts they could not communicate verbally.

Though the time the Strikers spent on the ground was rewarding, Honda had learned that their time in the air was anything but. They rarely took short trips and the long journeys could be extremely dull. That was why he had come up with constructive ways of filling his time.

Wherever they were going, Honda arranged to patch his personal computer into the data files of both Stephen Viens at the National Reconnaissance Office and those of Op-Center's computer chief, Matt Stoll. The NRO was the group that managed most of America's spy satellites. Because Viens was an old college chum of Stoll's, he had been extremely helpful in getting information for Op-Center when more established groups like military intelligence, the CIA, and the NSA were fighting for satellite time. Viens was later accused of forward-funding two billion dollars of NRO money into a variety of black ops projects. He was vindicated with Op-Center's help and recently returned to duty.

Before Striker headed to any territory, Viens set aside satellite time to do all the photographic recon that Colonel August needed. That imaging was considered of primary importance and was sent on the mission in Colonel August's files. Meanwhile, Stoll spent as much time as possible collecting electronic intelligence from the region. Police departments and the military did not share everything they knew, even with allies. In many foreign countries, especially Russia, China, and Israel, American operatives were often watched without their knowledge by foreign operatives. It was up to Op-Center to pick up whatever information they could and protect themselves accordingly. They did this by diverging from the agreed-upon routes and time schedules, using "dispensable" team members to mislead tails, or occasionally subduing whoever was following them. A host nation could not complain if the person they had sent to spy on an ally was later found bound and gagged in a hotel closet.

The ELINT Stoll had gathered was composed of everything from fax messages and e-mail to phone numbers and radio frequencies. Everything that came to or went from official sources or known resistance and opposition forces. These numbers, frequencies, and encryption codes were then run through programs. They were compared with those of known terrorists or foreign agents. If there were any possible "watchdogs or impediments" in the region, as mission planners referred to them, these scans helped to find and identify them. The last thing American intelligence chiefs wanted was to have undercover operatives photographed or their methods observed by foreign governments. Not only could that information be sold to a third party, but the United States never knew which friendly governments might one day be intelligence targets.

"Think Iran," Colonel August reminded them whenever they went on a joint mission with allies.

Honda had brought along a Striker laptop. The computer was equipped with a wireless, high-speed modem to download data Stoll was still collecting. Honda would memorize any relevant data. When Striker reached India, the computer would be left on the transport and returned to the base. Colonel August would keep his laptop to download data. Where they were going, the less Corporal Honda had to carry the happier he would be.

As the new intelligence was dumped into Honda's computer, an audio prompt pinged. It was alerting him to an anomaly that Stoll's program had picked up at Op-Center. Honda accessed the flagged data.

The Bellhop program on the air force's "Sanctity" satellite continually scanned the cell phones and radios that used police bands. Op-Center and the other U.S. intelligence agencies had these numbers for their own communications with foreign offices. It was a simple matter to hack the computers and look for other incoming calls.

The Bellhop had picked up a series of point-to-point calls made on a police-registered cell phone. It was coded "field phone" in the Bellhop lexicon. Most of the calls were placed over a five-month period from Kargil to the district police headquarters in Jammu, coded "home phone." During that time there was only one call to that field phone from the home phone. Stoll's program, which integrated Op-Center intel with NRO data, indicated that the call was placed less than one second before the Kashmir-focused ClusterStar3 satellite recorded an explosion in a bazaar in Srinagar.

"Damn," Honda muttered.

Honda wondered if Colonel August or General Rodgers had been informed about a possible terrorist attack. The fact that a police cell phone made a call to the site an instant before the explosion could be a coincidence. Perhaps someone was phoning a security guard. On the other hand there might be a connection between the two. Honda unbuckled himself from the uncomfortable seat and went forward to inform his commanding officers. He had to walk slowly, carefully, to keep from being bucked against his teammates by the aircraft's movements in the turbulent air.

August and Rodgers were huddled together over the general's laptop when he arrived.

"Excuse me, sirs," Honda said. He had to shout to be heard over the screaming engines.

August looked up. "What have you got, Corporal?"

Honda told the two officers about the explosion. August informed Honda that they were just reading an e-mail from Bob Herbert about the blast. It provided what few details anyone had about the attack. Then Honda informed his superiors about the phone calls. That seemed to grab General Rodgers's interest.

"There were two calls a day for five months, always at the same time," Honda said.

"Like a routine check-in," Rodgers said.

"Exactly, sir," Honda replied. "Except for today. There was just one call and it was made to the field phone. It was placed a moment before the explosion that took out the temple."

Rodgers sat back. "Corporal, would you go through the data file and see if this calling pattern is repeated, probably from field phones with different code numbers? Outgoing calls to one home phone and one or none coming back?"

"Yes, sir," Honda replied.

Honda crouched on the cold, rumbling floor and raised one knee. He put the laptop upon it. He was not sure what the officers were looking for exactly and it was not his place to ask. He input the code number of the home phone and asked for a Bellhop search. Colonel August's hunch was correct. He told them that in addition to this series there were seven weeks of calls from another field phone in Kargil. They were made twice a day at the same times. Before that there were six weeks of calls from another field phone, also two times daily. Thirteen weeks was as far back as these Bellhop records went.

"New Delhi must have had civilian agents tracking a terrorist cell," Rodgers said.

"How do you know that?" August asked. "The calls may just have been field ops reporting in."

"I don't think so," Rodgers told him. "First of all, only one of the calls on Corporal Honda's list was made from the home phone to the field phone."

"That was the one made at the time of the explosion," August said.

"Correct," Rodgers replied. "That would suggest the officers in charge of the recon did not want field phones ringing at inopportune moments."

"I'll buy that," August said.

"There's more than that, though," Rodgers said. "When Pakistan was knocked out of Kargil in 1999, the Indian Special Frontier Force knew that enemy cells would be left behind. They couldn't hunt them down with soldiers. The locals would have known if strangers were moving through a village. And if the locals knew it members of the cell would have known it. So the SFF recruited a shitload of locals to serve in their Civilian Network Operatives unit." The general tapped his laptop. "It's all here in the intelligence overview. But they couldn't give the recruits normal militia radios because, that close to Pakistan, those channels are routinely monitored by ELINT personnel. So the SFF gave their recruits cell phones. The agents call the regional office and complain about break-ins, missing children, stolen livestock, that sort of thing. What they're really doing is using coded messages to keep the SFF informed about suspected terrorist movements and activities."

"All right," August said. "But what makes you think the calls on this list aren't just routine field reports?"

"Because CNO personnel don't make routine field reports," Rodgers said. "They only report when they have something to say. There's less chance of them being overheard that way. I'm willing to bet that there are terrorist strikes to coincide with the termination of each of those series of calls. A target was hit, the cell moved on, the calls stopped being placed."

"Perhaps," August said. "But that doesn't explain the call to the temple right before the blast."

"Actually, it might," Rodgers told him.

"I don't follow," August said.

Rodgers looked up at Honda. "Corporal, would you please get the TAC-SAT?"

"Yes, sir."

Rodgers turned back to August. "I'm going to ask Bob Herbert to check on the dates of terrorist strikes in the region," he said. "I want to see if reports from field phones stopped coming in after terrorist strikes. I also want Bob to look into something else."

"What's that?" August asked.

Honda closed his laptop and stood. He lingered long enough to hear Rodgers's reply.

"I want to know what kind of detonator caps the SFF uses for counterterrorist strikes," the general replied.

"Why?" August asked.

"Because the Mossad, the Iraqi Al Amn al-Khas, Abu Nidal's group, and the Spanish Grapo have all used PDEs on occasion," Rodgers said. "Phone-detonated explosives."

THIRTEEN

Srinagar, Kashmir
Wednesday, 6:59 P.M.

It was nearly dark when Ron Friday returned to the bazaar. Though he was curious to see how the authorities here were handling the investigation he was more interested in what he might be able to find out about the attack. His life might depend on that information.

The rain had stopped and there was a cold wind rolling off the mountains. Friday was glad he had worn a baseball cap and a windbreaker, though the drop in temperature was not the reason he had put them on. Even from his room he could hear helicopters circling the area. When Friday arrived he found that the two police choppers were hovering low, less than two hundred feet up. In addition to looking for survivors, the noise echoing loudly through the square helped to keep onlookers from staying too long. But that was not the only reason the choppers were there. Friday guessed that they were also maintaining a low altitude to photograph the crowd in case the terrorist was still in the area. The cockpits were probably equipped with GRRs—geometric reconstructive recorders. These were digital cameras that could take photographs shot at an angle and reconfigure the geometry so they became accurate frontal images. Interpol and most national security agencies had a "face-print" file consisting of mug shots and police sketches of known and suspected terrorists. Like fingerprints, face-print photographs could be run through a computer and compared to images on file. The computer superimposed the likenesses. If the features were at least a 70 percent match, that was considered sufficient to go after the individual for interrogation.

Friday had worn the baseball cap because he did not want to be face-printed by the chopper. He did not know which governments might have his likeness on file or for what reason. He certainly did not want to give them a picture with which to start a file.

The blast sights had been roped off with red tape. Spotlights on ten-foot-tall tripods had been erected around the perimeters. Physically, the main market area reminded Friday of a gymnasium after a dance. The event was over, the place eerily lifeless, and the residue of activity was everywhere. Only here, instead of punch there were bloodstains. Instead of crepe there were shredded awnings. And instead of empty seats there were abandoned carts. Some of the vendors had taken their carts away, leaving dust-free spots on the ground in the shape of the stall. In the sharp light they resembled the black shadows of trees and people that had been burned on the walls of Hiroshima and Nagasaki by nuclear fire. Other carts had been simply abandoned. Perhaps the owners had not been there when the blast occurred and the hired help did not want to stick around. Maybe some of the sellers had been injured or killed.

Militiamen from the regular army were stationed around the perimeters. They were carrying MP5K submachine guns, very visible in the bright lights. Police were patrolling the square carrying their distinctive .455 Webley revolvers. Apart from discouraging looters—which did not really require exposed firearms—there was only one reason to haul out artillery after a strike. It was a means of restoring wounded pride and reassuring the public that the people in charge were still a potent force. It was all so sadly predictable.

Reporters were allowed to make their news broadcasts or take their pictures and then were asked to leave. An officer explained to a crew from CNN that it would be more difficult to watch for looters if a crowd gathered.

Or maybe they just did not want cameras recording their own thefts, Friday thought. He was willing to bet that many of the goods that had been left behind would be gone by morning.

A few people had come to the marketplace just to stare. Whatever they expected to see—broken bodies, the spectacle of destruction, news being made—it did not appear to fulfill them. Most left looking deflated. Bomb sites, combat zones, and car wrecks often did that to people. They were drawn to it and then repulsed. Maybe they were disappointed by a sudden awareness of their own bloodthirstiness. Some people came with flowers, which they laid on the ground beneath the tape. Others just left behind prayers for dead friends, relatives, or strangers.

At the destroyed police station and temple, building inspectors were moving through surrounding structures to determine whether they had been weakened or damaged in the blasts. Friday recognized them by their white hard hats and palm-sized echometers. These devices emitted either single- or multidirectional sound waves that could be adjusted to the composition of an object, from stone to concrete to wood. If the sound waves encountered anything that was inconsistent with the makeup of the material—which typically meant a breach—an alarm would sound and the officials would examine the site further.

Apart from the engineers there were the usual police recovery units and medical personnel working at all three sites. But Friday was surprised by one thing. Typically, terrorist attacks in India were investigated by the district police and the National Security Guard. The NSG was established in 1986 to act as a counterterrorist force. The so-called Black Cat Commandos handled situations ranging from in-progress hijackings and kidnappings to forensic activities at bomb sites. However, there was not a single black-uniformed NSG operative here. These sites were under the control of the brown-uniformed Special Frontier Force. Friday had never been to any bomb sites in Srinagar. Maybe this was the way responsibility for antiterrorist investigations had been parceled out, with the SFF getting the region nearest the line of control.

Friday was motioned along by one of the police officers. He would not be able to get into the rubble himself. But he could still come up with some sound ideas about how the attack was made. As he walked toward the place where the bus had exploded, Friday used his cell phone to call Samantha Mandor at the NSA's photo archives. He asked her to search the AP, UPI, Reuters, and other digital photograph files for pictures of sites struck by terrorists in Kashmir. He also wanted her to pull together any analysis files that were attached to the photographs. He probably had some of those in his own computer files back in his room. But he wanted information that was incident-specific. Friday told her to phone back the minute she had the photo and text archives.

The American operative neared the roped-off bus site. Unlike the two buildings, where the walls had kept people and objects from the street, the bus debris had been strewn everywhere by the powerful explosion. The bodies had been cleared away but the street was covered with metal, leather, and glass from the bus itself. There were books and cameras that the passengers had been carrying and travel accessories, clothing, and religious icons that had been packed in luggage. Unlike the buildings, this scene was a snapshot of the moment of impact.

Friday's cell phone beeped as he neared the red tape. He stopped walking and took the call.

"Yes?" he said.

"Mr. Friday? It's Samantha Mandor. I have the photographs and information you asked for. Do you want me to send the images somewhere? There are about four dozen color pictures."

"No," Friday said. "When was the last attack in Srinagar?"

"Five months ago," Samantha told him. "It was against a shipment of artillery shells that were en route to the line of control. The attack caused one hell of an explosion."

"Was it a suicide bombing?" he asked.

"No," Samantha said. "There's a microscopic image of liquid crystal display fragments that were found near ground zero. The lab analysis says it was part of a timer. They also said a remote sensor was found in the debris but that it was apparently not detonated."

That was probably part of a backup plan, Friday thought. Professionals often included a line-of-sight device to trigger the explosives in case the timer did not work or if the device were discovered before the timer could activate them. The presence of an LOS receiver meant that at least one of the terrorists was almost certainly in the area when the device exploded.

"What about the personnel at the bomb site?" Friday asked. "What kind of uniforms were they wearing?"

"There were National Security Guard officers as well as local police on the scene," the woman informed him.

"Any members of the Special Frontier Force?" Friday asked.

"None," she said. "There were additional assaults against military targets in Srinagar. They occurred six and seven weeks prior to that attack. National Security Guard officers were present there as well."

"Did anyone claim responsibility for those attacks?" Friday asked.

"According to the data file those two and this one were claimed by the same group," Samantha told him. "The Free Kashmir Militia."

"Thank you," Friday said. He had heard of them. Reportedly, they had the backing of the Pakistan government.

"Will you need anything else?" Samantha asked.

"Not right now," he replied and clicked off.

Friday hooked the cell phone to his belt. He would call his new boss later, when he had something solid to report. He looked around. There were no Black Cat Commandos here. Maybe that was significant, maybe it was not. Their absence might have been a territorial issue. Or maybe the NSG had been unable to stop the terrorists and the problem had been turned over to the SFF. Perhaps a former SFF officer had been named to a high government post. Appointments like that routinely led to reorganizations.

Of course, there was always the possibility that this was not routine. What kind of exceptional circumstances would lead to a department being shut out of an investigation? That would certainly happen if security were an issue. Friday wondered if the NSG might have been compromised by Pakistani operatives. Or maybe the SFF had made it look as though the Black Cats had been penetrated. Because budgets were tighter there was even more interagency rivalry here than there was in the United States.

Friday turned around slowly. There were several two- and three-story-high buildings around the market. However, those would not have been good vantage points for the terrorists. If they had needed to use the remote detonators, the carts with their high banners, awnings, and umbrellas might have blocked the line of sight. If there had been any cooked-food stands in the way smoke might also have obscured their vision. Besides, the terrorists would also have had the problem of renting rooms. There was a danger in leaving a paper trail, like the terrorists who charged the van they used to attack the World Trade Center in New York. And only amateur terrorists paid cash for a room. That was a red flag that usually sent landlords right to the police. Not even the greediest landlord wanted someone who might be a bomb maker living in their building.

Besides, there was no need to hide here. It would have been easy for a terrorist to remain anonymous in this busy marketplace day after day to case the targets, plant the explosives, and watch the site today. But Friday did wonder one thing. Why did the police station and the temple blow up at the same time while the bus did not explode until several seconds later? It was extremely likely that they were related attacks. It could have been that the timers were slightly out-of-synch. Or maybe there was another reason.

Friday continued walking to where the bus had been parked. Traffic had been diverted from Route 1A to other streets. He was able to stand in the broad avenue and look back at the site. This road was the most direct way out of here. It fed any number of roads. Pursuit would have been extremely difficult even if the police knew the individual or kind of vehicle they were looking for. He found the line-of-sight spot that would have been the ideal place to stand in case the timer failed. It was on the curb, near where the bus was parked. It was about four hundred yards from the target, which was near the maximum range for most remote detonators. Obviously, if a terrorist were waiting there for the blast, he would not have wanted the bus to blow up yet. He would have waited until after the temple explosion then moved a safe distance away. The bus explosion would have been scheduled to give him time to get away. Or else he had triggered the blast himself using the same remote he would have used on the temple.

But that still did not tell him why there were two separate explosions for the police station and temple. One large explosion would have brought both structures down.

Friday started back toward the other end of the market. When he got back to his room he would call the NSA. The market attack itself did not bother him. He did not really give a damn who ended up being in charge here. What concerned him were the Black Cats. These people would have access to intelligence about him and Striker once they went into the mountains. If there was even a possibility that the NSG was leaking, he wanted to make sure they were kept out of the circuit.

FOURTEEN

Kargil, Kashmir
Wednesday, 7:00 P.M.

As his motorcycle sped through the foothills of the Himalayas, Ishaq Fazeli wished he had one thing above all. He had left Apu's farm without eating dinner and he was hungry. But he did not want food. He had been driving with his mouth open—a bad habit—and his tongue was dry. But he did not want water. What he wanted most was a helmet.

As the lightweight Royal Endfield Bullet sped through the mountain pass, small, flat rocks spit from under the slender wheels. Whenever the roadway narrowed, as it did now, and Ishaq passed too close to the mountainside, the sharp-edged pebbles came back at him like bullets. He would even settle for a turban if he had the material to make one and the time to stop. Instead, Ishaq adjusted to driving with his face turned slightly to the left. As long as the pebbles did not hit his eyes he would be all right. And if they did he would be philosophical about it. He would still have his left eye. Growing up in the west, near the Khyber Pass, he had learned long ago that the mountains of the subcontinent were not for the weak.

For one thing, even during a short two-hour ride like this, the weather changes quickly. Brutal sunshine can give way to a snow squall within minutes. Sleet can turn to thick fog even quicker. Travelers who are unprepared can freeze or dehydrate or lose their way before reaching safety. Sunshine, wind, precipitation, heat and cold from fissures, caverns, and lofty tors—all rush madly around the immutable peaks, clashing and warring in unpredictable ways. In that respect the mountains reminded Ishaq of the ancient caliphs. They too were towering and imperious, answering only to Allah.

79

For another thing, the foothills of the Himalayas are extremely difficult to negotiate on foot, let alone on a motorcycle. The mountain range is relatively young and the slopes are still sharp and steep. Here, in Kashmir, the few paths one finds were originally made by the British in 1845 at the onset of the Anglo-Sikh Wars. Queen Victoria's elite mountain forces used the routes, known as "cuts," to flank enemy troops that were encamped in lower elevations. Too narrow for trucks, cars, and artillery, and too precarious for horses and other pack animals, the cuts fell into disuse at the time of the First World War and remained largely untraveled until the Pakistanis rediscovered them in 1947. While the Indians used helicopters to move men and matériel through the region, the Pakistanis preferred these slower, more secretive paths. The cuts peaked at around eight thousand feet, where the temperatures were too low at night and the air too cold to support simple bedroll camps or sustained marches.

Not that the hazards or the discomfort mattered to Ishaq right now. He had a mission to accomplish and a leader to serve. Nothing would get in the way of that. Not precipitous falls, or the hornetlike pebbles that wanted to send him there, or the sudden drop in the temperature.

Fortunately, the motorcycle performed as heroically as its reputation. More than a year before, Ishaq had taken the Royal Endfield Bullet from behind an army barracks. It was a beautiful machine. It was not one of the prized vintage bikes from the 1950s, made when the British company first set up its factory in India. But the machine was standard equipment of local military and police units. As such, it did not attract undue attention. And there were tactical advantages as well. Like all the Royal Endfield Bullets, the distinctive red-and-black motorcycle got exceptional mileage and had a maximum speed of nearly eighty miles an hour. The bike was durable and the 22 bhp engine was relatively quiet. At just under four hundred pounds the bike also caused very little stress on the cliffside portions of the road. And the low noise output was important as he made his way up into the foothills, where loud sounds could cause rock slides.

Ishaq saw small numbers carved in the side of the mountain. They indicated that the elevation was four thousand feet. The Free Kashmir Militiaman was behind schedule. He pushed the bike a little faster. The wind rushed at him, causing his cheeks to flutter. The noise they made sounded almost like the motorcycle engine. By the grace of the Prophet he and the machine had become one. He smiled at the ways of Allah.

Section 2E was near the high midpoint of the cuts. Pakistani troops had spent years mapping this region. When they retreated from Kargil, the troops left a large cache of weapons, explosives, clothes, passports, and medical supplies in a cave at the high point of the sector. Sharab and her team frequently retreated to the spot to replenish their stores.

Ishaq had kept an eye on his watch as he pushed higher into the hills. He did not want to keep Sharab waiting. That was not because their leader was intolerant or impatient but because he wanted to be there for her—whenever, wherever, and for whatever reason she needed him. A political professor with no prior field experience, Sharab's dedication and tactical ingenuity had quickly earned the respect and complete devotion of every member of the team. Ishaq was also a little bit in love with her, although he was careful not to let that show. He did not want her thinking that was the only reason he was with her. She liked to work with patriots, not admirers. Yet Ishaq often wondered if the leaders of the Free Kashmir Militia had asked her to lead this group because she was a woman. When ancient physicians used to cauterize the wounds of warriors it took five or more men to restrain the injured man—or one woman. For love of Sharab or fear of shaming their manhood, there was nothing the men in her cell would refuse to do.

A .38 Smith & Wesson was snug in a holster under his wool sweater. The handgun came to the FKM via the Karachi Airport security police, which had bought nearly one thousand of the weapons from the United States almost thirty years before. The weight of the loaded gun felt good against his ribs. Ishaq's faith taught him that it was only through the

81

Prophet and Allah that a man became strong. Ishaq believed that, passionately. Prayer and the Koran gave him strength. But there was also something empowering about having a weapon at your side. Religion was a satisfying meal that carried a man through the day. The Smith & Wesson was a snack that got him through the moment.

The road became bumpier due to recent rockfall from a cliff. The outside corners were also more precarious. To make things worse, a cool drizzle began. It nicked his face like windblown sand. But despite all this he pushed the motorcycle even harder. If the rain kept up and had a chance to freeze, the cut would become brutally slick. He also had to watch out for hares and other animals. Hitting one could cause him to skid. Still, he could not slow down. Not if he were going to reach the zone in time. They always met up here after a mission but never with such urgency. First, Sharab usually liked to go back to whatever house or hut or barn they had occupied in order to have a final talk with their host. She wanted to make sure that whoever she left behind understood that they would remain alive only as long as they remained silent. Some of the team members did not agree with her charity, especially when they were Hindus like Apu and his granddaughter. But Sharab did not want to turn the people against her. To her, whether they were Muslim or not, most of these farmers, shepherds, and factory workers were already Pakistani. She did not want to kill innocent countrymen, present or future.

The skies were dark and Ishaq flipped on his headlights. A powerful lamp illuminated the road almost two hundred yards ahead. That was barely enough visibility to allow him to keep moving at his current pace. Curves came up so suddenly that he nearly went off the cut twice. Every now and then he slowed for just a moment to keep from feeling like he could fly. That was a very real delusion at this height and these speeds. He also took that time to glance back. He wanted to make sure he was not being followed. With the hum of the engine echoing off the crags and valleys, the sputtering of his cheeks, and the knocking of the thrown pebbles, Ishaq would not necessarily hear the roar of a pursuing vehicle or helicopter. He had warned Apu to stay in the house and he had cut the telephone line. But still—one never knew how a man would react when a family member was in captivity.

Ishaq saw another roadside marker. He was at forty-five hundred feet now. He did not know exactly how far Sharab and the team would be able to go in the van. They were coming up another cut. Maybe they could get to five thousand feet before the road became too narrow to accommodate the truck. The roads joined a few hundred feet ahead. When he arrived, he would either see their tire treads or else wait for them at the cave. He hoped they were already there. He was anxious to know what had happened, what had gone wrong.

He prayed it was nothing that might keep them from him. If for some reason the others did not show up within twenty-four hours, Ishaq's standing orders were to get to the cave and set up the radio he carried in his small equipment case. Then he was to call the FKM base in Abbottabad, across the border in Pakistan. They would tell him what to do. That meant either he would be advised to wait for replacements or attempt to return home for a debriefing.

If it came to that, Ishaq hoped they would tell him to wait. Going home would mean climbing the mountains to the Siachin Glacier. Or else he would have to attempt to make his way across the line of control. His chances of surviving the trip were not good. FKM command might just as well order him to shoot himself at the cave.

As Ishaq neared the point where the two cuts converged he saw the truck. It was parked in the middle of the road. The flatbed was covered with an earth-tone tarp they carried and the cab was hidden beneath scrub. A smile fought a losing battle against the wind. He was glad they had made it. But that changed when his headlights found the team about two hundred yards ahead. As one they turned and crouched, ready to fire.

"No, it's Ishaq!" he cried. "It's Ishaq!"

83

They lowered their weapons and continued ahead without waiting for their teammate. Sharab was in front with the girl. Nanda was being urged forward at gunpoint.

That was not like Sharab.

This was bad. This was very, very bad.

FIFTEEN

Washington, D.C.
Wednesday, 10:51 A.M.

Bob Herbert was usually a pretty happy man.

To begin with, Herbert loved his work. He had a good team working beside him. He was able to give Op-Center personnel the kind of heads-up intelligence he and his wife never had in Lebanon. He was also happy with himself. He was not a Washington bureaucrat. He put truthfulness above diplomacy and the well-being of the NCMC above the advancement of Bob Herbert. That meant he could sleep at night. He had the respect of the people who mattered, like Paul Hood and Mike Rodgers.

But Bob Herbert was not happy right now.

Hank Lewis had phoned from the NSA to say that the latest information e-mailed from Ron Friday was being processed by decryption personnel. It would be forwarded to Herbert within minutes. While Herbert waited for the intel he did something he had been meaning to do since the Striker recon mission was okayed by the CIOC. He pulled up Ron Friday's NSA file on his computer. Until now, Herbert and his team had been too busy helping Mike Rodgers and Striker prepare for the mission to do anything else.

Herbert did not like what he saw in Ron Friday's dossier. Or rather, what he did not see there.

As a crisis management center, Op-Center did not keep a full range of military maps and intelligence in what they called their "hot box." The only files that were reviewed and updated on a four-times-daily basis were situations and places where American personnel or interests were directly involved or affected. Kashmir was certainly a crisis zone. But if it exploded, it was not a spot with which Op-Center

85

would automatically be involved. In fact, that was the reason Striker had been asked to go into the region and look for Pakistani nuclear weapons. Pakistani intelligence would not be expecting them.

Ron Friday was a very late addition to the mission. His participation had been requested over the weekend by Satya Shankar, minister of state, Department of Atomic Energy. Officially, one of Shankar's duties was the sale of nuclear technology to developing nations. Unofficially, he was responsible for helping the military keep track of nuclear technology within enemy states. Shankar and Friday had worked together once before, when Shankar was joint secretary, Exploration, of the Ministry of Petroleum and Natural Gas. Friday had been called in by a European oil concern to assess legal issues involving drilling in disputed territory between Great Indian Desert in the Rajasthan Province of India and the Thar Desert in Pakistan. Shankar had obviously been impressed by the attorney.

Since Op-Center was stuck with Friday, reading his file had not been a high priority for Herbert. Especially since the CIOC had already okayed Friday based on his Blue Shield rating. That meant Ron Friday was cleared to take part in the most sensitive fieldwork in foreign countries. Red Shield meant that an agent was trusted by the foreign government. White Shield meant that he was trusted by his own government, that there was no evidence of double-agent activity. Yellow Shield meant that he had been revealed to be a double agent and was being used by his government to put out disinformation, often without his knowledge or occasionally with his cooperation in exchange for clemency. Blue Shield meant he was trusted by both nations.

What the Red, White, and Blue rankings really meant was that no data had ever come up to suggest the agent was corrupt. That was usually good enough for a project overseer to rubber-stamp an individual for a mission. Especially an overseer who was new on the job and overworked, like Hank Lewis at the National Security Agency. But the Shield system was not infallible. It could simply mean that the agent had been too careful to be caught. Or that he had someone on the inside who kept his file clean.

Friday's file was extremely skimpy. It contained very few field reports from Azerbaijan, where he had most recently been stationed at the United States embassy in Baku as an aide to Deputy Ambassador Dorothy Williamson. There were zero communications at all from him during the recent crisis in the former Soviet Republic. That was unusual. Herbert had a look at the files of the two CIA operatives who had been stationed at the embassy. They were full of daily reports. Coincidentally, perhaps, both of those men were killed.

Friday's thin file and his apparent silence during the crisis was troubling. One of his superiors at the NSA, Jack Fenwick, was the man who had hired the terrorist known as the Harpooner to precipitate the Caspian Sea confrontation between Azerbaijan, Iran, and Russia. Herbert had not read all the postmortems about the situation. There had not been time. But Friday's silence before and during the showdown led Herbert to wonder: was he really inactive or were his reports made directly to someone who destroyed them?

Jack Fenwick, for example.

If that were true it could mean that Ron Friday had been working with Jack Fenwick and the Harpooner to start a war. Of course, there was always the possibility that Friday had been helping Fenwick without knowing what the NSA chief was up to. But that seemed unlikely. Ron Friday had been an attorney, a top-level oil rights negotiator, and a diplomatic advisor. He did not seem naive. And that scared the hell out of Herbert.

The decrypted NSA e-file arrived and Herbert opened it. The folder contained Friday's observations as well as relevant data about the previous antiterrorist functions of both the National Security Guard and the Special Frontier Force. It did not seem strange to Herbert that SFF had replaced the Black Cats after this latest attack. Maybe the SFF had jurisdiction over strikes against religious sites. Or maybe the government had grown impatient with the ineffectiveness of the Black Cats. There was obviously a terrorist cell roaming

Kashmir. Any security agency that failed to maintain security was not going to have that job for very long.

Either he or Paul Hood could call their partners in Indian intelligence and get an explanation for the change. Herbert's concerns about Ron Friday would not be so easy to dispel.

Herbert entered the numbers 008 on his wheelchair phone. That was Paul Hood's extension. Shortly before Op-Center opened its doors Matt Stoll had hacked the computer system to make sure he got the 007 extension. Herbert had not been happy about Stoll's hacking but Hood had appreciated the man's initiative. As long as Stoll limited his internal sabotage to a one-time hack of the phone directory Hood had decided to overlook it.

The phone beeped once. "Hood here."

"Chief, it's Bob. Got a minute?"

"Sure," Hood said.

"I'll be right there," Herbert said. He typed an address in his computer and hit "enter." "Meanwhile, I'd like you to have a quick look at the e-files I'm sending over. One's a report from the NSA about this morning's attack in Srinagar. Another is Ron Friday's very thin dossier."

"All right," Hood said.

Herbert hung up and wheeled himself down the corridor to Hood's office. As Herbert was en route he got a call from Matt Stoll.

"Make it quick," Herbert said.

"I was just reviewing the latest number grabs from the Bellhop," Stoll told him. "That telephone number we've been watching, the field phone in Srinagar? It's making very strange calls."

"What do you mean?" Herbert said.

"The field phone keeps calling the home phone in Jammu, the police station," Stoll said. "But the calls last for only one second."

"That's it?"

"That's it," Stoll told him. "We read a connect, a one-second gap, then a disconnect."

"Is it happening regularly?" Herbert asked.

"There's been a blip every minute since four P.M. local time, six thirty A.M. our time," Stoll told him.

"That's over four hours," Herbert said. "Short, regular pulses over a long period. Sounds like a tracking beacon."

"It could be that," Stoll agreed, "or it could mean that someone hit the autoredial button by accident. Voice mail answers nonemergency calls at the police station. The field phone may have been programmed to read that as a disconnect so it hangs up and rings the number again."

"That doesn't sound likely," Herbert said. "Is there any way to tell if the field phone is moving?"

"Not directly," Stoll said.

"What about indirectly?" Herbert asked as he reached Paul Hood's office. The door was open and he knocked on the jamb. Hood was studying his computer monitor. He motioned Herbert in.

"If the phone calls are a beacon, then the police in Kashmir are almost certainly following them, probably by ground-based triangulation," Stoll told Herbert. "All of that would be run through their computers. It will take some time but we can try breaking into the system."

"Do it," Herbert said.

"Sure," Stoll said. "But why don't we just call over and ask them what's going on? Aren't they our allies? Aren't we supposed to be running this operation with them?"

"Yes," Herbert replied. "But if there's some way we can accomplish this without them knowing I'd be happier. The police are going to want to know why we're asking. The Black Cats and selected government officials are the only ones who are supposed to know that Striker is coming over."

"I see," Stoll said. "Okay. We'll try hacking them."

"Thanks," Herbert said and hung up as he wheeled into Hood's office. He locked his brakes and shut the door behind him.

"Busy morning?" Hood asked.

"Not until some lunatic decided to set off fireworks in Srinagar," Herbert replied.

Hood nodded. "I haven't finished these files," he said, "but Ron Friday is obviously concerned about us having anything

89

to do with the Black Cats. And you're apparently worried about having anything to do with Ron Friday."

Paul Hood had not spent a lot of time working in the intelligence community and he had a number of weaknesses. However, one of Hood's greatest strengths was that his years in politics and finance had taught him to intuit the concerns of his associates, whatever the topic.

"That's about the size of it," Herbert admitted.

"Tell me about this police line blip," Hood said, still reading.

"The last home phone-to-field phone communication came a moment before the explosion," Herbert said. "But Matt just told me that the regular pulses from field to home started immediately after that. In ELINT we want three things to happen before we posit a possible connection to a terrorist attack: timing, proximity, and probable source. We've got those."

"The probable source being a cell that's apparently been working in Srinagar," Hood said.

"Correct," Herbert said. "I just asked Matt to try and get more intel on the continuing blips."

Hood nodded and continued reading. "The problem you have with Friday is a little dicier."

"Why?" Herbert asked.

"Because he's there at the request of the Indian government," Hood said.

"So is Striker," Herbert pointed out.

"Yes, but they've worked with Friday," Hood said. "They'll give Striker more freedom because they trust Friday."

"There's an irony in there somewhere," Herbert said.

"Look, I see where you're coming from," Hood acknowledged. "Friday worked for Fenwick. Fenwick betrayed his country. But we have to be careful about pushing guilt by association."

"How about guilt by criminal activity?" Herbert said. "Whatever Friday was doing in Baku was removed from his file."

"That's assuming he was working for the NSA," Hood

said. "I just put in a call to Deputy Ambassador Williamson in Baku. Her personal file says that Friday worked as her aide. He was on loan from the NSA to collect intelligence on the oil situation. There's no reason to assume the CIA involved him in the hunt for the Harpooner. And Jack Fenwick was playing with fire. He may not have told Friday what the NSA was really doing in the Caspian."

"Or Fenwick may have sent him there," Herbert pointed out. "Friday's oil credentials made him the perfect inside man."

"You'll need to prove that one," Hood said.

Herbert didn't like that answer. When his gut told him something he listened to it. To him, Hood's habit of being a devil's advocate was one of his big weaknesses. Still, from the perspective of accountability Hood was doing the right thing. That was why Hood was in charge of Op-Center and Herbert was not. They could not go back to the CIOC and tell them they called off the mission or were concerned about Friday's role in it because of Herbert's intuition.

The phone beeped. It was Dorothy Williamson. Hood put the phone on speaker. He was busy typing something on his keyboard as he introduced himself and Herbert. Then he explained that they were involved in a joint operation with Ron Friday. Hood asked if she would mind sharing her impressions of the agent.

"He was very efficient, a good attorney and negotiator, and I was sorry to lose him," she said.

"Did he interact much with the two Company men, the ones who were killed by the Harpooner's man?" Hood asked.

"Mr. Friday spent a great deal of time with Mr. Moore and Mr. Thomas," Williamson replied.

"I see," Hood said.

Herbert felt vindicated. Friday's interaction with the men should have shown up in his reports to the NSA. Now he knew the file had been sanitized.

"For the record, Mr. Hood, I do want to point out one thing," Williamson said. "The Company agents were not killed by one assassin but by two."

That caught Herbert by surprise.

91

"There were two assassins at the hospital," the deputy ambassador went on. "One of them was killed. The other one got away. The Baku police department is still looking for him."

"I did not know that," Hood said. "Thank you."

Herbert's gut growled a little. The two CIA operatives were killed getting medical attention for a visiting agent who had been poisoned by the Harpooner. Fenwick's plan to start a Caspian war had depended upon killing all three men at the hospital. Fenwick certainly would have asked Friday for information regarding the movements of the CIA operatives. And just as certainly that information would have been deleted from Friday's files. But after the two men were killed, Friday had to have suspected that something was wrong. He should have confided in Williamson or made sure he had a better alibi.

Unless he was a willing part of Fenwick's team.

"Bob Herbert here, Madam Deputy Ambassador," Herbert said. "Can you tell me where Mr. Friday was on the night of the murders?"

"In his apartment, as I recall," Williamson informed him.

"Did Mr. Friday have anything to say after he learned about the killings?" Herbert pressed.

"Not really," she said.

"Was he concerned for his own safety?" Herbert asked.

"He never expressed any worries," she said. "But there was not a lot of time for chat. We were working hard to put down a war."

Hood shot Herbert a glance. The intelligence chief sat back, exasperated, as Hood complimented her on her efforts during the crisis.

That was Paul Hood. Whatever the situation he always had the presence of mind to play the diplomat. Not Herbert. If the Harpooner was killing U.S. agents, he wanted to know why it did not occur to Ms. Williamson to find out why Friday had not been hit.

The deputy ambassador had a few more things to say about Friday, especially praising his quick learning curve on the issues they had to deal with between Azerbaijan and its neighbors. Williamson asked Hood to give him her regards if he spoke with Friday.

Hood said he would and clicked off. He regarded Herbert. "You wouldn't have gotten anywhere hammering her," Hood said.

"How do you know?" Herbert asked.

"While we were talking I looked at her c.v.," Hood said. "Williamson's a political appointee. She ran the spin-doctoring for Senator Thompson during his last Senate campaign."

"Dirty tricks?" Herbert asked disgustedly. "That's the whole of her intelligence experience?"

"Pretty much," Hood said. "With two CIA agents on staff in Baku I guess the president thought he was safe scoring points with the majority whip. More to the point, I'm guessing this whole thing sounds too clean to you."

"Like brass buttons on inspection day."

"I don't know, Bob," Hood said. "It's not just Williamson. Hank Lewis trusted Friday enough to send him to India."

"That doesn't mean anything," Herbert said. "I spoke with Hank Lewis earlier this morning. He's making decisions like a monkey in a space capsule."

Hood made a face. "He's a good man—"

"Maybe, Chief, but that's the way it is," Herbert insisted. "Lewis gets a jolt of electricity and pushes a button. He hasn't had time to think about Ron Friday or anyone else. Look, Hank Lewis and Dorothy Williamson shouldn't be the issues right now—"

"Agreed," Hood said. "All right. Let's assume Ron Friday may not be someone we want on our team. How do we vet him? Jack Fenwick's not going to say anything to anyone."

"Why not?" Herbert asked. "Maybe the rat-bastard will talk in exchange for immunity—"

"The president got what he wanted, the resignations of Fenwick and his coconspirators," Hood said. "He doesn't want a national trial that will question whether he was actually on the edge of a mental breakdown during the crisis, even if it means letting a few underlings remain in the system. Fenwick got off lucky. He's not going to say anything that might change the president's mind."

"That's great," Herbert said. "The guilty go free and the president's psyche doesn't get the examination it may damn well need."

"And the stock market doesn't collapse and the military doesn't lose faith in its commander-in-chief and a rash of Third World despots don't start pushing their own agendas while the nation is distracted," Hood said. "The systems are all too damn interconnected, Bob. Right and wrong don't matter anymore. It's all about equilibrium."

"Is that so?" Herbert said. "Well, mine's a little shaky right now. I don't like risking my team, my friends, to keep some Indian nabob happy."

"We aren't going to," Hood said. "We're going to protect the part of the system we've been given." He looked at his watch. "I don't know if Ron Friday betrayed his country in Baku. Even if he did it doesn't mean he's got a side bet going in India. But we still have about eighteen hours before Striker reaches India. What can we do to get more intel on Friday?"

"I can have my team look into his cell phone records and e-mail," Herbert said, "maybe get security videos from the embassy and see if anything suspicious turns up."

"Do it," Hood said.

"That may not tell us everything," Herbert said.

"We don't need everything," Hood said. "We need probable cause, something other than the possibility that Friday may have helped Fenwick. If we get that then we can go to Senator Fox and the CIOC, tell them we don't want Striker working with someone who was willing to start a war for personal gain."

"All very polite," Herbert grumped. "But we're using kid gloves on a guy who may have been a goddamned traitor."

"No," Hood said. "We're presuming he's innocent until we're sure he's not. You get me the information. I'll take care of delivering the message."

Herbert agreed, reluctantly.

As he wheeled back to his office, the intelligence chief reflected on the fact that the only thing diplomacy ever accomplished was to postpone the inevitable. But Hood was the boss and Herbert would do what he wanted.

For now.

Because, more than loyalty to Paul Hood and Op-Center, more than watching out for his own future, Herbert felt responsible for the security of Striker and the lives of his friends. The day things became so interconnected that Herbert could not do that was the day he became a pretty unhappy man. And then he would have just one more thing to do.

Hang up his spurs.

SIXTEEN

Siachin Base 2E, Kashmir
Wednesday, 9:02 P.M.

Sharab and her group left the camouflaged truck and spent the next two hours making their way to the cliff where the cave was located. Ishaq had raced ahead on his motorcycle. He went as far as he could go and then walked the rest of the way. Upon reaching the cave he collected the small, hooded lanterns they kept there and set them out for the others. The small, yellow lights helped Sharab, Samouel, Ali, and Hassan get Nanda up to the ledge below the site. The Kashmiri hostage did not try to get away but she was obviously not comfortable with the climb. The path leading to this point had been narrow with long, sheer drops. This last leg, though less than fifty feet, was almost vertical.

A fine mist drifted across the rock, hampering visibility as they made their way up. The men proceeded with Nanda between them. Sharab brought up the rear. Her right palm was badly bruised and it ached from when she had struck the dashboard earlier. Sharab rarely lost her temper but it was occasionally necessary. Like the War Steeds of the Koran, who struck fire with their hooves, she had to let her anger out in measured doses. Otherwise it would explode in its own time.

Nanda had to feel her way to the handholds that Sharab and the others had cut in the rock face over a year before. The men helped her as best they could.

Sharab had insisted on bringing the Kashmiri along, though not so they would have a hostage. Men who would blow up their own citizens would not hesitate to shoot one more if it suited them. Sharab had taken Nanda for one reason only. She had questions to ask her.

The other two blasts in the Srinagar marketplace had not been a coincidence. Someone had to have known what Sharab and her group were planning. Maybe it was a pro-Indian extremist group. More likely it was someone in the government, since it would have taken careful planning to coordinate the different explosions. Whoever it was, they had caused the additional explosions so that the Free Kashmir Militia would unwittingly take the blame for attacking Hindus.

It did not surprise Sharab that the Indians would kill their own people to turn the population against the FKM. Some governments build germ-war factories in schools and put military headquarters under hospitals. Others arrest dissidents by the wagonload or test toxins in the air and water of an unsuspecting public. Security of the many typically came before the well-being of the few. What upset Sharab was that the Indians had so effectively counterplotted against her group. The Indians had known where and when the FKM was attacking. They knew that the group always took credit for their attack within moments of the blast. The Indians made it impossible for the cell to continue. Even if the authorities did not know who the cell members were or where they lived, they had undermined the group's credibility. They would no longer be perceived as an anti–New Delhi force. They would be seen as anti-Indian, anti-Hindu.

There was nothing Sharab could do about that now. For the moment she felt safe. If the authorities had known about the cave they would have been waiting here. Once the team was armed and had collected their cold weather gear she would decide whether to stay for the night or push on. Moving through the cold, dark mountains would be dangerous. But giving the Indians a chance to track them down would be just as risky. She could not allow her group to be taken alive or dead. Even possessing their bodies would give the Indian radicals a target with which to rally the mostly moderate population.

Sharab wanted to survive for another reason, also. For the sake of future cells Sharab had to try to figure out how the Indian authorities knew what she and her team had been doing. Someone could have seen them working on the roof of the police station. But that would have led to their arrest and interrogation, not this elaborate plot. She suspected that someone had been watching them for some time. Since virtually none of the FKM's communications were by phone or computer, and no one in Pakistan knew their exact whereabouts, that someone had to have been spying from nearby.

She knew and trusted everyone on her team. Only two other people had been close to the cell: Nanda and her grandfather. Apu would have been too afraid to move against them and Sharab did not see how Nanda could have spoken with anyone else. They were watched virtually all day, every day. Still, somehow, one of them must have betrayed the group.

Ishaq was leaning from the cave about ten feet above. He reached down and helped everyone up in turn. Sharab waited while Ishaq and Ali literally hoisted Nanda inside. The rock was cool and she placed her cheek against it. She shut her eyes. Though the rock felt good, it was not home.

When she was a young girl, Sharab's favorite tale in the Koran involved the seven Sleepers of the Cave. One line in particular came to her each time she visited this place: "We made them sleep in the cave for many years, and then awakened them to find out who could best tell the length of their stay."

Sharab knew that feeling of disorientation. Cut off from all that she loved, separated from all that was familiar, time had lost its meaning. But the woman knew what the Sleepers of the Cave had learned. That the Lord God knew how long they had been at rest. If they trusted in Him they would never be lost.

Sharab had her god and she also had her country. Yet this was not how she had wanted to return to Pakistan. She had always imagined going home victorious rather than running from the enemy.

"Come on!" Samouel called down to her.

Sharab opened her eyes. She continued her climb toward the cave. The moment of peace had passed. She began getting angry again. She pulled herself inside the small cave and stood. The wind wailed around her going into the shallow cave, then whooshed past her as it circled back out. Two lanterns rocked on hooks in the low ceiling. Beneath them were stacked crates of guns, explosives, canned food, clothing, and other gear.

Except for Ishaq, the men were standing along the sides of the cave. Ishaq was reattaching a large tarp to the front of the cave. The outside was painted to resemble the rest of the mountainside. Not only did it help to camouflage the natural cave but it helped keep them warm whenever they were here.

Nanda was near the back of the cave. She was facing Sharab. The ceiling sloped severely and the Kashmiri woman's back was bent slightly so she could remain standing. There was a band of blood staining the ankle of her pants. The cuff must have worn the flesh raw yet Nanda had not complained. The corners of her mouth trembled, her breath came in anxious little puffs, and her arms were folded across her chest. Sharab decided that was probably an attempt to keep warm and not a show of defiance. They were all perspiring from the climb and the cold air had turned their sweat-drenched clothes frigid.

Sharab walked slowly toward her prisoner.

"Innocent people died today," Sharab said. "There will be no retribution, no more killing, but I must know. Did you or your grandfather tell anyone about our activities?"

Nanda said nothing.

"We did not destroy the temple and the bus, you know that," Sharab added. "You've lived with us, you must have heard us making plans. You know we only attack government targets. Whoever attacked the Hindus is your enemy. They must be exposed and brought to justice."

Nanda continued to stand where she was, her arms bundled around her. But there was a change in her posture, in her expression. She had drawn her shoulders back slightly and her eyes and mouth had hardened.

Now she was defiant.

Why? Sharab wondered. Because a Pakistani had dared to suggest that Indians could be enemies to Indians? Nanda could not be so naive. And if she did not agree, she did not want to defend her countrymen either.

"Samouel?" Sharab said.

The young bearded man stood. "Yes?"

"Please take care of dinner, including our guest," Sharab said. "She'll need her strength."

Samouel opened a frost-covered cardboard box that contained military rations. He began passing out the pop-top tins. Each of the shallow, red, six-by-four-inch containers was packed with basmati rice, strips of precooked goat meat, and two cinnamon sticks. A second cardboard box contained cartons of powdered milk. While Samouel handed those to the men Ali got a jug of water from the back of the cave. He added it to the powdered milk, pouring in skillful little bursts that kept the ice that had formed in the jugs from clogging the neck.

Sharab continued to regard Nanda. "You're coming with us to Pakistan," Sharab informed her. "Once you're there you will tell my colleagues what you refuse to tell me."

Nanda still did not respond. That seemed strange to Sharab. The dark-eyed woman had been talkative enough during the months at the farm. She had complained about the intrusion, the restrictions that had been placed on her, the militaristic leaders of Pakistan, and the terrorist activities of the FKM. It seemed odd that she would not say anything now.

Perhaps the woman was just tired from the climb. Yet she had not said anything in the truck either. It could be that she was afraid for her life. But she had not tried to get away on the mountain path or to reach any of the weapons that were plainly in view.

And then it hit her. The reason Nanda did not want to talk to them. Sharab stopped a few feet in front of the Kashmiri woman.

"You're working with them," Sharab said suddenly. "Either you want us to take you to Pakistan or—" She stopped and called Hassan over. Standing nearly six-foot-five, the thirty-six-year-old former quarry worker was the largest man on her team. He had to duck just to stand in the cave.

"Hold her," Sharab ordered.

Now Nanda moved. She tried to get around Sharab. She was apparently trying to reach one of the guns in the box. But Hassan moved behind Nanda. He grabbed her arms right below the shoulders and pinned them together with his massive hands. The Kashmiri woman moaned and tried to wriggle away. But the big man pushed harder. She arched her back and then stopped moving.

Hassan wrestled Nanda over to Sharab. The Pakistani woman felt the pockets of Nanda's jeans and then reached under Nanda's bulky wool sweater. She patted Nanda's sides and back.

She found what she was looking for at once. It was on Nanda's left side, just above her hip. As Nanda renewed her struggles, Sharab pulled up the sweater and exposed the woman's waist.

There was a small leather pouch attached to a narrow elastic band. Inside the pouch was a cellular phone. Sharab removed it and walked closer to one of the hanging lanterns. She examined the palm-sized black phone closely. The liquid crystal display was blank. Though that function had been disengaged the phone itself was working. It vibrated faintly, pulsing for a second and then shutting down for a second. It did that repeatedly. There was also a dark, concave plastic bubble on the top edge. It looked like the eye of a television remote control.

"Ali, Samouel, gather up weapons and supplies," Sharab ordered. "Do it quickly."

The men put down their meals and did as they were told. Hassan continued to hold Nanda. Ishaq watched from the side of the cave. He was waiting for Sharab to tell him what to do.

Sharab regarded Nanda. "This is more than just a cell phone, isn't it? It's a tracking device."

Nanda said nothing. Sharab nodded at Hassan and he squeezed her arms together. She gasped but did not answer. After a moment Sharab motioned for him to relax his grip.

"You could not have spoken to your collaborators without us hearing," Sharab went on. "You must have used the keypad to type information. Now they're probably tracking you to our base. Who are they?"

Nanda did not answer.

Sharab strode toward the woman and slapped her with a hard backhand across the ear. "Who is behind this?" the woman screamed. "The SFF? The military? The world needs to know that we did not do this!"

Nanda refused to say anything.

"Do you have any idea what you've done?" Sharab said, stepping back.

"I do," the Kashmiri woman said at last. "I stopped your people from committing genocide."

"Genocide?"

"Against the Hindu population in Kashmir and the rest of India," Nanda said. "For years we've listened to the promise of extermination on television, shouted outside the mosques."

"You've been listening to the radicals, to Fundamentalist clerics who shout extremist views," Sharab insisted. "All we wanted was freedom for the Muslims in Kashmir."

"By killing—"

"We are at war!" Sharab declared. "But we only strike military or police targets." She held up the cell phone and tapped the top with a finger. "Do you want to talk about extermination? This is a remote sensor, isn't it? We put you close to the site and you used it to trigger explosives left by your partners."

"What I did was an act of love to protect the rest of my people," Nanda replied.

"It was an act of betrayal," Sharab replied. "They moved freely because they knew we would not hurt them. You abused that trust."

Sharab's people took part in these acts primarily in the Middle East where they used their bodies as living bombs. The difference was that Nanda's people had not chosen to make this sacrifice. Nanda and her partners had decided that for them.

But morality and blame did not matter to Sharab right now. Nanda did not have the experience to have originated this plan. Whoever was behind this was coming and undoubtedly they would be well armed. Sharab did not want to be here when they arrived.

She turned to Ishaq. The youngest member of the team was standing beside the cartons eating his goat meat and rice. His lips were pale from the cold and his face was leathery from the pounding the wind had given it during his motor-cycle journey. But his soulful eyes were alert, expectant. Sharab tried not to think about what she was about to tell him. But it had to be done.

She handed Ishaq the cell phone. "I need you to stay here with this," she told him.

The young man stopped chewing.

"You heard what is happening," Sharab went on. "We're leaving but her accomplices must think we're still here."

Ishaq put down the tin and took the phone. The other men stopped moving behind them.

"It's very heavy," Ishaq said softly. "You're right. I think they've added things." He regarded Sharab. "You don't want the Indians to leave here, is that correct?"

"That is correct," Sharab replied quietly. Her voice caught. She continued to look into Ishaq's eyes.

"Then they won't leave," he promised her. "But you had better."

"Thank you," Sharab replied.

The woman turned to help the other men, not because they needed help but because she did not want Ishaq to see her weep. She wanted him to hold on to the image of her being strong. He would need that in order to get through this. Yet the tears came. They had been together every day for two years, both in Pakistan and in Kashmir. He was devoted to her and to the cause. But he did not have the climbing or survival skills the other men had. Without them they would not get across the mountains and the line of control and back to Pakistan.

The remaining members of the team pulled on the heavy coats they kept for extended stays in the cave. They threw automatic weapons over their right shoulders and ropes over their left. They put flashlights and matches in their pockets.

Ali took the backpack he had loaded with food. Hassan grabbed Nanda after Samouel gave him the backpack with pitons, a hammer, extra flashlights, and maps.

Then, in turn, each member of the party hugged Ishaq. He smiled at them with tears in his eyes. Sharab was the last to embrace him.

"I pray that Allah will send to your aid five thousand angels," Sharab whispered to him.

"I would sooner He send them to help you reach home," Ishaq replied. "Then I would be sure that this has not been in vain."

She hugged him even tighter then patted his back, turned, and stepped through the tarp.

SEVENTEEN

Srinagar, Kashmir
Wednesday, 10:00 P.M.

Ron Friday was in his small room when the phone on the rickety night table rang. He opened his eyes and looked at his watch.

Right on time.

The phone was from the 1950s, a heavy black anvil of a thing with a thick brown cord. And it really rang rather than beeped. Friday was sitting on the bed; after sending the encoded message to Hank Lewis he had turned on the black-and-white TV. An old movie was on. Even with English subtitles Friday had trouble following the plot. The fact that he kept dozing off did not help.

Friday did not answer the phone on the first ring. Or the second. He did not pick up until the tenth ring. That was how he knew the caller was his Black Cat contact. Tenth ring at the tenth hour.

The caller, Captain Prem Nazir, said he would meet Friday outside in fifteen minutes.

Friday pulled on his shoes, grabbed his windbreaker, and headed down the single flight of stairs. There were only twelve rooms at Binoo's Palace, most of them occupied by market workers, women of questionable provenance, and men who rarely emerged from their rooms. Obviously, the police turned a blind eye to more than just the gaming parlor.

The inn did not have much of a lobby. A reception desk was located to the left of the stairs. It was run by Binoo during the day and his sister at night. There was a Persian rug on a hardwood floor with battered sofas on either side. The windows looked out on the dark, narrow street. The smell of the potent, native-grown Juari cigarettes was thick here. The gaming parlor was located in a room behind the counter. A veil of smoke actually hung like a stage scrim behind Binoo's oblivious sister.

The heavyset woman was leaning on the counter. She did not look up from her movie magazine as Friday came down. That was what he loved about this place. No one gave a damn.

The lobby was empty. So was the street. Friday leaned against the wall and waited.

Friday had never met the fifty-three-year-old Captain Nazir. Atomic Energy Minister Shankar knew him and put a lot of trust in him. Friday did not trust anyone, including Shankar. But Captain Nazir's extensive background in espionage, first behind the lines in Pakistan in the 1960s, then with the Indian army, and now with the National Security Guard, suggested that the two men might enjoy a good working relationship.

Unless, that is, there were a problem between the NSG and the Special Frontier Force. That was the first order of business Friday intended to discuss with Nazir, even before they talked about the Striker mission to search for Pakistani nuclear missiles. Friday did not mind going on a sensitive mission for the Black Cats if they did not have the full trust and support of the government. Part of intelligence work was doing things without government approval. But he did mind going out if the Black Cats and the SFF were at war, if one group were looking to embarrass the other. A freeze-out of the NSG at the bomb site did not mean that was the case. But Friday wanted to be sure.

Captain Nazir arrived exactly on schedule. He was strolling in no particular hurry with no apparent destination, and he was smoking a Juari. That was smart. The officer was up from New Delhi but he was not smoking one of the milder brands that was popular in the capital. The local cigarette would help him blend in with the surroundings.

The officer was dressed in a plain gray sweatshirt, khaki slacks, and Nikes. He was about five-foot-seven with short black hair and a scar across his forehead. His skin was

106

smooth and dark. He looked exactly like the photographs Friday had seen.

Ron Friday obviously looked like his photographs as well. Captain Nazir did not bother to introduce himself. They would not say one another's names at all. There were still SFF personnel working in the bazaar. They might have set up electronic surveillance of the area to try to catch the bombers. If so, someone might overhear them.

The officer simply offered Friday his hand and said in a low, rough voice, "Walk with me."

The two men continued in the direction Captain Nazir had been headed, away from the main street, Shervani Road. The narrow side street where the inn was located was little more than an alley. There were dark shops on either side of the road. They sold items that did not usually turn up in the bazaar, like bicycles, men's suits, and small appliances. The street ended in a high brick wall about three hundred yards away.

Nazir drew on the nub of his cigarette. "The minister thinks very highly of you."

"Thanks," Friday said. He looked down and spoke very softly. "Tell me something. What happened today in the marketplace?"

"I'm not sure," Nazir replied.

"Would you tell me if you did?" Friday asked.

"I'm not sure," Nazir admitted.

"Why was the SFF handling the investigation instead of your people?" Friday asked.

Nazir stopped walking. He retrieved a pack of cigarettes from under his sweatshirt and used one to light another. He looked at Friday in the glow of the newly lit cigarette.

"I do not know the answer to that," the officer replied as he continued walking.

"Let me point you in a direction," Friday said. "Does the SFF have special jurisdiction over Srinagar or religious targets?"

"No," Nazir replied.

"But their personnel were on the scene and your people were not," Friday repeated.

"Yes," Nazir said.

This was becoming frustrating. Friday stopped walking. He grabbed Nazir by the arm. The officer did not react.

"Before I head north and risk my life, I need to know if there's a leak in your organization," Friday said.

"Why would you think there is?" Nazir asked.

"Because there was not a single Black Cat Commando at the scene," Friday told him. "Why else would you be shut out of the investigation except for security issues?"

"Humiliation," Nazir suggested. "You have conflicts between your intelligence services. They go to great lengths to undermine one another even though you work toward the same goal."

There was no disputing that, Friday thought. He had killed a CIA agent not long ago.

"The truth is, the SFF has been extremely quiet about their activities of late and we have been quiet about our operations, including this one," Nazir went on. "Both groups have their allies in New Delhi and, eventually, all the intelligence we gather gets shuffled into the system and used."

"Like a slaughterhouse," Friday observed.

"A slaughterhouse," Nazir said. He nodded appreciatively. "I like that. I like it very much."

"I'm glad," Friday replied. "Now tell me something I'm going to like. For example, why we should put ourselves into the hands of an intelligence agency that may be risking our lives to boost their own standing in New Delhi?"

"Is that what you think?" Nazir asked.

"I don't know," Friday replied. "Convince me otherwise."

"Do you know anything about Hinduism?" Nazir asked Friday.

"I'm familiar with the basics," Friday replied. He had no idea what that had to do with anything.

"Do you know that *Hinduism* is not the name we use for our faith. It's something the West invented."

"I didn't know that," Friday admitted.

"We are countless sects and castes, all of which have their own names and very different views of the Veda, the holy

108

text," Nazir said. "The greatest problem we have as a nation is that we carry our factionalism into government. Everyone defends his own unit or department or consulate as if it were his personal faith. We do this without considering how our actions affect the whole. I am guilty of that too. My 'god,' if you will, is the one who can help me get things done. Not necessarily the one who can do the best job for India." He drew on his cigarette. "The tragedy is that the whole is now threatened with destruction and we are still not pulling together. We need more intelligence on Pakistan's nuclear threat. We cannot go and get that information ourselves for fear of triggering the very thing we are trying to avoid—a nuclear exchange. You and your group are the only ones who can help us." Nazir regarded Friday through the twisting smoke of his cigarette. "If you are still willing to undertake this mission I will be the point man for you. I will go as far into the field as I can with maps, clearances, and geographical reconnaissance. The minister and I will make certain that no one interferes with your activities. He does not know the men who are coming from Washington but he has enormous respect for you. He considers you a member of 'his' sect. That is more than simply an honor. It means that in future undertakings of your own you will be able to call on him. To him the members of his team come before anything. But we must secure the intelligence we need to ensure that the team continues. The American force is going in anyway. I am here to make sure that you are still willing to go with them. I hope to be able to report that back to the minister."

Friday did not believe any man who claimed to put the good of the team before his own good. A minister who was running a secret operation with the Black Cats was looking to strengthen his ties to the intelligence community and build his power base. If he could spy on Pakistan today he might spy on the SFF or the prime minister tomorrow.

The fact that a politician might have personal ambition did not bother Friday. He had heard what Captain Nazir was really saying. Minister Shankar wanted Friday to go with Striker to make sure that the Americans were working for

109

India and not just for Washington. And if Friday did undertake this mission he would have a highly placed ally in the Indian government.

The men reached the brick wall at the end of the street and Nazir lit another cigarette. Then they turned around and started walking back to the inn. Nazir was looking down. He had obviously said what he had come to say. Now it was up to Friday.

"You still haven't convinced me that there isn't a leak in your organization," Friday said. "How do I know we won't go out there and find ourselves ass-deep in Pakistanis?"

"You may," Nazir granted. "That is why we cannot go ourselves. As for leaks, I know everyone in the Black Cats. We have not been betrayed in the past. Beyond that, I cannot give the assurances you ask for." Nazir smiled for the first time. "It is even possible that someone in Washington has leaked this to the Pakistanis. There is always danger in our profession. The only question is whether the rewards are worth the risks. We believe they are, for us—and for you."

That sounded very much like an introductory lecture from a guru at an ashram. But then, Friday should have expected that.

"All right," Friday said. "I'm in—with one condition."

"And that is?"

"I want to know more about today's attack," Friday said. "Something about it is not sitting right."

"Can you tell me exactly what is bothering you?" Nazir asked.

"The fact that the attacker detonated two separate charges to bring down the police station and the temple," Friday said. "There was no reason for that. One large explosion would have accomplished the same thing. And it would have been easier to set."

Nazir nodded. "I've been wondering about that myself. All right. I'll see what I can find out and I will let you know when we are together again—which will be tomorrow around noon. We can meet here and then go to lunch. I will bring the materials I'll be turning over to your team."

"Fair enough," Friday said.

110

The men reached the inn. Friday regarded the captain.

"One more question," Friday said.

"Of course."

"Why didn't you offer me a cigarette?" Friday asked.

"Because you don't smoke," Nazir replied.

"Did the minister tell you that?"

"No," Nazir told him.

"You checked up on me, then," Friday said. "Asked people I've worked with about my habits and potential weaknesses."

"That's right," Nazir told him.

"So you didn't entirely trust the minister's judgment about bringing me onboard," Friday pointed out.

Nazir smiled again. "I said I knew everyone in the Black Cats. The minister is not one of my commandoes."

"I see," Friday replied. "That was still sloppy. You told me something about yourself, your methods, who you trust. That's something a professional shouldn't do."

"You're right," Nazir replied evenly. "But how do you know I wasn't testing you to see if you'd notice what I did?" The captain offered his hand. "Good night."

"Good night," Friday said. He felt the flush of embarrassment and a trace of doubt as he shook Nazir's hand.

The Black Cat Commando turned then and walked into the night, trailing a thick cloud of smoke behind him.

EIGHTEEN

Alconbury, Great Britain
Wednesday, 7:10 P.M.

Mike Rodgers was looking at files Bob Herbert had e-mailed from Op-Center when the giant C-130 touched down at the Royal Air Force station in Alconbury. Though the slow takeoff had seemed like a strain for the aircraft, the landing was barely noticeable. Maybe that was because the plane shook so much during the trans-Atlantic flight that Rodgers did not realize it had finally touched down. He was very much aware when the engines shut down, however. The plane stopped vibrating but he did not. After over six hours he felt as if there were a small electric current running through his body from sole to scalp. He knew from experience that it would take about thirty to forty minutes for that sensation to stop. Then, of course, Striker would be airbound again and it would start once more. Somewhere in that process was a microcosm of the ups and downs and sensations of life but he was too distracted to look for it right now.

The team left the aircraft but only to stand on the field. They would only be on the ground for an hour or so, long enough for a waiting pair of hydraulic forklifts to off-load several crates of spare parts.

The officers of the RAF referred to Alconbury as the Really American Field. Since the end of World War II it had effectively been a hub of operations for the United States Air Force in Europe. It was a large, modern field with state-of-the-art communications, repair, and munitions facilities. Since every base, every field, every barracks needed a nickname, the Americans here had nicknamed the field "Al." Many of the American servicemen went around humming

112

the Paul Simon song, "You Can Call Me Al." The Brits did not really get the eternal American fascination with sobriquets for everything from presidents to spacecraft to their weapons—Honest Abe, Friendship 7, Old Betsy. But Mike Rodgers understood. It made formidable tools and institutions seem a little less intimidating. And it implied a familiarity, a kinship with the thing or place, a sense that man, object, and organization were somehow equal.

It was very American.

The members of Striker walked down the cargo bay ramp and onto the tarmac. Two of the Strikers lit cigarettes and stood together near an eyewash stand. Other soldiers stretched, did jumping jacks, or just lay back on the field and looked up at the blue-black sky. Brett August used one of the field phones standing off by the warehouse. He was probably calling one of the girls he had in this port. Perhaps he would bail on the team and visit her on the way back. The colonel certainly had the personal time coming to him. They all did.

Mike Rodgers wandered off by himself. He headed toward the nose of the aircraft. The wind rushed across the wide-open field, carrying with it the familiar air base smells of diesel fuel, oil lubricant, and rubber from the friction-heated tires of aircraft. As the sun went down and the tarmac cooled and shrunk, the smells seemed to be squeezed out of them. Whatever airfield in the world Rodgers visited, those three smells were always present. They made him feel at home. The cool air and very solid ground felt great.

Rodgers had his hands in his pockets, his eyes on the oil-stained field. He was thinking about the data Friday had sent to the NSA and the files Herbert had forwarded to him. He was also thinking about Ron Friday himself. And the many Ron Fridays he had worked with over the decades.

Rodgers always had a problem with missions that involved other governments and other agencies within his own government. Information given to a field operative was not always informative. Sometimes it was wrong, by either accident, inefficiency, or design. The only way to find out

113

for sure was to be on the mission. By then, bad information or wrong conclusions drawn from incomplete data could kill you.

The other problem Rodgers had with multigroup missions was authority and accountability. Operatives were like kids in more ways than one. They enjoyed playing outside and they resented having to listen to someone else's "parent." Ron Friday might be a good and responsible man. But first and foremost, Friday had to answer to the head of the NSA and probably to his sponsor in the Indian government. Satisfying their needs, achieving their targets, took priority over helping Rodgers, the mission leader. Ideally, their goals would be exactly the same and there would be no conflict. But that rarely happened. And sometimes it was worse than that. Sometimes operatives or officers were attached to a mission to make sure that it failed, to embarrass a group that might be fighting for the attention of the president or the favor of a world leader or even the same limited funding.

In a situation where a team was already surrounded by adversaries Mike Rodgers did not want to feel as if he could not count on his own personnel. Especially when the lives of the Strikers were at risk.

Of course, Rodgers had never met Ron Friday or the Black Cat officer they were linking up with, Captain Nazir. He would do what he always did: size them up when he met them. He could usually tell right away whether he could or could not trust people.

Right now, though, the thing that troubled Rodgers most had nothing to do with Friday. It had to do with the explosion in Srinagar. In particular, with that last call from the home phone to the field phone.

Other nations routinely used cell phones as part of their intelligence-gathering and espionage efforts. Not just surveillance of the calls but the hardware itself. The electronics did not raise alarms at airport security; most government officials, military personnel, and businesspeople had them; and they already had some of the wiring and microchips that were necessary for saboteurs. Cell phones were also extremely well positioned to kill. It did not take more than a

114

wedge of C-4, packed inside the workings of a cell phone, to blow the side of a target's head off when he answered a call.

But Rodgers recalled one incident in particular, in the former Portuguese colony of Timor, that had parallels to this. He had read about it in an Australian military white paper while he was on Melville Island observing naval maneuvers in the Timor Sea in 1999. The invading Indonesian military had given cell phones to poor East Timorese civilians in what appeared to be a gesture of good will. The civilians were permitted to use the Indonesian military mobile communications service to make calls. The phones were not just phones but two-way radios. Civilians who had access to groups that were intensely loyal to imprisoned leader Xanana Gusmao were inadvertently used as spies to eavesdrop on nationalistic activities. Out of curiosity, Rodgers had asked a colleague in Australia's Department of Defense Strategy and Intelligence if the Indonesians had developed that themselves. He said they had not. The technology had come from Moscow. The Russians were also big suppliers of Indian technology.

What was significant to Rodgers was that the radio function was activated by signals sent from the Indonesian military outpost in Baukau. The signals were sent after calls had indicated that one individual or another was going to be in a strategic location.

Rodgers could not help but wonder if the home phone had somehow signaled the field phone to detonate the secondary blasts. The timing was too uncomfortably close to be coincidence. And the continuation of the signal at such regular intervals suggested that the terrorists were being tracked.

Hell, it did more than suggest that, Rodgers told himself. And the more he thought about it, the more he began to realize that they might have a very nasty developing situation on their hands. The Pentagon's elite think tank, with the innocuous name of the Department of Theoretical Effects, called this process "computing with vaporware." Rodgers had always been good at that, back when the Pentagon still called it "domino thinking."

He had to talk to Herbert about this.

Rodgers called over to Ishi Honda. The communications man was lying on the tarmac with the TAC-SAT beside him. He came running over with the secure phone. Rodgers thanked him then squatted on the field beside the oblong unit and phoned Bob Herbert. He used the earphones so he could hear over the roar of landing and departing jets.

Herbert picked up at once.

"Bob, it's Mike Rodgers," the general said.

"Glad to hear from you. Are you at A1?" Herbert asked.

"Just landed," Rodgers said. "Listen, Bob. I've been thinking about this latest data you sent me. I've got a feeling that the Srinagar bombers have been tagged, maybe by someone on the inside."

"I've got that same feeling," Herbert admitted. "Especially since we've been able to place the calls from field to home before that. They originated at a farm in Kargil. We notified the SFF. They sent over a local constable to check the place out. The farmer refused to say anything and they could not find his granddaughter. Ron and the SFF guy are going over first thing in the morning, see if they can't get more out of him."

"None of this smells right," Rodgers said.

"No, it doesn't," Herbert said. "And there's something else. The farmer's daughter and son-in-law were resistance fighters who died fighting the Pakistani invasion."

"So the farmer certainly had a reason to be part of a conspiracy against the Free Kashmir Militia," Rodgers said.

"In theory, yes," Herbert said. "What we're looking at now is whether there is a conspiracy and whether it could have involved the district police station that was home for the cell phone. Matt Stoll's gotten into their personnel files and my team is looking at the backgrounds of each officer. We want to see if any of them have connections with antiterrorist groups."

"You realize, Bob, that if you find a link between the police and the Pakistani cell, we may have an unprecedented international incident on our hands," Rodgers said.

116

"I don't follow," Herbert replied. "Just because they might have known about the attack and decided not to prevent it—"

"I think it may have been more than that," Rodgers said. "There were three separate attacks. Only one of them conformed to the established m.o. of the Free Kashmir Militia, the bombing of the police station."

"Wait a minute," Herbert said. "That's a big leap. You're saying the police could have planned this action themselves? That the Indians attacked their own temples—"

"To coincide with the FKM attack, yes," Rodgers said.

"But an operation like that would have to involve more than just the police in Kashmir," Herbert pointed out. "Especially if they're tracking and going to attempt to capture the cell, which is apparently the case."

"I know," Rodgers replied. "Isn't it possible they do have help? From a group that is a little more involved than usual?"

"The SFF," Herbert said.

"Why not? That could be the reason they wanted the bazaar sealed and the Black Cats kept out," Rodgers said.

Herbert thought for a moment. "It's possible," he agreed. "But it's also possible we're getting ahead of ourselves."

"Better than being behind," Rodgers pointed out.

"Touché," Herbert said. "Look. Let's see what Ron Friday and his partner turn up in the morning. I'll bring Paul up to date and let you know when we have anything else."

"Sure," Rodgers said. "But while we're getting ahead of ourselves let's go one step further."

"All right," Herbert said tentatively.

"Striker is going in to Pakistan to look for nukes," Rodgers said. "What if we don't find very many or even none at all? Suppose the Indian government authorized the Srinagar attack just to rouse their population and pick a fight. A fight Pakistan cannot possibly win."

"You think they'll respond with a nuclear strike?" Herbert said.

"Why not?" Rodgers asked.

"The world wouldn't stand for it!" Herbert replied.

"What would the world do?" Rodgers asked. "Go to war against India? Fire missiles on New Delhi? Would they impose sanctions? What kind? To what end? And what would happen when hundreds of thousands of Indians started to starve and die? Bob, we're not talking about Iraq or North Korea. We're talking about one billion people with the fourth largest military in the world. Nearly a billion Hindus who are afraid of becoming the victims of a Muslim holy war."

"Mike, no nation on earth is going to condone a nuclear strike against Pakistan," Herbert said. "Period."

"The question is not condoning," Rodgers said. "The question is how do you respond if it happens. What would we do alone?"

"Alone?"

"More or less," Rodgers said. "I'm betting Moscow and Beijing wouldn't complain too loud, for starters. India nuking Pakistan leaves Moscow free to slam whichever republics they want with a limited nuclear strike. No more long wars in Afghanistan or Chechnya. And China probably wouldn't bitch too loud because it gives them a precedent to move on Taiwan."

"They wouldn't," Herbert said. "It's insane."

"No, it's survival," Rodgers said. "Israel's got a nuclear strike plan ready in case of a united Arab attack. And they'd use it, you know that. What if India has the same kind of plan? And with the same very powerful justification, I might add. Religious persecution."

Herbert said nothing.

"Bob, all I'm saying is that it's like the house that Jack built," Rodgers said. "One little thing leads to another and then another. Maybe it's not those things, but it's nothing good."

"No, it is nothing good," Herbert agreed. "I still think we're overreacting but I'll get back to you as soon as we know anything. Meantime, I have just one suggestion."

"What's that?" Rodgers asked.

"Make sure you sleep on the flight to India," Herbert said. "One way or another you're going to need it."

NINETEEN

Kargil, Kashmir
Thursday, 6:45 A.M.

Ron Friday was annoyed that the call did not come from Hank Lewis. It came from Captain Nazir. To Friday, that meant on this leg of the mission Friday was reporting to New Delhi and not to Washington. That suggested the Black Cats would be watching him closely. Perhaps the Indian government did not want him talking to the NSA or anyone else about whatever they might find here. At least, not before they went on the mission.

They were to go to a chicken farm in the foothills of Kargil. Apparently, an intelligence officer at Op-Center found a possible link between that location and the bazaar bombing. Op-Center did not tell Hank Lewis or their Black Cat liaisons why they thought the farm might be significant or what they believed that significance to be. All they said was that the situation in the bazaar was "atypical" and that the terrorists had to be taken alive. To Friday that translated as, "We aren't sure the terrorists did this and we need to talk to them."

The pair flew to the farm in a fast, highly maneuverable Kamov Ka-25 helicopter. Captain Nazir was at the controls. The compact sky-blue chopper was one of more than two dozen Ka-25s India bought from Russia when the Soviet Union collapsed and the military began cutting costs. Friday was not surprised to be riding in a military bird. A black National Security Guard chopper would stand out. But the skies here were full of Indian military traffic. Ironically, taking an air force craft was the best way to be invisible on Pakistani radar.

The men flew north at approximately two hundred feet, following the increasingly jagged and sloping terrain. Though their unusually low passage caused some agitation among sheep and horses, and curses from their owners, Nazir explained over the headset that it was necessary. The air currents here were difficult to manage, especially early in the morning. As the sun rose the lower layers of air became heated. They mixed violently with the icy air flowing down from the mountains and created a particularly hazardous navigation zone between five hundred and two thousand feet up. It troubled Friday that a single Pakistani operative with a shoulder-mounted rocket launcher could take out the Ka-25 with no problem. He hoped that whatever information Op-Center had received was not what the intelligence community called a "TM," a "tactical mislead," a lie precipitated by the desire to slow down pursuit by smoking out and eliminating the pursuers.

The two men reached the farmhouse without incident. Before landing, Captain Nazir had buzzed the small barn and then the wood-and-stone farmhouse. An old farmer came out to see what was happening. He seemed surprised as he shielded his eyes to look up at the chopper. Nazir came in lower until he was just above the rooftop.

"What do you think?" Nazir asked. "Is the farmer alone?"

"Most likely," Friday replied. Hostages who had been kept a short while tended to be highly agitated, even panicked. They wanted to get to someone who could protect them. Even if there were other hostages at risk, including close family members, self-preservation was their first, irrepressible instinct. Hostages who had been held a long while were usually just the opposite. They had already bonded with their captors and were very standoffish, frequently antagonistic. The man below them was neither.

Nazir hovered a moment longer and then set down on a nearby field. After the noisy forty-minute flight it was good to hear nothing but the wind. The cool breeze also felt good as they made their way to the farm. Nazir wore a .38 in a holster on his hip. Friday carried a derringer in the right pocket of his windbreaker and a switchblade in the left. The .22 gun did not pack much punch but he could palm it if necessary and easily use it to blind an assailant.

The farmer waited for the men to arrive. Friday made Apu

Kumar out to be about sixty-five. He was a small, slope-shouldered man with slits for eyes. His features seemed to have a trace of Mongolian ancestry. That was not uncommon along the Himalayas. Nomads from many Asian races had roamed this region for tens of thousands of years, making it one of the world's truest melting pots. One of the sad ironies of the conflict here was the fact that so many of the combatants had the same blood.

The men stopped a few feet from the farmer. The farmer's dark, suspicious eyes looked them up and down. Beyond the house was the barn. The chickens were still squawking from the flyover.

"Good morning," Nazir said.

The farmer nodded deeply, once.

"Are you Apu Kumar?" Nazir asked.

The farmer nodded again. This time the nod was a little less self-assured and his eyes shifted from Nazir to Friday.

"Does anyone else live here?" Nazir inquired.

"My granddaughter," the farmer replied.

"Anyone else?"

Kumar shook his head.

"Is your granddaughter here now?" Nazir asked.

The farmer shook his head. He shifted a little now. His expression suggested fear for his safety but now his body language said he was also tense, anxious. He was hiding something. Possibly about his granddaughter.

"Where is she?" Nazir pressed.

"Out," Apu replied. "She runs errands."

"I see. Do you mind if we look around?" Nazir asked.

"May I ask what you are looking for?" the farmer asked.

"I don't know," Nazir admitted.

"Well, go ahead," Apu said. "But be careful of my chickens. You've already frightened them once with your machine." He made a disdainful gesture toward the helicopter.

Nazir nodded and turned. Friday hesitated.

"What's wrong?" Nazir asked the American.

Friday continued to look at the farmer. "Your granddaughter is one of them, isn't she?"

Apu did not move. He did not say, "My granddaughter is one of who?" He said nothing. That told Friday a lot.

121

Friday approached the farmer. Apu started backing away. Friday held up his hands, knuckles out. The derringer was in his right palm where the farmer could not see it. Friday watched both the farmer and the farmhouse door and window behind him. He could not be absolutely certain no was one inside or that Apu would not try to get a gun or ax or some other weapon just inside.

"Mr. Kumar, everything is all right," Friday said slowly, softly. "I'm not going to do anything to you. Nothing at all."

Apu slowed then stopped. Friday stopped as well.

"Good," Friday said. He lowered his hands and put them back in his pockets. The derringer was pointed at Apu. "I want to ask you a question but it's an important one. All right?"

Apu nodded once.

"I need to know if you do not want to talk to us because you and your granddaughter support the terrorists or because they are holding her hostage," Friday said to him.

Apu hesitated.

"Mr. Kumar, people were killed yesterday when a bomb exploded in Srinagar," Captain Nazir said. "Police officers, pilgrims on the way to Pahalgam, and worshipers in a temple. Did your granddaughter have a hand in that or did she not?"

"No!" Apu half-shouted, half-wept. "We do not support them. They forced her to go with them! They left yesterday. I was told to be silent or they said they would kill her. How is she? How is my granddaughter?"

"We don't know," Nazir told him. "But we want to find her and help her. Have they been back here since the explosion?" Nazir asked.

"No," Apu said. "One man stayed behind when the others left. He called and claimed responsibility for an attack. I heard him. But then he left suddenly at around five o'clock."

"Suddenly?" Nazir asked.

"He seemed very upset after talking to someone else on the telephone," Apu told him.

"As if something had gone wrong?" Friday asked. That would certainly confirm what Op-Center was thinking.

"I don't know," Apu said. "He was usually very calm. I even heard him make jokes sometimes. But not then. Maybe something did happen."

"If you came to Srinagar with us, would you be able to tell us what these people look like?" Nazir asked.

Apu nodded.

Friday touched Nazir's arm. "We may not have time for that," the NSA operative said. Whatever is happening seems to be happening very quickly. "Mr. Kumar, were your visitors Pakistani?"

"Yes."

"How many of them were there and how long did they stay with you?" Friday asked.

"There were five and they stayed for five months," Apu told him.

"Did you hear any of their names?" Nazir asked.

"Yes," Apu said. "I heard 'Sharab' but no last names."

"Did they ever leave you alone?" Friday asked.

"Only in our bedroom," Apu told him. "One of them was always on guard outside."

"Did they ever mistreat you?" Friday asked.

Apu shook his head. He was like a prizefighter who kept getting peppered with jabs. But that was how interrogations needed to be conducted. Once the target opened up the interrogator had to keep him open. Friday looked over at the stone barn.

"Who took care of your chickens?" Friday asked.

"I did in the morning and Nanda—that's my granddaughter—she took care of them in the late afternoon," Apu replied.

"The Pakistanis were with you then?" Nazir said.

"Yes."

"How did your eggs get to market?" Friday asked.

"The Pakistanis took them," Apu replied.

That would explain how the terrorists had cased their target in Srinagar without being noticed. But it did not explain the field phone signal that came from here.

"Do you or your granddaughter own a cellular telephone, Mr. Kumar?" Friday asked.

Apu shook his head.

"What did she do in her free time?" Friday pressed.

"She read and she wrote poetry."

"Did she always write poetry?" Friday asked.

Apu said she did not. Friday sensed that he was on to something.

"Do you have any of the poetry?" Friday asked.

"In the room," Apu told him. "She used to recite it to herself while she worked."

Friday was definitely on to something. He and Captain Nazir exchanged glances. They asked to see the poems.

Apu took them inside. Friday was alert as they walked into the two-bedroom house. There was no one inside or anywhere to hide. There was hardly any furniture, just a few chairs and a table. The place smelled of ash and musk. The ash was from the wood-burning stove on which they also did their cooking. The musk, Friday suspected, was from their guests.

Apu led them to the bedroom. He took a stack of papers from the drawer in the nightstand. He handed them to Captain Nazir. The poems were short and written in pencil. They were about everything from flowers to clouds to rain. Nazir read the earliest.

```
It rained five days and flowers grew.
And they stayed fresh and new.
In my cart I kept a few
To sell to all of you.
```

"Not very profound," Nazir said.

Friday did not comment. He was not so sure of that.

The captain flipped through the others. The structure seemed to be the same in all of the poems, a "Mary Had a Little Lamb" cadence.

"Go back to the first," Friday said.

Nazir flipped back to the top sheet.

"Mr. Kumar, you said Nanda recited these poems while she worked?" Friday asked.

"Yes."

"Is she a political activist?"

"She is an outspoken patriot who was devoted to her parents," Apu said. "My daughter and son-in-law were killed resisting the Pakistanis."

"There it is," Friday said.

"I don't follow," Captain Nazir said.

Friday asked Apu to stay in the bedroom. He led Nazir back outside.

"Captain, there were five Pakistanis," Friday told him. "The woman mentions the number five in the first line of the first poem. The Pakistanis stayed here—she mentions that word too. She says something about her cart going to market. The Pakistanis sold the eggs for her. Suppose someone got her a cell phone. Suppose the line was open and monitored twenty-four/seven. You said the poems don't seem very profound. I disagree."

"She could have emphasized words that gave information to someone," Nazir said.

"Right," Friday said. "Doesn't the SFF maintain a group of volunteers from the general population? Civilian Network Operatives?"

"Yes."

"How does that system work?" Friday asked.

"Operatives are recruited in sensitive regions or businesses and visited on a regular basis, either at their place of employment or at home," Captain Nazir said. "They report unusual activities or provide other information they may have collected."

"What if an operative were to miss an appointment?" Friday asked. "What if Nanda failed to show up at the marketplace?"

Nazir nodded. "I see what you mean," he said. "The SFF would come looking for her."

"Exactly," Friday said. "Suppose at some point this woman, Nanda, had been recruited by the SFF. Maybe when the Pakistanis held Kargil, maybe after. If someone showed up with her cart in the bazaar, her SFF contact would have known that something was wrong. They might have arranged

125

to drop a field phone off in the barn where she was sure to find it."

"Yes, it's starting to come together," Nazir said. "The SFF sponsors the woman. She feeds them information about the cell and they decide to let the terrorists make their attack on the police station. At the same time the SFF enlarges the scope of that attack so the Pakistanis will take the blame for striking at religious targets. The SFF also seals off the site to clean up any evidence that might connect them to the other two explosions."

"But the job isn't finished," Friday said. "The terrorists realize they've been set up and are probably trying to get to Pakistan. They take Nanda with them in case they need a hostage."

"More likely a witness," Nazir pointed out. "The terrorists claimed responsibility for the explosion, probably before they knew the full extent of the damage. Nanda knows they were not responsible for the temple bombing. They need her to say that."

"Good point," Friday said. "Meanwhile, if she still has her cell phone with her, she may be signaling the SFF, telling them where to find them."

Nazir was silent for a moment. "If that is true, they probably haven't caught up with the terrorists yet," he said. "I would have heard about it. Which means we've got to get to them first. If the SFF executes the terrorists before they can be heard it will turn nearly one billion Hindus against Pakistan. There will be a war and it will be an all-out war, a holy war, with flame from the nostrils of Shiva."

"Shiva—the destroyer," Friday said. "A nuclear war."

"Provoked by the SFF and its radical allies in the cabinet and the military before Pakistan is equipped to respond," Nazir said.

Friday started running toward the Kamov. "I'm going to get in touch with Op-Center and see if they know more than they're telling," he said. "You'd better grab Mr. Kumar and bring him to the chopper. We may need someone to help convince Nanda she's on the wrong side of this thing."

As Friday hurried across the field he realized one thing more. Something that gave him a little satisfaction, a little boost.

Captain Nazir was not as smart as he had pretended to be back at the inn.

TWENTY

Washington, D.C.
Wednesday, 8:17 P.M.

For most of its history, the shadowy National Reconnaissance Office was the least known of all the government agencies. The spur for the formation of the NRO was the downing of Gary Powers's U-2 spy plane over the Soviet Union in May of that year. President Eisenhower ordered Defense Secretary Thomas Gates to head a panel to look into the application of satellites to undertake photographic reconnaissance. That would minimize the likelihood that the United States would suffer another humiliation like the Powers affair.

From the start there was furious debate between the White House, the air force, the Department of Defense, and the CIA over who should be responsible for administering the agency. By the time the NRO was established on August 25, 1960, it was agreed that the air force would provide the launch capabilities for spy satellites, the Department of Defense would develop technology for spying from space, and the CIA would handle the interpretation of intelligence. Unfortunately, there were conflicts almost from the start. At stake were not just budgeting and manpower issues but the intelligence needs of the different military and civilian agencies. During the next five years relationships between the Pentagon and the CIA became so strained that they were actually sabotaging one another's access to data from the nascent network of satellites. In 1965, the secretary of defense stepped in with a proposal that time and resources would be directed by a three-person executive committee. The EXCOM was composed of the director of the CIA, the assistant secretary of defense, and the president's science advisor. The EXCOM reported to the secretary of defense, though he could not overrule decisions made by the EXCOM. The new arrangement relieved some of the fighting for satellite time though it did nothing to ease the fierce rivalry between the various groups for what was being called "intelligence product." Eventually, the NRO had to be given more and more autonomy to determine the distribution of resources.

For most of its history NRO operations were spread across the United States. Management coordination was handled in the Air Force Office of Space Systems in the Pentagon. Technology issues were conducted from the Air Force Space and Missile Systems Center at Los Angeles Air Force Base in California. Intelligence studies were conducted from the CIA Office of Development and Engineering in Reston, Virginia. Orbital control of NRO spacecraft was initially handled by technicians at the Onizuka Air Force Base in Sunnyvale, California, and then moved to the Falcon Air Force Station in Colorado. Signals intelligence other than photographic reconnaissance was handled by the National Guard at the Defense Support Program Aerospace Data Facility at Buckley Air National Guard Base in Aurora, Colorado. The U.S. Navy's NRO activities were centered primarily on technology upgrades and enhancement of existing hardware and software. These duties were shared by two competing naval groups: the Space and Naval Warfare Systems Command in Crystal City, Virginia, and SPAWAR's Space Technology Directorate Division, SPAWAR-40, located at the Naval Research Laboratory across the Potomac River in the highly secure Building A59.

Though the NRO proved invaluable in bringing data back to earth, the management of the NRO itself became a nightmare of convolution and in-fighting. Though the government did not officially acknowledge the existence of the organization, its denials were a joke among the Washington press corps. No one would explain why so many people were obviously struggling with such rancor to control something that did not exist.

That changed in 1990 with the construction of a permanent NRO facility in Fairfax, Virginia. Yet even while the NRO's existence was finally acknowledged, few people had firsthand knowledge about its day-to-day operations and the full breadth of its activities.

Photographic reconnaissance operations director Stephen Viens was one of those men.

The consolidation of NRO activities under one roof did not end the competition for satellite time. But Viens was loyal to his college friend Matt Stoll. And he would do anything for Paul Hood, who stood by him during some difficult CIOC hearings about the NRO's black ops work. As a result, no group, military or civilian, got priority over Op-Center.

Bob Herbert had telephoned at four P.M. What he needed from Viens was visual surveillance of a specific site in the Himalayas. Viens had to wait two hours before he could free up the navy's Asian OmniCom satellite, which was in a geosynchronous orbit over the Indian Ocean. Even though the navy was using it, Viens told them he had an LAD—life-and-death—situation and needed it at once. Typically, the OmniCom listened to sonar signals from Russian and Chinese submarines and backed them up with visual reconnaissance when the vessels surfaced. That allowed the navy to study displacement and hull features and even to get a look down the hatch when it was opened. The satellite image was sharp to within thirteen inches from the target and refreshed every .8 seconds. If the angle were right the OmniCom could get in close enough to lip-read.

Working at the OmniCom station in the level four basement of the NRO, it was relatively easy for Viens and his small team to use the repositioned satellite to ride the field phone signal to its source. They pinpointed it to a site above the foothills at 8,112 feet. When Viens and his group had repositioned the satellite to look down on the site, dawn was just breaking in Kashmir. The rising sun cleared the mountains to the east and struck an isolated structure. It resembled a slender travertine stalagmite more than it did a mountain peak. Whatever it was, something remarkable was happening on its face.

There were over a dozen figures in white parkas on the eastern side of the peak. They were armed with what looked like automatic weapons. Some were climbing up the peak, others were rappelling down. They were all converging on a small mouth located near the base of the tor.

Viens quickly refined the location of the audio signal. It was not coming from the people on the cliff but from a stationary target. Probably from an individual or individuals inside the cave.

Viens immediately phoned Bob Herbert and redirected the signal to Op-Center.

TWENTY-ONE

Siachin Base 2E, Kashmir
Thursday, 7:01 A.M.

There is nothing like sunrise in the Himalayas.

The higher altitude and thinner, cleaner atmosphere allow a purer light to get through. Ishaq did not know how else to describe it. A photographer in Islamabad once told him that the atmosphere acted like a prism. The lower to the ground you were, the thicker the air blanket was and the more the sunlight was bent to the red. Ishaq was not a scientist. He did not know if that were true.

All the Pakistani knew was that the light up here was like he imagined the eye of Allah to be. It was white, warm, and intense. He wondered if the story of the mountain coming to Mohammad had originated in a peak like this one. For as the sun edged higher above the foothills below and the shadows shortened, the crags actually appeared to move. And as they moved their snow-covered sides glowed brighter and brighter. It was almost as though enlightenment were spreading throughout the land. Perhaps this was what the tale of the Prophet signified. The light of Allah and his Prophet was stronger than anything on this earth. And opening one's heart and mind to them made us as strong and eternal.

That was a comforting thought to Ishaq. If this were to be his last dawn at least he would die satisfied and closer to God. In fact, as he looked back over his life he had just one regret: that he might have to die here and now. He had wanted to be with his comrades when they returned to their homeland. But they had intentionally selected for their armory a cave that had no other direct line of sight nearby. It would have been difficult for anyone to spot the small outpost or to watch them while they were here.

Ishaq had stayed up all night preparing. Then he had watched the sun rise as he ate breakfast. He had not wanted to sleep. There would be time enough for that. Now, as he sat in the dark in the back of the cave, Ishaq heard scraping noises outside.

Sharab was right. They had been tracked here.

The Indians had been quiet at first. Now they were no longer taking pains to conceal their approach. They were probably wearing crampons and they sounded like mice outside a wall, scratching their way in. The sounds grew from a few scrapes along the rear and sides of the cave to constant noise and motion. From the shifting location of the sounds he could tell that the Indians were already within range of the mouth of the cave. They would probably lob teargas before charging in. If the cell had been here there would have been no escape.

Ishaq decided that this would be a good time to put on his gas mask. He slipped the Iranian-made unit on, tightened the straps over his head, and snapped the mouthpiece in place. His breath was coming in little bursts. He was anxious, but not because of what was going to happen. He was worried because he hoped he had done everything right. The Pakistani looked at the wooden crates lined with plastic. He had gathered them nearby, like wives in a harem, ready for a final embrace. It had been a simple process to attach detonators to individual explosives, leave them on the top of the crates, and make sure the receivers were facing him. But he had not been able to examine all of the explosives. They had been stored up here for nearly two years. Though it was dry and cold and dampness should not be a problem, dynamite was temperamental. The sticks they had used in Srinagar had been showing signs of caking. Moisture had gotten inside.

Still, everything should be all right. Ishaq had rigged seven bundles of dynamite with C-4 and remote triggers. All he needed was for one of the bundles to blow. He pulled off his heavy gloves and took the detonator in his right hand. He leaned back against the stone wall.

Ishaq's legs were spread straight out in front of him and his backside was cold. The folded canvas he was sitting on

133

was a bad insulator. Not that it mattered. He would not be sitting on it much longer.

The scraping stopped. He watched the tarp through the greenish tint of his facemask. Curtains of sunlight hung along the side walls of the cave. They shifted and undulated as the wind pushed against the tarp. The covering itself rattled against the hooks that held it in place.

Suddenly, the tarp dropped. Particles of ice that had collected on the outside flew, glistening in the sunlight. The shimmering beads died as two large, cylindrical canisters were lobbed in. They clanked on the cave floor and rolled toward Ishaq. They were already hissing and jetting thick clouds of smoke into the air and across the ground. Some of the gas unfurled sideways, and some of it was sprayed in his direction.

The Pakistani sat there, waiting calmly. The rolling green gas was still about fifteen meters away. The view to the nearest of the detonators remained unobstructed. He had a few more moments.

He began to pray.

Ishaq listened for the scraping to resume. After a moment it did, moving rapidly toward the front of the cave. He watched as the clouds of gas began to billow and roll aside as though people were moving through it. The gas had nearly reached the explosives.

It was time.

The Muslim continued his silent prayer as he pressed the blue "engage" button. A light on top of the small controller came on. Ishaq quickly pressed the red "detonate" button below it.

For a blessed moment the sun shined all around Ishaq and he felt as if he had been embraced by Allah.

TWENTY-TWO

Washington, D.C.
Wednesday, 9:36 P.M.

"What the hell just happened, Stephen?" Bob Herbert asked.

Op-Center's intelligence chief had pulled his wheelchair deep under the desk. He was leaning over the speakerphone as he watched the OmniCom image on his computer. What he had said was not so much a question as an observation. Herbert knew exactly what had happened.

"The side of the mountain just exploded," Viens said over the phone.

"It didn't just explode, it evaporated," Herbert pointed out. "That blast had to have been the equivalent of a thousand pounds of TNT."

"At least," Viens agreed.

Herbert was glad there was no sound with the image. Even just seeing the massive, unexpected explosion wakened his sensory memories. Tension and grief washed over him as he was reminded of the Beirut embassy bombing.

"What do you think, Bob? Was it set off by a sensor or motion detector?" Viens asked.

"I doubt it," Herbert said. "There are a lot of avalanches in that part of the world. They could have triggered the explosion prematurely."

"I didn't think of that," Viens admitted.

Herbert forced himself to focus on the present, not the past. Op-Center's intelligence chief reloaded the pictures the satellite had sent moments before the blast. He asked the computer to enhance the images of the soldiers one at a time.

"It looked to me like the climbers tossed gas inside," Herbert said. "They obviously believed that someone might be waiting for them."

"They were right," Viens said.

"The question is how many people were in there?" Herbert said. "Were the people who used that cave expecting the climbers? Or were they caught by surprise and decided they did not want to be captured alive?"

An image of the first soldier filled Herbert's monitor. There was a clear shot of the man's right arm. On top, just below the shoulder of the white camouflage snowsuit, was a circular red patch with a solid black insignia. The silhouette showed a horse running along the tail of a comet. That was the insignia of the Special Frontier Force.

"Well, one thing's dead for sure," Viens said.

"What's that?" Herbert asked.

"Matt Stoll just phoned to say he's not picking up the cell phone signal anymore," Viens told Herbert. "He wanted to see if we'd lost it too. I just checked. We have."

Herbert was still looking at the monitor. He saved the magnified image of the shoulder patch. "I wonder if the cell led the commandos there to throw them off the trail," he said.

"Possibly," Viens said. "Do we have any idea which way the Indian commandos would have come?"

"From the south," Herbert replied. "How long would it take you to start searching through the mountains north of the site?"

"It will take about a half hour to move the satellite," Viens said. "First, though, I want to make sure we're not wasting our time. If anyone left the cave they would have had to go up before they could go down again. I want to get the OmniCom in for a closer look."

"Footprints in the snow?" Herbert said as the secure phone on his wheelchair beeped.

"Exactly," Viens replied.

"Go for it. I'll wait," Herbert told him as he backed away from the desk so he could reach the phone. He snapped up the receiver. "Herbert."

"Bob, it's Hank Lewis," said the caller. "I've got Ron Friday on the line. He says it's important. I'd like to conference him in."

"Go ahead," Herbert said. He had been wondering what Friday would find at the farmhouse. He was hoping it did not confirm their fears of police or government involvement in the Srinagar market attack. The implications were too grim to contemplate.

"Go ahead, Ron," Lewis said. "I have Director of Intelligence Bob Herbert on the line with us."

"Good," Friday said. "Mr. Herbert, I'm at the Kumar farmhouse in Kargil with my Black Cat liaison. I need to know what other intel you have on the farmer and his granddaughter."

"What have you found out there?" Herbert asked.

"What?" Friday said.

"What did you find at the farm?" Herbert asked.

"What is this, 'I show you mine and you show me yours?' " Friday angrily demanded.

"No," Herbert said. "It's a field report. Tell me what you've got."

"I've got my ass on the front frigging line and you're sitting on your ass safe in Washington!" Friday said. "I need information!"

"I'm on my ass because my legs don't work anymore," Herbert responded calmly. "I lost them because too many people trusted the wrong people. Mr. Friday, I've got an entire team headed toward your position and they may be at considerable risk. You're a piece in my puzzle, a field op for me. You tell me what you have and then I'll tell you what you need to know."

Friday said nothing. Herbert hoped he was considering exactly how to word his apology.

After a few moments Friday broke the silence. "I'm waiting for that information, Mr. Herbert," he said.

That caught Herbert off guard. Okay. They were playing hardball with a hand grenade. He could do that.

"Mr. Lewis," Herbert said, "please thank your field operative for reconnoitering the farmhouse. Inform him we will

137

get our information directly from the Black Cat Commandos and that our joint operation is ended."

"You bureaucratic asshole—!" Friday snapped.

"Friday, Mr. Herbert has the authority to terminate this alliance," Lewis said. "And frankly, you're not giving me a reason to fight for it."

"We need each other out here!" Friday said. "We may be looking at an international catastrophe!"

"That's the first useful insight you've given me," Herbert said. "Would you care to continue?"

Friday swore. "I don't have time for a pissing contest, Herbert. I'll straighten you out later. We've learned that a Pakistani cell, part of the Free Kashmir Militia, stayed at the farm of Apu Kumar for about five months. The farmer's granddaughter, Nanda, is the only child of a couple who died fighting the Pakistanis. The girl wrote poetry the whole time the cell was here. It appears to have contained coded elements reporting on the cell's activities. She used to recite her poems aloud while she took care of the chickens. We suspect members of the Special Frontier Force heard what she was saying, probably by cell phone. She was with them when the bazaar attack in Srinagar took place and we believe the SFF was behind the temple bombing. We also believe that she is still with them, and might have the cell phone to signal SFF."

"She was signaling the SFF," Herbert replied.

"What happened?" Friday asked.

It was time to give Friday a little information, a little trust. "The Indian pursuit team was just taken out by a powerful explosion in the Himalayas," Herbert informed him.

"How do you know that?" Lewis asked.

"We've got ELINT resources in the region," Herbert said.

Herbert used the vague electronics intelligence reference because he did not want Lewis to know that he had satellite coverage of the region. The new NSA head might start pushing the NRO for off-the-books satellite time of his own.

"How many men were killed?" Lewis asked.

"About thirteen or fourteen," Herbert replied. "They were closing in on what appeared to be an outpost about eight thousand feet up in the mountains. The men, the outpost, and the side of the mountain are all gone."

"Were you able to ID the commandos?" Friday asked. "Were they wearing uniforms?"

"They were SFF," Herbert replied.

"I knew it," Friday said triumphantly. "What about the cell?"

"We don't know," Herbert admitted. "We're trying to find out if they got away."

Herbert looked at the computer monitor. Stephen Viens had just finished zooming in slowly on the northern side of the cliff. The resolution was three meters, sufficient to show footprints. The angle of the sun was still low. That would help by casting shadows off the side walls of any prints. Viens began panning the flattest, widest areas of the slopes. Those were the sections where people were likely to be walking in the darkness.

"If the cell did get away the SFF is not going to give up," Friday continued. "There's a possibility the SFF set them up to take the fall for the temple bombings in Srinagar."

"Do you have proof of that?" Herbert asked. He was interested that Friday had come to the same conclusion as he and General Rodgers.

"No," Friday admitted. "But the Black Cats would normally have handled the investigation and they were cut out of it by the SFF. They also obviously knew about the cell."

"That doesn't mean they were involved in the destruction of the temple," Herbert said. "The Free Kashmir Militia are known terrorists. According to Indian radio they already took credit for the bombing—"

"Whoever made that call may not have known the extent of the attack," Friday said.

"That could be," Herbert agreed. "I'm still not ready to declare them innocent. Maybe someone in the group betrayed them and rigged the extra explosions. But let's assume for the moment you're right, that the SFF organized the bombing to advance an agenda. What is that agenda?"

"My Black Cat partner believes it's a holy war," Friday said. "Possibly a nuclear holy war."

"A preemptive strike," Hank Lewis said.

Again, Herbert was encouraged by the fact that Ron Friday and the Indian Black Cat officer reached the same conclusions that he and Rodgers had. It meant there might be some truth to their concerns. But he was also discouraged for the same reason.

"We think the SFF forces used gas against the Pakistani stronghold," Herbert said. "Which would mean they wanted to try and capture them alive."

"A perp walk and confessions," Friday said.

"Probably. But I've got to believe the main reason the cell is running is not to save their own lives," Herbert said. "Even if they get back to Pakistan no one in India is going to take their word that they're innocent."

"They need the girl," Friday said.

"Exactly," Herbert said. "If she worked with the SFF to stage the attack, they need to get a complete public statement from her. One that doesn't look or sound like it's a forced confession."

"I'm missing something here," Lewis said. "If we suspect that this is going on, why don't we just confront the SFF or someone in the Indian government? Get them involved."

"Because we don't know who may already be involved in this operation and how high up it goes," Herbert said. "Talking to New Delhi may just accelerate the process."

"Accelerate it?" Lewis said. "How much faster can it possibly go?"

"In a crisis like this days can become hours if you're not careful," Herbert said. "We don't want to panic the people in charge. If we're right, the SFF will still try to capture the cell."

"Or at least Nanda," Friday said. "Maybe she's the one they're really after. Think about a teary-eyed Hindu woman going on television and telling the public how the FKM plotted to blow up the temple, not caring how many Hindu men, women, and children they killed."

"Good point," Herbert said. "What about the girl's grandfather? If the cell is alive and we can find them before the

140

SFF does, do you think he'd be willing to talk to her? To convince her to tell the public what she knows?"

"I'll make sure he's willing to talk to her," Friday said.

As they spoke the satellite camera stopped on what looked like it might be several footprints. Viens began zooming in.

"What are you thinking of doing, Bob?" Hank Lewis asked.

"We've already got two men on the ground and a field force on the way," Herbert said. "If I can get Paul to sign off on it, I'm going to ask General Rodgers to try and intercept the cell."

"And do what?" Lewis demanded. "Help avowed terrorists make it home safely?"

"Why not?" Friday said. "That might win us allies in the Muslim world. We can use them."

"America doesn't 'win' allies in the Muslim world. If we're lucky we earn their forbearance," Herbert said.

"A smart man knows how to work that too," Friday said.

"Maybe you'll get to show us how it's done," Herbert replied.

"Maybe," Friday replied.

The intelligence chief had worked with hundreds of field ops over the years. He had been one himself. They were a tough, thorny, independent breed. But this man was more than that. Herbert could hear it in his voice, the edge to his words and the confidence of his statements. Usually, men who sounded like Friday were what spy leaders called HOWs—hungry old wolves. Working on their own year after year they began to feel invisible to the host government and beyond the reach of their own government. They'd been out in the cold so long that they tended to bite anyone who came near them.

But Friday had not spent a lot of time on his own. He had come from an embassy post. That suggested something else to Herbert: an I-spy. The espionage game's equivalent of a bad cop, someone who was in this for themselves. Whatever Striker ended up doing in the field, if it involved Ron Friday Herbert would tell Mike Rodgers to watch him very, very closely.

141

"Bob?" Viens said on the speakerphone. "You still there?"

"I'm here," Herbert said. He told Lewis and Friday to hold the line.

"Are you looking at the monitor?" Viens asked.

"I am," Herbert said.

"You see that?" Viens asked.

"I do," Herbert replied.

There were footprints. And they were made during the previous night. The sun had not had a chance to melt and refreeze them. The cell had definitely left the cave and was heading north, toward Pakistan. Unfortunately, they could not tell from the jumble of footprints how many people were in the party.

"Good work, Stephen," Herbert said. He archived the image with the rest of them. "Have you got time to follow them?"

"I can track them for a bit but that won't tell you much," Viens said. "I looked at one of the overviews. We're going to lose the trail behind the peak about a quarter of a kilometer to the northwest. After that all we've got is a shitload of mountain to examine."

"I see," Herbert said. "Well, at least let's make sure they went as far as the turn. And see if we can get a better idea of how many people there were and maybe what they were carrying."

"I'm guessing they weren't carrying much," Viens said. "Three inches or so of snow cover, two inches of print. They look about the right depth for an average hundred-and-sixty-pound individual. Besides, I can't imagine they'd be carrying much more than ropes and pitons trekking through that region."

"You're probably right," Herbert said.

"But I'll see if we can't get a head count for the group," Viens said.

"Thanks, Stephen," Herbert said.

"Anytime," Viens replied.

Herbert clicked off the speakerphone and got back on with Hank Lewis and Ron Friday. "Gentlemen, we've definitely got the cell heading north," he said. "I suggest we table the political debate and concentrate on managing the crisis. I'll have a talk with Paul. See if he wants to get involved with this or whether we should abort the Striker mission altogether and turn the problem over to the State Department. Hank, I suggest you and Mr. Friday talk this over and see what you want your own involvement to be. Whether we stick to the original mission or work out a new one, it could get ugly out there."

"We'll also have to talk about what to tell the president and the CIOC," Lewis said.

"I have a suggestion about that," Herbert told him. "If you tag Mr. Friday as a loan-out to Striker as of right now, the NSA doesn't have to be involved in making that decision."

"That's a negative," Lewis told him. "I'm new on the job, Bob, but I'm not a novice. You let me know what Paul's thinking is and I'll make the call on our end."

"Fair enough," Herbert said. He smiled. He respected a man who did not pass the buck. Especially a buck this big.

"Ron," Lewis said, "I'd like you to talk to the farmer and to Captain Nazir. See if they're with you on a possible search-and-capture. I agree with Bob. Mr. Kumar can be very useful if we're able to locate his granddaughter."

"I'll do it," Friday said.

"Good," Herbert said. "Hank, you and I will talk after I've discussed this with Paul and General Rodgers. Mr. Friday— thank you for your help."

Friday said nothing.

Herbert hung up. He swore at the very thought of Ron Friday and then put him from his mind—for now. There were larger issues to deal with.

He made an appointment to see Paul Hood at once.

TWENTY-THREE

Kargil, Kashmir
Thursday, 7:43 A.M.

Before leaving the helicopter Ron Friday opened a compartment between the seats. He found an old backup book of charts in there. The chopper's flight plan was dictated by computer-generated maps. These animated landscapes and grid overlays were presented on a monitor located above the primary flight display screen between the pilot and copilot stations. A keypad beneath the monitor was used to punch in coordinates. Friday tore out the maps he wanted and shoved them in the pocket of his windbreaker.

As he headed back to the farm, Friday punched the air. He unleashed a flurry of strong, angry uppercuts that did not just hit the imaginary chin of Bob Herbert. The punches went through his new nemesis as he struck at the sky. Who the hell did Bob Herbert think he was? The man had been wounded in the line of duty. That entitled him to disability compensation, not respect.

The pismire, Friday thought. Bob Herbert was just a wage-slave drone in the hive.

Friday finished his flurry of blows. His heart was ramming his chest, his arms perspiring. Breathing heavily, he flexed his fingers as he stalked across the rocky, uneven terrain.

It's all right, Friday told himself. He was here, at the heart of the action, in control of his destiny. Bob Herbert was back in Washington barking orders. Orders that could easily be ignored since Lewis had not allowed him to be seconded to Op-Center. Friday put the self-pitying bureaucrat from his mind and concentrated on the work at hand.

Captain Nazir had gone inside with Apu Kumar. The Black Cat officer was looking around the house while Kumar

144

sat quietly on the tattered couch. Both men turned as Friday entered.

"What did they say?" Nazir asked.

"The Pakistani cell is alive and well and apparently moving north through the Himalayas," Friday told Nazir. "Op-Center and the NSA are considering a joint mission to try and apprehend the cell along with Mr. Kumar's granddaughter. They want to keep them all out of the hands of the SFF. Would the Black Cat Commandos and their allies in the government have a problem with an American-run search-and-recover mission?"

"Does your government believe there is a chance for a nuclear exchange?" Nazir asked.

"If they didn't think so, they would not even be considering a covert action," Friday replied. "It looks like your friends from the Special Frontier Force wanted that cell bad enough. Our ELINT resources caught a squad of them chasing the Pakistanis through the mountains."

"Where is the SFF squad?" Nazir asked.

"Waiting in line for reincarnation," Friday replied.

"Excuse me?"

"From what I gathered the commandos were caught by a Pakistani suicide bomber," Friday told him.

"I see," Nazir said. He thought for a moment. "The SFF presence supports what we were thinking, that they set this up."

"It sure looks that way," Friday said.

"Then yes," Nazir said. "The Black Cat Commandos would help you in any way we can."

"Good," Friday said. He walked over to Kumar. "We're going to need your help, too," he told the farmer. "Your granddaughter was apparently working for the SFF. Her testimony is the key to war and peace. If we catch up to them she must be made to tell the truth."

Apu Kumar rolled a slumped shoulder. "She is an honest girl. She would not lie."

"She's also a patriot, isn't she?" Friday asked.

"Of course," Apu agreed.

145

"Patriotism has a way of dulling the senses," Friday told him. "That's why soldiers sometimes throw themselves on hand grenades. If your granddaughter helped the SFF frame the Pakistanis for the destruction of a Hindu temple, she has to tell that to the Indian people."

Apu seemed surprised and gravely concerned. "Do you think that is what she's done?" he asked.

"We do," Friday told him.

"Poor Nanda," Apu said.

"We're not just talking about Nanda," Captain Nazir said. "If she does not tell what she knows then millions of people may die."

Apu rose. "Nanda could not have known what she was doing. She would never have agreed to such an outcome. But I will help you," he said. "What do you want me to do?"

"For now, get some warm clothes together and wait," Friday said. "If you have extra gloves and long johns, bring them too."

Apu said he would and then hurried to the bedroom. Friday walked over to a small table and pulled the maps from his pocket.

"Captain?" he said. It was a command, not a question.

"Yes?" Nazir replied.

"We need to make plans," Friday said.

"Flight plans?" Nazir said, noticing the charts.

"Yes," Friday replied.

But that was just the start. Whatever the mission and however it turned out, Friday would be in good stead with the Black Cat Commandos and his own friends and advocates in the Indian government. He was sure Hank Lewis would allow him to remain here when this was all over. And then Ron Friday would be free to nurture his ties to the nuclear and oil industries. That was where the nation's future lay.

That was where his own future lay.

TWENTY-FOUR

Siachin Base 3, Kashmir
Thursday, 9:16 A.M.

The call from Commander San Hussain did not surprise Major Dev Puri. Ever since he was informed of the top-secret plan to use the Pakistani cell, the major had been expecting to hear from the Special Frontier Force director at about this time. However, what Commander Hussain had to say was a complete surprise. Major Puri sat in his bunker for several moments after hanging up. For weeks, he had been expecting to play an important part in this operation: the quick and quiet evacuation of the line of control.

But Puri had not anticipated playing this role. The role that was supposed to have been played by the SFF's MEAN—Mountain Elite Attack Nation. That was the name of the original resistance force that worked to overthrow British imperial rule on the subcontinent.

The most important role.

Puri reached into a tin box on the desk. He plucked out a wad of chewing tobacco and placed it beside his gum. He began to chew slowly. Puri had been expecting to hear that the Pakistani cell had been captured in their mountain headquarters. After that, Puri's units were supposed to begin preparing for retreat. The preparations were supposed to be made quietly and unhurriedly, without the use of cell phones or radios. As much as possible should be done underground in the shelters and low in the trenches. The Pakistanis would notice nothing unusual going on. Devi's four hundred soldiers were supposed to be finished by eleven A.M. but they were not to move out until they received word directly from Hussain.

Instead, Commander Hussain had called with a much different project. Major Puri was to take half the four hundred soldiers in his command and move south, into the mountains. They were to carry full survival packs and dress in thermal camouflage clothes. Hussain wanted them to proceed in a wide sweep formation toward the Siachin Glacier, closing in as the glacier narrowed and they neared the summit. "Wide sweep" meant that the militia would consist of a line of men who came no closer than eyesight. That meant the force could be stretched across approximately two miles. Since radio channels might be monitored, Hussain wanted them to communicate using field signals. Those were a standardized series of gestures developed by MEAN in the 1930s. The Indian army adopted them in 1947. The signals told them little more than to advance, retreat, wait, proceed, slow down, speed up, and attack. Directions for attacks were indicated by finger signals: the index finger was north, middle finger south, ring finger west, and pinky east. The thumb was the indication to "go." Those hand signals were usually enough. The commands were issued by noncommissioned officers stationed in the center of each platoon. They could be overruled by the company lieutenants and by Puri himself, who would be leading the operation from the center of the wide sweep. In the event of an emergency, the men had radios they could use.

Puri picked up the phone. He ordered his aide to assemble his lieutenants in the briefing room. The major said he would be there in five minutes. He wanted top-level security for the meeting: no phones or radios present, no laptop computers, no notepads.

Puri chewed his tobacco a moment more before rising. Hussain had told him that the Pakistani cell had evaded capture and was thought to be heading to Pakistan. Four other bases along the line of control were activating units in an effort to intercept the terrorists. Each of the base leaders had been given the same order: to take the cell, dead or alive.

That option did not include their lone hostage, an Indian woman from Kashmir. Commander Hussain said that the SFF did not expect the woman to survive her ordeal. He did not say that she had been mistreated. His tone said something else altogether.

He wanted her not to survive.

Major Puri turned toward the door and left the shelter. The morning light was cold and hazy. He had checked the weather report earlier. It was snowing up in the mountains. That always produced haze here in the lower elevations. Nothing was clear, not even the walls of the trench itself.

Nor his own vision.

Major Puri had not expected to play that part either. The role of assassin. As he headed for the meeting it struck him as odd that a single life should matter. What he did here would contribute to the deaths of millions of people in just a day or two. What did one more mean?

Was he upset because she was Indian? No. Indians would die in the conflagration as well. Was he upset because she was a woman? No. Women would certainly die.

He was upset because he would probably be there when she died. He might even be the one to execute the commander's order.

He would have to look into her eyes. He would be watching the woman as she realized that she was about to die.

In 1984, when India was rocked by intercaste violence, Prime Minister Indira Gandhi ordered a series of attacks on armed Sikh separatists in Amritsar. Over a thousand people were killed. Those deaths were unfortunate, the inevitable result of armed conflict. Several months later, Mrs. Gandhi was assassinated by Sikhs who were members of her own bodyguard. Her murder was a cold-blooded act and a tragedy.

It had a face.

Major Puri knew that this had to be done. But he also knew that he wished someone else would do it. Soldiering was a career he could leave behind. The job of combatant was temporary. But once he killed, even in the name of patriotism, that act would stay with him for the rest of his life.

And the next.

149

TWENTY-FIVE

Washington, D.C.
Wednesday, 11:45 P.M.

Paul Hood was glad when Bob Herbert came to see him.

Hood had shut his office door, opened a box of Wheat Thins, and worked on the Op-Center budget cuts for the better part of the evening. He had left word with Bugs Benet that he was not to be disturbed unless it were urgent. Hood did not feel like end-of-the-day chitchat. He did not want to have to put on a public face. He wanted to hide, to lose himself in a project—any project.

Most of all Hood did not feel like going home. Or what passed for home these days, an undistinguished fifth-floor suite at the Days Inn on Mercedes Boulevard. Hood had a feeling that it would be a long time, if ever, before he regarded anything but the Hood house in Chevy Chase, Maryland, as home. But he and his wife, Sharon, were separated and his presence at the house created strife for her. She said he was a reminder of their failed marriage, of facing a future without a companion. Their two children did not need that tension, especially Harleigh. Hood had spent time with Harleigh and her younger brother, Alexander, over the weekend. They did things that Washingtonians rarely did: they toured the monuments. Hood had also arranged for them to get a personal tour of the Pentagon. Alexander was impressed by all the saluting that went on. It made him feel important not to have to do it. He also liked the kick-ass intensity of all the guards.

Harleigh said she enjoyed the outing but that was pretty much all she said. Hood did not know whether it was post-traumatic stress, the separation, or both that were on her mind. Psychologist Liz Gordon had advised him not to talk about any of that unless Harleigh brought it up. His job was to be upbeat and supportive. That was difficult without any input from Harleigh. But he did the best he could.

For Harleigh.

What he had been neglecting in all of this were his needs. Home was the biggest and most immediate hole. The hotel room did not have the familiar creaking and pipe sounds and outside noises he had come to know. There was no oil burner clicking on and off. The hotel room smelled unfamiliar, shared, transient. The water pressure was weaker, the soap and shampoo small and impersonal. The nighttime lighting on the ceiling was different. Even the coffeemaker didn't pop and burble the same as the one at home. He missed the comfort of the familiar. He hated the changes.

Especially the biggest one. The huge hole he had dug for himself with Ann Farris, Op-Center's thirty-four-year-old press liaison. She had pursued him virtually from the day she arrived. He had found the pursuit both flattering and uncomfortable. Flattering because Paul Hood and his wife had not been connecting for years. Uncomfortable because Ann Farris was not subtle. Whatever poker face Ann put on during press briefings she did not wear around Hood. Maybe it was a question of balance, of yin and yang, of being passive in public and aggressive in private. Regardless, her open attention was a distraction for Hood and for the people closest to him, like Mike Rodgers and Bob Herbert.

So of course Hood made the desperate mistake of actually making love to Ann. That had ratcheted up the tension level by making her feel closer and him feel even guiltier. He did not want to make love to her again. At least, not until he was divorced. Ann said she understood but she still took it as a personal rejection. It had affected their working relationship. Now she was cool to him in private and hot with the press in public.

How had Paul Hood gone from someone who reached the top of several professions at a relatively young age to someone who had messed up his own life and the lives of those around him? How the hell had that happened?

Ann was really the one that Hood did not want to see tonight. But he could not tell Bugs to keep only her out. Even if she did figure out that was what Hood was doing he did not want to insult her directly.

Ironically, the work Hood was doing involved cutting Ann and her entire division.

Hood was not surprised that Herbert was working this late. The intelligence chief preferred work to socializing. It was not politically correct but it was pure Herbert: he said that it was more of a challenge trying to get inside a spy's head than into a woman's pants. The rewards were also greater, Herbert insisted. The spy ended up dead, in prison, or incapacitated. It was a lesson Hood should have learned from his friend.

Hood was glad when Herbert came to see him. He needed a crisis to deal with, one that was not of his own making. The briefing that Bob Herbert gave Hood was not the low-intensity distraction he had been hoping for. However, the prospect of nuclear war between India and Pakistan did chase all other thoughts from Hood's mind.

Herbert brought Hood up to speed on the conversations he'd had with Mike Rodgers and Ron Friday. When Herbert was finished, Hood felt energized. His own problems had not gone away. But part of him, at least, was out of hiding. The part that had a responsibility to others.

"This is a sticky one," Hood said.

"Yeah," Herbert agreed. "What's your gut say?"

"It says to take this situation to the president and drop it square in his lap," Hood replied.

Herbert regarded Hood for a moment. "There's a 'but' in your voice," Herbert said.

"Actually, there are three 'buts' in my voice," Hood told him. "First, we're only guessing about what's going on. They're educated guesses, but we still don't have proof. Second, let's assume your intel is right. That there is a plot to start a war. If we tell the president, the president will tell State. Once you tell State, the world will know about it

152

through leaks, moles, or electronic surveillance. That could scare the perpetrators off—or it could accelerate whatever timetable they have."

"I agree," Herbert said. "The SFF and their allies would have insecurity issues instead of security issues. Typical when you're keeping information from your own country-men."

"Exactly," Hood said.

"All right. So what's the third 'but'?" Herbert asked.

"The fact that we may prove a nuclear attack plan is in place," Hood said. "If the United States exposes it we may actually give it impetus."

"I don't understand," Herbert said.

"In terms of military support and intelligence assistance, India has always leaned toward Russia," Hood said. "An entire generation of Indians considers the United States the opposition. Suppose we expose a patriotic plan. Do you think that will cause the Indians to kill it?"

"If it involves a nuclear exchange, yes," Herbert said. "Russia would come down on our side. So would China."

"I don't know if I agree," Hood said. "Russia is facing an Islamic threat along several of its borders. Op-Center just defused a crisis where the Russians were scared about Iran's access to Caspian oil. Moscow fought the mujahedin in Afghanistan. They're afraid of aggressive fifth-column activities in their own cities, in allied republics. We can't be sure they would back a Muslim nation against their old friend India. As for China, they're looking for allies in a move against Taiwan. Suppose India provided them with that, a kind of quid pro quo."

Herbert shook his head slowly. "Paul, I've been in this game a long time. I've seen videos of Saddam using gas and gunships against his own people. I've been to a Chinese execution where five men were shot in the head because they expressed dissenting political beliefs. But I can't believe that sane individuals would make a deal about nuclear strikes that will kill millions of people."

"Why not?" Hood asked.

"Because a nuclear exchange raises the bar for all of human conflict," Herbert insisted. "It says that anything goes. No one gains by that."

"Fair enough," Hood said.

"I still believe that we may have a radical group of Indian officials who may want to nuke Pakistan," Herbert said.

"Then valid or not, all three of my concerns point to the same thing," Hood said.

"We need more intel before we go to the president," Herbert said.

"Right," Hood said. "Is there any way of getting that electronically or from sources in the government?"

"There might be, if we had the time," Herbert said. "But we've got the Pakistani cell on the run in the mountains and the dead SFF commandos behind them. The Indians are not going to wait."

"Has anything been on DD-1 yet?" Hood asked. DD-1 National was the flagship station of Doordarshan, the Indian national television network. The broadcaster was also closely affiliated with Prasar Bharati, All India Radio, which was run and maintained by the Ministry of Information and Broadcasting.

"One of Matt's people is taping the newscasts," Herbert replied. "He's going to give me an assessment of how riled up people are and at what rate the media are adding to the whipping-up process."

"Can we go in and bust up their satellite?" Hood asked.

Herbert grinned. "They use five," he said. "INSAT-2E, 2DT, 2B, PAS-4, and ThaiCom. We can scramble them all if we have to."

"Good," Hood said. He regarded Herbert. "You're pushing for Striker to go in and grab the Pakistanis, aren't you?"

"Hell," Herbert said, "I don't want to just drop Mike and his people into the Himalayas—"

"I know that," Hood assured him.

"But I don't know if we have any other options, Paul," Herbert continued. "Whatever we think of what the Pakistanis have done, they have to get out to tell what they did not do."

"What would we do if Striker weren't headed toward the region?" Hood asked.

Herbert thought for a moment then shrugged. "What we did in Korea, Russia, and Spain," Herbert said. "We'd send 'em."

Hood nodded thoughtfully. "We probably would," he agreed. "Have you run this past Mike?"

"Not in so many words," Herbert said. "But I did tell him to sleep on the flight from Alconbury to Chushul. Just in case."

"How long is that leg of the trip?" Hood asked.

Herbert looked at his watch. "They've got another six hours or so to go," he said. "Four and change with a good tailwind and if we don't keep them on the ground in Turkey for more than a few minutes."

Hood clicked on the Op-Center personnel roster. He opened the file. "Matt is still here," he said, looking at the log-in time.

"He's going over the surveillance photos with Stephen Viens," Herbert said. "He hasn't left his desk since this started."

"He should," Hood said. "We'll need him to work on any ELINT that we need in the region."

"I'll have Gloria Gold spot him for a while," Herbert said.

Gold was the nighttime director of technical affairs. She was qualified to run tech operations though she did not have the same background in analysis that Stoll had.

"We also better get Lowell and Liz Gordon in on this," Hood said. Lowell Coffey was Op-Center's international legal expert. "We need to be up on Pakistani and Indian law in case they get caught. Psych profiles of the Pakistanis would also help. Did we get a detailed jurisdictional map of the region for Striker's missile search?"

"No," Herbert said. "That was going to be pretty tightly localized in Pakistani territory."

"We'll definitely need that, then," Hood said. "We're screwed if Striker stumbles into Chinese spheres of influence and gets caught."

"If Al George doesn't have those maps in archives I'll get them from State," Herbert said. "I've got a friend there who can keep his mouth shut."

"You've got friends everywhere." Hood grinned. It felt good to be part of a team that included people like Bob Herbert. People who were professional and thorough and there to support the team and its leader. It also felt good to smile. "What about Viens? How many satellites are there in the region?"

"Three," Herbert said.

"Will he be able to hold on to them?" Hood asked.

"That shouldn't be a problem," Herbert told Hood. "No one else is asking for intel from that region right now. Viens also has his entire team on rotation, so the satellite monitoring stations will always be manned. They can run three separate recons at once."

"Good," Hood said. He continued to look at the computer screen. There were other people he could call on if needed. Right now, though, he thought it was best to keep the number of people involved to a minimum. He would call Hank Lewis at the NSA and recommend that he do the same. He hoped that the new appointee would be content to let Op-Center run this as a "silent operation"—one in which the chain of command stopped short of involving the president.

Herbert left to get his personnel set up and to obtain the map. Hood called Coffey and tore him away from *Politically Incorrect.* Since Coffey's home phone line was not secure, Hood could not tell him what the late-night meeting was about. All he said was that the title of the TV show pretty well summed it up. Coffey said he would be there as soon as possible.

Hood thanked Coffey. He fished a few more Wheat Thins from the box and sat back. There was still a lot to do before he would authorize this mission. For one thing, Stephen Viens had to find the cell. Without that information they had nothing. Then Hood and Herbert would have to decide whether to land Striker as planned and then chopper them near the cell or try to jump them in. Parachuting would be extremely dangerous in the mountains due to the cold, wind,

156

and visibility. Perhaps they could get Ron Friday out there first to plant flares. But landing would also present a problem since Striker was expected in Srinagar for an entirely different mission. It might be difficult to break away from their hosts as quickly as Op-Center needed them to.

Besides, Hood thought, the fewer people who came into contact with Striker the better it would be for security. Lowell or Herbert could come up with a reason for them to have parachuted in. The Indian air force would have to go along with that or face the mission being scrubbed.

Hood thought about Rodgers and his team. He was proud to be working with them too. Regardless of how this unfolded it would be brutally difficult for Striker if they went forward. Thinking about it did not make Hood's own problems seem less immediate or important. Relativity never worked like that. Harleigh was traumatized by what had happened at the United Nations. Knowing that other people had lost their lives there did not make it any easier to deal with her condition.

But it did do one thing. It reminded Hood what courage was. He would not forget that in the hours and days ahead.

TWENTY-SIX

Washington, D.C.
Thursday, 1:12 A.M.

"We may have something!" Stephen Viens declared.

Gloria Gold was leaning forward in her chair. The excitement in Stephen Viens's voice came through clearly on the computer audio link. He was right. After methodically scanning the terrain for hours the cameras had detected a promising image.

"Hold on," Viens said. "Bernardo is switching us to infrared. The changeover will take about three minutes."

"I'm holding," said Gloria Gold. "Nice work," she added.

"Hold the back-patting," Viens said. "It still could be just a row of rocks or a herd of mountain goats."

"That would be a flock of mountain goats," the fifty-seven-year-old woman pointed out.

"Excuse me?" Viens said.

"Herds are domesticated animals," she said. "Flocks live in the wild."

"I see. Once a professor, always a professor," Viens teased. "But who will have the last laugh if we find out it's goats being led around by a Sherpa with a crook?"

Gloria smiled. "You will."

"Maybe we should bet on it," Viens said. "Your microcam against my lapel pin."

"No go," Gloria said.

"Why not?" Viens asked. "Mine has the range."

"And mine has the substance," she replied.

The NRO recon expert had once showed her the MIT lapel pin he had customized. It contained a dot-sized microphone made of molecules that resonated one against the other. It could broadcast sound to his computer audio recorder up to two hundred miles away. Her microcam was better than that. It broadcast million-pixel images to her computer from up to ten miles away. It was better and it was much more useful.

"Okay," Viens said. "Then let's bet dinner? The loser cooks? It's a fitting deal. Infrared image, microwave meals—"

"I'm a lousy cook," said Gloria.

"I'm not."

"Thanks, but no," said the thrice-divorced woman. For some reason Viens had always had a crush on her. She liked him too but he was young enough to be her son. "We'll make it a gentleperson's bet," she said. "If you found the Pakistanis, we both win."

Viens sighed. "A diplomat's deal. I accept, but under protest."

Tall, slender Gloria Gold smiled and leaned back in her chair. She was sitting at her glass-topped desk in Op-Center's technical sector. The lights of her office were off. The only glow came from the twenty-one-inch computer monitor. The halls were silent. She took a swig from the bottle of Evian water she kept on the floor. After knocking over a bottle and shorting her computer the night after she first came to work here, Gloria had learned not to keep anything liquid on her desk. Luckily her boss, Assistant Director Curt Hardaway— "the Night Commander," as they called him—admitted that he had once done that as well. Whether he had done that or not it was a nice thing to say.

The levity about the bet had been welcome. She had only been at this an hour but Viens had been working all day. And the elements in the image-feed from the NRO did look very promising. They were at five-meter resolution, meaning that anything down to five meters long was visible. The computer's simultaneous PAP—photographic analysis profile— had identified what it thought could be human shadows. Distorted by the terrain and angle of the sun, they were coming from under an intervening ledge. Infrared would ascertain whether the shadows were being generated by living things or rock formations. The fact that the shadows had shifted between two images did not tell them much. That could simply be an illusion of the moving sun.

The Op-Center veteran watched and waited. The quiet of night shift made the delay somehow seem longer.

The tech-sec was a row of three offices set farthest from the busy front-end of the executive level. The stations were so thoroughly linked by computer, webcam, and wireless technology that the occupants wondered why they did not just tear down the walls and shout to each other, just to make human contact now and then. But Matt Stoll had always been against that. That was probably because Matt did things in private he did not want the rest of the world to know about. But Gloria Gold knew his dark secret. She had spied on him one night using her digital microcam hidden on the door handle of his minirefrigerator.

Four or five times a day, Matt Stoll washed down a pair of Twinkies with Gatorade.

That helped to explain the boundless energy and increasing girth of Op-Center's favorite egghead. It also explained the occasional yellowish stains on his shirt. He chugged the Gatorade straight from the bottle. Even now, while Stoll was supposed to be resting on his sofa, he was probably reading the latest issue of *NuTech* or playing a hand-held video game. Unlike his former classmate Viens, Matt Stoll, with his sugar and Gatorade rush, defined the word *wired*.

Gloria's mind was back on the screen as the feed from the National Reconnaissance Office was refreshed. The mostly white image was now the color of fire. There were a series of yellow-white atmospheric distortions radiating from hot red objects along the bottom of the monitor.

"Looking good," Viens said. "Whatever is making the shadows is definitely alive."

"Definitely," Gloria said. They watched as the image refreshed again. The red spot got even hotter as it moved out from under the ledge. The bloblike shape was vaguely human.

"Shit!" Viens said. "Bernardo, go back to natural light."

"That's no mountain goat," Gloria said.

"I'm betting it isn't a Sherpa either," Viens added.

Gloria continued to watch as the satellite switched oculars. This changeover seemed to take much longer than the last.

The delay was not in the mechanical switch itself but in the optics diagnostics the satellite ran each time it changed lenses. It was important to make certain the focus and alignment were correct. Wrong data—off-center imaging, improper focus, a misplaced decimal point in resolution—was as useless as no data.

The image came on-screen in visible light. There was a field of white with the gray ledge slashing diagonally across the screen. Gloria could see a figure standing half beneath it. The figure was not a goat or a Sherpa. It was a woman. Behind her was what looked like the head of another person.

"I think we've got them!" Viens said excitedly.

"Sure looks like it," Gloria agreed as she reached for the phone. "I'll let Bob Herbert know."

Bob Herbert was there before the next image appeared.

The image that clearly showed five people making their way along the narrow ledge.

TWENTY-SEVEN

Kargil, Kashmir
Thursday, 12:01 P.M.

Ron Friday liked to be prepared.

If he were going into a building he liked to have at least two exit strategies. If he were going into a country he always had his eye on the next place he would go to out of choice or necessity. If he had a mission in mind he always checked on the availability of the equipment, clearances, and allies he might need. For him, there was no such thing as downtime.

After talking with Bob Herbert, Friday realized that it might be necessary for him and Captain Nazir to move into the mountains. He knew that the helicopter was good for travel at heights up to twelve thousand feet and temperatures down to twelve degrees Fahrenheit. They had enough fuel left for a seven-hundred-mile flight. That meant they could go into the mountains about four hundred miles and still get back. Of course, there was also the problem of having to set the chopper down at too high an altitude and having liquid-bearing components freeze. Depending on where they had to fly, it could be a long and unpleasant walk back.

Friday removed the detachable phone and kept it with him. Then he checked the gear they had onboard. There was basic climbing equipment but no cold-weather clothing. That might not be a problem, however. He had gone through Apu Kumar's things. There were some heavy coats. There were hats and gloves so those would not be a problem. His biggest concern was oxygen. If he and Captain Nazir had to do a lot of climbing at higher altitudes exhaustion would be a factor.

Perhaps Striker was bringing some of that gear with them. Friday would not know that or the location of the target area itself until he talked to Bob Herbert or Hank Lewis.

In the meantime, Friday reviewed maps with Captain Nazir to familiarize himself with the region. Apu was with them in the small kitchen area of his farmhouse, adding what firsthand knowledge he had of the region. He used to climb the foothills when he was younger.

Friday plotted a course from the Srinagar bazaar to the explosion in the mountains. He also mapped a route from the farm to the Himalayan blast site. There had been more than enough time for both the cell and the man from this farm to have reached the mountain site before the detonation. The question was where they would move from there. The cell only had to cover roughly twenty miles to go from the mountains to the Pakistani border. But they were a mountainous twenty miles that included both the line of control and the brutal Siachin Glacier. Reaching up to some eighteen thousand feet, the glacier would be difficult to climb under the best of circumstances. Tired and presumably pursued from the ground and possibly the air, the Pakistanis would need a miracle to get across.

The helicopter phone beeped while Friday was looking at topographic charts of the region. Nazir answered. It was Bob Herbert and Hank Lewis. He passed the phone to Friday.

"We've found the cell," Herbert said.

"Where are they?" Friday asked eagerly. He bent over the charts that were spread on the table. "I have seven to ten tactical pilotage charts each of the Muzaffarabad border region, the Srinagar border region, and the area from Srinagar to Kargil."

"They're in the Srinagar border region," Herbert said. "Just outside of Jaudar."

"What are the coordinates?" Friday asked as he went to that set and began flipping through the charts, looking for the village.

"Ron, we want you to go at once to thirty-four degrees, thirty minutes north, seventy-five degrees east," Lewis said.

"That's Jaudar," Friday said, looking at the map. "Is that where the cell is? In the village?"

"No," Lewis said. "That's where you'll rendezvous with Striker."

Friday stood up. "Gentlemen, I have a chopper here. I can be there in under an hour. Striker won't be landing for at least four hours. I might be able to get to the cell by then."

"So would your partner," Lewis reminded him.

"And?" Friday pressed.

"We haven't finished our security check on the Black Cat," Lewis said. "We can't take the risk that he'll turn the Pakistanis over to his people."

"That won't happen," Friday assured the new NSA chief. "I'll make sure of it."

"You can't guarantee that," Lewis said. "We also agree that Mr. Kumar should go with you and we can't be certain of his actions either. Mr. Herbert and I have discussed this and we're in agreement. You will meet Striker in Jaudar. They will have up-to-the-minute coordinates of the cell and the resources to get you and your companions into the mountains. If anything changes, we'll let you know."

"We're wasting time," Friday protested. "I could probably be in and out by the time Striker arrives."

"I admire your enthusiasm," Herbert said. "But the leader of the cell is cagey. They've been moving in shadows and beneath overhangs wherever possible. We don't know for certain what weapons they're carrying. They may have a rocket launcher. If you come after them in an Indian chopper they will probably shoot you down."

"If you tell us where they are we can circle wide and intercept them," Friday pointed out.

"There's also a chance that a Pakistani aircraft might try to slip in and rescue the cell," Herbert said. "We don't want to precipitate a firefight with an Indian aircraft. That could give the Indians even more ammunition to launch a major offensive."

Friday squeezed the phone. He wished he could strangle the deskbound bureaucrat. He did not understand field personnel. None of them did. The best field ops did not like sitting still. And the best of the best were able to improvise their way in and out of most things. Friday could do this. More than that, he wanted it. If he could grab the cell and bring them home he would have a chance to get in with their

Pakistani controllers. Having strong ties to New Delhi, Islamabad, and Washington would be invaluable to an operative in this region.

"Are we on the same page?" Herbert asked.

Friday looked down at the map. "Yes," he said. And as he looked he remembered something that Herbert had told him about the explosion. It had occurred at approximately eight thousand feet. That would put the cell on the southwest side of the range. Everything north of that, up through the glacier and the line of control, was at a higher elevation. Friday's grip relaxed. To hell with desk jockeys in general and Bob Herbert in particular.

"We'll brief you again when we have Striker's precise ETA and location," Herbert said. "Do you have any questions?"

"No," Friday replied calmly.

"Is there anything you wanted to add, Hank?" Herbert asked.

Lewis said there was nothing else. The NSA head thanked Friday and the men hung up. Friday returned the phone to its cradle.

"What is it?" Captain Nazir asked.

"What we've been waiting for," Friday said.

"They found the cell?" Nazir asked.

Friday nodded.

"And my granddaughter?" Apu asked.

"She's with them," Friday said. He did not know if she was or not, of course. But he wanted Apu with them. The farmer had harbored the enemy cell. If they needed to forestall any action by India, Apu's confession would play very well on Pakistani TV.

Friday looked at the map. Herbert had told him that the cell was sticking to the mountain ledges. That meant that if the chopper started following the line of the range at eight thousand feet and flew up one side and then down the other they were sure to encounter the cell. Friday glanced down at the inset conic projection and smiled. The round-trip was less than two hundred miles.

He would have them. And he would have that do-nothing Herbert.

"Come on," Friday said to Nazir.

"Where are we going?" the officer asked.

"To catch a terrorist cell," Friday replied.

TWENTY-EIGHT

Washington, D.C.
Thursday, 4:02 A.M.

Paul Hood's office was just a few steps away from Op-Center's high-security conference room. Known as the Tank, the conference room was surrounded by walls of electronic waves that generated static for anyone trying to listen in with bugs or external dishes.

Hood entered after everyone was already there. The heavy door was operated by a button at the side of the large oval conference table. Hood pushed it when he sat down at the head of the table.

The small room was lit by fluorescent lights hung in banks over the conference table. On the wall across from Hood's chair the countdown clock was dark. When they had a crisis and a deadline, the clock flashed its ever-changing array of digital numbers.

The walls, floor, door, and ceiling of the Tank were all covered with sound-absorbing Acoustix. The mottled gray-and-black strips were each three inches wide and overlapped one another to make sure there were no gaps. Beneath them were two layers of cork, a foot of concrete, and then another layer of Acoustix. In the midst of the concrete, on all six sides of the room, was a pair of wire grids that generated vacillating audio waves. Electronically, nothing left the room without being utterly distorted. If any listening device did somehow manage to pick up a conversation from inside, the randomness of the changing modulation made reassembling the conversations impossible.

"Thank you all for coming," Hood said. He turned down the brightness on the computer monitor that was set in the table and began bringing up the files from his office. At the same time, Bugs Benet was busy raising Colonel August on the TAC-SAT. In order to make sure Striker stayed in the loop, August and Rodgers were taking turns sleeping en route to Turkey.

"No problem," Lowell Coffey said. He had been pouring water from a pitcher into a coffee machine on a table in the far corner. The percolator began to bubble and pop. "The roads were empty. I managed to sleep on the way. Anybody think to get doughnuts?"

"That was your job," Herbert pointed out. "You were the only one who wasn't here." He maneuvered his wheelchair into his place at Hood's right.

"I've got mid rats in my office if you're hungry," said Liz Gordon as she settled in to Hood's left.

"No, thanks." Coffey shuddered as he sat across from Hood. "I'll stick to the coffee."

"You've got official military midnight rations?" Herbert asked.

"A three-course packet," Liz said. "Dried apricots and pineapple, jerky, and cookies. A friend of mine at Langley gave them to me. I think you've worked with her. Captain McIver?"

"We worked on some black ops stuff together," Herbert said. He smiled. "Man, mid rats. I haven't had them in years. They always hit the spot in the wee small hours."

"That's because you were tired and not selective," said the admittedly dilettantish Coffey.

Hood's data finished loading a moment before Bugs Benet called. Hood sent the files to the other computer stations around the table. Liz and Coffey scanned the files as Hood's assistant informed him that he had Colonel Brett August ready to be patched through from the C-130 Hercules. Hood put the telephone on speaker and looked across the table.

"We're ready to go," Hood said to the others.

Everyone came to attention quickly.

"Colonel August, can you hear me?" Hood asked.

"As clear as if you were in the cabin with us, sir," the Striker commander replied.

168

"Good," Hood replied. "Bob, you've been talking to New Delhi. Would you please bring everyone up to speed?"

Herbert looked at his wheelchair computer monitor. "Twenty-one hours ago there was an attack on a market in Srinagar, Kashmir," Herbert said. He spoke loud enough for the speakerphone to pick up his voice. "A police station, a Hindu temple, and a busload of Hindu pilgrims were destroyed. With intel from the NRO and from your NSA contact who happened to be on-site, we have reason to believe that the attack on the station was the work of the Free Kashmir Militia, a militant organization based in Pakistan. However, we suspect that the attacks against the Hindu sites may have been organized by India itself. We believe that elements in the Special Frontier Force, the cabinet, and the military may be trying to win public support for a quick, decisive nuclear strike against Pakistan."

No one moved. The only sounds were the hum of the forced air coming through the overhead vents and the crackling of the coffee machine as it finished brewing.

"What about the Pakistani terrorists?" Coffey asked.

"At this moment the cell is desperately trying to cross the Himalayan foothills—we believe to Pakistan," Herbert replied. "They have a prisoner. She's an Indian woman who apparently coordinated SFF actions to make the attack on the Hindu sites look like the work of the Pakistani Muslims. It is imperative that they reach Pakistan and that their hostage be made to tell what she knows."

"To defuse the outraged Indian populace that will otherwise be screaming for Pakistani blood," Liz said.

"Correct," Herbert said. "So far, the first attempt to capture the Pakistanis failed. SFF commandos were sent into the mountains. They were all killed. We do not know what other pursuit options are being considered or whether the cell has contacted Pakistan. We don't know what rescue efforts Islamabad may be attempting to mount."

"They'd probably be chopper HAP searches," August said.

"Explain," Hood said.

"Hunt and peck," August told him. "The cell would not risk sending a radio beacon to Pakistan or suggesting a rendezvous point. That would be too easy for an Indian listening post at the line of control to pick off. Pakistan doesn't have the satellite resources to spot the cell so they would have to fly in and crisscross suspected routes of egress. And they'd use helicopters instead of jets, to stay below Indian radar."

"Good 'gets,'" Herbert said.

"Paul, there's something that's bothering me," Coffey said. "Do we know for certain that the NSA operative was an observer and not a participant? This action may have been planned a couple of weeks ago, timed to draw attention from their attempted coup in Washington."

Coffey had a point. The former head of the NSA, Jack Fenwick, had been working to replace President of the United States Michael Lawrence with the more militant Vice President Cotten. It was conceivable that Fenwick may have helped to orchestrate this crisis as a distraction from the anticipated resignation of President Lawrence.

"We believe that Friday is clean, though right now we have him quarantined with an Indian officer," Hood replied. "I suspect that if Friday were involved with this he would be trying to get out of the region and keep us out as well."

"Which could also mean he is involved," Liz pointed out.

"In what way?" Hood asked.

"If you're suggesting, as I think you are, that Striker try to help the cell get home, it would be in Mr. Friday's interest to stay close to them and make sure they do not succeed."

"That could work both ways," Herbert said. "If Striker goes in after the cell we can also keep an eye on Friday."

"I want to emphasize here that we have not yet made a final determination on the mission, Colonel," Hood said. "But if we do try to help the Pakistanis the key to success is a timely intervention. Bob, you've been in contact with HQ Central Air Command."

"Yes," Herbert said. "We're dealing directly with Air Chief Marshal Chowdhury and his senior aide. I told the ACM that we may want to change the way we insert Striker."

"You're thinking about an airdrop," August said.

"Correct," replied Herbert. "I asked the ACM for jump gear. He said it will definitely be on the Himalayan Eagles

170

squadron AN-12. But I did not tell him what we may be asking you to do in the region. The good news is, whatever you do will be well shielded. The Indian military continues to be ultrasecretive about your involvement. The SFF and the other people behind the Srinagar attacks do not even know that Striker is en route to the region."

"What about the Indian officer who is with Mr. Friday?" Colonel August asked. "Are we sure we can trust him?"

"Well, nothing is guaranteed," Herbert said. "But according to Friday, Captain Nazir is not looking forward to the prospect of a nuclear attack. Especially when he and Friday are headed toward Pakistan."

"I was just thinking about that," August said. "Do you think you can include lead-lined long johns in the Indian requisition form?"

"Just get behind Mike," Herbert said. "Nothing gets past that sumbitch. Not even high-intensity rads."

There was anxious chuckling about that. The laughter was a good tension breaker.

"We've got Friday and Nazir en route by chopper to a town called Jaudar," Herbert said.

"I know where that is," Colonel August said. "It's southeast of the region we were supposed to be investigating."

"If we decide to move forward with a search and rescue, you'll be hooking up in the mountains north of there," Herbert said. "That's where we've pinpointed the cell."

"Colonel August, if we decide to go ahead with this mission you'll have to jump your people into the Himalayas near the Siachin Glacier, link up with the cell, and get them through the line of control," Hood said. "This is an extremely high-risk operation. I need an honest answer. Is Striker up for it?"

"The stakes are also high," August said. "We have to be up for it."

"Good man," Herbert muttered. "Damn good man."

"People, one thing I have to point out is that the Indians are not going to be your only potential enemies," Liz said. "You also have to worry about the psychological state of the Pakistani cell. They're under extreme physical and psychological duress. They may not believe that you're allies. The nature of people in this situation is to trust no one outside the group."

"Those are very good points and we'll have to talk about them," Hood told her.

"There's something else we'll have to talk about, Paul," Coffey said. "According to your file, the Free Kashmir Militia has acknowledged its involvement with at least part of this attack and with all of the previous attacks in Kashmir. Striker will be helping self-professed terrorists. To say that leaves us vulnerable legally is an understatement."

"That's absolute horseshit," Herbert said. "The guys who blew my wife up are still hanging out in a rat hole in Syria somewhere: Terrorists of warring nations don't get extradited. And the guys who help terrorists don't even get their names in the papers."

"That only happens to guerrillas who are sponsored by terrorist nations," Coffey replied. "The United States has a different form and level of accountability. Even if Striker succeeds in getting the cell to Pakistan, India will be within its rights to demand the extradition of everyone who had a hand in the attack on the bazaar, on the SFF commandos, and in the escape. If New Delhi can't get the FKM they will go after Striker."

"Lowell, India doesn't have any kind of moral high ground here," Herbert said. "They're planning a goddamn nuclear strike!"

"No, a rogue element in the government is apparently planning that," Coffey said. "The lawful Indian government will have to disown them and prosecute them as well."

The attorney rose angrily and got himself a cup of coffee. He was a little calmer as he sat back down and took a sip. Hood was silent. He looked at Herbert. The intelligence chief did not like Lowell Coffey and his disgust with legal technicalities was well known. Unfortunately, Hood could not afford to ignore what the attorney had just said.

"Gentlemen?" August said.

"Go ahead, Colonel," Hood said.

"We are talking about a possible nuclear conflagration here," August said. "The normal rules do not seem to apply. I'll poll the team if you'd like, but I'm willing to bet they say the same thing I'm about to. Given the stakes, the downside is worth risking."

Hood was about to thank him but the words snagged in his throat. Bob Herbert did not have that problem.

"God bless you, Colonel August," Herbert said loudly as he glared across the table at Coffey.

"Thank you, Bob," August said. "Mr. Coffey? If it's any help, Striker can always pull a Lone Ranger on the Pakistanis."

"Meaning what, Colonel?" Coffey asked.

"We can drop them off then ride into the sunset before they can even thank or ID us," August said.

Herbert smiled. Hood did, too, but inside. His face was frozen by the weight of the decision he would have to make.

"We'll get back to you later on all of this," Hood said. "Colonel, I want to thank you."

"For what? Doing my job?"

"For your enthusiasm and courage," Hood said. "They raise the bar for all of us."

"Thank you, sir," August said.

"Get some rest," Hood said. He clicked off the phone and looked across the table. "Bob, I want you to make sure we've got someone at the NRO watching the Pakistani border. If a chopper does come looking for the cell we have to be able to give Striker advance warning. I don't want them to be mistaken for a hostile force and cut down."

Herbert nodded.

"Lowell, find me some legal grounds for doing this," Hood went on.

The attorney shook his head. "There isn't anything," Coffey said. "At least, nothing that will hold up in an international court."

"I don't need anything that will work in court," Hood said. "I need a reason to keep Striker from being extradited if it comes to that."

173

"Like claiming they were on a mission of mercy," Coffey said.

"Yeah," Herbert interjected. "I'll bet we can find some UN peacekeeping status bullshit that would qualify."

"Without informing the United Nations?" Coffey said.

"You know, Lowell, Bob may have something," Hood said. "The secretary-general has emergency trusteeship powers that allow her to declare a region 'at risk' in the event of an apparent and overwhelming military threat. That gives her the right to send a Security Council team to the region to investigate."

"I'm missing how that helps us," Coffey said.

"The team does not have to consist of sitting Security Council personnel," Hood said. "Just agents of Security Council nations."

"Maybe," Coffey said. "But no one will accept the presence of a team consisting solely of Americans."

"It won't," Hood said. "India's a member of the Security Council. And there are Indians out there."

"Captain Nazir and Nanda Kumar," Herbert said. "Her own countrymen."

"Exactly," Hood replied. "Even if she's a hostile observer, at least she's present."

"Yeah. Since when does the Security Council agree on anything?" Liz pointed out.

"We may have to bring Secretary-General Chatterjee in on this once Striker is on the ground," Hood said. "Then we'll tell her what we know."

"And what if she refuses to invoke her trusteeship powers?" Coffey asked.

"She won't," Hood said.

"How can you be sure?" Coffey asked.

"Because we still have a press department," Hood said. "And while we do, I'll make sure that every paper on earth knows that Secretary-General Chatterjee did nothing while India prepared to launch nuclear missiles at Pakistan. We'll see whose blood the world wants then. Hers or Striker's."

I wouldn't bet the farm on that plan," Coffey warned.

Give me an option," Hood countered.

Coffey and Herbert agreed to have a look at the United Nations charter and brief Hood. Hood agreed to hold off contacting Chatterjee. Herbert left to follow up on the intel reports. Only Liz stayed behind with Hood. Her hands were folded on the table and she was staring hard at them.

"Problem, Liz?" Hood asked.

She looked at him. "You've had some run-ins with Mala Chatterjee."

"True," Hood said. "But forcing her hand or embarrassing her is not on the agenda. I'm only interested in protecting Striker."

"That isn't where I was going with this," she said. "You fought with Chatterjee, you fought with Sharon, and you've shut Ann Farris out." Her expression softened. "She told me about what happened between you."

"Okay," Hood said with a trace of annoyance. "What's your point?"

"I know what you think about psychobabble, Paul, but I want you to make sure you keep all of this on an issues level," Liz said. "You're under a lot of pressure from women. Don't let that frustration get transferred from one woman to another to another."

Hood rose. "I won't. I promise."

"I want to believe that," Liz said. She smiled. "But right now you're pissed at me, too."

Hood stood there. Liz was right. His back was ramrod straight, his mouth was a tight line, and his fingers were curled into fists. He let his shoulders relax. He opened his hands. He looked down.

"Paul, it's my job to watch the people here and point out possible problem spots," Liz said. "That's all I'm doing. I'm not judging you. But you have been under a lot of pressure since the UN situation. You're also tired. All I'm trying to do is keep you the fair, even-handed guy I just saw working things out between Bob Herbert and Lowell Coffey."

Hood smiled slightly. "Thanks, Liz. I don't believe the secretary-general was in danger, but I appreciate the heads-up."

175

Liz gave him a reassuring pat on the arm and left the room. Hood looked across the room at the crisis clock.

It was still blank. But inside, his own clock was ticking. And the mainspring was wound every bit as tight as Liz had said.

Even so, he reminded himself that he was safe in Washington while Mike Rodgers and Striker were heading into a region where their actions could save or doom millions of lives—including their own.

Next to that, whatever pressure he was feeling was nothing.

Nothing at all.

TWENTY-NINE

New Delhi, India
Thursday, 2:06 P.M.

Sixty-nine-year-old Minister of Defense John Kabir sat in his white-walled office. The two corridors of the Ministry of Defence offices were part of the cabinet complex housed in the eighty-year-old Parliament House Estate at 36 Gurdwara Rakabganj Road in New Delhi. Outside a wall-length bank of open windows the bright afternoon sun shone down on the extensive lawns, small artificial ponds, and decorative stone fountains. The sounds of traffic were barely audible beyond the high, ornamental red sandstone wall that enclosed the sprawling complex. On the right side of the grounds Kabir could just see the edge of one of the two houses of Parliament, the Lok Sabha, the House of the People. On the other side of this ministry annex was the Rajya Sabha, the Council of States. Unlike the representatives in the Lok Sabha, which were elected by the people, the members of the Rajya Sabha were either chosen by the president or selected by the legislative assemblies of the nation's states.

Minister Kabir loved his nation and its government. But he no longer had patience for it. The system had lost its way.

The white-haired official had just finished reading a secure e-mail dispatch from Major Dev Puri on his army's movements into the mountains. Puri and his people were frontline veterans. They would succeed where the SFF commandos had failed.

Kabir deleted the computer file then sat there reflecting on the crossroads to which he had brought his nation. It would be either the triumph or the downfall of his long career. It was a career that began with his rise through the military to captain by the age of thirty-seven. However, Kabir was frustrated by the weak social and military programs of Prime Minister Indira Gandhi. He was particularly upset when India defeated Pakistan in the 1971 war and failed to absolutely solidify their hold on Kashmir by creating a demilitarized zone beyond the line of control. He drew up a plan calling for a "zone of security." He wanted to use the villages on the Pakistani side for routine artillery, gunship, and bombing practice. He wanted to keep them unoccupied. What was the purpose of winning a war if the victor could not maintain security along its borders?

Not only was his plan rejected, but Captain Kabir was reprimanded by the minister of defence. Kabir resigned and wrote a book, *What Ails the Irresolute Nation,* which became a controversial best-seller. It was followed by *A Plan for Our Secure Future.* Within three months of the publication of the second book he was asked to become general secretary of the Samyukta Socialist Party. Within three years he was chairman of the national Socialist Party. At the same time he was appointed president of the All India Truckers' Federation. He led a strike in 1974 that crippled the highways and even railroad crossings, where trucks "broke down." That helped to trigger the establishment of Prime Minister Gandhi's "Emergency" in June 1975. That declaration enabled her to suspend civil liberties and incarcerate her foes. Kabir was arrested and held in prison for over a year. That did not stop him from campaigning for reform from his jail cell. Supported by union members and by Russian-backed socialist groups, Kabir was pardoned. The Russians in particular liked Kabir's advocacy of a stronger border presence against China. Kabir drew on his widespread grassroots support to have himself named deputy minister of industry. He used that post to strengthen his support among the working castes while restoring his ties to the military. That led to his appointment as minister of Kashmir affairs and his membership on the Committee on External Affairs. That was where he became good friends with Dilip Sahani. Sahani was the officer in charge of the Special Frontier Force in Kashmir. The men discovered they had the same concerns regarding the threat posed by both Islamic Fundamentalists and the nuclear research being conducted by Pakistan.

Two years ago, high-ranking officers and government officials who respected Kabir's Zone of Security plan got together and pressed the prime minister to name him minister of defence. Kabir asked the national commander of the SFF to come and work for him and then arranged for Dilip Sahani to take over that post. Together, the men plotted in secret. New Delhi was content to build its own nuclear arsenal as a deterrent and collect intelligence to assess the across-the-border threat. Kabir and Sahani were not. They wanted to make certain that Islamabad never had the opportunity to mount the very real threat of a jihad of mass destruction. With the unwitting help of the FKM cell and a young member of the SFF's Civilian Network Operatives, they were on the verge of realizing their dream. If the field commandos had succeeded in their efforts to capture and destroy the FKM, the goal would be just days if not hours away. Now they had to wait.

Major Puri would not fail them. He would close in on the terrorist cell and then kill them in a firefight. The CNO operative who was with them would tell the story as she saw it from the inside. Even if she died in the fight, she would reveal to Major Puri with her dying breath how the FKM attacked the temple and the bus. How the lives of those Hindus were the first sacrifices of the new jihad. The people of India would believe her because in their hearts they knew she was telling the truth. Her grieving grandfather would back up everything that she said. And then the Indian government would respond.

Of course, the president and prime minister would attack Pakistan as they usually did. With words. That was how nuclear powers were supposed to act. If they replied with weapons the results would be unthinkable. Or so the common wisdom went.

What the rest of the world did not realize was that Pakistan's leaders were willing to endure annihilation. They would sacrifice their nation if it meant the utter destruction

179

of India and the Hindu people. Islam would still have tens of millions of adherents. Their faith would survive. And the dead of Pakistan would live on in Paradise.

Kabir was not going to give Pakistan the chance to attack India. He was, however, perfectly willing to send them to Paradise. He intended to do that with a preemptive strike.

The team that was in charge of the Underground Nuclear Command Center was loyal to Minister Kabir. The key personnel had been carefully selected from among the military and SFF ranks. They would respond to dual commands issued by Minister Kabir and Commander Sahani. When those orders came, nothing on earth could turn them back.

Kabir's plan was to hit Pakistan before they had fully deployed their nuclear arsenal. He would use a total of seventy-nine Indian SRBMs. The short-range ballistic missiles each had a range of eight hundred kilometers. They constituted one-half of India's nuclear arsenal and were housed in silos located just behind the line of control. Eleven of those would hit Islamabad alone, removing it from the map and killing nearly 20 percent of the nation's 130 million people. In the days and weeks to come, radiation from the explosions would kill another 40 million Pakistanis. The rest of the SRBMs would strike at Pakistani military facilities. That included seven suspected silo locations in the Himalayas. Maybe the American team coming into the country would have found them. Maybe they would not. Regardless, their presence would be a powerful public relations tool for Kabir. It would show the world that India had reason to fear Pakistan's nuclear proliferation. The deaths of the Americans would be unfortunate but unavoidable.

Minister Kabir brought the remaining targets up on his computer. In addition to the mountains, SRBMs would be launched at each of Pakistan's air bases. Ten Pakistan Air Force bases were operational full-time. These were the "major operational bases" PAF Sargodha, PAF Mianwali, PAF Kamra, PAF Rafiqui, PAF Masroor, PAF Faisal, PAF Chaklala, PAF Risalpur, PAF Peshawar, and PAF Samungli. They would all be hit with two missiles each. Then there were eleven "forward operational bases" that became fully operational only during wartime. All of these would be struck as well. They were PAF Sukkur, PAF Shahbaz, PAF Multan, PAF Vihari, PAF Risalewala, PAF Lahore, PAF Nawabshah, PAF Mirpur Khas, PAF Murid, PAF Pasni, and PAF Talhar. Finally, there were the nine satellite bases used for emergency landings: PAF Rahim Yar Khan, PAF Chander, PAF Bhagtanwala, PAF Chuk Jhumra, PAF Ormara, PAF Rajanpur, PAF Sindhri, PAF Gwadar, and PAF Kohat. These were little more than landing strips without personnel to man them. Still, they would all be razed. With luck, the PAF would not be able to launch a single missile or bomber. Even if Pakistan did manage to land a few nuclear blows, India could absorb the loss. The leaders would have been moved to the underground bunkers. They would manage the brief conflagration and recovery from the UNCC.

When it was all over, Kabir would take the blame or praise for what happened. But however the world responded, Kabir was certain of one thing.

He will have done the right thing.

THIRTY

Ankara, Turkey
Thursday, 11:47 A.M.

The Indian air force AN-12 transport is a cousin of the world's largest aircraft, the Russian Antonov AN-225 Mriya. The AN-12 is half the size of that six-engine brute. A long-range transport, it is also one-third smaller than the C-130 that had brought Striker as far as Ankara. With the cargo section in the rear and an enclosed, insulated passenger cabin toward the front, the IAF aircraft is also much quieter. For that Mike Rodgers was grateful.

Rodgers had caught five solid hours of sleep on the final leg of the C-130 flight. He did that with the help of wax earplugs he carried expressly for that purpose. Still, the small downclick in sound and vibration was welcome. Especially when Corporal Ishi Honda left his seat in the rear of the small, cramped crew compartment. He ducked as he made his way through the single narrow aisle that ran through the center of the cabin. The team's grips, cold-weather gear, and parachutes were strapped in bulging mesh nets on the ceiling over the aisle.

The communications expert handed the TAC-SAT to General Rodgers. "It's Mr. Herbert," Honda said.

Colonel August was sitting beside Rodgers in the forward-facing seats. The men exchanged glances.

"Thank you," Rodgers said to Honda.

The corporal returned to his seat. Rodgers picked up the receiver.

"There are parachutes onboard, Bob," Rodgers said. "For us?"

"Paul's given the go-ahead for an expedited search-and-recover of the cell," Herbert said.

"Expedited" was spy-speak for "illegal." It meant that an operation was being rushed before anyone could learn about it and block it. It also meant something else. They were probably going to be jumping into the Himalayas. Rodgers knew what that meant.

"We have the target spotted," Herbert went on. "Viens is following them through the mountains. They're at approximately nine thousand feet and heading northwest toward the line of control. They're currently located thirty-two miles due north of the village of Jaudar."

Rodgers removed one of the three "playbooks" from under the seat. It was a fat black spiral-bound notebook containing all the maps of the regions. He found the town and moved his finger up. He turned to the previous page where the map was continued. Instead of just brown mountains there was a big dagger-shaped slash of white pointing to the lower left.

"That puts them on direct course for the Siachin Glacier," Rodgers said.

"That's how our people read it," Herbert said. "They can't be carrying a lot of artillery. It would make sense for them to head somewhere the elements might help them. Cold, blizzards, avalanches, crevasses—it's a fortress or stealth environment if they need it."

"Assuming it doesn't kill them," Rodgers pointed out.

"Trying to go through any lower would definitely kill them," Herbert replied. "The NSA intercepted a SIG-INT report from a Russian satellite listening in on the line of control. Several divisions have apparently moved out and are headed toward the glacier."

"Estimated time of encounter?" Rodgers asked.

"We don't have one," Herbert said. "We don't know if the divisions are airborne, motorized, or on foot. We'll see what else comes through the Russian satellite."

"Can General Orlov help us with this?" Rodgers asked.

Sergei Orlov was head of the Russian Op-Center based in St. Petersburg. General Orlov and Hood had a close personal and professional relationship. Striker leader Lt. Colonel Charles Squires died during a previous joint undertaking, helping to prevent a coup in Russia.

"I asked Paul about that," Herbert said. "He doesn't want to involve them. Russian technology helps drive the Indian war machine. Indian payoffs drive Russian generals. Orlov won't be able to guarantee that anyone he contacts will maintain the highest-level security status."

"I'm not convinced we can guarantee HLS status from the NSA," Rodgers replied.

"I'm with you on that," Herbert said. "I'm not sure Hank Lewis patched up all the holes Jack Fenwick drilled over there. That's why I'm giving information to Ron Friday on a need-to-know basis. He's moving up to Jaudar with a Black Cat officer and the grandfather of the CNO informant who's traveling with the cell."

"Good move," Rodgers said.

"We're also trying to get regular weather updates from the Himalayan Eagles," Herbert said. "But that could all change before you arrive. By the way, how are your new hosts treating you?"

"Fine," Rodgers said. "They gave us rations, the gear is all here, and we're on schedule."

"All right," Herbert said. "I'll give you the drop coordinates at H-hour minus fifteen."

"Confirmed," Rodgers said.

The general looked at his watch. They had three hours to go. That left them just enough time to pass out the gear, check it out, suit up, and review the maps with the team.

"I'll check back in when I have more intel for you," Herbert said. "Is there anything else you need?"

"I can't think of anything, Bob," Rodgers said.

There was a short silence. Mike Rodgers knew what was coming. He had heard the change in Herbert's voice during that last question. It had gone from determined to wistfulness.

"Mike, I know I don't have to tell you that this is a shitty assignment," Herbert said.

"No, you don't," Rodgers agreed. He was flipping through the magnified views of the region of the drop. Never mind the terrain itself. The wind-flow charts were savage. The cur-

184

rents tore through the mountains at fifty to sixty-one miles an hour. Those were gale-force winds.

"But I do have to point out that you aren't a part of Striker," Herbert went on. "You're a senior officer of the NCMC."

"Cut to the chase," Rodgers told him. "Is Paul going to order me to stay behind?"

"I haven't discussed this with him," Herbert said. "What's the point? You've disobeyed his orders before."

"I have," Rodgers said. "Kept Tokyo from getting nuked, if I remember correctly at my advanced age."

"You did do that," Herbert said. "But I was thinking that it might help if we had someone on-site to liaise with the Indian government."

"Send one of the guys the FBI tucked into the embassy," Rodgers said. "I know they're there and so do the Indians."

"I don't think so," Herbert replied.

"Look, I'll be happy to talk to whatever officials I have to from the field," Rodgers said. The general leaned forward. He huddled low over the microphone. "Bob, you know damn well what we're facing here. I've been looking at the charts. When we drop into the mountains the wind alone is going to hammer us. We stand a good chance of losing people just getting onto the ground."

"I know," Herbert said.

"Hell, if they didn't need to fly the plane I'd bring the Indian crew down with me. Let them help save their own country," Rodgers continued. "So don't even try to tell me that I shouldn't do what we're asking Striker to do. Especially not with what's at stake."

"Mike, I wasn't thinking about Striker or the rest of the world," Herbert replied. "I was thinking about an old friend with football-damaged, forty-seven-year-old knees. A friend who could hurt Striker more than help them if he got injured on an ice-landing."

"If that happens I'll order them to leave me where I land," Rodgers assured him.

"They won't."

185

"They will," Rodgers said. "We'll have to do that with anyone who's hurt." He hung up the receiver and motioned for Corporal Honda to come back and reclaim the TAC-SAT. Then he rose.

"I'll be right back," Rodgers said to August.

"Is there anything we need to do?" August asked.

Rodgers looked down at him. August was in an uncomfortable spot. Rodgers was one of the colonel's oldest and closest friends. He was also a superior officer. That was one of the reasons August had turned down this job when it was first offered to him. It was often difficult for the colonel to find a proper balance between those two relationships. This was one of those times. August also knew what was at risk for his friend and the team.

"I'll let you know in a few minutes," Rodgers said as he walked toward the cockpit.

Walked on rickety knees that were ready to kick some ass.

THIRTY-ONE

Jaudar, Kashmir
Thursday, 3:33 P.M.

The problem with flying an LAHR—low-altitude helicopter reconnaissance—in a region like the Himalayas is that there is no room for error.

From the pilot's perspective, keeping the aircraft steady is practically impossible. The aircraft shakes along the x- and y-axes, the horizontal and vertical, with occasional bumps in the diagonal. Keeping the chopper within visual range of the target area is also problematic. It's often necessary for the pilot to move suddenly and over considerable distances to get around violent air pockets, clouds that blow in and impede the view, or snow and ice squalls. Just keeping the bird aloft is the best that can be hoped for. Whatever intel the observer can grab is considered a gift, not a guarantee.

Wearing sunglasses to cut down on the glare, and a helmet headset to communicate with Captain Nazir in the noisy cabin, Ron Friday alternately peered through the front and side windows of the cockpit. The American operative cradled an MP5K in his lap. If they spotted the terrorists there might be a gunfight. Hopefully, a few bursts in the air from the submachine gun would get them to stop shooting and listen. If not, he was prepared to back off and snipe one or two of them with the 1ASL in the gun rack behind him. If Captain Nazir could keep the chopper steady, the large sharpshooter rifle had greater range than the small arms the terrorists were probably carrying. With a few of them wounded, the others might be more inclined to let Friday land and approach them. Especially if he promised to airlift them to medical assistance in Pakistan.

Apu was seated on a fold-down chair in the spacious cargo area. It wasn't so much a chair as a hinged plastic square with a down cushion on top. The farmer was leaning forward, peering through a hatchway that separated the cargo section from the cockpit. Apu wore an anxious look as he gazed out through the window. Friday was good at reading people's expressions. He was not just concerned about finding his granddaughter. There was a sense of despair in his eyes, in the sad downturn of his mouth. Perhaps Apu had been in the mountains as a young man. He had had some idea what was beyond the foothills. But Apu had certainly never gone this far, never this high. He had never gazed down at the barren peaks. He had never heard the constant roar of the wind over powerful 671 kW rotors, or felt that wind batter an aircraft, or experienced the cold that blasted through the canvas-lined metal walls. The farmer knew that unless they found Nanda the chances were not good that she would survive.

The chopper continued toward the line of control without any of the occupants spotting the terrorists. Friday was not overly concerned. They still had the southward trip along the other side of the range to go.

Suddenly, something happened that Friday was not expecting. He heard a voice in his helmet. A voice that did not belong to Captain Nazir.

"Negative zone three," said the very faint, crackling voice. "Repeat: negative zone three." A moment later the voice was gone.

Friday made sure the headset switch on the communications panel was set on "internal" rather than "external." That meant they were communicating only with the cockpit instead of an outside receiver.

"Who is that?" Friday asked.

Nazir shook his head slowly. "It's not control tower communication." The wheel was shaking violently. He did not want to release his two-handed grip. "Do you see that yellow button below the com-panel?" he asked.

"Yes," Friday said.

"That's the nosedome antenna," Nazir said. "Push it once then push on the external signal again."

Friday did. As soon as the button was depressed the voices began to come in more clearly. Other zones were checking in. There was also a blip on the small green directional map. The signal was coming from the northwest. Friday switched back to internal communications.

"We'd better check it out," Friday said.

"It cannot be a Pakistani search party," Nazir said. "They would not communicate on this frequency."

"I know," Friday replied. "The line of control isn't far from here. I'm worried that it could be an Indian unit moving in."

"A sweep coming down through different zones," Nazir said. "That would be a standard search-and-rescue maneuver. Should we do a flyover?"

"Why?" Friday asked.

"They may have intelligence on the cell's location that we do not," Nazir said. "The direction they are headed may tell us something."

"No," Friday said. He continued to look out the window. "I don't want to waste the time or fuel."

"What do we do if they contact us?" Nazir asked. "Radar at the line of control may pick us up as we near the end of the range. They may ask us to help with the search."

"We'll tell them we're on routine reconnaissance and were about to turn back to Kargil," Friday said.

Apu stuck his small, strong hand through the opening. He tapped Friday on the shoulder. "Is everything all right?" he yelled.

Friday nodded. Just then, about one hundred feet below, he saw snow billowing from under an overhang.

"Hold!" Friday barked at Nazir.

The helicopter slowed and hovered. Ron Friday leaned toward the side. The puffs of snow were concentrated in a small area and inching toward the north. They could be caused by an animal picking its way across the cliff or they could be the result of a wind funnel. It was impossible to tell because of the overhang. The sun was behind the top of the peak and unable to throw shadows behind or in front of the region.

"Do you see that?" Friday asked.

Nazir nodded.

"Take her down and away slowly," Friday said.

The chopper simultaneously began to descend and angle away from the cliff. As the target peak filled less and less of the window, the vastness of the range loomed behind it. The layers upon layers of brownish-purple mountains were a spectacular sight. Snow covered the peaks and Friday could actually see it falling on some of the nearer mountains, off-white sheets like stage scrims. The sun cut a rainbow through one of the storm centers. It was a massive arc, more brilliant than any Friday had ever seen. Though Friday did not have time to enjoy the view, it made him feel for a moment like a god.

They dropped nearly one hundred feet. As they did, three people came into view. They were slightly more than two hundred feet away. The three were walking close together. Each one was wearing dark, heavy clothing and carrying a backpack and weapon. They did not stop or look over at the helicopter until the rotor wash stirred the snow on the ledge beneath their feet. Given the parka tops they were wearing and the low rumble of the wind, Friday was not surprised they did not hear the chopper.

"Is Nanda there?" Apu asked.

Friday could not tell who the three people were. He was disappointed to see that only three of them had gotten this far. Unless—

"Take us back up and head north!" he shouted.

Captain Nazir pulled the U-shaped wheel toward him and the chopper rose. As it did, the tail rotor and starboard side of the cargo area were struck by short, hard blows. Friday could not hear them but he could feel the craft shudder. He could also see the thin shafts of white daylight appear suddenly in the bottom half of the cargo bay.

"What is it?" Nazir yelled.

"They think we are the enemy!" Apu shouted.

"It's a setup!" Friday snarled. "They broke into two groups!"

The chopper wobbled and Friday could hear the portside tail rotor clanging. The weapon fire from the stern had obviously damaged the blades. If they had not pulled up when they did the chopper would probably be plunging tail first into the rocky, mist-shrouded valleys below. As it was, Captain Nazir was having trouble keeping the Ka-25 steady and moving forward, much less gaining altitude. A moment later the chopper stopped climbing altogether.

"I'm losing her!" Nazir said. "And we're leaking fuel."

Friday looked at the gauge and swore. They had already off-loaded whatever gear they were carrying in the back. The only thing left was the fixed-winch. There was no extra weight they could push out. There probably was not time to get rid of it in any case.

Friday looked out the window as the chopper began to shudder violently. The rainbow vanished as the sun's angle changed. He no longer felt like a god but like a grade-A sucker. Of all the damn tricks to fall for. A freaking sleight of hand, a sucker punch. The operative studies the unthreatening team while a backup unit, either hidden or on another side, tears you a new exit.

"You're going to have to set us down anywhere you can!" Friday said urgently.

"I'm looking for a spot," Nazir said. "I don't see one."

A sudden fist of wind turned them nearly forty-five degrees so they were facing the cliff. A second burst of gunfire, this time from the group in front, tore at the undercarriage. The chopper lurched and dropped. They were at the top of a valley. Friday could not see what was below them because of a thick mist. But he did not want to go down there. He did not want to lose the cell and he did not want to be here when the nukes went off.

"I've got to go down while we still have power for a controlled landing," Nazir said.

"Not yet," Friday said. He unbuckled his seatbelt. "Apu, back up."

"What are you going to do?" Nazir asked.

191

"I'm going to crawl into the back," Friday said. "Do you have forward and aft mobility?"

"Limited," he said. "One of the tail rotors is still working."

"All right," Friday said. "If you can turn the stern toward the peak, Apu and I might be able to use the winch line to rappel to one of the ledges."

"In this wind?" Nazir exclaimed. "You'll be blown off!"

"The wind is blowing southeast, toward the cliff." Friday said. "That should help us."

"It could also smash you into the rocks—"

"We'll have to risk that!" Friday told Nazir. "I've got to reach the cell and tell them about the soldiers ahead."

"Even if you can get to the ledge, they'll gun you down," Nazir said.

"I'll send the old man out first," Friday said. "Nanda may recognize her grandfather's coat. Or they may see us as potential hostages. In any case, that might get them to hold their fire." Friday pulled out his switchblade and cut out the seatbelt. When the strap was free, Friday detached the radio and handed it to Apu. "With luck I'll be able to raise Striker. I'll tell them where we are and approximately where you set down. Striker will help us get to Pakistan and the Himalayan patrol can come and get you. You can tell them you were running independent recon but didn't find the cell."

Nazir did not look convinced. But there was no time to debate the plan and he did as Ron Friday asked. With his feet braced against the floor, his hands tight around the controls, Nazir carefully turned the chopper around and began edging it toward the cliff. As he did, Friday disconnected the communications jack but kept his helmet on. Then he swung through the hatchway between the seats.

"What is happening?" Apu asked. His flesh was paler than usual. Unlike the heated cockpit the cargo bay was damn cold.

"We're bailing," Friday said as he used the seatbelt to create a bandolierlike harness for Apu.

"I don't understand," Apu said.

"Just hang on," Friday said as he fastened the belt in front and then led the farmer to the winch. It was difficult to stand

192

in the bumping cargo bay so they crawled to the rear of the hold. The line was quarter-inch-diameter nylon wound around an aluminum spool. They remained on their knees as Friday unfastened the hook end from the eyelet on the floor.

"You're going to go out first," Friday said as he ran the line through the harness he had created.

"Go out?" Apu said.

"Yes. To your granddaughter," Friday told him. The American tugged on the line. It seemed secure. Then he motioned Apu back until the farmer was crouching on the hatch. "It's going to be a rough ride," Friday warned him. "Just grab the line, huddle down, and hold on until they get you."

"Wait!" Apu said. "How do you know that they will?"

"I don't, but I'll pray for you!" Friday said as he reached for the long lever that controlled the floor hatch. He pulled it. There was a jolt as the hatch began to open. Quickly, he grabbed the remote control that operated the winch. The line began unspooling as frigid air slipped over the doorway and slammed into the hold. "Tell them I'm coming next!" Friday shouted as Apu slid back.

Apu grabbed the line as Friday had said, hugging it to him as he slipped from the hold. With his free hand, Friday held the line himself and edged toward the open hatch. The wind was like a block of ice, solid and biting. He turned his helmet partway into the gale and watched through squinting eyes. As he expected, the wind lofted Apu up and out. It was a surreal vision, a man being hoisted like a kite. The chopper was about twenty-five feet from the cliff. It was listing to the starboard, where the rear rotor was out, and being buffeted up and down by the wind. But Nazir was able to hold it in place as Apu was swept toward the ledge. As Friday had hoped, the forward group went to retrieve him as the rear guard kept their weapons on the helicopter. The closer he got to the cliff, the more Apu was banged around by the wind as crosscurrents whipped down and across the rock face. But one of the cell members was able to grab him, while another cell member held on to his comrade. When everyone was safe, the cell member removed the winch line. Friday reeled it back in. He watched as the farmer spoke

193

with the others. One of the cell members raised and crossed his arms to the group in the rear. They did not fire at the chopper.

When the line came back in, Friday quickly ran it through the handle of the radio then strung it under his armpits and around his waist. He kept the radio against his belly and lay on his back. He wanted to go out feet first to protect the radio. He crab-walked down the open hatch, then pressed the button to send the winch line back out. He grabbed the line, straightened his legs, and began to slide down. The brutally cold air tore along his pants legs. It felt as if his skin were being peeled back. And then, a moment later, he was suddenly on a rocket sled. Because he was not onboard to control it, the line was going out faster than before and the wind was pushing even faster. The cliff came up so fast that he barely had time to meet it with his feet. Friday hit hard with his soles. He felt the smack all the way to the top of his skull. He bounced back then felt a sickening yank, then a drop, as the chopper lurched behind him.

"Shit!" he cried. He felt as if he had been slammed in the chest with a log. The line grew steel-taut as the chopper began to drop.

Hands reached for him from the ledge. The wind kept him buoyed. Someone held the radio while someone else tried to undo the line.

Suddenly, someone in front of him raised an AK-47 and fired a burst above his head. The nylon line snapped and the wind bumped Friday forward. More hands grabbed his jacket and pulled him onto the ledge. Because the wind was still battering him he did not feel as if he were on solid ground. He lay there for a moment as he sucked air into his wounded lungs. He was facing the valley and he watched as the helicopter descended in a slow, lazy spiral.

Then, a moment later, it stopped spiraling. The chopper fell tail first, straight and purposeful, like a metal shuttlecock. It picked up speed as it descended, finally vanishing into the low-lying clouds.

A moment later he heard a bang that echoed hollow through the valley. It was accompanied by a burst of orange-red that seemed to spread through the clouds like dye.

However, Ron Friday did not have time to contemplate the death of Captain Nazir. The hands that had saved him hoisted him up and put him against the wall of the cliff.

A woman put a gun under his chin and forced him to look at her. Her face was frostbitten and her eyes manic. Ice clung to the hair that showed beneath her hood.

"Who are you?" she demanded, screaming to be heard over the wind.

"I'm Ron Friday with American intelligence," he shouted back. "Are you the FKM leader?"

"I am!" she replied.

"Good," he said. "You're the one I'm looking for. You and Nanda. Is she with you?"

"Why?" she shouted.

Friday replied, "Because she may be the only one who can stop the nuclear destruction of your country."

THIRTY-TWO

Washington, D.C.
Thursday, 6:25 A.M.

"What the hell just happened?" Bob Herbert asked Viens.

Op-Center's intelligence chief was sitting at his desk in his darkened office. He had been watching the computer monitor with half-shut eyes until the image suddenly woke him up. He immediately hit autodial on his telephone and raised Stephen Viens at the NRO.

"It looks like a chopper went down," Viens said.

"Chopper," Herbert said. It was more a question than a statement.

"You were dozing," Viens said.

"Yes, I had my eyes closed," Herbert said. "What happened?"

"All we saw was the tail end of a chopper approach the cliff and lower a line with two men on it," Viens told him. "It looks like the cell took the men in and the chopper went down. We did not have a wide enough viewing area to be certain of that."

"Friday had a copter," Herbert said. "Could it have been him?"

"We don't know who was on the end of the line," Viens replied. "One of them looked like he might have been carrying a radio. It was an electronic box of some kind. It did not look like U.S. intelligence issue."

"I'll call you back," Herbert said.

"Bob?" Viens said. "If that was an Indian air force chopper they're going to know where it went down. Even if it wasn't, the explosion is going to register on their satellite monitors or seismic equipment."

"I know," Herbert said. The intelligence head put Stephen Viens on hold and called Hank Lewis's office. The NSA officer was not in yet. Herbert tried Lewis's cell phone but the voice mail picked up. He was either on that line or out of range. Herbert swore. He finally tried Lewis at home. He caught Lewis in the middle of shaving.

Herbert told the NSA chief what had happened and asked if he knew for certain whether Ron Friday was in Jaudar.

"I assume so," Lewis said. "I haven't spoken with him since our conference call."

"Do you have any way of reaching him?" Herbert asked.

"Only if he's in the helicopter," Lewis said.

"What about his cell phone?" Herbert pressed.

"We haven't tried that," Lewis said. "But on the move, in the mountains, it may be difficult."

"True," Herbert agreed. "And the radio?"

"We used a NATO frequency to contact him, but I don't have that info at home," Lewis said.

"Well, we can backtrack and raise him," Herbert said. "Thanks. I'll let you know when we have him."

Herbert ended the call and glanced at the computer clock. It was six thirty. Kevin Custer, Op-Center's director of electronic communications, would be in his office by now. Herbert called over.

Custer was a thirty-two-year-old MIT graduate and a distant relative of General George Armstrong Custer through the general's brother Nevin. Military service was expected in the Custer family and Kevin had spent two years in the army before taking a job at the CIA. He had been there three years when he was snatched up by Bob Herbert. Custer was the most chronically optimistic, upbeat, can-do person Herbert had ever met.

Custer told Herbert that he would get the information for him if he would hold the line. It wasn't even, "I'll get it and call you back." It was, "Don't go away. I'll have it in a second." And he did.

"Let's see," Custer said. "NSA log has the call coming through with input 101.763, PL 123.0 Hz, 855 inversion scrambling. I can contact the source of the call if you like."

"Put it through," Herbert said.

A moment later Herbert heard a beep.

"I'll get off now," Custer said. "Let me know if there's anything else."

"Actually, there is," Herbert said. "Would you ring Paul Hood and patch this call through?"

Custer said he would. The radio beeped again. Then a third time. Then a fourth.

"Bob, what is it?" Hood asked when he got on. He sounded groggy. He had probably been napping too.

"Viens and I just watched the Pakistani cell haul two people in from what looked like a downed chopper," Herbert said. The radio beeped a fifth time. "We're trying to ascertain if one of them was Ron Friday."

"I thought he was going to Jaudar," Hood said.

"Exactly," Herbert replied.

The radio beeped two more times before someone answered. It definitely was not Ron Friday.

"Yes?" said a woman's voice.

"This is 855 base," Herbert said, using the coded identification number. "Who is this?"

"Someone who has your radio and its operator," the woman replied. "I just saved him from death. But the reprieve may only be temporary."

The woman's accent definitely belonged to that region. Herbert would be able to place it better were it not for the screaming wind behind her. The woman was also smart. She had said only that she saved Friday's life. There was no reference to the rest of the cell or the other man they were holding. She had given Herbert as little information as possible.

Herbert hit the mute button. "Paul—I say we talk to her," he said quickly, urgently. "We need to let her know that Striker is on the way."

"This channel isn't secure, is it?" Hood asked.

"No," Herbert admitted.

"Friday will probably tell her that."

"He got there in an Indian chopper. They may not believe him," Herbert said. "Let me give her the overview."

"Be careful, Bob," Hood warned. "I don't want you telling her who we are, exactly."

Herbert killed the mute. "Listen to me," he said. "We are with American intelligence. The man you have works with us."

"He told me that his last name is Friday," the woman said. "What is his first name?"

"Ron," Herbert replied.

"All right," the woman said. "What do you want with us?"

"We want to get you home alive," Herbert said. He weighed his next words with care in case anyone was listening. "We know what happened in Srinagar. We know what your group did and did not do."

He did not have to say more. She would know the rest. There was a short silence.

"Why do you want to help us?" the woman finally asked.

"Because we believe there will be extreme retaliation," Herbert informed her. "Not against you but against your nation."

"Does your person Friday know about this?" she asked.

"He knows about that and more," Herbert informed the woman. "And he is not alone."

"Yes," the woman said. "We rescued an old farmer—"

"That is not what I mean," Herbert said.

There was another brief silence. Herbert could imagine the woman scanning the skies for other choppers.

"I see," said the woman. "I will talk to him. American intelligence, I do not know if I can take this radio with me," the woman went on. "If there is anything else I need to know, tell me now."

Herbert thought for a moment. "There is one more thing," he informed her. He spoke clearly and strongly so she would not miss a word. "We are helping you because inaction would result in unprecedented human disaster. I have no respect for terrorists."

"American intelligence," she said, using that as if it were Herbert's name. "I have lost nothing. If the world respected us before now, there would be no need for terrorism."

With that, the line went dead.

199

THIRTY-THREE

Mt. Kanzalwan
Thursday, 4:16 P.M.

Sharab could barely feel her fingers as she put the receiver back inside the radio. Despite the heavy gloves and the constant movement, the cold was beyond anything she had ever experienced. Her hands were numb when they were still, like dead weight. They burned when she moved them and blood was forced to circulate. It was the same with her feet. Her eyes were wind-blasted dry. Each blink of her icy lashes was agony.

But the worst pain was still the one inside. It had been strongest in those moments when the powerful winds slowed and the overhanging rock receded and the sun burned through the murderous cold. When survival was not a moment-to-moment concern and she had time to think.

Sharab had let herself be outsmarted by Indian security forces. She had let her nation, her people, and her fellow patriots down. That failure had cost brave Ishaq his life. And it had brought her and her small loyal militia to this precipice, to this flight. Her failure had made it unlikely that they would escape these mountains and tell the world the truth, that India and not Pakistan had been responsible for attacking the Hindu sites.

And yet, as it said in the Koran, "the wrongdoers shall never prosper." Perhaps Allah forgave her. It seemed as though He was looking out for her when this man dropped from the sky. Sharab did not like or trust Americans. They made war on Muslims around the world and they had traditionally curried favor with New Delhi instead of Islamabad. But she would not question the will of God. It would be ironic if this man were to provide them with salvation.

Ron Friday was still lying on his stomach. To the right, Nanda was huddled with her grandfather. Sharab would deal with them in a moment. She told Samouel to help pick the American up. Together, they pushed him back under the ledge, against the wall. It was even colder here because the sun was not on them. But there was less chance of them slipping off the ledge. Until Sharab heard what this man had to say, she did not want him falling to his death.

The man groaned as she pinned her forearm against his shoulder to help him stand.

"All right," Sharab said to him. "Tell me what you know."

"What I know?" Friday said. Puffy white breath and gasps of pain emerged from his mouth with each syllable. "To start with, you shot down our ticket out of here."

"You should not have come unannounced in an Indian helicopter," Sharab replied. "That was stupid."

"Unavoidable," Friday protested loudly.

The exclamation was followed by a painful wince. Sharab had to lean into the man to keep him from doubling over. She wondered if he had broken some ribs in the hard landing. But that was all right. Pain could be useful. It would keep him alert and moving.

"Never mind now," Friday said. "The main thing is that the Indian SFF set you up. They set Nanda up. She helped them blow up the temple and the bus. According to our intelligence, the SFF thought that would help solidify the Indian people behind the military. Nanda probably did not know that the Indian military intends to respond to the attack with a nuclear strike."

"For destroying the temple?" Sharab said. She was stunned.

"Yes," Friday said. "We believe certain militants will tell the populace that it's the first shot of an Islamic jihad against the Hindu people. Moderate government ministers and military officials may have no choice but to go along."

"You said you have intelligence," Sharab said. "What intelligence? American?"

"American and Indian," Friday said. "The pilot who brought me here was a Black Cat Commando. He had special information about SFF activities. Our people in Washington arrived at the same conclusion independently. That's why they're diverting the American strike force from their original mission."

"Which was?"

"To help the Indian military scout for possible Pakistani nuclear emplacements," Friday replied.

"They came to help India and now I'm supposed to trust them?" Sharab declared.

"You may not have a choice," Friday said. "There's something else. While we were searching for you we saw a force of Indian soldiers headed this way. They're moving in a wide sweep down from the line of control. You'll never get through them."

"I expected that after we killed their commandos in the mountains," Sharab said. "How many are there?"

"I could only see about one hundred soldiers," Friday told her. "There may be more."

"How many American soldiers are there and how will they find us?" Sharab asked.

"There are about a dozen elite soldiers and they've been watching you by satellite," Friday said.

"They can see us now?" Sharab asked.

Friday nodded.

"Then why did you have to search for us?" the woman pressed.

"Because they didn't want to tell me where you were," Friday said. "I'm with a different agency. There's mistrust, rivalry."

"Stupidity," she snarled. She shook her head. "Less than twenty soldiers against one hundred. When will the Americans be here?"

"Very soon," Friday said.

"How are they arriving?"

"By Indian transport, Himalayan Eagles squadron," Friday replied.

Sharab thought for a moment. Militarily, the American unit would not be much assistance. However, there might be another way that she could use them. "Can you contact the American unit?" she asked Friday.

"Through Washington, yes," he replied.

"Good. Samouel?"

"Yes, Sharab?" said the big man.

"I want you to wait here with Nanda," Sharab said. "I will lead the others down to the valley. A half hour after we leave you continue along the route we planned."

"Yes, Sharab," he replied.

Sharab turned to go over to where Nanda and Apu were speaking.

"Wait!" Friday said. "We're already outnumbered. Why do you want to split up?"

"If we contact the Americans by radio we can make sure the Indian ground troops also pick up the message," Sharab said. "That will draw them to us."

"What makes you think they'll be taking prisoners?" Friday asked.

"It does not matter, as long as we hold them there as long as we can," Sharab said. "It will leave the path clear for Samouel's group to get through. You said yourself that Nanda is the key to stopping the nuclear attack. She must reach Pakistan. Her people will listen to her confession, her testimony."

"How do you know she won't betray you?" Friday asked.

"Because I know something you don't," Sharab said. "The missiles your team is looking for? They are already in place. Dozens of them. They are in the mountains, pointed at New Delhi, Calcutta, Bombay. A strike against Pakistan will turn the entire subcontinent into a wasteland."

"Let me tell my superiors," Friday said. "They will warn the Indians not to strike—"

"Warn them how?" Sharab asked. "I have no proof! I don't know where the missiles are and my government won't reveal that information. I only know that missiles have been deployed. We staged attacks to distract the Indian military when elements were being moved into place." The woman took a breath, calmed herself. If she grew angry and began to perspire the sweat would freeze. "Unless Nanda wishes to

203

see her nation ravaged, she will have to cooperate with us. But that means getting her to Pakistan without the Indians killing her!"

"All right," Friday agreed. "But I'm going with her. She'll need protection. She'll also need international credibility. I was a witness to the blasts. I can make certain that officials from our embassy support her claims."

"How do I know you won't kill her?" Sharab cried. The winds had picked up and she had to shout to be heard over them. "You arrived in an Indian helicopter. How do I know you didn't want to take us back to Kargil? I only have your promises and a radio communication that could have come from anyone! These do not make you an ally!"

"I could have shot at you from the helicopter!" Friday yelled. "That makes me not your enemy."

Sharab had to admit that the American had a point. Still, she was not ready to believe him entirely. Not yet.

"You're wasting what little time we have," the man went on. "Unless you plan on killing me, I'm going with Nanda."

Sharab continued to hold Friday against the wall. His hot breath warmed her nose as she looked at him. His eyes were tearing from the cold but that was the only life in them. Sharab could not find anything else there. Not truth, not conviction, not selflessness. But she also did not see fear or hostility. And at the moment, that would have to be good enough.

"Samouel will run the operation," Sharab told Friday.

Friday nodded vigorously. Sharab released him. Samouel held Friday up until he was sure the American had his feet under him.

"Wait here," Sharab said, then turned.

With her back to the cliff wall Sharab edged toward Nanda. The Indian woman was crouched in a small fissure with her grandfather. She rose when Sharab arrived. She was wearing a heavy scarf across her face. Only her eyes were visible.

Sharab told Nanda that she would be traveling in one group, with Samouel, the American, and her grandfather.

"Why are you doing that?" Nanda asked.

When Sharab finished telling her everything Friday had said, she saw doubt and concern in Nanda's eyes. Perhaps the Indian woman did not know what the SFF and members of the military had been doing.

Unfortunately, Nanda's reaction told Sharab what she needed to know.

That the American's story could be true.

Nuclear war could indeed be just hours away.

THIRTY-FOUR

Washington, D.C.
Thursday, 6:51 A.M.

Paul Hood was not surprised that Bob Herbert had been blunt with the woman on the radio. Herbert's wife had been killed by Islamic terrorists. Working with the Pakistani cell had to be ripping him apart.

But what Herbert had told the woman, that he opposed her and her profession, was also a smart and responsible alliance tactic. Strangers tend to be suspicious of indulgence and flattery. But tell someone that you don't like them and are only working with them out of necessity and they tend to trust whatever information you give them.

"You okay, Bob?" Hood asked.

"Sure," he replied. "She got in a good one, though."

"So did you."

"She never felt it," Herbert said. "Zealots have skin like a tank. But it's all right," he went on. "I'm a big boy. I know how this works."

"Sometimes it just strikes a little close to the heart," Hood said.

"Yes, it does," Herbert agreed.

Hood had been through situations like this before with Herbert. The intelligence chief just had to work through it.

"We'll talk more about this later, Bob," Hood said. "Right now, I've got to brief the president. He'll need to know what we're planning."

The intelligence chief was silent for a moment. "I guess that's also bothering me, though. Whether we should really be doing this."

"What?" Hood asked. "Letting Striker go in?"

"Yeah."

"Give me an option," Hood said.

"Dump the problem in the president's lap," Herbert said. "Let him slug it out with the Indian government."

"He won't do that without proof," Hood said. "I'll tell him what our concerns are and what we're going to do about it. I know what he's going to say. He will okay having Striker on the ground for on-site intel, especially since the Indian government has authorized their being there. He's going to give us his blessings to go that far. The rest will be Mike's call."

Herbert was silent.

"But you're still uneasy," Hood said.

"Yeah," Herbert told him. "Let's just go over our command tent options again."

"All right," Hood said patiently.

"We've decided that the Indian government is probably out of the loop on this nuclear option," Herbert said. "So unless we get that Kargil woman, Nanda, in front of a TV camera to explain this was an inside job we have no proof to offer the president or the Indian people."

"That's it," Hood said. "We've also got Indian troops moving in to cut Nanda and the Pakistanis down."

"We assume," Herbert said.

"We have to assume it's search and destroy," Hood pointed out. "The SFF gains nothing by capturing the Pakistanis and letting the truth come out. We need to give the cell a chance to get home."

"God help us," Herbert said.

"Bob, there's a bigger picture than aiding terrorists," Hood said. "You know that."

"I know," Herbert said. "I just don't like it."

"The time it would take us to move this through diplomatic channels could cost the Pakistanis their lives," Hood said.

"And going ahead with this operation can cost Striker their lives," Herbert said.

"That's been true every time they've gone into the field," Hood reminded Herbert. "If Mike or Colonel August has any doubts about this action they can call it off at any time."

"They won't," Herbert assured him. "Not with what's at stake."

"That's probably true," Hood agreed.

"And not with the balls Mike's got," Herbert went on.

"It's more than that," Hood said. "He knows his people. Did he ever run that quote past you, the one from the duke of Wellington?"

"I don't think so," Herbert said.

"I was watching Striker drill one morning and I asked Mike how he could tell when he had pushed his people as far as they could go," Hood said. "He told me that Wellington had a simple way to determine when he had created the best fighting unit possible. 'I don't know what effect these men will have upon the enemy,' Wellington wrote, 'but, by God, they terrify me.' Mike said that when he felt his people were tough enough to scare him, that was when he stopped."

"Paul, I don't need to be reminded that Striker is the best," Herbert said. "But I'm worried about the jump into the Himalayas. I'm worried about the odds and having to trust terrorists. I'm worried about having no backup for them and, worse than that, no exit strategy."

"I'm worried about all that too," Hood replied. "I'm also aware that we have no other options."

The intelligence chief was quiet for a moment. The silence was uncomfortable. Hood felt as if Herbert were judging him.

Herbert must have felt that too. "I know we're doing what we have to do," he said. "It doesn't mean I have to like it." Herbert's voice was no longer angry or searching. It was resigned.

Herbert said that he would call the NRO to get the exact location of the cell and then give Striker a final update before H-hour. Hood thanked him and hung up.

Op-Center's director rubbed his eyes. Herbert had his personal demons but so did Hood.

Unlike the intelligence chief, Hood had never put his life on the line. He had been a mayor and a financial officer before taking this job. He had sent Striker into danger before but never into an armed conflict. To do that seemed cavalier, hypocritical, cowardly.

But, as Hood had told Herbert, it was also necessary. Paul Hood's personal issues could not affect his professional decisions. He had to be dispassionate. He owed the president and the nation that much.

Hood stopped rubbing his eyes. He was tired inside and out. It did not help that when this was over he had to deal with the closing of the press office. Fortunately, he would be able to minimize his contact with Ann Farris until then. Because this was a military action Hood would instruct her to institute a total press blackout on any Op-Center activities until noon. She would have to shut down the phones and computers. No press department staff would be permitted to answer their cell phones. Queries to the automated main number would go unreturned. As for Hood, he would go into the Tank with Bob Herbert, Liz Gordon, and Lowell Coffey until the crisis had passed.

Then Hood would give Ann Farris the bad news along with his complete attention.

He owed her that much.

THIRTY-FIVE

The Great Himalaya Range
Thursday, 4:19 P.M.

The parachutes were zero-porosity mixed-fabric PF 3000s "Merits." They had been selected for the Indian military in this region because they gave jumpers maximum control over their descent. If there were a sudden current in any direction the fabric would retain its shape and buoyancy. The canopies themselves were slightly elliptical with a tapered wing. That shape provided for the softest landings. First used militarily by the French air force, the Merits also provided the safest jump for novice parachutists.

The parachutes were stowed in slender Atom Millennium containers. They had classic plastic handle ripcords and narrow chest straps along with lightweight Cordura fabric exteriors. The thin straps and light weight would be relatively unrestrictive if Striker were forced to engage the enemy or the elements before doffing the backpacks. There was also an instant-collapse system operated by a rubber pull-string. That would allow the chute to be deflated immediately upon landing in the event of strong ground winds.

Rodgers and his team had unpacked and repacked the parachutes. They examined the fabric as well as the shroud lines and ring attachments. With elements of the Indian military apparently working at cross-purposes, Rodgers wanted to make certain the equipment had not been sabotaged.

Suited in the white Nomex winter gear they had brought with them, the Strikers were huddled next to the hatch before lining up. The team members were crouched to keep their balance in the bumping aircraft. In addition to their parachutes, each commando wore a hip holster with a Browning 9mm high-power Mark 2 pistol, a Kevlar bullet-proof vest, leather gloves, and climbing boots. The vests had side pockets for flashlights, flares, hand grenades, additional pistol magazines, and maps. Before jumping into the subzero environment the commandos would don the Leyland and Birmingham respirator masks they carried. These full-face masks included large, shatterproof, tinted eyepieces for wide visibility. Medic William Musicant had the added burden of a medical belt. This remarkably compact unit, devised by the Navy SEALs for use in Desert Storm, allowed him to treat a wide range of both fall- and combat-related injuries.

Rodgers reviewed photographs of the terrain with Striker. Viens had transmitted these images from the NRO computer directly to the Striker laptop. Rodgers had printed out two copies to pass around. The general had also printed out a second set of photographs that had just come in.

The team was going into what was referred to as a "high-contrast" terrain. That meant the landing would be problematic. The target area was a large, flat ledge approximately seventy meters by ninety meters. It was the only relatively large horizontal site in the region. The drawbacks were several large outcroppings of rock as well as steep drops on the northern and western sides. Sheer cliffs bounded the area on the south and east. Colonel August was also concerned about the winds. He pointed to the color photograph.

"Depending upon the strength of the winds in the area, this concave southeastern wall could create powerful outdraft," he said. "That could keep us from landing in the target zone."

"Unfortunately, the cell is moving along very narrow ledges," Rodgers said. "That's the only area where we can intercept them."

"Why do we have to catch them in the mountains?" Ishi Honda asked. In addition to his parachute the young corporal was carrying the TAC-SAT in a pouch on his chest.

Rodgers showed them the second photograph Viens had sent. It showed a line of dark shapes moving across a dreary terrain of wheat-colored scrub and patches of snow.

"These are Indian soldiers moving toward the target area," Rodgers said. "The NRO and Bob Herbert both put them at less than five miles from contact. There are up to two hundred of them, though we can't be sure. They obtained these pictures by hacking a Chinese satellite that watches the line of control. We can't pull back for a wider view."

"Which means that if we can't smuggle the cell through we will have to repel a much larger force," August told the group.

"For various reasons negotiation is not an option," Rodgers added. "We have to get past them one way or the other."

The general looked at the faces of his troops. With the exception of the medic, all of these soldiers had been in battle. Most of them had killed. They had shed the blood of others, usually at a distance. They had seen the blood of their teammates, which typically fanned their rage and made the blood of the enemy invisible. They had also faced superior odds. Rodgers was confident that they would give this effort everything they had.

Rodgers listened as Colonel August talked about the strategy they would employ upon landing. Typically, they would go behind enemy lines carrying mines. Two or three operatives would form a subgroup. They would go ahead and plant the mines along the team's route to protect them from enemies. They would also throw out substances such as powdered onion or raw meat to confuse and mislead attack dogs. They did not see dogs in the photographs and hoped that the animals were not part of the army units.

Since there were apparently four members of the cell, plus Friday and the two Indians, August had decided to go forward in an ABBA formation. There would be a Striker in front and behind each group of two Pakistanis. That would enable Striker to control the rate of progress and to watch the personnel they were escorting. Neither Herbert nor Rodgers expected any resistance from the cell, From everything they had been told, both groups wanted the same thing. To reach Pakistan alive. As for the Indian force, the American team was prepared to move at nightfall, wage a guerrilla campaign, or simply dig in, wait them out, and execute an end run when possible. They would do whatever it took to survive.

Striker had drilled for this maneuver high in the Rockies. They called it their red, white, and blue exercise. During the course of two hours their fingers had gone from red to white to blue. At least they knew what they would be facing. Once they reached the ground they would know how to pace themselves. The only uncertainty was what might happen on the way down. That was still what concerned Rodgers the most. They were approximately ten thousand feet up. That was not as long as most high-altitude, low-opening jumps. Those operations typically began at thirty-two-thousand feet. The HALO teams would go out with oxygen-heavy breathing apparatus to keep from suffering hypoxemia. They would also use barometric triggers to activate their chutes at an altitude of roughly two thousand feet above the target. They did that in case the jumper suffered one of two possible ailments. The first was barometric trauma, the result of air being trapped in the intestines, ears, and sinuses and causing them to expand painfully. The other was stress-induced hyperventilation, common in combat situations. Especially when jumpers could be aloft for as long as seventy or eighty minutes. That gave them a lot of alone-time to think, particularly about missing the target. At an average drift rate of ten feet for every hundred feet of fall, that was a concern for every jumper. Breathing bottled oxygen at a rapid pace due to stress could cause a lowering of blood carbon dioxide and result in unconsciousness.

Though neither of those would be a problem at this lower height, it was two thousand feet higher than they had practiced in the Rocky Mountains. And even there, then-Striker Bass Moore had broken his left leg.

Lean Sergeant Chick Grey was chewing gum, unflustered as always. There was a bit more iron determination and aggression in the eyes of waspish privates David George, Jason Scott, and Terrence Newmeyer. Corporal Pat Prementine and Private Matt Bud were popping gloved knuckles and shifting in place, as full of rough-and-tumble energy as always. And the excitable Private Walter Pupshaw looked as if he wanted to tear off someone's head and spit down the windpipe. That was normal for Striker's resident wild man. The other team members were calm with the exception of Sondra DeVonne and the green medic, William Musicant. Both Strikers seemed a little anxious. Musicant had limited combat experience and Sondra still blamed herself for events that led to the death of Lt. Colonel Charlie Squires. She had spent many months being counseled by Liz Gordon. But she had gone on other assignments with the team since then. While the young African-American woman was not as relaxed or go-get-'em as the others, Rodgers was certain he could count on her. She would not be here otherwise.

When they were ready, Rodgers picked up the phone beside the hatch. The copilot informed him that the plane would reach the target in less than five minutes. August lined up his team and stood at their head. After everyone had jumped, Rodgers would follow.

Since the aircraft was not typically used for jumping, there was no chute line or lights to indicate that they had reached the drop zone. August and Pupshaw opened the hatch while Rodgers remained on the phone with the cockpit. The air that surged in was like nothing the general had ever felt. It was a fist of ice, punching them back and then holding them there. Rodgers was glad they had the masks and breathing apparatus. Otherwise they would not be able to draw a breath from the unyielding wall of wind. As it was, August and Pupshaw were knocked away from the opening. The colonel and the burly private had to be helped back into position by the next Strikers in line.

Rodgers moved sternward along the fuselage, away from the hatch. The howl of the wind was deafening, bordering on painful. It would be impossible to hear the command to jump. The general went back three meters, as far as the phone cord would reach. He used his free hand to cover the left ear of his hood. He pressed down hard. That was the only way he could hear the copilot. Meanwhile, August motioned for each Striker to determine individual jump times by using the "blackout" system. That was the method employed for secret nighttime jumps. It meant putting the right hand on the shoulder of the jumper in front of them. When

214

the shoulder moved out from under someone's hand it was time for that person to go.

The wind pressed the Strikers' white uniforms toward the front of the plane. The soldiers looked like action figures to Rodgers. Every crease and fold seemed molded in place like plastic. The soldiers were leaning forward slightly to let the wind slide around them, though not so much as to allow it to batter the person behind them.

Seconds moved at a glacial pace. Then the word came that they were less than a half mile from their target. Then a quarter mile. Then an eighth of a mile.

Rodgers looked at the Strikers one more time. If they knew how difficult this jump was going to be they were not showing it. The team was still outwardly game and disciplined. He was beyond proud of the unit. Rodgers did not believe in prayer, though he hoped that even if some of the Strikers missed the target they would all survive.

August glanced at Rodgers and gave him a thumbs-up. Obviously the colonel could see the small plateau. That was good. It meant there was no snowfall in the drop zone. They would not be jumping directly over it but to the northwest. The copilot had calculated that the wind was blowing to the southeast at an average of sixty-three miles an hour. They would have to compensate so the wind would carry them toward rather than away from the target.

They passed over the plateau. August held up both thumbs. He had spotted the cell. Rodgers nodded.

A moment later Rodgers got the word from the cockpit. "Go!"

Rodgers motioned to August. As the team started moving through the hatch Rodgers shifted to the back of the line. The copilot emerged from the cockpit. He literally had to hug the port-side wall to get past the hatch before cutting to the starboard side to shut it.

Rodgers hoped he made it. The last thing the general saw before jumping was the small-built Indian flyboy tying a cargo strap to his waist before even attempting to crawl toward the sliding door.

Rodgers held his legs together and pressed his arms straight along his sides as he hit the icy mountain air. That gave him a knife-edged dive to get him away from the plane so he would not be sucked into the engine. He immediately reconfigured himself into an aerofoil position. He arched his body to allow the air to flow along his underside. At the same time he thrust his arms back and dipped his head to increase his rate of descent.

The general was now looking almost straight down. Almost at once he knew he was in trouble.

They all were.

THIRTY-SIX

The Great Himalaya Range
Thursday, 4:42 P.M.

At 4:31, Major Dev Puri's spotter, Corporal Sivagi Saigal, saw something that concerned him. He reported it to Major Puri. The officer was deeply troubled by what he heard.

Prior to leaving, he had been assured by the office of Minister of Defense John Kabir that reconnaissance flights in the region had been suspended. Neither Kabir nor Puri wanted independent witnesses or photographic evidence of what they expected to transpire in the mountains: the capture and execution of the Pakistani terrorists and their prisoner from Kargil.

The flyover of the Himalayan Eagle AN-12 transport was not only unexpected, it was unprecedented. The transport was over a dozen miles from the secure flight lanes protected by Indian artillery. As the spotter continued to watch the plane, Puri used the secure field phone to radio Minister Kabir's office. The major asked the minister's first deputy what the aircraft was doing there. Neither Kabir nor any of his aides had any idea. The minister himself got on the line. He suspected that the flyover was an independent air force action designed to locate and then help capture the Pakistani cell. He could not, however, explain why that mission would be undertaken by a transport. Kabir told Puri to keep the channel open while he accessed the transport's flight plan.

As he waited, Puri did not believe that the presence of a recon flight would complicate matters. Even if the cell were spotted, his unit would probably reach them first. Puri and his men would explain how the cell resisted capture and had to be neutralized. No one would dispute their story.

Kabir came back on in less than a minute. The minister was not happy. The AN-12 had gone to Ankara and had been scheduled to fly directly to Chushul. Obviously the aircraft had been diverted. The transport's manifest had also been changed to include parachutes in its gear.

A few moments later, Puri understood why.

"Jumpers!" he said into the radio.

"Where?" Kabir demanded.

"They're about one mile distant," the spotter told Puri. "They're using Eagle chutes," he said when the shrouds began to open, "but they are not in uniform."

Puri reported the information to Kabir.

"The Eagles must have spotted the cell," the minister said.

"Very possibly," Major Puri replied. "But they're not wearing Eagle mountain gear."

"They might have picked up an outside team in Ankara," Kabir replied. "We may have been compromised."

"What do we do?" Puri asked.

"Protect the mission," Kabir replied.

"Understood," Puri replied.

The major signed off and told his unit commanders to move their personnel forward. They were all to converge on the site where the parachutists were descending. Puri's orders were direct and simple.

The troops were to fire at will.

THIRTY-SEVEN

The Great Himalaya Range
Thursday, 4:46 P.M.

Ever since they competed on the baseball diamond back in elementary school, Colonel Brett August always knew that he would rise above his longtime friend Mike Rodgers. August just never expected it would happen quite this way and in a place like this.

Striker's delicately ribbed, white-and-red parachutes opened in quick succession. Each commando was jerked upward as the canopies broke their rapid descent. Some of the Strikers were hoisted higher than the others, depending on the air currents they caught. The wind was running like ribbons among them. Separate streams had been sent upward by the many peaks and ledges below. Though Mike Rodgers had been the last man out of the aircraft the general was in the middle of the group when the canopies had fully unfurled. Brett August ended up being the man on top.

Unfortunately, the view from that height was not what Colonel August had expected.

Almost at once, visibility proved to be a challenge. When the parachute tugged Colonel August up, perspiration from his eyebrows was flung onto the tops of his eyepieces. The sweat froze there. That was a high-altitude problem neither he nor General Rodgers had anticipated when they planned the jump. August assumed that frost was hampering the other Strikers as well. But that was not their greatest problem.

Shortly after jumping, Colonel August had seen the line of Indian soldiers converging in their direction. They were clearly visible, black dots moving rapidly on the nearly white background. He was sure that Rodgers and the others could see them too.

The Strikers knew enough to defend the perimeter once they landed. With the stakes as high as they were the Americans would not surrender. What concerned August was what might happen before they landed. Striker was out of range of ordinary gunfire. But the Indian soldiers had probably left the line of control well prepared. They were expecting to fight an enemy that might be positioned hundreds of meters away, on high ledges or remote cliffs. The Indian infantrymen would be armed accordingly.

There was no way for the colonel to communicate with the other members of the team. He hoped that they saw the potential threat and were prepared for action when they landed.

Assuming they did land.

As the seconds passed the descent proved more brutal than August had expected.

Seen from the belly of a relatively warm aircraft, the mountains had been awe-inspiring. Brown, white, and pale blue, the peaks glided slowly by like a caravan of great, lumbering beasts. But seen from beneath a bucking parachute shroud those same mountains rose and swelled like breaching sea giants, frightening in their size and rapid approach. The formations practically doubled in size every few seconds. Then there was the deafening sound. The mountains bellowed at the intruders, roaring with mighty winds that they snatched from the sky and redirected with ease. August did not just hear every blast of air, he felt it. The wind rose from the peaks two thousand feet below and rumbled past him. The gales kicked the shroud up and back, to the north or east, to the south or west, constantly spinning the parachute around. The only way to maintain his bearings was to try and keep his eyes on the target whichever way he was twisted. He hoped the winds would abate at the lower altitudes so that he and the other Strikers could guide their chutes to a landing. Hopefully, the peaks would shield them from the Indian soldiers long enough to touch down and regroup.

The mountains rushed toward them relentlessly. The lower the Strikers went the faster the sharp-edged peaks came toward them. The colors sharpened as the team penetrated the thin haze. The swaying of the chutes seemed to intensify as the details of the peaks became sharper. That was an illusion but the speed with which the crags were approaching was not. Three of the soldiers around him were on-course and had a good chance of reaching the plateau. The others would have to do some careful maneuvering to make it. Two were in danger of missing the mountain altogether and continuing into the valley below. August could not tell which Strikers were in danger since the winds had lifted some of the chutes more than others and thrown them out of jump order. Whoever they were they would have to contact the rest of the team by radio and link up as soon as possible.

As they neared to within one thousand feet of the target, August heard a faint popping sound under the screaming wind. His back was facing the Indian infantry so he could not be certain the sound came from them.

A moment later August was sure.

The air around them filled with black-and-white cloudbursts. They were flak rockets used against low-flying aircraft. The shells were fired from shoulder-mounted launchers like the Blowpipe, the standard one-man portable system of the Indian army. They fired metal pellets in all directions around them. Within a range of twenty-five meters, the fifty-seven shots in each shell hit with the force of .38-caliber bullets.

August had never been so helpless in his life. He watched as the first shell popped among the parachutists. It was followed moments later by another, then by one more. The canopies obscured his view of the Strikers themselves. But he saw how close the bursts came. There was no way his people were not being peppered with the hollow steel shells.

It did not occur to August that the shrapnel could take him down. Or that he could miss the plateau.

He forgot the cold and the wind and even the mission.

All that mattered was the well-being of his team. And there was nothing he could do to ensure their safety right now. August's eyes had darted from canopy to canopy as the rockets burst around them. Five of the lowest shrouds were heavily perforated within seconds. They folded into their own centers and dropped straight down. A moment later the chutes turned up, like inverted umbrellas, as the Strikers below dragged them through free fall.

Two parachutes in the middle of the group were also damaged. They dropped with their cargo onto another two canopies directly below. The shrouds became tangled in the swirling winds. The lines knit and the jumpers spun with increasing speed toward the valley below.

Even if the soldiers themselves had not been hit by shrapnel there was no way for them to survive the fall. August screamed in frustration. His cry merged with the wailing wind and filled the sky above him.

The attack left just himself and three Strikers still aloft. August did not know who they were. He did not know if they had been struck or if they were even alive. At least now they were below the line of the intervening mountains. They were safe from additional ground fire.

There was a fourth burst. It exploded white-and-black above and in front of August. He felt two punches, one in the chest and another in his left arm. He looked down at his chest. There was dull pain but no blood. Perhaps the vest had protected him. Or perhaps the colonel was bleeding underneath the fabric. He did not feel anything after the initial hit and his heart rate seemed the same. Both good signs. In his heart he was too sick over the Strikers he had just lost to care. But he knew he had to care. He had to survive to complete this mission. Not just for his country and the millions of lives in the balance, but for the soldiers and friends whose lives had just been sacrificed.

There were only a few hundred feet to the plateau. He watched as two of the Strikers landed there. The third missed by several meters, despite the efforts of one of the commandos to grab him. August used the guidelines to maneuver toward the cliff wall. He was descending rapidly but he would still rather hit the peak than miss the ledge.

August's left arm began to sting but he kept his attention on the cliff. He had dropped below the mountaintops. The tors were no longer hazards. They were once again towering, stationary peaks that surrounded and protected him from Indian fire. The enemy now was the valley on two sides of the plateau and the outcroppings of rock that could snap his back if he hit one. The updraft from the cliff slowed August, allowing him to guide the parachute down. He decided to stick close to the steep cliff and literally follow it down, thus avoiding the sharp outcroppings toward the center. Every time the wind would brush him toward the valley he would swing himself against the rock wall. The air rushing up the cliff gave him extra buoyancy. August hit the plateau hard and immediately jettisoned the chute. The shroud crumpled and scooted across the ledge, catching on a three-meter-tall boulder and just hanging there.

Before examining himself for injuries, Brett August stripped off his mask and mouthpiece. The air was thin but breathable. August looked across the plateau for the other Strikers. Medic William Musicant and Corporal Ishi Honda were the two who had made it. Both men were near the edge of the plateau. Musicant was on his knees beside the radio operator. The medic had removed the compact medical belt he wore. Honda was not moving.

The colonel got to his feet and made his way over. As he did he felt his chest under his vest. It was dry. The pellet had not gone through the garment. His arm was bleeding but the freezing air had slowed the flow considerably. He ignored the wound for now. Try as he might he could not clear his mind of the other Strikers. Sondra DeVonne. Walter Pupshaw. Mike. The others.

He concentrated on the Strikers who were just a few meters away. And he forced himself to think about what was next. He still had his weapons and he had his assignment. He had to link up with the Pakistani cell.

As August reached the men he did not have to ask how Honda was. The radio operator was panting hard as blood pumped from beneath his vest. The medic was trying to clean two small, raw wounds on Honda's left side. August could not see Honda's dark eyes behind his tinted eyepieces. The frost had evaporated and misted them over.

"Is there anything I can do?" August asked Musicant.

"Yeah," the medic said urgently. "There's a portable intravenous kit in compartment seven and a vial of atropine sulfate in twelve. Get them. Also the plasma in eight. He's got two more holes in his back. I've got to get him plugged and stabilized."

The colonel removed the items. He began setting up the IV. From triage classes he remembered that the atropine sulfate was used to diminish secretions, including blood loss. That would help stabilize the patient if there were internal bleeding.

"Is your arm all right, sir?" Musicant asked.

"Sure," August said. "Who was that you tried to reach at the ledge?"

"General Rodgers," the medic replied.

August perked. "Was the general wounded?"

"He appeared to be okay," Musicant replied. "He was reaching out, trying to get over a few feet more. The goddamn current grabbed his chute. I couldn't get to him."

Then it was possible that Rodgers had survived. August would try and contact him by point-to-point radio.

"After the IV is ready you'd better try and get in touch with those Indian soldiers," Musicant suggested. "If I can stabilize Ishi we'll need to get him to a hospital."

August finished setting up the small IV tripod beside Honda. Then he uncapped the needle. He would use Honda's radio to contact Op-Center and brief them. He would give Herbert their position and ask him to relay a call for medical assistance. But that was all he would do. He and Musicant could not wait here, however. They still had a mission to complete.

When the IV setup was finished August reached for Honda's TAC-SAT. Musicant had already removed the pack and set it aside. The reinforced backpack had taken some hits along one side but the telephone itself appeared to be undamaged. August wondered if Honda had taken pains to protect it, even at the cost of his own life.

Just then, Corporal Honda began to convulse.

"Shit!" Musicant said.

August watched as the radio operator coughed. Flecks of blood spattered his cheek.

"Ishi, hang on," Musicant yelled. "You can do it. Give me another minute, that's all I'm asking."

Honda stopped panting and coughing. His entire body relaxed.

"Take off his vest!" Musicant yelled. Then the medic grabbed for his medical belt and reached into one of the pockets. He withdrew a hypodermic and a vial of epinephrine.

Colonel August began unfastening Honda's vest. As he bent over the stricken soldier he noticed a stream of red seeping out from between the noncom's spread legs. Honda had to have been losing blood at an incredibly fast pace for it to pool that far down.

August watched as the blood crept to below Honda's knees. When the colonel pulled the vest away he found the front underside to be sticky with blood. The pellets from the Indian projectiles had gone up the corporal's torso through his lower back and emerged through his chest. Honda must have been near ground zero of one of the blasts.

Musicant knelt beside Ishi Honda. The medic spread his knees wide so he was steady beside the patient. Then he pulled aside Honda's bloody shirt and injected the stimulant directly into Honda's heart. August held the radio operator's hand. It was cold and still. Blood continued to pool on the ledge. Musicant leaned back on his heels and waited. Honda did not respond. His face was ashen from more than just the cold. The colonel and the medic watched for a moment longer.

"I'm sorry," Musicant said softly to the dead man.

"He was a good soldier and a brave ally," August said.

"Amen," Musicant replied.

August realized how tightly he was holding Honda's hand. He gently released it. August had lost friends in Vietnam. The emotional territory was bitterly familiar. But he had never lost nearly an entire squad before. For August, that loss was all there in the still, young face before him.

Musicant rose and had a look at August's arm. August was surprised how warm the last few minutes had left him. Now that the drama had ended his heart was slowing and blood flow was severely reduced. The cold would set in quickly. They had to move out soon.

While Musicant cleaned and bandaged the wound the colonel turned to the TAC-SAT. He entered his personal access code and the unit came on. Then he entered Bob Herbert's number. As August waited to be connected he removed the radio from his equipment vest.

He placed another call.

One that he prayed would be received.

THIRTY-EIGHT

Washington, D.C.
Thursday, 7:24 A.M.

"Have we heard anything yet?" Paul Hood asked as he swung into Bob Herbert's office.

The intelligence chief was drinking coffee and looking at his computer monitor. "No, and the NRO hasn't seen them yet either," Herbert said. "Still just the Pakistanis."

Hood looked at his watch. "They should be down by now. Has the transport landed yet?"

"No," Herbert replied. "The pilot radioed the tower in Chushul. He said that the cargo had been delivered but nothing more."

"I don't expect they stuck around to verify that our guys touched down," Hood said.

"Probably not," Herbert agreed. "That close to the Pakistani border I'm guessing the plane just turned south and ran."

"Hell, why not," Hood said. "We're only trying to stop their country from being involved in a nuclear war."

"You're stealing my cynicism," Herbert pointed out. "Anyway, they probably don't know what's at stake."

As Herbert was speaking the phone beeped. It was the secure line. He put it on speaker.

"Herbert here."

"Bob, it's August," said the caller. It was difficult to hear him.

"Colonel, you've got a lot of wind there," Herbert said. "You'll have to speak up."

"Bob, we've had a major setback here," August said loudly and slowly. "Indian troops from the LOC peppered us with flak on the way down. Most of our personnel were neutralized. Musicant and I are the only ones on the plateau.

227

Rodgers missed but he may have reached the valley. We don't know if he's hurt. I'm trying to reach him by radio."

"Say again," Herbert asked. "Two safe, one MIA, rest dead."

"That's correct," August told him.

The intelligence chief looked up at Hood, who was still standing in the doorway. Herbert's face looked drawn. He muttered something in a taut, dry whisper. Hood could not make out what Herbert was saying. Perhaps it was not meant to be heard.

But Hood had heard what August said.

"Colonel, are you all right?" Hood asked.

"Mr. Musicant and I are fine, sir," August replied. "I'm sorry we let you down."

"You didn't," Hood assured him. "We knew this wasn't going to be an easy one."

August's words were still working their way into Hood's sleep-deprived brain. He was struggling for some kind of perspective. Those lives could not simply have ended. So many of them had only just begun. Sondra DeVonne, Ishi Honda, Pat Prementine, Walter Pupshaw, Terrence Newmeyer, and the rest. Hood's mind flashed on their faces. Dossier photos gave way to memories of drilling sessions he had watched, memorial services, barbecues, tackle football games. It was not the same as the death of one man. Hood had been able to focus on the specifics of losing Charlie Squires or Bass Moore. He had concentrated on helping their families get through the ordeal. The scope of this tragedy and of the personal loss was both overwhelming and numbing.

"What's your assessment, Colonel?" Hood asked. His voice sounded strong, confident. It had to for August's sake.

"We'd still like to try and intercept the cell," August went on. "Two extra guns may help them punch through somewhere along the line."

"We're behind you on that," Hood said.

"But there are a lot of infantrymen headed our way," August went on. "Can you contact the Pakistanis and let them know what happened?"

"We'll try," Hood said. "The Pakistani leader has Friday's phone. She is not the most cooperative person we've dealt with."

"Does she know we're coming?" August asked.

"Affirmative," Hood told him.

"Has there been any arrangement with her?" August asked.

The colonel was asking who would be calling the shots once they linked up. "The cell commander and I did not have that conversation," Hood told him. "Use your own initiative."

"Thank you," August said. "One more thing, sir. We're looking at darkness and some heavy winds and cold coming in. I hope you have a contingency plan in place."

"We were just working on that," Hood lied. "But we're still counting on you and Corporal Musicant to pull this one through."

"We'll do our best," August assured him.

"I know that. We also need you two to stay safe," Hood said.

August said he would. He also said he would inform Op-Center if he managed to raise Mike Rodgers. Then he signed off. Hood disengaged the speakerphone. There was a long moment of silence.

"You all right?" Hood asked Herbert.

Herbert shook his head slowly. "We had thirteen people out there," he said flatly.

"I know," Hood said.

"Kids, mostly."

"This was my call," Hood reminded the intelligence chief. "I gave the operation the go-ahead."

"I backed you up," Herbert replied. "Hell, we had no choice. But this is a price they should not have had to pay."

Hood agreed but to say so seemed pathetic somehow. They were crisis management professionals. Sometimes the only barrier between control and chaos was a human shield. As iron-willed as that barricade could be, it was still just sinew and bone.

Hood moved behind the desk. He looked down at the computer. Logic aside, he still felt hollow. Hood and the others had known going in that there were risks involved with this mission. What galled him was that an attack from allied ground forces was not supposed to be one of those risks. No one imagined that the Indian military would shoot at personnel jumping from one of their own aircraft, suspended from the parachutes clearly identified as those belonging to the Indian air force. This phase of the operation was only supposed to pit trained professionals against severe elements. There was going to be a chance for most if not all the Strikers to survive. How did it go so wrong?

"Colonel August was right about us needing a backup plan," Herbert said. "We went off the playbook. We've got to get to work and give him—"

"Hold on," Hood said. "Something's not right."

"Excuse me?" Herbert replied.

"Look at this satellite image," Hood said.

Herbert did.

"The terrorist cell is still moving beneath the overhanging ledges, just as they've done since sunup," Hood said. "But they've also got a little elbow room now. They have these shadows to move in." Hood pointed at the jagged areas of blackness on the monitor. "See how the shadows are lengthening as the sun sets behind the Himalayas?"

"I see," Herbert said. "But I don't get your point."

"Look at the direction of the shadows relative to the sun," Hood told him. "The cell is moving in a westerly direction. Not northwesterly. That's different from before."

Herbert stared for a moment. "You're right," he said. "Why the hell would they be doing that?"

"Maybe there's a shortcut?" Hood suggested. "A secret path through the glacier?"

Herbert brought up the detailed photographic overviews from NASA's Defense Mapping Agency. These photographic maps were marked with coordinates and were used to target satellites. Herbert asked the computer to mark the area that Viens was studying now. Hood leaned over Herbert's wheelchair and looked closely at the monitor as a faint red cursor began to pulse on the region the cell was crossing.

"There's no shortcut," Herbert said. "What the hell are they doing? They're actually taking a longer route to the line of control."

"Will August still intercept them?" Hood asked.

"Yes," Herbert said. The intelligence chief pointed to a region slightly north of where the cell was. "Brett came down here. He's heading southeast. He'll just be meeting them a lot sooner than we expected." Herbert studied the map. "But this still doesn't make sense. This route isn't going to take the Pakistanis through more accessible terrain. It's farther from the LOC, it's not at a lower altitude, and it doesn't look easier to negotiate."

"Maybe they've got a weapons cache or another hideout along the way," Hood suggested.

"Possibly," Herbert said. He went back to the live NRO image. "But they were relatively close to the border where they were. Why would they want to give the Indians more time to catch them?"

The interagency phone line beeped. Herbert punched it on speakerphone. "Yes?" Herbert said.

"Bob, it's Viens," said the caller. "It's getting dark in the target area. The light is now down enough for us to switch to heat-scan without being blinded. We'll be able to track the cell easier."

"Go ahead," Herbert said. He hit the mute button on the phone.

Herbert and Hood continued to look at the overhead map. Hood was studying the area at the foot of the plateau.

"Bob, if we move the satellite will we be able to look into this valley?" Hood asked, pointing at a grid marked "77."

"I don't know," Herbert told him. He glanced over at his boss. "Paul, I want to find Mike too. But we only have the one satellite in the region. Do we want to tie it up looking for him?"

"Mike could have lost or damaged his radio in the fall," Hood said. "If he's alive there might be something he can do for Brett. We need every resource we can get over there."

"Even if they're two thousand vertical miles and God knows how many as-the-crow-flies miles away?" Herbert asked.

"We don't know for certain where Mike is," Hood pointed out. "We need to find out."

Before the intelligence chief could consider what Paul Hood had said, Viens came back on the line.

"Bob, are you looking at the new satellite photos?" Viens asked.

Herbert killed the mute function. "No," he replied and immediately jumped back to the feed from the OmniCom. "Is there a problem?"

"Maybe," Viens said. "Even when the cell was under the ledge we always caught a glimpse of a head or arm so we knew we still had them. What do you see now?"

Herbert and Hood both leaned closer to the monitor as the image formed. The picture looked psychedelic, like something from the sixties. Hot, red shadows were spilling out along a field of green-colored rocks and snow.

The shadows of only three people.

"What the hell's going on there?" Herbert asked.

"I don't know," Viens admitted. "Some of the terrorists could have been lost along the way."

"It's also possible they turned on Friday and the Indian officer," Herbert thought aloud. "Maybe there were casualties. We should try and get them on the radio."

"No," Hood said. "Contact August and let him know there are three individuals ahead. Tell him they may be hostile and that he is to use discretion whether to shadow rather than engage. Stephen, can you get me a look at grid 77 on file map OP-1017.63?"

"I'll bring that map up, see if it's in the OmniCom's focal range," Viens replied. "It'll only take a minute."

"Thank you," Hood said.

Herbert shook his head. "What reason would the cell have for attacking Friday?" he asked.

"Maybe it was Friday who turned against the cell," Hood said. Then he straightened. "Wait a minute," he said. "It

232

could be possible that none of the above happened."

"What do you mean?" Herbert asked.

"Ron Friday must have told the cell that the Indian soldiers were coming toward them," Hood said.

"Right," Herbert said.

"The Pakistanis could not know there was a threat until Friday joined them," Hood went on. "They did not know that getting Nanda to Pakistan was the only way they might be able to stop a nuclear exchange. What would you do with that knowledge, especially if you were also told that an American strike force was coming to link up with you?" Hood said. "If you were smart and bold and probably a little desperate you would try something unexpected."

"Like splitting your forces and using one group to draw the Indian soldiers away," Herbert said.

"Right. Which means that the other four people may be somewhere else, probably holding to the original course," Hood said.

"If that's true, it means we don't want August and Musicant linking up with the splinter group, since they're probably going to want to draw fire from the Indians," Herbert said.

"Correct. Bob, let August know what we're thinking," Hood said. He leaned back over the computer and returned to the NASA map. "Stephen, I need to see into that valley."

"I've got your map up now," Viens said. "I'm looking to see if the coordinates are in the OmniCom computer."

Meanwhile, Herbert punched in Striker's TAC-SAT number. "Paul, you can't be thinking what I think you are," Herbert said.

"I'm sure I am," Hood informed him.

"Assuming he's all right, you don't even know if you can talk to him," Herbert said.

"One thing at a time," Hood said.

"I can do it!" Viens shouted. "I'm sending up the order now. No guarantees about cloud cover and visibility, Paul, but I'll have you in the valley in ninety seconds."

"Thank you," Hood said.

"What are we looking for?" Viens asked.

"A parachute," Hood said. "One that may have Mike Rodgers on the end of it."

THIRTY-NINE

The Mangala Valley
Thursday, 5:30 P.M.

During the Strikers' descent, the AN-12 had made a quick turn to the south. A powerful downdraft from the fast-departing transport had driven Mike Rodgers toward the center of the parachutists. As a result, he was protected from the main thrust of the flak attack. But Rodgers had heard the explosions. He had seen the results as his teammates fell around him. By the time the general had guided himself toward the target, only he and one other striker were still aloft. Despite the heroic efforts of one of the strikers on the ledge, Rodgers had failed to reach the plateau. He had struck his shins and then his right hip and torso on the ledge. Fortunately, his equipment vest took the brunt of the chest hit. But Rodgers was dropping too fast and was not able to hold on. He was also unable to see what happened to the last aloft teammate. At least that chute was on the correct side of the plateau. If he or she were able to disengage from the chute it would probably be all right.

As the rock target disappeared from view, Rodgers studied the terrain immediately below. He had not given up trying to join the others and looked for a ledge he could reach. Unfortunately, Rodgers could not stay as close to the mountain as he would have liked. There were so many rough out-croppings that he ran the risk of snagging and ripping the parachute. Reluctantly, he made the decision to ride the chute to the valley.

While Rodgers descended, he looked for signs of other parachutes below. He had seen the Strikers fall and did not think any of them could have survived the plunge. If he were able to land near them he could be certain. Rodgers refused

235

to think about the soldiers who were almost certainly lost. There would be time to grieve later. All that mattered now was the mission and Rodgers had to find a way of getting back into it.

The currents diminished the lower Rodgers dropped. As he descended into the valley the shroud stopped its side-to-side swaying. The officer hung as straight as a plumb line, protected by the mountains from the fierce winds that raced through the outer range. He floated down through the wispy clouds.

Rodgers glanced at his large, luminous watch. He had been aloft for nearly fifty minutes. He was at a low enough altitude to remove his breathing apparatus and goggles. He strapped them to his belt. The water vapor in the clouds condensed on Rodgers's exposed face. It cooled the hot perspiration on his forehead and cheeks, invigorating him. Below him the clouds began to thin. He could see the terrain rushing up.

This was not going to be easy.

Technically, the formation below was a valley. It was an elongated lowland between two mountain ranges. A shallow, fast-running river cut through the center. To Mike Rodgers, however, the small, barren formation was just a rocky depression in the rugged foothills. The sloping, sharp-edged terrain made a soft landing impossible and a safe landing problematic at best. At least the air was calm. He could work the chute to try to avoid the most precarious spots.

As he dropped under the last level of clouds he saw the first of the Striker parachutes. It was bunched like an orchid in the middle of the river. The Striker was apparently below it. A moment later Rodgers saw the other chutes. Two of them were tangled together at the foot of one of the mountains. The Strikers were sprawled beside them. Their cold-weather outfits were smeared with blood. He saw the fourth Striker beyond and above them. The canopy was caught on a small outcropping about thirty feet up. Sondra DeVonne was suspended close beneath it. She was rocking gently at the end of the shroud lines.

Don't think about this now, Rodgers warned himself. He had to look ahead, at the cause for which these soldiers had sacrificed their lives. Otherwise there would be many more casualties.

Further beyond, to the south, he saw smoke curling up from behind a turn in the valley. Something had either exploded or crashed there. He did not think it was the AN-12. If the aircraft had been hit, the Strikers probably would have heard and certainly would have seen it go down. He glanced briefly to the north. He could see the foot of the glacier ahead. That was why this valley was so damned cold. The glacier had probably cracked this place from the mountains eons ago.

The ground was coming up quickly. As much as he did not want to hit the slopes, Rodgers did not want to land in the water. With the sun setting, his suit would freeze in a matter of minutes. He also did not want to hit one of the ragged slopes bordering the river. That was a good way to rip his cold-weather uniform or break some bones. Unfortunately, the cliffs tapered so sharply toward the river there was not much of a bank to land on.

That left him one other option. It was one that Rodgers did not want to take. But the choices in war were never easy. The general made his decision and forced it to go down.

Rodgers guided himself toward the downed parachute that had blossomed in the lake. The fabric straddled the shore on the eastern side. There were glints of ice around the edges still in the water. The shroud looked as though it would be stiff enough to take his fall without dumping him into the river. Hopefully, Rodgers would be able to stay on his feet and jump to the narrow shore before the canopy folded altogether.

With just seconds to impact, Rodgers positioned himself over the chute. On one side he could see an arm lying underwater. The flesh was blue-white. Rodgers did not want to land on the Striker's body. He kept his eyes on the other side of the canopy.

The target site loomed larger and larger. Its rapid approach created the distinct sensation that gravity had really grabbed Rodgers. Now he felt as if he were falling, not floating.

Rodgers landed lightly on the canopy. The rigid fabric gave in the middle where he landed, but the fringes remained flat. Rodgers managed to remain on his feet. He immediately popped his chute and let it blow away. He turned to the side nearest the shore. It took just over a second for the canopy to sink enough for water to begin flowing over the sides. By that time Rodgers had stridden several steps and leaped over the water to solid ground. The foot of the brownish-white granite cliff was less than four feet away. Rodgers walked toward it so that he could see further along the valley.

Landing on the shroud had caused it to drift slightly down-river. As Rodgers looked back he saw a body lying facedown underwater. The dead Striker's clothing was bloated by the water. The shroud lines were the only things moving.

Rodgers did not move him. He did not have time. He reached into his equipment vest and opened a flap to retrieve his radio.

At least, what was left of it.

Mike Rodgers looked at the unit in his gloved hand. The faceplate was shattered. Yellow and green wires were stick-ing up from the cracked plastic. Several shards of black cas-ing along with broken chips were rattling in the bottom of the radio. The unit must have been damaged when Rodgers's right side collided with the ledge.

Rodgers glanced at the dead striker's equipment vest. The radio pouch was underwater. Even if he took off his uniform to keep it dry and retrieved the radio, it was not likely to work. He looked downriver at the tangled parachutes of the other two Strikers. The partly inflated canopies were rolling back and forth in the brisk wind. The bodies beyond were on the narrow, rocky stretch of dry land on his side of the river. Rodgers jogged toward them. His right side and his leg hurt but he refused to let that slow him down.

Private Terry Newmeyer and Corporal Pat Prementine lay inert at the other end of the chutes. Newmeyer was on his right side. Rodgers gently rolled him to his back. His uniform and cheek were soaked with thick, nearly frozen blood. Like his body, Newmeyer's radio was crushed. It looked as if it had caught a piece of shrapnel. The general gave the dead man's shoulder a gentle pat then moved over to Prementine. The corporal was sprawled on his back. One eye was shut, the other was half-open. Prementine's left arm was lying across his chest, the right was twisted beneath him. But his radio seemed intact. Removing it from the pouch, Rodgers turned toward the valley wall. As he walked toward the cliff, the general switched the radio on. The red light on the top right corner glowed. At least something else in this goddamn valley was still alive, Rodgers thought bitterly.

The general raised the radio to his lips. He pressed "speak."

And he hoped the Indian army was not monitoring this frequency.

FORTY

The Great Himalaya Range
Thursday, 5:41 P.M.

Brett August and William Musicant had begun moving southward along the plateau. A fierce, cold wind was blowing toward them as the air cooled and the thermal currents stopped rising. The men had to put their goggles back on to keep their eyes from tearing as they worked their way toward the ledge some four hundred meters ahead. According to the NRO, that was the northern artery of the same ledge the Pakistani cell was traveling on.

The colonel halted when the TAC-SAT beeped. He crouched and picked up the receiver. It was Bob Herbert. The intelligence chief instructed the men to wait where they were.

"What's going on?" August asked.

"There's a chance the cell may have divided," Herbert informed him. "The group that's coming toward you may be bait to draw the Indian soldiers to the northwest."

"That would make sense," August said.

"Yes, but we don't want you to be caught in the middle of that," Herbert said. "There's also a chance that there may have been a struggle of some kind. We just don't know. We want you to proceed to a forward point that you can defend and then wait there."

"Understood," August said. The point where the plateau narrowed would be ideal for that.

"Paul has asked Stephen Viens to have a look around the area northeast of the plateau," Herbert went on. "We have reason to believe the rest of the cell may be headed that way."

"That's where Mike went down," August said.

"I know," Herbert said. "Paul's thinking is if we can locate Mike he can help us find the branch cell—"

A firm, low, intermittent beep began to sound in a pocket of August's equipment vest.

"Bob, hold on!" August interrupted. "I've got an incoming point-to-point radio transmission."

"Careful, Brett," Herbert said.

The colonel set the phone down. He plucked his radio from the equipment vest and punched it on. He would not let himself hope that it was a Striker. More likely it was someone who'd found one of the radios or an Indian army communications officer cutting into their frequency.

"Atom," August said. That was the code name he had selected. It was derived from the first initial of his last name. The Strikers used code names when they were uncertain about the origin of a call. If any of them were taken prisoner and forced to communicate they would use a backup code name based on the initial of their first name.

"Atom, it's Reptile," the caller said.

August did not feel the wind or the cold. The world that had felt so dead suddenly had a faint pulse.

"Are you okay?" August asked.

"Yeah," Rodgers replied. "But I'm the only one. You?"

"Midnight and I are fine," he replied. As he was speaking, August pulled the area map from a vest pocket. These were specially marked with coded grids. He laid it on the ground and stepped on one end while he held the other. "Do you have your map?" August asked.

"Getting it now," Rodgers said. "I'm at 37–49."

"Three-seven-four-nine," August repeated. "I copy that. Are you secure at that location?"

"I seem to be," Rodgers replied.

"Very good," August said. "I'm going to relay that information home. We may have new instructions."

"Understood," Rodgers said.

Colonel August set the radio on the map and picked up the TAC-SAT receiver. As he did he gave Musicant a thumbs-up. The medic smiled tightly. But at least it was a smile.

"Bob, it was Mike," August said. "He's safe in the valley, about three miles from the foot of the glacier."

"Thank you, Lord," Herbert said. "Other survivors?"

"Negative," August told him.

"I see. All right, Colonel," Herbert said. "Set up your perimeter, hang tight, and tell Mike to do the same. I'll pass the update to Paul."

"Bob, keep in mind that there is some very rough terrain out here and it's going to get dark and cold pretty fast," August said. "If we're going to send Mike on any search-and-recon missions, he's only got another forty minutes or so of visibility."

"I'm aware of the situation," Herbert said. "Tell him to get a good look at the landscape. We'll get back to you ASAP."

August hung up the TAC-SAT and briefed Rodgers. The general was his usual stoic self.

"I'll be okay down here," Rodgers replied. "If I have to move north it's a pretty straight shot to the glacier. I'll just follow the river."

"Good. Is your suit intact?" August asked.

"Yes," Rodgers replied. "There's only one thing I need. It's probably the same thing you need."

"What's that?" August asked.

Rodgers replied, "To find whoever sold us out and make them regret it."

FORTY-ONE

Washington, D.C.
Thursday, 8:30 A.M.

Paul Hood was on the phone with Senator Barbara Fox when the interoffice line beeped.

Now that the mission was beyond the point of recall, and politics would not get in the way of international security, Hood briefed the senator on the status of Striker and its mission. Several years before, the senator had lost her own teenage daughter in a brutal murder in Paris. Hood had expected her to respond with compassion and to give her support to the personnel who were still in the field.

She did not. The senator was furious.

"Op-Center took too much responsibility in this operation," the woman charged. "The other intelligence agencies should have been involved to a much greater extent."

"Senator, I told the CIOC that we have a crisis requiring immediate attention," Hood said. "I said we were involving the NRO and the NSA to the extent that time and on-site manpower permitted. You did not object to our handling of this at that time."

"You did not outline the specifics of the danger," she replied, "only the gravity of the threat."

"We did not know the specifics until we were in the middle of this," Hood pointed out.

"Which is exactly my point," she replied. "You sent resources into this situation without adequate intelligence. And I mean that in every sense of the word, Mr. Hood."

The interoffice line beeped again.

"Do you want me to pull the remaining assets out?" Hood asked the senator. Hell, he thought. If she was going to criticize his judgment he might as well leave the rest of the mission in her hands.

"Is there another way of resolving the crisis?" she asked.

"Not that we've come up with," Hood replied.

"Then unfortunately we are married to the scenario you've mapped out," the senator said.

Of course, Hood thought. It was now a no-lose situation for the politician. If it worked she would grab the credit for involving the CIOC at this juncture, for saving the lives of the rest of the Strikers as well as countless Indians and Pakistanis. If the mission failed Hood would take the full hit. This was not the first crisis the two had been through together. But it was the first one of this magnitude and with this high a price tag. Hood was disappointed that she was looking for a scapegoat instead of a solution.

Or maybe he was the one looking for someone to blame, he thought. What if the senator was right? What if he had fast-tracked this operation simply because Striker was en route and it seemed relatively risk-free at the onset? Maybe Hood should have pulled the plug when he learned how risky the jump itself would be. Maybe he had let himself become a prisoner to the ticking clock he feared instead of the things he knew for certain.

The interoffice line beeped a third time.

Years before, Chad Malcolm, the retiring mayor of Los Angeles, gave Hood some of the best advice he had ever received. Malcolm had said that what any good leader did was take information in, process it, and still react with his gut. "Just like the human body," the mayor had said. "Goes in through the top and out through the bottom. Any other way just isn't natural."

Senator Fox informed Hood that the CIOC would take up this "fiasco" in an emergency session. Hood did not have anything else to say. He clicked the senator off and took the call.

"Yes?" Hood said.

"Paul, we've got him," Herbert said. "Brett spoke with Mike."

"Is he okay?" Hood asked.

"He's fine," Herbert replied. "He landed in the valley at the foot of the plateau."

"Bob, thank you." Hood wanted to shout or weep or possibly both. He settled for a deep sigh and a grateful smile.

"While I was waiting for you to pick up the phone I called Viens," Herbert told him. "Instead of searching for Mike I've got him looking to see if the cell broke off. The way I read my map, there's a point between where Ron Friday joined the cell and where Colonel August is now that would have been perfect for the Pakistani group to split. If one team headed straight toward Pakistan, they would have had a relatively short distance of about nine or ten miles to cross. The two barriers they would face there were the line of control and the Siachin Glacier. But if Indian soldiers have been moved from the LOC to this new forward line, that would leave the border relatively clear."

"Which makes the glacier the big impediment," Hood said.

"Right. But that makes stamina instead of greater numbers the big obstacle," Herbert pointed out. "Under the circumstances, that's the challenge I'd choose to face."

"I agree," Hood said.

"The good news is, Mike is at the foot of the glacier," Herbert went on. "If we find a second group of Pakistanis, he has a good shot at intercepting them."

Hood brought up the map on his computer. He studied it for a moment. "Who's in touch with Mike?"

"Brett is," Herbert said.

"Bob, we're going to have to have Mike move out of the valley now," Hood said.

"Whoa," Herbert said. "You want him on the glacier before we know for sure that the Pakistanis are even there?"

"We don't have a choice," Hood replied.

"We do," Herbert protested. "First, we find the cell. Second, if they exist, we see which way they're going. If they're coming toward the valley, and we've sent him up the glacier, we'd be committing him to some pretty unfriendly terrain for nothing."

"I'm looking at the relief map of the region," Hood said. "They have to take the glacier. The valley route adds another twelve miles or so to the trek."

"Twelve relatively flat, easy miles," Herbert added. "Listen to me, Paul. That glacier is over eighteen thousand feet high."

"I see that."

"The cell was seven thousand, three hundred feet up in the mountains when Friday caught up with them," Herbert went on. "They would have to be out of their minds to go up when they could go down to a valley that's just two thousand feet above sea level."

"Certainly the Indian army would assume that," Hood said.

"Maybe," Herbert said.

"No, they'd have to," Hood insisted. "Think about it. If your manpower were depleted at the LOC would you reinforce the valley exit or the glacier? Especially if you thought the cell was moving in another direction altogether?"

"I just think it's premature to send Mike up there," Herbert said. "Especially if he just ends up walking back down with the cell. What we need to do is have Viens find the cell and see which way they're going. Then we can decide."

"If Viens finds them and if there's time to get Mike up there," Hood said. "The satellite has a lot of terrain to cover."

"Then here's an alternate plan," Herbert said angrily. "Why don't we just have August hold an AK-47 on the group that's heading his way and make them tell him what their plans are?"

"Would you trust what they tell you?" Hood asked.

That obviously caught Herbert by surprise. He was silent.

"Think about it logically, Bob," Hood continued. "If the cell divided they won't want to run into a sizable Indian force. That means taking the glacier route, which is where they would need Mike's help the most. If he doesn't start out now there's a chance he may not catch them."

" 'If,' " Herbert said. " 'Would.' 'May.' There's a lot of conjecture there, Paul. An awful lot."

"Yeah," Hood agreed. "And Barbara Fox just ripped me a new one for letting this mission out of the gate without sufficient intel. Maybe I did. Nuclear war is pretty serious stuff. But right now the goal is very clear. The key person isn't Mike, it's that girl from Kargil. And the mission is to get her safely to Pakistan. If there is a second group of Pakistanis and they go over the glacier, we can't afford to have Mike stuck in the valley or racing to catch them. He's our strongest, maybe our only asset. We need him in play."

"All right, Paul," Herbert said. "It's your call. I'll have Brett relay your orders to Mike."

"Thank you," Hood said.

"But I'm not with you on this one," Herbert added sharply. "My gut isn't telling me much because it can't. It's tied in a big goddamn knot. But my brain is telling me that before we send Mike up that glacier we need more time and intel to properly assess the situation."

Herbert hung up.

Slowly, Paul Hood replaced the receiver. Then he turned to his computer and diminished the map of the Himalayas. He switched programs to receive the direct feed from the NRO.

The OmniCom was just completing its retargeting and a barren, brown-and-white image began to fill the screen. Hood watched through tired eyes as the pixels filled in. Right now he wished that he were there, in the field with Mike Rodgers. The general had an organization solidly behind him, people praying for him, honor and pride at the end of the day, whichever way events took him.

But no sooner did Paul Hood stumble onto that thought than two others bumped it aside. First, that he had no right to be thinking about himself. Not after the sacrifice Striker had made or the risks Mike Rodgers, Brett August, and the others were taking.

Second, that he had to finish the operation he had started. And there was only one way to do that.

With resolve greater than that of the people who had started it.

FORTY-TWO

The Great Himalaya Range
Thursday, 6:42 P.M.

Brett August had become a soldier for two very different reasons.

One was to help keep his country strong. When August was in the sixth grade he read about countries like England and Italy that had lost wars. The young New Englander could not imagine how he would feel saying the Pledge of Allegiance each morning, knowing that the United States had ever been defeated or was under the heel of a conquering nation.

The other reason Brett August became a soldier was that he loved adventure. As a kid he grew up on cowboy and war shows on television, and comic books like *GI War Tales* and *4-Star Battle Tales.* His favorite activities were to build snow forts in the winter and tree forts in the summer. The latter were carefully woven together from the limbs shorn from poplar trees in the backyard. He and Mike Rodgers took turns being Colonel Thaddeus Gearhart at Fort Russell or William Barrett Travis at the Alamo, respectively. Rodgers liked the idea of acting a young officer dying dramatically as he battled vastly superior numbers.

The reality of everything August had anticipated was different from the way he had always imagined them.

The greatest threats against the United States were not from forces outside our borders but from those within. He had seen that when he returned from captivity in Vietnam. There were no honors awaiting him. There was condemnation from many of August's old acquaintances for having fought in an immoral war. There was condemnation from some corners of the military because August wanted to go back and finish the job he had started. They wanted to bomb the Cong into submission. The melting pot of America had become the melting point. People fighting rather than learning from their differences.

As for adventure, there was valor but little drama or glory in slaughter and captivity. Death was not big and flamboyant, it was ugly and lonely. The dying did not pause to salute the proud flag of Colorado or Texas but screamed about his wound or cried for a loved one a world away. Fear for himself and his friends made it impossible for August ever to feel anything but unadorned gratification whenever his patrol returned to base.

At the moment, August was driven by just one force: the battle-seasoned resolve of a professional soldier. Even his survival instinct was not that strong. Most of his unit were dead. Living with that loss was going to be difficult. He wondered, unhappily, if that was why William Barrett Travis had reportedly charged the Mexican army single-handedly at the onset of the battle for the Alamo. Not due to courage but to spare himself the pain of having to watch his command fall.

August decided this was not the time to think of hopeless charges. He needed to be in the here-and-now and he needed to win.

Poised behind a jagged-edged boulder twice his size, August watched the narrow, curving ledge just ahead. His visibility was only about fifty yards due to the sharp turn in the ledge. Soon darkness would be a problem. The sun was nearly down and he would have to put on his night-vision goggles. He wanted to wait in order to save the batteries. They might be forced to fight the Indian skirmish line before night's end.

Musicant was behind an even larger boulder. It was situated twenty-odd yards to August's left. Between them the Strikers could set up a crossfire between the end of the ledge and the plateau. No one would be able to get through without identifying themselves and being disarmed, if necessary.

To August's right was the TAC-SAT. He had switched the phone from audio to visual signal in order to maintain a position of silent-standing. The visual signal was on dim. If it shined, the light would not be seen from the other side of the boulder.

A steady wind blew from behind the men. It raised fine particles of ice from the plateau and swept them from the peaks. The icy mist rose in sharp arcs and wide circles, flying high enough to glimmer in the last light of the sun before dropping back to the dark stone. August was glad to see the airborne eddies. They would limit the visibility of anyone coming along the ledge.

August was crouched against the cold stone when the TAC-SAT flashed. He snatched the receiver without taking his eyes from the ledge.

"Yes!" he shouted. He had to press a hand against his hood to shut his open ear.

"Brett, it's Bob. Anything?"

"Not yet," August replied. "What about with you?"

"We need you to radio Mike," Herbert said. "We think a splinter cell might be headed toward the Siachin Glacier. Viens is looking for them. In the meantime, Paul wants Mike to head up there."

"That's a helluva trek," August said.

"Tell me about it," Herbert replied. "If there is a separate group, Paul's afraid Mike will miss them unless he leaves now. Tell Mike that if Viens spots them we'll pass along their location."

"Very good," August replied. "And if this cell knows anything I'll let you and Mike know."

"Fine," Herbert said. "I've tried to raise them on the radio but they're not answering. Listen, Brett. If Mike doesn't think he can do this I want to hear about it."

"Do you really think Mike Rodgers would turn down an assignment?" August asked.

"Never," Herbert said. "That's why I need you to listen between the lines. If there's a problem, tell me."

"Sure," August said.

August hung up and slipped the radio from the belt. Mike had the best "poker voice" in the United States armed forces. The only way August might find out if he had a problem with a mission was to ask him outright. Even then, Rodgers might not give him an answer.

Rodgers answered and August gave him Hood's instructions.

"Thank you," Rodgers replied. "I'm on it."

"Mike, is it doable without more gear? Herbert wants to know."

"If I don't answer the radio again, it wasn't," the general replied.

"Don't be an ass-pain," August warned.

"If you can feel your ass you're doing a lot better than I am," Rodgers replied.

"Point, Rodgers," August told him. "Stay in touch."

"You, too," Rodgers replied.

August switched the radio to vibrate rather than beep. Then he slipped it back into his belt. He was still watching the ledge. The wind had grown stronger over the past few minutes. The ice crystals were no longer blowing in gentle patterns. They were charging past the boulder in sharp diagonal sheets. The fine particles struck the cliff and bounced off hard at a right angle. They created the illusion of a scrim hanging in front of the ledge.

Suddenly, a dark shape appeared behind the driving ice. It was blacker than the surrounding amber-black of sunset. It did not appear to be holding a weapon, though it was too dark to be certain.

August motioned to Musicant, who nodded that he saw it.

For the colonel the rest of the world, the future, and philosophy vanished. He had only one concern.

Surviving the moment.

FORTY-THREE

The Great Himalaya Range
Thursday, 6:57 P.M.

Sharab had lost all sense of time. She knew that they had been walking for hours but she had no idea how many. The woman's thighs burned from the struggle of the upward and then downward trek, and her feet were blistered front and back. Every step generated hot, abrasive pain. Sharab did not know how much longer she could continue. Certainly getting down to where she believed the Indian army was situated would be virtually impossible. She would have to find some way of slowing the enemy down from up here.

The men behind her were not faring any better. They had discarded their flashlights and heavier shoulder-mounted weapons. They had also left behind all but a few of the explosives they planned to use to attract the attention of the Indian soldiers. They'd eaten the food so they would not have to carry it. The water had frozen in their canteens and they had left those behind as well. When they were thirsty they simply broke off the icicles they found in small hollows. All they carried were a rifle with a pocketful of shells as well as a handgun apiece and two extra clips. If there were an army coming toward them, Sharab knew she would not be able to overcome them. All she could hope to do now was draw them off and delay them long enough to give the American, Nanda, and the others a chance to get to Pakistan.

Surviving was also increasingly unlikely. If the Indians did not kill them the elements would.

Sharab even had some question now whether they would even find this elusive Indian army. They had heard some kind of artillery fire earlier. She wondered if the elite American unit had landed and engaged the enemy. She hoped not. The last thing she wanted was to send the Indians back to the line of control. That would only cause the military to bring in reinforcements. On the other hand, if any of the Americans had managed to land, that was good. They could certainly use the help fighting the Indians.

Unfortunately, Sharab could not find out what had happened. The radio she had used to communicate with Washington had become such a burden that she had left it behind.

Particles of wind-blown ice coated her wool hood and clung there. The cold had already numbed her scalp and frozen her sweat-soaked hair. The weight of the hood was such that it kept her head bent forward. That was good. It protected her eyes and cheeks from the sting of the ice pellets.

Sharab was feeling her way along the cliff and also using it for support. Ali was behind her, holding the hem of her parka. Every now and then she felt a tug as he halted or stumbled. Hassan was behind Ali. Sharab knew he was still there because she could hear him praying.

As the ledge widened, Sharab heard another sound. At first it sounded like a sudden, sharp quickening of the wind. But then she heard it again, louder. It was not the wind. Someone was shouting.

Sharab stopped and raised her eyes. She shielded them with her hand and peered ahead.

The young woman saw a cottage-sized boulder with something large moving behind the right side. Sharab could not make out what it was. She replayed the howl in her mind. Asian black bears and deer did not live this high. Perhaps it was a wild pig or goat.

It could also be a man.

It howled again. Sharab pulled off her hood and turned her right ear toward the boulder. She also removed her glove, tucked it in her left pocket, and drew the handgun from her right pocket.

"Who are you?" the figure shouted.

Sharab backed away. "Who wants to know?" she shouted back. The woman was surprised at the effort it took to yell. It actually caused her heart to race. Her voice sounded flat in the close, cold air.

"We are with the man who joined you before," the other man said. "Where is he?"

"Which man?" Sharab asked. "There were two." The man was speaking in English with an American-sounding accent. That was encouraging.

"We only know about one of them," the speaker said.

"What was his name?"

The man hesitated. Obviously, someone was going to have to make the first move to prove who they were. It was not going to be Sharab.

"Friday," the man said.

Sharab stepped forward again very tentatively. "He is not with us!"

"What happened to him?"

"He left," she replied. "Let's talk face-to-face."

"Come closer with your hands raised," the American said.

The speaker did not step from behind the boulder. It was the woman's turn to trust him.

Sharab protected her eyes again and tried to look past the boulder. She saw a second, smaller boulder off to the right but no sign of any other men. There could not be that many soldiers behind the two rocks. But the two boulders would provide good cover for a crossfire.

Sharab told Hassan and Ali to stay where they were. They nodded. Both men had drawn their weapons and were huddled close to the rock. Ali had moved out slightly to provide her some backup.

"If anything happens to me, fight your way out of this," she added. "You must keep the Indian army occupied."

The men nodded again.

The speaker was a few hundred yards away. Sharab did not put her gun away. She raised her hands shoulder-high and began moving toward the nearest boulder. It was difficult to see because of the blowing ice and she had to turn her face toward the side. Her scarf had fallen away and was whipping behind her. The ice particles lashed her flesh. Her cheek felt as if it were on fire. Sharab finally had to lower her left arm to protect it. There was no mountainside to lean against so her sore feet were taking all of her weight. She shambled from side to side to keep from putting all of her weight straight down. At least the terrain was level. That made it easier on her leg muscles.

Her eyes tearing from wind and pain, Sharab staggered the last few yards to the boulder. She fell against it and her knees just shivered and unlocked. She began to slide down the side. Strong, gloved hands reached around and helped to hold her up. She was still holding the gun. But even if Sharab had wanted to defend herself, her finger was too cold to pull the trigger.

A man in white winter gear pulled her behind the boulder. He sat her down and used his body to protect her from the wind. He bent close to her ear.

"Are you the leader?" he asked.

"First tell me who you are," Sharab said. She was barely able to say the words. Her lips were trembling.

"I am Colonel August of the U.S. Striker team," he said.

"I am the leader of these FKM fighters," Sharab replied weakly. She squinted across the dark plateau. She saw another man crouched there.

"That's Mr. Musicant, my medic," August said. "If any of your people need attention, I'll send him over."

"I think we're all right, except for the cold," the woman said. "Fingers, feet, mouth."

The man leaned nearer. He exhaled hotly on her lips. It felt good. He did it again.

"How many men have you?" Sharab asked.

"Three," he replied.

She fired him a look. "Just three?"

He nodded.

"The sounds we heard—?" she asked.

"Indian ground fire," he said. "It took out most of my team. Where is Mr. Friday?"

"We split the group," Sharab told him. "He is with the other half. They went in another direction."

"Over the glacier?" the colonel asked.

Sharab nodded.

"Is that how they're getting back to Pakistan?" August pressed.

The woman did not answer immediately. She looked up into his face. He was wearing goggles and she could not see his eyes. His mouth was straight, unemotional. His skin was pale but rough. He was definitely an American and he had seen some hardship.

"What will you do with the information?" she asked him.

"The third survivor of our drop landed in the valley," August replied. "He'll try and link up with your teammates."

"I see," she said. "Yes. The others are going to try and stay on the glacier until they are home."

"Do you have any way of contacting them?" August asked.

She shook her head.

"And what were you trying to do?" he asked. "Draw the Indian soldiers away from the other group, toward the northwest?"

"Yes," Sharab said. "We're carrying explosives. We thought we could attract their attention, maybe cause some rock slides."

"That won't be necessary," August informed her. "The Indian force is heading toward us. It'll be pretty tough for them to get up here so we'll be able to keep them busy while they bring in choppers from the LOC." August reached for his radio. "Do you and your men need food or water?"

"Food would be nice," she admitted.

August left the radio in his belt. He opened a vest pocket and removed several sticks of jerky. "Give some to your teammates and ask them to join us," he said as he handed her the flat, wrapped servings. "We should set up a defensive perimeter on this plateau. The Indians saw us come down here. I'm pretty sure that if we wait they'll come to us. That will give us a chance to rest, especially if they wait until morning to come after us."

"All right," Sharab said.

She started to stand. August helped her up. As he did, she looked up at him. "I'm sorry about your people."

"Thank you," he replied.

"But be consoled," she said. "Their death in the service of our people will earn them a place in Paradise. 'The steadfast who do good works, forgiveness and a rich reward await them,' " Sharab assured him.

The American smiled tightly. He left the woman supporting herself against the rock while he retrieved his radio.

Sharab winced as she put weight back on her swollen feet. She began hobbling back toward the ledge. But at least now she knew one thing that she did not know a few minutes ago.

The pain would end very soon.

FORTY-FOUR

Washington, D.C.
Thursday, 10:30 A.M.

It had been a grueling ninety minutes for Paul Hood. But then, suffering was relative, he told himself. He was in no physical danger. His children were safe. That helped him to keep his situation in perspective.

After his disagreement with Bob Herbert, Paul Hood had asked Liz Gordon, Lowell Coffey, Ann Farris, and political liaison Ron Plummer to come to his office. Hood had wanted to tell them what had happened to Striker. He also needed to mobilize them at once. Liz would have to put together grief counselors for Op-Center personnel as well as family members of the fallen Strikers. Coffey would have to be prepared to deal with any legal ramifications that might arise from recovering the bodies. And for the first time in years Ann would have to do nothing. As far as domestic officials and foreign governments were concerned, Op-Center would stand by the original mission profile. The team had been sent into Kashmir at the request of the Indian government to search for nuclear missile sites. Striker had been shot accidentally by Indian soldiers who were looking for the Pakistani terrorists. If Ann owed anyone at one of the major news outlets any favors she could tell them what Op-Center was saying to government officials. That, and nothing more. Ann was thoroughly professional and supportive. If she suspected there was anything wrong between her and Hood she did not show it.

Only the president had been told the truth. Lawrence and Hood had spoken briefly before the others had come to Hood's office. The president seemed neither shaken nor pleased by what Hood told him. Lawrence said only that he supported the plan from this point forward. The president's "no comment" did not surprise Hood. It would give him the room to praise or lambaste the NCMC at the end of the day, depending upon how things went.

President Lawrence did suggest, however, that the Pakistani ambassador to Washington be told the truth at once. He did not want Islamabad or Ambassador Simathna issuing statements about America's anti-Muslim activities or pro-India bias. If Mike were to show up with the cell after that it would taint the validity of the operation. It would seem as if America had forced Nanda to lie to repair bridges with Pakistan and the Muslim world.

Hood gave that job to Ron Plummer. He also wanted Plummer to stay with the ambassador, ostensibly to brief him on all the latest developments. In fact, Hood wanted to make certain the truth did not leak out prematurely. He was afraid that India might respond with a massive strike in the region. Since the terrorists were still on the run, and still being blamed for all the bombings, New Delhi would have the moral high road and world opinion on their side.

As the meeting was ending Hood received a call from Bob Herbert.

"I just spoke with Brett August and I've got some good news," Herbert informed him. "He's linked up with the cell."

Hood motioned for Ron Plummer not to leave and to shut the door. The small, slender political liaison closed the door behind Lowell Coffey. Plummer remained standing.

"Thank God for that," Hood said. "Bob, Ron's in here with me. I'm putting you on speakerphone."

"Okay," Herbert said. "Anyway, we were right," he went on. "The Pakistanis did spin off another group. Nanda Kumar and her grandfather are part of it, along with Ron Friday and one Pakistani. And you were correct, Paul. They're headed across the Siachin Glacier."

"Did Brett talk to Mike?" Hood asked.

"Not yet," Herbert replied. "They've got electrostatic interference from an ice storm on the plateau. Brett says the ice comes in waves. He's going to keep trying for a window."

Hood suddenly felt very guilty about his warm office and fully functional telephone.

"Paul, I have a suggestion," Herbert said. "I think we should ask the Pakistanis for help in extracting the teams. After all, it's their butts we're hauling out of the fire."

"We can't do that," Plummer told him.

"Why not?" Herbert asked.

"If the situation is as tense as Paul's described, an incursion by the Pakistani air force would only make it worse. It would give the Indian military more incentive to attack."

"At least then it would be a conventional fight," Herbert said.

"Not necessarily," Plummer said, "especially if there are Pakistani silos somewhere in the mountains. Also, we'd be giving Pakistan foreknowledge of a possible nuclear strike. That might encourage Islamabad to hit first."

"A jihad," Hood said.

"The clerics might call it that," Plummer said. "For the generals it would simply be a responsible tactical maneuver. The situation is hair-trigger enough without throwing more partisan armies into the fray."

"What about the United States sending additional forces into the mountains?" Hood suggested.

"That's not going to happen," Herbert said gravely. "Even if the Joint Chiefs and the president okayed a strike force out of Turkey or the Middle East, it would take hours for them to get there."

"There's one thing I'm missing here," Plummer said. "Why do we need a military response? Can't we let India know what their Special Frontier Force unit did? I'm sure that very few government officials knew about the plot to frame the terrorists."

"I'm sure it was a very tight conspiracy," Hood agreed. "The problem is we have no idea who was in it."

"Someone is obviously tapped into the Op-Center–New Delhi pipeline," Herbert said. "How else could they have known about Striker's mission? Anyway, before the bombing the moderate Indians might have done something. But Kev Custer has been monitoring the TV and radio broadcasts over there. There's a fast-growing grassroots movement in support of the militants."

"Meaning that moderates may be afraid to speak out," Hood said.

"Exactly," Herbert said.

"What about the United Nations secretary-general?" Plummer said. "You know her, Paul. Forget the bad blood between you. She's Indian. She'll have a very good reason to get out the facts about the attack."

"Mala Chatterjee?" Herbert said. "She's so soft on terrorism her speeches turn even bleeding hearts into a lynch mob. She flapped her lips while hostages were being assassinated in the Security Council."

"Chatterjee has far too many enemies of her own," Hood agreed. "At this point her involvement would only make things worse."

"I'll say it again, Paul. Maybe the Russians would be willing to help rein India in," Herbert said. "They want to be seen as serious peacemakers."

"Possibly," Hood said. "But even if we went to them, wouldn't time be a problem?"

"Time and recent history," Plummer said. "Pakistan has very close ties with Afghanistan. There are still a lot of Russian leaders who would like to see both countries pounded flat."

"But a continued stalemate between India and Pakistan means a continued weapons buildup," Herbert said. "Money talks. New Delhi would still have to buy weapons and matériel from Moscow."

"True, but then there's the point that Paul raised," Plummer said. "The same debate that we're having would keep the Kremlin busy for days if not longer. We don't have that kind of time."

"Well, Ron, I'm kind of running dry and getting a little frustrated," Herbert snapped.

"And I'm just doing the devil's advocate thing, Bob," Plummer replied defensively. "We can run some of these proposals up the flagpole in Moscow and at the Pentagon, but I don't see any of them getting the kind of support we need."

"Unfortunately, that's the problem with crisis management instead of crisis prevention," Hood said sadly. "Once you're in it there are not a lot of options."

"I count exactly one," Herbert said.

The intelligence chief was right, of course. With all the resources the United States had at its disposal, there was only one asset standing between India, Pakistan, and a possible nuclear exchange. One asset currently out of touch, underequipped, and on his own.

General Mike Rodgers.

FORTY-FIVE

The Siachin Glacier
Thursday, 9:11 P.M.

During the flight from Washington, Mike Rodgers had read a number of white papers on the Siachin Glacier. The most interesting was written by a Pakistani intelligence officer.

Dubbed "the world's highest battleground" by both the Indian and the Pakistani press, the Siachin Glacier has no strategic value. Long claimed by Pakistan, the glacier reaches nearly eighteen thousand feet in height, the temperatures drop below minus thirty-five degrees Celsius, and the near-constant blizzards and lack of oxygen make the region "sub-human," as one Indian report put it. No one lives there and no one crosses it on foot.

The glacier became a war zone in 1984 when Indian intelligence officers began showing up in the region. Their thinking, apparently, was to force Pakistan to assign human resources to the region, thus making them unavailable for war in habitable Kashmir and along the line of control. However, Pakistan discovered the presence of the Indian reconnaissance teams early in the process thanks to a mountaineering advertisement that appeared in an Indian magazine. The full-page ad showed recent photographs of the region without naming it. The text offered experienced climbers excellent compensation and the adventure of a lifetime to help lead tours through "uncharted territories." Pakistani counterespionage operatives began tracking and capturing the Indian recon teams. The conflict escalated and soon the region was drawing resources from both sides of the dispute. Nearly twenty years later, thousands of troops and aircraft from both sides were assigned to patrol the massive formation.

If they were out there now, Rodgers could neither see nor hear them. He had been in many isolated places during his long military career but he had never experienced anything like this. Standing at the foot of the glacier he was not just alone, surrounded by mountain and ice, but he could only see as far as his flashlight let him. And he was unable to get anything but static on his radio. He shined the light up the sloping white ice. The foot of the glacier reminded him of a lion's paw. There were long, large lumps of dirty white ice about ten feet high with crevasses between them. They led to a gently sloping area that rose higher and higher into the darkness. The formation made him feel fragile and insignificant. The glacier had probably looked exactly like this when the first humans were tossing sticks and berries at each other from trees in the valley.

Suddenly, Rodgers's radio beeped. He grabbed it quickly. "Yes?"

"The target is up there," said the caller.

The transmission was broken and the voice was barely recognizable. But Rodgers had no doubt that it was Brett August. The colonel did not know how long he would be able to transmit. So he got right to the heart of the communication without wasting words.

"Copy that," Rodgers said.

"Team of four," August said. "Girl and grandfather, Friday, and one cell member."

"I copy," Rodgers said again. "I'm at the foot of the zone. Should I go up now?"

"If you wait till sunup you may miss them," August said. "I'm sorry."

"Don't be," Rodgers said.

"Will try and keep enemy busy," August went on. His voice began to break up. "Storming here—cell exhausted. Ammo low."

"Then bail out," Rodgers said. "I'll be okay."

August's response was lost in static.

"I've got a good head start," Rodgers went on. He was shouting each syllable, hoping he would be heard. "Even if they enter the valley now they won't catch up to me. I'm ordering you to pull back. Do you read? Pull back!"

There was no response. Just a loud, frustrating crackle.

Rodgers turned down the volume and kept the channel open for another few moments. Then he shut the radio off to conserve the batteries and slipped the unit back in his belt.

Rodgers hoped that August would not try to stick this one out. Going back down the mountain might not be an option for August and the others. But finding a cave and building a fire would be a better use of their energies than hanging on to a slope and trying to draw the Indian army toward them. Unfortunately, Rodgers knew the colonel too well. August would probably regard retreat as abandonment of a friend as well as a strategic position. Neither of those was acceptable to August.

The plateau was also the place where the Strikers had died. That made it sacred ground to August. There was no way he would simply turn and walk away from it. Rodgers understood that because he felt the same way. It made no sense to fight for geography without strategic value. But once blood had been spilled there, one fought for the memory of fallen comrades. It validated the original sacrifice in a way that only combat soldiers could understand.

Rodgers took a moment to walk along the bottom of the glacier. It did not seem to matter where he started. He had to pull himself up one of the "toes" and start walking.

There were collapsible steel bipoint ice crampons in his vest. Rodgers removed them and slipped them over his rigid boots. The two-pronged claws on the bottoms would allow for a surer grip on the ice.

He strapped them on and removed the pitons from another pocket. He would hold them in his fists and use them to assist his climb. He would not take the time to hammer them in unless he had to.

Before he left, Rodgers secured the flashlight in his left-hand shoulder strap. There were powerful cadmium batteries in the specially made lights. The bulb itself was a low-intensity scatter-beam in front of a highly polished mirror. They would definitely last through the night. As he rested the toe of his left boot on the "toe" of the glacier, he took one last look up the mountain of ice.

"I'm going to beat you," he muttered. "I'm going to get up there and finish the job my team started."

Rodgers's eyes continued up through the darkness. He saw the stars, which were dimly visible through the wispy clouds. Time seemed to vanish and Rodgers suddenly felt as if he were every warrior who had ever undertaken a journey, from the Vikings to the present. And as he jabbed the base of one crampon into the ice and reached up with a piton, Mike Rodgers no longer saw stars. He saw the eyes of those warriors looking down on him.

And among them the eyes of the Strikers looking after him.

FORTY-SIX

Washington, D.C.
Thursday, 12:00 P.M.

The embassy of the Islamic Republic of Pakistan is located in a small, high-gated estate on Massachusetts Avenue in northwest D.C.

Ron Plummer drove his Saab to the gate, where a voice on the other end of the intercom buzzed him through. He headed up the curving concrete driveway to a second security checkpoint at the back of the mansion.

Plummer pulled up to the white double doors and was greeted by a security guard. The man was dressed in a black business suit. He wore sunglasses, a headset, and a bullet-proof vest under his white shirt. He carried a handgun in a shoulder holster. The man checked Plummer's ID then directed him to a visitor's spot in the small lot. The guard waited while Plummer parked.

As he hurried back to the mansion, Ron Plummer ran a hand through his untamed, thinning brown hair and adjusted his thick, black-framed glasses. The thirty-nine-year-old former CIA intelligence analyst for Western Europe was not just feeling the pressure of his own part in this drama. The political and economics officer was also aware of how many things had to go right or the Indian subcontinent would explode.

The National Crisis Management Center had not had a lot of dealings with the Pakistani embassy. The only reason the ambassador, Dr. Ismail Simathna, personally knew them was because of Paul Hood and Mike Rodgers. After the men had ended the hostage stalemate at the United Nations, Simathna asked them to visit the embassy. Plummer was invited to join them. The ambassador claimed to be paying his respects to a brave and brilliant American intelligence unit. Among the many lives they had saved were those of the Pakistani ambassador to the United Nations and his wife. But Hood and Plummer both suspected that Simathna simply wanted to meet the men who had embarrassed the Indian secretary-general. That feeling was reinforced when the visit received considerable coverage in the Islamabad media. Hood was glad, then, that Plummer had come along. Op-Center's PEO gave the appearance of substance to a meeting that was conceived to make a statement about India's ineffective contribution to world peace.

The security officer turned Plummer over to the ambassador's executive secretary. The young man smiled pleasantly and led Plummer to Simathna's office. The white-haired ambassador came out from behind his glass-topped desk. He was wearing a brown suit and a muted yellow tie. The sixty-three-year-old ambassador had been a frontline soldier and bore a scar on both cheeks where a bullet had passed through his jaw. He had also been an intelligence expert and a professor of politics and political sociology at Quaid-E-Azam University in Islamabad before being tapped to represent his nation in Washington, D.C. He greeted Op-Center's political officer warmly.

Plummer had not told Ambassador Simathna why he needed to see him, only that it was urgent.

The men sat in modern armchairs on the window side of the office. The thick bullet-proof glass muted their voices. As Plummer spoke he sounded almost conspiratorial.

The ambassador's lean face was serious but unemotional as Plummer spoke. He leaned forward, listening quietly, as Plummer told him about the Striker operation from conception to present, and Hood's fears about the actions of India's SFF. When Plummer was finished, the ambassador sat back.

"I am disappointed that you did not come to me for intelligence on the nuclear situation in Kashmir," the ambassador said.

"We did not want to impose on your friendship," Plummer replied. "It means a great deal to us."

"That was thoughtful of you," he replied with a little smile. "But you have come to me now."

"Yes," Plummer replied. "For your advice, your confidence, your patience, and most of all your trust. We believe we have a good chance to keep this under control but the hours ahead will be extremely difficult."

"One could describe nuclear brinkmanship in those terms," the ambassador said softly. "Your Strikers were quite brave, going into the mountains the way they did. And the surviving members give me hope. Nations are not monolithic, not even India and Pakistan. When people care enough about one another great things can be accomplished."

"Paul Hood and I share your optimism," Plummer said.

"Even at this moment?"

"Especially at this moment," Plummer replied.

Throughout the exchange Plummer had watched the ambassador's dark eyes. Simathna's mind was elsewhere. Plummer feared that the ambassador was thinking of alerting his government.

The ambassador rose. "Mr. Plummer, would you excuse me for a few minutes?"

Plummer also stood. "Mr. Ambassador, one more thing."

"Yes?"

"I don't wish to push you, sir, but I want to make certain I've made the situation clear," Plummer said. "It is vital that your government take no action until our people in the field have had a chance to extract the Indian operative."

"You have made that quite clear," the ambassador replied.

"There is the very real danger that even a leaked word could turn this into a self-fulfilling nightmare," Plummer added.

"I agree," Simathna assured him. The tall Pakistani smiled slightly and started toward the door.

"Mr. Ambassador, please tell me what you're going to do," Plummer implored. The American was going to feel very foolish if Simathna were going to get an aspirin or visit the lavatory. But Plummer had to know.

"I am going to do something that will require your assistance," Simathna replied.

"Anything," Plummer said. "What can I do?"

The ambassador opened the door and looked back. "You must give me something that you just requested of me."

"Of course," Plummer told him. "Name it." While the PEO waited he replayed the conversation in his mind on fast-forward, trying to remember what the hell he had asked the ambassador for.

"I need your trust," Simathna said.

"You have it, sir. That's why I came here," Plummer insisted. "What I need to know is if we're on the same tactical page."

"We are," Simathna replied. "However, I have access to footnotes that you do not."

With that, the Pakistani ambassador left his office and quietly shut the door behind him.

FORTY-SEVEN

The Siachin Glacier
Thursday, 10:57 P.M.

Ron Friday's anger kept him from freezing.

The NSA operative was not angry when he started this leg of the mission. He had been optimistic. He had effectively taken charge of the mission from Sharab. Even if the woman survived her encounter with the Indian army, Friday would be the one who led the cell into Pakistan. The triumph would be his. And the journey appeared feasible, at least according to the Indian military reconnaissance maps he had taken from the helicopter. The line of control did not appear to be heavily guarded at the Bellpora Pass. The region was extremely wide and open and easy to monitor from the air. Captain Nazir had told Friday that anyone passing through the jagged, icy region risked being spotted and picked off. So Friday and his group would have to remain alert. If the cell was still in the pass during a flyover, they would find a place to hide until it was finished.

However, Friday became less enthusiastic about the operation as the hours passed. He was accustomed to working alone. That had always given him a psychological advantage. Not having to worry about or rely on someone else enabled him to make fast tactical turns, both mentally and physically. It had been the same with his romantic relationships. They were paid for by the hour. That made them easy, to the point, and, most importantly, over.

Samouel was holding up well enough. He was in the lead. The Pakistani was deftly poking the ground with a long stick he had picked up, making sure there were no pockets of thin ice. Friday was directly behind him. There were two unlit

271

torches tucked under his right arm. They were made with sturdy branches the men had picked up before the tree line ended. They were capped by tightly wound strangler vines. The thick vines glowed rather than burned. Friday had stuffed very dry ryegrass between the vines to serve as primers. The torches would only be used in an emergency. Friday had five matches in his pocket and he did not want to waste them.

Nanda and her grandfather were at the rear of the line. Nanda herself was doing all right. She was a slight woman and she lost body heat quickly. But she had a fighting spirit and would have kept up the pace if not for Apu. The elderly farmer was simply exhausted. If not for his granddaughter the Indian probably would have lain down and died.

As darkness had descended over the ice and the temperature had fallen, Friday had become increasingly disgusted with the Kumars. He had no tolerance for Apu's infirmity. And Nanda's devotion frustrated him. She had a responsibility to end the crisis she had helped cause. Every minute they spent nursing Apu across the glacier slowed their progress and drained the energies of Nanda, Friday, and the other man.

The farmer's life just did not matter that much.

Friday had taken a last look around before night finally engulfed them. The group was on a flat, barren expanse. To the right, about a half mile distant, the blue-white glacier rose thousands of feet nearly straight up. The surface appeared to be rough and jagged, as though a mountain-sized section had been ripped away. To the left the terrain was much smoother, probably worn down by ages of rain and runoff from the mountains. It sloped downward into what looked like a distant valley. Friday could not be certain because a mist was rising from the lower, warmer levels of the glacier.

Not that it mattered. Pakistan was ahead, due north. And unless Ron Friday did something to speed up this group's progress they would not get there in time, if at all.

Friday took out his small flashlight and handed it to Samouel. The batteries would probably not last until sunrise. Friday told the Pakistani to get a good look at the terrain and then shut the light off until he absolutely needed it again. Then the American dropped to the left side of the loose formation. The air was still and the night was quiet. The glacier was protecting them from the fierce mountain winds. Friday waited for Nanda and her grandfather to catch up. Then he fell in beside the woman. She was holding Apu's hand close to her waist and walking slightly ahead of him. With each step Nanda stopped and literally gave her grandfather a firm but gentle tug across the ice. She was breathing heavily and Apu was bent deeply at the waist.

"We're not going to make it at this rate," Friday said.

"We'll make it," she replied.

"Not in time," Friday insisted. He did not know that for a fact. But saying it emphatically would make it sound true to Nanda.

Nanda did not respond.

"If either side drops a nuclear missile anywhere in the mountains, this glacier will become a freshwater lake," Friday pointed out. "Let me leave Samouel with your grandfather. You come with me. When we reach Pakistan we can send help."

"Leave my grandfather with one of the men who held us captive?" she said. "I can't trust a man like that."

"Circumstances have changed," Friday said. "Samouel wants to save his people. That means protecting your grandfather."

The young woman continued to help her grandfather along. Friday could not see her expression in the dark. But he could hear the farmer's feet drag along the ice. Just the sound had an enraging quality.

"Nanda, I need your cooperation on this," Friday pressed.

"I am cooperating," she replied evenly.

"You don't understand," Friday said. "We have no idea what's happening in the outside world. We need to get you across the line of control as quickly as possible."

Nanda stopped. She told her grandfather to rest for a moment. The farmer gratefully lowered himself to his knees while the woman took Friday aside. The American told Samouel to keep moving. Friday would find him by the bursts from the flashlight.

"If we leave the terrorist and my grandfather here, no one will come back," Nanda said. "I know this border region. There will be a great deal of tension on both sides of the glacier. No one will want to make any unnecessary or provocative military moves. Samouel will leave without him."

"We'll send a civilian helicopter back here," Friday said. "The American embassy can arrange it quickly."

"They'll be dead by then," Nanda told him. "My grandfather is pushing himself as it is. If I leave he'll give up."

"Nanda, if you don't leave, two nations may cease to exist," Friday pointed out. "You played a key role in this. You have to set it right."

The young woman was silent. Friday could not see her in the blackness but he could hear her breathing. It had slowed somewhat. Nanda was thinking. She was softening.

She was going to agree.

"All right," she said. "I'll do what you ask but only if you stay and help my grandfather."

That caught Friday by surprise. "Why?"

"You know how to survive out here," Nanda replied. She placed her hand on the unlit torches for emphasis. "I think I saw a valley to the west. You will be able to get him down there in the dark, find shelter, warmth, and water. Promise me you'll take care of him and I'll go ahead with Samouel."

The perspiration on the American's face was beginning to freeze. It was a strange feeling, like candle wax hardening. The insides of his thighs were badly chafed and his lungs hurt from the cold air they had been breathing. The longer he stood here the more aware he became of how vulnerable they were. It would be easy to stand still a moment too long and die.

Friday set the two torches down and removed the glove from his right hand. He scratched the frozen sweat from his cheeks and forehead. Then he slipped his hand into his coat pocket. Nanda was Friday's trophy. He had no intention of staying behind or being dictated to.

274

He removed the pistol from his pocket. Nanda could not see it or know what he was going to do. If he put a bullet in the farmer's head Nanda would have no choice but to press on, even if only to bring Friday to justice. Friday, of course, would argue that Apu was distraught about holding the others back. He had tried to reach the gun to end his own life. There was a fight. It went off.

Friday hesitated. He considered the possibility that a shot might attract the attention of the Indian soldiers from the line of control. But he realized that the many peaks and winding ice valleys would make the sound impossible to pinpoint. And those ice peaks were far enough away so that a shot would probably not bring loose sections crashing down. Especially if the blast were muffled by the parka of the dead man.

Friday walked around Nanda. "All right," he said with finality. "I will take care of your grandfather."

FORTY-EIGHT

Washington, D.C.
Thursday, 1:28 P.M.

Ron Plummer was not a patient man. And that had been a great help to him throughout his career.

Intelligence officers and government liaisons could not afford patience. They had to have restless minds and curious imaginations. Otherwise they could not motivate their people or themselves to look past the obvious or accept impasses. However, they also needed to possess control. The ability to appear calm even when they were not.

Ordinarily, Ron Plummer was also a calm man. At the moment his self-control was being tested. Not by the crisis but by the one thing a former intelligence operative hated most.

Ignorance.

It had been nearly forty-five minutes since Ambassador Simathna left the office. Plummer had sat for a few minutes, paced slowly, sat some more, then stood and walked in circles around the large office. He looked at the bookcases filled with histories and biographies. Most were in English, some were in Urdu. The wood-paneled walls were decorated with plaques, citations, and photographs of the ambassador with various world leaders. There was even one of Simathna with United Nations Secretary-General Chatterjee. Neither of them was smiling. The PEO hoped that was not an omen. He stopped in front of a framed document that hung near the ambassador's desk. It was signed in 1906 by Aga Khan III, an Indian Muslim. The paper was an articulate statement of objectives for the All-India Muslim League, an organization that the sultan's son had founded to oversee the establishment of a Muslim state in the region. Plummer wondered if

276

that was the last time Indian and Muslim interests had coincided.

Plummer saw his own reflection in the UV glass. The image was translucent, which was fitting. A political liaison had to have enough substance to know what he stood for but enough flexibility to consider the needs of others. He also had to have the skill to intermediate between the different parties. Even good, sensible, well-intentioned men like Hood and Simathna could disagree strongly.

Plummer glanced at his watch. Paul Hood would be waiting for an update. But Plummer did not want to call Op-Center. For one thing, the political liaison had nothing to report. For another, the embassy was certainly wired with eavesdropping devices. The office and phones were surely bugged. And any number Plummer punched into his cell phone would be picked up by electronic pulse interceptors. These devices were about the size and shape of a pocket watch. They were designed to recognize and record only cell phone pulses. Thereafter, whenever that number was used within the listening range of the embassy's antennae, Pakistani intelligence—or whomever Islamabad sold the data to— could hack and listen in on the call. It was one thing when cell phone users accidentally intercepted someone else's conversation. It was different when those calls were routinely monitored.

Plummer considered what Ambassador Simathna might be up to. Plummer decided on three possibilities. He certainly would have reported the intelligence to the chief executive of the republic, General Abdul Qureshi. Either Islamabad or the embassy might then draft a press release condemning New Delhi for their duplicity. The Indians would vehemently deny the charges, of course. That would rally the people around their respective leaders and ratchet tensions even higher. Especially at Op-Center, which would surely be cited by Islamabad for having provided them with the information.

The second possibility was that there would be no press release. Not yet. Instead, Qureshi and the generals of Pakistan's National Security Council would plan a swift, merciless nuclear strike against India. They would attempt to destroy as many missile installations as possible before releasing the intelligence Op-Center had provided. That would drag the United States into the conflict as a de facto ally of Pakistan.

Hood and Plummer had known that those were both possibilities. They simply hoped that reason would triumph. On the whole, Ambassador Simathna was a reasonable man.

That allowed Plummer to hold out hope for a third possibility, what he called "the one-eighty." It was an option the experts never considered, a development that popped up one hundred and eighty degrees from where the common wisdom had staked its tent. It was the Allies invading Normandy beach instead of Calais during World War II, it was Harry Truman beating Thomas Dewey for the presidency in 1948.

Simathna's parting words, about there being a footnote that only he could access, gave Plummer hope for a one-eighty.

The door opened while Plummer was reading the ninety-year-old paper signed by Khan.

"I often stand where you are and gaze at that document," the ambassador declared as he entered the room. "It reminds me of the dream for which I am an honored caretaker."

The Pakistani shut the heavy door and walked toward his desk. The ambassador seemed to be a little more distracted than before. That could be a good thing or a bad thing for Plummer. Either diplomacy had triumphed and Islamabad would give Mike Rodgers time to try to finish the mission. That meant the ambassador would be the hero or the scapegoat. Or else the children of Aga Khan III were about to write a new Muslim League document. One that would be blasted into the history books by plutonium 239.

Simathna walked quickly behind his desk. He gestured toward a chair on the other side. Plummer sat after the ambassador did. Simathna then turned a telephone toward the American political liaison.

"Would you please call Mr. Hood and ask him to connect you to General Rodgers," Simathna said. "I must speak with them both."

Plummer sat forward in the armchair. "What are you going to tell them?" he asked.

"I spoke with General Qureshi and the members of the National Security Council," the ambassador told him. "There was deep concern but no panic. Preparations are quietly being made to activate defense systems and policies already in place. If what you say about the Indian woman is true, we believe the situation need not escalate."

"How can Op-Center help?" Plummer pressed.

Ambassador Simathna told Plummer what the Pakistani leaders had discussed. Their plan was more than a one-eighty. It was an option that Plummer never could have thought of.

Plummer also realized that the plan carried an enormous risk. The Pakistanis could be looking for an ally in the war against India. If the ambassador were misleading Plummer about their intent, the Pakistani proposal would put the United States at the epicenter of the conflagration.

Literally.

Fortunately or unfortunately, all Ron Plummer had to do was make the call.

Paul Hood was the one who had to make the decision.

FORTY-NINE

Washington, D.C.
Thursday, 1:36 P.M.

Paul Hood was stealing a slice of pizza from his assistant's desk when the call came from Ron Plummer. Hood asked Bugs to have Bob Herbert join him. Then he hurried back to his desk to take the call.

"What have you got?" Hood said as he picked up. He heard the slight reverberation sound that indicated he was on speaker. Hood engaged his own speaker option.

"Paul, I'm here with Ambassador Simathna," Plummer said. "He has a proposal."

"Good afternoon, Mr. Ambassador," Hood said. "Tell me how we can help you."

Herbert wheeled in then and shut the door behind him.

"First, Director Hood, I want to offer my condolences on the tragic loss of your Striker unit, and my government's appreciation for what they were attempting to accomplish," Simathna said.

"Thank you," Hood replied. The ambassador sounded a little too compassionate. He had obviously figured out that the team had not been in the region to help stop Indian aggression.

Herbert was a little more blunt. The intelligence chief made an up-and-down motion with his fist.

"Second, my government has a plan that may assist General Rodgers and his personnel," Simathna went on. "As I have already explained to Mr. Plummer, it will require an understanding with your government that details of the operation must remain confidential."

"I am not in a position to speak for the government, only my small corner of it," Hood said. "If you tell me your idea

I will immediately confer with people who are in a position to offer those assurances."

Paul Hood was dying inside. Vital seconds and quite possibly lives were slipping away while he and Ambassador Simathna postured. But this was how the dance was done.

"The plan we propose is that your group proceed to a nuclear missile site that our military has erected in the glacier," Simathna said. "It is a remotely operated site with video cameras monitoring the interior. The Indian woman can make her broadcast from inside the silo."

Hood stared at Bob Herbert. Mike Rodgers was being invited to visit one of the silos Striker had originally been sent to find. The irony of the proposal was almost painful. What was difficult to process, however, was the dangers inherent in the plan.

"Mr. Ambassador, would you excuse me a minute?" Hood asked.

"Given the situation I would not take much longer than that," Simathna replied.

"I understand, sir, but I need to confer with one of my associates," Hood replied.

"Of course," Simathna said.

Hood punched the mute button. "What do your instincts tell you, Bob? Are they using us?"

"Man, I just don't know," Herbert admitted. "My gut says that the team needs to get to the nearest, warmest refuge as soon as possible. The more I looked at photographs of the glacier the more I started thinking they'll never be able to cross it without more gear and supplies than they're carrying. And the weather reports for the region suck. It's going to be around ten below zero before midnight. But I have to tell you, of all the places they could go, a Pakistani nuclear silo would be my absolute last choice."

"I agree with all of that," Hood replied. "The problem is we also have to get Nanda Kumar on-camera as fast as possible."

"Nanda, yes," Herbert said. "The problem is Mike and Ron Friday. If the Pakistanis get them on video there's no telling what bullshit story Islamabad might concoct. They could kill the audio, release the video to the news media, and say that Mike and Friday are there as technical advisors. How's that going to play in India, Russia, China, and God knows where else? An American general and intelligence officer working closely with Pakistani nuclear missiles?"

"They'd say we were in on the Pakistani operation from the start," Hood said. "I'm just not seeing any other viable options."

Herbert shook his head. "Nothing's jumping out at me either."

"Then let's move this along and just watch our step," Hood told him. "The first thing we have to do is try to get Brett on the line. Let's see if he can even contact Mike."

"I'm on it," Herbert said.

"I'll get the coordinates of the missile silo from Simathna," Hood told him. "Then I'll call Hank Lewis, Senator Fox, and the president and let them know what we want to do."

"You won't get support from Fox or the president," Herbert said.

"I know, but I don't think they'll shut the operation down," Hood replied. "We're already in this too deep. If Mike and Friday cross the line of control with the Pakistani cell, Islamabad will say the United States was helping them escape. That would be nearly as damaging."

Herbert agreed. He turned and wheeled himself into a corner of the office and punched the TAC-SAT number into his wheelchair phone.

Meanwhile, Paul Hood got back on the line with Ambassador Simathna. Hood turned off the speakerphone so his conversation would not interfere with Herbert's call.

"Mr. Ambassador?" Hood said.

"I am here," Simathna replied.

"Thank you for holding, sir," Hood said. "We agree that your proposal should be pursued."

" 'Pursued,' " the ambassador replied. "Does that mean you are also considering other courses of action?"

"Not at the moment," Hood said.

"But you might," the ambassador pressed.

"It's possible," Hood agreed. "Right now we're not even certain we can contact General Rodgers, let alone get him to the silo. We also don't know the condition of his party."

"I appreciate your uncertainty but you must understand my concern," the ambassador said. "We do not wish to give out the location of our defensive silo unless your officer is going to use it."

The conversation was becoming an exercise in hedging, not cooperation. Hood needed to change that, especially if he were going to trust Mike Rodgers's fate to this man.

"I do understand, Mr. Ambassador," Hood said.

Suddenly, Herbert turned. He shook his head.

"Hold on, Mr. Ambassador," Hood said urgently. He jabbed the mute button. "What is it, Bob?"

"Brett can't raise Mike," Herbert told him.

Hood swore.

"All he gets on the radio is heavy static," Herbert went on. "Sharab tells him the winds won't cut out for another five or six hours."

"That doesn't help us," Hood said.

Hood thought for a moment. They had thousands of satellites in the air and outposts throughout the region. There had to be some way to get a message to Mike Rodgers.

Or someone with him, Hood thought suddenly.

"Bob, we may be able to do something," Hood said. "Tell Brett we'll get back to him in a few minutes. Then put in a call to Hank Lewis."

"Will do," Herbert said.

Hood deactivated the mute. "Mr. Ambassador, can you stay on the line?"

"The security of my nation is at risk," Simathna said.

"Is that a 'yes,' sir?" Hood pressed. He did not have time for speeches.

"It was an emphatic yes, Mr. Hood."

"Is Mr. Plummer still with you?" Hood asked.

"I'm here, Paul," Plummer said.

"Good. I may need your help," Hood said.

"I understand," Plummer replied.

"I'm putting you on speaker so you can both be a part of what's going on," Hood said.

The ambassador thanked him.

Simathna sounded sincere. Hood hoped he was. Because if Simathna did anything to jeopardize Rodgers or the mission, Hood would know about it immediately.

Ron Plummer would make sure of that.

FIFTY

The Siachin Glacier
Thursday, 11:40 P.M.

It was the last thing Ron Friday expected to feel.

As he neared the kneeling body of Apu Kumar, Friday felt the cell phone begin to vibrate in his vest pocket. It could only be a call from someone at the National Security Agency. But the signal absolutely should not be able to reach him out here. Not with the mountains surrounding the glacier, the distance from the radio towers in Kashmir, and the ice storms that whipped around the peaks in the dark. The friction of the ice particles produced electrostatic charges that made even point-to-point radio communications difficult.

Yet the phone line was definitely active. Absurdly so, as if he were riding the Metro in Washington instead of standing on a glacier in the middle of the Himalayas. Friday stopped and let the gun slip back into his pocket. He reached inside his coat, withdrew the phone, and hit the talk button.

"Yes?" Friday said.

"Is this Ron Friday?" the caller asked in a clear, loud voice.

"Who wants to know?" Friday asked incredulously.

"Colonel Brett August of Striker," said the caller.

"Striker?" Friday said. "Where are you? When did you land?"

"I'm with Sharab in the mountains overlooking your position," August said. "I'm calling on our TAC-SAT. Director Lewis gave us your number and the call code 1272000."

That was the correct ID number for the NSA director in coded communications. Still, Friday was suspicious.

"How many of you are there?"

"Only three of us," August informed him.

"Three? What happened?" Friday asked.

"We were caught in fire from the Indian army," August told him. "Is General Rodgers with you?"

"No," Friday replied.

"It's important that you watch for him and link up," August said.

"Where is he?" Friday asked.

"The general reached the Mangala Valley and is headed east," August said. "Satellite recon gave him your general position."

"The valley," Friday said. His eyes drifted to where Samouel was moving through the darkness. "That's just ahead."

"Good. When you link up you are to proceed to these coordinates on the pilot's map you're carrying," August went on.

"Hold on while I get it," Friday said.

The American crouched and set the phone on the ice. He pulled the map and a pen from his pocket. Friday tried to read the map by the green glow of the cell phone but that was not possible. He was forced to light one of his torches. The sudden brightness caused him to wince. He tried jamming the branch into the glacier but the surface was too solid. Apu reached over and held it for him. Friday remained crouching with the map spread before him.

"I'm set," Friday said as his eyes adjusted to the light.

"Go to seventeen-point-three degrees north, twenty-one-point-three degrees east," August told him.

Friday looked at the coordinates. He saw absolutely nothing on the map but ice.

"What's there?" Friday asked.

"I don't know," August told him.

"Excuse me?"

"I don't know," August repeated.

"Then who does?" Friday demanded.

"I don't know that either," August admitted. "I'm just relaying orders from our superiors at Op-Center and the NSA."

"Well, I don't go on blind missions," Friday complained as he continued to study the map. "And I see that following the coordinates you gave me will take us away from the line of control."

"Look," August said. "You know what's at stake in the region. So does Washington. They wouldn't ask you to go if it weren't important. Now I'm sitting up here with my forces depleted and the Indian army at my feet. I've got to deal with that. Either I or William Musicant will call back in two hours with more information. That's about how long it should take you to reach the coordinates from the mouth of the valley."

"Assuming we go," Friday said.

"I assume you'll follow orders the same way my Strikers did," the colonel said. "August out."

The line went dead. Friday shut his phone off and put it away. Arrogant son of a bitch.

Nanda's voice rose from the darkness. "What is it?" she asked.

Friday continued to squat where he was. The heat of the torch was melting the ice beside him but the warmth felt good. The woman obviously had not seen what he was about to do before the telephone vibrated.

"The know-it-alls in Washington have a new plan for us but they won't tell us what it is," Friday said. "They want us to go to a spot on the map and wait for instructions."

Nanda walked over. "What spot?" she asked.

Friday showed her.

"The middle of the glacier," she said.

"Do you know what might be out there?" Friday asked.

"No," she replied.

"I don't like it," Friday said. "I don't even know if that was Colonel August on the line. The Indian army might have captured him, made him give them the code number."

"They didn't," a voice said from the darkness.

Friday and Nanda both started. The American grabbed the torch and held it to his left. That was the direction from which the voice had come.

A man was walking toward them. He was dressed in a white high altitude jumpsuit and U.S. Army equipment vest, and he was carrying a flashlight. Samouel was trailing slightly behind him. Friday shifted the torch to his left hand. He slipped his right hand back into the pocket with the gun. He rose.

"I'm General Mike Rodgers of Striker," said the new arrival. "I assume you're Friday and Ms. Kumar."

"Yes," the woman replied.

Friday was not happy to have company. First, he wanted to be sure the man was who he claimed to be. Friday studied the man as he approached. He did not appear to be Indian. Also, his cheeks and the area around his eyes were windblasted red and raw. He looked like he could be someone who walked a long way to get here.

"How do you know that it was actually August who called me?" Friday demanded.

"Colonel August spent several years as a guest of the North Vietnamese," Rodgers said. "He didn't tell them anything they wanted to know. Nothing's changed. Why did he contact you?"

"Washington wants us to go to a point northeast of here, away from the line of control," Friday replied. "But they didn't tell us why."

"Of course not," Rodgers said. "If we're captured by the enemy we can't tell them where we're headed." He removed his radio and tried it. There was only static. "How did Colonel August contact you?"

"TAC-SAT to cell phone," Friday replied.

"Clever," Rodgers said. "Is he holding up all right?"

Friday nodded. As long as August kept the Indians off their trail, he did not care how the pack animal was holding up.

Rodgers walked over to Apu and offered him a hand. Water had begun to pool around the Indian's feet.

"I suggest we start walking before we freeze here," Rodgers said.

"That's it, then?" Friday said. "You've decided that we should go deeper into the glacier?"

"No. Washington decided that," Rodgers replied. He helped Apu to his feet but his eyes remained on Friday.

"Even though we don't know where we're going," Friday repeated.

"Especially because of that," Rodgers said. "If they want to keep the target a secret it must be important."

Friday did not disagree. He simply did not trust the people in Washington to do what was best for him. On top of that, Friday loathed Rodgers. He had never liked military people. They were pack animals who expected everyone else to obey the pack leader's commands and conform to the pack agenda, even if that meant dying for the pack. Standing up to captors instead of cooperating for the good of all. That was not his way. It was the reason he worked alone. One man could always find a way to survive, to prosper.

Nanda and Samouel both moved to where Rodgers was standing with Apu. If the Indian woman had decided to continue on to the line of control, Friday would have gone with her. But if she was joining Rodgers, Friday had no choice but to go along with them.

For now.

Friday extinguished the torch by touching it to the melted ice. The water would freeze in seconds and he could knock the ice off if they needed the torch again.

The group continued its trek across the ice with Samouel in the lead and Rodgers and Nanda helping Apu. Friday kept his right hand in his pocket, on the gun. If at any point he did not like how things were going he would put them back on their original course.

With or without General Rodgers.

FIFTY-ONE

The Himachal Peaks
Thursday, 11:41 P.M.

It had been an arduous day for Major Dev Puri and the two hundred men of his elite frontline regiment. This was supposed to be a straightforward sweep of the foothills of the Great Himalaya Range. Instead, it had become a forced march sparked by surprising intelligence reports, unexpected enemies, evolving strategies, and constantly changing objectives.

The most recent shift was the riskiest. It carried the danger of drawing the attention of Pakistani border forces. Because of Puri's mission, it would be much easier for the enemy to cross the line of control at Base 3.

The Indian soldiers had been marching virtually without rest since they left the trenches. The terrain was merely rugged to start. Then the higher elevations brought cold and walls of wind. The successful attack on the paratroopers had given the force a much-needed morale boost as they continued to search for the Pakistani cell. But darkness and sleet had battered them as they ascended. Now they were looking at a climb that was going to tax their energies to the limit. Then there was the unknown factor: the strength and exact location of the enemy. It was not the way Major Puri liked to run a campaign.

Nearly eight hours before, the Indian soldiers had begun closing ranks at the base of the Gompa Tower in the Himachal cluster of peaks. The latest intelligence Puri had received was that American soldiers were jumping in to help the terrorists get through the line of control to Pakistan. That was where the parachutists had been headed. The Pakistani cell was almost certainly there as well. There was no way forward except through the Indian soldiers. The Pakistanis were undoubtedly exhausted and relatively underarmed now that the Americans had been stopped. Still, Major Puri did not underestimate them. He never took an enemy for granted when they had the high ground. The plan he and his lieutenants had worked out was to have twenty-five men ascend the peak while the rest covered them from the ground with high-powered rifles and telescopic sights. Twenty-five more would be ready to ascend as backup if needed. One or another of the teams was bound to take the cell. One or another of the teams was also likely to take casualties. Unfortunately, Defense Minister Kabir did not want to wait for the Pakistanis to come down. Now that Americans had been killed there would be hard questions from Washington and New Delhi about what had happened to the paratroopers. The minister was doing his best to stall air reconnaissance from moving in to locate and collect the American remains. He had already informed the prime minister that Major Puri's team was in the region and would pinpoint them for the Himalayan Eagles. What Kabir feared was that air reconnaissance might locate the Pakistanis as well as the paratroopers. The defense minister did not want the cell to be taken alive.

Using night glasses and shielded flashlights, the Indian troops had been deploying their climbing gear. They had detected faint heat signatures above and knew the enemy was up there waiting. Unfortunately, flyovers would not help them now. The fierce ice storms above made visibility and navigation difficult. And blind scatter-bombing of the region was not guaranteed to stop the cell. There were caves they could hide in. Besides, there were very holy, anchoritic religious sects and cliff-dwelling tribes living in the foothills and in some of the higher caves. The last thing either side wanted was to collaterally destroy the homes or temples of these neutral peoples. That would force them or their international supporters into political or military activism.

The Indian soldiers were nearly halfway into the preparations to scale the cliff when Major Puri received a surprising radio communiqué. Earlier in the day a helicopter on routine patrol had reported what looked like the wreckage of an aircraft in the Mangala Valley. However, there was no room for the chopper to descend and search for possible survivors. Major Puri had dispatched a four-soldier unit to investigate. Two hours before, the men had reported the discovery of a downed helicopter. It looked like a Ka-25. But the aircraft was so badly burned they could not be certain. Puri called the Base 3 communications center. They checked with the air ministry. There were no choppers on special assignment in the region.

Because the chopper went down in the narrow valley, rescue personnel would not be dispatched until the following day. A parachute drop at night was too risky and, in any case, there were no survivors.

An hour later, Puri's group found the remains of ten American paratroopers. Major Puri relayed that information to the defense minister. The minister said he would sit on that information until after the cell had been taken. He had already come up with a scenario in which, regrettably, Puri's soldiers had mistaken the Americans for Pakistanis and had shot the team down.

What surprised the Indian reconnaissance team was what they discovered on the body of one of the Americans. The soldier, a black woman, was hanging from a ledge by her parachute. There was a point-to-point radio in her equipment belt. Occasionally, the red "contact" light flashed. Someone in the communications link was trying to contact her or someone else in the link. That meant not all the soldiers had been killed. Unfortunately, the Indian soldiers could not confirm that. All they got on the radio was static.

Puri expected that he would find those soldiers in the cliffs above, with the Pakistanis. But the Mangala Valley unit had employed infrared glasses in a scan of the region. They had come up with a different scenario.

"We're detecting a very strong heat source several miles to the northeast," Sergeant Baliah, the leader of the reconnaissance unit, had reported. "There is a singular heat source on the glacier."

"It could be some of the native people," Puri said.

292

Several groups of mountain dwellers lived in the upper foothills of the ranges that surrounded the glacier. They often hunted at night after small game and the larger gazelles had returned to their dens and warrens. They also used the darkness to set traps for predators that hunted in the early morning. The Tarari did not eat the wolves and foxes but used their fur for clothing. The traps also kept the animals from becoming so numerous that they depopulated the region of prey.

"It's a little far west for them," Baliah remarked. "The heat signature is also less than we would get from a string of torches. I'm wondering if it might be some of the Americans. If their equipment was damaged in the jump, they might have built a campfire."

"How far is 'several miles'?" Puri asked.

"Approximately four," Baliah responded. "What I don't understand is why the Americans would have left the valley. The weather is much more temperate there. They could not have failed to see the ice."

"The survivors might have found the wreckage of the helicopter and anticipated a recon team. They moved on," Puri suggested.

"But then why would they have left the radio?" the sergeant wondered aloud. "They could easily have gotten it down. Then no one would know there were survivors."

"Maybe we were meant to find it," Puri said. "That way they could feed us miscommunications." Yet even as the major said that, he knew it did not make sense. The Americans could not have known that a reconnaissance unit was en route to the site.

Puri began to consider likely scenarios. The helicopter was probably in the valley to support the clandestine American operation. Perhaps it was there to extract the soldiers when their mission was completed. That was why there was no immediate flight profile. Perhaps the Americans were only supposed to link up with the Pakistanis and see them as far as the border.

And then it hit him. Maybe that was still the objective.

"Sergeant, can you make your way to that heat source double-time?" Major Puri asked.

"Of course," Baliah replied. "What do you think is going on, sir?"

"I'm not sure," Major Puri told him. "It's possible that some of the Americans survived the drop and joined the Pakistani cell on our plateau. But other paratroopers may have been blown clear of the valley."

"And you think the two may be trying to stay in touch point-to-point in order to find each other?" Sergeant Baliah asked.

"That's possible," Puri replied.

The major looked up at the plateau his men were getting ready to climb. The peak was dark but he could see the outline by the way it blocked the clouds above. Except for the presence of the American paratroopers he did not know for certain that the cell was up there. What if they were not? What if the American drop had been a feint? The shortest way to Pakistan from this region was across the Siachin Glacier, Base 3 sector.

Right through his command.

"Sergeant, pursue the Siachin element," Puri decided. "I'm going to request immediate air support in that region."

"At night?"

"At night," Puri said. "Captain Anand knows the region. He can get a gunship to the target. I want you there in case an enemy is present and he digs in where the rockets can't get him."

"We're on our way, sir," the sergeant replied. "We'll have a report in two hours or so."

"That should be about the time the chopper arrives," Puri said. "Good luck, Sergeant."

Baliah thanked him and clicked off.

The major walked over to his communications officer and asked him to put in a call to the base. Puri would brief Captain Anand and get the air reconnaissance underway. Puri would make certain that the operation be as low-key as possible. Anand was to take just one chopper into the field and there would be no unnecessary communications with the base. Even if the Pakistanis could not interpret the coded messages, a sudden increase in radio traffic might alert them that something was going on.

While the major waited for Captain Anand he told the lieutenant in charge of the ascent to finish the preparations but to put the operation itself on hold. They could afford to wait two hours more before risking the climb. The Pakistanis on the plateau were not going anywhere.

If there really were Pakistanis on the ledge.

FIFTY-TWO

The Siachin Glacier
Friday, 12:00 A.M.

When Mike Rodgers was in boot camp, his drill instructor had told him something that he absolutely did not believe.

The DI's name was Glen "the Hammer" Sheehy. And the Hammer said that when an opponent was punched during an attack, the odds were good that he would not feel it.

"The body ignores a nonlethal assault," the Hammer told them. "Whatever juices we've got pour in like reserves, numbing the pain of a punch or a stab or even a gunshot and empowering the need to strike back."

Rodgers did not believe that until the first time he was in a hand-to-hand combat situation in Vietnam. U.S. and Vietcong recon units literally stumbled upon each other during a patrol north of Bo Duc near the Cambodian border. Rodgers had suffered a knife wound high in the left arm. But he was not aware of it until after the battle. One of his friends had been shot in the butt and kept going. When the unit returned to camp and the medics had put the survivors back together, one of Rodgers's buddies gave him a black bandanna with a slogan written in red grease pencil. It said, "It only hurts when I stop fighting."

It was true. Moreover, there was no time to hurt. Not with more lives depending upon you.

The reality of losing the Strikers was with Rodgers every moment. But the pain had not yet sunk in. He was too busy staying fixed on the goal that had brought them here.

Rodgers was leg-weary as his group made its way across some of the starkest landscape Rodgers had ever encountered. The ice was glass-smooth and difficult to navigate. Nanda and Samouel slipped with increasing regularity. Rodgers was glad he still had his crampons, heavy though they were. Rodgers continued to help Apu Kumar along. The farmer's left arm was slung across Rodgers's neck and they were on a gradual incline. Apu's feet had to be dragged more than they moved. Rodgers suspected the only thing that kept the elderly man moving at all was a desire to see his grand-daughter reach safety. The American officer would have helped the farmer regardless, but he was touched by that thought.

That was not a sentiment Ron Friday seemed to share.

Friday had stayed several paces behind Rodgers, Apu, and Nanda. Samouel continued to hold the point position, turning the flashlight on at regular intervals. At just under an hour into the trek, Friday stepped beside Rodgers. He was panting, his breath coming in wispy white bursts.

"You realize you're risking the rest of this mission by dragging him along," Friday said.

Though the NSA operative spoke softly, his voice carried in the still, cold air. Rodgers was certain that Nanda had heard.

"I don't see it that way," Rodgers replied.

"The delay is exponential," Friday continued. "The longer it takes the weaker we become, slowing us down even more."

"Then you go ahead," Rodgers said.

"I will," he said. "With Nanda. Across the border."

"No," she said emphatically.

"I don't know why you're both so willing to trust those bastards in Washington," Friday went on. "We're at our clos-est approach to the border. It's just about twenty or thirty minutes north of here. Troops have probably been pulled out to man the incursion line."

"Some," Rodgers agreed. "Not all."

"Enough," Friday replied. "Heading there makes more sense than going another hour northeast to God-knows-where."

"Not to the guys we report to," Rodgers reminded him.

"They're not here," Friday shot back. "They don't have on-site intelligence. They aren't in our shoes."

"They're not field personnel," Rodgers pointed out. "This is one of the things we trained for."

"Blind, stupid loyalty?" Friday asked. "Was that also part of your training, General?"

"No. Trust," Rodgers replied. "I respect the judgment of the men I work with."

"Maybe that's why you ended up with a valley full of dead soldiers," Friday said.

Mike Rodgers let the remark go. He had to. He did not have the time or extra energy to break Friday's jaw.

Friday continued to pace Rodgers. The NSA agent shook his head. "How many disasters have to bite a military guy in the ass before he takes independent action?" he asked. "Hell, Herbert isn't even a superior officer. You're taking orders from a civilian."

"And you're pushing it," Rodgers said.

"Let me ask you something," Friday went on. "If you knew you could cross the line of control and get Nanda to a place where she could broadcast her story, would you disobey your instructions?"

"No," Rodgers replied.

"Why?"

"Because there may be a component to this we're not aware of," Rodgers replied.

"Like what?" Friday asked.

"A 'for instance'?" Rodgers said. "You flew out here with an Indian officer instead of waiting for us to join the cell, against instructions. Well, you hate taking orders. Maybe you were being headstrong. Or maybe you're working with the SFF. It could be that if we follow your short hop toward the border we'll end up not reaching Pakistan at all."

"That's possible," Friday admitted. "So why didn't I cut you down back at the valley? That would have made certain I get things my way."

"Because then Nanda would have known she's a dead woman," Rodgers told him.

"Can you guarantee that won't happen if she crawls across a glacier with you?"

Rodgers did not answer. Friday had a sharp, surgical mind. Anything the general said would be sculpted to support Friday's point of view. Then it would be fired back at him. Rodgers did not want to do anything that might fuel doubts in Nanda's mind.

"Think about this," Friday continued. "We're following the directions of Washington bureaucrats without knowing where we're going or why. We've been running across the mountains for hours without food or rest. We may not even reach the target, especially if we carry each other around. Have you considered the possibility that's the plan?"

"Mr. Friday, if you want to cross the line of control you go ahead," Rodgers told him.

"I do," Friday said. He leaned in front of Rodgers. He looked at Nanda. "If she goes with me, I'll get her to Pakistan and safety."

"I'm staying with my grandfather," the woman said.

"You were ready to leave him before," Friday reminded her.

"That was before," she said.

"What changed your mind?"

"You," she replied. "When my grandfather was kneeling and you walked over to him."

"I was going to help him," Friday said.

"I don't think so," she said. "You were angry."

"How do you know?" he asked. "You couldn't see me—"

"I could hear your footsteps on the ice," she said.

"My footsteps?" Friday said disdainfully.

"We used to sit in the bedroom and listen to the Pakistanis on the other side of the door," Nanda told him. "We couldn't hear what they were saying but I always knew what they were feeling by how they walked across the wooden floor. Slow, fast, light, heavy, stop and start. Every pattern told us something about each individual's mood."

"I was going to help him," Friday repeated.

"You wanted to hurt my grandfather," Nanda said. "I know that."

"I don't believe this," Friday said. "Never mind your grandfather. Millions of people may go to hell because of

299

something you did and we're talking about footsteps."

Mike Rodgers did not want to become involved in the debate. But he did not want it to escalate. He also was not sure, at this point, whether he even wanted Ron Friday to stay. Rodgers had worked with dozens of intelligence operatives during his career. They were lone wolves by nature but they rarely if ever disregarded instructions from superiors. And never as flagrantly as this. One of the reasons they became field operatives was the challenge of executing orders in the face of tremendous odds.

Ron Friday was more than just a loner. He was distracted. Rodgers suspected that he was driven by a different agenda. Like it or not, that might be something he would have to try to figure out.

"We're going to save Nanda's grandfather as well as those millions of people you're concerned about," Rodgers said firmly. "We'll do that by going northeast from here."

"Damn it, you're blind!" Friday shouted. "I've been in this thing from the start. I was in the square when it blew up. I had a feeling about the dual bombers, about the involvement of the SFF, about the double-dealing of this woman." He gestured angrily at Nanda. "It's the people who pull the strings you should doubt, not a guy who's been at ground zero from the start."

Friday was losing it. Rodgers did not want to waste the energy to try to stop him. He also wanted to see where the rant would lead. Angry men often said too much.

Friday fired up his torch again. Rodgers squinted in the light. He slowed as Friday got in front of them and faced them.

"So that's it, then?" Friday said.

"Get out of the way," Rodgers ordered.

"Bob Herbert barks, Mike Rodgers obeys, and Op-Center takes over the mission," Friday said.

"Is that what this is about?" Rodgers asked. "Your résumé?"

"I'm not talking about credit," Friday said. "I'm talking about what we do for a living. We collect and use information."

"You do," Rodgers said.

"Fine, yes. I do," Friday agreed. "I put myself in places where I can learn things, where I can meet people. But we, our nation, need allies in Pakistan, in the Muslim world. If we stay on this glacier we are still behind Indian lines. That buys us nothing."

"You don't know that," Rodgers said.

"Correct," Friday said. "But I do know that if we go to Islamabad, as Americans who saved Pakistan from nuclear annihilation, we create new avenues of intelligence and co-operation in that world."

"Mr. Friday, that's a political issue, not a tactical military concern," Rodgers said. "If we're successful then Washington can make some of those inroads you mention."

With Apu still clinging to him, Rodgers started moving around Friday. The NSA operative put out a hand and stopped him.

"Washington is helpless," Friday said. "Politicians live on the surface. They are actors. They engage in public squabbles and posturing where the populace can watch and boo or cheer. We are the people who matter. We burrow inside. We make the tunnels. We control the conduits."

"Mr. Friday, move," Rodgers said.

This was about personal power. Rodgers had no time for that.

"I will move," Friday said. "With Nanda, to the line of control. Two people can make it across."

Rodgers was about to push past him when he felt something. A faint, rapid vibration in the bottoms of his feet. A moment later it grew more pronounced. He felt it crawl up his ankles.

"Give me the torch!" he said suddenly.

"What?" Friday said.

Rodgers leaned around Friday. "Samouel—don't turn on the light!"

"I won't," he said. "I feel it!"

"Feel what?" Nanda said.

"Shit," Friday said suddenly. He obviously felt it too and knew what it meant. "Shit."

Rodgers pulled the torch from Friday. The NSA agent was surprised and did not struggle to keep it. Rodgers held the torch above his head and cast the light around him. There was a mountain of ice to the right, about four hundred yards away. It stretched for miles in both directions. The top of the formation was lost in the darkness.

Rodgers handed the torch to Nanda.

"Go to that peak," he said. "Samouel! Follow Nanda!"

Samouel was already running toward them. "I will!" he shouted.

"My grandfather—!" Nanda said.

"I'll take him," Rodgers assured her. He looked at Friday. "You wanted power? You've got it. Protect her, you son of a bitch."

Friday turned and half-ran, half-skated across the ice after Nanda.

Rodgers leaned close to Apu's ear. "We're going to have to move as fast as possible," he said. "Hold tight."

"I will," Apu replied.

The men began shuffling as quickly as possible toward the peak. The vibrations were now strong enough to shake Rodgers's entire body. A moment later, the beat of the rotors was audible as the Indian helicopter rolled in low over the horizon.

FIFTY-THREE

The Siachin Glacier
Friday, 12:53 A.M.

The powerful Russian-made Mikoyan Mi-35 helicopter soared swift and low over the glacier. Its two-airman crew kept a careful watch on the ice one hundred and fifty feet beneath them. They were flying at low light so the chopper could not be easily seen and targeted from the ground. Radar would keep them from plowing into the towers of ice. Helmets with night-vision goggles as well as the low altitude would allow them to search for their quarry.

The Mi-35 is the leading attack helicopter of the Indian air force. Equipped with under-nose, four-barrel large-caliber machine guns and six antitank missiles, it is tasked with stopping all surface force operations, from full-scale attacks to infiltration.

The aircrew was pushing the chopper to move as quickly as possible. The men did not want to stay out any longer than necessary. Even at this relatively low level the cold on the glacier was severe. Strong, sudden winds whipping from the mountains could hasten the freezing of hoses and equipment. Ground forces were able to stop and thaw clogged lines or icy gears. Helicopter pilots did not have that luxury. They tended to find out about a problem when it was too late, when either the main or the tail rotor suddenly stopped turning.

Fortunately, the crew was able to spot "the likely target" just seventy minutes after taking off. The copilot reported the find to Major Puri.

"There are five persons running across the ice," the airman said.

"Running?" Major Puri said.

"Yes," reported the airman. "They do not appear to be locals. One of them is wearing a high-altitude jump outfit."

"White?" Puri asked.

"Yes."

"That's one of the American paratroopers," Puri said. "Can you tell who is with him?"

"He is helping someone across the ice," the airman said. "That person is wearing a parka. There are three people ahead. One is in a parka, two are wearing mountaineering gear. I can't tell the color because of the night-vision lenses. But it appears dark."

"The terrorist who was killed in the mountain cave was wearing a dark blue outfit," Puri said. "I have to know the color."

"Hold on," the airman replied.

The crew member reached for the exterior light controls on the panel between the seats. He told the pilot to shut down his night-vision glasses for a moment. Otherwise the light would blind him. The pilot and copilot disengaged their goggles and raised them. The copilot turned the light on. The windshield was filled with a blinding white glow reflected from the ice. The airman retrieved his binoculars from a storage compartment in the door. His eyes shrunk to slits as he picked out one of the figures and looked at his clothing.

It was dark blue. The airman reported the information to Major Puri.

"That's one of the terrorists," the major said. "Neutralize them all and report back."

"Repeat, sir?" the airman said.

"You have found the terrorist cell," Major Puri said. "You are ordered to use lethal force to neutralize them—"

"Major," the pilot interrupted. "Will there be a confirming order from base headquarters?"

"I am transmitting an emergency command Gamma-Zero-Red-Eight," Puri said. "That is your authorization."

The pilot glanced at his heads-up display while the copilot input the code on a keyboard located on the control panel. The onboard computer took a moment to process the data.

Gamma-Zero-Red-Eight was the authorization code of Defense Minister John Kabir.

"Acknowledge Gamma-Zero-Red-Eight authorization," the pilot replied. "We are proceeding with the mission."

A moment later the pilot slid his goggles back into place. The copilot switched the exterior lights off and replaced his own night-vision optics. Then he descended through one hundred feet to an altitude of fifty feet. He flipped the helmet-attached gunsights over his night-vision glasses, slipped his left hand onto the joystick that controlled the machine gun, and bore down on the fleeing figures.

FIFTY-FOUR

The Siachin Glacier
Friday, 12:55 A.M.

Mike Rodgers's arm was hooked tightly around Apu's back as he looked out on terrain that was lit by the glow of the helicopter's light. The American watched helplessly as Nanda fell, slid, and then struggled to get up.

"Keep moving!" Rodgers yelled. "Even if you have to crawl, just get closer to the peaks!"

That was probably the last thing Rodgers would get to say to Nanda. The rotor of the approaching chopper was getting louder every instant. The heavy drone drummed from behind and also bounced back at them from the deeply curved slope of ice ahead.

Ron Friday was several paces ahead of Nanda and Samouel was in front of him. Before the lights from the helicopter were turned off, Rodgers saw both men look back then turn and help the young woman. Friday was probably helping her to further his own cause of intelligence control or whatever he had been raving about. Right now, however, Mike Rodgers did not care what Ron Friday's reasons were. At least the man was helping her.

Friday was wearing treaded boots that gave him somewhat better footing than Nanda. As the lights went out, Friday scooped the woman up, tugged her to her feet, and pulled her toward the peak.

Though the ice was dark again Rodgers knew they were not invisible. The aircrew was certainly equipped with infrared equipment. That meant the nose gun would be coming to life very soon. Rodgers had one hope to keep them alive. The plan required them to keep going.

An instant later the nose gun began to hammer. The air seemed to become a solid mass as the sound closed in on all sides. Rodgers felt the first bullets strike the ice behind him. He pulled Apu down and they began to roll and slide down the incline, parallel to the icy wall.

Hard chips of ice were dislodged by bullets hitting the ice. Rodgers heard the "chick" of the strikes then felt hot pain as the small, sharp shards stung his face and neck. Time slowed as it always did in combat. Rodgers was aware of everything. The cold air in his nose and on the nape of his neck. The warm perspiration along the back of his thermal T-shirt. The smell and texture of Apu's wool parka as Rodgers gripped him tightly, pulling him along. The fine mist of surface ice kicked up as he and Apu rolled over it. That was to be the means of their salvation. Perhaps it would still help Nanda and Ron Friday. Rodgers stepped out of himself to savor all the sensations of his eyes, his ears, his flesh. For in these drawn-out moments the general had a sense that they would be his last.

The two men hit a flat section of ice and stopped skidding. The fusillade stopped.

"On your knees!" Rodgers shouted.

The men were going to have to crawl in another direction. It would take the gunner an instant to resight the weapon. Rodgers pulled Apu onto his knees. The two men had to be somewhere else when fire resumed.

The men were crouching and facing one another in the dark. Apu was kneeling and half-leaning against Rodgers's chest. Suddenly, the farmer clutched the general's shoulders. He pushed forward. With nothing behind him, Rodgers fell back with Apu on top of him.

"Save Nanda," Apu implored.

The gunning restarted. It chewed up the ice and then drilled into the back of the farmer. Apu hugged Rodgers as the bullets dug into the older man's flesh. The wounds sent damp splashes onto Rodgers's face. He could feel the thud of each bullet right through the man's body. Rodgers reflexively tucked his chin into his chest, bringing his head under

307

Apu's face. He could hear the man grunt as the bullets struck. They were not cries of pain but the forced exhalation of air as his lungs were punctured from behind. Apu was already beyond pain.

Rodgers brought in his knees slightly and kept himself buried beneath Apu's body. He was thinking now and not simply reacting. And Rodgers realized that this was what Apu had wanted. The farmer had sacrificed himself so Rodgers could stay alive and protect Nanda. The devotion and trust inherent in that gesture made them as pure as anything Rodgers had ever experienced.

Rodgers heard several bullets whistle by his head. He felt a burning in his right shoulder. One of the shots must have grazed him. His arm and back warmed as blood covered his cold flesh.

Rodgers lay still. Their flight and Apu's sacrifice had kept the helicopter occupied for a short time. Hopefully, it had been long enough for Nanda, Friday, and Samouel to reach the peak.

The gunfire stopped. After a few moments the sound of the helicopter moved over Rodgers's head. The chopper was heading toward the icy slopes. It was time for Rodgers to move.

Apu was still holding him. Rodgers grasped the elbows of the man's parka and gently pulled them away. Then he slid to the right, out from under the dead man. Blood from Apu's neck trickled onto Rodgers's left cheek. It left a streak, like warpaint. The elderly man had not given his life in vain.

Rodgers got to his feet. He paused to remove the dead man's parka then ran toward the slope. The helicopter was moving slowly and the American paced it. He stayed behind the cockpit and out of view. He was waiting for the Mi-35 to get a little closer. That was when things should start to happen.

The nose gun began to spit fire again. The red-yellow flashes lit the slope like tiny strobes. Rodgers could see Nanda and the two men running along the curving base, away from the aircraft. The gentle turn in the slope kept the chopper from having a clear shot.

The chopper slowed as it moved closer to the slope. The guns fell silent as the chopper tracked its prey. Flying this close the pilots had to consider rotor clearance, winds, and propwash. Rodgers hoped those were the only things the pilots were worried about. That would be their undoing.

Rodgers reached the base of the ragged slope. He felt his way along. The winds from the tail rotor were savage, like waves of ice water. Rodgers shielded his eyes as best he could. He would be able to see as soon as the guns resumed firing. He was going to have to move quickly when they did.

The chopper continued to creep along the glacier. The throaty sound from the rotors knocked loose powder from the crags. Rodgers could feel it hitting his bare cheeks.

That was good. The plan might work.

A few moments later the guns came to life. Rodgers saw the cliff light up and started running toward the others. As he expected, this close to the slope, the sound of the guns and the rotor shook particles of ice from the wall. The area around the helicopter quickly became a sheet of white. And the flakes did not fall. The winds kept them whipping around in the air, adding layer upon layer. Within moments visibility had diminished to zero.

The guns shut down just as Rodgers raced around the front of the helicopter. Even with their night-vision goggles, the crew would not be able to see him or their quarry.

Rodgers had judged the distance between himself and the others. He guided himself toward them by running a hand along the slope. Though his legs were cramping he refused to stop.

"We've got to move!" Rodgers shouted as he neared the spot where he had seen the group.

"What's happening?" Nanda cried.

"Keep going!" Rodgers yelled.

"Is my grandfather all right?" she demanded.

From the sound of her voice Rodgers judged the woman to be about thirty yards away. He continued running hard. A few seconds later he bumped up against one of the refugees. Judging from the height of the individual it was Friday. They had stopped. Rodgers made his way around him. The general reached for Nanda, who was next in the line. The woman was facing him.

"Grandfather?" Nanda shouted.

"Everyone move!" Rodgers screamed.

In a crisis situation, an individual's fight-or-flight mechanisms are in conflict. When that happens, the shout of an authority figure typically shuts down the combative side. A harsh command usually closes it just enough to let the survival instinct prevail by following the order. In this case, however, Rodgers's cry killed Nanda's flight response. Friday stopped moving altogether as Nanda became as combative as Rodgers.

"Where is he?" the woman screamed.

"Your grandfather didn't make it," Rodgers said.

She screamed for the old man again and started to go back. Rodgers stuffed Apu's parka under his arm then grabbed Nanda's shoulders. He held them tight and wrestled her in the opposite direction.

"I won't leave him!" she cried.

"Nanda, he shielded me with his body!" Rodgers shouted. "He begged me to save you!"

The young woman still grappled with him as she attempted to go back. Rodgers did not have time to reason with her. He literally hoisted Nanda off her feet, turned her around, and pulled her forward. She fought to keep her feet beneath her, but at least those struggles kept her from fighting with him.

Rodgers half-carried, half-dragged the woman as he ran forward. She managed to get her balance back and Rodgers took her hand. He continued to pull her ahead. She went with him, though Rodgers heard her sobbing under the drone of the oncoming chopper. That was fine, as long as she kept moving.

The slope circled sharply toward the northeast. Samouel was still in the lead as they rushed to stay out of the helicopter's line of sight. But without the added drumming of the guns to dislodge fresh ice particles, the pilot would soon be able to see them. Rodgers was going to have to do something about that.

"Samouel, take Nanda's hand and keep going!" Rodgers said.

"Yes, sir," Samouel said.

The American held the woman's arm straight ahead as the Pakistani reached behind him. He found Nanda's hand and Rodgers released her. The two continued ahead. Rodgers stopped and Friday ran into him.

"What are you doing?" Friday asked.

"Give me the torches and the matches. Then go with them," Rodgers said as he took Apu's parka from under his arm.

The NSA operative did as he was instructed. When Friday was gone, Rodgers took one of the torches, lit it, and jammed it into a small crack in the slope. Then he hung Apu's coat on a crag just behind it. Removing his gun from his equipment vest, Rodgers moved away from the ice wall. He got down on one knee, laid the torch across his boot to keep it dry, then pointed his automatic up at a sixty-degree angle. That would put his fire about sixty feet up the cliff. He could not see anything above twenty feet or so but he did not have to.

Not yet.

Within moments the helicopter crept around the curve in the glacier. The pilots stopped to kill their night-vision goggles. Otherwise, the fire would have blinded them. They switched on their exterior light, illuminating the side of the cliff. As soon as the chopper opened fire on what they thought was one of the terrorists, Rodgers also began to shoot. His target were bulges of ice nearest the top of the chopper. The nose gun ripped up the torch, dousing the flame. The roar also tore away more surface ice. At the same time Rodgers's barrage sent larger ice chips flying into the rotor. The blades sliced the ice into a runny sleet that rained down on the cockpit. The slush landed on the windshield and froze instantly.

The chopper stopped firing.

So did Rodgers.

While the chopper still had its lights on, Rodgers briefly considered taking a shot at the cockpit. However, since Afghanistan and Chechnya, the Russians had equipped many of the newer Mikoyan assault choppers with bullet-proof glass to protect them from snipers. Rodgers did not want the flashes from his muzzle to reveal his position.

The general crouched in the open, waiting to see what the helicopter would do. He calculated that it had been in the air at least ninety minutes. The pilot had to allow for at least another ninety minutes of flying time to return to base. That would strain the Mi-35's fuel supply. It would also put extreme stress on the chopper's thermal tolerance, especially if the crew had to fight an ice storm each time they fired their nose gun. Even though the windshield would defrost in a minute or two, the ice would chill the external rotor casing.

Rodgers watched as the chopper hovered. His heart was thumping double-time due to anticipation and cold. Except for being a hell of a lot warmer, Rodgers wondered if the young shepherd David felt the same after letting his small pebble fly against the Philistine champion Goliath. If successful, David's gamble could result in victory for his people. If it failed, the boy faced an ugly, obscure death in the dusty Vale of Elah.

The chopper's exterior lights snapped off. The glacier was once again in darkness. All Rodgers could do now was wait and listen. It took exactly fifteen heartbeats for him to hear what he had been waiting for. With a sudden surge of power, the Mi-35 turned and swung back along the glacier. The beat of the rotor retreated quickly behind the wall of ice.

Rodgers waited to make certain that the helicopter was really gone. After another minute or so the glacier was silent. Slipping his gun into his vest, he took the matches from his jacket pocket and lit the torch. He held it ahead of him. The flame cast a flickering orange teardrop across the ice. It dimly illuminated the ice wall. And with it, the fallen torch and the shredded parka.

"Thank you, Apu, for saving me a second time," Rodgers said. Throwing off a small salute, he turned and followed the others to the northeast.

FIFTY-FIVE

Washington, D.C.
Thursday, 4:30 P.M.

Paul Hood watched the clock turn on his computer. "Make the call, Bob," he said.

Bob Herbert and Lowell Coffey III were both in the office with Hood. The door was closed and Bugs Benet had been told not to interrupt the men unless the president or Senator Fox was calling. Herbert picked up the wheelchair phone to call Brett August. Coffey was seated beside Herbert in a leather armchair. The attorney would be present for the remainder of the mission. His job was to counsel Hood regarding international legal matters that might come up. Coffey had already strongly informed Hood that he was very unhappy with the idea on the table. That an American military officer was leading a team consisting of a Pakistani terrorist, an NSA agent, and what amounted to two Indian hostages. And he was taking them into what was apparently a Pakistani nuclear missile site that had been erected in disputed territory. The idea that this constituted an ad hoc United Nations security council team still wasn't working for him.

Hood agreed that Ambassador Simathna's plan was not a great idea. Unfortunately, it was the only idea. Bob Herbert and Ron Plummer both backed Hood up on that.

The TAC-SAT number Herbert had to input included not just the number of the unit but a code to access the satellite. This made it extremely difficult for someone to reach the TAC-SAT or use it if they found it. Hood waited while Herbert finished punching in the lengthy number.

As Hood had expected, he had not heard from the president and the members of the Congressional Intelligence

Oversight Committee. Over ninety minutes ago, Hood had e-mailed them a summary of the Pakistani plan. According to executive assistants to both President Lawrence and Senator Fox, they were still "studying" Op-Center's proposal. After a short, angry debate with Coffey, Hood decided not to tell the president or Fox what kind of Pakistani military facility Rodgers was visiting. He did not want the CIA crawling all over sources in the region to try to find out what was out there. Coffey argued that with events moving beyond their direct control, Hood had a responsibility to give the president all the facts and hearsay at his disposal. And then it was up to the president, not Hood, to decide whether to call in the CIA. Hood disagreed. He had only Simathna's say-so that there was a nuclear site out there. Hood did not want to legitimize a possible Pakistani ploy by routing it through the White House and thus making it seem valid. Moreover, news of a possible nuclear silo might trigger an Indian strike while Rodgers was out there. That, too, could serve Pakistani purposes by forcing the United States into a confrontation with India.

Even with the edited report he had presented, Hood did not expect to hear from the president or Fox before H-hour. If the operation failed, they would say that Hood had been acting on his own. It would be Oliver North redux. If the Striker mission succeeded they would quickly jump onboard, like the Soviets declaring war on Japan in the waning hours of the Second World War.

After all that Paul Hood had done to help President Lawrence, he would have liked more support. Then again, when Hood saved the administration from a coup attempt he was doing his job. Now the president was performing his own duties. He was stalling. President Lawrence was using the delay to create a buffer of plausible deniability. That would protect the United States from possible international backlash if the Kashmir situation exploded. The abandonment was not personal. It only felt that way.

Hood did not have the luxury of time. He had told Mike Rodgers that he would hear from Brett August in two hours. Two hours had passed. It was time to place the call.

Op-Center's director had rarely felt this isolated. There were usually other field personnel or international organizations backing them up, whether it was Interpol or the Russian Op-Center. Even when he was dealing with the terrorists at the United Nations, Hood had the backing of the State Department. Except for the nominal support of the new head of the NSA, and the help of Stephen Viens at the NRO, they were alone. Alone and trying to stop a nuclear war, a world away, with a cell phone. Even the National Reconnaissance Office was not able to help much now. The towering peaks of the glacier blocked the satellite's view of much of the "playing field," as intelligence experts called any active region. Ice storms blocked the rest. Viens had not even been able to verify there was anything but ice at the coordinates the Pakistani ambassador had provided.

Herbert and August had not spoken for nearly an hour. Herbert had not wanted to distract him. Hood hoped there was someone at the other end of the TAC-SAT to take the call.

Colonel August answered quickly. Herbert put the conversation on the speakerphone. Except for the shrieking winds behind him, the colonel's voice was strong and clear.

Ron Plummer and the Pakistani ambassador were still on Hood's line. As Hood had promised, he left that speakerphone on as well.

"Colonel, I'm with Paul and Lowell Coffey," Herbert told him. "We also have the Pakistani ambassador and Ron Plummer on the other line. You are all on speaker."

"I copy that," August said.

August would know, now, not to say anything that might compromise American security objectives or operations.

"What's been happening there?" Herbert asked.

"Apparently, nothing," August said.

"Nothing at all?" Herbert asked.

"We can't see much now because of the ice storm and darkness," August told him. "But the Indians turn on lights occasionally and as far as we can tell there are still roughly two hundred soldiers at the foot of the plateau. We saw them making preparations for an ascent and then they just stopped about ninety minutes ago. They seem to be waiting."

"For backup?" Herbert asked.

"Possibly, sir," August said. "The delay could also be weather related. We've got a nasty ice storm kicking around us. It would not be a fun climb. Sharab says the winds usually subside just after dawn. The Indians could be waiting for that. With diminished winds they could also bring in low-altitude air support. Or the Indians could just be waiting for us to freeze."

"You feel you're in no immediate danger?" Hood asked.

"No, sir, we don't appear to be," August informed him. "Except for the cold we're all right."

"Hopefully, we'll be able to move you out before too long," Herbert said. "Colonel, we'd like you to raise Mike and his team. If they've arrived at the coordinates, and only if they are at the coordinates, tell them that they have reached an underground Pakistani nuclear missile site. The site is unmanned and operated remotely. Tell them to stand by and then call me back. The ambassador will provide us with passwords that will enable the team to enter the silo. Once inside they will receive instructions on how to access video equipment that the Pakistani military uses to monitor the facility."

"I understand," August said. "I'll contact General Rodgers now."

"Let us know if he has not reached the coordinates and also report back on the condition of his team," Herbert added.

August said he would, then signed off.

Hood did not know whether anything Ambassador Simathna had said to this point was true. But after Herbert hung up, the Pakistani said something on which they both agreed.

"The colonel," Simathna said, "is a courageous man."

FIFTY-SIX

The Siachin Glacier
Friday, 2:07 A.M.

Exhausted and freezing, Rodgers and his team reached the coordinates Brett August had provided.

Rodgers had half-expected to find a field with a temporary Pakistani outpost. Perhaps a few mobile missile launchers, landing lights for helicopters, and a camouflaged shed or two. He was wrong. They found some of the most inhospitable terrain they had yet encountered. Rodgers felt as though he had stepped into some Ice Age environment.

A circle of surrounding peaks enclosed an area of about ten acres. The team had walked through a large, circular, apparently artificial tunnel to get through the wall. Starting very close to the ground, the slopes jutted out at steep angles. At some time in the past slabs of ice must have broken from the facades and covered the ground. Or perhaps this was an ice cave and the roof had simply collapsed. The field itself was extremely rough and uneven, covered with rough-edged lumps of ice and slashed with narrow, jagged fissures. The harshness of the terrain suggested it did not get much sun. There did not appear to be the kind of smoothness that came with melting and refreezing. They were also at a much higher altitude than they were at the mouth of the valley. He doubted that temperatures here got much above zero degrees Fahrenheit.

Samouel and Friday were still relatively alert but Nanda was numb. Shortly after the Mi-35 turned and left, the woman had fallen quiet. Her muscles and expression had relaxed and she seemed almost in a trance. She moved along as he tugged her hand. But she had a rubbery, unfocused gait. Rodgers had seen this kind of emotional shutdown in

Vietnam. It usually occurred after a GI had lost a good buddy in combat. Clinically speaking, Rodgers did not know how long the effects lasted. But he did know that he could not count on afflicted soldiers for days thereafter. After everything that had happened, it would be tragic if they could not even get Nanda to tell her story.

Samouel and Friday had been walking a few paces ahead of Rodgers and Nanda. After the men had a chance to light their torches and flashlights and shine them along the walls and ground, they walked over to the general. Friday handed Rodgers the cell phone.

"Here we are," Friday said angrily. "Now the question is where the hell are we?"

Rodgers released Nanda's hand. She stared into the darkness as Rodgers went to check the time on the cell phone. The cold was so intense that the liquid crystal screen cracked. The digital numbers vanished instantly.

"Well done," Friday said.

Rodgers did not respond. He was angry at himself too. The cell phone was their only link to the outside world. He should have foreseen what the intense cold would do. He closed the phone and put it in his pocket, where it would be relatively warm. Then he turned to Nanda. He warmed her exposed cheeks with his breath and was heartened when she looked at him.

"Look around, try and find out why we've been sent here," Rodgers said to the men.

"Probably to die," Friday said. "I don't trust any of these bastards, not the Indians or the Pakistanis."

"Or even your own government," Samouel said.

"Oh, you heard?" Friday said. "Well, you're right. I don't trust the politicians in Washington either. They're all using us for something."

"For peace," Samouel insisted.

"Is that what you were doing in Kashmir?" Friday demanded.

"We were trying to weaken an enemy that has oppressed us for centuries," Samouel told him. "The stronger we are the greater our capacity to maintain the peace."

"Fighting for peace, the great oxymoron," Friday said. "What a crock. You want power just like everyone else."

Rodgers had let the discussion go on because anger generated body heat. Now it was time to stop. He moved between the men.

"I need you to check the perimeter," Rodgers said. "Now."

"For what?" Friday asked. "A secret, open sesame passage? Superman's Fortress of Solitude?"

"Mr. Friday, you're pushing me," Rodgers said.

"We're in a big, cold shooting gallery thanks to the bureaucrats but I'm pushing you?" Friday said. "This is a freakin' joke!"

The cell phone buzzed in Rodgers's pocket. The general was grateful for the interruption. He had been getting ready to end the conversation by knocking Friday on his ass. It was not a logical Hegelian solution but it would have worked for Rodgers. Big time.

The general pulled the phone out and shielded it with his high collar.

"Rodgers here!"

"Mike, it's Brett," August said. "Have you reached the coordinates?"

"Just got here," he said. "Are you okay?"

"So far," August replied. "You?"

"Surviving."

"Stay warm," August replied.

"Thanks," Rodgers said.

The general closed up the phone and put it back in his left pocket. His fingers were numb and he kept his hand there. Friday and Samouel had stuck the torches in a narrow fissure and were warming themselves around it. Both men looked up when the phone call ended.

"That was short," Friday said.

"Op-Center needed to confirm that we're here," Rodgers said. "We'll get the rest of the plan ASAP."

"Does Op-Center already have the plan or are they getting it from somewhere in Pakistan?" Friday asked.

"I don't know," Rodgers admitted.

"We're being set up," Friday said. "I can feel it."

"Talk to me about it," Rodgers said. The man might not be likable but that did not mean he was wrong.

"Jack Fenwick used to have a word for operatives who accepted partial codes or portions of maps," Friday said. "The word was 'dead.' If you can't control your own time, your own movements, it means that someone else is."

"In this case there's a reason for that," Rodgers reminded him. "Security issues."

"That reason serves Islamabad and Washington, not us," Friday said. "Fenwick would never have cut this kind of deal with a hostile government."

All covert operatives were cautious. But there was something about this man that seemed paranoid. Maybe the strain of the trek had worn them both thin. Or maybe Rodgers's earlier impression was right. The son of a bitch was distracted. Maybe his distrust of Washington went further than he had admitted.

Fenwick was like that too.

"Did you have a lot of contact with Director Fenwick?" Rodgers asked.

The question seemed to surprise Friday. It took him a moment to answer.

"I didn't work closely with Jack Fenwick, no," Friday said. "He was the director of the NSA. I'm a field operator. There is not a lot of overlap in our job descriptions."

"But you obviously had some contact with him," Rodgers said. "You were stationed in Azerbaijan. That was where he worked his last operation. He had some personal, hands-on involvement with that."

"We talked a few times," Friday acknowledged. "He asked for intelligence, I got it for him. There was nothing unusual about that. Why do you ask?"

"You put a lot of faith in your instincts," Rodgers said. "We all do when we're in the field. I was just wondering if your instincts ever told you that Fenwick was a traitor."

"No," Friday said.

"So they were wrong," Rodgers pressed.

Friday made a strange face, as though he were repulsed by the thought of having been wrong.

Or maybe Friday was disturbed by something else, Rodgers thought suddenly. Maybe the man could not admit his instincts were wrong because they had not been wrong. Maybe Friday had known that Jack Fenwick was attempting to overthrow the government of the United States. Yet Friday certainly could not admit he knew that either.

The implications of Ron Friday's silence were disturbing. One of the keys to Fenwick's plan had been starting an oil war between Azerbaijan, Iran, and Russia. To help that along, CIA operatives based in the U.S. embassy had to be murdered. The killer of one of those agents was never found.

The phone beeped again. Rodgers and Friday continued to look at one another. Friday's hands were still warming over the fire. Rodgers had his right hand in his pocket. As they stood there they shared a subtle alpha male exchange. Friday started to withdraw his right hand from the fire. He apparently wanted to put it in the pocket where he kept his gun. Rodgers poked his right hand further into his own pocket so it bulged. Friday did not know where the general kept his weapon. It happened to be in his equipment vest but Friday apparently did not realize that. Friday's right hand remained exposed.

In the meantime, Rodgers answered the phone. "Yes?"

"Mike, are you in a clearing hedged by ice?" August asked.

"Yes," Rodgers replied.

"All right," August said. "Look to the northwest side of the clearing. At the base of one of the slopes you should see a perfectly flat, white slab of ice about two yards by two yards."

Rodgers told Friday to pick up one of the torches. Then he told Samouel to sit with Nanda. Together, Rodgers and Friday walked toward the northwest side of the clearing.

"We're on our way over," Rodgers said. "Brett, any idea what the shape is of the chunk we're looking for?"

"Bob didn't say," August replied. "I guess 'slab' means flat."

The men continued walking across the uneven terrain. It was difficult to keep their footing because of all the small pits, cracks, and occasional patches of smooth ice. Rodgers remained several steps behind Friday. Even if Rodgers did not stumble, a man with a lit torch could be a formidable opponent.

Suddenly, Rodgers saw a piece of ice that fit the dimensions August provided. They walked toward it.

"I think we have it!" Rodgers said.

"Good," August told him. "You're going to have to move that and then wait for me to call back."

"For what?" Rodgers asked.

"For the code that will open the hatch underneath," August said.

"A hatch to what?" Rodgers asked.

"To an unmanned Pakistani nuclear missile facility," August told him. "Apparently the Pakistanis use a video setup to monitor the place. You're going to use that equipment to make your broadcast."

"I see," Rodgers said. "Hold on."

Mike Rodgers felt a chill from inside. The setting no longer appeared prehistoric. It suddenly seemed calculated, like a theme park attraction. The ice was real but it had probably been arranged to look uninviting and confusing, to discourage ground traffic or overhead surveillance. Pakistani soldiers must have camped here in camouflage tents for months, possibly years, working on the silo and the setting. The Pakistani air force would have flown in parts and supplies, probably solo excursions at night to lessen the chance of discovery. If they were telling the truth, it was an impressive achievement.

Rodgers kicked the edge of the slab with his toe. It was heavy. They were going to need help. The general turned. He motioned for Samouel to bring Nanda and join them.

Just then, Rodgers noticed movement along the dimly lit wall behind Samouel. Shadows were shifting on the ice near the northeast slope. The movement was being caused by the torchlight. But the shadows were not being cast by the mounds of ice. The shadows of the ice piled near the walls were moving up and down. These shadows were creeping from side to side.

Right beside the entrance to the enclosure.

"Friday," Rodgers said quietly but firmly, "kill the light and move away from me fast."

The urgency in Mike Rodgers's voice must have impressed Ron Friday. The NSA operative shoved the torch into a fissure headfirst and jumped to his left, away from Rodgers.

"Samouel, get behind something!" Rodgers shouted.

The general's voice was still echoing through the enclosure as he ran forward. Rodgers was afraid the phone would fall from his pocket so he tucked it into his equipment vest. A moment later he tripped on a small pit and banged his left shoulder on a chunk of ice. Instead of getting up again he moved ahead on all fours, crablike. It was the only way to negotiate the uneven terrain without falling. He kept moving toward where he had last seen Samouel and Nanda. He did not feel pain. The only thing that mattered was getting to Nanda. And hoping that he was wrong about what he saw.

He was not.

A moment later the fire of automatic weapons sent deep pops and dull sparks bouncing from the icy walls.

FIFTY-SEVEN

Washington, D.C.
Thursday, 5:00 P.M.

Hood's office was supernaturally silent when Herbert's phone beeped. His heart had begun to race just moments before, as though he knew the call was coming. Or maybe he was just getting more anxious as the minutes crept by. Even if nothing was happening, Herbert did not like being out of touch.

The intelligence chief jabbed the audio button. Wind screamed from the tiny speaker. It seemed to draw Herbert into the Himalayas. Or maybe he was feeling something else. A sense of exposure. The sound was being sucked from Herbert's armrest to the speakerphone on Hood's desk. The intelligence officer was unaccustomed to working with an audience. He did not like it.

"Go ahead," Herbert shouted.

"Bob, I think something just happened at the missile site," Colonel August informed him.

Herbert fired a glance at Hood's phone. Then he looked at Hood. Herbert wanted his boss to mute the damn thing.

"Mike's ass is on the line," Herbert said through his teeth.

"The damage is already done," Hood said softly as he nodded toward the speakerphone on his desk where the Pakistani ambassador was still on the line. He raised his voice. "Colonel, what's the situation?" Hood asked.

"I'm not certain, sir," August said. "I heard gunfire and shouting. Then there was nothing. I hung on for a few minutes before deciding to call. I thought I could use the downtime to get the codes in case Mike came back on."

"Colonel, was there any indication who might be firing at who?" Herbert asked.

"No," August replied. "Before it started, all I heard was someone shouting for the others to duck and take cover. I assume it was General Rodgers."

"Are you still secure?" Herbert asked.

"Nothing has changed here," August replied.

"All right," Herbert said. "Hold on."

Hood turned to the speakerphone. "Mr. Ambassador, did you hear the colonel's report?"

"Every word," Ambassador Simathna replied. "It does not sound like a happy situation."

"We don't know enough to say what the situation is exactly," Hood pointed out. "I do agree with Colonel August about having the codes ready to give to Mike Rodgers. Perhaps if he can get inside the silo—"

"I cannot agree." Simathna interrupted.

"Why is that, sir?" Hood asked.

"Almost certainly those are Indian troops attacking the general's group," Simathna said.

"How do we know they aren't Pakistani troops protecting the site?" Herbert asked.

"Because the mountain troops that monitor the glacier have remained on our side of the line of control," Simathna informed him. "They were told of your incursion."

" 'Our' incursion," Herbert said. He did not even attempt to conceal his disgust. "There's a Pakistani on the team."

"He is under the command of an American military officer," Simathna reminded him.

"How do we know your mountain troops obeyed their instructions?" Herbert pressed.

"I am telling you they have," Simathna replied.

Hood scowled and dragged the back of his thumb across his throat. He was telling Herbert to kill the discussion he had opened. Herbert would rather kill the ambassador. They were trying to save this man's country from vaporization and he would not do a thing to help Mike Rodgers.

"Mr. Ambassador," Hood said, "we have to assume that General Rodgers and his people will prevail. When they do they'll need to get into the silo as quickly as possible. It would be prudent to give Colonel August the codes."

"Again, I cannot allow that," Simathna replied. "It is unfortunate enough that our enemies may learn of this strategic site. But at least the safeguards are still in place."

"What safeguards?" Hood asked.

"Removing the ice block on top of the silo will trigger a timed explosive within the hatch," the ambassador told him. "Unless the proper code is entered within sixty minutes the bomb will detonate. It will trigger a series of conventional explosions that will destroy the surface area."

"Killing the enemy but leaving the silo intact," Herbert said.

"That is correct," the ambassador told him.

"Mr. Ambassador, we are still facing a nuclear attack on Pakistan," Hood pressed.

"We understand that, which is why we must protect our silos from discovery," Simathna told him.

That remark got Herbert's attention. It got Hood's attention, too, judging from his expression. The ambassador had just revealed that there were other silos, probably in other remote areas. That was not an accident. He had wanted Op-Center to know that, and to know it now.

Herbert knew it would be pointless to ask how many silos there were or where they were located. The question was whether revealing that information to New Delhi would trigger an immediate nuclear strike against the region or whether it would force India to stand down. Probably the latter. If Indian intelligence did not already know about the silos they would not know where to strike. Perhaps that was why Simathna had mentioned it. The information would sound more authentic if it were leaked to New Delhi from a branch of U.S. intelligence.

Of course, as with everything else Simathna told them, Herbert had no way of knowing if this were true. For all they knew, there was only the one silo. And there was no way of knowing if there were even a missile inside. Perhaps it was still in the process of being built.

"Ambassador Simathna, I'm going to ask Colonel August to free up his telephone line now," Hood said. "He'll let us know as soon as he hears from General Rodgers."

Hood looked at Herbert. Herbert nodded and told August to sign off until he had reestablished communication with Rodgers. Then Herbert punched off the telephone and sat back.

"Thank you," Simathna said. "Please try to understand our position."

"I do," Hood insisted.

So did Herbert. He understood that Rodgers and August were risking their lives for people who weren't going to do anything to help. He had been in this business long enough to know that covert operatives were considered expendable. They were at the front line of disposable assets.

Except when you knew them.

When they had names and faces and lives that touched yours every day.

Like Rodgers and August.

Like Striker.

The room was silent again, and still.

Except for the desperate racing of Herbert's heart.

FIFTY-EIGHT

The Siachin Glacier
Friday, 2:35 A.M.

White and red flares exploded in the skies above the clearing. Rodgers could now see the soldiers who were firing at them. They were a handful of Indian regulars, probably out from the line of control. The four or five men took up positions behind ice formations near the entrance.

Rodgers immediately dropped to his belly and began wriggling through the broken terrain. Friday was behind the slab at the entrance to the missile silo. He was firing at the Indians to keep them down. Rodgers watched the entrance for signs of additional troops. There were none.

The flares also enabled Rodgers to see Samouel and Nanda. The two were about thirty feet away. They were lying on their sides behind a thick chunk of ice. The barricade was roughly three feet tall and fifteen feet wide. The Pakistani was stretched out behind the woman. He was pushing her face-first against the ice, his arm around her, protecting her on all sides. Rodgers did not have the time to contemplate it, but the irony of a Pakistani terrorist protecting an Indian civilian operative did not escape him.

Bullets pinged furiously from the top of the formation. The onslaught showered the two with ice. As the barrier was whittled down Samouel looked around. Mike Rodgers was behind and slightly to the right of the two. The Pakistani did not appear to notice him.

"Samouel!" Rodgers yelled.

The Pakistani looked over. Rodgers sidled to his right, behind a boulder-shaped formation. He wanted Nanda as close as possible, in case they managed to get inside the silo.

"Come back here!" Rodgers shouted. "I'll cover you!"

Samouel nodded. The Pakistani pulled Nanda away from the ice and bundled her in his arms. Crouching as low as possible, Samouel ran toward Rodgers. The general rose and fired several rounds at the Indians. But as the light of the flares began to fade, and the last streaming embers fell to earth, the soldiers stopped shooting. Obviously, they wanted to conserve both their flares and their ammunition. Though Rodgers kept his automatic trained on the entrance there was no further exchange of gunfire. The ice walls kept even the wind outside. An eerie stillness settled on the enclosure. There was only the crunch of Samouel's boots on the ice and a deep, deep freeze that caused the exposed flesh around Rodgers's eyes to burn.

Samouel and Nanda reached the ice boulder. The Pakistani slid to his knees beside Rodgers. He was breathing heavily as he sat Nanda with her back to the ice. The young woman was no longer in the near-catatonic state she had been in earlier. Her eyes were red and tearing, though Rodgers did not know whether it was from sadness or the cold. Still, they were moving from side to side and she seemed to be registering some awareness of her surroundings.

Samouel moved toward Rodgers. "General, I saw something when the flares went off," Samouel panted.

"What did you see?" Rodgers asked.

"It was directly behind the place where you and Mr. Friday were," the Pakistani said. "On one of the lower ledges of the slopes, about nine or ten feet up. It looked like a satellite dish."

An uplink, Rodgers thought. Of course.

"Maybe that has something to do with why we were sent to this place," Samouel continued.

"I'm pretty sure it does," Rodgers said. "Was the dish out in the open?"

"Not really," Samouel said. "It was set back, in a little cave. About five or six feet it seemed." The Pakistani shook his head. He sighed. "I can't say for sure that it was a dish. There was white lattice, but it could have been icicles and a trick of the light."

"Would the site have been visible from the air?" Rodgers asked.

"Not from directly overhead," Samouel told him.

Rodgers glanced back. It was too dark to see the ice wall now. But what Samouel just said made sense. If there were a video setup somewhere inside the Pakistani missile silo, then there had to be an uplink somewhere on the outside. The dish or antenna did not have to be on the top of a peak. All the dish needed was an unobstructed view of one area in the sky. A single spot where a communications satellite, possibly Russian or Chinese built-and-launched, was in geosynchronous orbit. The cables connecting the relay to the silo would probably be relatively deep inside the ice wall. Whoever designed an uplink for this area would not want the wiring too close to the surface. Melting ice might expose the cables to wind, sleet, or other corrosive forces, not to mention leaving it visible to passing recon aircraft.

"Tell me something, Samouel," Rodgers said. "You wired some of the bombs and remote detonators for Sharab, didn't you?"

"Yes," Samouel said softly.

"Do you have experience with radios?" Rodgers asked.

"I have worked with all kinds of electronics," the Pakistani told him. "I did repair work for the Islamabad militia and—"

"On handsets too?" Rodgers interrupted.

"Walkie-talkies?" Samouel asked.

"Not just walkie-talkies," Rodgers said. He stopped for a moment to gather his thoughts. His questions and plans were racing ahead of the answers. "What I mean is this. If there is a satellite dish on the ledge would you be able to hook a cell phone to it?"

"I see," Samouel replied. "Is it a government cell phone with safeguards of any kind?"

"I don't think so," Rodgers said.

"Then I can probably rig something as long as you can expose the satellite cable," Samouel told him.

"What kind of tools would you need?" Rodgers asked.

"Not more than my pocket knife, I would imagine," Samouel said.

"Very good," Rodgers said. "Now tell me more about the ledge. Was there any way to get to the dish? Ledges, projections, handholds."

"I don't think so," Samouel told him. "It looked like a straight climb up a smooth wall."

"I see," Rodgers said.

The general had become slightly disoriented in the dash to save Nanda. He needed to get his bearings again. He turned himself completely around so he was facing what he believed was the back of the enclosure. He crouched on the balls of his feet.

"Friday, are you still at the slab?" Rodgers yelled.

Friday was silent.

"Say something!" Rodgers screamed.

"I'm here!" Friday said.

Rodgers pinpointed Friday's voice. He kept his eyes on the dark spot. At the same time, he reached into his vest and removed the cell phone. He gave the unit to Samouel.

"If Colonel August calls, tell him to keep the line open," Rodgers told Samouel.

"What are you going to do?" the Pakistani asked.

"Try and get to that dish," Rodgers replied. "How are you set for ammunition?"

"I have a few rounds and one extra clip," Samouel told him.

"Use them sparingly," Rodgers said. "I may need the cover when I start up the slope."

"I will be very careful," Samouel promised.

Mike Rodgers flexed his cold, gloved fingers then put his hands on the ground. He was anxious. A lot was riding on what he knew to be a long shot. He was also concerned about Ron Friday, about something the NSA operative had said earlier. Even if they got through this impasse Rodgers wondered if a deadlier one lay ahead. But that was not something he could afford to worry about now. One battle at a time.

After pausing to take a long, calming breath, the general once again began moving crablike across the rugged terrain.

FIFTY-NINE

The Siachin Glacier
Friday, 2:42 A.M.

Ron Friday listened as someone approached. He assumed it was either Rodgers or Samouel.

Probably Rodgers, the NSA operative decided. The go-get-'em warrior. The general would have a plan to salvage this mission. Which was fine with Friday. No one wanted a nuclear war. But barring such a plan, Friday also cared about getting the hell off this glacier and into Pakistan. And then from Pakistan to somewhere else. Anywhere that was upwind from the fallout that would blanket the Indian subcontinent.

Friday wanted out of here not because he was afraid to die. What scared him was dying stupidly. Not for a trophy or a jewel but because of a screwup. And right now they were in the middle of a massive screwup. A side trip that should never have happened. All because they had trusted the bureaucrats in Washington and Islamabad.

Friday waited behind the slab. The Indians must have heard the movement too because fresh gunfire pinged around the perimeter. There was not a lot of it. They were obviously conserving ammunition. They fired just enough to keep the person low and on the move.

Friday peered out at the blackness. His own weapon was drawn. His nostrils and lungs hurt from the knife-edged cold. His toes and fingertips were numb, despite the heavy boots and gloves. If he were shot, he wondered how long it would take the blood to freeze.

But most of all Friday was angry. It would not take much for him to point the gun at Rodgers and pull the trigger. The NSA operative was trying to figure out if anything could be gained by surrendering to the Indians. Assuming the Indians would not shoot the group out of hand, they might appreciate the American bringing them one of the terrorists who had attacked the marketplace. Surrender might well trigger the feared Indian nuclear strike against Pakistan. It might also save him from dying here.

The figure arrived. It was Rodgers. He crawled behind the slab and knelt beside Friday.

"What's going on?" Friday asked.

"There might be a way to get Nanda's confession on the air without entering the silo," Rodgers said.

"A silo. Is that what this place is?" Friday asked.

Rodgers ignored the question. "Samouel thinks he saw a satellite dish about ten feet up the slope," Rodgers continued.

"That would make sense," Friday replied.

"Explain," Rodgers said.

"When the flares came on I got a good look at the wall over the entrance," Friday said. "From about ten feet up on this side they'd have a clear shot across the opposite slope."

"That's what I was hoping," Rodgers said. "If there is a dish there, and we can get to the satellite cable, Samouel might be able to splice a connection to the cell phone."

The men heard movement from the other side of the clearing. Friday did not think the Indians would move against them. They would wait for the helicopter to return. But they might try to position themselves to set up a cross fire. If the Indians got Nanda the game was over. So were their own lives.

"We're going to have to get a good look at the dish before we do anything," Friday said.

"Why?" Rodgers asked.

"We need to see where the power source is," Friday said. "This is a good spot for a battery-driven dish. Oil companies use them in icy areas. The power source doubles as a heater to keep the gears from freezing. If that's the case, we don't have to go up to the ledge. We can expose the line anywhere and know it's the communications cable."

"But if the power source is inside the silo we have to get to the dish and figure out which cable it is," Rodgers said.

"Bingo," said Friday.

"I'll tell you what," Rodgers said. "You stay down and keep your eyes on the ledge."

"What are you going to do?"

Rodgers replied, "Get you some light."

SIXTY

The Siachin Glacier
Friday, 2:51 A.M.

Mike Rodgers moved to the far end of the clearing. He stopped when he reached the slope. Crouching and moving as quietly as possible he made his way along the wall. He wanted to be far enough from the slab so that Friday was protected. He did not need to be protected from what Rodgers was planning but from how the Indians might respond.

Rodgers hoped that Friday got a good look at the dish. Chances were good that Rodgers himself would not be seeing much. He would be busy looking for a place to hide.

The general stopped about twenty yards from Friday. That was a safe distance. He opened his jacket and removed one of the two flash-bang grenades he carried. The weapon was about the size and configuration of a can of shaving cream. He removed his gloves and held them in his teeth. Then he put his right hand across the safety spoon and slipped his left index finger through the pull-ring. He placed the canister on the ground and squatted beside it. Rodgers moved his right foot along the ground to make sure where the ice cliff was. He would need that to guide him. Then he pulled the ring, released the spoon, and rose. He turned and put his bare left hand against the slope. He felt his way around the thick bulges and barren stretches. He wanted to move quickly. But if he fell over something he might be exposed when the grenade went off.

Rodgers counted as he moved. When the general reached ten, the nonlethal grenade went off.

The nonlethal flash-bang grenade was designed to roll in a confined area, distracting and disorienting the occupants with a series of magnesium-bright explosions and deafening bangs. In this case, Rodgers was hoping the grenade would brighten the perimeter just enough for two things. For Friday to see the dish and Rodgers to find a place to duck.

There was a series of round-topped ice formations three feet ahead. They were about waist high and as thick as a highway pylon. They had probably once been much taller but looked as if they melted and refroze daily, gaining in girth what they lost in height. Rodgers did not run for them. He dove.

Rodgers hit the ground hard. He lost his breath, his gloves fell from his teeth, and he did not quite reach the barricade. But he got close enough so that he was able to scramble across the ice in a heartbeat. Fortunately, the heartbeat was still a measure of time he could use as bullets from Indian rifles chewed up the ice where he had been standing. As soon as he was down and safe he looked over at Ron Friday. Crouched behind the slab, the operative gave him a thumbs-up. Rodgers glanced at the ledge. There was a large black casing behind the base of the dish. Rodgers was glad Friday knew what it was. He himself would have had to go up and pry the cover off to try to read the cables.

As the light of the grenade died Rodgers looked over at Samouel and Nanda. The Pakistani was still lying down. But he had turned to look back at the other men. Rodgers needed to get him over with Nanda and the cell phone. This was probably the best time to do it.

Rodgers took out his weapon and indicated to Friday to do the same. Then he moved to the far side of the ice barricade. That gave him the clearest line of sight to Samouel. He held up three fingers. The Pakistani understood. He was to move out on a count of three. Rodgers gave the man a moment to prepare.

Samouel moved Nanda away from the boulder where they were lying. The Pakistani helped her to her knees and then to a crouching position. She seemed to be cooperating, aware of what she must do. Samouel looked toward Rodgers. The general quickly extended his fingers one at a time. At three, Samouel got up and pulled Nanda with him. She was in front, the Pakistani shielding her with his body. As the two ran forward, Rodgers and Friday immediately stood and began firing toward the Indians. The infantrymen were out of range but obviously did not know that. They ducked down immediately, giving Samouel time to cover most of the distance to the silo entrance.

As darkness enveloped the clearing a few more shots were fired from the Indian side.

"Don't return fire!" Rodgers shouted to Friday.

The general was afraid of hitting Samouel and Nanda in the dark.

The men listened to the crunch of the approaching boots. The gait was near but uneven. That was due, possibly, to the icy, unknown terrain. The sound skewed toward Rodgers's right, away from the silo. He crept to that side of his position and waited.

A few seconds later someone dropped beside Rodgers. The general reached out to pull whoever it was to safety. It was Nanda. Still on his knees, Rodgers wrapped his arms around her. He literally hauled her in and around him. Then Rodgers turned back to his right. He heard grunting a few feet away. The general crept over. He found Samouel near the front of the barricade. The Pakistani was on his belly. Rodgers grabbed the man under his arms. His bare right hand felt a thick dampness. The general pulled Samouel back behind the stumps of ice.

"Samouel, can you hear me?" Rodgers said.

"Yes," the Pakistani replied.

Rodgers felt around the man's left side. The dampness was spreading. It was definitely blood.

"Samouel, you're wounded," Rodgers said.

"I know," Samouel said, "General, I've 'screwed up.' "

"No," Rodgers said. "You did fine. We'll fix this—"

"I don't mean that," Samouel said. "I . . . lost the telephone."

The words hit Rodgers like a bullet.

Suddenly, gunfire erupted from the left. The short burst had come from Ron Friday.

"Our buddies are on the move again!" Friday said.

"Get down!" the general shouted.

Rodgers had no time for them. He reached into his vest and removed one of the two cylindrical "eight ball" grenades he carried. Those were the ones no one wanted to find themselves behind, the shrapnel-producing grenades. Without hesitation the general yanked the pin, let the no-snag cap pop off, and stiff-armed the explosive across the clearing. He did not want to kill the Indians but he could not afford to waste time. Not with Samouel injured.

Rodgers ducked and pulled Nanda down. Several seconds later the eight ball exploded, echoing off the walls and shaking the ground. Even before the reverberations stopped, Rodgers had pulled the nine-inch knife from his equipment vest. He had immediately begun prioritizing. Stop the Indians. Stop Samouel's bleeding. Then he would worry about the phone.

"Don't bother with me," Samouel said. "I'm all right."

"You're hit," Rodgers said.

The general cut into the man's coat. He put his right hand through the opening. He felt for a wound.

Rodgers found it. A bullet hole just below the left shoulder blade. He reached out to the right and felt for his gloves. He found them, cut out the soft interior linings, and placed them on the wound. He pressed down hard. He could not think of anything else to do.

The clearing was silent as the reverberation of the grenade subsided. There were no moans from the other side, no shouting. There was just deadly silence as time and options slipped away. Without the cell phone they could not communicate with August or hook up to the dish. Finding the unit in the dark would be time consuming, if it was even possible. Going out with a torch was suicide. And if they lost Samouel, none of it even mattered.

It had been a good plan. Ironically, they would have been better off following the instincts of a man who might well be a traitor.

Mike Rodgers crouched there, his arms held low. He continued to press on the makeshift bandage, hoping the blood on the underside would freeze. When that happened he would have to try to recover the phone, even if it cost him his life.

As Rodgers waited, his right elbow knocked into something in his belt.

He realized at once what it was.

Possible salvation.

SIXTY-ONE

Siachin Base 3, Kashmir
Friday, 3:22 A.M.

The Mikoyan Mi-35 helicopter set down on its small, dark pad. The square landing area was composed of a layer of asphalt covered with cotton and then another layer of asphalt. The fabric helped keep the ice from the lower layer from reaching the upper layer.

No sooner had the pilot cut the twin rotors than he received a message over his headset.

"Captain, we just received a message from Major Puri," the base communications director informed him. "You're to refuel, deice, and go back out."

The captain exchanged a disgruntled look with the copilot. The cockpit was poorly heated and they were both tired from the difficult flight. They did not feel like undertaking a new mission.

As the pilot looked over, he glanced past his companion. Through the starboard window of the cockpit he could already see ground crews approaching. There were two trucks crossing the landing area. One was a fuel tank, the other a truck loaded with high-volume hoses and drums of a solution of sodium chloride–ferric ferrocyanide.

"What is the objective?" the captain asked.

"The cell you were tracking before," the BCD replied. "One of Major Puri's units has them cornered. The unit estimates that there are four individuals but they do not know how heavily armed they are."

The captain felt a flush of satisfaction at the news. Although he had admired the way one man, armed with a pistol, had driven them back, he did not like being outsmarted.

"Where are they?" the captain asked. At the same time he punched up the topographical map on the computer.

"The Upper Chittisin Plateau," the officer replied, and provided the coordinates.

The pilot entered the figures. The criminals had simply followed the mountain. It was a particularly high, cold, inhospitable section of the glacier. He wondered if they had gone there intentionally or ended up there by accident. If intentionally, he could not imagine what was there. Perhaps a safe house of some kind, or a weapons cache.

Whatever it was, he could take the chopper around the glacier on the southwest side and be there in forty-five minutes.

"When we find them, what are our orders?" the captain asked.

"You are to retrieve Major Puri's team and then complete your previous mission," the BCD informed him.

The captain acknowledged the order.

Ten minutes later he was in the air heading toward the target. This time, he would not fail to exterminate the terrorists.

SIXTY-TWO

The Siachin Glacier
Friday, 3:23 A.M.

Samouel's blood was beginning to freeze. Rodgers felt it in his fingertips. They were the only part of his hands that had stayed warm.

As soon as that happened he picked up his knife and leaned close to Nanda. "I want you to come with me," he said.

"All right," she replied.

Together, they crept across the area between the ice barricade and the entrance to the silo.

"I'm coming in with Nanda," Rodgers said in a loud whisper. He did not want Friday thinking it was the Indians circling around.

"Is everything all right?" Friday asked.

"Samouel's been hit," Rodgers told him.

"How bad?"

"Bad," Rodgers said.

"You dumb bastard," Friday said. "And I'm even dumber for following you assholes."

"I guess so," Rodgers replied. He sidled next to Friday and handed him the knife. "If we're through with your debriefing, I'm going back to get Samouel. Meantime, I need you to start digging me a hole in the ice along the side of the silo entrance."

"That's how you're planning to get to the cable?" Friday asked.

"That's how," Rodgers admitted.

"It could be ten feet down!" Friday exclaimed.

"It won't be," Rodgers said. "The ice melts and refreezes out here. The conduit probably cracks a lot. They would not put it so far down that they couldn't reach it for repairs."

"Maybe," Friday said. "Even so, digging through three or four feet of ice is going to take—"

"Just do it," Rodgers told him.

"Up yours," Friday replied. "If Sammy boy croaks we're dead anyway. I think I'm going to have a talk with our Indian neighbors. See if we can't work something out."

Rodgers heard the knife clunk on the ice.

A moment later he heard the blade scrape the ice.

"I'll do it," Nanda said as she began chopping.

That caught Rodgers by surprise. Her voice sounded strong. It was the first indication he had that she was "back." It was their first bit of luck and the timing could not have been better.

Rodgers could not see Friday but he could hear his harsh breathing. The general had his right hand in his coat pocket. He was prepared to shoot Friday if he had to. Not for leaving them. He had that right. But he was afraid of what a cold, tired, and hungry man might say about their situation.

Ron Friday's breathing stayed in the same place. Nanda's action must have shamed him. Or maybe Friday had been testing Rodgers. Sometimes, what a man did not say in response to a threat said more, and was more dangerous, than a saber-rattling reply.

"I'll be right back with Samouel," Rodgers said evenly.

The general turned and recrossed the small area between the two positions. The Indians maintained their silence. Rodgers was now thinking they had been advance scouts for another party. Their orders were obviously to keep the enemy pinned until backup could arrive. Hopefully, that would not be for another half hour or so. If everything else went right in his improvisation, that was all the time Rodgers would need.

Samouel was breathing rapidly when Rodgers reached him. The general was not a doctor. He did not know whether that was a good thing or a bad thing. Under the circumstances, breathing at all was good.

"How're you doing?" Rodgers asked.

"Not very well," Samouel said. He was wheezing. It sounded as if there were blood in his throat.

"You're just disoriented by the trauma," Rodgers lied. "We'll fix you up as soon as we're done here."

"What can we do without the cell phone?" Samouel asked.

Rodgers slipped his arms under the Pakistani. "We still have my point-to-point radio," the general told him. "Will that work?"

"It should," Samouel replied. "The wiring is basically the same."

"That's what I thought," Rodgers said. "I'm going to get us to the cable and pry the back from the radio. Then you're going to tell me how to hook it to the satellite dish."

"Wait," Samouel said.

Rodgers hesitated before lifting him.

"Listen," Samouel said. "Look for the red line underground. Red is always the audio. Inside the radio, find the largest chip. There will be two lines attached. One leads to the microphone. The other to the antenna. Cut the wire leading to the antenna. Splice the red wire from the dish to that one."

"All right," Rodgers replied.

"You understand all that?" Samouel asked.

"I do," Rodgers assured him.

"Then go," Samouel said.

The Pakistani's voice had become weaker as he spoke. Rodgers did not argue with him. Pausing only long enough to squeeze Samouel's hand, Rodgers turned and hurried back to the slab.

SIXTY-THREE

The Siachin Glacier
Friday, 3:25 A.M.

Nanda did not remember much of what had happened since the helicopter had attacked them. She knew that her grandfather had died. But it seemed as if after that her mind had drifted. She was awake but her spirit had been elsewhere. The shock of her grandfather's death must have dulled her kundalini, her life force. That forced the Shakti to take over. Those were the female deities that protected true believers in times of strife. Using their own secret mantras and mandalas, the mystical words and diagrams, the Shakti had guarded her life force until Nanda's own depleted natural energies could revive it.

The shock of the latest explosions and the rattling gunfire had accelerated the process. General Rodgers's high-intensity activities of the last few minutes had finished it. Whatever alertness Nanda had always felt when she was dealing with the SFF had come back to her. And she was glad it had. The young woman's return seemed to have defused whatever tensions had been building between Rodgers and his fellow American.

Nanda continued to chisel, hack, and pry at the ice. She worked from left to right, cutting new inroads with her right hand while scooping out ice chips with her left. At the same time she felt for anything that might be a cable or a conduit. With their luck they would find one and it would be made of steel or some compound they could not break through.

Whatever the outcome, the activity of chopping the hard ice felt good for the moment. It helped keep her blood flowing and kept her torso and arms relatively warm.

Rodgers had only been gone a minute or two before returning. He came back alone.

"Where's your boy?" Friday asked.

"He's not doing too well," Rodgers admitted. "But he told me what to do." The general moved close to Nanda. "Hold on a second," he said. "I want to check the dig."

Nanda stopped. She could hear General Rodgers feeling along the perimeter of the slab.

"This is good," he said. "Thanks. Now I need you both to move back, over by the slope. Lie there with your feet to your chin, arms tucked in, hands over your ears. Leave as little of yourself exposed as possible."

"What are you going to do?" Nanda asked.

"I have one more of those flash-bang grenades I used earlier," Rodgers said. "I'm going to put it in here. Enough of the force will go downward. The heat of the explosion should melt the ice for several feet in all directions."

"Did our terrorist friend tell you what to do if the cable is inside two-inch-thick piping?" Friday asked.

"In that case we bury the hand grenade I have," Rodgers said. "That should put a good-sized dent in any casing. Now go back," he went on. "I'm ready to let this go."

Her hands stretched in front of her, Nanda knee-walked toward the slope. The ground was sharp and lumpy and it hurt. But she was glad to feel the pain. Years before, a potter, an artisan of the menial Sudra caste in Srinagar, had told her that it is better to feel something, even if it is hunger, than to feel nothing at all. Thinking of her own suffering and her dead grandfather, Nanda finally understood what the man had meant.

When she reached the wall, Nanda curled up on the ice the way Rodgers had instructed.

It did not escape Nanda's notice that the American had taken a moment to thank her for the work she had done. In the midst of all the turmoil and doubt, the horror of what had been and what might lie ahead, his word smelled like a single, beautiful rose.

That was the pretty image in the young woman's mind as the ground heaved and her back grew hot beneath her clothes and the roar blew through her hands, ringing her skull from back to jaw.

SIXTY-FOUR

The Siachin Glacier
Friday, 3:27 A.M.

Rodgers did not go as far from ground zero as the others. He knew that the explosion would not hurt him, though it would be hot. But he was counting on that. His exposed fingers were numb and he was going to need them warmed to work. He went as far as the edge of the slab and sat there with his knees upraised and his face buried between them. He used the insides of his knees to cover his ears. His arms were folded across his knees. He was braced for quite a bump when the grenade went off.

Rodgers made certain that the knife was back in his equipment vest and the radio was secure in his belt before he sat down. And he leaned to his left side as much as possible. Hopefully, if the blast knocked Rodgers over, he would not fall on the radio.

The in-ground explosion was even more potent than Rodgers had imagined. The ice beneath him rolled but did not knock Rodgers over. But the blast did take an edge of the slab off. Rodgers could hear the chunk as it whistled upward. The sound was shrill enough to cut through the surf-loud roar of the detonation itself. It came down somewhere to the left. Rodgers imagined the Indians initially thinking they had been attacked by a mortar shell. After a moment they would probably realize that the enemy had detonated another flash-bang grenade.

There were a series of lesser flashes and whiplike cracks as the grenade continued to fire. Before they died, Rodgers made his way over to the site. The explosion had cut a hole in the ice roughly four feet by four feet. Melted ice filled the excavation. Near the center was a severed cable.

While the last embers of the grenade still burned on the edge of the hole, Rodgers flopped on his belly and grabbed the dish-side end of cable. There were three wires bundled together inside a half-inch-thick plastic cover. One of the wires was red, another was yellow, and the third was blue. Rodgers removed his knife and pried the red one from the others. He cut the wet edge off and quickly scored the rubber sides of the wire with the tip of the knife. As he was finishing, the light from the last embers was fading.

"Friday, matches!" he said.

There was no answer.

"Friday!" he repeated.

"He's not here!" Nanda said.

Rodgers looked back. It was too dark to see that far. Either the NSA operative was hiding until he saw which way this went or, anticipating failure, he was making his way to the Indian side of the clearing. Whichever it was, Rodgers could not afford to worry about him. He laid the cable down so the exposed end was out of the melted ice. Then, moving quickly but economically, with a level of anxiety he had never before felt, Rodgers removed the map from his vest pocket. He unfolded the sheet away from the dying ember so it did not create a local breeze. Then he held his breath, leaned forward, and touched the edge of the map to the barely glowing thread of magnesium. He was afraid that if he touched the ember too hard it would be extinguished. Too light and the map would not feel it.

The fate of two nations had been reduced to this. One man's handling of the first and most primitive form of technology human beings had embraced. It put forty thousand years of human development into perspective. We were still territorial carnivores huddling in dark caves.

The paper smoked and then reddened around the edges. A moment later a small orange flame jumped triumphantly across the printed image of Kashmir. That seemed fitting.

"Nanda, come here!" Rodgers said.

The woman hurried over. Assuming the Indians did not move on them, the duo was safe for now. The remaining section of slab would afford them enough protection as long as they did not move from here.

Rodgers handed Nanda the paper when she arrived. He removed his coat, set it on the ice beside the hole, and told Nanda to put the map on it. He said the coat would not burn but he needed to find something else that would.

"Very quickly," he added.

"Hold on," Nanda said.

The young woman reached into her coat pocket and removed the small volume of Upanishads she always carried. She also removed the documents she was supposed to plant on the terrorists to help implicate them when they were captured.

"These devotionals will save more souls than the Brahmans ever imagined," she said.

Obviously, Nanda was experiencing some of the same spiritual and atavistic feelings Rodgers was. Or maybe they were both just exhausted.

As the papers burned, the general withdrew the radio from the belt loop and laid it on the coat. He bent low over it.

The radio was made of one vacuum-formed casing. Rodgers knew he would not be able to break that without risk of damaging the components he needed. Instead, he stuck the knife into the area around the recessed mouthpiece. Rodgers carefully pried that loose. The wire behind it, and the chip to which it was attached, were what he needed to access.

Still listening for activity from across the clearing, Rodgers used the knife to fish out the chip that was attached to the mouthpiece. He could not afford to sever the chip from the unit. If he did that, the chip itself would have no power source. That power came from the battery in the radio, not from the battery behind the satellite dish. He had to make sure he cut the right one to splice. He pulled the mouthpiece out as far as it could go and tilted the opening toward the light. Twenty years ago, this would have been a hopeless task. Radios then were crammed with transistors and wires that were impossible to read. The inside of this radio was relatively clean and open, just a few chips and wires.

Rodgers saw the battery and the wire that hooked the microchip and mouthpiece to it. The other wire, the one that led to the radio antenna, was the one he needed to cut.

Carefully placing the radio back on the coat, Rodgers used the knife to slice that wire as close to the radio antenna as possible. That would give him about two inches of wire to work with.

Crouching and using the tip of his boot as a cutting surface, Rodgers scored and stripped that remaining piece of wire. Then he picked up the scored cable from the satellite dish. He used his fingernails to chip the plastic casing away. When a half inch of wire was exposed, he twisted the two pieces of copper together and turned the unit on. Then he backed away from the radio and gently urged Nanda toward it.

It was the unlikeliest, most Frankenstein monster–looking, jury-rigged device that Mike Rodgers had seen in all his years of service. But that did not matter. Only one thing did.

That it worked.

SIXTY-FIVE

Washington, D.C.
Thursday, 6:21 P.M.

It was something Ron Plummer had never experienced. A moment of profound euphoria followed by a moment so sickening that the drop was physically disorienting.

When the call came from Islamabad, Ambassador Simathna listened for a moment then smiled broadly. Plummer did not have to wait for the call to be put on speakerphone to know what it was.

Mike Rodgers had succeeded. Somehow, the general had gotten the message to the Pakistani base that monitored the silo. They had forwarded the message to the Pakistani Ministry of Defense. From there, the tape was given to CNN and sent out to the world.

"My name is Nanda Kumar," said the high, scratchy voice on the recording. "I am an Indian citizen of Kashmir and a civilian network operative. For several months I have worked with India's Special Frontier Force to undermine a group of Pakistani terrorists. The Special Frontier Force told me that my actions would result in the arrest of the terrorists. Instead, the intelligence I provided allowed the Special Frontier Force to frame the Pakistanis. The terrorists have been responsible for many terrible acts. But they were not responsible for Wednesday's bomb attack on the pilgrim bus and Hindu temple in the Srinagar market. That was the work of the Special Frontier Force."

Ambassador Simathna was still beaming as he shut the phone off and leaned toward a second speakerphone. This was the open line to Paul Hood's office at Op-Center.

"Director Hood, did you hear that?" the ambassador asked.

"I did," Hood replied. "It's also running on CNN now."

"That is very gratifying," Simathna said. "I congratulate you and your General Rodgers. I do not know how he got the woman's message through but it is quite impressive."

"General Rodgers is a very impressive man," Hood agreed. "We'd like to know how he got the message through ourselves. Bob Herbert tells me that Colonel August is unable to raise him. The cell phone must have died."

"As long as it is just the cell phone," Simathna joked. "Of course, the Indians will certainly claim that Ms. Kumar was brainwashed by the Pakistanis. But General Rodgers will help to dispel that propaganda."

"General Rodgers will tell the truth, whatever that turns out to be," Hood said diplomatically.

As Hood was speaking the other phone beeped. Simathna excused himself and answered it.

The ambassador's smile trembled a moment before collapsing. His thin face lost most of its color. Ron Plummer did not dare imagine what the ambassador had just been told. Thoughts of a Pakistani nuclear strike flashed through his desperate mind.

Simathna said nothing. He just listened. After several seconds he hung up the phone and regarded Plummer. The sadness in his eyes was profound.

"Mr. Hood, I'm afraid I have bad news for you," the ambassador said.

"What kind of bad news?" Hood asked.

"Apparently, the slab on top of the silo was removed or significantly damaged during General Rodgers's actions," Simathna said.

"Don't say it," Hood warned. "Don't you frigging say it."

Simathna did not have to. They all knew what that meant.

The defensive explosives around the silo had been automatically activated. Without someone inside the silo to countermand them, they would detonate in just a few minutes.

SIXTY-SIX

Washington, D.C.
Thursday, 6:24 P.M.

Paul Hood could not believe that Mike Rodgers had gone this far, worked whatever miracle he had conceived, only to be blown up for something that could be prevented. But to prevent it they would have to reach him. Though Hood, Herbert, and Coffey sat in silence, frustration under the surface was intense. Despite the technology at their disposal, the men were as helpless as if they were living in the Stone Age.

Hood was slumped in his leather seat. He was looking down, humbled by this uncharacteristic sense of helplessness. In the past there had always been another play in the book. Someone they could call for assistance, time to move resources into position, at the very least a means of communication. Not now. And he suspected that Mike or Nanda or the others had used up their guardian spirit quota stopping a nuclear war. Hood did not think it would help to pray for their salvation now. Maybe their lives and the lives of the Strikers were the price they had to pay. Still, Hood did ask quietly that whatever Christian, Hindu, or Muslim entities had gotten them this far would see them a little further. Paul Hood was not ready to lose Mike Rodgers. Not yet.

"Maybe Mike and the girl did their business and left the area," Coffey suggested.

"It's possible," Herbert said. "Knowing Mike, though, he would continue to broadcast for a while. They may have no way of knowing that their message got through."

Coffey scowled.

"Even if they did leave, I'm not sure they would have gone far enough," Herbert went on.

"What do you mean?" Coffey asked.

"It's dark, dead-of-night where they are," Herbert said. "My guess is that after all they've been through, Mike would have wanted to find a place to bunk down until well after sunrise. Let the area warm a little. If anyone was wounded, in whatever went on out there, Mike might have wanted to take time to perform first aid. The bug in the juice is we don't know exactly how much time is left before the blast. Obviously, Mike accessed the silo somehow to make the transmission. The explosives were armed when he moved the slab. That means we're well into the countdown."

"I can't believe those bastards in Pakistan can't shut the process down," Coffey said.

"I do," Herbert replied. "And I'll tell you what's happening right now. I've been thinking about this. I'll bet they put together a network of underground silos out there, all linked by tunnel. Right now the missile is automatically shifting to another site."

"You mean like an underground Scud," Coffey said.

"Exactly like that," Herbert replied. "As soon as it's out of range the silo and whoever found it go kablooey. No evidence of a missile is found among the residue. They can claim it was some kind of shelter for scientists studying the glacier, or soldiers patrolling the region, or whatever they like."

"None of which helps us get Mike out of there," Coffey said gravely.

The phone beeped as Herbert was talking. Hood picked it up. It was Stephen Viens at the National Reconnaissance Office.

"Paul, if Mike is still out in the Chittisin Plateau, we've got something on the wide-range camera he should know about," Viens said.

Hood punched on the speakerphone and sat up. "Talk to me, Stephen," he said.

"A couple of minutes ago we saw a blip moving back into the area," Viens said. "We believe it's an Indian Mi-35, possibly the same one they tangled with before. Refueled and back for another round."

While Viens had been speaking, Hood and Herbert swapped quick, hopeful looks. The men did not have to say anything. There was suddenly an option. The question was whether there was time to use it.

"Stephen, stay on the line," Hood said. "And thank you. Thank you very much."

Moving with barely controlled urgency, Herbert scooped up his wheelchair phone and speed-dialed his Indian military liaison.

Hood also did something. Inside, in private.

He speed-dialed a silent word of thanks to whoever was looking after Mike.

SIXTY-SEVEN

The Siachin Glacier
Friday, 4:00 A.M.

Rodgers was crouched behind the slab, his gun drawn as he looked across the clearing. He had allowed the fire to die while Nanda continued to make her broadcast. Although the Indians had not moved on them, he did not want to give them a target if they changed their minds. He could think of several reasons they might.

If Nanda's message had gotten through, the soldiers certainly would have let Rodgers know by now. The Indians would not want to risk being shot any more than he did. Their silence seemed to indicate that either the Indians were waiting for Rodgers to slip up or for reinforcements to arrive. Possibly they were waiting for dawn to attack. They had the longer-range weapons. All they needed was light to climb the slopes and spot the targets. It could also be that the Indians were already moving on them, slowly and cautiously. Ron Friday may have gone over to rat out their position in exchange for sanctuary. That would not surprise Rodgers at all. The man had given himself away when he registered no surprise about why Fenwick had resigned. Only Hood, the president, the vice president, the First Lady, and Fenwick's assistant had known he was a traitor.

But Friday knew. Friday knew because he may have been the son of a bitch's point man in Baku, Azerbaijan. For all Rodgers knew, Friday may have had a hand in the attacks on the CIA operatives who had been stationed there. One way or another, Ron Friday would answer for that. Either he'd hunt him down here or end their broadcast with a message for Hood.

With the fire gone, however, Mike Rodgers had another

concern. He had sacrificed his gloves and jacket for the cause. His hands were numb and his chest and arms were freezing. If he did not do something about that soon he would perish from hypothermia.

He took a moment to make sure that Nanda was protected from gunfire by what remained of the slab. Then he crept back to where he had left Samouel behind the ice barricade.

The Pakistani was dead.

That did not surprise Rodgers. What did surprise him was the sadness he felt upon finding the lifeless body.

There was something about Samouel that did not fit the template of an objective-blinded terrorist. In the Pakistani's final moments, while he should have been praying for Allah to accept his soul, Samouel was telling Rodgers how to splice the dish to his radio. Along with Samouel's dogged trek alongside two historic enemies, that had touched Rodgers.

Now, in death, Samouel was even responsible for saving Rodgers's life. The general felt grateful as he removed the dead man's coat and gloves. Stripping the bodies of enemies had always been a part of warfare. But soldiers did not typically take even things they needed from fallen allies. Somehow, though, this felt like a gift rather than looting.

Rodgers knelt beside the body as he dressed. As the general finished, his knees began to tickle. At first he thought it was a result of the cold. Then he realized that the ground was vibrating slightly. A moment later he heard a low, low roar.

It felt and sounded like the beginnings of an avalanche. He wondered if the explosions had weakened the slopes and they were coming down on them. If that were the case the safest place would not be at the foot of the slopes.

Rising, Rodgers ran back toward Nanda. As he did, he felt a rumbling in his gut. He had felt it before. He recognized it.

It was not an avalanche. It was worse. It was the reason the Indians had been waiting to attack.

A moment later the tops of the surrounding ice peaks were silhouetted by light rising from the north. The rumbling and roar were now distinctive beats as the Indian helicopter neared. He should have expected this. The soldiers had radioed their position to the Mi-35 that had tried to kill them earlier.

Rodgers slid to Nanda's side and knelt facing her. He felt for her cheeks in the dark and held them in his hands. He used them to guide his mouth close to her ear, so she could hear over the roar.

"I want you to try and get to the entrance while I keep the helicopter busy," Rodgers said. "It's not going to be easy getting past the soldiers but it may be your only hope."

"How do we know they'll kill us?" she asked.

"We don't," Rodgers admitted. "But let's find out by trying to escape instead of by surrendering."

"I like that," Nanda replied.

Rodgers could hear the smile in her voice.

"Start making your way around the wall behind me," he said. "With luck, the chopper will cause an avalanche on their side."

"I hope not," she replied. "They're my people."

Touché, Rodgers thought.

"But thank you," she added. "Thank you for making this fight your fight. Good luck."

The general patted her cheek and she left. He continued to watch as the chopper descended. Suddenly, the Russian bird stopped moving. It hovered above the center of the clearing, equidistant to Rodgers and the Indians. Maybe twenty seconds passed and then the chopper suddenly swept upward and to the south. It disappeared behind one of the peaks near the entrance. The glow of its lights poured through the narrow cavern.

Rodgers peeked over the slab. The chopper had landed. Maybe they were worried about causing an avalanche and had decided to deploy ground troops. That would make getting through the entrance virtually impossible. He immediately got up and ran after Nanda. He would have to pull her back, think of another strategy. Maybe negotiate something with these people to get her out. As she had said, they were her people.

But as Rodgers ran he saw something that surprised him.

Up ahead. Three of the Indian soldiers were rushing from the clearing. They were not going to attack. They were being evacuated.

What happened next surprised him even more.

"General Rodgers!" someone shouted.

Rodgers looked to the west of the entrance. Someone was standing there, half-hidden by an ice formation.

All right, Rodgers thought. He'd bite. "Yes?" the general shouted back.

"Your message got through!" said the Indian. "We must leave this place at once!"

Everything from Rodgers's legs to his spirit to his brain felt as though they had been given a shot of adrenaline. He kept running, leaping cracks and dodging mounds of ice. Either Ron Friday had gotten to him with a hell of a sell job or the man was telling the truth. Whichever it was, Rodgers was going with it. There did not seem to be another option.

Looking ahead, Rodgers watched as Nanda reached the entrance. She continued on toward the light. Rodgers arrived several moments later. The Indian soldier, a sergeant, got there at the same time he did. His rifle was slung over his back. There were no weapons in his gloved hands.

"We must hurry," the Indian said as they ran into the entrance. "This area is a Pakistani time bomb. An arsenal of some kind. You triggered the defenses somehow."

Possibly by tinkering with the uplink, Rodgers thought. Or more likely, the Pakistani military wanted to destroy them all to keep the secret of their nuclear missile silo.

"I can't believe there were just two of you," the sergeant said as they raced through the narrow tunnel. "We thought there were more."

"There were," Rodgers said. He looked at the chopper ahead. He watched as soldiers helped Nanda inside and he realized Friday had deserted them. "They're dead now."

The men left the entrance and ran the last twenty-five yards to the chopper. Rodgers and the sergeant jumped into the open door of the Mi-35. The aircraft rose quickly, simultaneously angling from the hot Pakistani base.

As the helicopter door was slid shut behind him, Rodgers

staggered toward the side of the crowded cargo compartment. There were no seats, just the outlines of cold, tired bodies. The general felt the adrenaline kick leave as his legs gave out and he dropped to the floor. He was not surprised to find Nanda already there, slumped against an ammunition crate. Rodgers slid toward her as the helicopter leveled out and sped to the north. He took her hand and snuggled beside her, the two of them propping each other up. The Indians sat around them, lighting cigarettes and blowing warmth on their hands.

The cabin temperature inside the helicopter was little higher than freezing, but the relative warmth felt blissful. Rodgers's skin crackled warmly. His eyelids shut. He could not help it. His mind started to shut down as well.

Before it did, the American felt a flash of satisfaction that Samouel had died on something that was nominally his homeland. Silo, arsenal, whatever Islamabad called it, at least it was built by Pakistanis.

As for Friday, Rodgers was also glad. Glad that the man was about to die on the opposite side of the world from the country he had betrayed.

Joy for a terrorist. Hate for an American.

Rodgers was happy to leave those thoughts for another time.

SIXTY-EIGHT

The Siachin Glacier
Friday, 4:07 A.M.

Ron Friday had been confused, at first, when he saw the chopper leave the clearing.

His plan had been simple. If Eagle Scout Rodgers had managed to come out on top of this, Friday would have told him that he had gone off to the side to watch for an Indian assault. If the Indians had won, as Friday expected, he would have said he had been trying to reach them to help end the standoff.

Friday had not expected both sides to reach some kind of sudden détente and leave together. He did not expect to be stranded on the far side of the clearing where the drumming of the chopper drowned out his shouts to the men. He did not expect to be stranded here.

But as Ron Friday watched the chopper depart he did not feel cheated or angry. He felt alone, but that was nothing new. His immediate concern was getting rest and surviving what remained of the cold night. Having done both, he could make his way back to the line of control the next day.

Where he had wanted to go in the first place.

Accomplishing that, Friday would find a way to work this to his advantage. He had still been a key participant in an operation that had prevented a nuclear incident over Kashmir. Along the way he had learned things that would be valuable to both sides.

Friday was slightly northeast of the center of the clearing when the light of the rising chopper disappeared behind the peaks. He had only seen two people join the Indians. That meant one of them, probably Samouel, was dead near the entrance to the silo. The Pakistani would no longer need his

362

clothing. If Friday could find a little niche somewhere, he could use the clothes to set up a flap to keep out the cold. And he still had the matches. Maybe he could find something to make a little campfire. As long as life remained, there was always hope.

A moment later, in a chaotic upheaval of ice and fire, hope ended for Ron Friday.

SIXTY-NINE

The Himachal Peaks
Friday, 4:12 A.M.

Crouched against the boulders on the edge of the plateau, Brett August and William Musicant were able to see and then hear a distant explosion. It shook the ledge and threw a deep red flush against the peaks and sky to the northeast. The light reminded August of the kind of glow that emerged from a barbecue pit when you stirred the dying coals with a stick. It was a wispy, blood-colored light that was the same intensity on all sides.

August watched to see if a contrail rose from the fires. He did not see one. That meant it was not a missile being launched. The blast came from the direction in which Mike Rodgers had been headed. August hoped his old friend was behind whatever it was rather than a victim of it.

The inferno remained for a few moments and then rapidly subsided. August did not imagine that there was a great deal of combustible material out there on the glacier. He turned his stinging, tired eyes back to the valley below. Down there were the men who had killed his soldiers. Shot them from the sky without their even drawing their weapons. As much as the colonel did not want the situation to escalate, part of him wanted the Indians to charge up the peak. He ached for the chance to avenge his team.

The ice storm had stopped, though not the winds. It would take the heat of the sun to warm and divert them. The wind still swept down with punishing cold and force and a terrible sameness. The relentless whistling was the worst of it. August wondered if it were winds that inspired the legends of the Sirens. In some tales, the song of the sea nymphs drove sailors mad. August understood now how that could happen.

The colonel's hearing was so badly impaired that he did not even hear the TAC-SAT when it beeped. Fortunately, August noticed the red light flashing. He unbuttoned the collar that covered his face to the bridge of his nose. Then he turned up the volume on the TAC-SAT before answering. He would need every bit of it to hear Bob Herbert.

"Yes?" August shouted into the mouthpiece.

"Colonel, it's over," Herbert said.

"Repeat, please?" August yelled. The colonel thought he heard Herbert say this was over.

"Mike got the message through," Herbert said, louder and more articulately. "The Indian LOC troops are being recalled. You will be picked up by chopper at sunrise."

"I copy that," August said. "We saw an explosion to the northeast a minute ago. Did Mike do that?"

"In a manner of speaking," Herbert said. "We'll brief you after you've been airlifted."

"What about the Strikers?" August asked.

"We'll have to work on that," Herbert said.

"I'm not leaving without them," August said.

"Colonel, this is Paul," Hood said. "We have to determine whose jurisdiction the valley—"

"I'm not leaving without them," August repeated.

There was a long silence. "I understand," Hood replied.

"Brett, can you hold out there until around midmorning?" Herbert asked.

"I will do whatever it takes," August said.

"All right," Herbert told him. "The chopper can pick up Corporal Musicant. I promise we'll have the situation worked as quickly as possible."

"Thank you, sir," August said. "What are my orders regarding the three Pakistanis?"

"You know me," Herbert said. "Now that they've served their purpose I'd just as soon you put a bullet in each of their murderous little heads. I'm sure my wife has the road upstairs covered. She'll make sure the bus to Paradise gets turned back."

"Morality aside, there are legal and political considerations as well as the possibility of armed resistance," Hood cut in.

"Op-Center has no jurisdiction over the FKM, and India has made no official inquiries regarding the rest of the cell. They are free to do whatever they want. If the Pakistanis wish to surrender, I'm sure they will be arrested and tried by the Indians. If they turn on you, you must respond however you see fit."

"Paul's right," Herbert said. "The most important thing is to get you and Corporal Musicant home safely."

August said he understood. He told Hood and Herbert that he would accept whatever food and water the chopper brought. After that, he said he would make his way to the Mangala Valley to find the rest of the Strikers.

Hanging up the TAC-SAT, August rose slowly on cold-stiffened legs. He switched on his flashlight and made his way across the ice-covered ledge to where Musicant was stationed. August gave the medic the good news then went back to where Sharab and her two associates were huddled. Unlike the Strikers, they had not undergone cold-weather training. Nor were they dressed as warmly as August and Musicant.

August squatted beside them. They winced as the light struck them. They reminded the colonel of lepers cowering from the sun. Sharab was trembling. Her eyes were red and glazed. There was ice in her hair and eyebrows. Her lips were broken and her cheeks were bright red. August could not help but feel sorry for her. Her two comrades looked even worse. Their noses were raw and bleeding and they would probably lose their ears to frostbite. Their gloves were so thick with ice that August did not even think they could move their fingers.

Looking at them, the colonel realized that Sharab and her countrymen were not going to fight them or run anywhere. August leaned close to them.

"General Rodgers and Nanda completed their mission," August said.

Sharab was staring ahead. Her red eyes began to tear. Her exposed mouth moved silently. In prayer, August suspected. The other men hugged her arms weakly and also spoke silent words.

"An Indian helicopter will arrive at sunup," August went on. "Corporal Musicant will be leaving on it. I'm going to make my way back to the valley to find the rest of my team. What do you want to do?"

Sharab turned her tearing eyes toward August. There was deep despair in her gaze. Her voice was gravelly and tremulous when she spoke. "Will America . . . help us . . . to make the case . . . for a Pakistani Kashmir?" she asked.

"I think things will change because of what happened over the last few days," August admitted. "But I don't know what my nation will say or do."

Sharab laid an icy glove on August's forearm. "Will . . . you help us?" she pressed. "They . . . killed . . . your team."

"The madness between your countries killed my team," August said.

"No," she said. She gestured violently toward the edge of the plateau. "The men . . . down there . . . killed them. They are godless . . . evil."

This was not a discussion August wanted to have. Not with someone who blew up public buildings and peace officers for a living.

"Sharab, I've worked with you to this point," August said. "I can't do any more. There will be a trial and hearings. If you surrender, you will have the opportunity to make a strong case for your people."

"That will not . . . help," she insisted.

"It will be a start," August countered.

"And if . . . we go back . . . down the mountain?" the woman asked. "What will you do?"

"I guess I'll say good-bye," he replied.

"You won't try . . . to stop us?" Sharab pressed.

"No," August assured her. "Excuse me, now. I'm going back to join the rest of my unit."

August looked at the defiant Pakistani for a moment longer. The woman's hate and rage were burning through the cold and physical exhaustion. He had seen determined fighters during his life. The Vietcong. Kurdish resistance fighters. People who were fighting for their homes and families. But this furnace was a terrifying thing to witness.

Colonel August turned and walked back across the slippery, windswept ridge. Tribunals would be a good start. But it would take more than that to eradicate what existed between the Indians and the Pakistanis. It would take a war like the one they had barely managed to avoid. Or it would take an unparalleled and sustained international effort lasting generations.

For a sad, transient moment August shared something with Sharab.

A profound sense of despair.

SEVENTY

Washington, D.C.
Tuesday, 7:10 A.M.

Paul Hood sat alone in his office. He was looking at his computer, reviewing the comments he planned to make at the ten A.M. Striker memorial.

As promised, Herbert had persuaded the Indians to bring choppers from the line of control to collect the bodies of the Strikers. The leverage he used was simple. The Pakistanis agreed to stay out of the region, even though they claimed the valley for their own. Herbert convinced New Delhi that it would be a bad idea for Pakistanis to collect the bodies of Americans who had been killed by Indians. It would have made a political statement that neither India nor the United States wished to make.

Colonel August was in the valley to meet the two Mi-35s when they arrived late Friday afternoon. The bodies had already been collected and lined up beneath their canopies. August stayed with the bodies until they had been flown back to Quantico on Sunday. Then and only then did the colonel agree to go to a hospital. Mike Rodgers was there to meet him.

Hood and Rodgers had performed too many of these services since Op-Center had first been chartered. Mike Rodgers inevitably spoke eloquently of duty and soldiering. Heroism and tradition. Hood always tried to find a perspective in which to place the sacrifice. The salvation of a country, the saving of lives, or the prevention of war. The men invariably left the mourners feeling hope instead of futility, pride to temper the sense of loss.

But this was different. More than the lives of the Strikers was being memorialized today.

369

New Delhi had publicly thanked Op-Center for uncovering a Pakistani cell. The bodies of three terrorists had been found at the foot of the Himachal Peaks in the Himalayas. They appeared to have slipped from a ledge and plummeted to their deaths. They were identified by records on file at the offices of the Special Frontier Force.

Islamabad had also publicly thanked Op-Center for helping deter a nuclear strike against Pakistan. Though Indian Defense Minister John Kabir had been named by Major Dev Puri and others as the man behind the plot, Kabir denied the allegations. He vowed to fight any indictments the government might consider handing down. Hood suspected that the minister and others would resign, and that would be the end of it. New Delhi would rather bury the reality of any wrongdoing than give Pakistan a more credible voice in the court of world opinion.

Hood even got a thank-you call from Nanda Kumar. The young woman called from New Delhi to say that General Rodgers had been a hero and a gentleman. Although he had not been able to save her grandfather, she realized that Rodgers had done everything he could to make the trek easier for him. She said she hoped to visit Hood and Rodgers in Washington when she got out of the hospital. Even though she was technically an Indian intelligence operative, Hood had no doubt that she would get a visa. Nanda's broadcast had made her an international celebrity. She would spend the rest of her life speaking and writing about her experience. Hood hoped that the twenty-two-year-old was wise beyond her years. He hoped she would use the media access to promote tolerance and peace in Kashmir, and not the agendas of India or Nanda Kumar.

The praise from abroad was unique. Even when Op-Center succeeded in averting disaster, Hood and his team were typically slammed for their involvement in the internal affairs of another nation—Spain or the Koreas or the Middle East or anywhere else they handled a crisis.

Despite the praise coming from abroad, Op-Center took several unprecedented hits on the home front. Most of those came from Hank Lewis and the Congressional Intelligence

Oversight Committee. They wanted to know why General Rodgers had left the Siachin Glacier without Ron Friday. Why Striker had jumped into a military hot zone during the day instead of at night. Why the NRO was involved in the operation but not the CIA or the full resources of the NSA, which had an operative on-site. Hood and Rodgers had gone over to Capitol Hill to explain everything to Lewis and to Fox and her fellow CIOC members.

They might just as well have been speaking Urdu. The CIOC had already decided that in addition to the previously discussed downsizing, Op-Center would no longer be maintaining a military wing. Striker would be officially disbanded. Colonel August and Corporal Musicant would be reassigned and General Rodgers's role would be "reevaluated."

Hood was also informed that he would be filing daily rather than semiweekly reports with CIOC. They wanted to know everything that the agency was involved with, from situation analyses to photographic reconnaissance.

Hood suspected the only thing that protected Op-Center at all was the loyalty of the president of the United States. President Lawrence and United Nations Secretary-General Mala Chatterjee had issued a joint statement congratulating Paul Hood for his group's nonpartisan efforts on behalf of humanitarianism and world peace. It was not a document the CIOC could ignore, especially after Chatterjee's bitter denunciation of the way Hood had handled the Security Council crisis. Hood could not imagine the kind of pressure Lawrence must have applied to get that statement. He also wondered how Chatterjee really felt. She was a pacifistic Indian whose nation had tried to start a nuclear war against its neighbor. Unless she was steeped in denial, that had to be difficult for her to reconcile. Hood would not be surprised to hear that she was resigning her post to run for political office at home. That would certainly be a good step toward peace in the region.

All of which served to make this a very different time, a very different memorial service. It was the last time Paul Hood and the original Op-Center would do anything as team-

371

mates. The rest of them would not know that yet.

But Paul Hood would. He wanted to say something that addressed a new loss they would all soon be feeling.

He reread the opening line of his testimonial.

"This is the second family I have lost in as many months . . ."

He deleted it. The statement was too much about him. Too much about his loss.

But it did start him thinking. Although he was no longer living with Sharon and the kids, he still felt as though they were together in some way. If not physically then spiritually.

And then it came to him. Hood knew the line was right because it caught in his throat as he tried to say it.

Hood typed with two trembling index fingers as he tried to see the computer monitor. It was blurry because he was blinking out tears over what was supposed to be just a job.

"This I have learned," he wrote with confidence. "Wherever fate takes any of us, we will always be family. . . ."

Tom Clancy's
Op-Centre

Created by
Tom Clancy and Steve Pieczenik

THE INTERNATIONAL BESTSELLER

Situated in Washington, Op-Centre is a beating heart of defence, intelligence and crisis-management technology, run by a crack team of operatives both within its own walls and out in the field. When a job is too dirty, or too dangerous, it is the only place the US government can turn.

But nothing can prepare Director Paul Hood and his Op-Centre crisis-management team for what they are about to uncover – a very real, very frightening power play that could unleash new players in a new world order . . .

A powerful profile of America's defence, intelligence and crisis-management technology, *Tom Clancy's Op-Centre* is the creation of Tom Clancy and Steve Pieczenik – inspiring this novel, as well as the special NBC Television presentation.

ISBN 0 00 649658 X

Tom Clancy's Op-Centre

Mirror Image

Created by
Tom Clancy and Steve Pieczenik

THE INTERNATIONAL BESTSELLER

The Cold War is over. And chaos is setting in. The new President of Russia is trying to create a new democratic regime. But there are strong elements within the country that are trying to stop him: the ruthless Russian Mafia, the right-wing nationalists and those nefarious forces that will do whatever it takes to return Russia back to the days of the Czar.

Op-Centre, the newly founded but highly successful crisis management team, begins a race against the clock and against the hardliners. Their task is made even more difficult by the discovery of a Russian counterpart . . . but this one's controlled by those same repressive hardliners.

Two rival Op-Centres, virtual mirror images of each other. But if this mirror cracks, it'll be much more than seven years' bad luck.

A powerful profile of America's defence, intelligence and crisis management technology, Tom Clancy's Op-Centre *is the creation of Tom Clancy and Steve Pieczenik – inspiring this and other gripping novels.*

ISBN 0 00 649659 8

Tom Clancy's
Op-Centre

Games of State

Created by
Tom Clancy and Steve Pieczenik

THE INTERNATIONAL BESTSELLER

In the newly unified Germany, old horrors are reborn. It is the beginning of Chaos Days, a time when neo-Nazi groups gather to spread violence and resurrect dead dreams. But this year Germany isn't the only target. Plans are afoot to destabilize Europe and cause turmoil throughout the United States.

Paul Hood and his team, already in Germany to buy technology for the new Regional Op-Centre, become entangled in the crisis. They uncover a shocking force behind the chaos – a group that uses cutting-edge technology to promote hate and influence world events.

A powerful profile of America's defence, intelligence and crisis management technology, Tom Clancy's Op-Centre *is the creation of Tom Clancy and Steve Pieczenik – inspiring this and other gripping novels.*

ISBN 0 00 649844 2